OF DARKNESS AND LIGHT

By Ryan Cahill

THE BOUND AND THE BROKEN

The Fall
Of Blood and Fire
Of Darkness and Light

OF DARKNESS AND LIGHT

BOOK TWO OF
THE BOUND AND THE BROKEN

RYAN CAHILL

OF DARKNESS AND LIGHT

BOOK TWO OF THE BOUND AND THE BROKEN SERIES

First edition: December 2021

ISBN 978-1-8383818-6-8

www.ryancahillauthor.com

Cover Design by: Stuart Bache

Edited by: Sarah Chorn
Illustrations by: Aron Cahill
Map by: Keirr Scott-Schrueder

OF DARKNESS AND LIGHT

BOOK TWO OF
THE BOUND AND THE BROKEN

RYAN CAHILL

OF DARKNESS AND LIGHT

BOOK TWO OF THE BOUND AND THE BROKEN SERIES

First edition: December 2021

ISBN 978-1-8383818-6-8

www.ryancahillauthor.com

Cover Design by: Stuart Bache

Edited by: Sarah Chorn
Illustrations by: Aron Cahill
Map by: Keirr Scott-Schrueder

To Dad, for teaching me there is nothing more important in the darkness than a ray of light.

The Story So Far

The following is meant only as a quick, high-level refresher of the events in *The Fall* and *Of Blood and Fire*, rather than a full synopsis. As such, I will gloss over many important occurrences and characters during this recap, and some – in a few cases – are not mentioned at all. I will try to catch you up on the events and characters that are the most important to *Of Darkness and Light*.

This refresher will contain spoilers.

The Fall

Every four hundred years since the dawn of time, the Blood Moon – a time when the veil between gods and mortals is at its thinnest – casts its light over the world. But when the Blood Moon rose in the year two-six-eight-two After Doom, everything changed.

It was on this night that ***The Order*** *was betrayed by those who had sworn to protect it, and their fortress city of* ***Ilnaen*** *was laid siege by the forces of* ***Fane Mortem*** *– a mage of immense power.*

Upon discovering the betrayal ***Alvira Serris,*** *the Archon of the* ***Draleid*** *– warriors who were soulbound to great dragons – attempted to ensure the safety of The Order's council. But Alvira arrived in the council chamber to discover that her closest friend and First Sword of the Draleid,* ***Eltoar Daethana****, had aligned himself with the traitors. In the ensuing battle, Eltoar with the aid of two* ***Fades*** *– dark servants of the traitor god,* ***Efialtír*** *– and his dragon,* ***Helios****, slew Alvira and the dragon to which she was bound.*

Feeling the sickly Taint of blood magic radiating from the city of Ilnaen, the ***Knights of Achyron*** *– a pious order of knights sworn to the warrior god, Achyron – travelled through the Rift to drive back the forces of* ***the Shadow****. But they were too late. The city was already lost, the Archon was dead, and The Order had fallen. Only seventeen* *knights survived the battle of Ilnaen, and they returned to their temple, broken and shattered.*

Amidst the raging battle, ***Coren Valmar*** *– an apprentice Draleid – and her dragon, Aldryn, fought for their lives against those they had once called brothers and sisters. Under instructions from her master, Coren and two other Draleid,* ***Dylain*** *and* ***Farwen****, raced to Ilnaen's western hatchery to secure the dragon eggs held within. But she was too late. Dylain's dragon, Soria, was slain in the fighting while Coren and Farwen were lucky to escape the tower with their lives.*

While walking through the wreckage of the western hatchery, Eltoar Daethana discovered the Uraks had betrayed their word and had destroyed the dragon eggs that rested within the tower. Seeing this enraged Eltoar. When he stumbled upon Dylain fighting for his life against a group of ***Uraks****, Eltoar slaughtered the beasts, utilising the dark power of blood magic to do so. However, once Dylain discovered Eltoar's betrayal of The Order and denounced him, Eltoar slew Dylain in a fit of rage. Struggling to come to terms with his betrayal of those closest to him, Eltoar watched as* ***Fane Mortem*** *took advantage of the thin veil between worlds and, emboldened by the powers given to him by Efialtír, ripped the continent of Epheria in half.*

Of Blood and Fire

In the aftermath of **The Fall**, **Brother-Captain Kallinvar** and his knights find the last Sigil Bearer – a young man close to death, who is to take the last remaining Sigil of Achyron and finally restore the Knights of Achyron to their full strength.

Four hundred years after the events of The Fall, Fane Mortem now rules the **Lorian Empire** and holds dominion over the High Lords of the South. After the events in The Fall, the continent of Epheria is split in two, divided along the centre by both the **Darkwood** and **The Burnt Lands.** Only nine Draleid have survived the centuries since The Fall, but they now support the empire and have taken on the name **Dragonguard.**

Our story begins in **The Glade**, one of seven villages that lie at the very edge of the province of Illyanara, in Epheria.

On the cusp of his eighteenth summer, **Calen Bryer** will soon take part in The **Proving** – a trial of courage and skill that not at all survive. But as he waits, he struggles to come to terms with the death of his brother, **Haem.** Haem was killed two years prior when he led the town guard in chase of Uraks – monstrous creatures with grey and brown skin, heavy muscles, and a thirst for blood – who had attacked The Glade.

While Calen is preparing for The Proving, his sister, **Ella**, is preparing to leave The Glade entirely. Secretly, Ella is in love with a young man named **Rhett Fjorn** – Haem's best friend and the man that her father, **Vars**, blames for Haem's death.

When time for The Proving finally comes, Calen, along with his friends **Dann Pimm** and **Rist Havel**, enter Olm Forest together. While in Olm Forest, Calen, Rist, and Dann face many obstacles. On the first night, they are attacked by a bear which they successfully kill and skin to bring back the pelt. However, on the second night, the trio are set upon by another group – **Fritz Netly**, Denet Hildom, and Kurtis Swett. While attempting to steal the bear pelt Fritz injures Rist with an arrow and drives Calen, Rist, and Dann further into Olm Forest.

With Rist injured and the group exhausted, the journey back through Olm Forest is a long and slow one. On the way back, Rist, Calen, and Dann cross paths with two Uraks. In the ensuing battle the boys manage to slay the beasts, more from luck than skill. It is here that Rist has the first inkling of his ability to touch the **Spark** – the source of magic in the world – but he keeps it quiet, afraid of what the others might say.

Upon arriving back at The Glade with the head of an Urak, the group faces an inquest, led by one of the village elders, **Erdhardt Hammersmith.** After the inquest, Calen, Dann, and Rist are declared victors of The Hunt, and Calen dances with the girl he pines after, Anya Gritten, while listening to music from a Narvonan bard called **Belina Louna.**

A few days after the celebrations, Calen's father gifts him an elven sword that he himself was given a long time ago. After receiving the sword, Calen goes with Dann and Rist to the nearby town of Milltown to deliver a shipment of weapons and armour for Vars, and to spend some of their winnings.

While in Milltown, Calen purchases a silk scarf for his mother before meeting back up with Rist and Dann at The Two Barges inn. At the two barges, Calen and Dann play a game of axe throwing with a group of men from **Drifaien** – **Alleron, Baird, Kettil, Leif, Fell, Audun**, and **Destin**. While playing axes, Calen is approached by a young man named **Erik**. After showing immense skill at the game, Erik unceremoniously leaves. Seeing that Erik left his mantle behind, Calen went after him to return it.

Outside the inn, Calen, Erik, and Erik's father and brother – **Aeson** and **Dahlen** – have a violent encounter with empire soldiers, which results in Calen killing a man for the first time. Calen, Dann, Rist, Erik, Aeson, and Dahlen flee into Olm Forest.

Meanwhile, back in The Glade, unaware of what has happened, Ella and Rhett finally set off on their journey to **Berona**, leaving only letters behind.

In Olm Forest, the group are saved from an Urak attack by **Asius**, a **Jotnar** – giant – with pale blue skin, and a natural affinity for the Spark. Later that night, camped in Olm Forest, Calen hears a voice calling to him from within a satchel that is in Aeson's possession, whispering the words 'Draleid' and '**n'aldryr**'.

With the knowledge that the empire might continue looking for them, and could potentially threaten their families, Calen, Dann, and Rist sneak off in the night and ride back to The Glade.

Unbeknownst to Calen, Aeson is aware of the voice Calen heard and believes him to be the first free Draleid since The Order fell. With this knowledge, Aeson sends Asius and the other Jotnar to deliver messages to their Allies in preparation for war against the empire. Then, Aeson, Dahlen, Erik and **Therin** – an elf, thought by Calen to only be a bard, but in truth is a lot more – ride after Calen, Rist, and Dann.

Now back in The Glade, Calen, Rist, and Dann separate to go and seek out their own families. Calen finds that his parents are being questioned by imperial soldiers. He recognises two of the soldiers from the fight outside The Two Barges – a man in a red cloak, **Inquisitor Rendall**, and a man in a black cloak, **Farda Kyrana**. In the altercation that follows, Rendall kills Calen's father, and Farda kills Calen's mother. It is only by Aeson, Erik, Dahlen, and Therin's intervention that Calen escapes.

After escaping back into Olm Forest, Calen confronts Aeson as to why the empire is chasing them. Aeson reveals that within his satchel is a dragon egg. This revelation changes everything, as not a single Epherian dragon egg has hatched in the four centuries since The Fall. But the egg that Aeson has in his possession is not an Epherian dragon egg; it is a dragon egg from the northern icelands of Valacia. Believing his entire family dead, including Ella, and the empire chasing him, Calen agrees to go with Aeson and the others to **Belduar** – a city of legend that has defied the empire for centuries. Unwilling to let their friend go alone, Dann and Rist also join the group.

In the city of Camylin, Aeson meets an acquaintance and arranges for letters to be sent across the continent to his allies, informing them that he has found the Draleid that will be bound to the dragon within the egg, and readying them for the rebellion to come. That night, the group are attacked by empire soldiers and chased through the streets of Camylin. During the attack, Rist and Dahlen are separated from the rest of the group and are subsequently attacked by a Fade, who takes Rist captive and leaves Dahlen unconscious.

Meanwhile, Ella and Rhett have also arrived in the city of Camylin, only just missing Calen and the others. It is here that Rhett receives a letter from his uncle, **Tanner Fjorn.** In the letter, Tanner tells Rhett that he has purchased a ticket for both Rhett and Ella to travel north, from the port of Gisa. Due to Epheria being split by The Burnt Lands and the Darkwood, almost all travel between the North and South is done by ship. There are only two ports in the South that make this journey, **Gisa** and **Falstide.** As Rhett and Ella could never have afforded a ticket for the relatively safe journey from Gisa to Antiquar, they had initially intended to travel the breadth of Illyanara and sail along the Lightning Coast from Falstide to Bromis.

When Dahlen re-joins the group in the woods outside Camylin, Calen blames him for Rist's capture, and a split forms between the two young men. That night, the dragon egg hatches for Calen, revealing a small white-scaled dragon whose consciousness and soul are indelibly intertwined to Calen's.

Back in The Glade, Farda Kyrana learns of Ella's existence from Fritz Netly, despite Inquistor Rendall insisting that Calen's entire family was dead. Farda sends soldiers to both Gisa and Falstide in search of Ella and also sends Fritz along with the soldiers.

When Calen and the others reach the city of Midhaven, they learn that the empire has set up a blockade around the city of Belduar, which forces them to change their plans and instead travel through a mountain pass at the edge of the Darkwood. On the way, Calen learns that due to his connection with the dragon he has the ability to touch the Spark. This is also when he learns his first words of the Old Tongue and decides on the dragon's name: **Valerys** – Ice.

When in the Darkwood, the group are set upon by Uraks. During the fight, Calen draws heavily from the Spark and almost kills himself, but is saved by Therin and the group are rescued by a patrol of Elven rangers. After the rescue, the Elven captain, Thalanil, fails to convince Aeson to seek refuge in the elven city of Aravell – a secret city at the heart of the Darkwood that has been hidden from the world since The Fall. Instead, five elven rangers – **Ellisar**, **Gaeleron**, **Vaeril**, **Alea**, and **Lyrei** – swear oaths to protect Calen with their lives.

On the journey through the mountain pass, Therin reveals to Calen that Aeson was once a Draleid and that his dragon, Lyara, was hunted down and killed by the empire. With Lyara's death, Aeson is now known as **Rakina** – 'one who is broken', or to the elves, 'one who survived.'

While Calen and his group travel along the mountain pass, Ella and Rhett are stopped by empire soldiers along the merchant's road to Gisa. When the soldiers learn Ella's name, a fight breaks out and Rhett is killed. Ella only survives when **Faenir** – the wolfpine that her family raised – appears and kills the last two soldiers.

In the mountain pass, exhausted from the constant training he is being put through by Aeson and Therin, Calen is visited by the Fade, who discovers that the dragon egg has now hatched. With the knowledge that the Fade now knows the egg has hatched, Aeson pushes the group even harder to reach Belduar.

Thousands of miles away, in the embassy for the **Circle of Magii** in Al'Nasla, Rist awakens in a room to be greeted by a mysterious man by the name of **Brother Garramon**, who proceeds to tell Rist that he is in fact a fledgeling mage, and has the power to touch the Spark.

Upon arriving at Belduar, Calen and his group are greeted by **King Arthur Bryne** and his close friend and advisor, **Lord Ihvon Arnell**. Soon, Calen, along with Asius, Arthur, and Aeson, is brought to the **Durakdur** – one of the four kingdoms of the **Dwarven Freehold** – to speak to the dwarven rulers: **Queen Kira of Durakdur, Queen Elenya of Ozryn, King Hoffnar of Volkur**, and **Queen Pulroan of Azmar**. Calen, Asius, Aeson, and Arthur journey through an intricate tunnel network to Durakdur on a dwarven machine known as a **Wind Runner**, that is piloted by a skilled navigator called **Falmin Tain**.

After the meeting with the dwarven rulers – which ended in a heated shouting match between Calen and Queen Kira – assassins attack Durakdur and attempt to kill Calen, Aeson, Asius, and the dwarven rulers. When the attack is thwarted, Calen, Asius, and Aeson race to Belduar to ensure the safety of Arthur Bryne. Before they board the Wind Runner, Queen Kira arrives with a small army of her Queensguard and travels with Calen and the others to Belduar.

While Calen and the others journey through the mountain, Ihvon Arnell opens the entrance to the mountain pass and allows the Fade, along with a force of imperial soldiers, into the city of Belduar. Upon realising that the Fade had used the memories of his dead wife and child to manipulate him, Ihvon has a change of heart and realises that he has made a terrible decision and sounds the city bells to warn of the attack.

By the time Calen and the others arrive in Belduar, the city is already under attack. Many of the **Bolt Throwers** – enormous crossbows that have long protected Belduar from the Dragonguard – are in flames and the streets are flooded with imperial soldiers. They fight their way through the city, finding Ellisar, Dann, and Therin along the way.

When they finally reach the great hall, they find that the Fade has killed Arthur and holds Arthur's son, **Daymon**, captive. In the fight that ensues, Ellisar is killed and Dann is badly wounded, before Valerys finds his fire and burns the Fade from the world. In the aftermath of the battle, Daymon is crowned king of Belduar.

However, the victory is short lived as **Tarmon Hoard** – the new Lord Captain of the Kingsguard – informs Daymon that the imperial forces that had been holding the blockade are now marching towards Belduar, and the Dragonguard are with them.

In the city of Gisa, Ella and another survivor of the attack on the merchant's road, **Shirea**, mourn over those they lost, finally deciding to continue on to the North using the two tickets that Tanner had purchased for Rhett and Ella. After initially running into trouble bringing Faenir aboard the ship at Gisa, Ella is helped by an unknown stranger – Farda.

Contents

N
W
E
S
Valacia
Antigan Ocean
Dracaldryr
Azmar
Durakdur
Beldvar
Midhaven
Milltown
Wolfpine Ridge
Camylin
Olm Forest
Erith
Pirn
Stormwatch
Skyfell
Ironcreek
Lostwren
VALTARA
Myrefall
Marin Mount
Arthyn Plair
Aeling
Oberwall
VARSUND
Torebon
Ballmar
Aonar
Aonan Wood
Longwood
Orilon
Vaer Leon
Bay of Light
Arisfall
Longforge
Narvona
Ardan
EPH

Sea of Stone
catagan
Kolmir
fort harken
Merchant's Reach
Dead Rock's Hold
highpass
Khergan
Lightning Coast
Elkenrim
Steeple
Berona
Greenhills
holm
Gildor
Bromis
Ravensgate
MAR DORUL
Arginwatch
Easterlock
copperstille
The Burnt Lands
LYNARION
The Darkwood
Kingspass
Argonan Marshes
falstide
peargall
Baylomon
Driftstone
Aylia
narrith
Heart Stead
Stonehelm
Veloran Ocean
Cardend
tower of Ilragorn
lensa
Hirane
ARKALEN
Aerilon
yarrin
Karvog
Seaside
The Stormwood
Bayfort
Land's End

CHAPTER ONE

THE WALLS

Belduar - Winter, Year 3080 After Doom

need to stop the bleeding.

Calen dropped to his knees. His heart pounded as he pushed the dwarf up against the hard stone of the battlements. The sword had come through on the left side of the dwarf's stomach, just where the plate gave way to the chain mail. Calen took the dwarf's hand and pushed it up against the wound, blood streaming through his fingers.

"I need you to keep pressure on it. Can you hear me? Put pressure on it!"

The dwarf gave a weary nod. His eyes were glazed over, and his breathing was shallow.

He's losing blood too fast.

"Nock arrows!"

Calen heard Tarmon Hoard's voice, as the Lord Captain of the Kingsguard bellowed into the night. He stood about a hundred feet off on Calen's right, King Daymon beside him in full plate armour. The new king had insisted on being at the front.

It had taken the imperial forces five days to reach the city. The defenders of Belduar had managed to stop the empire's advances at the third wall of the Outer City. Two well executed tactical retreats had minimised the loss of life as the Belduaran forces abandoned the first and second walls. There was now only one more wall between them and the Inner Circle.

"Ready, hold..."

Calen clapped his hands over his ears as the buildings behind him erupted in a ball of flames. The explosion sent pieces of slate and stone streaming in all directions. He shivered from the chilling screams as debris crushed armour and bone. The imperial mages had started the bombardment after they had taken the first wall. The Belduaran mages and those few mages in the Freehold who had any battle experience had managed to keep the worst of the strikes at bay, but they couldn't stop them all.

"Hold... Loose!"

The *whooshing* sound of arrows sliced through the air as they rained death on the imperial soldiers below. Calen pulled his eyes away from the dwarf, scanning the ramparts. "Vaeril... where are you...?"

The elves hadn't left his side for most of the battle, but Calen had lost them during the last wall assault. He had always been told of the honour and glory of battle. But this was chaos.

Vaeril would be able to heal the wound. But the dwarf didn't have the time to wait.

"It's all right. You'll be all right."

Calen reached out to the Spark. He felt the strands wrapping around each other, twisting and turning as they moved, resonating energy. The warmth of Fire called out to him. He pulled on it, drawing the threads inward, channelling them into the tip of his blade. He had to cauterise the wound. It would put the dwarf at a higher risk of infection once it blistered, but they could worry about that later. First, he needed to stop the blood loss. That's what his mother had always told him. *Deal with the most urgent problem first; worry about everything else later.*

Calen watched as the tip of his sword glowed an incandescent orange, the steel changing colour as he funnelled the threads of Fire into it. "This is going to hurt..."

The dwarf's eyes showed a moment of lucidity as he realised what was about to happen. He gulped, but gave a short nod. "Do it..."

The sound of more ladders clattering against the outer stone of the wall resonated in Calen's ears. There was a *click* as hooks dug into the stone, fixing the heavy ladders in place. They were preparing the next wall assault. He needed to do this, *now*.

He pulled back the area of the chain mail where the links had been broken by the sword. With a quick nod to the dwarf, Calen pushed the tip of his sword through the exposed area of mail and directly onto the open wound. The acrid smell of seared flesh hit the back of his throat before the sizzling sound touched his ears. The dwarf didn't scream. The muscles in his jaw were clenched, and Calen could see the pain in his eyes, but he didn't scream.

"Your name?" Calen asked, pulling the sword away.

"I am Orin, *Draleid,*" the dwarf said between deep breaths, his face twisted in a grimace.

It didn't come as a surprise to Calen that the dwarf knew who he was. Everyone within the walls knew his face ever since Daymon's coronation.

"Calen." Erik's voice cut through the din of the battle as he clasped his hand onto Calen's shoulder, his face painted with a mixture of dirt and blood. "I was worried we'd lost you on the last ladder assault. Are you all right?"

Calen gave a nod to Orin before standing up. The dwarf let out a sigh as his head rested against the battlements.

"I'm all right. Have you seen any of the others?"

"I haven't seen them since we retreated from the second wall."

Calen sighed. The tactical retreats from the first and second walls had been planned, and they had worked, but many had still died. Nothing could have prepared him for this. The city was consumed in blazing infernos – arrows rained down everywhere he looked, while fireballs tore through the sky, turning stone to smouldering rubble. All those hours spent practising sword forms, and yet it seemed there was nothing but luck that separated the living from the dead.

"Ladders! Ready, brace!"

Calen glanced at Erik, who nodded, gripping his swords and turning towards the battlements.

"Orin, can you stand? I need you to stand." Calen picked up the dwarf's double-sided axe that rested by his feet and pushed it into his hands.

"Aye, Draleid. I will stand with you. May your fires never be extinguished."

"And your blade never dull."

The dwarf gave Calen a weak smile as he dragged himself to his feet, using the shaft of his axe for leverage.

The night's breeze whipped at Calen's face as he looked along the length of the ramparts. To his left and to his right, Belduaran soldiers stood shoulder to shoulder with the dwarves of the Freehold Kingdoms, cutting lines, tipping ladders, and preparing themselves for what was to come. Calen couldn't help but feel a chill run down his neck at the sight of it.

After Kira had come to Belduar's aid during the Fade's attack, Hoffnar, Pulroan, and Elenya had committed to doing the same. Without their help, the city might have already fallen. It may have taken four hundred years, but the dwarves of the Lodhar Freehold had finally left their mountain kingdoms. Calen was sure that in itself would make a fine story for Therin to tell one day.

Calen looked down over the city in front of him, and on to the rolling valleys beyond. The city was in ruins, several sections of the first wall were completely collapsed, and most of the buildings were smouldering piles of rubble. Beyond that, the night was illuminated by the campfires of the empire's army. An endless sea of torches and braziers. It was as though the entirety of the North had been emptied into the valleys below Belduar.

How are we to stand against this?

Calen's moment of inner panic was broken as the imperial soldiers reached the top of their ladders and flooded over onto the walls. As they had done many times that night.

He took a deep breath as a reddish-black helmet rose from the other side of the wall. Waiting until he saw the white of the soldier's eyes, Calen shifted forward, driving his blade through the man's exposed neck. He grimaced as blood sprayed from the wound and spluttered out over the man's lips. Calen watched the soldier's body go limp as he pulled the blade free. It hung there for a moment before collapsing backwards, plummeting to the ground below.

Before Calen could take a breath, another soldier took the man's place, thrusting his sword forward as he crested the wall. Calen jerked backwards, losing his balance as he attempted to avoid the strike. He caught himself, just in time to see Orin bury his axe in the man's chest. The dwarf pulled the soldier, still attached to his axe, up and over the rampart, slamming him into the stone floor. He jammed his foot into the man's neck, using it as leverage to heave his axe free. Without saying a word, the dwarf turned back toward the battlement, swinging his axe in an arc, slicing through the imperial soldiers who were attempting to scale the top of the wall.

Calen felt a warning from Valerys scratch at the back of his mind. He threw himself to the side, slamming his back against the wall, only just avoiding the imperial soldier's lunge.

In a flash of white, the young dragon swooped down from where he had been hanging in the sky. His claws tore through the soldier's armour as if it were made of parchment. Calen felt Valerys's anger as the dragon ripped out the man's throat. It burned in him, clouding his mind. Their anger was one. He shook his head, trying to focus. He needed his mind to be clear. Erik caught his eye, a stiff gaze with a raised eyebrow saying, "You all right?"

Calen gave a short nod in response.

A shiver ran down Calen's spine as the entire city was consumed by an earth-shattering roar from the skies above. He lifted his head just in time to see a river of orange-red flames burning through the sky straight towards him. The screams and shouts of men and dwarves all called out the same thing.

"Dragons!"

A heavy weight slammed into Calen's side. It lifted him off his feet, out of the way of the streaming dragonfire, and brought him crashing down onto the cold stone of the ramparts.

The screams were the first thing he heard. Shrieks of men and dwarves as the dragonfire engulfed them, the flesh melting from their bones. The acidic taste of vomit touched the back of Calen's throat. He could taste it on his tongue and smell it in his nostrils. But he choked it back down, his shoulders trembling.

Calen lifted himself to an upright position, staring out across the ramparts that had held so many souls only moments before. There was nothing left. Just charred, crumpled corpses. The stench of their still-crackling skin hung heavy in the air. The stone was scorched to a charcoal black, and large chunks of the wall had been knocked free from the force of the blast. The dragon roared again, like thunder tearing its way through the sky.

Calen panicked for a moment until he felt Valerys picking at the back of his consciousness. The young dragon was crouched on a nearby rooftop, shuffling from side to side, his eyes fixed on the sky. *Thank the gods.*

"Calen, we need to move. There's another one coming down!"

Another one?

Calen turned his gaze to the sky. Horror peeled through him as three gargantuan shadows soared overhead, their silhouettes outlined by the silver light of the moon above, and the incandescent glow of the burning city below. They were enormous. Each of them easily over a hundred feet long from head to tail. Even as he stared, one of the massive shapes pulled away from the others, twisted with deceptive speed, and plummeted straight for the wall.

"Fall back! To the Keep! Protect the King!" Tarmon Hoard's voice rose above the chaos, deep and strong. *At least the king is still alive.*

Erik turned to Calen, his eyes wide. "Calen?"

"We need to get Orin, we can't…" Calen stumbled over his words as realised where Orin had been standing. Nothing but char and ash remained there now. *May your fires never be extinguished and your blade never dull.*

Erik grabbed Calen by the arm and dragged him to his feet, pushing him along the ramparts towards the stairway to the streets below. "We need to go, *now!*"

Calen stumbled sideways as another soldier with the black lion of Loria emblazoned on his chest leapt up over the wall, swinging his sword in wild sweeps. Calen hesitated, his mind shrouded by the image of all those corpses, their charred, blackened skin crackling and snapping.

Focus.

He brought his sword up in time to block the soldier's swing, directing the momentum towards the open side of the wall that looked down into the yard below. The force of the soldier's swing carried him forward, off balance. Calen shoved him with his elbow, sending the man tumbling over the edge. The soldier's landing was marked not by a crash, but by the silence of his screams.

Calen pushed on. Everything was madness. As the defenders abandoned the walls, the imperial soldiers flooded onto them. An endless sea of red and black.

"We're not going to make it down. There's too many," Erik said, drawing up alongside Calen, resignation in his voice.

Valerys scratched at the back of Calen's mind. He knew what the dragon wanted to do.

No.

There was a defiance, a rumble of disagreement. But Valerys stayed where he was, his body pressed down against the slate roof of a nearby building, surveying the battle. If Valerys had used his fire to clear a path for Calen and Erik, it would have been like lighting a beacon to the empire. Those three dragons overhead would rip him apart like a plaything.

A thought sprang into Calen's mind. He turned to Erik. "Do you trust me?"

"I..." Erik's eyes narrowed. "Why?"

"Yes or no?"

"Yes."

"When we land, back-to-back, all right?" Calen wrapped his arm around Erik's shoulder and reached out to the Spark, drawing on threads of Air. A cool sensation tickled his skin as he pulled the threads into him.

I hope this works.

"When we land—" Erik was cut short as Calen gripped him tighter, dug his heels into the stone, and launched them both off the edge of the wall.

Chapter Two

A New King

Calen grappled with Erik as they fell. He needed to hold on.

"Trust me!" he shouted, the words muffled by the wind as they plummeted through the air.

Calen tried to focus, to stay calm. He held onto the threads of Air, swirling them around himself and Erik. The ground approached at a rapid pace. Calen suddenly questioned his decision.

Please, let this work.

As they drew closer to the yard below, Calen pushed against the ground with the threads of Air. He needed to slow them down. It was working. They were slowing – but not fast enough. He drew deeper, pulling more of the Spark into himself. They were only twenty feet from the ground. He pushed again, slowing them down further. But still *not enough.*

Ten feet.

Five feet.

At the last moment, Calen whirled the threads of air around himself and Erik, swelling them into a sphere. He closed his eyes and, just as they were about to land, he slammed the ball of air into the ground below, trying desperately to break their fall.

They hit the ground with a thud, the sound of cracking stone filling Calen's ears. His knees and back ached, but he was not in enough pain to signify any broken bones. Calen opened his eyes to a cloud of dust and stone shrouding the air. Erik knelt beside him, a sword in one hand, his other hand pressed against the ground. They knelt in a small crater that had not been there before the jump.

"Don't… do that… again," Erik said through short huffs as he lifted himself to his feet.

The sounds of battle drifted through the greyish-brown cloud of dust. The harsh clatter of steel on steel, the wailing screams of dying men, the thunderous explosions of the Lorian mages as they wrought destruction on the city. Footsteps.

A group of imperial soldiers leapt through the shroud of dust, howling battle cries as they charged.

"Back-to-back!" Erik roared, slamming his back into Calen's. "Be patient, wait for an opening."

With that, they were engulfed.

Calen swung his sword upward, blocking a strike from one of the onrushing soldiers before knocking the man to the ground with the flat of his boot. He brought his blade across his body, slicing a path of blood along another man's chest. No matter how many soldiers fell, more simply piled in on top. It wasn't long before Calen's arms were like lead, each stroke of his sword taking more and more energy.

As the cloud of dust around them began to settle, Calen saw the chaos that surrounded them. The dwarves and the Belduarans had formed up in multiple lines at every main street that led into the courtyard, stemming the flow of Lorian soldiers that poured down from the walls and through the now-open gates. Patches of Belduaran soldiers were still scattered throughout the encroaching mass of the Lorian army, fighting tooth and nail to get to their companions. Calen and Erik were stuck in the middle of it all. The realisation set a coil of dread in Calen's stomach.

Trying his best to still the fear that shivered through his veins, Calen parried a side swipe from a Lorian soldier, only to watch the man crumple to the ground as Valerys dropped from the sky, tearing into the man's back. A rumble of satisfaction touched the back of Calen's mind. The dragon's usually shimmering white scales were marred with a mixture of blood and greyish dust, but his lavender eyes pierced through. *Thank you.*

"We need to get to one of those lines." Erik pointed towards a line of Belduaran troops that had blocked off the street that led towards the great bridge. They moved as quickly as the thick of battle would allow. Having Valerys by their side made it easier. Even though he was a tenth the size of the dragons that soared through the sky above the city, the Lorian soldiers still gave him a wide berth. They were not like the people of the South. These people knew dragons. They knew first-hand what they were capable of.

Calen and Erik cut their way through the Lorian soldiers in front of them, pushing towards the Belduaran line, picking up stragglers as they went. Calen couldn't help but turn his head towards the sky every few feet. The three dragons above were taking turns diving towards the city, rivers of flame pouring from their open jaws. The occasional bolts of lightning shot up from different places across the city – mages trying desperately to do something, *anything* to stop the onslaught from above. They didn't stand a chance. Wherever lightning flashed, was bathed in dragonfire seconds later. Once a mage gave away their position, that was it.

The same happened with the Bolt Throwers – those massive crossbows that were fixed atop all the towers in Belduar. They might have made a difference if so many of them had not been destroyed during the Fade's attack. They had been specifically targeted that night. Less than a quarter of the original number remained. It was not enough to fight back.

The fighting was thickest as they approached the Belduaran line. The tide of red and black leather was stemmed by the purple cloaks of the Kingsguard. Calen watched as the men in shimmering plate carved holes through the Lorian soldiers, their resolve never wavering. They were every bit as impressive as they looked. For every man they lost, they took ten with them.

"It's the Draleid!" King Daymon's voice rose over the fog of battle. "Tarmon, get them in here!"

The Lord Captain sat on the back of a massive bay stallion, purple cloak billowing behind him. "Kingsguard. Break rank, bring the Draleid in!"

With that, the solid wall of Kingsguard burst outward, like a raging river escaping a dam. They crashed down on top of the Lorian soldiers, their swords sweeping arcs of blood into the air. For a moment, it seemed as though nothing could stand in their way. But almost as quickly as they had burst through the Lorian mass, they were being cut down, engulfed by the sheer number of imperial soldiers. They didn't stand a chance; they were only breaking rank to give Calen, Valerys, and Erik a chance.

Calen looked to Erik, his mouth a grim line. They needed to take advantage of the Kingsguard's push. They couldn't let those men die in vain. Tightening his grip on the hilt of his sword, Calen pushed forward. Valerys weaved in and out of the combat as they moved, tearing at any Lorian soldiers who left themselves exposed.

Tarmon Hoard himself was on the ground at the front of the line, hurrying Calen through. "Draleid, quick, we can't hold on like this. We need to get back into rank."

The Kingsguard fell in behind them as the Lord Captain shuffled them through, falling back into a solid line with incredible efficiency.

"Calen, Erik. I can't say how happy I am to see you are all right." Daymon dropped from the back of his bay stallion with poise, making his way over towards Calen. Up close, the young king looked mightily impressive. A very different sight from the timid young man Calen had met only recently. His plate armour was polished to a mirror-like finish, with a golden trim along its edges. A regal, purple cloak fluttered at his back, attached to massive, ornate pauldrons on each of his shoulders. The symbol of Belduar – a crossed axe and sword with a lonely mountain in the background – was emblazoned in gold across his breastplate.

Lord Ihvon Arnell, who stood behind the king, gave Calen a short nod of recognition. He was a stark contrast to the man who had seemed awkward in the slim fitting navy doublet Calen had met him in. He looked as though he was born to his armour. The heavy plate that rested on his shoulders seemed to soften the scowl that had been set on his face the past few days. As if the simplicity of battle relieved him of the burdens that came with the royal court.

"As we are you, Your Majesty," Erik said, responding to the king. "Have you seen my father or brother?"

A look of concern crossed Daymon's face. "Last I saw them, they were holding back the Lorians, on the second wall, just before our retreat."

Erik nodded, turning his gaze toward the ground.

Calen grimaced, but stepped forward. "What is the plan, Your Majesty?" It felt strange for him to add the title. Arthur had always waved it away with disdain. But Daymon was not Arthur, and Daymon did not correct him.

"Tarmon, we are to make for the keep, correct?"

"Yes, Your Majesty. The dwarves managed to reconstruct some of the Bolt Throwers that surround the keep, and we have placed our most powerful mages on the walls of the Inner Circle. If we can make it there, we should be able to hold them off. I will leave some of the Kingsguard to cover our retreat."

There was a hesitant look on Daymon's face, but he did not object.

It didn't sit right with Calen, leaving men to die just so a chosen few might be able to live. He made to interject, but was cut short when a deafening roar ripped through the sky above, echoed by two more. Beside him, Valerys shrieked, his eyes tracking the dark night.

The dragons flew low overhead, their scales glistening in the fires of the city, the deep reverberations of their wingbeats shaking the air. A sharp gust of wind followed as the dragons passed, rippling the flames that consumed the surrounding buildings.

"What in the gods…"

"They're heading for the keep!" a voice called out.

Before anybody could respond, all three dragons unleashed devastating torrents of fire down upon the Inner Circle of Belduar, igniting the air like a blazing sun. The sheer power was like nothing Calen had ever seen, and it terrified him to his core. Every hair on his body stood on end, and his heart sank into the pit of his stomach. Even over the din of battle, he could hear the howls and wails as they echoed through the mountain city. The narrow flagstone streets carried the screams of the dying for hundreds of feet before they faded.

A surge of strength filled Calen as a massive bolt from one of the Bolt Throwers sliced through the air and hammered into the side of one of the dragons. The dragon tumbled, shrieking wildly. But Calen's surge of strength was dashed when one of the other dragons spun sharply and engulfed the top of the tower in flames, turning the Bolt Thrower into a charred mess.

The city is lost.

"Your Majesty… I…" A weight seemed to hold Tarmon's throat as the hulk of a man attempted to process what was happening. "We need to make for the Wind Tunnels. We… we need to retreat. I fear the city is lost."

"We are not cowards!" Daymon snapped, shoving his hands into the Lord Captain's chest. He was not as large as Tarmon, but he cut an intimidating figure in his burnished plate. "This city has never been taken. Not in over two thousand years. I will not be the one who sees that change!" The king clenched his jaw, veins pulsed at the side of his head, and there was a touch of crimson in his face. "I will not! I will not spit on my father's grave!" Daymon slipped his fingers into the armholes of Tarmon's armour and pulled the man close. "Do you hear me? I—"

Calen rested his arm on Daymon's shoulder. "Is this what he would have wanted? To watch you, and every soldier in this city, die? To throw your lives away?"

Calen had to focus to keep his emotions in check. Images of his own father flashed through his mind. Images of his life… of his death.

"I…" The king's grip on Tarmon loosened.

"Their lives are more important than your legacy. You are their king. Protect them."

Daymon let go of Tarmon's armour, the colour draining from his face. He nodded at Calen before turning back to the Lord Captain. "Sound the retreat, Lord Captain. We make for the Wind Tunnels… The city is lost."

Chapter Three

Broken

orm up! Hold the line while the evacuation is underway!" Tarmon turned his horse, inspecting the wall of Kingsguard that stood across the entrance to the courtyard. Similar lines had formed at each of the six entrances that led from the main city into the courtyard of the Wind Tunnels. It would force the Lorian soldiers to focus their efforts into narrow passageways, where their numbers would count for less.

"My king. Go now, I will stay with the men. When the last of the main army has retreated down the tunnels, we will follow."

A flash of anger touched Daymon's face but was gone almost as quickly as it had appeared. "No, Tarmon. I will not allow it. You come with me. That is an order."

"I cannot. You are my king. But *they* are my men. I cannot ask them to do something that I am unwilling to do myself."

Daymon clapped his hands down on Tarmon's shoulders, looking him in the eye. "Dammit, Tarmon, don't be a fool! I need you!"

"I will follow you, my king. Once the men are to safety."

Daymon held Tarmon's gaze, his jaw clenched. After what seemed like an eternity, he whispered, just loud enough for Calen to hear, "Promise me you will come back. I can't lose you too."

"My king…"

"Promise me."

"You know I can't do that."

Daymon took his hands off Tarmon's shoulders, their eyes still locked. "Very well, Lord Captain. See to it this line does not break."

"It will not break, my king," Tarmon said as Daymon strode away towards the stone landing that fronted the nearest Wind Tunnel, flanked by ten Kingsguard either side.

Tarmon turned towards Calen. "You go too, Draleid. This is all for nothing if you die."

Calen made to object until he realised the man was right. The empire was here for him. They wanted Belduar crushed, but they were here to kill *him.*

"We will head to the nearest landing, Lord Captain. We will cover your retreat from there." Calen turned on his heels before Tarmon could argue, Valerys and Erik following behind him.

Throngs of archers were stationed along the edge of each of the five landings, the enormous Wind Tunnel openings at their backs. They would be used to cover the retreat of the Kingsguard, no doubt. *Or to slow the enemy down if they broke through the line.*

"Draleid, over here!"

Calen felt a flash of relief when he saw Vaeril standing on the landing nearest to him. As Calen looked to the elf, it was as though a fist closed around his heart. Images of Ellisar flashed through his mind. Images of the blade sweeping through the air. Of Ellisar's lifeless body slumping to the ground. Calen's breath trembled from his lungs. He pushed the thoughts to the back of his mind as he scaled the stairs to the landing.

Vaeril wore the same solemn expression that seemed to take permanent residence on his face.

"It's good to see you," Calen said, extending out his arm as they reached the top of the stairs. Vaeril reciprocated the gesture, wrapping his hand around Calen's forearm.

"As it is you, Draleid. And you Erik, and Valerys." Vaeril's formality showed through, with a slight bow as he spoke. "Erik, your father and brother are on the landing at the other end of the yard."

Calen could sense Erik's relief at the elf's words. "Thank you, Vaeril, that's welcome news."

"The others?" Calen asked, afraid to hear the answer. "Have you seen Alea or Lyrei? Gaeleron? Therin?"

"I have not seen any of them since we were separated."

Calen nodded, dread coiling in his stomach.

"I'm sure they've made it to one of the landings." The look in Erik's eyes didn't match the certainty of his voice, but Calen appreciated the words none the less. At least Dann was safe in Durakdur. He hadn't been too happy about being left behind, but he had been in no shape to fight.

Calen would not have seen Daymon approach were it not for the two rows of Kingsguard that marched on either side of him as he strode across the landing. "Calen, can I have a word?" The king waved his guard away as he spoke.

Calen nodded, moving towards the king. He was not sure if he would ever truly grow accustomed to seeing the crown atop Daymon's head. The young man had seen only two more summers than Calen himself. He was not the cocksure, charismatic monarch Calen had met on his arrival to Belduar. He was not Arthur. A melancholy sank into the back of Calen's mind at the thought of the fallen king. "What do you need, Your Majesty?"

"I need you to promise me something."

Calen didn't respond. He fixed his gaze on Daymon's, waiting for the king to continue. Promises were dangerous. And Calen had a feeling that promises to a king were even more so. He felt Valerys at the back of his mind. The dragon was peering over at them, his lavender eyes focused on Daymon, the frills on the back of his neck standing on end. Valerys did not trust Daymon.

"I need you to promise me that you will keep Tarmon alive. The man is too stubborn to do that himself. But… he and Ihvon are all I have left. I've sent Ihvon down the tunnels already, to coordinate the evacuation from that end. But I need Tarmon alive. I… need you to promise me."

There was a vulnerability in Daymon's eyes as he spoke. In that moment, he was not a king. He was a young man who watched his father die. He was Calen.

"I promise." Calen regretted the words as soon as they left his lips. But he had no choice. He understood Daymon. He felt his pain, viscerally.

"Thank you. These archers will stay with you until the last. They will help cover Tarmon's retreat. I'm sorry I cannot stay."

"Nonsense. Your people need their king."

There was a grim look on Daymon's face that told Calen he wasn't lying. He would rather stand there and fight than face the fallout afterwards. Calen thought he would probably feel the same if he were in Daymon's position.

"Captain Konar?"

"Yes, my king," replied a soldier who had suddenly appeared beside the two men.

"The command is yours. Calen, I will see you on the other side."

Calen nodded as the king walked off towards the massive Wind Runner that sat docked in the entrance to the Wind Tunnel.

"Move, move. Make way for the next Wind Runner," Ihvon shouted. He saw the looks on the soldiers' faces as they passed. Desolation. He was fighting it off himself. The battle had been going well… until the dragons appeared. What could they have done in the face of such raw power?

He had watched his men burn alive. Roasted like crabs in their shells of armour. The acrid stench of burning flesh clung to his nostrils, turning his stomach.

Even of the ones who had made it to 'safety', at least half carried some form of injury. Those who could walk on their own hobbled and stumbled their way down the steps that led from the platform. Others were missing limbs entirely, only stumps of knotted flesh where the wound had been cauterised by the medics on the field who had run out of antiseptic salve; they would probably still die, eventually.

Two men passed by carrying a dwarf on a stretcher made of wood and tarp. Even if Ihvon had not looked at the dwarf, her wails would have made Ihvon's skin crawl. She was a mess of charred skin covered in welts and blisters. The dwarf's armour around her chest had melted into her skin, crackling and bubbling as she was carried down the steps. Ihvon had to swallow the vomit that hit the back of his throat.

He had seen battle. He had fought the Uraks many a time. They were beasts of unnatural strength, capable of unfathomable ferocity and cruelty. But he had never seen the aftermath of dragonfire.

A weightlessness settled in his stomach as he took in the scene around him. If he had not been so weak, none of this would have happened. The Bolt Throwers would not have been sabotaged by that Fade. These men would not be dying… Arthur would still be alive.

"Forgive me, old friend…"

Calen watched as the Wind Runner launched down the tunnel.

"That's the last of them," Captain Konar, the man Daymon had called over before he left, said before turning to one of his soldiers. "Signal the retreat!"

The soldier pulled an ornate horn that was strung around his neck, up to his lips. He drew air into his lungs and released a deep bellow that resonated throughout the courtyard.

Nodding to Calen, Captain Konar moved over to the line of archers that stood at the edge of the landing. "Archers, ready!"

Calen looked along the other landings where more horns answered Captain Konar's call. Rows of archers stood on each landing, pulling arrows from their quivers, waiting to cover the retreat of the Kingsguard that had been holding back the tide of Lorian soldiers.

Calen watched as the Kingsguard at each entrance fell back. They were slow and methodical. They allowed the Lorian soldiers to crash off their shields as they inched backward, never giving too much ground at any one time. Their discipline in the face of chaos was incredible. Each group moved as a cohesive unit, never missing a step. But it was only a matter of time before they reached the end of the closed street and were backed fully into the open courtyard. Once that happened, the Lorian soldiers would flood in and swarm them.

So many of them will die. I need to do something.

Calen felt a rumble of recognition from Valerys, sheer defiance radiating from the dragon's mind as he stepped up beside Calen. Valerys's lips pulled back and his wings fanned out, a snarl forming in his throat.

The Kingsguard had reached the open courtyard; their slow, precise retreat was over. They were going to have to break and run now. He couldn't let them die.

"Erik, Vaeril. I need you to stay here."

"What? What are you—"

Without waiting for Erik to finish, Calen pushed past his companion and through the row of archers, bounding from the edge of the landing. He drew on threads of Air, as he had when he had thrown himself and Erik from the wall, and used them to soften his descent, feeling the stone crack under his feet. Valerys's wings beat ferociously as the dragon lifted himself from the landing. They would have to be quick.

The Kingsguard had broken at each of the entrances and now ran at full speed toward the Wind Tunnels, the Lorian soldiers flooding in after them. Calen heard breathing to his left. He turned to see Vaeril matching him stride for stride as they sprinted across the courtyard. The elf simply nodded and fixed his gaze ahead; there wasn't time to argue. They stopped in the centre of the courtyard. Calen wasn't sure if he would have the strength to do it from that distance. But he needed to be able to reach all the entrances. He couldn't leave any of them standing. "I'm going to bring the buildings down over the entrances."

Vaeril nodded. "I'll take the three on the right."

"Are you sure you can?"

"I am not just a healer, Draleid. I will take the ones on the right. Are *you* sure that you can take the ones on the left?"

Calen gave a shaky nod. He wasn't sure. He had never done anything like it before. Though, something had changed after the battle with the Fade. Ever since Valerys had discovered his fire, Calen felt… stronger. He closed his eyes. Reaching out to the Spark, he let his mind fade to an empty blackness, only illuminated by the interlaced strands of pulsing light that twisted and turned in on each other in the shape of a floating sphere.

He drew on threads of Earth, pulling them inward. They felt solid, rough, as though he were dragging chains of wrought iron through his mind. He would need them to break the stone. Then he pulled at threads of Air. Their cool touch tickled the edge of his consciousness, rippling through his body. He would need them to control the debris, to shift the breaking stone.

The energy of the Spark coursed through him, pulsating through his veins.

Don't take too much.

Opening his eyes, Calen pulled at the threads of Earth and Air, dragging them deeper into himself.

Only what you need.

His body thrummed with the power of the Spark. He felt it in his bones. Tasted it on his tongue. Heard it in every crevice of his mind. More than anything else, he was completely and utterly aware that it might destroy him; but he had no choice.

"Now!" Calen slowed his breathing as he weaved the threads of Earth through the buildings that flanked each of the first three entrances. *Please work.*

He started with the entrance farthest to the left. The one he had come through; the one where Tarmon Hoard had been. He needed to be careful. He couldn't try to shatter every stone; that might kill him. Instead, he focused on those along the bottom of the buildings, along the outer facing walls, the ones that kept the buildings upright. That still might kill him, but he had to try. He couldn't let all those men die.

As delicately as he could, Calen pushed the threads of Earth through every crack and crevice of the stone supports.

The warmth of the Spark burrowed its way into him, caressing the edges of his consciousness, tempting him to take more, to crush the buildings and drag them to the ground. Valerys roared in the back of his mind, urging him on. He felt the anger in the dragon, the will to crush all those who would harm his friends, his family. Calen blocked it out. *No.*

Valerys rumbled in disagreement, a fire burning inside the dragon.

As the buildings began to give way, Calen pushed with the threads of Air, forcing their walls to collapse inward, onto the street packed with Lorian soldiers. Once he felt the walls start to fall past the halfway point, he let go. Within seconds, the strength leeched from his body. His legs trembled under the weight of his own bones, and his lungs struggled to drag in air. He watched as giant blocks of stone plummeted down into the packed entrance, crushing the Lorian soldiers. A landslide of crashing stone muffled their screams and howls. Every soldier caught in those streets would be crushed or buried alive in rubble. Calen felt a sudden pang of anguish. *So many dead. What have I done?*

He pushed those thoughts down, dragging them into a dark corner of his mind where they could not reach him. Two more entrances still stood; he could not stop now. With a glance to his right, he saw that Vaeril had succeeded in bringing down his first entrance and had moved onto his second, the howls of dying men muffled by the thunderous crashing of stone.

Steadying himself as much as he could, Calen moved his attention to the second entrance. Some of the empire soldiers had already come through and out into the courtyard, but most of them had not yet pushed through the swell of bodies. He took a deep breath and, once more, wove the threads of Earth through the stone, weakening it everywhere he could, being careful not to draw too much. As the stone began to crumble, he pushed with Air. What had started as a warmth at the edges of his mind was now a searing pain that burned through his body, forcing him to drop down to one knee as the strength in his legs gave way. *I can't stop now. Just one more.*

As the crumbling buildings fell on the second entrance, Calen once again reached for the Spark. As the drain pulled at him, a wave of fear flooded into his mind from Valerys's, urging him to stop. *I must. They'll all die if I don't.*

Ignoring the pain that rippled through him, Calen kept pushing. He grasped at the threads of Earth, but they seemed to hang just out of reach. Again, he pulled at them only to feel the Spark burn through him, urging him onwards but giving him nothing in return. He threw his gaze towards the third entrance. More and more of the Lorian soldiers rushed through, swarming over the retreating Kingsguard, tearing into them as they ran.

"I have to..." Calen bit down on the inside of his cheeks with such force the coppery taste of blood coated his tongue. The pain had become so excruciating he thought it might steal his consciousness from him. It seared across his skin, as though his body stood bare before a blazing fire.

"Draleid. No, stop!" Vaeril clasped his arms around Calen, dragging him to his feet and causing him to involuntarily let go of the Spark. "You cannot. We need to run."

"I'm not letting them die." Calen shook his head. His vision had grown blurry, clouded by agony. "I—"

"They are already dead, and we need you to live."

Calen looked past Vaeril. The empire soldiers were now in full charge through the third entrance, carving a path through the retreating Belduarans.

"Go." Vaeril turned Calen and pushed him back towards the landing. Calen very nearly went crashing straight to the ground as he commanded his legs to obey him. He had released his hold on the Spark, but the pain subsided slowly, and the energy was already sapped from his bones. "I said go, Draleid!"

Calen looked over his shoulder, a horrific knot twisting in his chest as he watched the advancing Lorians cut down the Kingsguard as though they were blades of grass in a field. *I should have saved them...*

"Back to the Wind Runner!" Vaeril shouted. The elf tucked his arm under Calen's shoulder and pushed him onward towards the stone landing that fronted the Wind Tunnel. The drain from the Spark exhausted the little energy he had left. But he pushed through. He had been precise. Yet still, it sapped him. He had never drawn so heavily before; his legs felt as though they were made of lead, and his veins burned as though filled with molten fire.

But he still had not been able to save them.

"Almost there," Vaeril grunted, half carrying, half dragging Calen towards the landing.

Rage burned through Calen as they reached the foot of the steps that led to the landing. It wasn't his own, but at the same time, it was, and with it came a surge of energy that jolted him upright. An enormous pressure began to build at the back of his mind, flooding over from Valerys, the thrum of it resonating through him. The last time he had felt that pressure was in the great hall with the Fade.

A red-faced Erik greeted Calen and Vaeril as they reached the top of the steps. "Calen! What in the void was that? You can't just—" Erik stopped mid-sentence, reaching to catch Calen as he stumbled. "What's wrong? Are you all right?"

"I'll be fine. I'm just…" he panted, steadying himself. "That… took a lot out of me."

"Easy," Erik said, reaching his hand around Calen's shoulder, propping him up.

The pressure continued to build at the back of Calen's mind as Valerys circled the courtyard, just below the ceiling of rock, drawing parallel with the far wall. The pressure yielded only to a brief moment of clarity before Valerys opened his jaws. The fire that poured forth paled in comparison to the utter devastation the larger dragons had wrought throughout the city. But neither was it a trickling flame.

The dragon soared through the air, raining orange-red dragonfire down on the Lorian soldiers below. Men and women howled as the flames consumed them, melting steel, scorching leather, stripping skin from bones. The harrowing shrieks sent shivers rippling over Calen's skin. Even the soldiers who were not caught in the flames scattered in all directions, abandoning their chase, scrambling to escape their companions' fate.

The distraction did not last long, though. As soon as Valerys had stopped and turned back towards the landing, the soldiers began to regroup. But the momentary reprieve had given the Kingsguard the time they needed. They were already at the steps.

"Keep moving!" Erik shouted as soon as the Kingsguard reached the top of the landing, ushering them onward to the Wind Runner.

With a nod to Calen, Captain Konar signalled for the archers to cease firing and join the retreat.

Calen let go of Erik's support just as Valerys alighted on the landing in front of them. He dropped to one knee, placing his hands on either side of the dragon's head, his forehead touching Valerys's. A feeling of warmth washed over the back of his consciousness. "Draleid n'aldryr."

Calen hadn't intended to speak the words, but they felt right.

A rumble emanated from the dragon's throat in response.

"Navigator, are we ready to go?" Calen called out as Erik helped him back to his feet.

The Lorian soldiers were over halfway across the yard now.

"Aye, Draleid," came a familiar voice from aboard the Wind Runner, "and it's good t' see you again, too."

Calen turned to see the gangly form of Falmin Tain standing at the edge of the Wind Runner, one hand resting on the rope bridge that connected the Wind Runner platform to the stone landing.

"Falmin, it's good to see you." Calen let a soft smile touch his mouth at the sight of a friendly face, but he didn't let it linger for long. "We need to go. *Now.*"

"I'm ready when you are," the navigator said, giving him a wink before dragging his odd copper-sided glasses down over his eyes and returning to the front of the machine.

There was a *whoosh* as an arrow flew past Calen's head, cracking off the stone wall behind him. It was followed by several more, each one closer than the last. Some of the Lorian soldiers had stopped mid-chase and had drawn their bows.

Erik grabbed Calen by the shoulders and pushed him towards the rope bridge as Valerys lifted himself into the air and swooped past them towards the Wind Runner.

It was only about halfway across the bridge that it struck Calen. *Tarmon.*

"Erik, is Tarmon on board? Did he make it?"

"I didn't see him, Calen."

As if saying the man's name had summoned him, the broad frame of Tarmon Hoard came crashing up the steps of the landing.

"Go! Go! Go!" Tarmon bellowed as he dashed across the stone. A look of shock spread across the man's face as an arrow burst through his lower abdomen, sending him crashing to the ground in a heap. "Go!" he shouted again, lifting his head, his hands wrapped around the shaft of the arrow.

More arrows continued to slice through the air, clinking off stone, their shafts snapping. One or two caught the edges of Tarmon's pauldrons, sliding at an angle and bouncing off harmlessly.

Calen made to run back across the bridge towards Tarmon, but Erik held onto him. "Calen, we can't—"

"I'm not leaving here without him, Erik." Calen held Erik's gaze for only a fraction of a second before Erik started pushing him back along the bridge.

The Lorian soldiers crested the top of the steps just as Calen and Erik reached Tarmon. They both clasped their hands in the loops of Tarmon's armour, heaving him to his feet and dragging him towards the Wind Runner.

"You need to run!" Calen yelled without stopping, his own legs close to collapse. He glanced over his shoulder. *We're not going to make it.*

Some of the Lorian soldiers who had made it to the landing dropped to their knees and drew their bows. Calen kept moving, kept pushing Tarmon onward. But in the back of his mind, he waited for the void.

As he looked up, Calen saw Falmin dashing across the rope bridge. Vaeril was at his side, and Valerys swooped through the air towards them.

"Get down!" the navigator yelled, his hand outstretched. Calen felt that tickle at the back of his mind. He could see Falmin drawing from the Spark. He didn't have time to speak. He held onto Tarmon's armour and dragged the three of them to ground. They hit the stone just in time to avoid the vicious blast of Air that left Falmin's outstretched hand and swept across the landing. It crashed into the Lorian archers, lifting them off their feet, throwing them up into the air.

Hands clamped down on Calen's shoulders, pulling him to his feet. The rope bridge shook beneath him. Then, he felt the cold base of the *Crested Wave* as he dropped to his knees. A collective groan came from the mass of bodies squeezed onto the Wind Runner as Valerys crashed onto the platform beside Calen, not having enough time for a graceful landing. Barely a moment had passed before the vibrations rattled through Calen's bones.

"Hold on t' somethin'!" Falmin yelled, as the giant machine lurched into life and launched down the tunnel.

With more effort than he would have liked, Calen dragged himself to his feet. The *Crested Wave* was filled to the brim. Everywhere he turned his gaze, men and dwarves leaned on each other for support, their armour battered and stained crimson, their eyes glazed over. The soldiers heaved to and fro as the great machine catapulted through the never-ending system of tunnels beneath the Lodhar Mountains.

Calen watched for a moment as Vaeril removed the arrow from Tarmon's stomach.

"Very unlucky," the elf said, examining the wound. "More times than not, your armour would have taken that hit."

Calen felt the elf drawing from the Spark. A complex mix of threads: Fire, Water, Air, Earth, and Spirit. It pained his mind to even attempt to follow what the elf was doing.

Turning, he pushed his way through the densely packed bodies of exhausted soldiers. He stopped behind Falmin, resting his hand on the navigator's shoulder. "Thank you."

Falmin only grunted in response, stumbling to the left.

What's wrong with him?

Panic shot through Calen as Falmin's knees gave way beneath him, and he fell backwards into Calen's arms.

Dread coiled in Calen's stomach when his eyes fell on the arrow that jutted out through the front of Falmin's stomach, just below his ribs. He didn't have long to let the situation sink in as the Wind Runner lurched, its rings creaking, its momentum slowing. Calen's hair blew back over his face as the rushing wind pierced the protective shell that Falmin had been holding around the *Crested Wave*.

Without thinking, Calen stood up and reached out for the Spark. He felt Valerys's panic in the back of his mind as he drew threads of Air into himself. He needed to keep the machine going, or they would all die. His body groaned as he pulled at the Spark. He was already too weak, even with Valerys willing him on. But he had no choice.

He funnelled threads of Air into the Wind Runner, pushing it forward, shrouding it in a sphere of air. The rings began to spin at full speed once more. They were moving, but Calen had no idea where he was or where he needed to go. With every fork in the tunnel, he flipped a coin in his mind. Left. Then right. Left again.

He didn't know how much longer he could keep it up. It was taking all his focus simply not to crash.

He saw an opening ahead. *I don't know where that is. But it will have to do.*

"How do I slow this thing down?" he whispered, panic once again setting in. He pulled back, reversing his threads of Air, pushing against the flow. The giant machine heaved in response, a high-pitched creaking sound reverberating through the tunnel. It wasn't enough. They weren't slowing down fast enough.

"Hold on to something!"

Chapter Four

A Wolf Among Sheep

Ella's grip tightened on the rough rail that ran along the outer edge of the ship, the splintered wood grating against her hand. She closed her eyes and drew a slow breath in, filling her lungs with the salty morning air. The waves of the Antigan Ocean crashed off the ship's hull while the deckhands scuttled about, mopping the decks, checking the ropes, and carrying out whatever other tasks deckhands carried out. Ella had never been on a ship before, and the day-to-day activities of the vessel's crew were at the bottom of her current priorities.

She held her breath for a moment, allowing her chest to swell before exhaling slowly. As she inhaled again, the ship jerked forward, throwing her off balance and spraying a fine mist of sea water over her face. The cool touch of the misted water did little to help her current state. Her stomach lurched as it had done multiple times a day, every day, for the past five days.

"Gods dammit!" she muttered to herself as she bent at the waist, dipping her head down while her hands still clung to the banister. She inhaled slowly once more. *I hate ships.*

Ella heard the purposeful clip of footsteps against the wooden decking.

"Are you feeling unwell?"

She opened her eyes, turning her head to look at her new companion. She knew who it was already, of course. His words were as refined as every other passenger on this ship of ladies and lords – every passenger with the exception of her and Shirea; they stuck out like sore thumbs – but his voice had an added edge to it.

"I'm fine. I'm just not used to the sea is all." Ella drew herself to her full height, desperately trying not to let the discomfort in her stomach show on her face. She still wasn't sure how she felt about the man. He was the reason they had managed to even get on the ship in the first place, though they hadn't spoken since he had offered her and Shirea a place in his cabin. The last place Ella wanted to be was in the same cabin as a Lorian soldier. And if there was one thing Ella knew, it was that this man held absolutely no true concern for her wellbeing.

"I suppose your friend is feeling even worse. I don't think I have seen her above deck since we set sail." The cold didn't seem to bother him as he stood there in his shirtsleeves, his arms folded across the ship's rail, staring out over the crashing waves.

"She's been busy. We have a lot of planning to do before we get to Antiquar, and she likes to be prepared."

"I see," the man said, his bottom lip folding over his top one. "Farda Kyrana."

"Excuse me?"

"Farda Kyrana is my name. Typically, you would now respond with your own." Farda raised a curious eyebrow, holding Ella's gaze.

Suddenly, Ella's throat felt as dry as cotton. She couldn't use her own name, of that much she was certain. It wasn't safe. Farda was an empire soldier, and a high up one at that. Why else would the sailor's attitude have changed so quickly at the port in Gisa? She needed to be careful. The last time she told somebody her full name, her entire life changed. *I still don't know why. I need to know why.*

"Um... Ella Fjorn."

"Ella Fjorn. Are you sure?"

Ella's pulse quickened, and a sickly feeling set in her stomach. Did he know who she was? "I... of course I'm sure," she said, finding her composure. "What kind of question is that?"

To Ella's surprise, the man simply laughed and turned his head back out to the ocean. "I am only teasing you. You seemed as though you were uncertain. What business have you in Antiquar, Ella Fjorn?"

"I have family in Berona," she lied. "My uncle is in the city guard."

"Oh, he is? What is his name? Perhaps I know him."

Gods dammit. Why did I have to say that?

"Ta... Tanner." Ella stumbled over the words. Why had she given Tanner's real name?

Farda raised an eyebrow in surprise. "Tanner Fjorn?" The man's gaze lingered on her for a moment, as if he was going to challenge her. Finally, he shook his head, turning his eyes back out towards the ocean. "I wasn't aware Tanner had family in the South."

Ella froze. *He knows Tanner.*

An awkward silence descended between them as Ella pretended not to hear Farda, relief washing over her when she felt something nuzzling into her hip. *Just in time.* She reached down and ran her fingers through the coarse, greyish-white fur at the back of Faenir's neck, receiving a satisfied grumble in return. How such a massive wolfpine was able to sneak up on her, she would never know, but she was not going to complain.

Even Ella was surprised when Faenir's grumble turned to a deep growl as the wolfpine stepped between her and Farda. To Farda's credit, he didn't so much as flinch.

"I'm sorry," Ella said, pulling Faenir back. "He can be protective. It's probably time I feed him. Please, excuse me."

"Not at all," Farda replied, lifting his arms from the rail, standing up straight. He tilted his head, his eyes fixed on Faenir, which only made the wolfpine's growl grow deeper. "That is a trait to be admired."

Waiting until the girl had gone, Farda rested his hands against the rail of the ship. He winced as the glare from the morning sun reflected off the water's surface, right into his eyes. The girl was interesting. There was a steeliness in her he had not anticipated. And she knew Tanner; the High Captain of the Beronan guard. She was obviously not his family – which raised more questions – but she did not speak the name by chance. Tanner was a stubborn man, though Farda did have respect for him. He was a man who kept his word; those were few and far between.

At least the wolf explained what happened to the soldiers he had sent to watch over the merchant's road. Yet another thing he had not anticipated. If he had to kill the beast and take her captive, he would, but that was not his preferred way. He would get a lot more from her if he were able to court her trust. Besides, a prisoner was easier to transport when they walked into their prison of their own volition. The other girl, however… He would have to find a way to deal with her. She would only get in the way.

Farda's loose cotton shirt rippled in the breeze as he walked along the length of the main deck. Part of him felt naked without his armour and his cloak, but another part of him wished he would never have to wear them again.

He sighed as he looked out across the ship. It was enormous; over two hundred feet in length, with three massive masts that jutted upward into the sky. The vessel was an impressive piece of engineering. At the speed it was going, they would be in Antiquar by sunrise the next morning.

Ella pushed open the door to the cabin, recoiling as the smell of sweat and day-old sick hit the back of her throat. The sun at her back shone through the doorway, carving a wedge of light through the dimly lit room, illuminating the damp wooden floor and stained bedsheets of the dilapidated cabin. It had seemed the cost of the tickets from Gisa to Antiquar had more to do with the journey itself than it did any luxury or comfort that might be associated with it.

Faenir let out a whine, brushing up against Ella's hip as he stepped into the room. Closing the door behind her, Ella reached down and scratched the side of Faenir's jaw. "It's all right, boy."

"Ella?" Shirea's voice was rough, as if her throat had been rubbed with cotton. "Is that you?"

"It's me. How are you feeling?"

A sliver of light slipped through the closed curtain by Shirea's cot, highlighting the dark rings under the woman's sunken, bloodshot eyes. Shirea sat in the same place Ella had left her in earlier that morning: cross-legged in the bed, an iron braced wooden bucket in her lap. "I've been better."

Ella sat on the edge of the cot, snatching the waterskin that sat on the floor by Shirea's shoes. Unscrewing the lid, she pressed the nozzle to the woman's lips. "You need to keep drinking."

"It just keeps coming back up," Shirea said, waving the waterskin away.

"Which is precisely why you need to keep drinking."

Ella pushed the waterskin into Shirea's hands before lifting the wooden bucket from between the woman's legs and laying it on the ground. Vomit sloshed around in the bucket as she set it down, releasing the pungent aroma of half-digested food with renewed vigour. The combination of the sound and the smell turned Ella's stomach, and it was all she could do not to retch.

Shirea held the waterskin to her chest, but she didn't drink. Instead, she lifted her head and met Ella's gaze. Her voice was soft, barely a whisper. "How do you do it?"

"How do I do what?" Ella asked, pulling her eyes from Shirea's. Ella knew, of course, what the woman meant. But she wasn't sure her heart wouldn't shatter if she spoke about Rhett, if she said his name aloud. She would have taken a broken bone rather than feel the relentless pain that burned its way through her soul. As if sensing Ella's sorrow, Faenir sat down beside her, resting his head across her lap. Reaching down, Ella ran her hands through the fur on the back of the wolfpine's neck, receiving a low grumble in return. When Shirea did not answer, Ella let out a soft sigh. "I pull myself out of bed each day because it is the only thing I can do. Every breath hurts, but I take it anyway. Rhett..." Ella had to pause for a moment as Rhett's name lingered on her tongue. "Rhett is gone."

Ella's voice caught in her throat, and she pulled Faenir's head in tighter to her lap. "He is gone, but that does not mean I will not carry him with me for the rest of my life. When my brother, Haem, was taken from us, my mother told me and Calen that 'we honour the dead not by how we mourn their death, but by how we live on despite it.'"

"I like that," Shirea said, the weakest of smiles touching the edges of her mouth. A tear ran down the woman's cheek as she fidgeted with the nozzle of the waterskin. "Will it ever stop hurting, though?"

"I don't think so," Ella said, feeling a tear roll down her own cheek. There was no point in lying.

"Ella?"

"Yes?"

"Will you lie down with me? Just for a little while."

Ella might not have known Shirea for very long, but they were kin of a sort. Bonded by grief. "Of course."

Pale moonlight washed down over the ship as Farda stepped out onto the main deck. It was empty except for a few passengers who meandered about, minding their own business, enjoying the peace of the night. He preferred it that way. He had little to no inclination for small talk and particularly not with wealthy traders or nobles who spoke of nothing but peasants and coin.

The waters had calmed just before sunset, and now all he could hear was the swash of the waves as they rippled against the hull of the ship. It was a calming, if repetitive, sound.

Farda reached into his coat pocket, producing a small briar wood pipe and a circular tin of Greenhills tabbac. Opening the tin, he added three pinches into the chamber of the pipe, pushing each down with his index finger, adding a little more pressure each time. Once he was satisfied, he returned the tin. He had only taken a liking to tabbac in the last century, and particularly that grown in Greenhills; the dry heat so close to the Burnt Lands seemed to produce a stronger flavour.

Drawing in a thin thread of Fire, Farda created an ember in the chamber. Plumes of smoke drifted up and around his face, fading into the night as he took three long puffs of the pipe, pulling the air through to feed the burn. He watched as the incandescent, orange glow spread through the tabbac like the roots of a tree pushed through soil.

Without hesitation, Farda again pushed his finger into the smouldering tabbac. He felt a burning sensation as the orange embers touched his skin. He smelled the sharp scent of charred flesh as it hit the back of his throat. But he felt no pain. He sighed as he pulled his finger back, observing the charred black patches where the embers had burnt his skin.

Four hundred years had passed since he last felt pain. He could feel the irritation of steel as it dug into his skin, the pressure of a boot against his neck. But not pain. There was the ache in his bones that had never left him and no healer seemed capable of relieving. But *true* pain had been stripped from him when Shinyara was killed. Along with many other things.

When you blend something so completely, it is impossible for it to return to what it once was.

Pulling himself from his ponderings, Farda lit the pipe again. He took a large puff, releasing the cloud of smoke in a sigh.

As he approached the rail at the starboard side of the ship, the incessant swash of the waves was interrupted by a soft sobbing. In the dim light provided by the moon, he made out the vague features of a small woman standing against the exterior wall of one of the cabins. Her shoulders shook as she sobbed. He didn't have to see the person's face to know who it was. Despite what Ella had told him, he had lain awake listening to that noise the previous four nights as it echoed through the ship.

"Are you all right?" he said, approaching the woman. He took another puff of his pipe as the sobbing faded into a subdued sniffle.

"Oh," the woman said, rubbing the sleeves of her coat into her eyes, the occasional sniffle betraying her poor attempt at masking her current state. "I… I didn't see you there. You're the man who helped us onto the ship. What has you up at this hour?"

"Couldn't sleep. The pipe usually helps." Farda rested his elbows on the bannister and gazed out over the night-obscured water, the light of the moon adding a silvery glisten to the peaks of the undulating waves. He took another puff from the pipe, letting the smoke linger in his mouth for a moment before releasing. "Farda, is my name. Farda Kyrana."

"It's… it's nice to meet you, Farda. I'm Shirea." The woman moved away from the wall of the cabin as she spoke, joining Farda by the banister. She looked as though she were a wretch on the street in Al'Nasla. Her eyes were raw red, ringed with deep purple hollows, and small droplets of semi-dried blood were caked into the lines where her lips had dried and cracked. The woman had spent the entire trip emptying her stomach and crying herself to sleep. Farda wished he could hold sympathy for her. But *that* ability had been stripped from him, too. *One who is broken.*

"Do you smoke, Shirea?"

"I… I never have. But John did. He loved smoking tabbac. He said it always calmed him down, too." Shirea bit her top lip, moving her teeth side to side as though contemplating. Then she muttered to herself just loud enough for Farda to catch a few words. "How we live on despite it…"

"Excuse me?"

"Oh," Shirea said, shaking her head as though she had been lost in a dream. "Nothing. May I… May I try?"

Farda held the pipe out for Shirea to take, smoke streaming from his nostrils.

Shirea took the pipe in her hands, holding it by the stummel. She gave a slight sniffle before bringing the stem to her mouth and taking an ambitious puff. Within seconds, smoke billowed from her nose and mouth as she coughed and spluttered, bending over double.

"My apologies. I should have said not to inhale. Try again," Farda said, placing a hand on her back.

Shirea coughed again, smoke still wisping from her nostrils. "I'll try," she choked out.

Farda gave her a short nod, trying his best to form his lips into a smile. Her second attempt was better; she still coughed, but she did not choke and splutter like before.

"No, thank you," Farda said when she offered the pipe back to him. "You keep going. It will help calm you."

Shirea's eyes softened at Farda's words, a tentative smile creeping across her face. "Thank you."

As Shirea took another short puff of the pipe, Farda reached into his coat pocket, producing a thick gold coin. On one side was a roaring lion, the symbol of Loria. On the other, a crown. He knew it well. It was as much a piece of him as his eyes and ears. Even without looking, he knew every nick and every dent that marred its surface. He rolled the coin back and forth across his fingers, his gaze fixed on it.

"I've seen you toss that coin before. Why?"

Farda had been lost in his own thoughts. He hadn't noticed Shirea staring. She held the stummel of the pipe in both hands, cupping it, her teeth chattering as the wind rolled over the deck.

"Fate," Farda said as he rested the coin on his thumb and index finger. "Fate is fluid. It changes with every decision that is made. It is utterly out of our hands, and completely within our control at the same time."

Farda flicked the coin into the air.

Shirea looked confused. "I'm not sure what you mean."

Farda watched as her eyes followed the flight of the coin. It produced a metallic ringing noise as it flipped through the air, then gave a light *thump* as it settled into Farda's outstretched palm. He turned his gaze toward the coin. It landed with the image of a roaring lion staring back at him. *So be it.*

Farda moved quickly. He drew on threads of Air, pulling them through him. He closed them around Shirea's throat; that way she couldn't scream. She stumbled against the banister, gasping for air. The pipe dropped to the deck with a crack as Shirea grasped at her throat, desperately trying to pull air into her lungs.

Again, Farda wanted to feel sympathy. He yearned for it. But he felt nothing. He tightened the threads of Air around Shirea's neck, pulling them harder and harder until he heard a crack. Her body went limp. Farda reached out, catching her just before she hit the deck. He lifted her in one motion and tossed her lifeless body over the side of the ship. A splash signalled that she belonged to the ocean.

I do what must be done.

Farda reached down and picked up the pipe from the deck where Shirea had dropped it. He held it in one hand, his fingers cupped around the stummel. With thin threads of Fire, he reignited the tabbac, and took a deep puff. Smoke billowed into the night air as he walked back along the main deck towards his cabin.

Chapter Five

The Depths

Calen felt something nudging him, pushing into his ribs. He groaned as his sensations came rushing back, feeding his body with pain. Everything hurt. A deep rumble emanated from Valery's chest as the young dragon continued to push his snout into Calen's side.

"I'm all right, I'm all right," Calen said, coughing as he opened his eyes and pushed himself to an upright position. The air was so thick with grey dust he could barely see more than a foot in front of his own face. The only light was a soft blueish-green glow that drifted through the dusty haze. Calen quickly dismissed his thought to create a baldír. He didn't have the strength; steering the Wind Runner had sapped the last of his energy.

Reaching up, he grasped his hand around something rough and metallic; using whatever it was as leverage, he pulled himself to his feet. A sudden pain burned just below his ribs. He looked down to see two long gashes had ripped through his leather armour, their edges stained crimson. He shook his head, trying to loose the stiff grogginess clouding his mind and the ringing in his ears.

"Is anybody there?" he called, the words drifting through the air, accompanied by moans of pain, low grumbles, and the spluttering sound of men coughing as the dust mixed with blood in their throats. The sounds seemed to come from all around him.

Calen brought his hand to his face as a sudden flash of white light burned his eyes. Valerys leapt in front of Calen, his head lowered towards the light, his mouth pulled back in a snarl, and a deep growl reverberating in his chest.

"It's me, Draleid."

As the glare from the light dimmed, Calen made out Vaeril, a small baldír floating in front of him. The elf's face was so streaked with blood and dirt he looked almost unrecognisable.

A man stood beside Vaeril. He was taller than the elf, with shoulders that looked as though they were carved from stone. Calen recognised Tarmon Hoard immediately.

"You're both a sight for sore eyes," Calen said, trying to muster a half-smile as he fought the pain in his body. "Are you hurt?"

"We'll live," Tarmon replied, his mouth twisting into a grimace; his hand was pressed against the spot where the arrow had struck him.

"And you, Draleid?" Vaeril stepped closer to Calen, ignoring the fading rumble from Valerys's throat. "Were you injured?"

"I'm fine, Vaeril," Calen said, swatting the elf's hands away. "Have you found anybody else?"

"Not yet," Tarmon replied between short breaths. "We only came to a few minutes ago. The elf pulled me from the rubble."

With the newfound source of light, Calen took in his surroundings. They stood in a wide, open cavern, its surfaces smooth and angular. A multitude of tunnels were nestled into the rock all about the cavern, branching off deeper and deeper into the mountain. Small swaths of Heraya's Ward protruded from the rock at random places throughout the wide, open space, glowing with a dim bluish-green light. Bits of bent and shattered steel were strewn all over the ground: remnants of the *Crested Wave*.

The horrid mixture of death and dry earth tinged the air. Every few seconds, blood-chilling shrieks of pain broke through the blanket of low cries and moans that echoed throughout the cavern. Everywhere Calen looked, he saw crushed armour, gore, bodies, and severed limbs. Two men were impaled on a piece of shattered steel. A dwarf, long dead, lay a few feet away, both of his legs shorn at the knee. The acidic taste of vomit teased the back of Calen's throat, but he pushed it back down with a gulp. "We need to check for survivors."

Just as Calen spoke, he felt Valerys – who had begun wandering through the debris – scratching at the back of his mind urgently.

"Valerys has found someone." Calen waded through the debris from the crashed Wind Runner, Vaeril and Tarmon close behind him. He dropped to his knees as he reached Valerys, panic setting in when realised who the dragon had found. Erik was half buried in a mound of clay and bits of curved, bent metal.

Dirt bedded into Calen's fingernails as he dug away at the debris. "Erik! Wake up!"

A plume of clay and dust fountained into the air as Erik coughed and spluttered. His eyes were raw red and half-stuck together with dirt. "Calen?" His voice was weak as he choked out the word.

Tarmon dropped down beside Calen, tossing away some of the heavier bits of bent steel weighing Erik down.

"Don't move," Tarmon said, as his gaze fell on something. "Elf?"

"What's wrong?" The panic at the back of Calen's mind turned to dread when his eyes fell on two thin steel rods, one that jutted out through Erik's leg and another just above his hip.

Vaeril knelt beside Erik, the dirt crunching under his knee. He reached down and slid his hands beneath Erik's body, his eyes darting around, looking for something. "The rods are not connected to anything on the other side. On the count of three, I will need you to pull them both free. Then I will stop the blood flow and knit the wounds. Understood?"

Both Tarmon and Calen nodded. The Lord Captain of the Kingsguard looked a lot more certain than Calen felt. Taking in a deep breath, Calen steadied himself and wrapped his hands around the steel rod that jutted out just above Erik's hip. Erik let out a sharp gasp of pain. "Fuck, why don't you just stick another one in? That might actually hurt less."

"Shut up, or I will shut you up," Calen replied, raising his eyebrow as a question to see if Erik wanted to take him up on the offer.

Erik gave a weak smile that quickly twisted into a grimace of pain as Tarmon grasped the other steel rod. "Just hurry up and get them out of me."

Calen felt Vaeril drawing from the Spark, just as he did when he was healing Tarmon on the Wind Runner. Fire, Water, Air, Earth, and Spirit. Calen attempted to follow the threads as Vaeril spun them around each other, but the speed at which the elf worked was astounding. There was more to the Spark than simply pulling on the threads. There were so many intricate and complex ways it could be twisted, turned, and shaped. So many ways that each of the elemental strands could be combined. Therin had said healers were special. That a wound couldn't simply be healed – the healer had to understand precisely what it was they were healing.

"One," Vaeril said. "Make sure you pull it free in one clean movement."

Calen tightened his grip around the steel rod.

"Two."

Erik closed his eyes. His mouth twisted in the anticipation of pain.

"Three."

Erik howled as both Tarmon and Calen pulled at the steel rods, ripping them free of his body, but Vaeril did not hesitate. He set to work straight away, weaving his threads of the Spark in complex patterns. It was beyond anything Calen had ever seen. The wounds were so open that he could see inside, yet not a drop of blood flowed. Calen watched as muscle and tissue knitted itself together. Strands of thin red filament shot every which way across the wound, connecting on the other side. He stared in wonder as the wounds closed, and the holes were patched over by skin in the way that a spider weaves its web.

Vaeril collapsed as Erik let out a sigh of relief. The elf just about managed to catch himself with his left hand before he hit the ground.

"I am well," he said, as Calen reached out to grab him. "Healing is different from everything else. It takes more from you. I just need to rest, as does he."

Calen nodded in acquiescence as the elf propped himself up against a large boulder.

"We need to keep looking. More might need our help," Calen said, turning his attention towards Tarmon.

"Agreed, Draleid. There are bound to be more," Tarmon replied, bringing himself to his feet.

Calen grunted and dragged himself to a standing position. He had always been considered tall, but even he had to look up to talk to Tarmon. "Please, call me Calen."

Hours passed as they dug through the Wind Runner's wreckage in search of more survivors, finding far more than Calen had even dared hope. Calen looked around. Besides himself, Falmin, Vaeril, Erik, and Tarmon, just over sixty others had survived – sixty-two, to be precise. Twenty-three dwarves and thirty-nine men. Everyone sat around a large pile of Heraya's Ward they had gathered in the centre of the cavern to provide light; Vaeril couldn't have kept the baldír going indefinitely, and there was nothing they could burn. The blueish-green glow of the luminescent plant pulsated through the cavern, bathing everything in its strange light.

As happy as Calen was to find so many alive, there had been over two hundred souls on the *Crested Wave*. Over two hundred souls, and this was all that was left. So many dead. All but fourteen of Tarmon's Kingsguard. The magnitude of the loss pressed down on Calen, coiling knots in his stomach and constricting his throat. The only thing that stopped him from becoming lost in the depths of his own anguish was the touch of Valerys's mind against his.

The dragon stood by Calen's side, nuzzling his snout into the palm of Calen's hand, trying desperately to ease the sense of loss that held Calen in its grasp.

"Thank you," Calen whispered, the most fragile of smiles touching his lips as he ran his fingers over the scales of Valerys's snout. A feeling of comfort pressed against the back of his mind in response.

Groaning, Calen dropped down onto the hard-packed dirt. His muscles ached, his throat was dry, and a multitude of cuts laced his body. Valerys nestled in beside him, resting his scaled head on Calen's knee.

"Tis b'yond belief what you can do, elf." Falmin fingered the mottled patch of skin that covered where the arrow had come through his abdomen. Erik had found the navigator, unconscious, half buried beneath a mound of clay and steel.

Vaeril nodded in recognition. "I am sorry I could not do more. I am weak. For everything that healing gives to the victim, it takes twice over from the healer."

"Ah don' be worryin' 'bout that. Women love scars," Falmin said with a wink.

To his own surprise, Calen couldn't help but choke out a laugh as he watched Vaeril. The elf simply stared at Falmin, unsure what to say, an uncomfortable expression set on his face. "Falmin, I just wanted to say thank you. If you hadn't come back for us… well, we wouldn't be here."

"Aye," Tarmon said, shifting his weight in the dirt. "The Draleid—Calen," Tarmon corrected himself, "is right. We owe you our lives."

Erik nodded in agreement.

Falmin's face contorted into a look of genuine shock. "You owe me yer lives? Not a one o' us would be alive if it weren't for you. If the guard hadn't held the empire in the yard. If the Draleid hadn't steered the *Crested Wave* – may the gods care for her tiny metal heart. I think I already owe you m'life more times than I know, and I feel I'll owe you a lot more soon. Jus' scratch one offa the list."

"So," Erik said after a brief silence. "What are we going to do?"

The question hung in the air like a bad smell. Everybody had been thinking it, but nobody had said it out loud. They had no idea where they were. Even Falmin, without knowing the route that Calen took to get there, was at a loss.

"This place looks like what used t'be a waypoint. Long time ago by m'reckonin'. All o' those tunnels go somewhere," Falmin said, pointing across to the other tunnels that were set into the sides of the massive cave. "I say we just pick one. All o' the main tunnels have markers on 'em. If we can find one, I can probably get us to Durakdur. Maybe."

Calen perked up a bit at that. There was hope.

"We need to be careful," one of the dwarves, who had told Calen his name was Korik, said. The dwarf, a member of Kira's Queensguard, stood no taller than five feet and a crimson cloak hung over his shoulders. Korik's head was shaved clean, and his thick black beard was knotted with an array of gold and silver rings. His double-sided axe lay across his lap. "A lot of dark things roam the depths of these mountains: Uraks, wyrms, Depth Stalkers, kerathlin. There is a reason some of these tunnels were abandoned."

"What in the gods is a Depth Stalker?" Erik leaned forward, his forearms wrapped around his knees, his short blond hair reflecting the bluish-green glow of the flowers.

"Oh, they're nasty all right," Falmin said. "Some of 'em are as big as a house. Skulls like arrowheads, hides as thick as stone, and tails covered in spikes as long as yer arm. I ain't seen nothin' that'd chill your blood more than staring up at one of those things..."

A shiver ran the length of Calen's spine. The thought of running into a Depth Stalker didn't sit well with him. A light vibration emanated from Valerys, a low growl in response to Calen's fear. Sometimes Calen forgot that his mind was no longer solely his own.

"What's gotten into him?" Erik asked, tilting his head sideways at Valerys.

"Nothing. Don't think he likes the sound of a Depth Stalker."

Valerys's growl grew deeper.

"Whatever it is we do," Vaeril said, sitting forward, "we need three things – food, water, and rest."

"Aye." Falmin stretched his arms in the air. "I could sleep for days."

Calen had been ignoring the dull ache that had set into his body, the energy that had been leeched from him. Bringing down those buildings had taken a massive toll on him, and in truth, he wasn't sure if he would physically be able to stand back up if he tried.

"Agreed," came the deep voice of Tarmon Hoard. "First, we rest. Then we move. I will arrange guard shifts. Two hours sleep each, then switch. That is all the time we can afford. Is this agreeable?"

Tarmon was looking directly at Calen as he spoke. The man was young to be the Lord Captain of the Kingsguard, but he had seen at least ten more summers than Calen. Calen realised that Tarmon wasn't the only one looking to him. They all were. They were all looking to him to make the decision.

Feeling the weight that hung over Calen's shoulders, Valerys gave a grumble, lifted his head, and brought himself to his feet. The young dragon strode off towards the centre of the cavern, his lavender eyes watching over the tunnel entrances.

"Yes," Calen said, finally, with as much confidence as he could muster. "Valerys will stay on watch as well."

"I'll take first watch," Erik said, climbing to his feet. He was joined by Tarmon and some of the other men and dwarves. "I'll wake you in a few hours."

Calen kicked at a small rock as the group made their way through the tunnel. A few hours of sleep weren't nearly enough. Calen could have slept for days on end, but that wasn't an option.

"I don't think he has any idea where we're going," Erik whispered to Calen as Falmin examined a navigator glyph on the tunnel wall. "We've been walking for hours, and he seems to have no better idea of where we are."

"He has more of an idea than we do," Calen replied. Everything looked the same to him, but Falmin seemed to recognise some of the glyphs that had been etched into the smooth tunnel walls. "What else would you have us do? He's our best chance of getting out of here."

"I know." Erik let out a heavy breath and ran his hands through his hair. Calen wasn't used to seeing Erik anything other than calm. "I'm sorry… these tunnels, they just… They make my skin crawl. It feels like the walls are closing in."

Calen stopped in his tracks, resting his hand on Erik's shoulder. "We'll get through this, Erik. We just need to keep going. One foot in front of the other."

Erik nodded, his gazed drifting to the ground. "Yeah, you're right."

"Can I get that in writing?"

Erik let out a chuckle, raising his gaze to meet Calen's once again. "Shut up and get back to walking," he said, pushing Calen forward. "We'll never get out if we just keep standing around."

The small bunches of Heraya's Ward that grew in random places along the ground and tunnel walls provided just enough light for Calen to see a few feet in front of himself, but not much more than that. A baldír would have been a waste of energy, but it was still a tempting option. Just like Erik, Calen couldn't help but feel claustrophobic, staring forward into the endless depths of the tunnel, buried beneath miles of rock. His only true comfort came from Valerys, who padded along beside him, the ethereal light from the flowers painting his snow-white scales with a strange bluish-green hue.

"How are you feeling?" Vaeril asked as he stepped up beside Calen.

"Me? I'm fine," Calen lied. "What about you? The healing looked as though it took a lot out of you."

Vaeril raised a curious eyebrow. "What you did in the Wind Runner courtyard, it should have killed you. You have not known the Spark long enough to survive drawing so deeply from it."

"I wasn't sure it wouldn't." Calen shrugged, a resignation in his voice. "I'm still not sure how it didn't."

"I have never seen a Draleid before, and I have not learned much of their ways with the Spark, but I believe it may have something to do with Valerys. We may ask Therin or Rakina Aeson when we arrived back in Durakdur. I'm sure one of them will know more."

Calen gave a weak smile as he pondered the idea, his eyes falling on Valerys. As he thought about Therin and Aeson, a question popped into his mind. "Vaeril?"

"Yes?"

"Why do the other elves of the Aravell hate Therin?"

Vaeril sighed. "They do not hate him..."

"They ignore him, Vaeril. They scowl at him. Gaeleron shows nothing but disdain for him. He doesn't even attempt to hide it. It is only you who does not."

Vaeril's eyes tracked along the ground as they walked, not meeting Calen's gaze. Calen could see the thoughts ticking over in the elf's head. "They do not hate him. They see him as having no honour. To an elf, that is as good as not existing."

"But… Why?"

"That is a story that would take a long time to tell. And I was not alive when it happened, so my account may be inaccurate."

"We have time," Calen said, gesturing at the endless tunnel that lay before them, shrouded in darkness, only patches illuminated by the luminescent flowers. He was tired of people keeping things from him.

"Very well," Vaeril replied. Calen saw Erik shuffle a little closer, his ears perking up to hear what Vaeril was about to say. "I have told you the start of the story before, when we were in the Aravell. I shall tell you again. When The Order fell and Fane Mortem took power in Al'Nasla, a great purge began. The empire hunted the Jotnar to extinction, or so they thought, and they drove the dwarves underground. We elves, and small groups of your people, stood against them. Enormous battles were fought across Epheria. Many, many lives were lost. But in the end, the combined power of the empire and the treacherous Dragonguard was too much for us."

"What happened?" interrupted Erik, who had moved closer as Vaeril talked and was now walking with them.

"A divide," Vaeril said, a deep sadness in his eyes. "In our history, we refer to it as The Breaking. Our people split into two factions. One of which believed the war was no longer theirs, and they abandoned the other races of Epheria."

"And the other?" Erik asked, leaning in closer.

"I am part of the other. We believed we could not just leave Epheria to fall to Fane. We needed to do something."

"But what about Therin?" Calen interjected, growing tired of hearing the same story.

"Therin had to make a choice. The elves of Lynalion, or the elves of the Aravell."

"And he chose Lynalion?" There was a look of shock on Erik's face. Calen didn't speak, but dread churned in his stomach. Surely Therin hadn't chosen to abandon the continent. To leave it in Fane's hands.

Vaeril sighed. "He chose neither. Therin's beliefs aligned with the elves of Aravell, but his duty was, first and foremost, to all elves. You see, to me, Therin's choice was the most honourable. He chose what he knew would be exile, so as not to encourage the breaking of our people. To the others, he was a coward, leaving his people to stumble alone in their darkest hours. Honour is a delicate thing. What one elf views as honourable, another might see as despicable."

"There's something up ahead," one of the soldiers called out from the front of the group.

Sure enough, as Calen lifted his head, he could see a speck of yellow light in the distance. "What do you think it is?"

"Hopefully, a way out," Erik answered with a shrug. "But I suppose we'll find out soon enough."

The further the group walked, the larger the yellow light became, growing and growing until it became clear that it emanated from a chamber at the end of the tunnel.

"Draleid, you're gonna wanna see this," Falmin called back from the head of the group as he stepped into the chamber.

As Calen, Erik, and Vaeril approached the mouth of the chamber, the Belduaran soldiers – who had been walking at the front of the group – stepped aside to let them pass. Calen couldn't help but feel more than a little uncomfortable at the chorus of "Draleid" and "my lord" that left the soldiers' lips as they gave a slight bow of their heads.

Dipping his head towards the ground, Calen made his way past the soldiers and into the chamber, trying his best to avoid the amused smile he knew sat on Erik's face.

Once inside, Calen could see the source of the yellow light that had shone through the tunnel: an enormous, luminescent flower similar to Heraya's Ward. The flower sat in the centre of the hexagonal chamber, which stretched about fifty feet from side to side. The walls of the chamber were smooth and angular, carved straight into the rock of the mountain, like most dwarven architecture. On the far side, past the luminescent flower, was a massive stone doorway with glyph markings carved all along its edges, inlaid in gold.

On either side of the doorway stood two enormous golden statues that stretched from the floor to the ceiling of the cavern. Both statues were identical: dwarves in sharp-cut plate armour, the heads of their axes resting at their feet, with their arms crossed over the pommels.

"I didn't see one this colour in Durakdur," Calen said, holding his hand just a few feet from the glowing flower that sat in the middle of the room. The yellow light was mesmerising. "It's incredible."

"By Hafaesir's hammer."

Calen turned to see Korik and the other dwarves entering the chamber. Each of them dropped to one knee as they caught sight of the yellow flower and the enormous, statue-framed doorway.

"It's always drama with dwarves," Falmin muttered, rolling his eyes. Shaking his head, the navigator walked off to the other side of the chamber, toward the massive stone door.

"Do you know this place?" Calen asked as he approached Korik and the other dwarves.

"I cannot be certain," the dwarf answered, his voice laced with awe. "But I believe it to be an entrance to Vindakur, the jewel of the Freehold. We lost contact with them centuries ago. Every scouting party we sent was met with collapsed tunnels, swarms of kerathlin, or Uraks. We had thought this place lost. In all the texts, Vindakur is the only city in the Freehold where the Heraya's Ward takes this colouring."

"Could it be, truly?" another dwarf asked, stepping past Korik, his eyes fixed on the enormous stone doorway.

"Aha!"

All eyes turned to Falmin, who stood by the massive stone door, his hands on his hips and a triumphant look on his face. Yellow light flooded through the parting stone that was now split in two, each of the halves receding into the walls that framed it.

Falmin shrugged as Calen and the others approached the opening passageway. "I figured I'd make meself useful, while you lot were blabberin'. There was a lever over there. Just had to pull it."

"I—" Calen was cut short as Erik stepped between him and Falmin.

"What in the…" Erik's voice petered out as he tilted his head sideways, gazing at what lay on the other side of the stone door.

The cool light of the moon washed over the rubble as Rendall picked his way through the remains of the collapsed building. Belduar had finally fallen. For centuries, it had been a thorn in the empire's side. It had withstood attack after attack. Many dragons had fallen to those monstrous crossbows, wickedly brilliant inventions of the dwarves. The Fade may not have succeeded in taking the new Draleid, but destroying those machines was the gift that turned the tide.

The new Draleid. Rendall's laugh echoed through the empty ruins of the city, mixing with the crackling of the still burning fires. The boy from the village was the Draleid. He would not have believed it if the Fade had not confirmed it. However dark and twisted that creature was, it didn't lie. It had no need to. Rendall would have killed the boy on the spot had he known.

He *tssked* as he kicked aside a pile of crumbled rock. The scouts hadn't found the bodies of any civilians. Not one. No women, no children, no old or infirm. The Belduarans must have evacuated them before the battle. Down those tunnels they made sure to collapse as they retreated.

The grotesque corpse of a Belduaran soldier was splayed out on the ground at Rendall's feet. The metal that had once protected him, now fused to his bones. The molten steel had peeled away most of the man's charred and blackened skin.

Rendall's face twisted into an unimpressed grimace as he tapped his boot on the misshapen corpse. Dragons were an effective weapon, but they never left enough people alive to interrogate. Rendall enjoyed interrogating people. There was something about seeing a person reach their breaking point, and seeing how far you could push the limits of the body. Some crumpled with a simple flogging – crude, but effective. Others required more… nuance. They were his favourite.

Some men gritted their teeth and set their jaws when Rendall threatened to take their limbs or peel the skin from their bones. It always surprised him how many of them truly believed he would not follow through on his threats. He enjoyed the fear in their eyes when they realised they were wrong.

"Inquisitor, sir."

Rendall let out a sigh as he stood with his hands on his hips, his red cloak billowing in the dust laden breeze. "What is it, Captain?"

"We found a live one, sir. An elf."

Rendall snapped his neck around. He made no attempt to hide the wicked grin that spread across his face. Before him stood three soldiers in the red and black of the Lorian empire, steel breastplates stained with dirt and blood. But at their feet, with its knees in the dust, was an elf.

Its long brown hair was crusted with blood, and a thin scar ran down its right cheek. There was a stump of mottled flesh where its left hand should have been. It was not fresh, but it still looked raw. A wound from a previous battle, most likely the recent attack. Cold hatred burned in the elf's eyes as it stared back at Rendall.

"Good," Rendall said, hunching down in front of the elf. "There is fight in you. I will enjoy stripping it away, piece by piece."

Rendall gave the elf a quick wink before rising to his feet. "Don't keep it with the other prisoners. Take it to my tent and secure it there. This one will require special attention."

"Sir." The soldier nodded before dragging the elf away.

I will find your secrets.

Eltoar leaned back with his eyes closed, letting the wind roll off his face and rush through his hair. He took a deep breath in through his nose, shifting slightly where he sat at the nape of Helios's neck. Opening his eyes, he looked out over the blazing pile of ruin and rubble that had once been the city of Belduar, the flames illuminating the night. A slight pang of guilt twisted in his heart. He had now helped raze two of the most beautiful cities that had ever existed. Images of Ilnaen's white walls crumbling flashed through his mind. The screams of the dying. The acrid smell of charred flesh. The taste of ash and blood tingeing the air.

He pushed it all away, banishing it to the darkest corners of his mind. And that was where it would stay.

Swallowing the lump in his throat, Eltoar reminded himself how many of the Dragonguard had fallen to Belduar's giant crossbows over the centuries. The bolts fired by those dwarven contraptions travelled at speeds only matched by lightning. He clenched his hands into fists at the thought of the dragons falling from the sky, blood streaming behind them. In truth, even those giant crossbows should never have stopped the Dragonguard. But in their hubris, they had underestimated them. This time, Eltoar had not repeated past mistakes. This attack had been swift and uncompromising. It had not hurt that the Fade had destroyed enough of those contraptions during its initial attempt to capture the Draleid, that their bolts could not fill the sky.

Eltoar pulled himself from his own head, letting out a tired sigh. *Land down beside Lyina and Karakes.* Helios rumbled in response before gliding left and dropping into a nosedive.

Eltoar smiled at the sudden change of direction and sheer drop. Nothing in the world had ever come close to riding on Helios's back when the dragon flew freely. The power, speed, and elegance were unmatched by anything in the known world. He let his mind flow freely into Helios's, feeling every subtle motion of the wind. The slight pull of the current, the chill in the air, the subtle vibrations elicited by Helios's wingbeats. He could feel it all.

Through Helios's keen eyes, he could see Lyina down below, tending to Karakes – the red scaled dragon had taken one of Belduar's bolts through the shoulder during the battle. He would live, but Eltoar could almost sense the pain radiating from the majestic creature.

Almost as quickly as he had dropped, Helios pulled level just above the ground with a single powerful beat of his wings, sending spirals of dust and ash sweeping into the air. Eltoar leapt from the dragon's back, cushioning his landing with threads of Air. *I will send for some food. Rest, my soulkin. You have earned it.*

Helios dipped his enormous head so the tip of his snout rested just in front of Eltoar, who reached up and rested the palm of his hand on the dragon's black scales. "Myia elwyn er unira diar." *My heart is always yours.*

A feeling of comfort and warmth radiated from Helios's mind to Eltoar's before the enormous dragon curled himself up and lay on the ground, his eyes fixed on Lyina and Karakes.

"How is he?" Eltoar asked as he approached his sister-in-arms.

Lyina was a human of old Lorian descent. Her bronzed skin was unmarred by the passage of time, while her dark blonde hair was tied at the back of her head. Just like Eltoar, she wore the white plate armour of the Dragonguard, gilded at the edges, with a black flame emblazoned across the chest.

She let out a sigh as she turned to Eltoar. "He's all right – lucky, really. If the big lummox had pulled up when I said, then I wouldn't be here patching up his shoulder."

A deep growl resonated from Karakes as the red dragon's lips curled back into a snarl, baring his teeth. Karakes wasn't quite as large as Helios, but he was not far off, over a hundred and fifty feet from head to tail.

"Oh, pipe down," Lyina hissed, before turning back towards Eltoar. The woman seemed half-mad sometimes, but she was a warrior of incredible skill, and she had stood by Eltoar in the darkest of days. "He'll be fine. He just needs to rest."

"See to it that he gets it. We ride north at daybreak."

Lyina responded with a firm nod, before turning around to *tssk* at Karakes.

With that, Eltoar headed for the Dragonguard command tent. It was not difficult to find; the rest of the army tended to avoid setting their tents within a mile of the Dragonguard and their dragons.

Just like the Dragonguard's armour, the large tent's canopy was a brilliant white with a trimming of gold and a black flame stitched into each side. The tent stood over fifty feet by fifty feet, with a rectangular flag at its peak fluttering in the wind. Even in the pale moonlight, Eltoar could see the two symbols that occupied the flag: the black lion of Loria and the flame of the Dragonguard.

Fane had been true to his word. The Dragonguard were not tethered, whipped, and commanded like the Draleid had been by The Order. It was true that Fane often called on them, but it *was* different. On the field of battle, they were their own, and in life, they were the arbiters of their own fate. Gone were the days when the council of The Order demanded fealty, when the Draleid and their bound dragons were forced to heel to the whims of tempestuous and childish rulers.

But had the price been worth the reward? That was a question Eltoar asked himself every day, and it was one he saw in the eyes of his brothers and sisters. Nine. That was how many of the Dragonguard remained. Hundreds had joined their ranks at Ilnaen, and twice that number had fought on the other side. Now, only nine were left.

Not a single dragon egg had hatched since that night – until now. Not one of them had been able to understand why the eggs had not hatched, but maybe this… maybe something had changed. They needed to find this new Draleid and his dragon. They *needed* to understand.

Eltoar entered the command tent to find Pellenor shirtless on the floor, his legs folded, and his eyes closed. Pellenor was a gangly dark-skinned man, built from wiry muscle. Apart from the cropped beard he wore, there was not a hair on his head.

"Did you sense anything?" the dark-skinned man asked.

"I did not," Eltoar replied as he poured himself a cup of water from the large crystal flask that sat on the table to his right. "Has the Inquisitor reported yet?"

"Not yet." Pellenor opened his eyes and tilted his head at Eltoar, his eyes narrowing. "You are troubled."

"I am fine," Eltoar snapped. Pellenor always seemed to pick up on even the most subtle of Eltoar's moods. It was equal parts useful and irritating. At that moment, it was more the latter than the former. "Where is Meranta? I did not see her outside."

Pellenor didn't react to the change of subject. He simply raised an eyebrow, which only served to frustrate Eltoar further. He curled his bottom lip but acquiesced. "She went hunting. Better to hunt now, while she can, than thin the herd. There is never any telling when livestock might run low."

Eltoar nodded, draining his water in one mouthful, then refilling the cup. He tried his utmost to keep his mind from fixating on the new Draleid, but that was easier said than done. Why had that egg hatched when none of the others had? That dragon could be the key to truly rebuilding what was lost. They needed to find it.

"What's he frowning about?" Lyina asked as she walked into the tent, rubbing the blood off her hands with a thick cloth.

"He's fretting over the hatchling and its Draleid," Pellenor answered without missing a beat.

Eltoar shot Pellenor a scowl but stopped himself from speaking. How the man had any idea what was inside Eltoar's head was a mystery. But he always seemed to know, whether Eltoar told him or not. "I am not fretting. I am curious, that is all."

A knowing smile touched Lyina's face as she gave Pellenor a playful wink. The two of them were bad enough on their own, but together, Eltoar found them infuriating. Fane had questioned why, of all the Dragonguard, Eltoar had chosen Lyina and Pellenor as his right and left wings. At times like these, Eltoar asked himself the same question. But in truth, the answer was obvious: they were skilled, they were loyal, and above all else, they reminded him of what once was. Where the others had changed, Pellenor and Lyina had stayed the same. They had not allowed what happened at Ilnaen to eat away at them, piece by piece. They had stayed true to who they were, choosing not to look back but to look forward instead.

Of the other Dragonguard, Ilkya and Voranur had grown cold over time; apathy seemed to be the only emotion they could muster towards others. Death had become a part of them. Their captain, Jormun, was worse still. Eltoar only wished the man tended towards apathy, but instead, he was pure bloodlust. Eltoar could feel the darkness that loomed over Jormun's soul; it was a tangible thing. Over the years, he had consumed Essence at an unsustainable rate, and he was not the man he had once been.

In truth, Eltoar rarely saw the other three Dragonguard. The last he had heard, Erdin had flown west, towards Arda; Luka had gone to Karvos; and Tivar hadn't left Dracaldryr in nearly a hundred years. Eltoar couldn't blame them for their absence. Darkness had loomed large over them all since Ilnaen, or 'The Fall' as it had become so commonly known. That name clamped like a vice around his heart and left a bitter taste on his tongue.

It was at least an hour before the messenger arrived from the Inquisition to give his report. He was a scrawny young man who barely fit in his leathers and had a weaselly face with a scrunched nose. There was an awkwardness in the way he held himself. He quite clearly did not bring good news. If it were good news, then he would not be there at all; Inquisitor Rendall would have come himself. That scheming rat would never miss an opportunity to heap praise upon himself.

"Well?" Eltoar said after the young man had stood at the entrance to the tent without speaking for almost two minutes. Eltoar pushed himself back in his chair, letting out an impatient sigh. Lyina leaned against a tent pole some five feet away, and Pellenor was where he had been since Eltoar had arrived, sitting on the ground with his legs folded.

"I emm..." The young soldier swallowed hard before straightening has back. "I am here to provide a report from Inquisitor Rendall, sir."

"Go on," Eltoar said, gesturing for the soldier to speak.

"The emm..."

"The commander doesn't like men who can't finish their sentences," Lyina said with a shrug. "I'd get on with it if I were you."

The young man swallowed hard. "Inquisitor Rendall reports that there was no sign of the Draleid within the city walls, my lord. He believes the Draleid escaped to the Dwarven Freehold through the tunnels."

Eltoar clenched his jaw before standing up. "First," he said, walking toward the young soldier, "I am not a lord." The soldier looked up at Eltoar with what could only be seen as terror in his eyes. Eltoar was more than aware of the intimidating figure he cut with his broad shoulders and sharp jaw, along with the white plate armour he wore, the black flame of the Dragonguard on its breastplate. He knew of the rumours that flooded the common army. Tales of how the Dragonguard's souls were as dark as a Fade's. How their dragons feasted on the bones of those who failed the empire. Eltoar did not care for the rumours, but they did have their uses. "Second, is he *sure* the Draleid has retreated into the Freehold?"

"Yes, my lo—". The man shook. His lips trembled, and he was back to stumbling over his words. "He is sure."

Eltoar eyed the young man and pulled on threads of Air. He funnelled the threads towards his ears, amplifying the sounds around him. He narrowed the threads, focusing until an erratic thumping noise filled his ears. The soldier's heart pounded as though he were climbing a mountainside in full plate. *There's something you aren't saying.* "Very well. Leave us."

The soldier didn't need to be told twice. A look of pure relief flashed across his eyes, and he was gone from the tent before Eltoar could even begin to contemplate whether he should have given him to Helios as a plaything. That would have been one way to send a message to that infernal Inquisitor.

"Have that messenger and Inquisitor Rendall followed. They are scheming something, and I want to know what," Eltoar said once the messenger was out of earshot.

"It will be done," Pellenor replied, rising to his feet without even unfolding his legs. "I believe you are right. There is definitely something left untold in this story."

"Any ideas?" Eltoar asked, raising an eyebrow.

Pellenor puckered his lips in thought. "He may not have found the boy or the dragon, but he did find something, or *someone,* he believes will lead him to them."

"You got all that from a shit-scared soldier who barely spoke more than four sentences?" Lyina scoffed, shaking her head. "I swear you just make these things up, Pellenor."

The corners of Pellenor's mouth pulled back in amusement. Not quite a smile – the man rarely ever truly smiled – but Eltoar definitely saw amusement. "No, Lyina. I 'got all that' from centuries of studying inquisitors, watching how they operate, seeing how they react to particular situations, and applying a semblance of logic." There was a momentary pause as a silence filled the air between the two Dragonguard. "That and I received a message from one of my informants. They saw this particular Inquisitor having a one-handed elf dragged to his tent." Eltoar watched as Pellenor gave a mocking bow and exited the tent.

"That bastard," Lyina said, throwing her gaze to the sky.

CHAPTER SIX

WORDS OF SHADOW

Dahlen took a moment to steady himself. The Heart of Durakdur may as well have been an infirmary. It was packed with wounded, men and dwarves alike, some of whom had no right to be alive, such was the extent of their wounds. Two dwarves carried a man on a cot past Dahlen. His arm had been severed at the shoulder, and his face and neck were a mess of crackling, blackened skin. His screams sent a chill down Dahlen's spine.

He was sure that on a normal day, the Heart of Durakdur would have been an amazing sight to see. It was a city inside a city, inside a mountain. He imagined the hustle and bustle of the mountain kingdom, the smells of freshly baked bread and roasted barley floating through the air, mingling with the metallic tinge of the forge. But that was not what lay around him. The air did not smell of freshly baked bread or roasted barley. It smelled of sweat, steel, and charred flesh. It was heavy and nauseating. The putrid scent clung to the back of his throat, so thick that it was almost a taste.

It was not the squeak of wheel axles and the laughter of children that drifted into his ears. It was the screams of dying men and dwarves and the sobbing of their loved ones. And all of it was bathed in the soft bluish-green glow of those odd flowers.

Everything had happened so fast in Belduar. As soon as the dragons began torching the city, it was chaos. Soldiers just turned and ran. They dropped their swords and their shields, and they ran as fast as their legs could carry them. Dahlen didn't blame them. What use was a sword and a shield against a beast that can rain fiery death from the sky? Against a monster that can melt steel and peel the skin off a man's back with its breath? Dahlen held his hands out in front of himself. They didn't tremble, but that was only because he had trained them not to. Fear still held his heart in its grasp.

His father sat beside him on a low stone wall. Aeson had barely spoken since it became clear that Erik and Calen hadn't made it to Durakdur. He just sat in silence.

Therin approached them from across the yard. Even in the midst of all the madness, the elf walked with poise, his greenish-brown cloak drifting lazily behind him. The blue-green light of those strange flowers gave his silver hair an ethereal look, as if he were a spirit.

The elf greeted Dahlen and Aeson with his mouth drawn in an unyielding line. "Aeson, they are ready for us."

Aeson nodded, rubbing his hands together as he stood. He placed a hand on the shoulders of both Dahlen and Therin, drawing them in close. "Whatever is said in there, we are going after Erik and Calen. They are still alive and somewhere in this network of tunnels. I can feel it."

Therin's face betrayed no emotion. "As can I. I am with you, Aeson. We *will* find them."

The despair that had previously been set into Aeson's face gave way to a weak smile. "We will. For now, let us go talk with kings and queens."

No guards stood at the entrance to the council chamber. Which seemed odd to Dahlen, but he supposed that nobody had the time, or the inclination, to bother with those things at the minute.

Therin pushed open the door and made his way inside the chamber, gesturing for Aeson and Dahlen to follow.

Dahlen wouldn't have thought it possible, but the atmosphere in the chamber was even worse than it had been in the courtyard. There were no screams or wails, though. Silence ruled here. The air smelled of leather and incense, not of charred skin, but there was a weight that held it down, a despondency.

The rulers of the Dwarven Freehold sat slumped in their thrones, perched upon a raised dais. Not one of them even lifted their chin to acknowledge the new entrants. Behind the dais, set in six alcoves, were statues of the gods, as regal and as judgemental as ever. Dahlen noted that Hafaesir was positioned next to Heraya. He already knew that was typical of dwarven culture, from his father's teachings, but it was still strange to see.

King Daymon was slouched on a short wooden bench that rested against the wall to the left, his plate armour still adorning his shoulders. Even dented and stained with dried blood, the armour, with its gold trim and massive pauldrons, looked every bit fit for a king.

The king's new chief advisor, Ihvon Arnell, stood in front of the bench, his arms crossed and his brow furrowed. The giant, Asius, sat in the middle of the floor, his massive legs folded, his pale, whitish-blue skin shimmering in the flowerlight. He seemed the only one in the room who wasn't showing an outward display of emotion.

"May your fires never be extinguished and your blades never dull," Therin pronounced, giving a slight bow at the waist towards the queens and king of the Dwarven Freehold. The dwarves muttered a response.

"Your Majesty." Therin repeated his slight bow, his eyes fixed on Daymon. "Have you come to some kind of agreement?"

One of the dwarves seated on a throne stirred. The streaks of grey that ran through her blonde, braided hair marked her as Pulroan, queen of Azmar. The elder dwarf sighed as she heaved herself into a less slumped position. "Of a sort, master elf."

Therin raised his eyebrow, a curious look on his face.

"They will give my people refuge." Daymon's voice held a bitter twist at the end. "But they will not even consider a plan to retake the city."

"Enough dwarven lives have been lost on this day!" one of the other dwarven queens shouted, still clearly seething in anger from an earlier argument. Dahlen guessed her to be Queen Elenya of Ozryn. Her fire-red hair and the short axe strapped to her belt gave her away. That meant the still silent queen was Kira of Durakdur, with King Hofnar of Volkur sitting to her left.

"My people have perished too, lest you forget, Queen Elenya. And now the city of Belduar no longer stands guard over your little… *burrows*." Daymon's eyes narrowed as he spoke, his words dripping with indignance. "We—"

"What my king is trying to say," Ihvon interrupted, a softness in his eyes as he glanced at Daymon, "is that although we are eternally grateful for the refuge you provide our people, we cannot simply sit back and be content with the loss of our home. Would you give up Durakdur so easily? Or Ozryn? All we ask is that you acknowledge our need to retake Belduar."

A palpable silence hung in the air, filling the room like a thick fog. Not one person dared be the first to make a sound. Dahlen did not know much of etiquette when it came to royal courts, but he would hazard a guess that it was not common for an advisor to interrupt his king.

All eyes were on Daymon, but he said nothing. His gaze was fixed on Ihvon. Something unheard passed between them, but Dahlen could only guess at what it was. When it was clear Daymon wasn't going to openly chastise Ihvon, Pulroan spoke.

"That is very well, Lord Arnell, but right now, we are in no position to plan an attack. Which you well know. I am surely not the only one who walked past the courtyard full of screaming wounded while on their way to this chamber. We are crippled. We had to collapse all the Wind Tunnels to Belduar just so the empire couldn't follow us back to Durakdur. For now, we must regroup. We must gather our strength. Then, and only then, can we contemplate taking back your city."

Ihvon grimaced, dipping his head in a slow bow. Dahlen thought he saw a momentary scowl on the man's face. He had not spoken kindly of dwarves in the king's drawing room; it must have hurt him to grovel so.

It was Daymon who responded, pulling himself to his feet. He cut a striking figure at full height, his armour coated with blood and dirt. "It is easy to speak these words when you sit upon a throne with your people safe in their homes!"

Kira snapped herself into an upright position, her eyes ablaze. "We understand your position, oh king without a kingdom, but remember where you stand. You are here due to the deeds of those who came before you.

We do not take you simply on the merit of your father and his father before him. Each must prove their own worth. And you have a lot more to prove before you can speak to us in the way you do. You are correct – this is *our* home, and you would do well to remember that!" Kira's chest rose and fell with deep breaths.

Daymon did not respond. Fury seeped from every inch of him as he stormed from the chamber, not waiting for his advisor to follow. Ihvon gave an apologetic look towards Pulroan but glared when his eyes fell on Kira. The man gave a short bow as he exited the chamber, inclining a nod toward Aeson and Therin.

Pulroan let out an exhausted sigh as she shifted in her throne. Her eyes burned into the back of Kira's head, who sat in petulance, gazing at a spot on the far wall. "Therin Eiltris, Aeson Virandr. I am sorry that this was your reception. But at least you now know the state of affairs. What will be your part in this?"

"We leave after we rest, Your Majesty," Aeson said, much to the queen's surprise. "My son, Erik, and the Draleid have not returned. They were on the last Wind Runner to leave Belduar. I believe something went wrong, and they are somewhere within the network of tunnels. I would be much obliged if you could provide us with a guide."

"It will be done, Rakina. Our people owe you that much," Pulroan said, a hint of curiosity in her voice. "But as you know, the tunnel network is vast, and it runs all throughout the Lodhar Mountains. And there are things other than dwarves that roam the depths of these mountains."

"We understand, Your Majesty."

"Very well," Pulroan said, a mass of wrinkles forming around her frown. "Your guide will be ready in the morning. Now, if you would be so kind as to leave us. There are things we must discuss."

"At once, Your Majesty. And thank you."

The queen gave a brief nod of acknowledgement before turning to say something to Elenya.

They had just left the council chamber when Asius caught up with them. "Aeson, I will not be able to accompany you in your search. I will instead reach out to clan Fenryr of the Angan. I believe they will be able to aid us in the search for the Draleid and your son, should you not be successful."

"The shapeshifters?" Aeson replied. "If you feel it best."

"The Fenryr are an honourable clan, and they are in my debt. Journey safe, my friend."

"Asius," Therin said as the giant made to leave, "if you do have difficulty with the Fenryr, tell them that the son of the Chainbreaker is lost, and he needs them."

The giant raised an eyebrow in curiosity, but simply gave a nod. "As you say, I will do, Therin Eiltris, son of Alwin Eiltris." With that, Asius strode off across the courtyard, his massive legs sweeping in great strides.

"I will meet you here in the morning," Therin said, turning to Aeson and Dahlen. "There are a few things I must see to."

Aeson and Dahlen made their way across the courtyard, the natural acoustics of the mountain city echoing the screams of the dying. Dahlen stopped in his tracks as he spotted a man draped in a black, hooded cloak staring at them from across the yard. He stood unmoving amidst the wounded and the dying. His face was obscured by his hood, but his gaze made the hairs on the back of Dahlen's neck stand on end. Even as Dahlen noticed him, the man didn't move, didn't even avert his gaze.

"Dahlen? What are you doing?"

"Nothing, I…" The man had disappeared. *Did I imagine him?* Dahlen continued after his father, checking over his shoulder as he did. There would not be much sleeping tonight.

"What do you mean, Calen didn't make it?" Dann leapt from the side of his bed, a wince letting Therin know the boy's wounds had not yet entirely healed. They hadn't been able to spare any healers before the battle, and Dann had been left in Durakdur, much to his chagrin.

"He and Erik, along with Vaeril and Gaeleron, never made it back down the Wind Tunnels. We believe something went wrong, but that they are alive."

"How do you know they're alive? And why are you only telling me this now? You've been back for hours!" Dann's face seemed to quickly switch between anger and worry. The boy was usually so cocksure. Therin hadn't ever seen him like this.

"It is a… *feeling*. It is difficult to explain unless you can touch the Spark. But all things are connected, and sometimes, you can *sense* things. I haven't told you until now because I have had things to attend to." Therin said no more, letting the silence linger in the air.

"We're going to find him," Dann whispered, almost to himself.

"Yes, we are."

"It wasn't a question, Therin. We're *going* to find him. I can be ready in half an hour." Dann snatched up a leather bag from beside his bed and began to stuff in whatever was within reach.

"Settle yourself," Therin said, looking at the mess of knotted flesh on Dann's shoulder. The tissue looked raw and angry. "We leave in the morning. In the meantime, let me take a look at that wound."

The boy was irritating at the best of times, but Therin couldn't help but feel a small spark of admiration for him.

The man crept into the room without eliciting so much as a creaking whisper from the floorboards. He was garbed in all black from head to toe, with a hooded cloak pulled tightly around his shoulders that hung just past his knees. Two knives were strapped to a belt that was wrapped across his chest, and a double-edged short sword sat at his hip. He drifted across the room, carefully making his way towards Daymon's bed.

The low rasp of a sword being drawn from its scabbard cut through the silence that had previously consumed the room. Only a moment passed before that sound was replaced with the soft thud of a blade ripping through a duck feather stuffed blanket.

Obscured by darkness, Ihvon couldn't help but let out a deep laugh.

"Almost," he said, rising from the chair where he sat in the corner. The man leapt backwards. Ihvon had been sitting in the dark room long enough for his eyes to adjust to the dim light, long enough to see the scowl on the assassin's face. There was a moment when the man's feet shifted, that Ihvon thought he might run. Instead, he pushed his right foot forward and charged.

"Good," Ihvon said, cracking his neck side to side as he stepped forward to meet the assassin. He left his blade in its scabbard until he would need it.

The man in black lunged, twisting as he stabbed his blade towards Ihvon's stomach. Ihvon sidestepped, deflecting the blade downward with his steel vambraces. He felt the crunch of bone as he brought his elbow back up, slamming it into the assassin's nose. The assassin reeled from the force of the blow, his free hand clasping his broken and bloody nose.

"You think you can come in here? Into my king's bedchamber, and murder him in his sleep?" Ihvon tilted his head down to look at the assassin, who was doubled over, stumbling backward.

The assassin lunged again, swinging his sword in an arc. Ihvon ducked the blow and came back up to slam his fist into the man's already broken nose, sending him crashing to the ground. The man scrambled to his feet, gathering himself, tucking his free hand into his cloak. Ihvon's darkness-adjusted eyes caught the glint of steel as the knife sliced through the air. He twisted to avoid the projectile, but felt a sting as it nicked his cheek. He pursed his lips, giving a slight shrug of his shoulder. "Not bad, but I'm done playing games."

Ihvon ripped his sword from its scabbard, bounding across the floor, clearing the distance to the assassin in seconds. The assassin thrust with his sword, and Ihvon parried the first two strikes with ease. With the third one, he sent the man's sword clattering to the ground. In one smooth motion, Ihvon lifted his foot and planted it square in the man's chest.

Ihvon didn't wait for him to land. He leapt after him, holding his knee against the assassin's stomach, feeling a crack in the man's ribs as they hit the ground. Without hesitation, Ihvon buried his sword into the man's shoulder, not stopping when he felt the crack of bone. The assassin's scream echoed throughout the stone room.

"Make no mistake. You are not leaving this room alive. That will not happen. But you will determine how painfully you die. Speak."

The man choked, gasping for air.

"You want me to lift my knee? I can do that." Ihvon lifted his knee just enough for the man to take in air.

"Your king will be—" The man screamed again as Ihvon twisted the sword in his shoulder.

"Don't fucking test me." Ihvon pulled the other knife from the belt across the man's chest. "Which ear?"

The man's eyes gaped. "Wh… what?"

"Which ear is your favourite? I'll take the other one."

The man hesitated. Ihvon didn't. The knife was sharp. The assassin's right ear came away smoothly, though his screaming would start to wake others sooner or later.

"The next thing I take won't be an ear. Speak."

"It was the Queen. Elenya."

Ihvon nodded. An answer was an answer.

"May The Mother embrace you," he said, driving the man's knife through the soft tissue at the side of his head.

"Do you think he's telling the truth?" Daymon asked, striding into the room with Dahlen Virandr at his side. The young man had tipped them off. He'd said he'd seen a strange person in the Heart, watching Daymon. All these years had taught Ihvon one thing. When it comes to the safety of your king, no reaction is an over-reaction. *I'm sorry, my friend. I will protect Daymon until my dying breath.*

"I truly do not know, Your Majesty. He might have been lying to save his skin. He might not have been. But one thing is for sure," Ihvon said, pulling the blade free from the man's head as he rose to his feet, "there is more going on in this city than we realised."

Dahlen sat on the low stone wall that ringed the fountain at the centre of the square, right in front of the massive set of thick wooden doors that separated the Heart from the rest of the city. In the middle of the fountain, the statue of Heraya pouring the Waters of Life looked down over the yard. Tales of the gods had always interested him more than any other stories during his father's teachings. It was said the gods were an old race, the ones who had given life to the known world. The Jotnar called them the Enkara.

Subtle nuances in dwarven worship had always intrigued Dahlen. Like in common worship, Heraya was "The Mother", the giver of life and the receiver of the dead. Varyn was "The Father", the protector of all things and the provider of the sun. Though, in Dwarven worship, Heraya seemed to be the only god besides the dwarves' patron god – Hafaesir, "The Smith" – deemed worthy of a statue outside the council chamber.

Pulling himself from his thoughts, Dahlen cast his gaze over the empty courtyard. It looked nothing like it had the night before. Most of the injured had been moved out over the course of the night, as the Heart was no place to treat the wounded. Some had been moved to makeshift infirmaries within the bounds of Durakdur, but others had been transported further into the mountain, to the cities of Volkur, Azmar, and Ozryn.

With the wounded gone and the smooth stone washed clean, the putrid aroma of charred flesh and sweat had been replaced by the overpowering antiseptic smell of brimlock sap. The sharp, medicinal scent stung the back of Dahlen's nostrils as he drew in a deep breath.

The faint crashing sound of the waterfall from the main city drifted in past the gates, echoing through the empty Heart. That was one thing that had taken Dahlen by surprise: the way sound travelled in the city. It almost gave him a claustrophobic feeling, the way it resonated through the labyrinth of tunnels and massive chambers. This only served to emphasise the fact that the city itself was surrounded by miles of solid rock. Take away the elaborate golden domes, the sweeping arches, the diamond encrusted colonnades, and all the other wonders of dwarven construction, and they essentially sat in a giant tomb.

Dahlen laughed uneasily at that thought. The tunnels would be worse. He was never a fan of tight spaces, but neither was he a fan of sitting around on his backside. He would be glad to keep moving. And besides, Erik was out there. He would not sit around while his brother needed him.

The footsteps of the two elves reached Dahlen's ears long before they turned the corner and entered the courtyard. Alea and Lyrei were usually full of life. They seemed to have a habit of making Dann jump through hoops just for the fun of it, which gave Dahlen no small amount of enjoyment. But now, they both wore sombre expressions that left no room for joy.

"We will be leaving soon?" Alea asked, swinging her satchel down onto the ground in front of her feet.

Each elf carried a white bow with a leather quiver slung across her back and a slightly curved sword at her waist, almost identical to the one that Calen used. Their long green cloaks draped down over their brown leather armour. The two-part cuirass of their armour was moulded from thick leather, with intricate patterns woven throughout. The shoulders of the cloaks dropped effortlessly between the slats of their articulated pauldrons.

"As soon as my father returns with the guide Queen Kira promised."

Lyrei nodded before taking a seat beside Dahlen on the low stone wall.

"Is everything all right?"

"We should not have allowed ourselves to be separated from the Draleid."

"You cannot blame yourself for that. It was a battle, the city was on fire, and we were being overrun."

"You do not understand." Lyrei sighed and dropped her eyes to the stone floor.

Dahlen didn't respond. She was right; he didn't understand.

"Gaeleron and Vaeril never returned," Alea said, her arms folded across her chest, her forehead creased in worry.

"They may be with Calen and Erik. My father and Therin are convinced they are alive."

"Perhaps. I hope the Draleid is alive. Things have been set in motion. Pieces on a board that haven't moved in centuries. We will have to face what is to come, with or without the Draleid at our side. I, for one, would rather it was *with.*"

Dahlen nodded in response. He didn't know what to say. He couldn't shake the feeling of resentment that niggled at the back of his mind. He had trained his whole life – he and Erik both. They had followed their father through everything. Spent their childhoods holding swords, learning to fight. Then, when it came down to it, he had to fall in line behind someone who stumbled upon them by accident. It just didn't feel right. It also didn't help that Calen seemed intent on blaming him for losing Rist. *Not that I had a choice.*

The clink of dwarven chain mail rang through the air as Aeson approached, a fully armoured dwarf at his side and a small army walking in his wake. The sound of fifty or so armoured boots reverberating against the rock walls of the Heart only served to emphasise how devoid of people it was.

"Nimara, this is my son, Dahlen." Aeson grasped Dahlen's shoulder as he introduced him to the dwarf who stood at his father's side. The dwarf stood about a foot shorter than Dahlen. Her blonde hair was tied back in a braid that was laced with gold, bronze, and silver rings. Her heavy, angular armour sat over a coat of glistening chain mail, and a twin-bladed axe was nestled in a loop across her back.

"May your fire never be extinguished and your blade never dull, Nimara."

The dwarf smiled and repeated the greeting before making the same exchange with the elves.

Dahlen tilted his head towards Aeson's entourage, raising a questioning eyebrow. "The dwarves don't trust us on our own?"

"Actually," Aeson replied, "besides Nimara, they are volunteers. It seems the title of Draleid still holds considerable weight with the dwarven people. They each wanted to aid in the search. There were many more, but I had to turn them away. We can't bring an army on a search through that maze of tunnels."

"We're not late, are we?" Dahlen turned to see Dann and Therin approaching from across the courtyard. Therin's mottled brownish-green cloak drifted behind him, his silver hair shimmering in the flowerlight. The elf never seemed to move with anything short of elegance. Dann was garbed in full hunting leathers, with his bow slung across his back. He seemed to have recovered from his wounds in remarkable time. *Maybe one of the healers got to him.*

"Therin," Aeson smiled, pulling the elf into a tight embrace. Releasing Therin, Aeson turned to Dann, an apologetic look in his eye. "Dann, I'm sorry. But you can't come with us. The tunnels are no place for someone without training, and you're still injured. It's too dangerous."

"I'm coming." Dann just stood there, his eyes fixed on Aeson's, unblinking.

"I'm sorry Dann, you can't—"

Dann moved with surprising speed, drawing level with Aeson. "I said, I'm coming. You will have to stick a knife in me to keep me from going after Calen. I'm not letting you convince me to leave *another* friend behind."

Dahlen swallowed subconsciously. A palpable tension filled the air as everyone's attention was fixed on Dann and Aeson.

Aeson's gaze did not falter. His piercing blue eyes met Dann's stare, matching its intensity with ease. Dahlen's father was a warrior. His shoulders were solid, his stance was wide, and his jaw was set. He should have cut a far more intimidating figure than Dann. But at that moment, there was nothing to separate them. Dahlen couldn't help but admire Dann's tenacity.

"Very well," Aeson said, finally, with a subtle upturn of his lips.

Dahlen thought he saw Alea and Lyrei release the breaths they had both been holding. In fact, he felt himself do the same.

Dann nodded, waiting for a moment before he backed away from Aeson and went over to greet the elves. Therin watched after him, smiling with admiration.

Dahlen was caught by surprise when his father touched his shoulder.

"*You*, truly, are not coming with us."

Dahlen just stood there, dumbstruck. What was he saying? "Of course I am. What are you talking about?"

"After what happened last night – the attempt on Daymon's life – I need someone to be my eyes here. Someone I can trust. Someone who can handle themselves and keep Daymon alive."

Dahlen felt his temper flaring, threatening to take over. "Dad, I'm going after Erik. If he's still alive, then—"

"Then I will find him. I'm not doing this to punish you. When we bring Erik back, and Calen, and Valerys, we will need the dwarves and King Daymon behind us. There is a war coming, Dahlen, and we need our allies in one piece. This is what we have been fighting for. Please, do this for me."

"Yes, sir," Dahlen said, before turning to storm off towards the gates that led out into the main city.

CHAPTER SEVEN

THE CIRCLE

A sliver of soft orange light drifted through the window as the sun set over the aptly named *Sea of Stone*. The sweeping mountainscape seemed to flow endlessly into the horizon. Its sandy-brown peaks dominated the skyline; some were thin and jagged, some broad and flat-topped. There was something unique in the beauty of its discordance. It was not natural, that much the Scholars of the Circle agreed upon; it was created by the Spark aeons ago. But for what purpose? That was the unanswered question.

The view from that window was probably the only redeeming quality of the room in which Rist sat. It was small and sparse with bare walls and stiff wooden chairs. Only four of those chairs were filled, though, by Neera, Tommin, Lena, and himself. Garramon had told him it was not common for initiates or apprentices to be schooled or trained outside the High Tower in Berona. But it did happen on occasion when the initiate was sponsored, as Garramon had sponsored him. He still couldn't wrap his head around it. *Me… a mage.* It still seemed far too much like one of the old bards' stories Calen loved so much – so far detached from the reality he had known. He had not gotten much of a chance to speak with the others yet, to ask them about the Circle. Garramon did not allow him much in the way of free time. That seemed to be a drawback of being sponsored by a *Guide*. A lot more was expected of you; their name was on the line.

A lectern stood at the very front of the room, and behind it perched a sour-faced man with narrowed eyes and a long grey robe that fell over his shoulders, stopping just past his knees. His grey robes marked him as a Lector, a member of the Scholars, and four ranks above initiate.

"Initiate… *Initiate*?"

It took a moment longer than it should have for Rist to realise the Lector was talking to him. "I'm sorry, Brother Pirnil, I—"

Rist sensed the man reaching for the Spark before he felt the searing pain shoot up his back. He clenched his jaw and dropped his hand under the table, twisting it into a fist as the blood trickled from the newly opened cut on his back. Rist bit his lip. It would be a while before the pain subsided. He should know. It would not be long before the cut healed and scarred over, taking its place beside its seven brothers and sisters – reminders that a mage could never lose focus or disobey their superiors.

"To lose your focus…" Brother Pirnil raised one eyebrow as he stepped out from behind the lectern and ambled towards Rist, all the while seeming to look down his nose at him. There was a pleased expression on the man's face when he noticed Rist's clenched fist. That seemed to be the only time Rist saw even a semblance of contentment on the man's stiff, rat-like face: when he saw pain.

"Is to lose your life," Rist continued, through gritted teeth.

"Good. Now, as I have already asked, in what year did the liberation of the free peoples of Epheria begin?

"In the year two-six-eight-two After Doom, sir."

"Good." Irritation flickered across Brother Pirnil's face at Rist's correct response. He couldn't inflict pain for a correct response. "And who was the leader of the traitors at that time?"

"I…" Rist closed his eyes and readied himself. He felt Pirnil reach for the Spark. *What's one more?* But the usual pain did not come.

"Alvira Serris, Brother Pirnil. She was the last tyrant to lay claim to the title of Archon, and she was slain by the venerable High Captain of the Dragonguard, Eltoar Daethana. The ruler of the Lorian Kingdom at the time was Eric Ubbein, defeated by the emperor himself. The elves in their hubris were pushed back into Lynalion, their cities destroyed. The stain of the Jotnar was cleaned from the land, and the Southern kingdoms were brought to heel, sir." Neera sat up straight, her spine pressed against the back of the stiff wooden chair, a smug grin on her face. She had probably seen a summer or two more than Rist, and brown apprentice robes were draped over her shoulders. She did not have a coloured trim on her robes, which marked her as a first-grade apprentice – an apprentice who had not yet earned their colour. If not strictly beautiful, she was certainly handsome, as loath as Rist was to admit it. Her eyes were a deep brown, almost black, matching her hair. If she didn't give off such an air of self-importance, Rist probably would have found her attractive – maybe.

Brother Pirnil nodded, giving an impressed upturn of his lip. "Quite right, apprentice."

All of a sudden, Neera let out a stifled screech, barely audible through gritted teeth, but Rist saw her fingernails sink into the wooden desk in front of her. He knew the pain well. Not all the Lectors seemed to relish pain in the way Brother Pirnil did. In that, he was unique. But none of them hesitated to utilise it as an *educational tool.*

"But as we speak of hubris," Brother Pirnil said, strolling towards the front of the room as if he had not just sliced a gash in Neera's flesh, "we must be sure to keep our own in check."

"Yes, Brother Pirnil. Thank you for your teachings." If Neera's words seemed submissive, the venom in her voice said otherwise. Her glare could have burned holes in the Lector's back as he made his way to the front of the room, and she did nothing to hide it. Trying to understand a woman was an exercise in futility. Instead of stilling her, the pain and open chastisement seemed only to stoke her boldness. Rist did not always understand Neera, but there was something in her that he admired, if only a bit.

Reaching the lectern, Brother Pirnil turned to face the room, a satisfied grin creeping onto his face when he noticed Neera glaring. "We are done for the day. For tomorrow, remember the pain we endure for repeating our mistakes is often tenfold the initial pain."

Before Brother Pirnil had even finished speaking, Neera leapt to her feet, swung her satchel over her shoulder, and strode from the room. Tommin and Lena were not far behind her, but there was notably less urgency in their movements. They each wore the plain brown robes of an apprentice. Rist was the only one of the four who had not yet earned his robes, though it didn't bother him much. They had been initiates for at least a year or so before they earned their robes; he had only been in the embassy a few weeks. There would be time yet. For now, though, Garramon had asked Rist to report to him at the end of the day.

The corridors of the embassy of the Circle of Magii were decorated much the same as Rist's room: pragmatically, to the point of austerity. The walls and floors were carved from solid stone. Windows were set into the stone at regular intervals, just enough so as to provide adequate light, but not so much as to allow an unnecessary amount. A solid wooden chair sat outside each door, as stiff and as hard as the day was long. Not all meetings or lessons finished within the allotted time, and a chair to wait on was simply the sensible thing. It was far from the intimate and homely way his mother decorated and much closer to his taste, and yet… He found himself missing the warm hearth, fur blankets, and mugs of Arlen root tea. Missing home.

As he made his way through the long, drab corridors, the only thing that seemed in any way flamboyant was the gilded black carpet that ran the length of every floor. It was inlaid with intricate patterns of red and gold that flowed into images of lions and dragons, nestled beneath trees or soaring over mountains. In truth, it was quite a fantastic piece of craftsmanship. No matter which corridor Rist found himself in, the carpet was there. The same images never seemed to repeat. Every few feet was a new story. There wasn't enough coin in all the villages to afford something so incredible.

Rist pulled his pensive gaze from a particularly elaborate scene of two golden dragons fighting as a man walked past him, a long green robe with silver markings draped over his shoulders. Green was the colour of the Consuls, the advisors and diplomats of the Circle of Magii. The silver markings, however, denoted his rank as a High Mage, or High Consul within the green affinity. The hierarchy of the Circle was one of the first things Brother Pirnil had taught him. *'It is important to know one's place,'* Rist could hear the man saying.

Rist dropped his head into a deep bow, as was appropriate for someone of the High Consul's status. "High Consul."

Without stopping, the man gave a curt tilt of his head accompanied by an indecipherable grunt. That was all Rist had come to expect from anyone in the Circle embassy, except for Garramon. That being said, Rist had met but a handful of High Mages from the various affinities, and this was the first one who had even acknowledged he was alive. He was sure Dann would have a funny quip to make about that if he were here.

Rist was only an initiate. He had not yet earned even his brown robes, never mind his colours. Grey, black, white, green, yellow, and red, for the Scholars, the Battlemages, the Healers, the Consuls, the Craftsmages, and the Inquisition.

Rist stopped when he reached the door to Garramon's study, a sturdy oak door with the insignia of The Circle – two thin concentric circles with six smaller solid circles set into them at evenly spaced intervals – emblazoned across it in shimmering gold. He gave two solid knocks and took a step back.

"Enter."

Garramon's study was perhaps the most lavishly decorated room in the entire embassy, at least of the rooms Rist had seen. An enormous bookcase, made from a deep brown wood that Rist did not recognise, consumed the western wall, stocked to the brim with books and scrolls that looked twice as old as Rist, and then twice again. A large marble fireplace, the sides of which were carved into two roaring lions standing on their hind legs, was set into the wall opposite the bookcase. The fireplace was not lit, but the white marble on the inside was blackened from previous use. Two leather armchairs sat in front of the fireplace, and Garramon's desk was at the back of the room, about three feet out from the wall, a sturdy wooden chair on either side.

Garramon stood in front of his desk, conversing with a man in a black hooded cloak. He was of Garramon's affinity, a Battlemage. The silver markings on his cloak meant he was also the same rank as Garramon: a High Mage, or Exarch among the Battlemages. He was solidly built, with broad shoulders and a strong jaw. In any other circumstance, Rist thought the cloaked man would have dominated the room, but in this case, he seemed almost… meek. Despite the fact that he and Garramon were of the same rank, the man's shoulders were drooped, and he shuffled his feet as if eager to leave. The entire scene was… *odd*.

Garramon's lips were pursed as if he were contemplating something, and the creases along his brow let Rist know that whatever news he was receiving was not to his liking. Neither man acknowledged Rist as he entered, nor did they cease their conversation.

"And they are increasing in frequency?"

"Yes, my—" the man's eyes flitted to Rist and then back to Garramon. "Yes. We receive new reports each day. The Uraks grow bolder as we get closer to the Blood Moon. Many towns along the base of Lodhar and Mar Dorul are attacked weekly, daily in some cases. In the South they can barely—"

"We should discuss this later. We will need to inform the Grand Council and the emperor." There was a tone of finality in Garramon's words. The man bowed, a little more deeply than Rist would have expected from an equal, and then strode past Rist without a word.

A warm smile spread across Garramon's face as he turned to acknowledge Rist. "My apologies. There are some troubling events occurring across the continent. Please, take a seat." Garramon made his way around to the other side of the desk and dropped himself gracefully into his seat. "How goes your history class with Brother Pirnil? He is stern, but there is a lot to learn from him."

"Yes, good," Rist lied as he sat down in the wooden chair, ignoring the sharp pain that ran the length of his back from Brother Pirnil's *history* lesson. "He is very wise. Brother Garramon?"

"Yes, initiate?"

"I… em, I've been meaning to ask you. I know I've brought it up a few times but… have you heard back from any of the messages that were sent to my family?"

With a smile, Garramon reached inside his long black cloak, producing a small cream envelope held shut with a beeswax seal that Rist immediately recognised. It was all Rist could do to not snatch it straight from Garramon's hands.

"My parents!" Rist said, louder than he had intended.

"Indeed." Garramon handed the letter over to Rist, the soft smile never leaving his face. "Go ahead. You can open it."

Rist didn't need a second invitation. He peeled open the beeswax seal, taking care not to rip the envelope. His heart could have stopped when his eyes fell on his mother's handwriting. A strange tingling filled his stomach, like butterflies flapping their wings. He was nervous. He had felt more alive in the past few weeks than he ever had before. Touching the Spark had lit a fire in him. In his mind, the mundane life of the Glade threatened that feeling, for some reason. He didn't want to go home. But he missed his mother and father more than anything.

Our dearest son,

I can't put into words how relieved we were to receive your letter. When you left, we were terrified. With everything that happened… We're just happy you're all right.

We are doing well here. The soldiers have protected us from the Uraks and the bandits. There have been more bandits on the roads since that man started calling himself a Draleid, stirring up trouble. I'm not sure what we'll do if things get worse. Hopefully, the soldiers stay. We received word from High Lord Castor Kai in Argona. He says that he will send soldiers himself, to fend off the bandits and the Uraks. But we're not holding out hope.

We hope they are treating you all right up there. A mage? Your father had to read that part of your letter to me four times before I stopped calling him a liar. We are both so very proud of you, but the North is not safe. Promise us you will be careful. If we had the coin, we would come to you straight away. We promise we will try our best. Please keep writing. Tell us everything that goes on in your days.

Dann's parents have written him a letter as well. It's in the envelope. We hope Calen is all right. We pray to Varyn and Heraya for him each night.

All our love,
Mam and Dad.

There was an apologetic look on Garramon's face. "We have not received any other letters. Our officers were unable to find any of your friends, and the hawk we sent to Belduar did not return, I'm afraid. But unfortunately, that is to be expected."

Calen and Dann. The thought of his friends sent Rist's stomach lurching. They would think him lost, or worse. He needed to let them know he was all right, but how?

Garramon's words floated through Rist's head, taking a moment to register. "Why is it to be expected that the hawk wouldn't return from Belduar?"

Garramon's expression reminded Rist that his level of informality was not common.

"Why is it to be expected, Brother Garramon?" he corrected himself.

"There is a lot of unrest across Epheria. Uraks are appearing in large numbers, attacking villages and murdering travellers on the roads near to the mountains. But in the South, things are worse. War has broken out between our great nation and the kingdom of Belduar."

Rist couldn't hide the look of shock that spread across his face. News was hard to come by. He still hadn't been allowed to roam the streets of the city, and the guards and mages in the embassy were hardly known for their gossip. The news that Belduar and Loria were at war was among the last things Rist had wanted to hear. Belduar was where Aeson had been bringing the others before they got separated.

"Don't worry, my child. *War* is a generous term. The city has fallen, and the kingdom has been brought to heel. It is just a matter of time before the soldiers root out the new child king."

A coil of dread twisted in Rist's stomach, and a wave of anguish swept over him. He was not a true believer in the gods, but right then and there he prayed to all six that Calen, Dann, and the others had never made it to Belduar.

"The more troublesome news," Garramon continued, "is of the man who calls himself a Draleid."

"Draleid?" Rist's mind instantly flitted back to Therin's stories, particularly the one he had told during the Moon Market that spring. "The ones from the stories?"

"Traitors to Epheria." Garramon scowled, his eyes becoming cold and hard. The man took a breath, his face softening. "When controlled properly, as in the case of the Dragonguard, dragons and the ones bound to them can be of great use. But when they are bound to someone like this man, they are a danger to us all. Even now, the dragon is not even half grown, and it has cost thousands of lives. Many more will be lost until it is brought under control or stopped."

There was so much to process. Rist slowed the thoughts in his mind, pushing away those that were unimportant. Questions were all well and good, but unless you asked the right ones, you would never get the answers you were looking for.

"But how did they get a dragon egg? And how did it hatch? From the stories I know, an egg hasn't hatched since… well, since The Fall."

Garramon gave a short *tssk*. Rist saw a touch of impatience in the man's eyes.

He would have to be careful. Where he grew up, the empire was not exactly… *loved.* He didn't always share the same sentiments as those in the villages. The empire had done nothing in particular to him, and his father's inn had always done well, but sometimes he didn't realise how his upbringing steered his way of thinking. He often forgot where he now stood: in Al'Nasla, the capital city of the Lorian Empire. He had to learn to conceal his initial thoughts. To pick his words carefully. He knew well that he was a sheep nestled snugly inside a den of wolves. "I mean, since the Liberation."

A smile touched the edge of Garramon's lips at Rist's words, his early impatience pushed to the back of his mind. "These are questions we are currently searching for the answers to, my child. But more pressingly, I have something for you."

"You do?" Rist needed to be cautious. At first, he had been swept up in it all. Magic. The empire. A whole new world of possibilities. But the more time he had to think, the more his common sense started to creep through. *Keep asking questions. If he is telling lies, questions are his worst enemy.*

"I do."

Garramon bent down under his desk, shuffling a few things around. When he emerged, he held a brown bundle of folded clothing in his arms. Garramon set the bundle down on the desk. He didn't say a word. He just looked at Rist, expectancy on his face.

That can't be. "My robes?"

Garramon nodded slowly, his mouth spreading into a subdued grin of pride.

"I…" Rist didn't know what to say. Those robes were the first *real* step. They were the first tangible thing bringing him into the Circle. He was now an apprentice. "But why? I have only been here a matter of weeks."

"With war on the horizon, we do not have the time that we would usually give to new initiates. Needs must." Garramon said, rising to his feet. The man stepped out from behind his desk and placed a hand on Rist's shoulder. "I am proud of you, Rist. You have come a long way in a short time. And I believe that with dedication, you will wear the black with pride. I am proud to be your Guide. Now, shall we try on those robes?"

Rist's heart stopped. "Black? But I haven't decided my affinity. How could I—"

Garramon's laugh cut through Rist's words.

"Calm yourself, apprentice. It is not the apprentice who chooses his acolyteship. It is the Guide, for you can never truly see yourself. But I see you, and I see what you can become – a Battlemage.

CHAPTER EIGHT

AWOKEN

The glow of the lanterns illuminated the stone walls as Kallinvar walked along the edge of the sparring chamber, his hands clasped behind his back, his eyes narrowed in focus.

The sparring chamber within the Temple of Achyron was easily two hundred feet in length and at least a hundred feet from side to side. Stone walkways divided it into ten large, sand covered sparring pits, one for each chapter. Nothing hung on the walls except for sconces and weapon racks; a sparring chamber had no need for ornamentation.

The sound of steel on steel rang through Kallinvar's ears as he skirted the edge of the sparring pit that was dedicated to The Second, the knights chapter under his command. On any other morning, he would have joined his brother and sister knights in training. But Lyrin had not yet returned from his journey to Camylin. That left nine knights, an odd number. Ten chapters, ten knights in each. That had always been the way.

With the exception of Kallinvar's knights, the massive chamber was empty. He preferred it that way. It was not that he did not appreciate the company of his brothers and sisters of the other chapters, but he liked to able to focus when he observed the sparring. Any weaknesses addressed then could save a life later.

A loud crash drew Kallinvar's attention. Young Arden stood over Ildris, who lay on his back in the sand, Arden's sword pressed against his neck. Arden had come along quickly since they found him only two years gone. *The last Sigil Bearer. Nearly four hundred years to recover from that night in Ilnaen and rebuild the knighthood.*

Physically, Arden was a specimen. His chest and shoulders were thick and broad, and his muscles were dense. By Kallinvar's gauge, he was almost six and a half feet in height. As he stood over Ildris now, his short brown hair was matted to his face with sweat and his bare chest heaved up and down in slow, measured strokes. Well, his chest would have been bare, were it not for the green Sigil at its centre, appearing as though it were a shimmering metallic tattoo. The Sigil of the Knights of Achyron – a downward-facing sword, set into a sunburst.

The young man had impressed Kallinvar at every turn. Not just with his skill in combat, but in his learning and his comprehension. He was already a fine Brother Knight, but he would become a great one. Of that, Kallinvar had no doubt.

"Yield," Arden said, his arm firm and unshaking as he held the blade to Ildris's neck.

"Never."

Arden smiled as he lowered his sword and held out his hand.

Ildris laughed, clasping Arden's outstretched hand, using it as leverage to pull himself to his feet. "You're getting better."

"Oh, I am? Why, thank you, *Brother Knight.*" Arden gave a mocking bow as he spoke.

"Again," Kallinvar shouted, levelling a disapproving glare at Arden and Ildris.

Both knights stiffened, the laughter gone from their faces. "Yes, Brother-Captain."

Kallinvar nodded. A kinship between his knights was important. They needed to be willing to bleed for each other, and to die for each other if Achyron demanded it. But they could not afford to grow slack, not with the Blood Moon so close. He held his gaze over the two knights for a moment before continuing on to watch over the other sparring sessions.

Sister Ruon and Brother Tarron were locked in a fierce exchange, their swords ringing out across the stone as they fought with a fury. Ruon, Tarron, and Ildris had been with him the longest. Since before. Before their numbers had been decimated at The Fall. Achyron had asked a heavy price of them that night. Of one hundred knights, only seventeen had returned from that battle, a battle they had lost to the Shadow. In truth, their chapter had suffered the least, making up four of the seventeen survivors: Ruon, Tarron, Ildris, and Kallinvar. The Fourth, The Eighth, and The Ninth had been completely wiped out, sent to rest in Achyron's halls. Kallinvar sighed. The scars ran deep. He looked out over the training ground. With the exception of the survivors from that night, most of those before him had been knights for less than a century. It had been over seven hundred years since Kallinvar himself had first accepted the Sigil. For seven hundred years, he had served the will of Achyron. The Sigil would not permit him to die. Not that he would permit himself to either. To serve under The Warrior was the greatest honour a man could ever receive.

Kallinvar's eyes fell on Brother Mirken and Sister Sylven. Flashes of green light pulsed from their Soulblades as the weapons collided in mid-air. Soulblades were weapons wrought from Spirit. They were pure energy that did not exist until called upon by a knight. The Soulblade was the weapon of the knighthood, gifted by the warrior god himself. Some mages or Draleid who were powerful enough could imitate it. They called them níthrals in the Old Tongue. But whatever they chose to call them, they did not understand the power of a *true* Soulblade, wrought from the soul of Achyron himself.

"Care to join, Brother-Captain?" Varlin called from the other side of the sparring pit. Sweat rolled down the woman's face as she leaned on the pommel of her sword, the tip of the blade buried in the sand. Varlin had a strong frame, layered with smooth muscle. The sides of her head were shaved, and the remainder of her straw-blonde hair was tied into a plat that ran down the back of her head in the style of her native Valtara. She was a warrior even before she had received the Sigil, a blademaster. Kallinvar had found her almost a hundred years ago, during the Valtaran uprising. She was exactly where the Grand Master had said she would be: in a field of bodies, about two hundred miles north of the Marin Mountains, at the base of an old willow tree, still clinging to life like a cornered hound.

Kallinvar smiled. "I still have bruises from the last time we sparred, Sister Varlin. You can continue to take your anger out on Brother Daynin, if it pleases you."

Brother Daynin glared at Kallinvar, a hint of a smile at the corner of his lips as he mouthed the words, "I will get you for this."

Footsteps of steel on stone echoed down the wide staircase at the far end of the chamber. "Brother-Captain Kallinvar, I see I've arrived just in time to teach you a few lessons in swordsmanship."

Kallinvar rolled his eyes as Lyrin descended the staircase. Lyrin had accepted the Sigil less than seven years past. He was a strong young man, almost a match for Arden in both strength and skill. His shoulder-length brown hair was meticulously groomed, to a point that it looked almost unnatural. *His hair is just about the only thing he is meticulous about.* Etiquette was not Lyrin's strong suit, and he could do with learning a lesson or two.

"Lyrin. I trust your trip to Camylin went as expected, then?"

"Indeed, Brother-Captain. The Thieves Guild in Camylin was happy to take our gold. We will receive weekly reports."

"Very good," Kallinvar said, rolling his shoulders back, feeling the stretch. The thrum of Kallinvar's Sigil coursed through his body as he called on his Soulblade. A white-hot sensation burned in his chest, where the Sigil had fused with him all those years ago, strands of pulsing green light rushing from either side of his hand. The strands wrapped and weaved around each other, melding together to form something greater.

Kallinvar didn't have to look to know that his fingers grasped the glowing green handle of his Soulblade. The piercing light had dissipated, and in its place was a low, pulsing glow. Kallinvar's Soulblade took the shape of a double-edged greatsword. It was as solid as if the green pulsing light had been cut from steel, though unlike steel, a Soulblade could draw blood from a Fade, and it could rip the dark creature's soul from the world of the living.

Lyrin's shoulders sagged, and he let out a resigned sigh.

Let's teach you some etiquette.

Kallinvar dropped himself into the firm leather chair that sat behind his stone-carved desk. Like the rest of the Great Temple, Kallinvar's study was cut from solid stone. The multitude of beeswax candles bathed the room in a soft, warm light, not that there was much to illuminate. Besides his desk and chair, all that resided in the room was a bookcase stocked with ancient texts, a long stone bench against the far wall, and a tapestry that depicted the day the Knights of Achyron had been formed. It was a simple room. Kallinvar enjoyed simplicity; life was complicated enough. He let out a sigh and wiped the sweat from his brow, his white cotton shirt clinging to his chest, weighed down with sweat from his sparring session with Lyrin. The young man was a good swordsman, but he still had a lot to learn.

"Brother-Captain Kallinvar."

Kallinvar straightened his back, seating himself properly in his chair. "Grandmaster Verathin. I was not aware that I should have expected you tonight."

"At ease, Kallinvar, we have known each other far too long for all of this formality," Verathin said, as he seated himself on the stone bench opposite from Kallinvar. "Are you well?"

Kallinvar narrowed his eyes. It was true, he and Verathin had known each other for a long time – since Kallinvar first took the Sigil – and they had grown to be close friends, but Verathin was a formal person. He always had been.

"I am," Kallinvar said cautiously.

Verathin laughed. "No, old friend. I am not here to simply see how you are doing."

Kallinvar did not speak, letting silence hang in the air, urging Verathin to continue.

"You have not changed in all these centuries," Verathin said, the slightest of smiles touching his face. Verathin held Kallinvar's gaze for a few moments before continuing. "The Blood Moon is upon us once more. It will taint the sky red within a year, and its effects will linger even longer."

Kallinvar grimaced at the thought. It had been four hundred years since the last Blood Moon, a time when the power of blood magic was heightened and when the traitor god could cast his hand into the world and grant terrible power to his followers. That was when The Order fell, the empire rose, and when his brothers and sisters died.

"We have known it was coming, and we have prepared. Our time has come once again. Also, I have received reports of which I first held suspicion, but as of now, I am sure." Verathin must have seen the curiosity in Kallinvar's eyes, for he did not wait for a response. "A new dragon has hatched."

Every hair on Kallinvar's body stood on end. A hatchling hadn't been born since The Fall. Nine Dragonguard still lived, and they were powerful enough, but if more eggs were starting to hatch, Fane Mortem and the empire would become unstoppable. "How is this possible?"

"I am not sure. But if the reports are true, the dragon – and its Draleid – do not fight for the empire and, in turn, the traitor god."

Draleid. It had been a long time since Kallinvar had heard that word. But it only served to raise even more questions. "Forgive me for my lack of knowledge, Grandmaster, but again, *how*?"

Verathin shook his head. "I do not know, Brother-Captain. But it is something we must ascertain."

Kallinvar sat back in his chair. *This could change everything. A Draleid not loyal to the empire.*

"If the Draleid and the dragon are not loyal to the empire… we must protect them," Kallinvar said. "They will be powerful allies against the coming Shadow."

"Agreed. And to that end, there are some things we must discuss."

Arden didn't think the Tranquil Garden would ever cease to amaze him. In truth, there wasn't a single thing that hadn't amazed him in the two years since he had taken the Sigil, but walking through the garden held its own sense of wonder. Beneath his leather boots, the ground was soft and pliable, covered by a carpet of varicoloured moss that played home to a multitude of insects and small animals. Around him, the long delicate branches of the Hallow trees whirled and spiralled in all directions, twisting and coiling in on themselves, tracing along the roof of the enormous cavern. Even the roots sprouted from the ground in seemingly random places, twisting into whirlpool shapes with lanterns hung on their ends. Overhead, the lush green of the canopy was interspersed with clusters of vibrant purple flowers that hung down over the branches, glowing with a dim light. There was no place in all of Epheria that filled him with such a sense of peace.

"Shit..."

Arden laughed as Lyrin's face twisted into a grimace of pain. A large blackish-blue bruise had already formed along the length of his friend's forearm, and the long, thin cut that ran along his cheekbone was raw and red. They had come to the Tranquil Garden after sparring to rest their bones in Heraya's Well. "You knew what you were doing."

Lyrin shrugged. He winced as he touched his finger against the cut on his cheek. "I'm going to beat him one day, mark my words."

"Sure you are," Arden said, tilting his head back and rolling his shoulders until he felt a crack. He closed his eyes and took a moment to let the sounds of the garden drift into his ears. The birdsong that floated through the air was as constant as the burbling of the many tiny streams that meandered through the garden like a network of cobwebs, all finding their way to Heraya's Well, a luminescent pool at the garden's centre.

"Are you coming?"

Arden opened his eyes again, just catching sight of a small orange and blue bird darting between the canopy of the trees above. "Sorry, I just needed a moment."

The rumbling sound of falling water softened most other noises as the two knights approached Heraya's Well. The ground fell away at the edges of the pool, with tangled strands of moss and dangling roots hanging down, brushing the surface of the shimmering water. Hundreds of tiny threadlike streams fed into the pool from all sides, tumbling down over the edge. The water held within the pool was like nothing else Arden had ever laid eyes on. It shimmered in a wide variety of vivid blues, as if the water itself were alive. Patches of the pool were as dark as the ocean at night, and laced through those patches of darkness were coruscating clusters of lighter, more vibrant blues.

"Do you think it is truly Heraya's Well?" Lyrin said, crouching down onto his haunches and running his hand through the water of one of the tiny streams. "The true *Waters of Life…*"

"Had you asked me that question two years ago, I would have said no. But now…" Arden traced his fingers over his sweat-soaked shirt, following the lines of the Sigil he bore on his chest. The Sigil that was burned into his flesh and fused with his soul. The Sigil that saved his life. "… now, I need no more proof that the gods stretch their fingertips into this world. Come, we don't have long before supper."

Arden tossed his clothes in a loose pile at the edge of the pool, and then slowly lowered himself into the water. He felt it immediately, the cooling sensation that flooded his body as he submerged himself. Every ache, every pain and minor irritation dissipated at the water's touch, melting away. The clusters of bright, vivid light swarmed around his body, pulsating as they touched his skin.

"It feels incredible," Lyrin said, the water shimmering around him as he dropped into the pool. "I think—"

"Five minutes," Arden said, cutting across Lyrin.

"Five minutes what?"

"Hold that thought for five minutes. Just five minutes of peace, Lyrin."

"I'll show you damned peace…"

Arden chuckled to himself as he closed his eyes and tossed his head back in the water, just letting himself float.

Not three minutes had passed when the silence was broken. "Ahem."

"Lyrin, I said *five* minutes."

"Brother Arden, Brother Lyrin."

Arden nearly leapt out of his skin when he recognised the voice. He snapped his eyes open and dropped his feet to the bottom of the pool. "Grandmaster Verathin, my apologies. We were rejuvenating after sparring. How may we serve?"

The Grandmaster stood at the edge of the pool, a white mantle draped over his shoulders with the Sigil of Achyron emblazoned across its front in a dark green. He was a tall man with a sharp jaw and short brown hair speckled with flecks of white. He always seemed to have a serious look in his eyes, as though he were weighing up everything he saw. Watching and judging. The Grandmaster was not alone. Watcher Gildrick, one of the priests of the temple, stood by his side. His robes were a dark green with a trim of white. The Watchers were a particular group of the Priests of Achyron, who were tasked with overseeing the knights and guiding them on their path. Arden liked Gildrick; he was a good man.

"That is perfectly all right, Brother Arden," Grandmaster Verathin said. "Heraya's Well is for us all. When you have finished, you are both required in the Heart Chamber. I have sensed a minor convergence of the Taint near a small town in the North – Helden. You will be going through the Rift."

"Yes, Grandmaster," Arden and Lyrin both replied at the same time.

"Good, we shall await you in the chamber."

With that, Verathin and Gildrick made their way back through the garden, leaving the two knights standing in Heraya's Well. Lyrin immediately broke out into laughter. "That was brilliant. '*Grandmaster Verathin, my apologies*'. Serves you right."

Arden shot him a look that could kill. "Shut your mouth or I'll drown you."

"You can't drown me in here. It's the *Waters of Life*. Emphasis being on *life*."

"So, you'll just keep drowning indefinitely then?"

Lyrin snapped his mouth shut at that, pursing his lips inward as he realised the flaw in his thinking. "So… shall we go?"

Chapter Nine

Shadows Rising

rother-Captain Kallinvar, Grandmaster Verathin, and Watcher Gildrick were all waiting in the Heart Chamber by the time Arden and Lyrin arrived.

The Heart Chamber resided at the centre of the great temple of Achyron, hence its name. Arden had stepped foot within its stone walls on but a handful of occasions. The Heart Chamber was mostly used for sending knights through the Rift, and Arden had not yet had the honour of undertaking such a journey. The Rift was reserved for when rapid action was needed. When time was the difference between lives saved and lives lost. And that was why the hairs on the back of Arden's neck were standing on end.

"Brother Arden, Brother Lyrin, welcome." Watcher Gildrick folded his arms across his chest and dipped his head slightly.

Arden nodded his head in return, with Lyrin following suit.

"Welcome, my brothers," Grandmaster Verathin said, his sharp eyes moving quickly between the two knights. "Watcher Gildrick?

Watcher Gildrick nodded, turning to address Arden and Lyrin. "We have been receiving reports for a few weeks now that the Bloodspawn have been raiding many of the villages along the foothills of Mar Dorul, with recent sightings near Helden," Watcher Gildrick added, looking towards Kallinvar and Verathin. "With Grandmaster Verathin sensing a convergence of the Taint so close to the town, it is highly likely that Helden is in imminent danger."

Brother-Captain Kallinvar stepped closer to Arden and Lyrin. "If the town is in danger from Bloodspawn, you are to eliminate the threat. Understood?"

"Understood, Brother-Captain." Lyrin gave a nod, turning to Arden with a half-smile.

"Yes, Brother-Captain," Arden said, closing his hand into a fist and bringing it to his chest. "For Achyron."

A deep sense of pride swelled in Arden's chest as Kallinvar's eyes locked on his. Even more so than Verathin, Brother-Captain Kallinvar was a legend. Arden could not count the number of stories he had heard about Kallinvar from the elders of Ardholm and even from the Watchers. He was one of the few survivors of The Fall, and it was said he was the greatest warrior ever to bear the Sigil. It was Kallinvar, along with the other knights of The Second, who had saved Arden and given him a second chance in the world. Arden would not let him down.

A shiver ran through Arden's body and a deep thrum resonated from his Sigil as a green orb appeared in the air behind Grandmaster Verathin, materialising as if from nothing. Before Arden's eyes, the orb flattened, spreading out into a wide disc over ten feet in diameter. As the disc spread, its centre grew darker until it was as black as night. After a few seconds, only the outer rim of the floating disc retained its green colour, and everything else within was dark as obsidian, rippling as though it were the surface of a lake.

The Rift.

Arden took a step forward, his legs moving on their own. Every beat of his heart resounded in his chest and sent a rippling shiver across his skin. He took a deep breath, a slight quiver betraying him as he exhaled. The Rift was a power given only to the Grandmaster. A portal that could send a knight, as long as they were encased in their Sentinel armour, anywhere in the known world in a matter of moments. Arden's mouth grew dry as his eyes traced the rippling lake of black that hung in the air, its green outer rim shimmering. It wasn't fear that gripped him; it was reverence. To step through the Rift was to feel the touch of a god – the god that had pulled him from death's door: Achyron.

"Step forward, Brother Arden, Brother Lyrin." Grandmaster Verathin moved to the side, allowing Arden and Lyrin to take their place before the rippling pool of black that hung in the air. "I will open the Rift ten miles south of Helden so as not to alert the Bloodspawn. It is your charge to protect the people of that town and any others around it. May The Warrior guide your hands. The duty of the strong is to protect the weak."

"The duty of the strong is to protect the weak," Arden and Lyrin replied, stepping forward. Taking a deep breath, Arden called to the Sigil of Achyron that was fused with his chest, summoning his Sentinel armour, a gift to the knights from Achyron himself. The thrum of the Sigil resonated through his body as it answered his call. An ice-cold sensation spread from his chest, sweeping through his bones and over his skin as the Sentinel armour poured forth from the Sigil. He watched as the molten green liquid spread down his arms and over his fingertips before hardening and taking shape. Within moments, he was covered from head to toe in smooth, overlapping plates of dark green. Power surged through the armour. Arden felt as though he could grind stone to dust beneath his boots. The Sentinel armour was stronger than any metal and lighter than a floating feather. It was armour wrought from Achyron's own Spirit.

"For Achyron," Kallinvar said, giving a slight tilt of his head.

"For Achyron," Arden and Lyrin replied.

Taking the sword and sword belt that Watcher Gildrick offered him, Arden fixed his gaze on the rippling lake of black that hung, suspended, in the air, its outer rim a vivid green hue. He had heard the other knights describe how it felt to step through the Rift, to feel its icy embrace wrap around your soul. He turned to Lyrin, seeing the man encased head to toe in shimmering green, the Sigil of Achyron emblazoned across his chest in a brilliant white, matching the cape that fell from his shoulders. No words needed to be said. Arden moved forward, hesitating only for a second before plunging into the darkness-obscured depths of the Rift.

An implacable chill swept over his body, seeping through his armour, prickling his skin, and leeching the warmth from his bones. For a moment, he felt as though he were back in the forest, blood pouring through his fingers, death standing over him, waiting patiently for his soul. Then he was through.

Arden's breath plumed out in front of him as it met with the icy embrace of winter air. Grandmaster Verathin had said he would open the Rift a little under ten miles to the south of Helden. Arden questioned that distance; they had been walking for hours through the darkness-enveloped forest, and there seemed no end in sight. The only sounds that pierced the eldritch silence of the dense wood were those of the frost-crusted leaves and twigs crunching and snapping beneath the weight of Arden's and Lyrin's armoured boots.

"How far do you think it is?" Lyrin asked, his breath misting as he spoke, all but his head encased in his Sentinel armour.

"Can't be much longer—"

Crack.

Arden snapped his head around, staring into the vast emptiness of the forest. He ripped his sword from the scabbard at his hip, the hairs on the back of his neck standing on end, and his blood shivering through his veins. If a Fade or the Bloodspawn had set a trap for them, they had walked into it like lambs to slaughter.

"Can you see anything?" A sharp rasp let Arden know that Lyrin had drawn his sword as well.

The pounding of Arden's heart resounded in his head, the rushing blood thumping in his eardrums with each beat.

Crack.

Something moved in the darkness, leaves crunching beneath its charge. Stilling the fear that had crept into the back of his mind, Arden lunged forward, sweeping his blade in a wide arc. He could see little in the dark forest haze, but he felt the resistance as steel met skin and bone, and the release as the blade sliced clean through.

With a heavy thud, the body of their attacker crumpled to the ground, the force of its charge carrying it forward into the trunk of a tree. Squawks and flapping wings echoed preternaturally through the night as birds jettisoned from the canopy above. Then there was silence.

"What is it?" Lyrin whispered.

"A doe," Arden said, letting out a sigh as he knelt beside the body. He ran his gauntleted hand along the deer's side, stopping as he came to the stump of its neck. He had taken the poor creature's head clean off. Arden's heart sank, and his voice dropped to a whisper. "Forgive me, Heraya. Welcome her into your arms." Letting out a heavy sigh, Arden rose to his feet. "Let's keep moving."

Arden's gaze flitted from side to side as they continued through the forest, his senses heightened. Every snapping branch and rustling leaf made his hand twitch on the pommel of his sword. The susurration of the arthritic branches overhead crashed through his eardrums like breaking waves.

"Arden?" Lyrin's voice pierced through the cacophony of sound, almost causing Arden to leap out of his skin. "What do you think?"

"About what?" Arden asked, his eyes still scanning the depths of the surrounding forest.

"About what Watcher Gildrick said. The reports of the Bloodspawn attacking the villages at the foot of Mar Dorul, more and more each day. Do you think they are true? Do you think the Shadow truly is rising?"

Arden shrugged. "That's why we're here. We will find out when we get to the town, I suppose. I hope it is not, but…"

Snap. Arden wrapped his fingers around the hilt of his sword, pausing only when a fox flitted across the ground at his feet.

"And have you heard the rumours of the Draleid?" Lyrin said, ignoring the fox. He had that usual excitement in his voice when he thought he knew more about something than someone else.

"I have, though surely they are not true." Arden let his fingers loosen, but kept them hovering over the sword's pommel. He narrowed his eyes, turning back to Lyrin. "What have you heard, Lyrin?"

"Not much."

Arden didn't take the bait. He simply raised an amused eyebrow and turned his gaze back to the darkness-shrouded forest path ahead, allowing the eerie sound of nocturnal bird calls and the rustling of foliage to fill the void of conversation.

"Oh, you're no fun," Lyrin huffed after a few minutes of waiting for Arden to break and ask him more questions. "When I was in Camylin, I heard rumours of Lorian soldiers arriving at the port in Gisa. Thousands of them. Days later, the empire had set up a blockade on Belduar."

"And? The empire has been trying to take Belduar since The Fall."

"And, not days ago, three of the Dragonguard reduced the city to smouldering ash. How long has it been since the Dragonguard have actually flown south of the Burnt Lands? Why did they come this time? The network has been tight on any news coming from the battle. But you can take my word for it, there is a new Draleid, and the empire wants them dead."

"I—" A high-pitched scream in the distance cut Arden short. He hadn't even realised they had stepped out from the confines of the forest. Up ahead, what he could only assume was the town of Helden was covered in flames.

"It came from the town," Lyrin shouted, breaking into a sprint. Arden followed him. As they drew closer to the town's outskirts, the screams grew louder, rippling through the night, accompanied by the crackling of burning wood and the clang of steel. Helden didn't seem a particularly large town, maybe big enough to house one or two thousand people at most. Now, nearly all those people filled the streets. Helden's buildings were a mix of stone and stout logs with thatched roofing. It was the thatched roofing that allowed the fires to burn so furiously, pluming smoke and embers into the air.

In the midst of the chaos, a man caught sight of Arden and Lyrin suited in full Sentinel armour, swords strapped to their belts. Arden could see in his eyes that it took all his courage to stop and call out to them. "Please, they're just—"

An enormous spear shot out from one of the side streets, bursting through the man's chest and sending him crashing to the ground, splattering the dirt with dark gore. Following the spear, several hulking figures rushed from the shadows cast by the blazing inferno of the town. Each carried blackened blades that radiated a red glow at their base. Leathery grey skin pulled tightly at the creatures' dense muscle, rippling as they moved. Bloodspawn – Uraks.

"I guess we have our answer." As Lyrin spoke, molten green metal rose from the collar of his Sentinel armour, moving up his neck and over his head, before settling, taking the shape of a smooth helm with slits for eyes that shimmered with a green light.

Arden followed suit, calling forth his own helm before charging towards the Bloodspawn. Choosing his target, he summoned his Soulblade, feeling the familiar burn in his hand as the Sigil responded. Tendrils of green light burst from his fist, twisting and turning like the roots of a tree. They wrapped around each other, joining together to form a sword of shimmering green light.

As the first Urak approached, Arden dropped his shoulder and lunged forward, charging into the massive creature's chest before it could strike back. While the beast was off balance, Arden pushed off his back foot to close the distance between them and drove his now fully formed Soulblade through the beast's sternum. The creature wailed in agony as Arden pulled his Soulblade free from its chest. It dropped to the ground, the life draining from its eyes.

Spinning on his heels, Arden brought his Soulblade around, deflecting a strike from one Urak, then ducking below a swipe from another.

"Move!" Lyrin shouted, leaping onto the back of the beast that had swiped at Arden. His glowing green Soulblade lit up the night around them as he brought the hilt above his head, then drove the blade down into the creature's skull. Lyrin leapt from the Urak's back as it crashed to the ground, plumes of dust and ash spiralling into the air.

Without missing a beat, Lyrin hit the ground and moved straight towards one of the two remaining Uraks, his Soulblade gripped firmly in hand.

A howl erupted on Arden's right. The other Urak charged at him, roaring as it swung its blackened blade through the air. The beast's red eyes shone almost as brightly as the gemstone set into its blade.

With the power of the Sentinel armour surging through him, Arden turned and met the creature's charge. He caught its first strike with his Soulblade, before parrying a second with such force that the beast's blade was knocked free of its grasp. Arden closed the distance between them in a fraction of a second. He ducked the Urak's flailing arm, sidestepped, then brought his boot down on the side of its knee. He felt the dense bone snap under the force of his boot, and the creature collapsed onto its good knee, howling in pain.

Arden flipped his Soulblade into reverse grip, rested his left hand on the pommel, and drove the blade down through the back of the creature's neck. Blood fountained from the wound as the creature collapsed, lifeless, on the ground.

"Arden," Lyrin called, standing over the body of the other Urak. "There are more. I can sense them."

"As can I."

Knights of Achyron could sense Uraks and any other Bloodspawn in the same way they could sense the Taint of blood magic, for they were one and the same. Arden could feel it now, a sickly, oily sensation that crept into the back of his mind. The horrid feeling oozed through the town like an infection in a festering wound. It was all around them, hanging heavy in the air, seeping into the soil, and bleeding into the minds of the weak. But there was something… *more*, towards the eastern edge of the town.

Arden turned as a blood-chilling shriek rang out from a nearby building, a shriek that carried enough fear to cause the hairs on the back of his neck to rise.

"Go," Lyrin shouted to Arden, "I will push on."

Arden nodded in response. The shriek had come from a tavern with a sign outside that read 'The Foot of the Hill'.

Drawing strength from his Sentinel armour, Arden leapt up the flight of wooden steps that fronted the tavern's main entrance. Dropping his shoulder, he crashed through the door, sending bits of shattered wood and splinters in all directions. Bodies littered the inn's common room, charred and broken, strewn about the floor as though the building had been hit by a hurricane of wind and fire.

On the opposite side of the room, by the bar, the wall had almost completely collapsed, leaving a gaping hole to the night beyond. But it was not the gaping hole that held Arden's attention. The air caught in his chest when he saw what stood over the crumpled body of what looked to be the innkeeper.

Bloodmarked.

Arden had never seen a Bloodmarked before. According to Watcher Gildrick, no one had in at least two centuries. But even had he not recognised it from the paintings in the textbooks, he would have known it by the Taint that radiated from its twisted, black heart. The looming beast stood nearly ten feet tall, the top of its head scraping the ceiling of the tavern's common room. Smoke drifted from sets of glowing red runes that covered its thick leathery hide, carved directly into the monster's flesh. Its fingers were twisted into claws of obsidian black that looked as though they could rend steel with ease. For all that it had in common with what it once was, an Urak, the Bloodmarked looked as though it was an entirely different creature altogether. The beast's glowing red eyes locked on Arden as it turned to find the source of the shattered door.

"Pain is the path to strength," Arden whispered to himself before charging towards the twisted creature. He cast a momentary glance at the body of the innkeeper, checking for any signs of life. A sense of relief hit him when he caught the slight rise and fall of the man's chest. *The duty of the strong is to protect the weak.*

Just as Arden was about to launch himself at the creature, he felt it pulse with a sudden burst of the Taint. It swung its arms outward, stretching them behind its back then slamming them together, giving off the sound of a thunderclap. A wave of concussive force erupted from the beast's hands, so powerful Arden could see it visibly ripple through the air and strip the wood from the floor.

The wave crashed into Arden's chest, launching him backwards through the air, sending him crashing into the stone fireplace that was set into the wall behind him. Even encased in his Sentinel armour, Arden's back and legs ached, and a shooting pain lit up his spine. Were it not for the armour, the blow would have snapped him in half.

"Pain is the path to strength," Arden repeated, the iron tang of blood coating his tongue. He gritted his teeth and dragged himself to his feet, calling on his Soulblade once more – in the shock of the blow, he had released it. Spirit burned through him as the weapon formed in his right hand, its green glow striking against the red light that emanated from the Bloodmarked's runes.

Clenching his jaw, Arden once more stilled his fear and charged towards the Bloodmarked. This time, when the beast unleashed its shockwave of blood magic, Arden was ready. He leapt out of the way, jumping onto one of the few upright tables in the common room that stood outside the shockwave's reach. The wood creaked under his weight, but he didn't need it to hold. The table gave an audible groan as he bent his knees and launched himself towards the Bloodmarked. He could feel the Taint begin to well in the creature as it prepared to strike again.

Swinging his arm, Arden launched his Soulblade through the air. The creature howled in pain as the shimmering blade sunk into its shoulder, searing through its rune-marked flesh.

But as the beast howled, it reached out and snatched Arden from the air, wrapping its clawed hands around his armoured throat. Arden's entire body shivered, convulsing at the Taint that radiated from the enormous creature. He slammed his fists down on the Bloodmarked's arms, trying desperately to break free, but the beast did not so much as flinch, its grip growing tighter and tighter.

His heart pounding and his throat constricting, Arden reached out, trying to grab hold of his Soulblade, which was still lodged in the Bloodmarked's shoulder. But before he could reach it, the beast lifted him into the air and slammed him down into the ground with such force he almost lost consciousness.

Arden gasped for air. His lungs felt as though they were bound with rope, and his back burned with a pain that ran the length of his spine. He pushed himself up with one hand before something crashed into his side and sent him careening through the air. He came to a stop only when he smashed through the inn's wooden bar.

Again Arden scrambled for air, dragging it into his hungry lungs as he lifted himself to his knees, a ringing in his ears, his head spinning. The Bloodmarked stood over him, smoke drifting from its rune markings, its blood-red eyes fixed on his. Taint oozed from the creature, seeping from its bones.

But as the beast raised its hands to deliver the final blow, a shimmering green light burst from its gut, slicing through its thick hide as though it were paper.

The beast howled and thrashed, trying desperately to pull free from the blade. But the Soulblade held, lodged in its torso of dense bone and leathery, rune-marked skin. Then the blade shifted, ripping down through the beast's body, tearing it open from chest to groin. The runes across its body burned with a fierce light as the creature stumbled away from Arden, its blood and entrails spilling out onto the floor at its feet. Two steps and then it crashed to its knees before its runes lost all light and it collapsed to the floor.

Arden's heart pounded like a war drum. He took a deep breath and held it, savouring the sweet taste of air as it filled his lungs.

In the space where the Bloodmarked had stood, he saw Lyrin, his Sentinel armour glistening in the flames that shone through the holes in the building.

"The innkeeper," Arden said, panting, as Lyrin reached out his hand and dragged Arden to his feet.

"He's alive. This is worse than we feared." Lyrin nodded towards the mutilated body of the Bloodmarked that lay crumpled on the floor. Even lying there, the light of its runes faded to nothing and its body near shorn in half, the beast was monstrous. The people of this town never stood a chance.

Arden sighed, his bones aching as he knelt beside the innkeeper, checking the weak rise and fall of the man's chest. Lifting his head, Arden passed his gaze over the other charred and mutilated bodies that lay about the inn. "May Heraya take you in her arms."

Picking the innkeeper up in his arms, Arden carried him from the half-wrecked building, Lyrin following close behind. Stepping through the open passage where the door had once been, Arden lay the man down against the inn's outer wall. The buildings around them were still ablaze as the townsfolk ran about, carrying buckets of water and sacks of sand.

"There is more still to be done here. I can feel something... *else*," Arden said. The sickly sensation of the Taint still clung to the air, pulsating from somewhere deeper in the town. Arden could feel it probing at his mind, touching the edge of his consciousness with its oily tendrils.

"It lies further in."

"You," Arden called out to one of the men who had just emptied his bucket into the unquenchable flames of a nearby bakery.

The man turned at the call, but Arden saw fear in his eyes the moment he realised who had called him. It wasn't difficult for him to understand why; not many people in the past few centuries had seen a Knight of Achyron in Sentinel armour, never mind covered in the blood of a Bloodmarked. Arden called out to the Sigil. In a matter of moments, the green metal helm that covered his head had turned to liquid and receded into the main body of the Sentinel armour, allowing the man to see that Arden was, in fact, human. Though it seemed the sight of that alone only served to set a deeper fear into the man. *You always fear what you do not understand.*

"I am Arden of the Knights of Achyron. This is Lyrin. We are here to help you."

Judging by the look on the man's face, he was not entirely convinced, but Arden didn't have time to waste convincing him. "There are more of those creatures." Arden gestured to the Urak corpses that he and Lyrin had left strewn on the ground. "I need you to help this man so we can deal with them."

The fear never left the man's eyes, but he did not back away. Instead, he gave a weak nod, his body trembling. "I'll… eh… I'll look after him… I…"

Arden did not wait for the man to regain his composure. Calling his helm forth once more, he rose to his feet, and he and Lyrin set off towards the source of the Taint.

Bodies lay littered throughout every main street and side alley. Torn limb from limb, mutilated, beheaded. Arden watched as a group of women dragged the mangled body of a small child, his bones twisted and broken, out from under a toppled cart. The boy could not have seen more than six summers. The Bloodspawn cared little for who they slaughtered so long as they collected the Essence. Arden held his breath as he ran, releasing it when he had no other choice. No matter how many times he saw the brutality of death, the vomit in his stomach never ceased to rise.

A shiver ran through Arden's body as he and Lyrin turned a street corner and entered the town centre.

Gore and shattered bone decorated the ground everywhere he looked. Men, women, children. So many dead. The sound of crackling wood and the shouts of men and women echoed through the night as the townsfolk rushed to put out the fires that consumed their homes. But there, in that square, the air held an eerie silence.

"By the gods…" Arden followed the direction of Lyrin's stare.

A creature stood at the other side of the square, partly obscured by shadow. An Urak. Short, barbed horns protruded from its head, and a long sleeveless robe was draped over its broad grey shoulders. A red gemstone shimmered at the tip of the wooden staff it gripped in its fist. At the bottom of the staff was a blackened blade, slick with blood.

The creature did not move. It just stood there, its crimson eyes fixed on Arden and Lyrin. The Taint radiated from it, oozing forth in short pulses, causing the air to ripple. Arden's mind recoiled as the shroud of sickly Taint crawled along the dirt and seeped through the air. He shuddered, a coil of dread twisting in his stomach. He had never felt the Taint pulsate with such ravenous hunger before. He knew if he were to lower his guard, even in the slightest, it would consume his soul.

"A Shaman." Lyrin's voice held as much awe as it did contempt.

Just as Lyrin spoke, the Shaman's lips pulled back into an abhorrent grin, blood coating its jagged yellow teeth. The beast stared at them for a moment, Taint pulsating from its soul. But then, as though it had seen all it had wished to see, it turned and stepped back into the shadows.

Arden moved to rush after it, but Lyrin's arm caught him across the chest. "What are you doing? We need to kill it!"

"No. There aren't enough of us. Not to kill a Shaman."

Arden clenched his fingers into fists, rounding on Lyrin. "Then why is it running? We need to go after it!"

"It's not running," Lyrin said, none of his usual mirth in his voice. "It's gotten what it came for." Lyrin gestured towards the twisted and broken corpses that filled the square, feeding the ground with their blood. It had come to harvest.

"Gods dammit!" Arden pushed Lyrin's hand away and stepped out into the square, his eyes trailing over the bodies of the dead. And as he looked, anguish, rather than anger or fury, surged through him. "We should have been here sooner!"

"We did what we could. Many more would have died had we not been here."

"We should have done more!"

Lyrin closed the distance between them in a flash, clasping his hands on either of Arden's shoulders. "I know what you're feeling. But we can't save everyone, Arden. Many people are alive here today because we came."

"You, there." The voice cut through the tension. It sounded as though it came from someone who was accustomed to wielding authority, but it held a tremble, an uncertainty in itself. Arden and Lyrin turned to find three men standing behind them. Each of them wore steel breastplates over surcoats of murky brown. Their faces were streaked with soot, ash, and blood.

"Who are you?" one of the men said, stepping to the front. He was the man who had initially spoken. "We've not seen…" The man stumbled backwards as Arden called on the Sigil to remove his helm. "…*What* are you?"

Arden took a step closer to the three men. "We are the Knights of Achyron. We are here only to help."

Arden saw the uncertainty painted on the faces of each of the men. But one of the two who stood at the back took a tentative step forward.

"What are you doing?" one of the man's companions hissed. "They're—"

"They're the Knights of Achyron. Have you not heard the stories?" The man who had stepped forward gave one last glare towards his friend before turning to face Arden. "My name is Dilon, this is Kop, and our captain, Loril. We are members of the town guard. What's left of it…"

The captain, Loril, looked as though he was about to say something, maybe to chastise his inferior, but he did not speak. He just held his chin high in the air and attempted to look as though he were firmly in control of the situation. But the same tremble that betrayed his voice moved through his hands as well. Arden could only see one thing in the man's eyes: terror.

Arden gave Lyrin a look that said to take his helm off. It took a moment for him to understand, but then the metal that encased his head shifted to liquid and receded into the main body of his Sentinel armour. "What happened here?"

"They've raided from time to time, over the years," Dilon said, stopping to release a trembling breath. "But there were never many of them. In truth, we usually have more trouble with bandits. Tonight, though, there were so many. They came out of nowhere. I was on my watch in the western tower, and I turned around to see fire. Then the warning bells rang out. They just slaughtered everyone… I watched them burn that young girl alive… it just picked her up and… I…"

Tears rolled down Dilon's cheeks, carving rivers through the matted dirt that coated his skin. His words turned to a blubbering mess as the other town guard, Kop, pulled him into an embrace. "It's all right," Arden heard him say. "It's all right."

"What do we do?" the captain, Loril, said, approaching Arden. Even through soot and ash, his face was etched with fear. "We can't survive another attack like that. I saw what you can do. I saw how you fought them. Will you stay?"

"I'm sorry, we cannot," Lyrin said, his mouth drawing into a thin line. "Send word to the other towns. Tell them what happened here and ask them for aid."

"It would do no good," Loril replied. "All the towns and villages along the foot of the mountains are being attacked, and they do not have a man to spare."

"So, it is true," Lyrin whispered to Arden.

"It would appear so." Arden took a deep breath, holding it for a moment before releasing it. He turned to Loril, summoning his helm once more. "We must go and bring news of this to our commanders. I will ask that they send help. But in truth, I believe it is best that you pack your belongings and make for Berona."

A look of shock spread across the man's face. "Leave our homes? This we will not do."

"Then you will be dead before the next full moon," Arden replied, turning back towards the forest. He did not intend to sound callous, but it was a simple fact, so there was no point in pretending otherwise.

The surface of the water glistened and sparkled in the light from the sun as it rose over the mountains to the east. It gave the false impression that the morning was a warm one. An impression that was quickly eroded by the bitterness of the wind as it swept over the deck of the ship. At the very least, the breeze carried a refreshing mist of sea salt that served to somewhat replace the pungent aromas of a well-travelled ship.

Ella laughed as Faenir grumbled, shaking his body side to side to rid himself of the water that had splashed over the lip of the vessel. She tussled the fur on the top of his head. "Don't worry, it's not long now. I can see Antiquar in the distance. We'll be there in a few hours. We just need to find Shirea."

Shirea had not been in her cot when Ella woke. This was the first time over the course of the journey the woman had risen before Ella. It gave Ella a bit of hope that Shirea had started the long climb out of her grief.

It was a climb they both needed to make. Every morning when she woke, Ella fought a powerful longing to not leave the bed. She knew that if she stayed wrapped beneath her sheets, then she would become entangled in her own thoughts. She would drown in the darkness. If Shirea had gotten up early to watch the sunrise, perhaps she had beaten that longing for the first time. "Come on, Faenir. Let's see where she is."

Ella searched for just short of an hour but found no sign of Shirea. The ship was enormous. And it seemed that every single passenger had come up onto the deck early to watch the sun rise over Antiquar, which didn't make it any easier to find Shirea. *I probably just keep missing her.*

Ella took a moment to admire the island city of Antiquar as it bathed in the morning sun. With the exception of the port, the entire island was surrounded by enormous walls of sand-brown stone that blended seamlessly with the sheer cliff edges that sank into the sea. It was as though, at some point, the ground had risen and smoothed itself into city walls. Ella couldn't see any of the buildings over the gargantuan walls, but the rooves of the city's towers were covered in a mixture of orange and greyish-blue tiles that looked striking in the morning sun.

Masses of white sails filled the open water around the island, flooding in and out of the port. Antiquar's port was famous across Epheria. In honesty, Antiquar itself was famous. 'The cultural capital of the North'. At least, that's what all the storytellers said. *We'll have to spend a few nights there before we go to Berona.*

"Ella."

Ella hadn't heard Farda approach. She turned to see him standing on the deck behind her. His black cloak flapped in the breeze, partially covering a steel breastplate and sturdy leather trousers. She hadn't seen him dressed like that before. Like a soldier. It left a bitter taste in her mouth.

But there was something else that caught her attention. He had a look on his face – the look of somebody who was about to give bad news. She had seen that expression on her father's face more times than she could count. "Farda, what is it?"

"I'm sorry, Ella."

"What do you mean, you're sorry? What…" The realisation sank in. Ella stepped towards Farda, Faenir moving alongside her. A deep growl resonated from the wolfpine's chest, the hackles on the back of his neck standing on end. "Where's Shirea? What did you do?"

"Me?" Farda tilted his head sideways, an incredulous look on his face.

"Yes, you," Ella snapped, her chest trembling.

"A deckhand saw her last night, Ella. She threw herself overboard."

Ella felt as though a sack of stones had hit her in the stomach. Her mouth dried up, and a shiver ran from her shoulders down through her chest. "That's not true… She would never…" Ella's voice dropped to a whisper. "She was getting better…"

Farda took a step closer. "I am sorry, but it is true."

Ella let herself fall backward, connecting with the rail of the ship. She brought her hands up behind her neck and let herself slide to the deck. Hot tears burned at the corner of her eyes, carving paths down her cheeks.

Farda reached down, as though intending to wipe the tears from Ella's face.

"Get away from me!" Ella snapped, slapping the man's hand away.

"I didn't mean to—" Farda stopped mid-sentence, stepping backwards as Faenir moved in front of Ella, a deep snarl forming in the wolfpine's throat. Farda went to speak again, but as he did, Faenir's snarl grew deeper and the hackles on his back rose higher.

Ella didn't lift her head as the man walked away. She didn't say anything; she simply held her hands at the back of her neck and let her tears fall.

Ella had been keeping herself together over the past few days. She had nearly broken, more than once. It was like holding back an ocean. She hadn't known Shirea long, but having someone who understood the gaping hole in her chest had been a small comfort. That comfort, however, was gone now, and nothing stood between her and her mind's darkest thoughts.

So, she wept.

Chapter Ten

The Shadow of What Was Lost

Every hair on Calen's body stood on end as he looked through the now-open doorway.

"Vindakur." Korik stepped up beside Calen, pulling a closed fist across his chest, reverence in his eyes.

Through the doorway, Calen saw a city that made even Durakdur look as though it lacked for wealth. It was enormous – as if a section of the mountain had been hollowed out and one of the grandest cities in all of Epheria had been slotted into the space left behind.

Massive luminescent flowers all but covered the vast rock ceiling that sat hundreds of feet above the city, like a sky of incandescent yellow. All the buildings were cut from smooth grey stone, topped with rooves of gold and another whitish metal that reflected the yellow flowerlight in variegated patterns. Swooping archways and shimmering golden domes swept across the cityscape, looking as much like works of art as they did anything else.

"It's incredible," Calen said, stepping forward, Valerys moving beside him, the dragon's head tilting sideways curiously. Before them lay a long stone pathway that joined onto a massive flagstone street that ran straight through the city's centre. A long, raised platform of stone bisected the street. Along the platform, set at evenly spaced intervals, were enormous statues of dwarven soldiers, wrought from shimmering gold, crafted with such skill and meticulous attention it looked as though they would burst to life at any moment. "Korik, do you know if there would be another way out of the city, or a way back to Durakdur?"

"There should be other doorways at the edges of the city, much like this one, and Wind Tunnels as well. They might lead to more tunnels that could bring us back towards the Freehold. But in truth, I'm not sure. Until today, we thought Vindakur lost. The other tunnels and passages may well be destroyed."

"It's our only option," Tarmon said in a flat tone, looking back towards the group of men and dwarves. "We can't keep wandering these tunnels. Hunger and thirst will kill us before anything else does. Surely there will be something to orient us here. Maybe even Wind Runners."

The thought of finding an abandoned Wind Runner gave Calen a sudden jolt of hope.

"The Lord Captain speaks the truth," Vaeril added. "At the very least, there should be a source of water here. The city would not have been built without one."

"It's settled then," Erik said. "We go forward."

There was a moment of awkward silence after Erik spoke, and all eyes were focused on Calen.

Calen looked back over the ramshackle group of survivors that had been thrust together. Twenty-three dwarves, forty-three men, an elf, and a dragon. Beaten, broken, bloody, and tired. They looked to *him*. None of them sneered or averted their gaze. There was hope in their eyes. And he would not see that hope disappear. Not when so much of it had already been extinguished. Ignoring the dull aches that ran the length of his body, Calen moved forward.

"Let us go first. We don't know what waits for us here," Tarmon said, putting his giant hand across Calen's chest. Calen made to argue, but Tarmon moved ahead. "We should make for that tower," he said, pointing towards an enormous tower that jutted above the other buildings, near the centre of the city. "From the top of that tower, we should be able to see which tunnels are still standing."

Tarmon turned back towards Calen, meeting his gaze. Calen nodded.

With a smile and a short nod in reply, Tarmon moved out along the stone pathway. "Kingsguard, form up. Soldiers of Belduar, on our heels."

Only fourteen Belduaran Kingsguard had survived the Wind Runner crash. But despite everything they had been through since the retreat from Belduar, each of them fell in behind Tarmon without so much as a groan or complaint. They formed up into four lines and started across the pathway. Calen was in awe at how their purple cloaks and burnished plate armour still managed to look resplendent, even under the weight of all that blood and dust.

The surviving Belduaran soldiers – twenty-five in total – followed the Kingsguard across the bridge. The soldiers produced a few grumbles and complaints, but they did not hesitate.

"You next," Korik said, turning to Calen once all the Belduarans were out of the chamber. "We will take up the rear."

Calen took a moment to look over the dwarves who stood behind Korik. Each wore the sharp-cut armour of the dwarven kingdoms, their beards knotted with many rings of bronze, silver, and gold. Some wore the green and silver cloaks of Azmar, some the black of Ozryn or the crimson of Durakdur. Each of them had joined together to come to Belduar's aid. They had answered the call – his call – and now they were here.

"Let's go," Calen said, reluctantly, nodding to Falmin, Erik, and Vaeril. Vaeril's eyes were heavy with exhaustion, and his steps were laboured. Healing Erik, Falmin, and some of the other injured had taken a lot out of him, but he didn't argue or complain. He simply returned the nod and stepped out onto the pathway.

A low rumble rose beside Calen. Valerys was crouched low to the ground, the sound reverberating from his throat as he narrowed his eyes and stepped out in front of Calen as they followed Tarmon and the Kingsguard down the empty street in front of them. The dragon didn't trust this place, and his wariness seeped into the back of Calen's mind, sharpening his senses. Calen reached for the Spark, just to feel it. Just to make sure it was there if he needed. Not that he was sure he had the strength to actually use it.

As they made their way down the stone pathway and out onto the main street, Calen couldn't help but find himself awestruck as the city rose up around him. The buildings on either side of the street varied in height. Some were no bigger than The Gilded Dragon back in The Glade, while others rose a hundred or so feet into the air, their monstrous height still a long way off touching the flower-covered ceiling.

Up close, the intricately carved golden statues atop the street's central platform were even more incredible than they had been from the doorway. Each was unique. Each had a different face and different ornamentation on their armour. The craftsmanship was so detailed that Calen could make out each rivet in the golden coats of mail.

"There was a battle here," Erik whispered, his finger trailing over an aged bloodstain marring the side of a statue. "A long time ago."

"Aye, it's not exactly lookin' in tip-top shape," Falmin said, kicking a small stone across the empty, rubble-strewn street. "But… where are all the bodies?"

A shiver ran down Calen's spine. He had been so captivated by the grandeur of the city, he had not noticed the damage to the buildings. The rubble and debris strewn throughout the streets. There had most definitely been a battle here. But there wasn't a single body in sight. No rotting corpses or dusty skeletons. Nothing. *Where are the bodies?*

"May their fires never be extinguished and their blades never dull." Sorrow permeated Korik's voice as he and the rest of the dwarves spoke the lament.

"May their fires never be extinguished and their blades never dull," Calen repeated.

Calen's eyes flitted between the various side streets that connected onto the main thoroughfare, becoming acutely aware of the vast silence that hung like a fog over the gargantuan city. The sound of the party's footsteps was the only noise that echoed through the streets, dampened slightly by the blanket of flowers that coated the walls and ceiling of the enormous hollow within the mountain.

As they walked – the Belduarans ahead and the dwarves behind – Calen's eyes were drawn to a small grey building at the side of the street. A large section of the roof and wall had been destroyed, and most of the windows were smashed. Calen would not even have noticed it were it not for a symbol that was engraved just above the door: a triangle, pointing upward, with three smaller triangles set at each of its edges.

"The symbol of The Order," Vaeril said, his eyes following Calen's gaze. "And of the Draleid. The central triangle represents the dragons, and each of the smaller triangles signify the elves, the Jotnar, and the humans."

"The Order…" Calen whispered, almost to himself, his eyes remaining fixed on the symbol that was engraved above the door. "What is it doing here?"

"Before The Fall, The Order had many embassies throughout Epheria. Though, I do believe they were not quite as common in the dwarven cities." Vaeril raised an eyebrow, turning to Korik.

"No," the dwarf replied, eyeing the embassy with a hint of curiosity. "I was not even aware there had ever been an embassy for The Order in the Freehold. There was one in Kolmir, in the North. But the empire destroyed the entire city after The Fall. May their fires never be extinguished and their blades never dull."

The other dwarves echoed Korik's words.

A low rumble emanated from Valerys's chest as the dragon, head raised, stepped in front of Calen. A feeling of loss drifted from Valerys's mind, and the frills on the back of his neck rose. Something inside that building reeked of sorrow.

Valerys moved forward, beating his wings, lifting himself into the air. Each wingbeat echoed through the ghost city, reverberating off the stone as they would the walls of an empty valley. Within moments, the dragon had cleared the distance to the embassy of The Order and flown in through the gaping hole in the wall of the second storey.

"Valerys!" Calen called, his voice echoing eerily. "Dammit. I need to go after him."

Calen darted across the wide-open street after Valerys, not waiting for a response from the others. The heavy brass door of the embassy creaked as Calen leaned his shoulder against it and heaved it open. Whatever it was that Valerys had sensed on the second floor of the building, the dragon had now found it. The feeling of sheer loss that radiated from Valerys's mind almost brought Calen to his knees. *I'm coming.*

With the door open, Calen ran through the rubble-strewn hallway, bounding up the stairs as quickly as his legs would carry him. The walls of the building were stained crimson, deep furrows raking the stone.

The door at the top of the stairs no longer sat on its hinges. With a deep breath, Calen stepped into the room Valerys had found.

The room itself was deceptively large, at least twice as big as the common room of The Gilded Dragon, but not quite as big as that of The Traveller's Rest back in Camylin. Books, papers, notes, and all sorts of trinkets were strewn about the floor. Most of the furniture – with the exception of a long, stone desk – was shattered, large sections of the roof and walls had been completely destroyed, and piles of stone lay scattered about the floor. If the building had once held the same grandeur as the city itself, that time had long passed.

Calen found Valerys taking up most of the left corner of the room, curled around something on the floor. A wave of sorrow washed into Calen's mind from Valerys's, a soft whine escaping the dragon's throat.

"What is it?" Calen asked as he stepped closer to Valerys, reaching out his hand.

Before Calen's hand touched Valerys's white scales, the dragon pulled back his wing and lifted his head, providing Calen with a clear view of what had caused such sorrow: a shattered wooden chest along with the broken remains of four dragon eggs.

The sight of the broken fragments twisted a knot in Calen's chest and stole the air from his lungs. He dropped to one knee beside Valerys, resting his hand on the cool scales of the dragon's back. The eggs looked exactly as Valerys's had when Calen had first laid eyes on it, except with different colouring and accents along the ridges of the scales.

"I'm sorry," Calen whisper, letting his mind drift into Valerys's, doing all he could to provide the dragon with even the slightest of comforts.

Valerys reached down, touching the broken fragments of shell with the tip of his snout, his nostrils flaring. Calen's hands trembled as the loss Valerys felt tore through their shared soul. It was primal, visceral. It twisted coils of grief in Calen's stomach and swept shivers across his skin. Images flashed through Calen's mind. His mother, his father, Ella, Haem – all gone. That was Valerys's sorrow; the brittle remnants of his family lay before him. Shattered. Broken.

Shifting his body, Valerys stretched his neck into the air and let out a deep, heart-rending roar that rippled through the city like thunder, echoing against the cold stone. It was not a roar of anger or fury but of abject grief. The sound of the cry resonated through Calen's body, setting all his hairs on end. It tore at his heart and brought tears to his eyes. His shoulders slumped, and the strength fled from his muscles.

"What's happening?" Erik shouted as he and Vaeril burst into the room, swords drawn. "You can't just run off like that!"

Calen pulled himself to his feet, cupping his hands around his nose and digging his fingers in around his eyes, wiping away the tears that flowed freely. "Nothing..." Calen let out a heavy sigh as he looked back towards Valerys. The dragon still lay on the ground, his body sprawled protectively around the shattered shells. "Nothing we could have done anything about."

Both Erik and Vaeril must have seen the tears that rolled down Calen's cheeks, as they didn't push him for any further answers.

Avoiding Erik's and Vaeril's gazes, Calen moved over towards the stone desk at the centre of the room. The desk was mostly covered by scattered pieces of paper, dust, and bits of broken stone. But, buried under some sheets of destroyed paper, was a small envelope, sealed with crimson wax.

Brushing aside the dust and sheets of paper, Calen picked up the envelope, examining it. The wax seal held the symbol of The Order, and the envelope felt heavy, as though it held more than a note. Holding it in front of himself for a moment, Calen pulled at the edge of the wax seal. When it wouldn't pull away, he tore the envelope around the seal and tipped its contents out onto the desk. There was a clink as a circular pendant fell from the envelope, along with a letter that was folded over three times.

Reaching down, Calen picked up the pendant, turning it over in his hands. The back of the pendant was wrought from brass, with intricate spiral patterns worked into its surface, while the front was cut from obsidian, with white markings inside the black glass that depicted the symbol of The Order. Holding the pendant in his right hand, Calen picked up the letter and peeled it open.

My dearest Eluna,

I have left more. The pendant is the key.
Always remember, even in the shadow of what was lost, we can find light anew.

Your Archon, and your friend.
Alvira Serris

"Alvira Serris…" Calen whispered, his eyes lingering on the name. *The Archon of the Draleid. The one from Therin's stories.*

"Calen, we need to keep moving. The others are waiting for us outside."

Letting out a sigh, Calen folded the letter over and slipped it and the pendant into his pocket. "All right. Just give me a moment."

Turning, Calen moved towards Valerys, who still lay curled up around the shattered remains of the eggshells, a low whine emanating from the dragon's throat. The light from the yellow flowers that covered the ceiling shone through the open roof of the embassy, casting a golden hue across Valerys's white scales.

As Calen reached out to Valerys, he heard a *click-clack* noise, and he saw something out of the corner of his eye. One of the piles of stones had moved; he was sure of it.

"Draleid!"

Calen felt Vaeril reach for the Spark as he shouted. He snapped his head around to find himself staring at a spider-like creature, suspended three feet off the ground with threads of Air. The creature was the size of a hound, a jet-black claw that looked as though it could tear furrows into stone at the end of each of its eight legs. Its entire body was covered in a thin, chitinous armour as grey as stone. Four deep-black eyes were set into its head, and its mouth was framed by two large mandibles that looked as though they could snap bones.

"What in the gods is that?" Erik said, rushing to Calen's side.

"I don't know," Vaeril answered. Calen felt the elf pull on the threads of Air that encased the creature, eliciting a series of snaps and cracks as the stone-spider's shell collapsed inwards, and it fell to the floor, blue blood seeping into the stone. "But we need to go, *now*."

A warning flashed in the back of Calen's mind. He leapt to the ground, just in time to avoid Valerys's tail as it whipped through the air, colliding with another of the stone spiders. The force of the strike cracked straight through the creature's shell and hammered it against the wall.

Vaeril wasn't so lucky. Another of the stone spiders leapt from the shadows, one of its clawed legs slicing through Vaeril's calf. The elf howled as he dropped to one knee. But before the creature could follow up its initial attack, Vaeril pulled his sword from its scabbard and drove it down through the top of the monstrosity's shell, then pulled it free, letting the creature fall to the floor. As it fell, a repetitive clicking sound drifted on the air, like the sound of heavy rain on steel. It seemed to come from everywhere and nowhere all at once, reverberating through the dead city like rolling thunder.

Valerys stood still, his eyes alert and his head tilted to the side. The frills that ran along the back of the dragon's neck stood up straight and a low rumble resonated in his chest, dropping to a deep growl. Calen felt Valerys tugging at the back of his mind. Urgency. Anger. Fear.

"Kerathlin!" came a cry from the street outside.

"Valerys, go!" Calen turned to Vaeril and Erik as the dragon beat his wings and lifted himself out through the destroyed roof. "Come on," Calen said, reaching down and pulling Vaeril to his feet. "Can you walk?"

The elf nodded through gritted teeth, pushing Calen towards the doorway.

As Calen, Vaeril, and Erik sprinted down the stairs, more piles of stone began to shift where they lay, unfurling long legs tipped with jet-black claws.

"What in the gods did ya do?" Falmin shouted as Calen and the others burst from the doorway of the embassy.

All about the street, the dwarves had formed up in groups of threes and fours, stone-like kerathlin carcasses at their feet. But more than a few dwarven bodies lay still on the ground as well.

"They're everywhere..." Erik said, his voice almost a whisper.

Calen followed Erik's gaze. His heart sank into his stomach and dread flooded his veins with ice. Everywhere he looked, kerathlin awoke from whatever kind of hibernation they had been in. All along the rooftops, in the windows of buildings, along side streets and alleyways. He watched as the creatures shook the dust and rubble from their shells and rose to confront whatever had disturbed their nest.

A flash of grey-streaked across Calen's vision to his left as three kerathlin crashed into a group of dwarves. One dwarf fell, his armour sliced open like parchment, his blood spraying into the air. The other two dwarves fought valiantly until more kerathlin fell on them, washing over them like a river, ripping them to shreds.

"Run!" Korik shouted, pointing towards Tarmon and the Belduaran soldiers, who were a little further ahead. The dwarf's voice was barely audible above the ever-increasing *click-clack* of the kerathlin claws cracking against stone. Nobody argued. The entire group broke out into a sprint. The muscles in Calen's legs burned as he pushed them to carry him faster. Two hours' sleep had definitely not been enough. He was dropping behind the rest of the group.

As he ran, Calen cast his eyes behind him. He watched as thousands of the creatures spewed forth from doorways and side streets, climbing over each other, swarming into the street like a chitinous wave.

Erik, Falmin, and Vaeril were keeping pace with Calen, though Vaeril was pushing himself to the breaking point, blood streaming from the wound in his calf. A tingle at the back of Calen's mind made him notice the elf was funnelling threads of Spirit into himself. Calen was not sure what the elf was doing, but as long as it kept him on his feet, that was all that mattered.

More cries rang out up ahead as flashes of grey darted from the side streets, colliding with Tarmon and his men in a crash of claw and steel. The creatures were unlike anything Calen had ever seen. They moved like lightning, swarming over their prey.

"We have to help Tarmon and his men!" Calen shouted.

Erik gave a short nod, but his eyes held a sombreness, an acceptance. There was little chance they were leaving this place alive. Calen took a deep breath, letting Valerys's mind seep into his own as he charged. The dragon swooped through the air overhead, readying himself.

Many of the Kingsguard and Belduaran soldiers were already down, and they would not be getting back up.

Screams rose from behind, and Calen knew the kerathlin had caught some of the dwarves. He risked a glance over his shoulder. Only Korik and two others were still with him. But about ten feet behind them was an ocean of kerathlin. Thousands of them. They swept over the street and up the sides of buildings, never stopping.

Calen pushed his legs harder, fuelling them with fear. Erik, Vaeril, and Falmin matched his pace. They had almost reached Tarmon and his men. No more than seven of them still stood.

Fury flooded into the back of Calen's mind as Valerys crashed down on top of the kerathlin that surrounded the Kingsguard. A stab of pain seared through Calen's mind as a thick, black claw gouged a furrow into Valerys's side. The young dragon howled before clamping his jaws down on the creature, cracking its armoured shell, killing it instantly.

Valerys sent swaths of kerathlin crashing into the side of a building with a powerful swipe of his tail, shells snapping, stone shattering. Tarmon and the other Kingsguard rallied around the dragon, their swords drawn, guttural battle cries escaping their throats.

Piercing shrieks rang out as pillars of dragonfire poured forth from Valerys's jaws, roasting the kerathlin in their shells. But with every monster Valerys sent to the void, four more leapt from the ruins of the city. If this place was a kerathlin nest, the nest was waking.

I need to do something.

Calen reached out to the Spark, the drain sapping at him as soon as he did. His hands shook, sweat dripped from his brow, and that familiar pain seared through him, as though wrapping around his soul. He was already weak; he hadn't given himself any time to recover. But he had no choice. He needed to push through it. Once more, Calen reached for the Spark, driving past the pain, leaning into it. Pure energy pulsated through him as the elemental strands came to life in his mind. He pulled on threads of Air, the familiar cool sensation flooding his body.

He spotted a jagged piece of metal about two feet in length amongst the rubble of a ruined building. Calen wrapped the piece of metal with threads of Air and, with all the power he could muster, launched it from the ground, sending it through the air and crashing through the shroud of kerathlin. The monsters hissed and screeched as their shells were shattered and blue blood sprayed across the stone. Calen crashed to his knees, unable to hold his own weight as the drain burned through him, snatching at his soul.

"On your feet, Draleid." Calen recognised Korik's voice as the dwarf grabbed him underneath the arms and heaved him to his feet. He barely managed to stay upright as he stumbled over a pile of rubble, but he felt Valerys at the back of his mind, urging him on. The dragon had lifted himself back into the air and continued to pour dragonfire down over the onrushing kerathlin.

Calen felt Falmin – about five feet in front of him – reach for the Spark, pulling threads of Air into himself. The navigator lifted hundreds of the creatures off the ground, smashing them off the walls of the nearby buildings, clearing a path to Tarmon and the others.

"Keep going!" Erik roared as he reached Tarmon. "There's a bridge up ahead."

Tarmon's eyes flitted between the bodies of his fallen companions. All but four had fallen to the kerathlin, and one carried a heavy limp. With a look of regret, he wrapped the injured soldier's arm around his shoulder and ran.

As Calen and the others rushed towards the bridge, Valerys swooped past them. The pressure built in Calen's mind as the dragon called forth his dragonfire, kicked back his head, and carved a path of fire and fury through the swarm of kerathlin that washed over the street behind them.

"What is that?" Erik called out as they reached the foot of the bridge. On the other side was an island of rock, dominated by a massive mound at its centre. The island was surrounded by a chasm on all sides, with a sheer drop that seemed to descend endlessly to the centre of the world. It was connected to the rest of the city by four bridges set to its north, south, east, and west. The western and northern bridges were collapsed, but the others still stood.

Nobody answered. They kept running, getting over the bridge as fast as their legs could carry them, the *click-clack* of the kerathlin growing closer with every passing second.

Just as he made it to the other side of the bridge, Calen skidded to a halt. There was nowhere to go. The kerathlin had them trapped.

"Falmin, I need you."

The gangly navigator dashed over to Calen, gasping for breath. "What is it?"

"We need to bring the bridge down behind us, but I'm too weak to do it alone. If I weaken the stone, can you bring it down with Air?"

A grin spread across Falmin's face. "I like the way ya think. Let's be quick 'bout it."

Calen nodded and reached out for the Spark. It sat just out of reach, the twisting strands of light teasing him. He pushed deeper, closing his eyes, embracing the pain, and letting everything fade to black. When he felt the Spark, he pulled desperately on thin threads of Earth. Just enough, no more, no less. He dropped to his knees, the drain sapping at him. His legs were weak, and his mind was fuzzy.

"Draleid, are you all right?" Korik's hand pressed down on Calen's shoulder, a look of concern in his eyes. "They've reached the bridge."

"Aye," Calen said, giving the dwarf a slight nod. A gust of air swept over Calen as Valerys flew overhead, spinning sharply, doubling back. Calen felt a rush overcoming Valerys, the pressure building to a head. The dragon opened his jaws, unleashing a column of dragonfire down on top of the onrushing kerathlin as they swept over the bridge.

With Valerys's fire, a rush of energy surged through Calen's body. It wasn't much, but it was enough. He pushed the palms of his hands against the stone at the foot of the bridge. Focusing his mind, he drew on the Spark and funnelled threads of Earth into the stone. The swarm of kerathlin were halfway across, sweeping over the charred carcasses of their dead.

Calen felt for the bonds in the stone, probing, searching with the threads. He didn't have the strength to crumble them, even with the energy that flowed from Valerys. But if he could just weaken them…

Valerys landed on the ground beside Calen, a deep growl resonating from his throat. Calen felt the stone begin to crack as the threads of Earth weaved through the bridge. "Falmin, now!"

Threads of Air swept around the navigator, like a whirlwind only visible to those who could touch the Spark. Calen watched as the navigator pushed the threads into the air above the bridge, then brought them crashing down like a hammer on an anvil. The bridge shook with the force of the strike and many of the kerathlin were thrown over the edge, screeching as they plummeted into the chasm below. Clouds of dust hung in the air, and the enormous cavern was filled with a momentary silence as the bridge held, and a pang of fear shot through Calen's mind. *I didn't do enough.*

Then, with a thunderous crack, it collapsed. The deafening sound of cascading stone reverberated up the walls of the chasm, mixing with hissing shrieks as hundreds of the monstrous creatures fell into the abyss below.

"Over here! There's an entrance!" Tarmon shouted from beside the mound of rock at the centre of the small island.

"Draleid." Falmin tugged at Calen's arm. "We need t'go. The other bridge is still standin', and they won' be long in figurin' that out. The others are already gone inside."

The entrance to the mound of rock was a smooth circular tunnel, much like the ones that ran all throughout the mountain. It wasn't long before Calen, Falmin, and Valerys made it through the tunnel and stepped into the circular chamber at the centre of the rock formation.

The others stood at the centre of the chamber in front of a large pedestal, the top of which gleamed with yellow light. Around the edge of the chamber, four stone rings were embedded in the rock face. Each stood about twenty feet in diameter, ornamented with intricate pattern carvings with a glyph marking at the very top. A small set of stone stairs sat in front of each ring, leading up to its inner lip.

"What is this place?" Calen said, stepping up beside Tarmon and Korik, who stood beside the glowing pedestal.

"I…" Korik's words caught in his throat as he gazed around the chamber in awe. "I believe it to be a Portal Heart… but…"

"I don't mean to rush you, Korik, but those kerathlin won't take long to cross the other bridge." Erik shrugged his shoulders as he spoke, but there was a hardness in his voice.

"You're right. I am sorry. It is said that against the wishes of the other gods, The Smith granted the dwarves five Portal Hearts. A means of quick travel across the lands, a consolation for our inability to wield the Spark. But I thought them just legend."

"How do we use it?" Erik asked, an urgency in his voice.

"I… I don't know."

"Fuck!" Erik roared, kicking out at a loose stone on the ground. "We're trapped."

"The glyphs." Falmin stood by the pedestal at the centre of the room. He ran his hand over the source of the glowing yellow light at the top of the pedestal. It looked like a polished crystal, split into four quarters, each with a glyph marking. "Each o' these glyphs. They match the ones carved into the top o' the rings."

"Do you think you can work it out?" Calen asked, stepping closer to Falmin.

"Dunno, let's see." Without hesitating, Falmin placed his hand on top of one of the glyph crystals and pushed down. Calen's heart jumped as the crystal inched downward. But nothing happened. "Hmm… curious, that. Really thought that woulda done somethin'."

Erik stood beside Falmin, a dumbfounded look on his face. "Did you just press on a glowing crystal, in the middle of a dwarven ruin, with no idea what would happen?"

"No… I pressed down on a glowing crystal, in the middle of a dwarven ruin, with no idea *nothing* would happen."

Erik just stared at Falmin for a moment, then shook his head and walked back towards the entrance.

"Where are you going?" Calen asked, grabbing Erik's shoulder as he walked past.

"If we're going to die. I'm going to do it with my swords in my hands," Erik replied, shrugging off Calen's hand and walking over to stand at the entrance to the tunnel.

"A bit dramatic, isn' he?" Falmin said, shrugging as he pondered over the glyphs on the pedestal.

"Draleid, Erik is not wrong. If those kerathlin get through that entrance before we've figured out how to make the portals work, we will die here." There was a hard look on Tarmon's face.

Calen let out a sigh before nodding. He turned to the rest of the group. They each stared back at him, covered in sweat, dirt, and blood. Despair was etched into their faces, and a resignation sat in their eyes. Calen had brought them here, and now they looked at him as though they expected him to say something to stoke fire in their hearts. But he had no words.

As though reading Calen's mind, Tarmon leaned closer, whispering in his ear. "Words are pretty. But when it comes down to it, men follow actions, not words. We're with you."

Calen turned to look at Tarmon, but the man simply nodded, saying nothing more.

Returning the gesture, Calen pushed his fear down and summoned as confident a voice as he could muster. "Falmin, you keep working on the pedestal. Everyone else, to the entrance. We need to give him as much time as possible."

There were some groans and mumbles, but nobody argued. As each of the survivors made their way towards the entrance, Calen's eyes fell on the injured Kingsguard who Tarmon had helped across the bridge. Blood seeped out from under the man's breastplate, and he heavily favoured his right leg.

"Not you," Calen said, resting his hand on the man's shoulder. "You stay with Falmin."

"I can't just sit around and wait to die, Draleid. I will help."

"Yes, you will help. By making sure if anything gets past us, it doesn't get to Falmin. Understood?"

"Yes, my lord," the Kingsguard replied, not a hint of sarcasm or mockery in his voice. *I'm not a damned lord.*

"You too," Calen said, turning to Vaeril. "Don't argue about honour. You can't protect me if you're dead."

Vaeril hesitated for a moment before he nodded and limped back over towards Falmin and the injured Kingsguard. Calen could not understand how the elf was still standing at all. It had to be something to do with the threads of Spirit he continued to pull into his body. That was a question that could wait.

Tarmon bumped his shoulder off Calen's as they walked over toward the chamber entrance. "You handled that well." He said with a half-smile on his face before walking over to have a word with the other two Kingsguard.

Shaking his head at Tarmon's words, Calen knelt beside Valerys, running his hand along the dragon's scaled neck. "We won't die down here. I won't let that happen."

A rumble of agreement resonated in the back of Calen's mind as Valerys nuzzled his head into Calen's hand. Calen couldn't get over how much the dragon had grown since he had first emerged from that egg. When standing on all four limbs, Valerys's back was now at least the height of a powerful horse. His snout had elongated, and the horns and spines that framed his face had thickened and grown sharper. The end of his tail had begun to fan outward, small barbs at its edges. He grew stronger with each passing day. Calen leaned forward, resting his forehead against Valerys's. "Draleid n'aldryr."

A growl of agreement resonated in Valerys's chest, while a sensation of pure energy rippled through his mind, spilling into Calen's.

"They're coming!" Erik's call echoed through the stone chamber. The *click-clack* of kerathlin claws echoed down the tunnel, following Erik's words, slowly rising to a sound that mimicked rolling thunder. The walls of the chamber shook as the swarm washed over the outside of the dome.

Calen turned to Falmin, whose gaze was lost in the yellow glow of the crystal atop the pedestal. "We need you to solve that, or we're all dead."

"No fuckin' pressure!" the navigator shouted, turning back towards the pedestal.

Calen felt every beat of his heart as it thumped against his ribs, pumping the blood through his veins. He stood at the entrance to the tunnel, Erik and Tarmon to his left and the dwarves to his right. Valerys stood behind him, his teeth bared, a deep growl resonating from his chest.

"Stay together," Tarmon shouted. "We need to crowd the entrance, take away their numbers. Hold them off as long as we can—"

"Korik, gimme me a hand!" Falmin's shout cut across Tarmon.

"I'm a little busy here, navigator!"

"No, Korik. I literally need yer hand!"

Korik looked at Calen, who gave a sideways glance to Tarmon before turning back to the dwarf. "Go."

The dwarf groaned as he set off in a sprint towards the pedestal where Falmin stood.

Erik let out a sigh, spinning his swords around in anticipation, an eerie smile on his face. "I never thought this is how I'd die."

"In a cave, a kerathlin claw in your chest?" Tarmon asked, a hint of laughter at the edge of his words that unsettled Calen.

"No. Standing shoulder to shoulder with a Draleid, a dragon, two dwarves, and the Lord Captain of the Kingsguard of Belduar. It's a story, all right. Too bad there'll be nobody left to tell it."

A knot twisted in Calen's stomach. He could see the kerathlin now. The yellow light from the pedestal washed over their smooth stone-like shells as they streamed down the tunnel. Calen's blood froze in his veins as the creatures crashed over each other, hissing and clicking as they charged towards their prey.

Calen reached out to Valerys, letting their minds flood into one another. *I'm sorry. I should have done better.*

A fierce rage poured into Calen's mind as the dragon let out a roar so visceral it drowned out the thunderous drum of the kerathlin claws. Only one thing radiated from Valerys's mind: defiance. A sheer refusal to lie down and die.

Calen took a deep breath, holding it in his chest as he tightened his grip on his sword. He cast one final glance at the faces of those around him, the people who were prepared to die beside him. The people who had trusted him to lead them out of this labyrinth. Their expressions were grim – as they should be. He had failed them.

Calen stumbled as a deep *whooshing* noise resounded through the chamber and the ground shook beneath his feet. Plumes of dust burst from cracks in the ceiling above them, small pieces of rock coming loose and dropping to the floor.

"It works!" Falmin roared. "Quick, t'me!"

Calen glanced over his shoulder, terrified to take his eyes off the onrushing kerathlin. His jaw nearly fell to the floor when he saw that one of the rings was now filled with what looked to be an undulating pool of molten gold. A constant ripple moved from the centre of the pool as if a stone had been dropped through its newly formed surface. Calen looked at the ring and then back at the tunnel entrance.

"Come on, come on!" Falmin shouted. The others looked at Calen, waiting for permission to run for their lives.

This was their only chance.

"Run!" Calen roared, turning his feet towards the ring.

Falmin, Korik, Vaeril, and the injured Kingsguard stood on the top step of the gold-filled ring, their arms waving frantically. A massive chunk of rock cracked off the stone two feet to Calen's left. The kerathlin were coming through the dome. Calen kept running. They were only twenty feet from the ring.

He looked to his right. Sweat dripped from Tarmon and Erik as they ran. Their faces twisted in effort.

Fifteen feet.

Another rock fell from the ceiling, but this one knocked one of the Kingsguard onto his back. Calen moved to help the man, but he was too late. Two kerathlin fell through a newly formed hole in the dome above, landing on the man's chest, tearing through his armour with their clawed legs. The sight turned Calen's stomach, but he kept running. Valerys bounded ahead of him, landing next to Falmin.

Ten feet.

"Go through!" Calen shouted. He saw the hesitancy on Falmin's face. There was no point in waiting. It didn't matter where the ring led. They were dead if they stayed here. "Go, Falmin! Go!"

Falmin gave a frantic nod, then shuffled Korik through the shimmering pool of golden liquid that stood suspended within the ring.

Calen risked a look over his shoulder. The rest of the kerathlin had flooded into the chamber, hundreds of grey-shelled, arachnid-like creatures, their clawed legs cracking against the stone, hunger in their shimmering eyes. Calen watched in horror as another Kingsguard was taken by a falling rock, then devoured by the moving swarm.

Calen stopped at the top of the stairs; Falmin, Korik, Vaeril, and the injured Kingsguard had already gone through. "Go, go, go!" he shouted to Erik and Tarmon as he put his hands on their backs and shoved them through the ring. The two other dwarves were next.

"Valerys, go through!" The dragon did not argue, leaping straight through the ring.

The kerathlin had reached the bottom of the steps.

Calen turned his head and jumped through the ring.

Tarmon dropped to his knees, gasping for breath. His teeth chattered as a shiver ran down his spine. Passing through that ring was like jumping into the ocean in high winter. *Get off the ground. This isn't the time to be on the ground.*

Tarmon clenched his jaw, tightened his grip on the hilt of his sword, and dragged himself to his feet. The navigator stood to his left, shivering. Righkard, the elf, and the three dwarves stood with him. Erik Virandr was on one knee beside Tarmon, both his swords still held firmly in his hands. The young man was very much his father's son.

All seven of them stared at the shimmering pool of gold that filled the stone ring. It looked identical to the one they had come through only moments before.

The surface of the pool rippled as the dragon burst through from the other side. Its white scales gleamed in the golden light as it tucked its wings in close to its chest and spiralled through the air, alighting on a large stone about five feet in front of the ring. Tarmon took a moment to admire the creature. It had grown fourfold since he had first laid eyes on it. It had seemed almost fragile then. That was no longer the case. Its hind legs were thick and muscular, its chest had grown deeper, and its teeth looked as though they could cut through steel. He saw the way it had attacked the creatures in Vindakur. It had been ferocious. The dragon regarded him with pale, lavender eyes, so striking against its snow-white scales. *I'm glad you're on our side.*

The dragon gave a deep growl as the pool of molten gold rippled again, and this time the Draleid came crashing through.

"Turn it off!" The Draleid tumbled through the gate, rolling as his knees hit the ground at the bottom of the steps. He leapt to his feet, swinging his sword in an arc, slicing through the underbelly of a kerathlin that had leapt through the ring after him.

"Navigator, Korik!" Tarmon roared. "Turn off that damned ring!"

As Tarmon clenched his jaw and charged towards the Draleid, he saw Righkard and Erik doing the same. A second kerathlin came through the ring, and a third. Two quick flashes of steel and they lay lifeless at the bottom of the steps.

Heaving his greatsword through the air, Tarmon caught one of the kerathlin in mid-air, slicing the creature in half before it hit the ground. He spun again, aiming to bring his blade down across another of the spider-like monstrosities, only to watch as the dragon plunged from the air, shattering the creature's shell with one whip of its tail.

Tarmon roared, letting go of his sword as a burning sensation ripped through his leg. He felt something scraping against his bone as the claw was pulled back through the way it had come. Something hard collided with his back, sending him crashing to the stone floor. He rolled over just in time to hold the kerathlin above him, its mandibles crashing together as it attempted to tear him limb from limb. The creature hissed as its clawed leg slammed into the stone beside Tarmon's head.

The hissing stopped as the silvery tip of a blade burst through its belly. A thin stream of bluish-green blood flowed from the wound as the sword was pulled back, and the creature collapsed on top of Tarmon.

Heaving the carcass aside, Tarmon clasped the hand that was extended to him and leveraged it to pull himself to his feet. The golden pool held within the ring was gone, and only stone stood behind it now. Ten kerathlin were broken on the stone floor, their shells split and shattered, leaking bluish-green blood. One of the dwarves lay lifeless in the carnage, his plate shredded and his chest ripped open. Tarmon's heart clenched as his eyes fell on Righkard's lifeless body. The man had been with him since they were both children. *May The Mother embrace you.*

Tarmon turned to look at the man who had helped him up and found himself standing face-to-face with the Draleid. The young man's face was smeared with dark blood, deep purple circles hanging under his eyes. They had all been through a lot since the city had fallen, the Draleid more than most, but his gaze was firm and his hand steady. Tarmon wasn't sure who had changed more, the dragon or the Draleid.

"I owe you my life once more, it seems," Tarmon said, dipping his head in thanks.

"I do not doubt that you will repay the debt tenfold by the time we make it back to Durakdur," the Draleid answered, his mouth a thin, grim line. "I'm sorry about your men, Lord Captain. I will burn his body," the Draleid said, tilting his head towards Righkard, "if that is what you wish. I would not see him lie restless in this cave."

"I would appreciate that very much."

With a nod, the young man walked away to check on Erik Virandr and the dragon before moving on to the navigator and then to the dwarves. Tarmon watched him as he checked each one of them, not moving on until he was sure they were without injury. There was something about the young man. Something Tarmon did not see in many men with his kind of power. Despite the death and despite all the loss and pain, he cared.

Chapter Eleven

Home is Where the Heart is

ayne sat with one leg draped across the sill of the arched stone window and the other dangling over the edge. He bit his teeth into the flesh of the green apple he held in his hand, feeling its bittersweet juices roll out over his lips and down his chin. From the top of the Skytower, he had the perfect view of both the Rolling Mountains and the Antigan Ocean. The sun cast a dim orange-red glow over the horizon as it plunged into the water, tinting the white foam of the waves in a reddish hue. Valtara saw the best sunsets; he had decided that long ago. It was good to be home.

Gazing out over the ocean, Dayne tossed the half-eaten apple up in the air, letting it drop back into his hand without taking his eyes off the picturesque view. With three bites, he finished the meat of the apple, swallowing core and all, then swung himself back through the window and stepped onto the aged wooden floorboards of the room within. Standing there, with the floorboards creaking beneath his weight, he rested his hand over the pocket of his robes – the pocket that held Aeson Virandr's letter. He didn't need to open it. He had read it the best part of fifty times. He drew in a deep breath of air, held it for a moment, and then released it in a resigned sigh.

Dayne strode across the old room, swung open the door, and made his way down the three hundred and forty-seven limestone steps of the

Skytower. Once at the bottom, he reached out to the Spark and pulled on paper-thin threads of Air, just enough to do the job, not enough to draw attention. He pushed the threads of Air into the locking mechanism of the door that stood in front of him, shifting the pins as the key would have, sliding the bolt out of place, just as he had done hundreds of times before. With a click, the door opened, and Dayne released his hold on the Spark.

The central plaza was the beating heart of Skyfell's many markets. On a regular day it would be flooded with people dashing about in the high sun, haggling and bartering for the day's wares. But as the sun set over the ocean, washing the sandy-brown stone with a warm, red glow, the plaza was all but empty. All that remained were some rambling city folks, a few traders packing away their wares, and the gentle citrus aroma that drifted down from the city's orchards.

Pulling his robes closer to shield himself from the cool evening breeze, Dayne strode across the courtyard, making his way toward Redstone, the ancestral home of House Ateres. He didn't have long. Baren would be on his way to the council soon, and Dayne needed to speak to him before he left.

As cities went, Skyfell was as beautiful as any Dayne had ever known. It was a layered canvas of sweeping colonnades, enormous archways, and beautiful staircases built from a mixture of red and sandy-brown stone. The archways of Skyfell were famed for their gargantuan size and smooth, masterful aesthetics. The city had been built to such a large scale to accommodate the pride of Valtara: the Wyvern Riders. When Dayne was a child, he and his sister used to spend hours just sitting in the plaza watching the majestic beasts swooping in and out of the archways, alighting atop the colonnades and purpose-built landing platforms. It had been their favourite thing to do. A deep sadness welled in Dayne's heart as he looked up to empty skies. Those times were long gone, but the sheer scale and beauty of Skyfell's architecture remained.

A dark shadow passed over Dayne as he stepped beneath one of the massive archways. Dust crunched under his feet, whirling along the ground in sweeping clouds, whipped up by the breeze. It felt strange to be back. It looked the same as it always had, but it *felt* different. Not that it had ever been a happy place to begin with.

He passed the temples of Neron and Achyron, the two most prominent gods in Valtaran culture. Each of the temples was over a hundred feet high, fronted by enormous statues of their patron gods bracketed on either side by staircases that led to the temples' inner sanctums. Neron wore a smooth steel cuirass that flowed down into his armoured skirts. His legs were protected by a set of greaves that matched the vambraces on his forearms. Dayne had seen The Sailor depicted in many ways across Epheria – from a seafaring trader, to a ferocious pirate, to a powerful man with a long scraggy beard and a trident. But in Valtara, Neron was a warrior. He was the warden of the seas and the oceans and – along with Achyron – the protector of the Valtaran way of life.

On the other side of the wide, dusty street, the statue of Achyron stood similarly dressed at the front of his temple. In one hand, he held the valyna and in the other the ordo – the spear and circular, concave shield used by Valtaran warriors in battle. While Neron might have been depicted as a warrior in Valtaran culture, Achyron was *The* Warrior.

The statues had been carved by Irikes the sculptor millennia ago. It had taken him forty summers. And here they stood, even now, watching over the people of Valtara. Nations had risen and fallen, rivers had dried, mountains had been pulled from the earth, but Neron and Achyron stood, ensuring Valtara lived on. Dayne would ensure he did them proud.

The Warrior and The Sailor. By blade and by blood, I am yours.

The emptiness of the streets was not eerie to Dayne. It was nostalgic. The setting of the sun was the traditional time for evening meal in Valtara. There were very few reasons – one being war – that would excuse a Valtaran citizen from evening meal. It was a welcome respite from the drunken revelry and the dark, dingy corners of the other Epherian cities.

Dayne dropped his eyes to the ground as the sound of armoured footsteps echoed through the empty streets. Valtarans didn't wear armoured boots within the city unless they were at war.

"Does it ever rain here?" one of the imperial soldiers said as the patrol turned the corner. There were three of them, each armoured from head to toe in the ruby-red plate of the Inquisition Praetorians. *What is the Inquisition doing here?* Dayne stuffed his hands into the pockets of his robes, kept his head down, and walked past the patrolling soldiers. The empire kept a garrison in each of the major cities of Valtara since the rebellion, but the Inquisition were not a common sight.

"You there."

Dayne froze, dropping his hands to his sides. His fingers drifted to the pommel of the sword under his robes.

"I'm speaking to you," the soldier called, irritation in his voice.

Dayne puffed out his cheeks with a sigh, then turned. They shouldn't know him. There was no reason for them to know. But if they did... "Can I help you?"

The soldier who had spoken stepped forward. He wasn't particularly large and looked about five or six summers Dayne's junior, but his narrow eyes were cold, like a man who found his joy in abusing others. "Should you not be at evening meal?" The man's eyes scanned Dayne from top to bottom, his hand resting on the pommel of the sword that sat at his hip.

"I'm on my way now."

"To where?"

Bastards. The empire had no right to be questioning a Valtaran citizen for no reason, in the streets of Skyfell of all places. "To Redstone."

"*You* are of House Ateres?" The man widened his stance. Dayne felt the air change. As much as he would welcome the opportunity to take their heads from their shoulders, it would do him no good here.

"No, sir. My family are servants of House Ateres. We have a home on the grounds of Redstone."

The soldier pursed his lips. Dayne brought his hand to the front of his robes, closer to his sword, should the need arise.

"Come on, Jared, don't waste your time with a servant. The Inquisitor is expecting us."

The man ran his tongue over his front teeth, his cold stare still fixed on Dayne. "Don't dally. The streets aren't safe after dark." There was more than a hint of sarcasm in the soldier's voice as he turned to join his companions.

Dayne moved his hand away from his sword, letting his shoulders relax and his lungs exhale. He was no stranger to confrontation with Lorian soldiers, but he didn't have the time for it tonight. He picked up his pace as he weaved through the empty streets towards Redstone.

Two of the six major Valtaran houses called Skyfell their home, and House Ateres was one of them. They commanded wealth and respect, but most of all, power. The keep of Redstone lay at the edge of the city, backing onto the Abaddian cliffs that overlooked the Antigan Ocean. The keep was surrounded by its own thick walls that were manned night and day; it was a veritable fortress. Dayne looked up at the statues nestled into the alcoves along the walls of the place he had once called home. Each was carved in a likeness of one of the past heads of House Ateres, interspersed with depictions of the gods: Heraya, Varyn, Achyron, Elyara, Neron, and Hafaesir. As a child he used to look up and wonder at them, but now all he saw was the hubris of depicting House Ateres on the same level as the gods. *How the mighty have fallen.*

Dayne stopped about twenty feet from the gates, tilting his head back and closing his eyes. He took a deep breath, allowing air to fill his lungs to the point he felt a sharp pressure at the front of his chest, and held it. *Here goes nothing.*

With a long, slow exhale, Dayne opened his eyes, rolled back his shoulders, and approached the gates. An older man stood before the gates, conversing with the guards on duty.

"What business have you—" The older man cut his sentence short as realisation set into his face. The man looked far older than he had when Dayne left. In his naivety, Dayne hadn't truly expected him to look much different. Marlin Arkon was the steward of House Ateres; he was as close to family as was possible for someone not born of the blood. He practically raised Dayne. He had been a powerful man – skilled with a blade, quick with his mind, and his eyes missed nothing. His eyes, *they* had not changed. But patches of white now flecked his shoulder-length hair, and his skin was leathered, with more wrinkles than Dayne remembered.

Dayne turned his gaze to the ground. It was difficult to look the man in the eye after what he had done. He felt like a child again, shuffling his feet, awaiting punishment for knocking over the porcelain vase that had belonged to his mother. "I—"

"My boy, you are a sight for old and weary eyes."

At first, Dayne tensed up as Marlin wrapped his arms around him, drawing him into a fierce embrace. But then he closed his eyes and allowed a tired smile to touch his face.

"Where have you been all these years?"

Dayne didn't answer. He just stood there and slowly allowed himself to return the embrace.

Marlin pulled away and grasped Dayne by the shoulders, looking him over with a beaming smile. "You've grown into a fine man. I always said those shoulders would fill out."

"It's good to see you too, Marlin. It's been a long time." Dayne was loath to break the warmest embrace he had felt in many years. "Has Baren left yet?"

Marlin's welcoming smile drew up into a frown as he pulled back. "He has not. But I don't think now is a good time."

"I have to see him, Marlin."

The older man nodded absently, biting his top lip and shuffling back towards the gates. "Yes… come. Come inside, I believe he is in his study."

The two guards who stood at the front of the gates eyed Dayne askance as he followed Marlin into the keep, but they didn't move to stop him. He didn't recognise them. They were young, twenty summers at most, about the age he'd been when he left.

The garden was just as it had been when he was younger. A brownish-red flagstone pathway led through its centre with rows of orange trees on either side. Even in the dim light of the fading sun mingling with the newly emerging moon, the vibrant colour of the oranges stood stark against the deep green of the leaves. About a hundred feet ahead, at the other end of the garden, the main house stood twice as high as the walls that surrounded the keep. Its front was an intricate web of ornate columns and swooping archways. The higher windows were smaller, and some were occupied by statuettes. Aside from the main house, many other buildings resided within the grounds of Redstone: housing for the servants and the main garrison, food stores, dining halls, stables, and of course, a small temple.

At that time, the garden was mostly void of servants. Even servants did not miss evening meal unless they had a task of some import. The ones Dayne did see wore robes stained in the burnt orange and white colours of House Ateres. They each nodded at Marlin as they passed, dropping into a shallow bow, but they barely paid Dayne any heed whatsoever. Why would they? He was not dressed as though he was a man worthy of attention. His robes were a mixture of muted cream and white, wrinkled and worn from travel, and his face and hair were dirty and ungroomed. He looked like nothing more than a petitioner to Lord Ateres.

Dayne stopped in his tracks as a beautiful young woman hurried down the steps of the main house, heading straight for them. She wore a flowing orange robe, trimmed with white and cut off at the sleeves, along with a pair of thin, goatskin gloves. Marlin pursed his lips as he looked from Dayne to the young woman, a sigh of resignation escaping him.

"Marlin, you haven't seen…" The young woman stopped in her tracks, her head tilting and eyes widening as her gaze fell on Dayne. "That couldn't be…"

As the woman drew closer, Dayne could make out her features more clearly. She was a lot taller than he remembered, maybe only just shorter than he was. Her frame was lean, with noticeable muscle on her shoulders and arms. The sides of her head were shaved, and her hair, the colour of deep mahogany, was tied into a plat that ran down the back of her head. Numerous tattoos ran along her arms and neck. That didn't surprise Dayne. Tattoos were an integral part of Valtaran culture. But what did catch him off guard were the quartets of black rings on each of her forearms, bisected by solid black lines. *She has become a master of both the spear and the sword.* Dayne could do nothing to hide the smile on his face as his eyes traced over the lines. When he eventually pulled his eyes away from the markings on the woman's arms, he found her face to be an indecipherable mixture of warmth, fury, and concern.

"Alina, I—"

Dayne felt a crack in his jaw as Alina's hand caught him hard across the face. He barely had time to understand what was happening before she shoved him in the chest, causing him to stumble off balance.

"How dare you!" she said, almost under her breath, her voice trembling. But not with fear – with fury. "You have no right…"

"You look beautiful." His words seemed to take her by surprise, as though she had already planned exactly the way this conversation was going to pan out and he had thrown a stone into the middle of things. He couldn't help but smile, a tear forming at the corner of his eye, but he held it back. "You have grown so much… so beautiful, and so strong." Dayne touched his hand to his tender face, cracking his jaw side to side.

Alina's breathing grew shallow, and Dayne could see the shake in her hands and shoulders. "I…"

He winced as she charged towards him, only to feel her arms wrap around his back and her head bury itself in his chest. The sound of her gentle sobbing broke his heart.

"You're alive…"

"I'm sorry, Alina… I didn't have a choice…"

Alina's grip around Dayne's back loosened as she pulled away and looked at him properly for the first time. Her eyes were red, and her cheeks were marked where her tears had rolled. "You're alive," she repeated. There was a flash of motion, and Dayne felt another crack in his jaw.

An anger rose inside him. "What was that for?"

"For leaving us." Alina's fiery expression seemed to soften the longer she held his gaze.

"What was the hug for?"

"For coming back."

"I've missed you every single day."

"And I've wished you dead for leaving us, but… you're home now."

"I need to see Baren."

Alina's expression shifted. Dayne cursed himself for being so blunt. Why was he such an idiot? Alina drew in a deep breath and tucked her thumb into her clenched fist. She had always done that as a child when trying to holding back her irritation. "He's leaving for the council soon."

"I know. Which is why I need to see him *now*." There would be time to make his apologies to Alina later. They had a lot of time to catch up on. It was incredible to see her grown. She truly had become a beautiful woman, and fierce.

Alina's eyes narrowed. "Marlin, can you please see Dayne to Baren's study?"

"Alina, I know where the study is. Will you walk with me?"

"It has been a long time, *brother*. Your memory might not hold true. Now, I have some things to see to. You will stay for breakfast in the morning?" It was not a question. Alina turned on her heels, heading off towards the temple. She was exactly how he remembered their mother; they could have been twins.

"That actually went better than I thought it was going to," Dayne said, turning to Marlin who had a dumbstruck look on his face.

"You thought that went well?" the steward said.

"You didn't?" Dayne replied, laughing. "Can you please bring me to my brother, Marlin?"

The old steward gave a reluctant nod, pursing his lips.

Like the gardens, the main house of Redstone had not changed much. Marlin walked Dayne through the colonnade at the front of the house and into the entrance hall. Antechambers were common in Valtaran homes, but that was not the case in Redstone. There was no need for one, as the gardens served that purpose. A wave of nostalgia washed over Dayne as he looked about the hall. Oil lamps hung from brackets on the walls and sat atop pedestals, providing a consistent light throughout. The ceiling of the entrance hall stretched up at least a hundred feet in the air, supported by enormous columns of red stone. The ceiling was ornamented with square shaped stone panels, each one depicting a different point in Valtaran history. At least, the points that House Ateres were involved in.

Marlin led Dayne up the stone staircase on the left side of the hall. He had walked those steps many times as a child, up to his father's study. *Now Baren's study*. It still felt strange to think of it like that. Dayne ran his hand along the ornately carved stone banister that framed the right-hand side of the staircase. It felt coarse to the touch, his fingers slipping over the same little pockets of cracked stone he remembered. A wall ran along the left side of the staircase, with alcoves set into it at regular intervals. The contents of the alcoves alternated between oil lamps and busts of Dayne's ancestors. The heads of House Ateres.

"I must warn you… he is not in the best of moods today. An imperial Inquisitor arrived this morning." It was still strange to see the furrows in Marlin's skin, carved by the passing of time. "He has been sour ever since."

"Why are they here, Marlin?"

"In truth, my lord. I do not know, but I do not think I would be far off if I were to think it had something to do with the rumblings of the battle at Belduar. The word about the keep is that the empire razed the city to the ground, and they have been sending Battlemages and Inquisitors to every corner of the South to 'keep the peace.'"

My lord. "I do not deserve that title, Marlin."

"As you say, my lord," Marlin said with a grin.

Dayne laughed under his breath; time may have ebbed away at the man's appearance, but nothing had dulled his mind.

Once they reached the stone landing of the second floor, Marlin led Dayne to the large stained wooden doors he knew so well. Dayne reached out, running his fingers along the thick brass hinges that fixed the door to the wall, then down along a rough-cut groove where the wood was pale and splintered. Dayne had made that cut himself when he had seen little more than nine summers. It had been an accident, of course, but Marlin had set him to a week in the orchards nevertheless.

"Baren is inside, my lord."

Dayne took a deep breath in through his nose, filling his lungs. His right foot tapped nervously on the landing. Puffing his cheeks out, he stepped forward and pushed open the door to Baren's study.

The study was perhaps the one thing that was *not* the same as Dayne remembered. His father had always filled it with beautiful paintings and works of art, and there had been three soft couches in the centre of the room for conducting business and so the children could read in comfort. Now, though, the room was austere in its simplicity. The paintings and sculptures were gone, as were the couches. Bookshelves lined the western wall, while an array of old Valtaran weapons hung on the opposite side. A heavy desk sat on the far side of the room, just in front of the open window that looked out over the ocean. A solitary wooden chair sat behind the desk, with two more in front. Baren stood, looking out the window as the sun began its descent into the horizon, his back to the doorway.

Baren was only eighteen when Dayne left. There was no way of telling what kind of man he had become, but he had always been the more compassionate between the two of them. *I hope you haven't changed too much, brother.*

Baren wore a simple blackened steel cuirass over a burnt orange tunic that flowed down into armoured skirts. It was tradition for the heads of the Houses to attend the council dressed for war, with the exception of their boots. Just like Alina, four black rings were tattooed on both his left and right forearms, with a black line running through the first to the last rings. The markings of a spearmaster and a blademaster; Dayne had only earned two rings of each marking before he left Valtara. Though, the blood he had shed in the time since then would have earned him full markings twice over.

Baren didn't turn to see who had entered the study. Only a slight tilt of his head gave away that he had even heard the door opening. "I will be leaving in a moment, Marlin. What is it?"

"It's not Marlin… brother."

"No…" Baren turned to look at Dayne, who still stood at the entrance of the study. "That's not possible… It's been—"

"Twelve years, four months, eleven days." Dayne took two steps towards the heavy desk. "I have not stopped counting, and I have never forgotten."

Baren still stood by the window, a look of confusion and shock etched into his face. He rounded the heavy desk and moved towards Dayne. Without thinking, Dayne scanned the room. His brother had no weapons, but his sword rested on his desk. The obvious exit was through the doors he had just come through, but the gates would be closed in seconds if Baren sounded the alarm. The drop from the window would be a couple of hundred feet, but he could soften the landing with threads of Air and disappear into the water. That would be his escape route. *Stop it. I won't need an escape route. Just stop being who you are.*

Dayne took another step forward as Baren reached out his hand, his fingertips brushing Dayne's cheek. The coarse, calloused tips of a soldier's hand. "How… where have you been all these years?"

"That is a very long story, brother. One I can tell you tonight, after the council. But for now, there is something more important."

"More important than learning my brother is alive? I think not." Baren cupped Dayne's face in his hands and pressed their foreheads together.

"Father would have been proud of the man you've become, Baren." That seemed to catch Baren off guard. He pulled away. It had not been Dayne's intention to do so. His words were simply the truth. But twelve years living the way he had, he didn't always consider the sensitivities of things before he spoke.

"I'm sorry," Dayne said, reaching out to his brother. "I didn't mean to… it is true though – he would be proud."

"It's all right…" There was a forlorn look in Baren's eyes as he spoke. "Where did you go, Dayne? We thought you were dead. We needed you."

"I've been everywhere but where I wanted to be, brother. I wasn't given a choice."

"But you are here now," Baren said, a smile spreading across his face. As Baren spoke, Dayne could see a tear glistening at the corner of his brother's eye. Baren reached out, wrapped his arms around Dayne, and squeezed. "That is all that matters, Dayne. You are here." After a few moments, Baren pulled back, his smile still spread wide. "I would stay, but I need to go to the council. I'm sorry. The Inquisition are here along with Consul Rinda.

I can't escape it. But when I come back, we will drink and feast until the sun rises and sets again. And then you can tell me everything." Baren clasped Dayne's shoulders, his eyes glistening, gazing at Dayne as though he looked upon a ghost. "You are here."

"That's all right, brother. I know you have questions, and I will give you answers. For now, just know that I didn't leave you of my own will. Before you go, you need to read this." Dayne pulled Aeson Virandr's letter from the pocket of his robes and handed it to his brother. "It is from Aeson Virandr."

In an instant, the smile was gone from Baren's face. "Aeson Virandr?" He threw the letter back at Dayne. His eyes were narrowed, and his breathing shallow. "What a fool I am! To think you had come back to us."

"I did come back, Baren. I'm not going anywhere!"

"But you didn't come back for *us*, Dayne. Did you?"

"Baren. Read the letter."

"You came back at the whim of the man who broke our family."

"Baren. Read the gods damned letter!"

"I don't need to read the gods damned letter, Dayne!" Baren swept his hand across his desk, sending its contents crashing to the floor. "Aeson Virandr wants another rebellion. Am I right? What else could he want? All he has ever wanted is Valtaran blood for his cause. I don't have time for this."

"I need you to trust me, Baren."

"Trust you? I hardly know you." The words stung Dayne, and Baren's eyes softened a little as he looked at his brother. "I'm sorry, but it is true. You haven't been here. You don't know what it's been like."

Dayne grabbed Baren by the shoulders. He hadn't stopped to truly examine his brother, which was something Dayne tended to do as soon as he met anyone at all. Baren's face was marked with more furrows than someone who had only just seen their thirtieth summer should have had, though his eyes were still keen and bright. *Good, the burden of leading has not broken you, brother.* "I am sorry I haven't been here. But I cannot change the past. I can only look forward. I need you to trust me."

Baren bit his lip, letting out a sigh of frustration. "Fine. When I get back from the council. We will talk, and you will tell me everything."

"Agreed. I will meet you here when the council has ended."

Baren made to leave, but Dayne clasped him by the shoulders once more and pulled him into an embrace. "I've missed you."

Dayne forced himself to stop biting his lip as he leaned against the cold stone wall, looking out over the moonlit ocean that stretched endlessly towards the horizon. He closed his eyes, letting the soft sound of waves as they crashed against the rockface, again and again, drift to his ears.

To be home. It wasn't a thought he had ever truly contemplated. He had barely entertained the idea, even after receiving Aeson's letter. It was too risky, not just for him, but for Alina, and Baren, and Marlin too. It was impossible to predict what the empire would do if they found him not just alive, but returned to Redstone. He pushed the thought from his mind. Baren would be back soon, and then they would talk.

With a deep sigh, Dayne pulled his gaze from the window and turned back into the study that had once been his father's, but now belonged to Baren. To stand at the head of House Ateres was a burden Dayne should have taken himself. It was not fair for Baren to have had to carry it.

When Baren had left for the council, Dayne collected everything his brother had knocked to the floor and replaced it on the heavy wooden desk that sat just before the large window: a pen, an inkwell, a few stacks of parchment, and a wax seal.

"The seal of House Ateres," Dayne muttered as he clasped his hands around the bronze handle of the seal. His father had used that seal – the wyvern of House Ateres – to mark each and every letter he sent. The empire had forbidden the flying of House banners in Valtara after the rebellion, but the seal had been his father's quiet 'fuck you'. Dayne couldn't fight the smile that slipped onto his face at the sight of the wyvern embossed onto the seal.

The sound of footsteps marching down the hall pulled Dayne from his nostalgia. He tilted his head, reaching out to the Spark, channelling the sound on thin threads of Air. At least eight pairs of feet, four of them armoured. The Inquisition guards and the Inquisitor. *No... Baren, you didn't.*

Dayne flashed his gaze towards the open window. He could be gone before they reached the door. The muscles in his legs twitched, his instincts urging him to run. But he fought them back; he had run from his family once, and he would not do it again.

Taking a deep breath, he steadied himself. His fingers rested on the pommel of his sword; it was all he could do not to rip it from its scabbard. But he had to trust Baren. He had to. Family was all he had now. It was all he ever had.

Seconds passed like hours as Dayne waited for the footsteps to reach the door of the study. He set his feet and let the threads of Air drift into his ears, amplifying even the slightest of sounds.

"We want him alive." The words were spoken in a hushed whisper, but Dayne heard them as though the man was shouting in his ear. The man's accent was strange. He had a Lorian twang in his voice, but he was not originally from Loria – Arkalen, maybe? It didn't matter.

Without any more of a warning, the door burst open. The three Praetorians Dayne had crossed earlier charged into the room, swords drawn. Behind them stood a tall man in red robes with light-blonde hair and gaunt cheeks – the Inquisitor. His face was expressionless, but there was something about the way he stared that put Dayne on edge.

Before Dayne could make out the others behind them, the Praetorians charged, attacking from three directions.

Leaping over the table, Dayne ripped his sword from its scabbard just in time to block the first strike, nimbly ducking beneath the blade of the soldier to his left, and narrowly deflecting the third blow with threads of Air, his heart pounding in his chest.

Inquisition Praetorians were well trained, they moved together, they held their guard, and they struck hard. But Dayne had killed many of them before, and he would kill many more.

With a swift kick, Dayne took one of the soldier's legs from under him. But before he could drive his blade through the man's exposed neck, a thread of Air sent his sword flying from his hands. He didn't have to look to know the Inquisitor had wreathed himself in threads of Air.

Rolling to the side to avoid the arcing blade of one of the two standing Praetorians, Dayne pulled on threads of Earth and Air. He pushed the threads of Earth into the breastplate of the fallen soldier, forcing it to collapse inward. The sound of snapping bones sent a shiver down his spine as the steel crushed the man's chest like brittle wood. *Two more.*

Without hesitation, Dayne wrapped the threads of Air around one of the valyna that hung on the wall at the opposite side of Baren's study. The long spear came loose without much effort, soared through the air, and burst through the chest of the Praetorian to his right. The surprise in the man's eyes left a melancholy in Dayne's mind. A man should know how and why he died. *One more.*

Dayne pulled harder on the threads of Air, dragging the valyna through the man's chest and into his open hands. He caught the haft of the spear mid-flight, his fingers slipping on the blood, and rammed its butt-spike into the last Praetorian's throat. The force of the blow sent the soldier crashing to the ground, gasping for air, blood spilling out over his hands. *Just the Inquisitor left.*

Spinning on his heels, Dayne dropped the tip of the long spear to the mage's throat. Sweat dripped from Dayne's forehead, and he felt the blood pulsing through his veins. In that moment, he could see the four others who had accompanied the soldiers, and a knot formed in his throat. Baren and Alina stood behind the Inquisitor, along with two of the Redstone guard in their burnt orange skirts and bronze cuirasses. A weightlessness set into Dayne's stomach as he looked at his brother and sister. Silence hung in the air as he stared into their eyes, and they stared back.

"Dayne Ateres, by order of the Imperial Inquis—" The Inquisitor's eyes rolled to the back of his head, and he collapsed in a heap as Dayne cracked him across the skull with the side of the heavy steel spike at the end of the valyna. He would have killed the wretch, but they needed more time to prepare, and a dead Inquisitor would have brought the empire hammering down on them in full force.

Dayne turned to his brother and sister, letting the valyna fall to the floor. "Baren… Alina… How could you?"

"How could we?" Baren snapped, taking a step closer to Dayne. "You left me no choice, Dayne. I didn't want this, but it is my responsibility to protect this House now. To protect Valtara… even against my brother. I cannot just throw away Valtaran lives as our parents did."

Fury ignited inside Dayne. "Don't you dare speak of them in that way!" He took a step towards Baren. Subconsciously, he pulled at the Spark. Threads of Fire and Air. "You know nothing of the sacrifices they made. Nothing!"

"And where were you to teach me?"

Dayne didn't have the slightest idea of how to respond. In truth, he had not been sure what to expect. He knew the risks of bringing Aeson's letter to his brother, or at least he had thought he did. He turned his gaze towards Alina. She met it without flinching, but she did not speak. Was this how she felt, too?

"Don't look at her," Baren said. "Look at me, Dayne. Answer me—" Baren collapsed to the ground, his legs buckling beneath him. Dayne stared in disbelief at the sight of Alina standing over their brother, her sword drawn, its pommel smeared with Baren's blood.

"Alina… what did you do?"

Alina ignored Dayne and instead turned to address the two Redstone guards who stood at her side. "Prop him up against the door." The two guards snapped to attention at her command, even giving a short bow as they strode past her, ignoring Dayne entirely, and went to prop Baren up against the doors to the study.

"Alina, what is going on?"

"We don't have time for questions right now, brother. Come with me if you want to live."

The cool breeze drifted through the docks, rippling the sails of the ships as they pulled in to moor. It was a welcome respite from the heat of the afternoon sun.

"Well?" Ella said, her patience wearing thin.

The sailor raised a curious eyebrow, tilting his head. "Are you sure you can handle this, little lady? Wyrm's Blood will put hairs on yer chest for sure." The man puffed out his bottom lip into a pout, looking down at Ella. "Would be a shame."

Ella twisted her tongue in her mouth, clenching her jaw. It was a reflex more than anything else, one that helped her hold her tongue and kept her from saying things she would regret. Her mother had taught her to do it ever since she was young. *'Hold your tongue like that for five seconds. If you still want to say what you thought about saying after that, then say it.'* Surprisingly, it tended to work quite well. "It doesn't seem to have put any hairs on your chest. Are you sure it works?"

A chorus of laughter broke out from the other sailors who had been lying out in the afternoon sun. The man's face turned a bright red.

"You better watch your mouth," he said, leaning forward.

"Or you'll what?" Ella raised an eyebrow, tilting her head at Faenir, who stood by her side, his nose wrinkled in a soundless snarl.

"One silver mark. Then get out of here. You're more trouble than you're worth."

"Silver? That stuff isn't worth any more than five coppers."

"Seven coppers," the man said, letting out an irritated sigh.

Good, you're willing to negotiate. "Six."

"Seven."

"Five."

"Fine," he said, thrusting the waterskin into Ella's hand. "Take it and get lost."

Reaching into her pocket, Ella pulled five copper marks from the purse she had taken from the dead soldiers on the road to Gisa and pushed them into the sailor's outstretched hand. "Pleasure doing business with you."

The man simply grunted and turned back to the other sailors, receiving many a mocking laugh as he did.

"Good boy," Ella said, ruffling the fur on the top of Faenir's head. "Now, let's go find a nice spot to drink this."

Ella sat at the edge of the dock, the tips of her toes just barely grazing the water's surface. Occasionally a wave crashed against the underside of the wooden dock and the sea spray would mist into the air, tickling her cheeks.

The waterskin sloshed as Ella brought it to her nose. She recoiled at the sharp scent that wafted from its nozzle. A low grumble emanated from Faenir, who sat curled up at her side, his eyes fixed on the waterskin.

"What?" Ella said, frowning at the wolfpine. "It's not that bad. You can have some if you want."

Faenir grumbled in response before tucking his head down on top of his paws.

"Chicken." Ella shook her head as she took another whiff of the noxious spirit. It might not physically put hairs on her chest, though she was less sure of that after smelling it, but it would certainly dull her senses, which was precisely what she wanted. Ella brought the nozzle of the waterskin to her lips and took a large mouthful of the horrid liquid. It burned. She coughed and spluttered as she attempted to choke it down. "Shit… what is this made of?" she muttered, her lips, mouth, and throat still burning.

The sailors behind her laughed as they unloaded the wares from their ship. She turned to glare at them only for the vapours of the spirit to catch in her throat, causing her to cough against her will, which only made them laugh harder. A sharp, rising growl from Faenir shut them up as Ella turned her attention back to the open water.

With a sigh, she tussled the fur at the nape of Faenir's neck and took another swig from the skin, smaller this time. She fought the urge to cough, grimacing as the spirit burned its way down her throat. She would not give the sailors the satisfaction of seeing her cough again. It might be a horrid drink, but it was working. She already felt a warmth flooding her, smoothing the edges of her consciousness, and at the very least, she had finally found something that tasted worse than ale.

Shirea had killed herself. Thrown herself overboard less than a day from reaching land. Ella clutched the waterskin tighter at the thought. Had Shirea truly felt so alone that she thought death was her only option? Ella drew in a deep breath and let it out in a slow, purposeful sigh. She closed her eyes as the breeze lifted the sea spray up onto her face and just sat there, not thinking, not speaking, just sitting. She had no inclination to explore the city, not anymore.

Ella took another swig from the waterskin. It burned less this time.

"You hear about the girl that fisherman found?" one of the sailors who had laughed at her shouted. He was talking to one of his companions as they heaved crates of linens from the deck of their ship down onto the docks. Ella nearly choked on another mouthful of the Wyrm's Blood. *Shirea?*

"Aye. Found her this morning, so he did. All wrapped up in his fishing nets. Poor thing must have fallen and snapped her neck. I heard the bones were shattered."

A shiver ran down Ella's spine. She slowed her breathing but didn't turn her head. Best not to let them know she was listening.

"Maybe… I'm not sure how you would do that just falling overboard… maybe she pissed off the wrong person?"

"Or maybe she hit a rock. There's not always a story behind everything, Dunk."

Faenir's head shot up, and his ears perked. Ella was so engrossed in the conversation that she hadn't heard the footsteps approaching along the wooden dock.

"Ella?"

Ella jumped at the sound of Farda's voice, losing her grip on the neck of the waterskin and letting it drop into the water below. "Shit…" she said in a low whisper, before turning back towards Farda. "What?"

"I just wanted to see if you were all right. I hadn't meant to upset you on the ship. I just thought it best that you heard the news from me, rather than some deckhand."

Ella narrowed her eyes. "How did you find me?"

"You're the only person sitting on the docks with a seven-foot wolf at your side."

A slight growl rumbled in Faenir's chest. The wolfpine lifted his head, his nose wrinkling as he looked at Farda.

Ella pulled herself to her feet, patting invisible dust from her dress. Although her face was all measure of calm, her heart raced, and her chest tightened. Farda was over a head taller than she was, but she made sure to hold his gaze. "The deckhand who saw Shirea jump overboard, what colour was his hair?"

"Excuse me?" Farda said, the surprise evident on his face.

"What colour was his hair?"

"What does that matter?"

"It matters."

"It was brown. He had blue eyes. No more than twenty-five summers. And he had an odd twitch in his right cheek. Would you like to know the colour of his smallclothes?"

Ella kept her eyes locked on Farda's. She had seen that deckhand. He had swabbed the deck each morning for hours. "He's a wolfpine."

"What?"

"Faenir is a wolfpine, not a wolf."

"My apologies. I will try to remember." If Farda was taken aback by her abruptness, he didn't show it. "I have concluded my business here in Antiquar and arranged a carriage to Berona. Would you care to join me? It is more than a few weeks' travel to Berona, and it is dangerous for anyone to travel alone. Besides, I could do with some decent conversation."

A knot formed in Ella's stomach as she returned Farda's gaze. "I may stay here a few days more. Thank you, but I will make my own way to Berona."

Ella thought she saw a flash of irritation on the man's face, but it was gone before she could be sure. "Nonsense. I can hold off a few days if you wish to see more of the city."

Part of her wanted to lie to him, to make up some excuse as to why she could not travel with him. Every minute they spent together was another minute when he might poke holes in her story. But as little as she trusted the man, his was the only face she knew in the North. And he had gotten her and Faenir onto that ship. At the very least, he would be useful if they ran into any problems. "All right, I will travel with you. But I do want to stay at least one more night. I've never been to Antiquar before."

"No," Farda said, smiling, "I can't imagine you have. Not many people have the coin to travel often between the North and the South."

Ella gave Farda a weak smile. He always seemed to be probing, as if he were only looking for her to reveal the lie he already knew she was telling. What would she do when they got to Berona and Tanner told Farda she was not his niece? What then? She would deal with that when the time came. *I need to focus on what's in front of me. I need to get to Berona first, and he is the quickest way there.*

"Okay, we shall stay one more night. I will have the carriage ready to leave by sunset tomorrow," he said, turning on his heels. "I'm sure the wolf can keep up on foot. For now, I'm hungry. Food?"

Wolfpine. Faenir growled at Farda's back as the man walked back towards the city streets.

"I don't trust him either, but he is our best bet to make it to Berona," Ella said, crouching down and running her hand through the fur at the back of Faenir's neck. "Besides, as Mother always says, 'don't look a gift-horse in the mouth'. A free carriage to Berona, and protection. If he tries anything, you can deal with him."

Faenir nuzzled the top of his head into Ella's hand as if agreeing, a soft rumble emanating from his throat.

With one last look back towards the ocean and the sailors who were unloading their ship, Ella puffed out her cheeks and followed after Farda.

CHAPTER TWELVE

STORMSHOLD

Moonlight washed over the streets of Skyfell as Dayne, Alina, and the two Redstone guards raced through the city. With each step, vibrations jolted through Dayne's legs as his sandal-clad feet pounded against the smooth sandy-brown stone. His lungs burned, and sweat dripped from his brow.

He couldn't take his eyes from the back of Alina's head. Where was she taking him? What just happened? There would be plenty of time for questions once they got wherever they were going, but for now, he just had to trust her.

Taking a deep breath, Dayne urged his legs to move faster. It would not be long before somebody stumbled across Baren and the Inquisitor lying unconscious in the study with the dead Praetorians. Once that happened, there would not be a safe place in the city.

"We're almost there," Alina called back. "Try and keep up."

Dayne just grunted, glancing quickly over his shoulder to see if there was anyone behind them. The streets were empty, as they would be at that time of night. But there would still be patrols. And four people armed to the hilt sprinting through the city streets would no doubt draw their attention.

After a few minutes, the smell of salt water and fish permeated the air, and the soft susurration of breaking waves reached Dayne's ears. She was taking him to the port.

Even before they turned the corner towards the port, Dayne could see the enormous masts and white sails jutting up through the gaps in the buildings. Turning the corner at the end of the street, they stepped through a massive, sweeping red-stone archway.

The port stretched hundreds of feet in length and swept around in an enormous semi-circle, with enough mooring spots and docking berths to house over a hundred ships at any one time. A large area of smooth stone skirted the docks, interspersed with areas of gravelled rocks and flower beds. Wooden stalls covered by tarp canopies stretched the length and breadth of the port. Most of the buildings that faced out toward the water were fronted by colonnade porches or multicoloured awnings to provide some relief from the harsh sun during the day. There was barely a soul in sight except for a few dockhands and the occasional drunken sailor trying to find his way back to whatever inn he was staying at.

"This way," Alina said, tilting her head towards a mooring about fifty feet along the docks to the right. Dayne nodded and followed on her heels.

Alina stopped in front of a small ship that held a single sail and a solitary row of oars. "Get on."

Dayne hesitated, stopping just short of the mooring. "Alina, where are you taking me?"

"I will explain on the way. Just trust me."

"My trust is running a little thin right now."

Alina grasped the fabric at the neck of Dayne's robes, wrapping it up into her fist, and drew her gaze level with his. "You are not in chains because of me. Get on that damned ship now or I will kick you into the water myself."

Dayne couldn't hide the smile that spread across his face, which only seemed to irritate Alina even further.

"What?" she said, her jaw clenching.

"I'm proud of you," he said with a shrug, stepping past her and onto the ship.

Just as his foot elicited a creak from the wooden decking of the ship, Dayne yelped, something hard cracking him in the back of his head. It was not a strong enough blow to do any real damage, but it would certainly leave a bruise. He turned just in time to see Alina storming off towards one of the men who stood at the other end of the ship.

The smile didn't disappear from Dayne's face as he reached his hand back to feel the lump already forming at the back of his head. But he did throw a dark stare at the two Redstone guards who stood behind him, barely attempting to conceal their laughter. There had been a time where no man or women in Skyfell would have dared laugh at a member of House Ateres, though Dayne barely fit that title anymore.

After a minute or two, the deckhands began to move around the ship, releasing the moorings and getting the oars ready. The vessel lurched as it started off into the water. Dayne had missed the feeling of near weightlessness as the floor shifted beneath him and the feel of the spray drifting up into the air, dancing across his skin. He closed his eyes and took a deep breath, letting the scent of the sea fill his nostrils and the wind roll over his skin. It had been so long.

"You might want to get some sleep. It will be a few hours before we arrive."

Dayne opened his eyes as Alina draped a blanket over his shoulder. "I would rather sit and talk."

Alina pulled her mouth up into a weak smile. "There will be plenty of time for that, brother. There is a lot we must talk about. But for now, rest."

Dayne pulled the blanket from across his shoulder, watching as his sister strode off towards the other end of the ship. He dropped himself to the deck, resting his back against the gunnel. Pulling the blanket across himself, Dayne couldn't help but stare at Alina. The last time he had laid eyes on her, she had been a child, constantly crying any time he left for longer than a day, clinging to him like a shadow. He barely even recognised the woman who stood before him, barking orders at one of the soldiers.

Then he saw it, at the back of her neck, the tattoo of a sunburst. The mark of one who had given the gift of life. She was a mother. A sickly feeling sank to the pit of Dayne's stomach, and he found himself praying to Heraya. *Please, let it have been a girl. Please.*

Dayne woke to the feeling of a hand tugging at his shoulder.

"It is time, brother. We are here."

He opened his eyes to see Alina crouched in front of him, her left hand resting on his shoulder. He would have stayed there forever if time would have allowed it. *I will never leave you again. I promise.*

With a sigh and a half-smile, Dayne pushed the blanket off and rose to his feet. Night still dominated the sky, and the waters around them were lit by nothing but the light from the moon and the shimmer of the stars. In front of the ship, a sheer rock face rose for thousands of feet into the dark, stretching off to both the left and the right. Dayne knew this place. There was nowhere else they could have travelled to in that time. "Are you going to tell me why we're at Stormwatch?"

"You will see," Alina replied, not taking her eyes off the rock face that stood about two hundred feet in front of them.

"I'm getting tired of you saying that." Looking up, Dayne took in the jagged peaks of the cliff that were illuminated by the silvery light of the moon. The fortress city of Stormwatch had once been the focal point of Valtara's dominance of the seas. It had allowed them to control the flow of trade between the northernmost and southernmost regions of the continent, while also being a powerful tactical location. So high and so thick were the walls, no army could summit them. Bedded into the mountainside, with the sea at its front, it was impenetrable. The only access point was the port, which sat thousands of feet below the city walls. But when the empire quashed Dayne's parents' fledgling rebellion, they had no need to get inside the city. They had not wished to capture it, only to destroy it.

The empire made them watch – Dayne, his father, and his mother – from the deck of a Lorian ship as the Dragonguard bathed the city in dragonfire. It lasted for hours. Most of the men and women within the city did not die from the fire. They died from the heat and the smoke. Cooked alive and suffocated. He had always tossed up in his head which he would have preferred. The fire seemed quicker. Dayne still heard the screams at night when he slept. He still heard the blood-chilling howls as the fire stripped skin from bone and set men's lungs ablaze.

Now, the city lay empty. Not so much as a solitary flame could be seen in any of the windows, the only exception being the flame of the lighthouse that sat at the very top of the keep, warding off ships from the rocks.

It's not a city. It's a grave. Even when the ship began to tack right, Dayne did not take his eyes from the outline of the enormous fortress that stood empty in the side of the mountain, illuminated by nothing more than the light of the moon.

The ship skirted the rock face in silence for just over a half hour, the only sounds being the oars as they dipped in and out of the water and the grunts of the men as they heaved back and forth.

"There," Alina said, pointing out into the dark night towards a patch of moonlit rockface where the waves seemed at their most furious.

Dayne squinted, using his hand to keep the spray out of his eyes. "Alina, what are you…" He almost hadn't seen it. Just where Alina had pointed, precisely where the waves crashed against the rocks like they were trying to break through, sat the mouth of a small cave, only just managing to catch the light of the moon. "You're joking? You can't sail that close to the rocks, not by moonlight. It's suicide."

A smile spread across Alina's face, breaking into a slight laugh.

Dayne stood back to his full height, his eyes opened wide. "You're not joking."

"I am not."

"Alina, we are going to die."

"You have been away too long, brother. Where is your sense of the sea? Are you even Valtaran anymore?"

He knew she meant them in jest, but Alina's words stung. "Valtaran or not, that cave mouth is barely any larger than this ship, and it's near impossible to steer."

"Then you better hold on to something," she said with a shrug.

Dayne puffed his cheeks out and tilted his head backwards. "Let's get this over with. I have skirted death for too long anyway."

"That's the spirit," Alina said, laughing as she clasped her hands down on Dayne's shoulders. "Trust me, it will be worth it."

Dayne gave his sister a placating smile before grasping a rope that was tied around the mast. He gave it a tug to ensure it was fastened securely, then set his feet, firmly considering the possibility that Alina had lost her mind entirely.

It didn't take long before the waves began to push against the hull of the ship, lifting it up and carrying it closer to the sheer rock face. The waves were small at first, and the captain was able to adjust his course without too much difficulty. But as they got closer to the cave mouth, the waves increased in both size and ferocity, crashing against the hull, one after another, each time threatening to capsize the ship. The ocean rose as the ship swung from side to side, dark water flooding the deck.

Dayne looked over at Alina, thinking he could discern a touch of worry on her face, but it was gone in an instant, replaced with a cold glare as she stared down the ocean.

As they approached the cave mouth, a tangible fear made its home in Dayne's heart. They would not make it. The water level in the cave rose and fell in massive vicious sweeps. There was not a doubt in his mind that any ship caught within would be dashed against the walls, and its crew would be lost to the bottom of the ocean.

"Alina," he roared, trying to raise his voice above the crashing waves. "We need to turn back!"

The smile on her face as she turned toward him was unsettling. "Have a little faith, brother."

She has gone mad. They would be smashed to pieces if one of those waves caught them. Dayne could not see a scenario where the ship actually made it through in one piece. *I need to do something.*

Just as Dayne began to reach for the Spark, he felt someone else do the same. By instinct, he dropped his right hand to his sword belt, where he grasped at nothing – his sword still lay on the floor of Baren's study. He pulled even harder at the Spark, drawing in threads of Water and Air. He let their cool touch wash over him. *Who is it?*

Dayne cast his eyes across the crew of the ship, but he couldn't sense the Spark in any of them. He should have felt it earlier, when he boarded, but maybe they had masked themselves.

It was at that moment he realised it wasn't coming from the ship – it was coming from within the cave. He could see them now: the threads of Water, Air, and Spirit. Whoever it was, stood within the cave, out of sight, weaving their threads into the water around the ship. The waves began to calm, only a bit at first, but after a few moments they were no more than gentle swells.

Straightening his legs and standing up to his full height, Dayne threw a questioning glance at Alina.

"I told you to have faith," she said with a knowing smile. She seemed to smile a lot, but it was never a smile that held any happiness.

Dayne ran his hands through his hair, feeling the water as it built up against his fingers and dripped down onto the deck. He could already feel the salt bedding into his skin. It was comforting, in a way. Familiar.

Shaking out his robes, he stepped up beside Alina. "I think there may be a few things you are not telling me."

"I hold no more secrets than you," she said with a blank look in her eyes. Sighing, she let a frown touch the corner of her mouth. "I'm sorry. It's been a long time. There are a lot of things I always told myself I would say to you if I ever saw you again. I just…"

"I understand."

They stood there in silence at the front of the ship while the mouth of the cave swallowed them whole. The cave's mouth was fifty feet across at its widest point, and the ship's mast barely cleared its rocky roof.

"I'm only going to ask one more time, what—" Dayne stopped mid-sentence as the ship passed through the cave mouth and entered into an enormous open cavern, the largest he had ever seen.

The cavern stretched hundreds of feet up into the air and two or three times that again either side, illuminated by braziers and the pale moonlight that drifted in through openings at the very top. In front of them were several ships about the same size as the one they were on, and a few even larger – warships – sat tied to the moorings of a newly constructed dock. Past the dock, throngs of people hustled about stone streets, moving in and out of a series of colonnades that supported larger structures – homes, shops, halls.

Above the first layer of colonnades, running in broad sweeping strokes across the cavern, were terraces carved straight into the rock, each tier rising up and up, stacking on top of the next. It took Dayne a moment to notice the windows set at regular intervals along the terraces. They were homes. Enormous staircases snaked upward through the terraced mountain homes, breaking off at multiple points, feeding into what Dayne presumed was a web of tunnels.

Two long walkways jutted into the middle of the water, extending out from the docks. Each of the walkways ended with a small platform, and on each platform stood a hooded figure in orange robes. Dayne could feel the Spark radiating from them.

"How..."

Overhead, a series of ferocious roars resounded through the air. Way up at the top of the cavern, beyond the highest terrace, soaring between alcoves set into the cavern walls, were wyverns. Hundreds of them. He knew his mouth hung open, but he didn't care.

He watched as one of the wyverns leapt from an alcove, dove for fifty feet, then unfurled its wings, changing direction in an instant. The beautiful creature was covered in scales of gleaming red, about twelve feet from head to tail, with two powerful hind legs, and forelimbs that spread out into its wings. Its neck was thick and muscular, while its head was slightly flat with an arrowhead-like shape.

Dayne stood there, just watching the wyverns swooping across the roof of the cavern. Every now and again, he caught sight of a rider sat astride one of the creatures. He had grown up dreaming of becoming a wyvern rider – the vanguard of the Valtaran army. But for whatever reason, wyverns only ever accepted female riders. There were logistical reasons, of course. Most wyverns were not large enough to take flight with a fully grown man on their backs. But even outside of that, there had never been a male wyvern rider, something his younger sister had always reminded him of.

With a floating feeling in his stomach and a tear welling in his eye, Dayne turned to his sister. A smile sat on her face, and for the first time, he saw unbridled happiness. "Alina… how is this possible?"

"I never stopped believing you would return, and Valtara will never stop fighting. As I said, we have much to discuss."

Without a thought, Dayne wrapped his arms around Alina. He held her so tightly his muscles ached, but he didn't move to stop the tears that ran down his cheeks. "I love you, little sister."

Dayne felt the laughter in Alina's chest before she pulled him in tighter again. "I love you too, brother. Now, show me that letter."

Chapter Thirteen

Something to Fight For

s Alina and her guard led Dayne through the streets of the cavern, he couldn't help but notice the colours of each major house were on display in one place or another.

To Dayne's left, a man who was clearly a fisherman – judging by the noxious odour that wafted from his clothes, and his long scraggy beard – walked past wearing a belted tunic coloured in the pale blue of House Koraklon. Behind the man was a woman dragging along a small child whose face was beetroot-red as she tugged against her mother's grasp. Both wore the green and gold of House Deringal.

Across the street, a man in the red robes of House Herak sat on a stone bench chatting to another man in the black of House Vakira, while a woman in Thebalan yellow listened in with her arms folded and her face twisted in a disapproving look.

"Alina," Dayne called, pulling close to his sister, lowering his voice. "How is this? I see all the Houses here."

"We do not fight for House Ateres or House Vakira, brother." A weak smile touched the corner of Alina's mouth. "We fight for Valtara. One nation."

A thousand questions floated through Dayne's mind. The infighting between the houses was legendary. Even during the rebellion, they had been at each other's throats over whose flag would be carried at the front of the army or hang from the walls of a captured city. It had always been the way. His father had often cited it as a major reason the rebellion failed. *'You cannot win a war when you are fighting enemies from the outside and from within.'*

Alina led Dayne to a short stone staircase that veered off from the main street towards a large rectangular building that rose three storeys off the ground. The building consisted of pale grey stone, with no embellishments whatsoever, much like the rest of the hidden city. It was clear everything in this place was built solely for function.

The entrance to the large rectangular building was flanked by two guards in traditional Valtaran armour – smooth, bronze-hued steel cuirasses that flowed down into armoured skirts. They each wore a large helmet that covered most of their face and neck, with almond-shaped slits for eyes and a thin opening that dropped sharply from their nose to the base of the helmet. Their arms were protected by a set of steel vambraces, while their legs were guarded with steel greaves that ran into lightly armoured boots, built for flexibility. *They are ready for war.*

Each guard held a circular ordo shield in one hand, a valyna in the other, and a short sword strapped at their hip. But it was the colouring of the cloth in their armoured skirts that attracted Dayne's attention. One wore skirts of pale blue to represent House Koraklon, and the other wore the yellow of House Thebal – old enemies. Growing up, Dayne could not remember ever seeing warriors of House Koraklon and Thebal in the same room together, at least not with both of them leaving alive.

"Your weapons," the Koraklon guard said, stepping in front of Dayne as they reached the top of the staircase.

Without a thought, Dayne reached out to the Spark, pulling threads of Air into himself. It was always better to be safe than sorry. His brother had just betrayed him, and he would be a fool if he didn't believe that Alina might do the same, though he hated himself for thinking that way.

"You won't be coming in without handing them over, brother," Alina said with a shrug as she handed her sword to the guard who wore the Thebalan colours. The two Redstone guards who had accompanied them from Skyfell did the same.

Dayne puffed out his cheeks before acquiescing with a reluctant nod. It was not like he had many weapons on him anyway; he had left his sword in Baren's office, and he had not carried a spear in a long time. Reaching down to his belt, Dayne pulled the two knives from their sheaths at his hip before producing three more from within his robes. "Don't lose those, please. I'm quite fond of them."

The Koraklon guard just grunted at Dayne as he took the knives, then nodded him on.

"In here," Alina said after they had spent a few minutes walking down a maze of winding stone corridors with nothing adorning the walls save for just enough oil lamps to provide light.

The room where she led him was large enough to fit twenty people. Its grey stone walls were drab and lifeless, and twelve uncomfortable-looking wooden chairs sat around a heavy oak table that ran lengthways through the room, six on each side. The fireplace set into the far wall, behind the end of the table, crackled with a low flame, warming the room and tingeing the air with the aroma of burning wood. The door before Dayne was the only way in or out of the room. The two Redstone guards took up positions on either side of it, standing as straight as tree trunks.

"Are you coming?" Alina called from within, standing beside the table, her arms folded, a single eyebrow raised.

Dayne had a rule: never go into a room that only had one way out, and if you did, never let anybody stand between you and that way out. He hadn't broken that rule since the day he had deemed it necessary, twelve years ago.

Taking one more look at Alina, Dayne stepped over the threshold, walking past the guards and taking the chair closest to the door, on the right side of the table. His first opinion was proven correct: the chair was indeed uncomfortable. The wood was hard and roughly sawn, grating against his skin. It would have benefitted from a cushion of some sort.

"Not quite up to your standards, brother?" Alina asked with a laugh. "We don't exactly have the spare coin to waste on luxury."

"I wouldn't quite consider a cushion to be luxury," Dayne said with a shrug before folding his arms across his chest.

"You have been gone too long." Alina's expression didn't change. "Wait here."

With Alina gone and the room empty, Dayne let his shoulders sag. He sat there, leaning back slightly in his chair, his eyes staring at nothing in particular, the sound of crackling wood fading into the back of his mind. He was home. It was not the homecoming he had hoped for, but at least he was finally there. Slipping a small, round-backed throwing knife from where it had been strapped to the inside of his sleeve, Dayne started flipping it across his fingers. His mother had always said he had fidgety hands. He had never admitted it to her face, but of course, she was right. It helped him think. And at that moment, he needed help thinking.

Dayne couldn't get Baren's words out of his head. *'You left us here, alone.'*

Not a day had passed in over twelve years where Dayne hadn't felt guilt tear strips from his heart for having left his brother and sister that day. The more logical side of him said he had never had a choice. If he had not left, the empire simply would have killed them all. Usually, Dayne listened to the more logical side of his mind, but Baren's words ate at him. Regardless of how he rationalised it, he had left them alone. If Baren was an angry young man who had turned towards the empire for help, that was Dayne's fault because he had left Baren with no one else to turn to.

At the sound of footsteps coming down the hall, Dayne slipped the knife back into the strap under his sleeve and once again folded his arms.

Striding into the room, Alina tossed an apple towards Dayne and took a bite out of the one in her other hand. "Still your favourite?

Dayne nodded, shaking his head in disbelief that she had remembered – she had been so young when he left.

Alina pulled out the chair opposite Dayne and took a seat, resting her elbows on the table. "You listen first, then you talk, understood?"

"Understood." No matter how hard he tried, Dayne couldn't get over the woman his sister had become. Their parents would have been proud, of that he had no doubt.

Alina sat back in her chair, the top of her foot tapping methodically against the air. She took another bite of her apple, the orange glow from the fireplace casting shadows across her face. "Things have not been easy. With mother and father dead and you gone, our House was in tatters, as were all that stood by us – Thebal, Deringal, Herak. High Lord Loren consolidated every shred of dropped power. He stood on our necks."

Guilt pushed against Dayne's heart. He should have been there. Exile or not, he should never have left. But then again, what could he have done? One man, under threat of death. "I'm sorry."

Alina frowned. Dayne could see the concentration on her face as she forcibly stopped the slight twitch in her foot. "Being sorry soothes nothing but your own ego, brother. Be better."

The words stung, but Dayne could not find fault in them. He would be better. He could not fix the past, but he could help forge the future. "What did you do?"

"It was not me. It was Baren. He was head of the House, and he took it upon himself to piece our world back together. He made deals with Loren and brokered peace among some of the Houses. It was not a peace that would last, but it didn't need to be. It just needed to survive long enough so we could get back on our feet. At first, it was better. But over time, Baren became so buried in the politics of the Houses that it consumed him. At some point, it became more about showing, taking, and holding power than it was about protecting family. I don't think he ever saw the wrong in the things he did – even now." Alina paused for a moment, staring up towards the ceiling, a slight tremble in her breathing. "He asked me to wed High Lord Loren's son, to 'strengthen the bonds between our families.' Though, it was less a question and more of a command."

"He did what?" Dayne could do nothing to hide the surprise on his face, leaning forward, cracking his fist down on the table. "He had no right, Alina!"

Alina raised her hand in the air. "It doesn't matter. What is done is done. I never wed the grimy little bastard anyway. Not after he found out I already had a lover." Alina's voice trembled, and she buried her nails into the wooden arms of the chair, exposing some of the lighter wood underneath. "Baren… He…"

Dayne leaned forward. A shiver ran the length of his body, and a sick feeling set into his stomach.

"He was furious when he found out about Kal…" The tremble in Alina's voice grew stronger. "Not that I was hiding him, but…" Alina clenched her jaw, lowering her head. "He had Kal murdered, Dayne. He doesn't think I know, but I tracked down the filthy wretch who did it. It didn't take long to find out who had hired him." Alina lifted her head, her eyes growing cold and vacant. "I still can't get the sight of it out of my dreams. Kal's body lying there, lifeless and cold… all the joy and laughter drained from his heart. All to make sure I would wed Loren's son… All for 'the glory of the House.'" Alina fixed her gaze on Dayne, her voice taking on a sombre tone. "I should have killed him before we left Redstone… I should have just…" Tears streamed down Alina's cheeks, her eyes red and raw. Her fists were clenched so tightly that a thin stream of blood rolled through her fingers and dripped onto the stone floor. "I will kill him, Dayne." It was a simple statement of fact.

Dayne swallowed hard. "Alina… the Marking of Life… I…"

"It was a boy," she said through muffled sobs. "I was with child when Baren killed Kal… He found out soon after."

An emptiness consumed Dayne. A hollow filled his chest, and his heart felt as black as coal. This had been his fault. If he had not left them alone, if he had not left them to fend for themselves in a den of wolves. "Alina, I—"

"You're what? You're sorry?" Alina rose from her seat, glaring down at Dayne. Her skin glowed in the light from the fire, and her eyes burned with a fury. "It doesn't matter how many times you say it, Dayne. You weren't there. You weren't there when Baren murdered Kal, and you weren't there when he took my newborn son and handed him over to the empire, just like our father did with Owain. Just like every family must with their first-born son since the rebellion!"

Dayne got to his feet, holding his arms out wide. Alina was so close to him that he had to push his chair back just to stand up. "I swear—"

Alina shoved him in the chest before he could finish his sentence. "It doesn't matter what you swear! I don't know you. I haven't known you since I was barely up to your hip. The meaning of your word must be earned. I'll tell you what *I* swear." Alina dug her hand into the pocket of her robes, producing the letter he had given her. Aeson Virandr's letter. She ripped it open, shoving it in his face. "Aeson Virandr wants another war? Another rebellion?" She threw the letter into the air, ignoring it as it drifted to the ground. "He will have his fucking war! But I swear to you that I will feed the soil with Baren's blood. I swear to you that Valtara will either be free, or it will burn. I will never again feel another boot on Valtara's neck. And I will find my son."

Alina's chest heaved back and forth as she drew trembling breaths through her nose. She stared at Dayne for a moment. Then, letting out a heavy sigh, she wiped the tears from the right side of her cheek, replacing them with a splattering of blood from the cuts her fingernails had sliced into the palm of her hand. "I will leave in the morning. There are things that must be put in place. I think it is best if you lie low until I am back. I cannot say how the other members of the council will react to finding out that Dayne Ateres is alive."

With that, Alina left the room, slamming the door behind her. Dayne stood there for a moment, letting everything sink in before dropping back onto the hard wooden chair. As he sat, he became acutely aware of everything in the room. The sound of the crackling fire as it crumbled in on itself. The smell of dust and charred wood that hung heavy in the air. The thin line of ants that marched their way from a crack in the far wall towards a piece of stale bread that had fallen in the corner. It was easier to focus on the small things around him than on the gaping hole in his chest.

He had thought he had considered everything when he received Aeson's letter. He had mulled everything over in his mind, thinking up every possible scenario. Most of them hadn't ended well, but he had never expected this. He had never expected Baren to turn on Alina. Nor had he expected Alina to have had a child, though perhaps that was because she had still been a little girl in his mind. A little girl that used to follow him around like a shadow. She was not a child anymore, that was for sure.

"I will make things right," he muttered to himself, clenching his hand into a fist. He might never be able to rid himself of guilt, or fill the void in his heart, but he could fight. For Alina. For Valtara. For Baren.

Alina slammed the door shut as she stormed into her bedchamber. Gods damn him. Damn him for leaving her. Damn him for making her love him, and damn him for making her hate him. Was it possible to both love and hate someone?

Why had he not come back sooner? Why had Aeson's letter compelled him to come home when his family had not?

Alina roared, kicking out at a wooden stool as she did, a jolt of pain shooting through the top of her foot as it connected, knocking the stool to the ground. "Fuck!"

She let out a frustrated sigh, resting her back against the closed door and sliding to the ground. Tears still burned her eyes and rolled down her cheeks. She could taste the mixture of salt and runny snot on her lips. She had not intended to show her hand so quickly, but seeing Dayne again had brought out everything within her: anger, fear, love, loss. He would have found out eventually; he had always seen the things others had not. Besides, she refused to hide her Mark of Life anymore. She refused to hide who she was. Wherever her son was, wherever he slept at night, whatever roof he lay under, he was still her son, and she would find him.

Slowing her breathing down in an effort to calm herself, Alina ran her hands through her hair, then took a deep breath in through her nose, producing an involuntary snivel. Reaching up, she wiped away the mixture of snot and tears from her face, rubbing it into her orange robes, giving a disdainful look at the streaks of red that ran through the mixture. She had forgotten her nails had cut into the palms of her hands earlier.

Alina shook her head, then puffed out her cheeks. Bloodstains on her robe were the least of her concern. There would be plenty more blood on the path she was walking down.

For now, she needed to know her brother's true mettle. She needed to see if he felt the same fire that burned in her belly. Would he be willing to die for his people? To burn for them if need be? They all had to be willing if they were to truly start a new rebellion. It would take a different kind of courage to face dragons. Or a different kind of stupidity – she had not yet decided.

CHAPTER FOURTEEN

LIGHT AT THE END OF THE TUNNEL

The dirt and clay that coated the tunnel floor crunched under Calen's feet as he pushed one foot in front of the other, wincing as a particularly large patch of Heraya's Ward shimmered blueish-green light into his eyes. The yellow flowers they had seen in Vindakur and in the Portal Heart on the other side of the ring had dwindled in number the further they walked, and the bluish-green colour they knew from Durkadur had slowly returned. He wasn't sure how long they had been walking after coming through the ring. Days? A week? Without being able to see the sun rise and set, the only thing he had to go by was when the group stopped to sleep: six times. Surely that meant six days had passed?

Calen grunted as a sharp pain rumbled in his stomach. He swallowed hard. The only food they had come across were small rat-like creatures with six legs and grey mushrooms that grew through the cracks in the tunnels' smooth surface.

The mushrooms tasted the way shit smelled. The first time Calen had eaten one he had spewed all over the ground, losing what precious scraps of food he had already eaten that day. The rats weren't too bad as long as they were burnt to a crisp. But they were scrawny and had little meat on their bones. If they didn't find a way out of the tunnels soon, they would starve – of that, Calen had no doubt. But for the moment at least, they were alive.

Only eight of them had made it through the ring, including him and Valerys. Eight. Calen's empty stomach wrenched in pain at the thought of how many had fallen to the kerathlin. Those horrible spider-like monstrosities had shredded through them mercilessly. Images of the swarm flooding over the city streets had haunted Calen's dreams ever since, the screams and the *click-clack* of claws echoing through his mind.

He clenched his jaw, pushed his thoughts down, and kept moving. There would be time to mourn once he had seen the others to safety. His duty was to those who still lived. He owed them that much.

Calen felt a grumble in his mind from Valerys. Each passing day in the never-ending enclosed space had set an anxiousness in the dragon. Not that the tunnels were tiny by any measure. Each of them was large enough for a Wind Runner to travel through, except for a few that seemed solely for the purpose of foot travel. Though, what was a small or large amount of space was vastly different to Calen than it was to Valerys. Dragons were creatures of legend, meant to soar through open skies, not to be hemmed in on all sides by endless tunnels of smooth rock.

The idea a dragon could feel anxiety in the same way people did was not something Calen had ever considered. But they most definitely did. The anxiety that consumed Valerys bled into Calen, seeping into his mind and body. Valerys's emotions were Calen's; they were one and the same. His stomach turned as the walls closed in, sweat glistened on his palms, his heartbeat fluttered erratically, speeding up, then slowing down, and an uncontrollable tremble had crept into his breathing. It was as though his own mind were closing in on itself, and it paid no heed to the fact that he would be trapped beneath the weight. But despite it all, he would not change a thing. He would not leave Valerys to suffer alone. A burden shared was a burden halved.

"Another dead end," Erik said as they came to an abrupt halt. With a slow sigh, he rested his hands on the wall of rock that closed off the end of the tunnel. "We've been at this for days… This place is a maze. What if it doesn't lead to the surface and we're just walking around aimlessly?" Panic crept into Erik's voice as he spoke, quickly followed by resignation as his shoulders slumped. "We're dead men."

"We will find a way out. Have faith, our journey is not yet finished," Vaeril said, handing Erik a waterskin. "Don't take too much. I haven't sensed water in a while. I'm not sure how long we will need it to last."

From time to time, Vaeril had been able to sense underground pools of water with the Spark. Just like the food, there was never much water in one place, but it had been enough to keep them from dying of thirst.

"Our journey? Our journey is dead and buried!" Dark purple circles ringed Erik's eyes, and dried dirt matted his skin. Calen sensed the same level of agitation from him as he did from Valerys. The same agitation that rose inside himself. "And now we have no water? What's the damn point?" Erik threw the waterskin against the floor and slammed his back against the wall of the tunnel in frustration.

"Calm yourself, Erik," Tarmon said, his hand resting on Erik's shoulder. "We *will* find a way out, and we *will* find more water. The only way we will die down here is if we give in to our darkest thoughts."

Erik wheeled around, glaring at Tarmon. "Calm myself? Do you not see where we are? This is not some foe we can just cut our way through. We're going to die down here, slowly, buried under miles of stone, and there's not a damn thing we can do about it!" Erik's chest heaved, trembling as the words left his mouth, and he stood there in silence, his gaze locked on Tarmon's. "How are you all right with this?"

"He's not." Calen said, stepping forward, all eyes turning towards him. Ever since Calen had known Erik, the man had never once faltered. He had always been sure of himself, always willing to lay his life down. To see him now, like this, felt wrong. "None of us are, Erik. But I, for one, am not ready to just lay down and die."

Erik turned his stare to the dirt-packed ground, ran his tongue over the front of his teeth, and slid down the wall of the tunnel, nodding absently as he did. "Sorry… I don't know what's happening to me. I'm just…"

"It's all right," Tarmon replied, snatching up the discarded waterskin and handing it back to Erik. "There are demons within us all that we must face. They only ever surface when we are at our lowest because they are not strong enough to challenge us at our highest. Now, drink. We will rest here for a while, I think." Tarmon glanced towards Calen as though he expected confirmation. Calen ignored the hulking man's expectant gaze and dropped himself to the ground. These decisions were not his. He had not earned them, he did not want them, and he certainly was not the one who should be making them.

With a stiff argument from his muscles, Calen rested his back against the wall of the tunnel, just beside a small glowing patch of Heraya's Ward. His legs and back ached, and his eyes were tacky from the dirt and dust in the tunnels. He ran his fingers through his matted hair, digging them into his temples in an effort to relieve the pressure that was building up in his head. Valerys padded over to him and lay at his side, nuzzling his head into Calen's shoulder. Calen felt the uneasy sensation settling back into his mind, mixing with a warm comfort. A chaotic blend. *It will be okay. We will find a way out.*

"Y'all right?"

Calen hadn't seen Falmin approach, but the navigator hunched down in front of him, his spindly fingers wrapped around the neck of an outstretched waterskin. Regardless of the situation, Falmin never seemed to lose the arrogance in the way he moved. His cotton shirt was a mess of dirt marks and bloodstains, and dents covered the strange copper-sided glasses that sat atop his usually pristine, slicked back hair, which was now filthy and bedraggled. But despite this, there was a smirk on his face and a self-assured look in his eye.

Calen took the skin from Falmin. Relief flooded through him as the cold water touched his cracked lips and soothed the dryness in his throat. "Yeah..." he said with a sigh. "I'm just tired, and there doesn't seem to be an end in sight."

"Could be worse," Falmin said as he took the waterskin back from Calen.

"Worse?"

"You could 'ave no legs," Falmin said with a shrug, standing back up to full height.

"I..." Calen just stared at Falmin for a moment before he shook his head as he allowed himself a laugh that descended into a dry cough. "How do you do it?"

"How do I do what?" the navigator asked, setting himself down on the other side of Calen.

"Make jokes, when..." Calen didn't finish his sentence. Falmin tracked Calen's eyes as they roamed the depths of the tunnel, and he seemed to understand his meaning.

"I don't suppose you've ever been captured by the Imperial Inquisition, Draleid?" Falmin nodded when Calen gave a weak shake of his head. "Well, it turns out one of the only things they can't take from you is your sense of humour." Falmin reached his hand down, wrapping his fingers around the bottom of his shirt, lifting the fabric to reveal a twisted mess of scarred and burnt flesh. The man's stomach looked as though it had been flogged with a red-hot poker, then raked a hundred times with a knife. Just the sight of it knotted Calen's stomach. "Besides, there is nothing more important in the darkness than a ray of light." With just a hint of a smile, Falmin pulled himself to his feet, took the waterskin from Calen's hands, and made his way over to Korik and the other surviving dwarf, Lopir.

Calen closed his eyes, resting his head against the cold tunnel wall. *There is nothing more important in the darkness than a ray of light.* The words brought a calm over him. He wasn't sure why, but they did, and as they did, that calm seeped into Valerys. It was the first time Calen felt the dragon's mind at ease since they had set out through the tunnels. His own mind – though it grew harder and harder to separate the two – melted away as his aching body urged him to sleep. He gave a long, deep yawn, running his hand along Valerys's smooth, scaled neck. If he had learned one thing in the tunnels, it was how to fall asleep in as little time as possible.

Click-clack.

A shiver shot through Calen's back as he lurched forward at the sound. His heart slammed against the walls of his chest, and every hair on his body stood on end. Erik and Tarmon were on their feet. Erik gripped both of his swords so tightly his knuckles were pale. Korik and Lopir stood back-to-back, fear painted on their faces. Even Falmin's usually cool demeanour was broken; he bit his lip and his eyes flitted around the walls of the tunnel. That sound had nearly been the end of them all.

Calen felt Vaeril reach for the Spark as the elf bounded over to him and Valerys. "They might just be passing in the tunnels around us..." he whispered, just loud enough for Calen to hear over the sound of kerathlin claws clicking against the rock. Vaeril's words failed to soothe Valerys's panic and anxiety, which came flooding back like a cascading waterfall.

Click-clack, click-clack.

Calen leapt to his feet. A horrid skin-crawling feeling rippled through him, prickling his skin and setting a tremble into his hands. Fear and panic flooded over from Valerys as the dragon shook his head side to side, high-pitched whines escaping his throat. Images of the kerathlin flitted through Calen's mind. Thousands of the hideous creatures moving in a chitinous wave. Black claws. Crushing mandibles. Blood.

Calen could feel Valerys pushing him towards the Spark, urging him to draw from it as heavily as he could. It was everything Calen could do to hold Valerys's panic at bay. To stop it from consuming him.

"Valerys, it's all right." Calen's voice trembled as he clasped his hands to either side of Valerys's head, staring into the dragon's lavender eyes. "I need you to—" Calen grunted as Valerys's mind pushed harder against his own, clawing at the Spark, reaching for threads of Earth and Air, his desire to kill the kerathlin overriding everything else. "—I need you to stop. We'll bring the whole tunnel down."

"Where's it coming from?" Tarmon whispered, his knees bent, and his sword already drawn.

"All around us," Korik replied, his eyes scanning the tunnel walls.

"There must be thousands of them..." Erik's voice trailed off, swallowed by the drumming clicks of kerathlin claws.

The tension that permeated the air was so palpable everyone seemed to jump out of their skin when Valerys let out a deafening screech. He stamped his feet, smoke streaming from his nostrils, as he flicked his tail back and forth, cracking it against the wall of the tunnel. Fear and panic radiated from the dragon's mind, so powerful it threatened to overwhelm Calen completely.

Calen pulled Valerys's head towards him, pushing his forehead down against the dragon's snout. "It's all right. It's all right." Without thinking, Calen pulled at threads of Spirit. He had seen Vaeril use threads of Spirit to calm horses, but would it work on dragons? He didn't have much choice. He pulled on the thin threads of Spirit, weaving them into Valerys's mind, attempting to soothe the dragon's agitation. It seemed to work. Calen could feel Valerys's heart begin to slow and his breathing start to level off. Around them, the tunnel walls trembled from the vibrations of the kerathlin as they scuttled unseen through the spaces around them.

"What's wrong with him?" Erik's eyes were still fixed on the walls around them as he leapt over to Calen's side.

"It's everything," Calen said, still holding his head against Valerys's snout. "The tunnels, the noise—ahh." Calen clasped his right hand to the side of his head as a sharp pain shot through him. He had lost his concentration and in doing so had released the threads of Spirit he had been weaving through Valerys's mind. The pain was a blinding flash that blocked out all sound and light. His eyes saw nothing but white, and the only thing that he could feel or hear was Valerys. Panic flooded the dragon's mind. Calen could feel every tiny thing Valerys felt. His pain, his fear, his helplessness. Their minds were as one. Images, flashes of thought, streaked through their mind. The fear of never seeing the open world blended with the indomitable clicking of kerathlin claws. It was like the walls were closing in on them, crushing them, squeezing the air from their lungs, breaking off their wings. A single note shrieked through their head, a piercing noise that grew louder and louder until it reached a crescendo. Their panic twisted, melting into a white rage.

"Aaahhh!" Calen's shout was accompanied by a deafening roar from Valerys. Calen felt a shockwave leaving him. A shockwave of Earth and Air that erupted in all directions, rippling through the air, crashing into the rock. Everyone around him was thrown to the ground or slammed against the walls by the force of the wave. The tunnel shook, and cracks spread through the roof, giving way to clouds of stone dust and shards of rock bouncing off the floor. Calen didn't remember reaching out to the Spark, but he felt the threads. Earth and Air. He was wrapped in them, and so was Valerys. The mixture of rough iron and cool ice peeled through his body as the energy of the Spark surged. He felt Valerys's energy as much as he did his own; there was no separation between the two. Larger cracks began to spread through the stone as the threads of Earth and Air intensified. Calen had no control; Valerys kept pushing, drawing deeper and deeper from the Spark.

"Calen!" Calen felt hands on his shoulders and something pushing against his mind. Threads of Spirit. "Calen!" It was Vaeril's voice, faint, but recognisable. "You need to focus. Be strong, reach out with your mind. You need to calm him."

Valerys.

Calen could feel Valerys, his panic and his anger. He wanted to kill the kerathlin. To crush them inside their shells and smell the air as they burned. *Valerys, you need to stop. You're going to kill us.* There was a flash of recognition from Valerys. *I know you're scared, but I'm here.* Calen emptied his mind. He focused only on Valerys and the Spark. He let the threads of Air and Earth flow through him, reaching out, drawing in threads of Spirit. *Hear me. Please. Draleid n'aldryr, Rakina nai dauva.* Dragonbound by fire, Broken by death. Therin hadn't taught him those last few words, he just… knew them, as though they had been buried deep in his mind – or in Valerys's.

Something stirred in Valerys at the words. The blinding flash began to peel away, and the voices of Calen's companions flooded into his ears. His hands were still clasped on either side of Valerys's head, and as his vision slowly returned, he found himself staring directly into the white dragon's pale lavender eyes. Dirt crunched beneath him as he dropped to his knees. Valerys's head pressed down against his neck, a soft whine escaping the dragon's throat.

"I'm here," Calen said with a sigh, his body sagging. "Everything is going to be all right."

Vaeril and Erik were at Calen's side in seconds.

"What in the name of the gods was that?" Erik's eyes were wide with a blend of fear and concern.

"I… I don't know. Valerys was scared, and he…" Calen pulled Valerys's head in tighter, letting the relief sweep through him. He drew in a deep, dust-filled breath, held it, then released it slowly. They had come so close to the entire tunnel collapsing on top of them.

"Well, at least he scared off those fuckin' stone bugs," Falmin called out, hunkered down a few feet away with his hand against the wall of the tunnel. "The noise is gone and the walls ain't shakin' no more."

Calen listened intently. He heard nothing. There was no *click-clack* of the kerathlin claws or vibrations in the stone. Only silence… and… something else. A sound he picked up while the threads of Air and Spirit still lingered in him. A soft *whooshing* whistle that flowed through the tunnels. It was familiar, yet odd. Tentatively, Calen reached out with threads of Air, intensifying the sound in his ears. A surge of urgency flared in his mind as he realised what the sound was. "I think I know how to get out of here."

Chapter Fifteen

Old Friends

he tunnel ahead seemed to stretch on to the end of time. It forked and split, like the roots of a tree weaving their way through the mountain. With each step, he doubted himself. Was it really the wind he was hearing? How could he be sure? He could ask Falmin or Vaeril. But something told him he was right. It wasn't like they had much choice either way, so he just put one foot in front of the other. Again and again. Every muscle in his body cried out for something soft to lie down on and a warm bath to relax in. He yearned to see the sun setting and rising. The indeterminate passing of time only served to intensify every emotion and dim all hopes of escape. At least in Durakdur, there had been clocks in every room. It was not the same as seeing the light of the sun, but it was something.

Calen scratched at an itch on his head as he walked. Dirt was matted into his hair and bedded under his fingernails, as though he had been digging graves with his bare hands. It was a good thing he couldn't see his own face, because if he looked anything like the others, then he probably wouldn't have recognised himself. At least he couldn't smell anything. He had no doubt they all smelled like shit, but the only thing that filled his nostrils was the earthy scent of dirt.

"So, what is it we are *following*?" Erik asked, drawing up level with Calen's hurried pace, dark circles still ringing his eyes.

"It's hard to explain," Calen said in between breaths. He rubbed his hands up and down his arms as they walked, trying to stave off the cold that had begun to set into the air the closer they got to the source of the whistling. "It's the Spark. With the right amount of Spirit and Air… I can just… hear the wind? I can follow it and hear it changing as the tunnels open out and change shape. The closer we get to the way out, the more it changes. It's not far now."

"Not bad, Draleid," Falmin said, his lower lip curling over his top lip in a pout. "In the guild, we call it the drift. The flowing currents of air that pass through the tunnels. Though, I've never had to use it to find my way before. Impressive."

Calen couldn't help but feel a slight swell of pride at the navigator's words. It didn't seem that he gave out praise very often, so Calen didn't intend on wasting it.

The cold wasn't the only change as they progressed through the tunnel. The patches of Heraya's Ward that had been so reliable in their supply of light, grew scarce as they pressed on. Their eyes managed for a while, adjusting to the increasingly dim tunnels, but eventually they needed to create light. Calen had a feeling there were more than a few things they didn't want to cross in the darkness of these tunnels.

The baldír that floated at the head of the group was weak, giving off just enough light to show them where they were going and no more. Calen couldn't afford to give it any more of his strength. Even as it was, barely more than a flickering candle, keeping it alight burned a lethargy through him. Valerys's episode had leeched the energy from them both; Calen still felt the drain sapping at him.

Vaeril had offered to light the way instead, but his body was still too weak. Calen could see it in the elf's eyes. Fresh streams of blood appeared every few hours where the scab on his leg stretched and broke. He acted as though the wound didn't bother him much, but Calen knew better, and he wasn't about to let the elf risk himself any more than he already had.

The only other person capable of touching the Spark was Falmin. The navigator's command of Air was almost effortless, but he didn't seem to understand much outside the manipulation of that single elemental strand, which seemed strange to Calen. He had never truly seen the elemental strands as separate entities. Each one was clear and unique, but they always seemed intertwined. Either way, Falmin could not help, and Calen would have to do it himself. Taking a deep breath of cool air, he gritted his teeth and pushed more energy into the baldír, illuminating the path ahead. He would have done almost anything to just lie down and sleep. To let his weary body rest. But he couldn't. He needed to get the others out of the tunnels. He would not let them die. *Almost there.*

Every few paces Calen turned his attention back towards Valerys. He felt the dragon's weariness and anxiety. It was subdued now, but still there, lingering at the edge of his consciousness. Valerys lifted his head so his eyes were looking into Calen's. Calen felt the shame, like a blanket of misery, that wrapped itself around the dragon. Shame at allowing himself to lose control, and for putting Calen and the others in danger. It was so very heavy. "Don't worry, we're nearly out of here," Calen whispered, forcing a weak smile.

The lack of warmth, rest, and food was wearing on them all. As much as Calen could feel it in his own muscles and lungs, he saw it in the others. Valerys was the worst off. They had scarcely found enough food to feed themselves, but feeding Valerys was a whole other story. Mushrooms and rats were not enough for a dragon, even one who was still young. His steps were laboured, his mind foggy. Calen could feel the pain and cramps spreading throughout his body; if they didn't get him some real food soon… it was best not to think about it. Calen could sense the point that he thought was the tunnel mouth. Soon.

"The end is near." Tarmon panted, resting his hand on the wall of the tunnel.

Falmin dangled his gangly arm over Tarmon's shoulder as the soldier stopped to give his lungs a rest. "Don't be so negative. I reckon you've got a few more years left in ya," Falmin said with a grin.

Tarmon just stood there, shaking his head in disbelief, a weary smile daring to touch the corner of his lips as the gangly navigator strode ahead of him. Again, the navigator was the only one who seemed capable of mustering anything more than a grumble. The rest of them just trudged through the now frost-covered tunnel, their heads down and their teeth chattering. They kept moving forward.

Calen crossed his arms, tucking his hands into his armpits, clamped his jaw shut to stop the chattering, and pushed one foot after the next.

After a while, Calen's breath plumed out in front of him, and the floor of the tunnel gained a firmer crunch under a soft blanket of frost.

Erik's voice broke Calen out of his trance-like state. Left foot, right foot, left foot. "Light! Up ahead! There's an opening!"

Calen pulled his gaze from the frosted tunnel floor as a feeble cheer echoed through the group. Erik was right. A small speck of white light sat at the end of the tunnel, and now that Calen was focusing, he could sense the change in the air. It was the tunnel mouth they had been searching for. He sighed as he let go of the thin threads of Air he had been holding, relief flooding through him as he did. He had only drawn in the thinnest threads he possibly could – just enough to follow the air – but still they had ebbed away at him, slowly eroding the last vestiges of his energy.

The group's pace quickened to somewhere between a swift stagger and a laboured strut. Any faster and they would die of exhaustion before they got there; any slower and they would die of hunger.

As they got closer, the speck of light grew and grew, until it stood as a clear doorway, nearly twelve feet high and fifteen feet wide. At least, it used to be a doorway. Heaps of rubble were strewn about the tunnel floor, and the remnants of a gigantic stone doorframe still clung to the tunnel mouth on either side. It looked as though it had been broken through from the outside by an immense blast. Past the ruined doorway was a canvas of black and white, flecked with deep green. A blanket of snow dotted with needle leafed trees yielded only to the blackest of night skies, only illuminated by the pale light of the full moon that had drifted into the tunnel. Even without his hearing augmented by threads of Air, Calen heard the hoots of an owl echo into the tunnel mouth. A smile crept onto his face.

The bitter wind snapped at Calen's face as he stepped out through the ruined doorway, the snow coming just short of his knees. He didn't care. He closed his eyes and filled his lungs. The air was cold, crisp, and it burned a little in the back of his throat. "Damn, that's good."

He felt Valerys's agreement as the dragon collapsed in the snow, a wave of relief washing over Calen's mind like a flood. He could feel the cool touch of the snow on Valerys's scales as if they were his own, the sensation of the fresh air filling his lungs, and the sense of freedom that came with spreading his wings.

Erik dropped to his knees beside Calen, the snow coming up past his hips. He ran his dirt covered fingers through his hair, a wide, relief filled smile spreading across his face. "I didn't think we were going to get out." He looked up at Calen, the sombreness in his eyes in stark contrast to the mirth in his smile. "I really didn't, Calen."

A warmth filled Calen from top to bottom as he looked down at Erik and across at the others – they had done it. They were free. The relief that set into him was so great it sent a tingling shiver through his body. He reached out his hand and grasped Erik by the forearm, pulling him to his feet. "We're out, Erik." He pulled Erik into a tight embrace, squeezing so hard he feared that one of the two of them might break. "We're out."

"Thank you," Erik whispered, pulling away from Calen but looking him in the eyes.

Calen nodded, a broad smile spreading across his face. They had not stopped running since Belduar. How much time had passed? How many weeks? It was impossible to tell. But they had made it.

"Pity we're all gonna freeze t'death now," Falmin said with a shrug, his hands tucked firmly under his armpits.

"Do you ever shut up?" Tarmon walked out past Calen and Erik, his hands set on his hips as he looked out into the night.

"Where do you think we are?" Vaeril asked, the elf's gaze following Tarmon's.

"Korik, Lopir, do either of you have any idea?" Calen turned to the two dwarves. To his surprise, he found that they still stood in the collapsed doorway that had once marked the entrance to the tunnels. It was difficult to be sure beneath their knotted beards of golden, silver, and bronze rings, but they seemed hesitant to step out from the tunnel. Scared, even. The hairs on the back of Calen's neck stood on end and his body tensed, his hand dropping to the pommel of his sword. "What's wrong?"

It took a moment for Korik to meet Calen's gaze. "Belduar was the first time we had ever stepped outside of the Freehold. We were born and raised beneath the stone of Lodhar."

Calen let the tension drain from his body, sighing with relief. He pulled his hand away from his sword and pushed his way through the snow, ignoring the biting wind. He stopped just short of where Korik and Lopir stood in the doorway and reached out his hand. "You do not take your steps alone. Wherever we are now, we are all strangers here. But at least we are together."

Korik and Lopir exchanged a glance. With Lopir giving a short nod, they both stepped from the doorway. Korik reached out his hand, wrapping his fingers around Calen's forearm. "We are with you, Draleid."

"And we are with you."

So many had died, but they had made it.

"There is a village," Tarmon shouted, his voice carrying through the night.

"How far?" Calen called back, pushing his way through the snow to step up beside Tarmon. He followed the man's line of sight, his eyes falling on a small splattering of orange lights far below, off in the distance. It wasn't until that moment that Calen realised how far up the mountain they were.

"It's about four hours' walk by my guess. Though that is just a guess. And it won't be enjoyable. In this kind of darkness, this mountainside is extremely dangerous terrain, and we can't risk using one of your light orbs because we don't know who – or what – might be out here with us. But we don't have a better option."

Calen didn't notice Vaeril stepping up beside them, looking down at the small village at the base of the mountain. "The Draleid and I can lead the way. Has Therin taught you how to use *moonsight?*"

Calen shook his head. Moonsight was not something that had ever come up in his lessons with Therin – lessons that had ended far sooner than they should have. He found his mind lingering on Therin, the elf he had once thought to be nothing but a storyteller. An elf, he now knew, was so much more than that.

"Moonsight," Vaeril continued, "is using threads of Fire and Spirit to augment your vision. It doesn't quite give you the same sense of sight as you would have during the day, but it is far better than wandering through the darkness. Watch me and follow."

Calen nodded, biting the corner of his lip as he watched Vaeril reach for the Spark. The elf drew on thin threads of Fire and Spirit, just like he had said. Calen matched him, following his every movement as he weaved the threads through his eyes and mind. The warmth of the Fire felt soothing in Calen's bones as he pulled it through him; Fire always had the strongest hold over him, calling for him to draw on more. He ignored that urge as he followed Vaeril, who worked slowly to allow Calen to follow. In the back of his mind Calen felt Valerys watching them with great interest; he didn't have to look to know that a pearlescent set of pale lavender eyes were fixed on him from where Valerys lay, his white scales blending seamlessly into the snow.

As Calen followed Vaeril's threads, mimicking the elf's motions, a shiver ran down his spine. His vision changed gradually. The world became brighter, and he no longer saw blotches of darkness-obscured shapes, but clear outlines and features. Vaeril's face seemed as clear as day, and Tarmon's armour shimmered in the dim glow of the moonlight. But there was more to it than that; as everything around him grew clearer, the lights and objects in the distance seemed to blur into a muddled haze. It was more than a little disorienting.

"How does it feel?" Vaeril asked, tilting his head as he did. The moonlight gleamed in the elf's eyes as it would in the eyes of a kat.

"It feels… strange."

"It does," Vaeril agreed, "but you will get used to it. You need to be careful when you use moonsight. You will be sensitive to flashes of bright light, and you won't be able to see anything more than a hundred feet away. It's a trade-off."

Calen nodded absently, pushing his fingers into the creases of his eyes as he did when trying to clear his vision in the morning after a long sleep. Nothing changed. The world around him was as bright as day, though it did not have the same vibrancy. The colours seemed duller, washed out. "Why didn't you show me this in the tunnels?"

"A baldír was better suited to the tunnels. Moonsight only benefits the wielder. There is a time and place for everything."

"We should get moving," Tarmon said, "before we all freeze to death."

With the threads of Fire flowing through him, Calen had all but forgotten about the snow and the freezing wind that surrounded them. The Fire had driven the cold from his bones. But he was all too aware that those around him did not benefit from the same luxury. When the cold was added to the hunger and the sleep deprivation, the mountainside was a dangerous place to be. They needed to get to shelter as fast as they could.

"Calen and I will lead the way," Vaeril said, turning to Calen for confirmation.

Calen didn't think he would ever come to terms with Vaeril and Tarmon looking to him for these things – or anyone, for that matter. It was not long ago his mother was telling him to clean up after himself in the mornings after he ate bread, or his father was sighing at him for overworking a horseshoe. Wordlessly, Calen gave a nod, eager for something to distract him from thoughts of his family.

The journey down the side of the mountain was slow. The thick blanket of snow made every step a precarious one. Even with moonsight, it was nearly impossible for Calen to tell if he would find solid footing with his next step. Tarmon and Erik had more than a few close calls where they caught their feet on loose stones or fallen branches. Thankfully, they had managed to right themselves before any damage was done, but the danger was very real.

The threads of Fire might have kept the cold from Calen's skin, but they held no such sway over the damp that seeped through his boots and trousers, soaking him as he trudged down the mountain.

Calen had seen snow before, of course. It snowed most winters in the villages. Not all, but most. When it did snow, it was nothing like this. Calen had never seen snow rise more than a few inches off the ground. And in the centre of The Glade, where footfall was higher, the snow tended to melt away by mid-morning.

The muscles in his hips and legs burned as he dragged them through the dense blanket of icy white, the snow seeming to pull at him, as though trying to suck him in, making his steps feel laboured and heavy, sapping the energy from his bones. They might have been free of the tunnels, but nothing had changed. It was still the same motion – left foot, right foot, left foot, right foot. The others must have felt much the same, for barely a word was spoken as they slogged through the now waist-high snow.

While Calen held onto moonsight, everything around him was illuminated in a dull glow – a faded version of daylight. But the lights of the village in the distance were nothing but a blur. It was the strangest sensation. He just had to keep moving. Left foot, right foot. "Erik?"

"Not long now," Erik said through chattering teeth. "I can make out the houses and smoke rising from the chimneys. Oh, the things I would do for a warm fire and a tankard of ale."

As Calen looked ahead at the blurred horizon and picked out the blotch of orangey-red light that he figured was the village, he began to salivate. Not so much at the idea of a fire and a tankard of ale, like Erik. But at the thought of warm food and a bed. His back and neck stiffened at the thought of sleeping on something that was not hard rock.

More than anything else, he was looking forward to not having to walk until his blisters had blisters and those blisters had scabbed over into callouses. He could not remember the last day that did not involve walking. And every day that involved walking, held pain.

A snap of branches came from a cluster of trees about fifteen feet to the left of the group. Valerys leapt into the air, his ever-growing wings lifting him high into the night, spraying a fine mist of snow behind him. Calen felt Valerys's hunger in the back of his mind, aching, twisting. The sound had come from a deer. Valerys could smell it, which meant Calen could too. The scent of its damp fur clung to the air, drifting along the wind.

Go, but be careful. A half-hearted rumble of acknowledgement came back. Unlike Vaeril or Tarmon, Valerys had not intended to wait for permission. However hungry Calen was, Valerys was three times that again. It would do him well to eat some meat. Mushrooms and strips of rat were not enough for a dragon.

"Where's he going?" Erik called as he picked up his pace and drew level with Calen, the slightest touch of worry in his voice.

"He's going to eat. There's deer out there."

"I could use some deer. Would he be willing to get some for the group?"

While holding onto moonsight, Calen could easily make out the grin that sat on Erik's face. Erik knew as well as he did that once Valerys got a hold of food, sharing was not taken under consideration.

"Move no further," a voice called.

Without thinking, Calen dropped his hand to the pommel of his sword and reached for the Spark. A tingling sensation ran through the back of his neck as Vaeril and Falmin did the same. He didn't have to look to know the others had drawn their weapons.

"Who goes there?" Tarmon answered, his fingers wrapped around the hilt of his greatsword. For a moment, no response came, just the empty whistling of the wind as it swept over the mountainside, sprinkling the air with snow dust. But then Calen saw them with the help of his moonsight – soldiers, emerging from the trees, surrounding them. Calen counted ten in total, four ahead and three on either side. Vaeril saw them too. Calen felt him reaching for threads of Air.

The soldiers wore heavy furs draped over coats of black, riveted chain mail with thick hoods obscuring their faces. Each of them carried a circular shield of layered wood painted a deep blue, with a domed iron boss at the centre. Some form of angular short sword hung at their hips, but most of them carried a long spear or wicked-looking axe, while three carried bows. It was difficult to determine the finer details with his moonsight-augmented eyes, but one thing Calen could tell: they were armed for war, not for hunting.

"Tarmon, there are ten of them," Calen whispered, just loud enough for the man to hear over the whistling wind. "Four ahead, three on either side. They're armed."

Tarmon nodded in reply, not turning his head towards Calen. The group of men drew in closer from each side until Calen was sure they were visible to the rest of the group. The three with bows held their ground.

"We can take them quickly," Erik said, drawing up beside Calen, his two swords drawn. There was not a hint of hesitation in his voice or warmth in his eyes. "Can you deal with the archers?"

Calen looked around at his companions. The snow was only just short of Korik and Lopir's chests; exhaustion had set into the dwarves' eyes, and the cold had turned their faces a pale blue. Falmin, Tarmon, and Erik shivered ceaselessly, and their teeth chattered with every breath they took. They didn't have the time to be standing around. Calen could feel the uneasy tension in the air. They had spent so long wandering through those tunnels, hungry, exhausted, close to the void. All it would take was the wrong word and his companions would happily tear through anyone who stood between them and a warm meal.

One of the men from the other group broke away and stepped out through the snow holding a hefty twin-bladed axe with an edge that glinted in the light of the moon. "It is not you who will be asking the questions. What are you doing in these lands?"

"We are just passing through," Tarmon answered, lowering his sword. "We don't want any trouble. Just a bed and a warm meal."

"Just passing through?" the man scoffed. "Nobody *just passes through* Mount Helmund. Who *are* you?"

"Mount Helmund?" Falmin muttered. "We're in Drifaien…"

Calen couldn't make sense of what he had just heard. Drifaien was in the far south, over a thousand miles from Belduar. *That's not possible.*

Tarmon pressed on as though the revelation had not affected him. "We are travellers. We mean no harm, and we are happy to talk beside a warm fire, but if we stay out here arguing much longer, we will freeze to death."

"That is not our problem, *traveller.* We came dressed for the weather, as you should have. I—" A thunderous roar cut through the man's words as Valerys swooped down in a cloud of snow, greeted by gasps and shouts of shock from the men around them.

The dragon's scales shimmered in the moonlight, blending in and out of sight with the snow. Valerys dropped the broken body of a stag into the snow, blood dripping from his jaws, steam rising from wherever the droplets fell to the ground. The frills on his back stood on end, like the hackles of a threatened wolfpine.

A deep, rumbling growl resonated from the dragon's armoured chest as he craned his neck from side to side, weighing up the enemies before of him. Fury rose in Valerys, along with a ball of pressure threatening to build. *No. Not yet. We need to wait.*

Valerys's head snapped around to glare at Calen, his teeth bared as a disagreement seeped from one mind to another. Valerys did not believe the risk in waiting was worth taking. But the pressure dissipated, even if the threatening growl remained.

Calen stepped up beside Valerys, sheathing his sword as he did. He reached for the Spark, pulling on threads of Air and Spirit. Just as he had seen the mage do at Daymon's coronation, he weaved the threads into his voice as he spoke, sweeping his words through the gelid air so that all the men could hear him. "I am Calen Bryer, first of the free Draleid. This is Valerys, and these are my companions. We have come here, not by choice, but by necessity. We are hungry, tired, and sick of death. Please, a warm fire, some food, and a bed. That is all we ask."

The man at the front of the group moved forward a few steps and pulled back his hood. Calen couldn't make out his face; his beard was thick, and his hair dragged down past his shoulders.

The man started to laugh, a deep, bellyaching laugh that echoed across the mountainside. It was not the response Calen had expected. It set a strange, uneasy feeling in his stomach, and he tightened his grip on his sword.

Letting his laugh die down, the man hefted his axe up and slid it into place on his back. "By the gods, you have a fucking dragon. The last time we met, all you had was a purse full of coins and a deft hand with an axe."

"Calen?" Erik's voice held the same question that Calen's mind did.

"I'm not sure…" Calen narrowed his eyes as he stared at the man. Even with moonsight, he couldn't make out the face past the thick beard. But something about him was familiar. "It couldn't be… Alleron, is that you?"

It couldn't be, could it? Calen had only met the man once, in The Two Barges, right before everything happened. But he *had* been from Drifaien.

"As I live and breathe… Get over here." Alleron stepped forward and grasped Calen's forearm, though he gave Valerys a sidelong glance as he did. A deep growl still resonated from the dragon's chest as his eyes narrowed, watching Alleron's every move. *He is a friend.*

Valerys's eyes narrowed even further in response. Calen ignored the dragon. A smile crept across his face as he looked into Alleron's eyes. He released the Spark, allowing the moonsight to drift away. The world grew darker around him, but his eyes felt like they were his own again. He wrapped his fingers around Alleron's forearm, returning the gesture with enthusiasm.

"You…" Calen stifled a disbelieving laugh; after so long wandering that labyrinth of tunnels, part of him had lost hope. He did not know the man well, or at all, really, but Calen couldn't help but feel a sense of relief at the sight of him. When they had met in Milltown – that seemed so long ago – there had been something about him that spoke to Calen, something genuine. "You are a sight for sore eyes. I—"

"No," Alleron said, raising his hand. "By the look of you—" Alleron paused for a moment, again turning his gaze towards Valerys, who had calmed somewhat. "And by the look of *him,* you have many stories to tell, but that can wait. You'll not last long out here in this cold. You are lucky we were patrolling out here. Come, the village of Katta is not far, we can shelter there for the night."

"Thank you," Calen said, closing his eyes for a moment, savouring the first drop of good news he had heard in weeks. All at once, his body sagged as though an enormous weight had been lifted from his shoulders, and he could finally rest. He relished the thought of a good night's sleep and some real food. "Please, lead the way."

The journey to the village was filled with an uneasy tension. Calen, Erik, and Alleron were the only ones who talked as they slogged through the blanket of nearly waist-high snow. The others eyed the soldiers askance the entire way; the time in the tunnels had put them on edge. He couldn't blame them; the lack of sleep and food combined with the constant fear of the kerathlin had put him on edge as well.

Korik and Lopir stayed huddled together as they trekked, only exchanging a few brief words, low enough so nobody else could hear. Falmin and Tarmon were similarly quiet, which was a first for Falmin, at least. He was almost as bad as Dann when it came to keeping his mouth shut. Though, judging by the way he shivered and the repetitive clicking sound that came from his chattering teeth, the cold was having an effect on his usually wagging tongue. After all, there was hardly a pound of fat on the man's gangly body; nothing to keep the harsh wind at bay. That same wind bit at the exposed skin on Calen's face the second he released the Spark. The thin threads of Fire and Spirit required to use moonsight did not cause much of a drain on him, but combined with hunger and exhaustion, even they were difficult to maintain.

Of them all, though, it was Vaeril who seemed the most uneasy. He did not allow himself to stray more than five feet from Calen at any point, and the entire time Calen felt the elf holding on to the Spark. Calen glanced back at him more than once to try and reassure him with a look, to tell him they were safe, they were with friends. But the snow had begun to fall again, and it was difficult to tell if Vaeril could even see the expressions on his face.

The Drifaienin soldiers, for their part, kept their distance from the group. They walked in two columns on either side, cutting their way through the snow with practised efficiency. They did not shiver and shake like Calen and his companions did. Cloaks of thick fur draped down over their chainmail, and the insides of their hoods were lined with a soft padding. The reason they kept their distance was no puzzle. They hardly walked five or ten feet without throwing sidelong glances at Valerys. The dragon marched through the snow at Calen's side, a low grumble perpetually resonating from his throat. He was no bigger than a horse, but horses did not have wings, they weren't covered in armour, they did not have teeth and claws that could rend steel, and they certainly could not breathe fire.

A smile touched Calen's lips as he looked at Valerys. They were bound by a magic older than the ground beneath their feet or the moon in the sky. In everything they did, they could feel each other. If they were separated by mountain and sea, Calen was sure he could point his hand in Valerys's direction. They were two halves of a whole. Though, as Valerys grew, so too did his influence in Calen's mind. If Calen had not been able to hold Valerys's panic at bay in the tunnels, the dragon's mind would have overwhelmed him. It was something he would have to be careful about.

After they spent some time trudging through the snow, the flickering torches of Katta came into view. The village itself was about as large as the Glade. The houses comprised thick wooden logs, with blankets of snow set heavy across their rooves. The only paths through the snow were those trodden by frequent footfall. Tall, oil-burning torches fixed into wooden stands stood at regular intervals along the trodden paths, chasing the shadows back into the night. A palpable sense of relief flooded through Calen's mind at the sight of the village up close.

Alleron stopped about twenty feet short of the village, just in front of a large two-storey building with a sign out front that read The Brazen Boar. A slightly bitter aroma of ale drifted from the inn. "Food, a warm bath, and a bed. I will see to it you have all three here. The barn is on the other side. It will be as good a place as any for the dragon to sleep. I'll take you there now. Alwen can bring the others to the inn." Alleron waved over one of his men, a tall, brooding man with a stony look in his eyes and a head of long blonde hair that fell in curls. He explained to the man what was to be done and set him about his task.

Turning back to Calen, Alleron took another look at Valerys, who returned his curious stare. A long moment passed where Alleron and the dragon held each other's gaze, but then the man shook his head with a laugh. "Gods be damned… a dragon. Come on, it's best we get him inside, don't know how the people will react to a dragon skulking about at night."

Calen nodded. "Just give me a minute."

Falmin, Korik, and Lopir had followed Alleron's man, Alwen, without a second's hesitation. Food and heat were the only things on their minds. But Vaeril, Erik, and Tarmon still stood by Calen's side, and they made no motions to move. Each of them looked as though they stood with one foot on death's door. Their faces were tinted with a hue of pale blue, and it was clear that all of them were trying their best to suppress their bodies' desire to shiver.

"Go," Calen said, "it's been a while since any of us have had some decent food and a soft bed. I'm going to stay in the barn tonight with Valerys. I'll have some food brought out."

"Draleid, I don't—"

"Vaeril, *go.*"

In truth, Calen didn't want company. He didn't want a drink, or a conversation, or someone looking over his shoulder. He wanted nothing more than to collapse on the ground beside Valerys and sleep for days on end. He wanted five minutes on his own, without the gaze of others on his back. Watching him or expecting things of him.

The elf frowned in disapproval but did not argue. "As you wish, Draleid."

The elf gave a short bow of the shoulders and stormed off as much as his graceful stride would allow. As much as Calen had grown to like Vaeril, he was beginning to think he would never truly understand the way of elves. Their sense of humour was *interesting* at best, and he never seemed to say the right thing as far as they were concerned.

"Don't mind him," Erik said. "He's just a bit on edge. We all are. You sure you don't want one of us to stay with you?"

Calen shook his head. "I'll be fine. I can't leave Valerys out here on his own, and I could use the time myself."

"Suit yourself," Erik said with a shrug. "I'll have an ale for you. In fact, I might have three. Come on, Tarmon, let's see how well the Lord Captain of the Kingsguard holds his drink."

Tarmon threw a sideways frown towards Erik and rolled his eyes to the sky. "We won't be far, Calen. I will come and check on you in the morning. Sleep well."

When they had all made their way inside the inn, Alleron gestured for Calen to follow him around to the other side of the building where he pushed open the barn doors and ushered Calen and Valerys inside. "There should be more than enough room for the two of you. Normally, when the cold is this harsh, we keep the cows in the barn. But since the last Urak attack, there aren't any more cows. So, she's all yours. I'll have Mirrin bring you some blankets, hot water for washing, and some of whatever the cook has in the pot. Are you sure you wouldn't rather stay in the inn?"

"Thank you, Alleron. I will be fine in here."

Alleron hadn't exaggerated. The barn was large enough to fit a hundred people, never mind just himself and Valerys. It was nearly forty feet across and longer again in length, with piles of hay strewn about and a spacious loft overhead. The only light was the silvery wash of the moon that drifted in through the small rectangular windows on the second level. With a whoosh of air, Valerys half jumped and half swooped past Calen and Alleron, dropping himself down onto a large pile of hay in the corner of the barn. Calen didn't even try to hide his weak smile as Valerys rumbled contentedly, nestling himself into a comfortable position, a feeling of relief sweeping through the back of his mind.

"Calen." There was a serious tone in Alleron's voice – all the earlier warmth was not gone, but there was a definite change in his stance. "I need to know the truth. About you. About... *him*." Alleron nodded towards the half-asleep figure of Valerys in the corner of the barn. "About how you got here. We've heard the rumours. That a man in Illyanara has claimed himself to be Draleid and joined Belduar in declaring war on the Lorian Empire. From what we've heard, Battle Mages and Inquisitors have been dispatched to every High Lord in the

South with demands to have this *Draleid* captured and detained. My father is expecting one any day now in Arisfall."

"Your father?"

Alleron sighed, bringing his hand up to scratch at the back of his head, and dropped himself down onto a stack of hay. "My name is Alleron Helmund. My father is Lothal Helmund, High Lord of Drifaien."

A High Lord? Calen didn't know what to say. It's not as if he ever asked the question. But could any of the High Lords be trusted? From Therin's stories, and all other stories besides, the High Lords would sell their own grandmothers if they thought it might benefit them in any way. Even Castor Kai, High Lord of Illyanara. There were more than a handful of stories about how the Varsund War had started, and at least half of them laid the blame at his feet. Suddenly, Calen felt as though he were walking on a thin layer of ice, and any misstep could cause him to plummet through the surface. But even at that, there was something about Alleron that set him at ease. His conflicting feelings battled each other as Calen looked wordlessly at the man.

Alleron returned Calen's gaze without flinching. "I am not here to hand you over to the empire, though I doubt my father would hesitate to do so. Look, there seems to be a lot that both of us don't know. How about I get Mirrin to bring us some food, and we can talk? Nothing you say will leave this room unless you want it to. I swear by The Mother and The Father. However, I need to know who I have welcomed into my lands and what you plan on doing next."

Calen brought his hand to his face and scratched at the short, stubbly beard that had begun to form while he was in the tunnels. All he wanted was to eat and to sleep; even washing could wait until the morning. But it wasn't like he had much choice. He never seemed to have a choice; that was the way of things now. Becoming a Draleid had given him a strength he had never thought possible, but it had also tied chains around him, binding him to his path. He sighed, running his hands through his hair and twisting his neck to relieve some of the stiffness that had set in, two loud cracks signalling that he had done just that. "Okay… let's talk."

Large stone hearths roared on both sides of The Brazen Boar, bathing the crammed common room in a warm, orange light. Not even one of the long, heavy wooden tables was empty, and the air was tinged with the scent of fresh stew, sweat, and beer. Though, what decent inn didn't have a lingering smell of sweat and beer, Falmin wasn't sure. In unison with Erik, Lopir, and Korik, he slammed his short wooden cup down on the table with a definite crack. He puffed out his cheeks, grimacing as the golden-brown liquor burned its way down his throat. Whiskey – that's what the Drifaienin, Alwen, had called it when he set the bottle down at the table. It had a hell of a kick to it, but it warmed him up fierce quick. It was amazing what a strong drink could do to a man. Not more than a few hours before, everyone at the table had looked to be on the edge of the void. Some warm stew, a lively inn, and, most importantly, a few shots of whiskey later, and even the two dwarves looked like they were ready to submerge themselves in the snow again.

In truth, Falmin knew his body was done. His body didn't know it, thanks to the whiskey, but he did. He did not plan to leave whatever bed he stumbled into tonight until the sun had risen and set again over the horizon the next day. He also did not plan on ruining that delightful sleep by trying to outdrink two dwarves, a Drifaienin man who looked as though he had come out of the womb clutching that bottle of whiskey, and a young man who knocked the fiery liquid back with the enthusiasm of a babe at the tit of a wet-nurse. No. He was prone to doing foolish things, but he was not a fool. There would be plenty of time left in the world to burn the bad memories out of his brain with drink.

Falmin scrunched his mouth at the sight of Alwen tipping more whiskey into the wooden cups that lay about the table. Six cups. Five for those at the table, and one for the soldier who, Falmin was certain, had no intention of returning to drink it. The elf and the Draleid had never come in at all. Falmin had not expected them to, either. Whatever happened between the

Draleid and the dragon in the tunnels – it was something to do with the Spark, that was all Falmin could tell – it was clear the Draleid had been moving his legs through sheer strength of will ever since. Falmin would be surprised if the Draleid woke the next day before he did. And the elf was never more than five feet from the Draleid.

"In Drifaien, it is considered seven years bad sex if you close your eyes while drinking whiskey," Alwen said with a matter-of-fact look on his face as he pushed two of the wooden cups into the dwarves' hands. "Ten years if you choke on it." He said to Erik with a wink as he passed him his cup. Falmin shook his head as Alwen offered him a cup.

"No, no," Falmin said, lifting himself to his feet and slipping his fingers over the rims of the cup offered to him and the sixth unclaimed cup, snatching them up into his hand. "I'll take these t'go. My bed calls, and I've no desire t'watch you *choke on it.*"

Alwen laughed at first as Falmin moved away from the table. But out of the corner of his eye, Falmin watched the man's expression change. *That's it. Bit slow on the uptake. But you got there.*

Pushing his way through the throngs of drunken Drifaienin without spilling any of the whiskey from his two cups was almost as difficult as making it through those tunnels. A shiver ran through him as he stepped out onto the porch of the inn, where he was greeted by the brisk touch of snow-chilled air.

Tarmon Hoard was exactly where Falmin expected him to be. Not that he had expected him to be sitting on a wooden chair, barely sheltered from the blustering snow with a blanket drawn over his shoulders and his massive sword laid on the decking in front of him. But the chair he sat in faced out towards the barn where the Draleid slept.

The soldier was an interesting one. All men had something that motivated them. For most, it was coin… or women. Usually both. Sometimes other men, but that was simply personal preference. It was clear the first did not apply to the soldier; he was not the type. The second… possibly, but if that were true, he would either be eager to get back inside the inn, or eager to get back to Belduar – whatever was left of it. It didn't seem to be drink or a full belly either. No, he was one of them *honourable* types. Lord Captain of the Kingsguard. You don't get a title like that unless you've risked your life to save men who aren't worth saving. That's why they give you a title, to make sure you do it again. Falmin didn't understand it, but he supposed he respected it.

"Too warm for ya inside?" Falmin said as he pushed one of the cups of whiskey into Tarmon's unsuspecting hands.

Tarmon gave him a sidelong glance before wrapping his fingers around the wooden cup, his gaze never quite shifting from the barn. He brought the cup to his lips and took a mouthful of the burning liquor without so much as a grimace. "Tonight doesn't feel like a celebration to me."

Falmin sighed, resting his shoulder against one of the wooden posts that held up the porch roof. "No? I think survivin' those tunnels is a thing worth celebratin'," he said with a shrug. "Ya have to take the little victories, *Lord Captain.*"

Tarmon's expression didn't change, and he didn't turn to look at Falmin, either. He stared off through the blanket of falling snow towards the barn. He took another sip of his whiskey. "How many people do you think died in Belduar?" His voice was flat.

Falmin knew that tone well. It was the one a man used when he did not require an answer. Thousands had died. Crushed by falling rocks, disembowelled by Lorian steel, mangled, and burned alive by dragon-fire. The thought of it sent a shiver up his spine, but he tried to ignore it.

Tarmon must have recognised the silence. "How are the others?"

"Celebratin'." Falmin shrugged. He stared out at the snow that came down heavy over the village. He sighed. "They're all right. The young Virandr and the two dwarves are runnin' on empty. They'll drink 'emselves unconscious soon. I assume you know the elf isn't in there."

Tarmon nodded, suppressing a slight laugh. "He's been sitting on the porch of the barn since we got here. Won't go more than ten feet from the Draleid. Funny creatures, elves. Never thought I'd get to meet one. Then again, I never thought I would get to meet a Draleid, either."

Sure enough, through the drifting blanket of snowfall, Falmin made out the figure of the elf sitting cross-legged, his eyes closed, off to the side of the barn door. The extended lip of the porch roof was the only thing keeping him from being buried in snow. Falmin switched his gaze between the elf and Tarmon, suppressing a chuckle. The man didn't seem to notice the irony in his words. *Yeah, funny creatures.*

"What do you think of him, navigator?" Tarmon tilted his head just enough so Falmin could see the white of his eyes.

Falmin winced as a sip of whiskey seared its way down his throat. "Who? The elf?"

"The Draleid. What do you think of him?" Tarmon turned further until their eyes were locked. There was an intensity in his stare that Falmin couldn't quite place.

"Me? What does it matter what I think of 'im?"

"It matters, navigator. What has been set in motion cannot be undone. People are going to come for him and those with him."

The only things Falmin knew about the bond between dragons and Draleid, he knew from stories. Less than half of which were reliable and less than half again he believed true. What he did know was that this Draleid – Calen – was a tough young man, the kind who would die for a cause. Falmin could see it in his eyes; it was always the eyes that told you these things. "What do *you* think of him?"

Tarmon turned back into his chair, taking another sip of whiskey. "He's a good man."

"That's it? I thought I was about to get some inspirational speech." Falmin chuckled, taking another mouthful of the burning brown liquid. The liquor definitely added a second layer of warmth.

Tipping his head back, Tarmon downed the remainder of his cup and leaned back in his chair. "There aren't many good men left."

Chapter Sixteen

Secrets

endall sank his teeth into the peach's soft flesh, letting the juice roll over his fingers as he walked down the long stone stairwell. The Beronan dungeons had been the perfect location for the Inquisition headquarters in the city. So far beneath the ground, the cool chill that emanated from the walls helped to balance out the sweltering heat that came with being so close to the Burnt Lands.

Reaching the bottom of the stairwell, he dropped the carcass of the fruit on the ground and continued towards the interrogation halls. It was a little quieter than usual, but then again, that was to be expected with the rising number of Urak attacks across the empire. Many of the Inquisition had been dispatched to aid the Battlemages and to ensure order in the outer villages. After all, they were more than a match for those self-important black cloaks.

It didn't matter much either way. Rendall knew where he was going, and he knew what he would do once he got there. His initiate should be there already. The young man had potential. He did not possess the Spark, but that was not a problem; they could assign him a Seeker. The Inquisition was different to the rest of the Circle in that way. It was not the Spark that made an Inquisitor. A person could be capable of touching the Spark but be completely incapable of doing what needed to be done. That was what separated the Inquisitors from the others: the ability to do what needed to be done, in the name of the empire.

The initiate had arrived by boat from Falstide in the South only days before, after the little expedition Farda had seen fit to send him on. As far as Rendall was concerned, Farda was more than a little odd. He rarely spoke, seemed to always be distracted by nothing in particular, and had an irritating insistence on following that coin of his. Justicar or not, the man was a nuisance, and Rendall was entirely sure the man had sent his initiate on a wild goose chase simply to make a point.

The Beronan dungeons were a maze – they had been designed that way intentionally. Anyone who escaped their cell would then have to find their way through the haphazard web of corridors and hallways. More than a few escapees had been found as rotting corpses a month or so after their attempted escapes. But Rendall knew every turn like he did the freckles on his daughter's face. Every Inquisitor, and everyone who worked in the dungeons, was required to memorise the entire thing, lest they, too, be found shrivelled and rotting.

A right, followed by twenty feet straight, then a left, then the third hallway on the left, through the low archway, two lefts followed by three rights, up a staircase, and then the third corridor on the right.

He found his initiate just where he had expected to find him: sitting on the small wooden chair set outside interrogation room one-four-seven. *Good, you have memorised the map already.*

Rendall reached out to the Spark, drawing on threads of Spirit, weaving them into his voice, adding a touch of intimidation. "Initiate."

The young man leapt to his feet, keeping his arms straight down by his sides. "Inquisitor Rendall. Fritz Netly, sir. It is good to see you again, sir."

"Your name is not yet relevant, initiate. Nor will it be until you have earned your colours. You have brought what I asked for in the note?"

The young man gulped, and there was a slight shake in his hands, but all in all he seemed decidedly unperturbed. *Good.*

"Yes, sir, I have it here." The young man reached down on the other side of the wooden chair and produced a large leather satchel that Rendall knew well.

"Give it here," Rendall said, reaching out his hand and taking the red leather satchel by the strap at the top. "Now, come. It is time for your first lesson."

Rendall turned towards the thick wooden door set into the stone wall beside the chair, the numbers one, four, and seven nailed onto its front. He pulled a heavy iron key from his pocket, slotted it into the lock that sat midway down the door, and turned it until he felt the click. The door creaked as it opened just a fraction, with Rendall pushing against it to open it fully.

The heat hit him as soon as he opened the door. The warm smell of damp, sweat, blood, and excrement filled the air, that familiar metallic taste settling on Rendall's tongue. He had long since grown used to the putrid smells of the interrogation rooms, though the gagging noise that came from his initiate showed that it was not an easily acquired tolerance. The interrogation rooms were the only places in the dungeon that retained heat – again, they were designed that way. It ensured that anyone held in the interrogation rooms would not experience even a moment's respite.

The oil lamps on the corridor walls outside carved a wedge of light through the darkness that filled the room.

Gesturing for his initiate to follow, Rendall stepped into the dark room, allowing the heavy air to roll over his face. "Close the door behind you."

There was a moment's hesitation, but then the door creaked, and the already sparse light retreated from the room. A thud followed by a distinctive click signalled that the door was now securely closed.

"Well then, how are we?" Rendall said, as if to no one in particular, the sound of his boots against the stone floor echoing through the room. The sound of clinking chains was the only response.

Rendall reached out to the Spark, drawing in threads of Fire, feeling their heat lick his skin. Holding the threads, he lit the candles that sat in the alcoves about the chamber, bathing the room in a warm, but dim, orange light.

The interrogation rooms were simple. They were square in shape – ten feet long by ten feet wide. There were no windows or gutters, layers of insulation were stacked between the walls, and the only ventilation was through the cracks in the wooden door. Each room was equipped with a small metal table with foldable wheels and a long wooden bench big enough for a person to lie on.

Two panels were set into the stone floor at the centre of the room and two more into the ceiling directly above. The prisoners were kept in place by a set of manacles around their wrists that were linked by chains to the two panels on the floor.

"Wake up." Rendall flicked a thread of Fire across the back of the crumpled heap that lay in the centre of the room, eliciting only a stifled grunt. *Good, don't you lose that stubbornness just yet.* Rendall gestured to the table that sat in the corner of the room with foldable wheels. "Initiate, bring me that table."

While the initiate moved to fetch the table, audibly gagging as he did, Rendall cast his eyes over the prisoner. Thick scars laced the elf's back and shoulders, and the hardening skin still looked raw where Rendall had taken the nails from its fingers and toes. He had not truly expected that to break the elf – removing nails was fairly basic – but it had been convenient during the journey from Belduar.

The elf had been in room one-four-seven since they arrived in Berona about four days past. Rendall had made sure to have the creature sent straight there without a moment's rest. He found that often it wasn't pain that broke a man. No, it was a lack of hope. A man could endure excruciating pain as long as they held hope in their heart. That was something not all people realised. Interrogation was not about inflicting pain. It was about eradicating hope. And the first step towards eradicating hope was destroying any sense of time. Once time became impossible to determine, hope quickly dwindled.

"How has your day been?" Rendall asked, standing over the elf as it lay on the ground. Angry welts had begun to form on the wretched creature's right wrist where it had pulled tight against the manacle. The manacle on the elf's other arm had been a bit of a bother, considering that only a mottled lump of flesh remained of its left hand. Rendall had contemplated leaving it to just hang free, but he settled on having one of the acolytes fuse the manacle onto the elf's forearm with the Spark. Better safe than sorry.

"I'm going to have to get you to stand up. We simply won't be able to have a proper conversation with you lying down there."

Rendall reached out to the Spark once more, pulling on threads of Fire, Earth, and Air. He pushed the threads of Fire into the bolts that held the prisoner's chains to the two panels in the floor, heating them until they turned to liquid metal. Using threads of Earth and Air, he pulled the molten globs of metal and dragged them towards the two panels set into the ceiling. As they rose, they dragged the prisoner with them. At first, only his arms lifted into the air, and he dangled there like a puppet on a string; but as the chains reached their full length and tightened, they pulled his half-limp body off the floor.

Once the bolts reached the two panels on the ceiling, Rendall used the threads of Fire to cool them back down, pulling the heat into the air, fusing them in place. It was a useful design.

Now the elf hung in front of him, the manacles cutting into his wrists as he dangled there, his dark, greasy hair matted to his face and neck.

"I know you are awake, elf." Rendall nodded to the initiate who had just set the table in front of him. Reaching into the leather satchel that he still clutched in one hand, Rendall pulled out a large canvas wrap. He placed it down on the table and dropped the satchel on the floor. "Some men and women respond well to being broken down physically," Rendall said, pulling at the strings that kept the wrap secure. "Broken bones, beatings. Those kinds of things."

He heard the clinking of metal as the links in the prisoner's chains moved.

"I don't think you are as simple as that." With the knot in the string undone, Rendall proceeded to pull apart the wrap, letting it open across the table, the candlelight glinting off the instruments within. "No, I don't think so. Some people need to be broken down slowly. The layers need to be peeled back, so to speak. I think you're in that group. What do you think?"

The only sound that drifted through the chamber was the elf's slow, heavy breathing followed by the occasional low grunt as it shifted in discomfort.

"I agree," Rendall said, pulling a small steel paring knife from the wrap. He reached down into the satchel, producing a small leather-wrapped journal. "Take this," he said to his initiate, following the journal up with a pen and inkwell. "Take notes."

"Yes, sir."

"Now, back to you," Rendall said, walking over towards the elf. "Did you know I was nearly a healer? I could have been standing here in white robes, tending to your wounds. It's ironic, really, but that's where my talents lie." He shrugged, puffing out his lower lip. "But you know what, they still have a use." Rendall dropped his hand below the elf's chin, tipping it upwards so he could look directly into the elf's eyes. To its credit, it stared right back, delightfully defiant. "You see, no matter how much skin I peel from your back, I can just build it back and start again – it's wondrous what the Spark can do. This will not end, elf. For today though, there will be no questions."

Rendall pulled threads of Air into himself, using them to fix the prisoner in place in case he thrashed about. Slowly, he walked behind the elf, letting his purposeful steps reverberate off the walls. He brought the blade of the paring knife to the nape of the elf's neck, letting the cool steel rest against its skin. Angling the blade, he pulled down, letting it cut into the elf's skin, small streams of blood running down either side.

The elf didn't scream, but it would.

A creak echoed against the stone as the door of interrogation room one-four-seven opened, admitting the Inquisitor and his initiate into the hallway. Pellenor didn't move. His wardings of sight and spirit would keep him unseen so long as he stayed perfectly still, which, over the centuries, was an ability he had honed to mastery.

Pellenor couldn't help but be impressed. The Inquisitor and his initiate had been in the interrogation room for over four hours. That in itself was nothing to sniff at, seeing as most, if not all, the Inquisition interrogation rooms reached sweltering temperatures and reeked of death and shit. But what was most impressive was that by the time the Inquisitor and his apprentice left the interrogation room, Pellenor had not heard a single scream – not even so much as a muffled grunt. Either the elf had the mental fortitude of a god made flesh, or the poor wretch's soul was already broken to a point that pain no longer held the same meaning. Pellenor hoped it was the former and not the latter.

Pellenor watched as the Inquisitor spoke to his initiate then handed the young man a red leather satchel and dismissed him to his daily tasks. On any other occasion, Pellenor would have left, his information gathered. But he could sense something in the Inquisitor, in the way he always could with people. An eager anticipation wafted from the man. Whatever business Rendall had in the interrogation rooms was not yet complete. Sure enough, as the initiate turned the corner at the end of the hallway, Rendall waited a moment, strode across the hall, and slotted a key into the door of interrogation room one-four-eight. A creak signified the opening of the door, followed by a click as the door closed and the latch fell back into place.

Chapter Seventeen

A Wild Chase

he force of the blow vibrated through Aeson's forearm. He brought his second blade around and sliced through the Urak's arm, severing it at the elbow. The beast howled in pain, charging forward with its head, cracking Aeson on the bridge of his nose. A twinge of pain shot through him, and a flash of stars obscured his vision. Just as Aeson moved to drive his sword through the Urak's belly, he heard a *whoosh*. In a plume of blood, an arrow plunged into the soft tissue at the side of the Urak's head. The beast stumbled for a moment, then collapsed to the ground, blood seeping into the dirt.

Aeson turned to see Dann nock another arrow before firing it into the belly of a second Urak, following it up with another through the creature's neck. Aeson had underestimated the boy.

A roar to his left drew Aeson out of his thoughts as two Uraks charged him. He reached out to the Spark, praying to the gods that it would answer his call. A flash of relief swept through him as he felt it pulsating in the back of his mind. He grabbed hold without hesitation, pulling on threads of Air. He wove the threads around each other, whipping at the Uraks' legs, then slamming the beasts down onto the cold rock of the cavern floor. He wrapped the threads around a piece of shrapnel from the crashed Wind Runner and flung it through the abdomen of a third.

Around him, the fight seemed to be dying down. The two elves – Alea and Lyrei – fought like raging tempests. Wherever their blades swung, blood followed and Uraks fell. Calen had done well to have them oathbound to him; they were some of the finest warriors Aeson had seen since The Fall.

To the left side of the cavern, Aeson watched as Therin impaled a number of the beasts with threads of Earth, piercing their thick hides with long shards of sharpened rock. Nimara and her dwarves fared much the same. Those who had come with them were seasoned warriors. They had fought Uraks many a time – he could see it in the way they moved – but still, they had taken losses.

The Uraks had come upon them shortly after they discovered the remains of the crashed Wind Runner. The creatures must have smelled the death. The scent of blood, rotting flesh, and dirt clung to the air around the place.

"That's the last of them," Dann said, slinging his bow over his shoulders, the light from the patches of Heraya's Ward around them glistening off the fresh blood on his face. The boy had proven himself time and time again over the course of the weeks they had been searching the tunnels. He seemed a different person than the one Aeson had met in that village all those months ago. Though that should not have surprised him. A lot had happened since that night.

There was something in Dann's eyes, a steely determination that cut through all the usual jokes. Aeson suspected it had a lot to do with Calen and their other friend, Rist. Their bond was clear, and he knew all too well the things a person would do for the people they love.

Finding Calen was critical, but there was nothing in all Epheria that would stop him from getting to Erik. He could still feel him; it was not something he could explain, but he just knew they were both alive. Leaving Dahlen in Durakdur made sense for several reasons. They needed somebody to watch over Daymon, somebody they trusted. But Aeson would be lying to himself if he said he had not done it to keep Dahlen safe. He had already failed to protect one son; he could not let the same thing happen again. Dahlen and Erik were the only true things Aeson had left of his wife, Naia. Just thinking of her name twisted a knot in his stomach.

In the almost four hundred years since the fall of The Order, Aeson had never allowed himself to take a wife. What was the point? He would only have to watch them grow old and fade to dust. He could not have endured that kind of pain again. The death of his dragon, Lyara, still burned in the half-soul he had left.

That was all until he found Naia. Finding Naia was what made Aeson understand there were some people in the world who would walk into your life and just demand your love. Simply by existing, they changed everything.

But Naia's death had been like losing Lyara all over again. If Lyara had taken half of his soul with her to the gods' halls, then Naia had taken half of his heart. His sons were all he had left of her. He would protect them with every drop of blood in his body and every breath of air in his lungs. He would carve through armies and march over molten fire. *I will find you, Erik.*

"Aeson?" Dann raised an eyebrow, tilting his head to the side.

"They are alive. They moved on from here." Aeson said, running his tongue along the edges of his teeth as he cast his gaze over the crash site.

"You are certain?" Therin asked, wiping the sweat from his brow.

Aeson nodded. "We should search the dead, but I am certain. There are tracks over by the northern tunnel. I saw them before the Uraks attacked. Boot and claw marks."

"Calen..." Dann whispered, turning towards the northern tunnel without another word. The two elves followed closely behind.

Aeson went to call after him – they needed to stay together – but he felt a hand resting on his shoulder, staying him.

"Leave him," Therin said. "He is hurting, and he is yet too young to understand how to channel that grief."

Aeson let out a sigh. It irritated him how often Therin was right, but it tended to be the case. "If he dies down there, it's on you."

"I'll add it to the list. Let's search this place and get after him."

Aeson felt a pang of guilt as Therin walked off, issuing orders to Nimara and the other dwarves to search through the wreckage. He hadn't meant for his tongue to be sharp; he often forgot that Therin carried as much regret as he did.

"Gods dammit!" Dann slammed his hand against the tunnel wall, ignoring the ripple that jarred down through his arm. "Another dead end!" He threw his bow against the hard ground, flinching at the sound of snapping wood. "Fuck!"

Dropping his back against the wall, Dann slid down until he hit the ground. He drew in a deep breath and blew it back out as he ran his fingers through his dirt and dust matted hair, digging them into his scalp. He closed his eyes. He was sick to death of the blue glow from those damned dwarven flowers. Had the dwarves never heard of candles?

What was he going to do now? He couldn't stop. He would find Calen, and they would find Rist. Then maybe they could go home? He laughed a little at the idea, choking on the dust that lined his throat. The idea of Calen walking back into The Glade as if nothing had happened, a gleaming white dragon by his side. It would definitely be a sight.

He puffed out his cheeks, rubbing the bridge of his nose with his fingers, then digging them into the corner of his eyes, trying to dislodge the dirt that stuck there. He would love to see his father, though, and his mother. He had never thought missing home would be a factor for him. He was never a 'home bird'. But right then, at that moment, he would have given anything to go back.

Dann allowed his face to crack into a smile at the thought of him, Calen, and Rist drinking tankards of Lasch's mead on the steps of The Gilded Dragon a couple of summers back. There was nothing special about the memory. It was a normal day. The sun stayed high and shone bright, as it always did during the summer. They drank, they talked, and they stumbled home. It was one of his favourite memories, marred a little by the tongue-lashing his mother had given him when she found him half-asleep in his own vomit the next morning, but still good. He had never been so happy waking up in his own vomit. "I am coming for you. I promise..."

"Are you well?"

Dann opened his eyes to find Alea hunched down in front of him, her blonde hair hanging to the left side of her face and her golden eyes glittering in the blue light of the flowers. The elf's gaze was soft, full of concern. But the last thing Dann wanted to do was talk. Telling someone how scared he was of losing his friends would not change anything.

"I am," Dann said, tilting his head to the side, letting out a huff.

"We *will* find the Draleid."

Something inside Dann snapped. He lifted his head, matching Alea's gaze, his fists clenched by his side. "His name is *Calen*, Alea. I do not call you 'the elf', do I?" Almost as soon as the words left his mouth, Dann regretted them. His anger was not meant for her. It was meant for himself. "Alea, I'm…"

Dann would have preferred if the elf had stormed off in a rage. But no, instead, she looked him in the eye, and all he saw was hurt. He held his breath as she walked away towards the other side of the tunnel.

"… sorry." Dann sighed, rolling his eyes to the roof, and resting the back of his head against the cave wall. He saw Lyrei eyeing him askance out of the corner of his eye. He ignored her. He knew he was wrong; it would do him no good to start *another* argument.

The sound of footfalls echoed down the tunnel.

"About time we caught up with you. What are you doing on the…" Aeson's voice trailed off as he noticed the dead end. He drew in a deep breath through his nostrils, tilted his head back, and let out a deep regretful sigh. "Well, that's not what we wanted to find."

"Are you well, Dann?" Somehow, even in the dimly lit tunnel, covered in dirt and stone dust, Therin's silver hair still managed to look as pristine as ever. He glided over towards Dann, reaching down with his hand. With a huff, Dann grabbed Therin's hand and heaved himself to his feet.

"Yeah, I'm all right." Dann threw a sideways glance over toward Alea, which he was sure Therin caught, but the elf ignored it. "What do we do now, Therin?" Dann couldn't help the slight note of desperation that crept into his voice.

Therin looked at him, the picture of calm. "We will find a way. On my honour."

Dann noticed Alea and Lyrei turn sharply at Therin's words, their eyes wide in surprise. Calen had mentioned something to him about elves and honour before, when they were in Belduar, but he couldn't remember exactly what he had said. He could tell by the look in Therin's eyes, though, that the promise was as binding as a blood oath, maybe more so.

"These tunnels are like a spider's web." Nimara said, running her fingers through her braid laden with gold and silver rings. "It could take weeks to find the right path."

Twenty-five kills for a gold ring, ten for a silver, and one for a bronze. Dann had asked one of Nimara's soldiers about the rings on the first night. Nimara looked every bit the warrior in her sharp-cut plate armour, and that double-bladed axe hefted across her shoulder. But Dann had still thought twice before believing the dwarf. Most of the dwarves had two or three silver rings with a few bronze – some a bit more, some a bit less. But Nimara's braid held so many that she would not be hard pressed to open a jewellery shop in Camylin. Despite Dann's doubts, though, over the course of the past few weeks, Nimara had doubly lived up to the promise those rings gave.

"We don't have weeks," Aeson said, folding his arms. "We barely have enough food to see us back to Durakdur."

"Then we better start moving," Dann said, rolling up his sleeves. "There are nearly fifty of us here, and you and Therin have that magic of yours – it has to be good for something. If we split up, we can cover twice as much ground."

Aeson clamped his hand down on Dann's shoulder, holding him in place. "Patience. We will go after them, but first we have to come up with a real plan. We can't just keep pushing headfirst through these tunnels."

"I'm not waiting," Dann said, shrugging off Aeson's hand. "He would not wait to go after me. He's down here, and I'm going to find him."

"Dann." Therin stepped between Dann and Aeson, a level expression on his face. "We are low on food, there is very little water down here, and we need to rest. We are no good to Calen if we are dead. We can't just charge forward."

"It took us weeks to find this!" Dann roared, gesturing towards the wreckage of the Wind Runner. "They can't afford for us to waste time. He doesn't have weeks, Therin. He doesn't have weeks..."

Therin ran his hand across his chin and bit the corner of his bottom lip; Dann noticed he did that when thinking particularly hard on something. "We know where the wreckage is now. Nimara, how long would it take us to get back to Durakdur now that we know the way?"

"Four days at most," Nimara said. "And I'd reckon we could get a navigator as well. The chaos in the Freehold has likely died down by now. We will be able to move a lot quicker with a Wind Runner."

"Four days out and four days back," Dann corrected. "We can't afford it, Therin."

"We don't have a choice," Therin responded, a sombre look on his face.

"Of course, we have a damn choice!"

"Do you not think we want to just push through?" Dann hadn't seen Aeson move, but the man was in front of him, a fire in his eyes. Dann may have stood level with him in Durakdur, but that was different. He had never seen Aeson lose his cool, not in all the months they had travelled together. But the man that stood in front of him now was touching that line. His jaw was clenched, his right foot twisted in the dirt, and his breathing was long and drawn out with a slight tremble, like that of a man who was trying to stop himself from doing something he knew he shouldn't. "Calen isn't the only one we are tracking. My son is out there too. As are Gaeleron and Vaeril. You are not the only one who hurts."

A pang of guilt flashed through Dann as he glanced towards Alea and Lyrei. He was such an idiot. Alea had only tried to reassure him. Her friends were out there too, and he had been so lost in finding Calen that he had forgotten.

"You are not the only one who is chasing something. If you plan on coming with us, you better pull yourself together or all you'll be is a liability. We are going back to Durakdur, consolidating, and coming back here with a clear direction. You stay if you want." Without another word, Aeson stormed off down the tunnel, stopping only for a moment to talk with Nimara, who shouted for her soldiers to follow.

Dann stood where he was, his boots firmly planted on the dust-covered rock. He wasn't angry, and he wasn't upset – in truth, he didn't know what he was. But he just stood there.

"Come, Dann. I promised you on my honour that we would find them, and we will, but you have to trust us." Therin gave Dann a weak smile before he turned to follow Aeson, his greenish-brown cloak drifting behind him.

Dann looked to Alea and Lyrei. Alea mimicked Therin's weak smile, but Lyrei didn't so much as look at him. She just kept walking.

As they all walked away, Dann knelt and picked up his broken bow. He'd had it since he was twelve. It had been a bit big for him back then, but he had insisted on using it – not that he even had the strength to pull the string back at first. He let out a sigh, gripped the two pieces of split wood in his hand, and set off after the group. It wasn't as if he had many options.

Chapter Eighteen

All the King's Horses

ahlen tilted his head back as they walked, gazing in wonder at the blanket of Heraya's Ward that swept across the ceiling of the cavern, only broken by lines of brass piping fitted with thick nodules that sprinkled a seemingly never-ending supply of water over the crops. All around them, wispy stalks of barley and rye rose up, drinking in the bluish-green light that radiated from the flowers above.

"Marvellous, isn't it?" Oleg Marylin chirped. The emissary to the Dwarven Freehold was an odd man, but Dahlen enjoyed his company and was glad to hear he had insisted on coming along to Daymon's meeting with Queen Pulroan. "The flowers provide the crops with the same sustenance as the sun – wondrous! There is a reason it's named *Heraya's Ward*, you know – it's the lifeblood of the mountain. A gift from the goddess herself. Without it, surviving down here would be near impossible."

"It truly is fascinating," Dahlen agreed, reaching out, the hairy stems of the barley tickling his hands. He told no word of a lie; it truly *was* fascinating. Durakdur lay beneath miles and miles of rock, devoid of sunlight and rainfall, and yet the dwarves had found a way to grow thriving fields of crops. It also went a long way to explaining why The Mother was so revered among their people. "What of the water?"

"It's irrigated from the many streams within the mountain," Oleg said, panting to keep up with the brisk pace set by Ihvon and Daymon in front of them. "But mostly it comes from the great waterfall within the city. The whole system is ingenious, really."

"That it is..." Dahlen's voice trailed off as he looked up to the ceiling, his eyes tracing along the brass piping fitted into the rock.

The group walked in silence as they made their way through the underground crop field, Daymon and Ihvon at the front with four Kingsguard marching along either side, their purple cloaks drifting lazily behind them. It seemed a strange place for Pulroan to choose. A king and a queen meeting in a field of barley and rye. There had to be a reason for it. Likely to show Daymon who it was that controlled the food.

"We have to bide our time, my king," Dahlen heard Ihvon say as the man ran his hand across the top of his hairless head. "Whoever sent that assassin knows we know. They know he failed, and they will be worried about what he may have told us. We have the advantage. As soon as we go to the Freehold, we lose that advantage."

"What advantage does it give us?" Daymon replied, his tone curt. "I see no benefit in knowing my life is under threat and doing nothing. Pulroan may be able to help us."

"Because they do not know what we know. We must not show our hand too soon. We do not know what part Pulroan might play on all this."

"It's been weeks, Ihvon! And we know nothing new. We must confront them, head-on, as my father would have."

Ihvon let out a sigh. The look on his face said he knew he was fighting a losing battle. Dahlen had seen enough of these conversations to know they usually ended with Daymon losing his temper and dismissing both him and Ihvon. Which usually led to Dahlen going to the training yard and Ihvon going to the inn. The man's breath seemed to smell more of ale with each passing day. With all things said, Dahlen actually agreed with Ihvon. Pulroan may have seemed like a wise old queen, but he had long learned not to take people at face value.

"My king, our people are refugees here. Each of the four kingdoms provides them with safety, food, and shelter. What do you think would happen if, all of a sudden, we accuse Elenya? We need to be clever about this."

"You need to—"

"King Daymon, you have found your way I see." An intricate golden crown adorned the queen of Azmar's head, resting atop her braided grey-streaked blonde hair. She wore the customary dress of the dwarven rulers, an odd mixture of leathers and silks that made her look as though she were prepared both for battle and for court. Two Queensguard stood to either side of Pulroan, their sharp-cut armour glistening in the flowerlight, the green and gold cloaks of Azmar draped around their shoulders.

Daymon turned to Ihvon, irritation still etched into his face. "You may leave, Lord Arnell. I will speak with Queen Pulroan alone."

"Is that wise, my king?

"You question my wisdom now?" Daymon's eyes burned with an unspoken fury. "You may leave, Ihvon. And take Dahlen Virandr with you."

"But, my ki—"

"I said *leave.*" Daymon hissed the words through clenched teeth, his face softening as he walked towards Pulroan. Oleg Marilyn threw an apologetic glance back towards Dahlen as he and the Kingsguard followed after Daymon. "Your Majesty, it is good to see you. I most certainly did find my way…"

Dahlen didn't hear the rest of Daymon's sentence as the king strode away. A few moments passed where Dahlen thought Ihvon might disobey Daymon's instruction, but he just stood there, his jaw clenched as he watched after the young king. Dahlen had expected to see anger in the man's eyes, but instead he was surprised to find a deep, pensive sadness.

"That went well," Dahlen said, faking a half-smile, doing his best to break the tension that hung in the air.

Ihvon let out a heavy sigh. "Aye, as well as it has done every other day." He held his gaze on Daymon for a few more moments before turning his head to Dahlen. "Care to take a walk? There are a few things I need to see to, and I've noticed you haven't spent too much time exploring the city."

"I was actually on my way to the practice yard after the meeting with Pulroan."

Ihvon tilted his head to the side, a ponderous look in his eye. "Tell you what, I'll spar with you if you come with me afterwards."

Dahlen cocked an eyebrow. "Are you sure? I wouldn't say no to a sparring partner, but I won't be taking it easy."

A smile touched the corner of Ihvon's mouth. "So, we have a deal?"

Dahlen shrugged. "Will Daymon not need us later today?"

"He will not," Ihvon said, a frown painting his face. "He will be taking supper in his quarters tonight, and the guard is to be doubled, at his command."

Dahlen bit down on the back of his tongue, trying his best not to show his frustration. He should have been with his father, looking for Erik. But instead, he was nothing more than a glorified babysitter. What was worse, the king didn't even want him there. He was wasting his time while his brother needed him. "To the yard then?"

"Lead the way."

Two dwarves in sharp-cut plate armour stood at attention at the front of the training yard when Ihvon and Dahlen approached. Their crimson cloaks fluttered in the ever-present breeze that flowed through the city from the Wind Tunnels.

The Heart's training yard was usually reserved for the Queensguard alone. Ihvon resented the idea of having to ask permission from *dwarves*. He tried not to let his own feelings seep into his arguments with Daymon, but he held no such reservations when he was not counselling the young lad. He despised the idea of being indebted to anyone, but to these oath-breaking cave dwellers more than anything. The sooner they were able to get their people out of this damn mountain, the better. But until then, he would just have to bite his tongue. The ale helped with that, funnily enough. Most men Ihvon knew get rowdier with ale, but not him. Ale, a pipe, and a quiet corner; they had been his solace in this hornets' nest. He took a deep breath, holding it in his chest as he prepared to feign respect, but before he could speak, Dahlen stepped in front of him.

"Yoring, Almer." Dahlen tipped his head to the two dwarves without breaking stride, gesturing for Ihvon to follow.

"I—" Ihvon stopped for a moment, almost ready to argue, before shaking his head and following Dahlen. The dwarves gave him a short nod as he passed, to which he replied with a frown, holding his pace. Ihvon wasn't sure why he was surprised. Dahlen had spent most of his spare time training, and he was also Aeson Virandr's son – that certainly carried weight. "You know them?"

"I fought beside them on Belduar's second wall," Dahlen replied, as he tossed his satchel to the ground. "Yoring took an arrow to the knee. Almer and I dragged him to the Wind Runner. They let me use the yard when it's empty."

Ihvon nodded, grunting as he stretched his arms out as wide as he could before pulling them backwards until his shoulder-blades touched. A slight crack just below his right shoulder blade provided the relief he was looking for. He unhooked his sword belt from around his waist, pulled the blade free, and rested the scabbard against one of the wooden posts that framed the training yard. There was something about the weight of a blade in his hand that calmed him. It was the simplicity of it. No games, no politics, no pretending; just steel, sweat, and blood. If everything in life was as clear cut and straightforward as fighting, there would be no need of ale.

He let out a sigh as he tossed the sword from hand to hand, loosening his arms, letting his thoughts run riot in his head. Arguing with Daymon had become part of his morning routine. He should have been stronger with him. The boy needed guidance, now more than ever. But who was he to provide guidance? Especially to the son of the king he had failed. Arthur was dead because of Ihvon's weakness. And no amount of good deeds or unwanted advice would ever change that. *Stop it. Just stop it. What is done is done.*

"First blood?" Dahlen called out as he tossed his satchel to the ground.

You don't play around. All the better; a bit of sparring was exactly what Ihvon needed.

"I win, and I don't have to go touring the city with you."

Ihvon shrugged. "Agreed. What if I win?"

"I'll go drinking with you tonight."

"Agreed," Ihvon answered with a laugh.

Dahlen reached over his shoulders and pulled his two swords free from the scabbards across his back. Back-mounted scabbards simply didn't seem practical to Ihvon, but it seemed Aeson Virandr had passed his tastes to his children. Not that the young man who stood in front of him could be mistaken for a child of any sort. Ihvon had not personally seen him fight, but he had talked with more than a few soldiers who swore the young man had carved a river of blood through the Lorian forces during the attack on Belduar. *Tastes weren't the only thing Aeson passed to his sons.*

"Ready?"

Ihvon passed his sword back into his right hand, tightening and loosening his fingers on the grip, feeling the leather rub against his palm. He nodded.

Dahlen closed the distance between the two of them in a heartbeat, his eyes cold. Ihvon only just about blocked the young man's first two blows, stumbling off balance as he did. The third he sidestepped, then put some space between the two of them, which Dahlen closed down again in a matter of seconds. They moved like that for few minutes: Dahlen attacking, Ihvon retreating, neither of them truly trying to end the contest.

The determination in the young man's eyes matched the half-smile that touched the corner of his mouth. He was quick. His blades sliced through the air in a whir of steel, always moving. And he gave no signs of tiring.

It wasn't long before Ihvon's lungs burned and sweat dripped down his forehead and tacked his shirt to his chest. But with each minute that passed, he was learning. The young man always led with his left foot, he favoured his right hand, and he had absolutely no inclination towards self-preservation. And every so often, he struck with both of his blades at the same time, negating the advantage the two weapons gave him.

Ihvon let out an exaggerated puff as a heavy blow jarred his arms. He saw the smirk grow wider on Dahlen's face. Stepping backwards, Ihvon faked a wince as his right foot hit the stone. He let a limp creep into his step as he moved out of Dahlen's reach. Warriors like Dahlen and Aeson could smell blood. If the young man was anything like his father, he wouldn't be able to resist what he thought was a weakened adversary.

Dahlen took the bait like a wolf spotting a wounded deer. He lunged forward, again leading with his left foot. Ihvon twisted as the two blades came in; he caught them both in quick succession, letting the crash of steel vibrate through his arms. Then, as Dahlen leaned forward, Ihvon tightened his grip on the hilt of his sword and brought the pommel crashing up into Dahlen's nose.

The young man stumbled backwards, clearly dazed by the strike, unsure how his wounded deer had suddenly regained its footing.

Ihvon surged forward. He hammered the flat of his blade into Dahlen's arm, causing the man to lose the grip on his sword, letting it clatter to the floor. Smelling blood, Ihvon surged forward again. He caught Dahlen in the cheek with an elbow, then swung his opposite foot around and lifted the man's legs from under him.

Without a moment's hesitation, Dahlen snatched up his second blade and leapt back to his feet.

"Almost," Ihvon said with a knowing smile.

Dahlen's face twisted with confusion.

Ihvon brought his left hand to his face, rubbing his thumb along the bridge of his nose, indicating Dahlen to do the same.

Narrowing his eyes, Dahlen followed. Still clutching his sword, he brought his right hand up to his face and rubbed his wrist against the bridge of his nose.

"To first blood, no?" Ihvon said at the sight of the crimson mark that now coated the inside of Dahlen's wrist. He watched as the young man's shoulders dropped in realisation.

"To first blood," Dahlen repeated, dropping onto his haunches then rolling back onto the ground with a sigh.

"It was a good fight."

Dahlen nodded his head with pursed lips, reaching back and sliding his swords into their scabbards with practised ease.

Ihvon snatched up his sword belt from where it stood against the wooden post, fastened it around his waist, then replaced his sword into its scabbard. He then walked over to where Dahlen sat on the cold stone of the yard and reached out his hand. "I got lucky."

Dahlen furrowed his brow, a look of clear displeasure on his face. But he took Ihvon's hand, dragging himself to his feet. "Don't patronise me."

"I'm not," Ihvon said with a shrug. "Nine times out of ten, you win that fight. You move just like your father, and he is the best swordsman I have ever seen. Then again, he ought to be. He's had enough centuries to practise."

"Well, what happened this time, then?"

"You fought to win a sword fight. I fought to make you bleed. You didn't play to the rules. You must always be aware of why you are fighting, who you are fighting, and the minimum it will take to win that fight."

Dahlen scrunched his mouth and let out a sigh through his nose. "You faked your limp."

"I did," Ihvon said with a grin. "You must also be aware of your own shortcomings. So tonight, we have a drink. But today, there are a few things that must be done. Grab your satchel."

"Where are we going?"

Dahlen let the air fill his lungs, exhaling slowly as he walked. Queen Kira had ordered the Craftsmages of the Crafts Guild to carve out a new area at the edge of the city to house as many of the Belduaran refugees as possible. The new area was connected to the main city by a stone walkway that passed only about fifty feet from the enormous waterfall that dominated the mountain chasm. It was on this walkway that Dahlen found himself following closely behind Ihvon. Dahlen closed his eyes for a moment as he walked, letting the cool spray of the waterfall tickle the exposed skin on his face and arms. It was not just the touch of the spray, though. The sound of the crashing water dominated everything. It resounded through the air like rolling thunder, causing all other sounds to yield at its insistence. He could have stood on that bridge for hours. However, that would not happen today. With a sigh, Dahlen opened his eyes and moved to catch up with Ihvon.

"How many?" Dahlen asked as they approached the large passage that was cut into the rock face at the end of the walkway, the crashing water still calling for him to raise his voice to a half-shout.

"In Durakdur? About forty thousand, mostly the sick and infirm who couldn't travel further to the other cities. Overall, I'm not entirely sure. Belduar was home to over two hundred thousand souls before the attack. Though most of the citizens were evacuated before the battle, we lost many warriors during the fighting, and not all the elderly survived the journey. The Wind Runners are no small challenge for someone whose heart has already seen more than its fair share of summers. I truly do not know what we number now."

Ten men stood at the entrance to the refugee quarters, deep purple cloaks draped over burnished plate. Dahlen remembered the awe he had felt when he first laid eyes on the Kingsguard of Belduar. He had seen many great warriors on his travels with Erik and their father, but the Belduaran Kingsguard looked as though they had been pulled straight from the stories of old. What he felt now, though, was not awe but an unshakeable respect. He had seen them fight at the Battle of Belduar. They were no show ponies, dressed to frighten bandits. They were disciplined, brave, and fought like wolves. Had the Dragonguard not arrived, Dahlen had no doubt the Kingsguard would have held back the Lorian tide.

Dahlen gave Ihvon a sidelong glance at the sight of two pairs of dwarves standing on either side of the Kingsguard, crimson cloaks fixed around their shoulders.

"The Queen's insistence." A slight snarl touched Ihvon's words as he spoke. "Like penned animals who require herding."

Dahlen couldn't help but feel a pang of anger. What need was there for dwarven guards at a refugee camp for the sick and elderly?

"Lord Arnell," one of the soldiers said, stepping forward and giving a slight bow at the hip. Unlike the other soldiers, she did not wear a helmet. Her face had a harshness to it, and her dark hair was tied into braids at the back of her head.

"Captain Harnet, all is well?"

"It is, my lord," the soldier replied, throwing slight glances towards the two pairs of dwarves that framed the entrance. "The food rations arrived only moments ago. The dispensers should be just inside."

Ihvon nodded. "Thank you, Captain Harnet. Please, take this," he said, pushing a small purse into the captain's hand and folding her fingers around it. "For you and your guards. I know the past few weeks have not been easy."

The captain nodded, allowing a smile to touch the corners of her mouth. "You have my thanks, Lord Arnell."

Ihvon nodded in return before gesturing for Dahlen to follow him. Dahlen took one last look over the guards, his eyes lingering on the pair of dwarves who stood to the right of Captain Harnet's soldiers. The dwarves did not so much as turn to acknowledge his presence. They stood with their backs straight, the pommels of their axes pressed against the stone floor, the blades pulled flat against their chests. With a breath through his nose, he followed Ihvon through the passageway in the rockface.

The passageway travelled for about twenty feet. It was almost identical to the tunnel they had passed through when they first arrived in Belduar. The rock face was impossibly smooth, the ceiling rose to about seven feet, and the tunnel was around ten or twelve feet at its widest point. The sound of Ihvon and Dahlen's footsteps echoed against the stone, set to the backdrop of the crashing water that rumbled behind them.

A heavy wave of heat hit Dahlen head-on as he stepped out of the passage. It was accompanied by a tangy aroma that caused Dahlen to gag, his stomach lurching. He wasn't sure exactly what the smell was, but it was absolutely wretched.

"Sweat, soup, and shit," Ihvon said, folding his arms across his chest.

"What?"

"The smell. It's sweat, soup, and shit. The refugee quarters don't have the natural ventilation the rest of the city does. And with the number of people who are crammed in here along with the moisture from the waterfall out front, it gets pretty damp and hot."

"And the shit?"

Ihvon shrugged, pouting. "The sewage system isn't finished yet. I doubt they actually plan on finishing it at all, to be honest."

"But how will they expect people to live like this?"

The look on Ihvon's face told Dahlen all he needed to know.

Like the rest of the city, the refugee quarters were cut straight from the mountain itself using a combination of magic and dwarven machinery; at least, that is what Dahlen remembered overhearing the architect saying when he had met with Daymon in his quarters.

Dahlen stood at the top of a large stone staircase that fanned outward, descending into the refugee quarters. Out in front of him was an enormous street that stretched endlessly into the distance. The street was over a hundred feet wide and paved with smooth stone, and even then, it was not wide enough. It was like watching a colony of ants being funnelled through the eye of a needle. On either side, rising ever upwards, were rows and rows of doors set into the walls of the enormous cavern. An intricate web of staircases connected each level to the next, with a dizzying number of walkways sweeping over the top of the main street like the branches of a forest canopy. No human hands could ever have created it on their own. Dahlen's eyes strained as he looked upwards, unable to see where the rows of doors folded into the ceiling hundreds of feet above.

"Come," Ihvon said, setting off down the staircase. "Those wagons over there hold the new rations."

"And what are we to do?" Dahlen asked, following closely on Ihvon's heels.

"Help with handing them out," Ihvon replied with a shrug. "And ensure there are no riots."

"Riots?" Dahlen raised a questioning eyebrow as he pushed through the throngs of people. It was like trying to force the sea to part.

"The Craftsmages in the Dwarven Freehold," Ihvon said, shoving his way through the crowd, "do not have the knowledge and gifts they once did in the old times. The construction of these homes is still ongoing, there is little to no sanitation, and food is scarce. We are in a barrel of oil, my boy, and all it takes is a spark."

An uneasy feeling set into Dahlen's stomach as the surrounding crowds took on new meaning. He could see it in their faces when he looked closer. Most wore dark circles under their eyes, and their clothes were torn and ragged. The pungent smell that filled the endlessly long cavern made it near impossible to pick up any other aromas, but Dahlen would hazard a guess that not many of them had bathed in quite a while. Not all of them were old and infirm, but the majority were. Either too sickly, too old, or too poor to make the journey to the other cities.

Dahlen stopped in his tracks as he watched an elderly woman hobble by with only one leg, a long wooden crutch strapped under her left arm, layers of padding wrapped around the handle. He saw something different in the woman's eyes. It wasn't hunger, or despair, or rage. It was resignation, and it sparked an anger within Dahlen that surprised even him. This wasn't right.

"Come on," Ihvon said, tugging at his shoulder. "They start handing out the rations shortly."

"I thought you said most of the citizens were evacuated before the battle?" Dahlen planted his feet and met Ihvon's gaze.

Ihvon let out a heavy sigh, bringing his hand up to his face, closing his eyes and digging his fingers into his long beard. "They were. But not during the first attack, when the king… was killed. There was not enough warning to evacuate. The Lorians were not selective about whose flesh their blades cut."

Dahlen watched as the old lady hobbled off, swallowed by the crowd. But again, the closer he looked, the more he saw. Men, women, children, all missing limbs, deep scars bedded into their flesh, anguish in their eyes. They had not even been soldiers. The injured soldiers were housed separately on the other side of the city, deeper into the mountain, so their screams did not disturb the others.

Dahlen's mind flashed back to the Heart, just after the battle in Belduar. Images washed through him. The dwarf whose plate of armour had been melted into his flesh by dragonfire. The man carried on a cot, only shattered bone and blood where his legs had once been. The lifeless bodies sprawled all about the enormous courtyard, blood seeping into the cracks, not enough medics to even contemplate the dignity of the dead.

The screams of the dying echoed through his head. He tried to push them away, but they were etched into his mind. He heard them even when he slept. Bone-chilling, blood-curdling screams. The howls of men and women who knew death would take them, slowly, painfully. Dahlen's breath caught in his chest, and a nauseous feeling set itself in his stomach. The palms of his hands were slick with sweat, and his mouth dried to a barren wasteland. The screams resounded in his head, growing louder and louder, rising to a horrifying crescendo.

"Dahlen?"

The touch of Ihvon's hand on his shoulders sent a shiver through Dahlen's body and dragged him out of his own mind.

"Are you all right?" Ihvon's eyes narrowed, as though he was trying to see something *more.*

"Yes, I'm—" Dahlen grunted as a man with horrific burns on his face knocked into his shoulder. "I'm all right."

Tilting his neck backwards, eliciting a sharp crack, Dahlen puffed out the air from his lungs, feeling his heartbeat pounding in his veins. He pushed the thoughts from his head. He could deal with them later.

Dahlen followed after Ihvon, pushing through the crowds until, in a matter of seconds, he stood in a small clearing. Four wagons occupied the centre of the clearing, each over fifteen feet long, with iron bands that held up canopies of thick canvas. Teams of men and women in purple livery scurried about, unloading large crates, casks, and boxes.

Belduaran soldiers ringed the open space, separating the crowds from the supplies. Each of them wore thick leather armour with teardrop shaped shields strapped to their arms.

"Lord Arnell, it is a pleasure," one of the men in purple livery said, striding past Dahlen to bend deeply at the waist in front of Ihvon.

Ihvon gave a short nod in return. Dahlen had noticed a slight twitch at the corner of the man's mouth any time somebody said the words 'Lord Arnell'.

"We are nearly ready, Mister Gromsby?"

"Indeed, we are, my lord. Though everyone is a little on edge after the other day."

"That is to be expected. How is the young woman? And the child?"

The man's shoulders drooped, and his gaze fell to the floor as he gave a soft shake of the head.

"Gods dammit," Ihvon whispered loud enough that only the three of them could hear. He let out a heavy sigh, clasping his hand behind his neck. "Please, send someone to find her family for me. When they have been found, let me know."

"It will be done, my lord. My apologies, but I must get back to the rations."

Ihvon gestured for the man to continue with his business. "Dammit," he repeated.

"What happened the other day?" Dahlen wanted to snatch the question out of the air and take it back as soon as he saw the look on Ihvon's face. It was a look he had seen on his father's face before: guilt. A deep, tangible guilt.

Ihvon sighed, biting the top of his lip. "For some reason, a rumour got around that there was not enough food. Some of the people decided to storm the wagons. A soldier reacted and knocked one of the men unconscious with his shield. There was a bit of a fight, nobody was killed but… in the panic afterwards, a young woman was trampled by the crowd. She had a small child."

A knot twisted in Dahlen's stomach. "That's…" Dahlen couldn't seem to find the words. "It's not your fault."

Ihvon gave a weak smile in return. "Come, let's give a hand."

CHAPTER NINETEEN

WINTER'S TOUCH

alen jolted upright, his chest heaving, his heart pounding, sweat dripping down the sides of his face and neck. His dreams had felt so vivid, so real. Images of dragons soaring through the sky, bolts of lightning stripping stone from buildings, blazing infernos that spread for miles. It felt as though he was there. He closed his eyes, trying his best to slow his breathing. Then he felt Valerys. The dragon's thoughts crashed into his own like a boulder rolling down a hill. They were the same as his. Panic, fear, loss. Calen could feel Valerys's urgency, as though he feared for Calen's life. They had shared the dream.

Valerys craned his neck around, nuzzling his snout into the side of Calen's head as they lay there in the hay pile.

"It's all right. It was only a dream. It was only a dream." Calen tried to calm the dragon as he ran his hand along the scales at the back of Valerys's neck. The words didn't calm the dragon entirely, but Valerys's fear subsided a little. Calen didn't blame him; it had felt *so* real. "Draleid n'aldryr, Valerys. Myia nithír til diar." *My soul to yours.*

The words came to him as naturally as breathing, though he was not sure how he knew them. Therin's lessons in the Old Tongue had not been as frequent as Calen had liked. He had only picked up bits and pieces. He did not remember learning that phrase, but he knew it. It was the strangest thing. Where was the language coming from?

"Is it you?" Calen looked into Valerys's pale lavender eyes, searching them.

The dragon returned Calen's stare, tilting his head to the right. They stayed like that for a few seconds before Calen gave a weak smile, pushed his thoughts to the back of his mind, and dragged himself to his feet.

Calen rubbed the palms of his hands into the corner of his eyes, trying to loosen the stickiness that always came with the morning. Still, as tired as he was, he was determined to see the sun rise over the mountains in the east. He wasn't sure how long they had been down in the tunnels. Weeks, at least two, maybe three… maybe four. But in the dim flowerlight, surrounded by miles and miles of rock, with no end in sight and the *click-clack* of the kerathlin claws ever in the back of his mind, weeks had felt like months. He hadn't wanted to say it to Erik, but he, too, had doubted whether they would ever find their way out. Were it not for Valerys pushing him on, he wasn't sure he would have been able to keep going.

Calen made his way to the wooden ladder that hung from the loft of the barn. Grabbing one of the rungs, he climbed up, his muscles aching with each movement. Once he had dragged himself to the top, he walked over to the nearest of the rectangular windows that held a view of the mountains to the east. Even then, while the world was still shrouded in the dark of the receding night, Calen could see the glow of the morning sun drifting over the horizon, accompanied by the trill of birdsong.

'It is the simple things, boys. It is the simple things that bring the greatest pleasure.' Calen remembered his father's words as they, along with Haem, watched the sun rise over Wolfpine Ridge not four summers gone. He missed them both fiercely, as he did his mother, Ella, and Faenir. Even the slightest thought of them set a knot in his stomach and sent a shiver through his veins. If he had not gone back that day…

He felt Valerys tugging at his mind. Images flashed across his eyes, pushing everything else to the back. Images of home, memories that he had not thought of in years. Haem teaching him how to hold a sword. His mother wiping his knee clean after he had fallen from the tree outside Erdhardt Hammersmith's home. Riding on his father's shoulders as they went to help Ella train Faenir. They were the purest of memories, and they set a warmth in his heart, if only for a moment. Calen brought his hand to his face, wiping silent tears away as they rolled down his cheeks. *Thank you.*

A rumble in the back of his mind emanated from Valerys. And just as it did, the soft orange glow of the sun crested the snow-capped mountain peaks in the distance, casting a beautiful orange light over the landscape. For a while, Calen did not move. He just stood there and let the warm touch of morning gently kiss his skin as it rolled over the world of white and green, glittering against the snow and frost. The simple beauty of a sunrise was a luxury he would not soon take for granted again.

He allowed himself a few more moments of uninterrupted peace before he had to face the day. He knew what he needed to do; his mind was set and it would not be changing.

Calen climbed back to the ground floor of the barn, snatched a half-eaten piece of bread that he hadn't had the stomach to finish the night before, and pulled on the clean shirt and trousers Alleron had arranged for him.

"You need to stay here for a bit," Calen said as he turned to Valerys, who still lay curled up in the pile of hay where Calen had left him, his ever-growing wings folded over himself. The dragon craned his neck into the air at the sound of Calen's voice, his lavender eyes fixed on Calen, giving a half-hearted rumble of disagreement. Calen couldn't blame him. He had been trapped in those tunnels for weeks and now Calen was asking him to stay inside even longer. But Valerys did not put up much of a fight; he knew that he could not be seen by the villagers. From what Alleron had said the night before, the empire had sent mages to every High Lord in the South, and more Lorian soldiers were arriving at Gisa and Falstide by the day. It did not take a scholar to recognise that the empire was using the Battle of Belduar and the appearance of the 'rebel Draleid' to solidify its position in the South.

The emissary had not yet arrived in Drifaien, but rumours had travelled fast from the other provinces. They could not trust the villagers to keep Valerys a secret.

"We will leave at nightfall, and the skies will be yours." Calen reached out, running his hand along the length of Valerys's snout, feeling the cool touch of the armour-like scales. A sense of comfort drifted from Valerys, followed by a reluctant acquiescence. "I will be back shortly."

While Valerys nestled his head back down into the hay, Calen picked up his sword and scabbard. He moved his fingers along the masterfully crafted leatherwork of green and brown, gently, as though it might break at any moment. Holding the scabbard in his left hand, he wrapped his right hand around the sword's grip and pulled the blade out five or six inches. He smiled as his eyes traced the intricate swirls that decorated the blade that had once belonged to his father – all that Calen had left of him. Calen slid the sword back into its scabbard and strapped the sword belt around his waist before bounding over to where his filthy clothes and leather armour still lay by one of the hay piles. Pushing his dirt-coated shirt aside, he dug his hands into the pocket of the trousers, a sigh of relief escaping him when he felt the soft unmistakable touch of the silk scarf. It looked as beautiful as it had the day he bought it. As red as the leaves that sat on the trees in The Glade, ready to fall at autumn's touch, with vines of gold and cream woven throughout it.

Standing back to his full height, Calen pulled one end of the silk scarf through a loop on his sword belt at his right hip, then tied it in a knot, before doing the same to the other end. It was a short scarf, so it didn't hang much, and that way he would not fear losing it. Either way, the idea of his mother sitting next to his father was a nice thought.

Taking a deep breath, Calen tilted his head back and let it out in a long puff. He made his way over to the barn door they had come in the night before, pushing it open just a crack before stepping out and closing it behind him.

Despite the glare of the morning sun, Calen most definitely felt winter's touch as the air swept over his skin, pushing through his thin shirt and causing every hair on his body to stand on end. He took a deep breath in through his nostrils, letting the frosty air fill his lungs. Despite the cold, it was a welcome change from the thick, dusty air that hung in the tunnels.

Another welcome change was the trill of morning birdsong that danced through the village, reminding him of home.

The sky above was clear, but a blanket of white coated the ground, the patrol routes of the village guard clearly marked out by carved paths of melted snow. The snowfall also covered every rooftop as far as Calen's eyes could see, with thick plumes of white and grey smoke drifting lazily from chimneys.

"It is a cold morning."

Calen almost leapt from his skin at the sound of Vaeril's voice. He turned to find the elf sitting cross-legged to the left of the barn door, still wearing his leather armour with his green cloak draped over his shoulders. His sword and white-wood bow were laid out in front of him. "Vaeril? What are you doing? You didn't stay out here all night, did you?"

Despite his legs being tangled together, the elf rose to his feet with a smoothness and a grace that Calen would never have been capable of imitating – even in his dreams.

"No, not all night. I spent some time walking the perimeter of the village. It is surrounded by forest on all sides but the north, with enough homes for four or five hundred. There seem to be guard patrols throughout the night. I spotted six separate groups of—"

"Vaeril, stop, stop. Why were you walking the perimeter of the village at night in the snow?"

"We needed to know where we are and what we might face. I couldn't do it during the day," Vaeril said with a shrug.

"I meant why were you doing it *at all*? Wait – what do you mean you couldn't do it during the day?"

Vaeril frowned. "My *kind* are not usually welcome in your lands. Belduar was different. They were used to us, but out here…"

Calen felt like an idiot. He had spent so long with Vaeril, Therin, and the other elves that the thought had not even come into his head. But he did remember Therin saying the same thing outside Camylin. "Vaeril, I'm sorry I didn't realise."

Vaeril shook his head and pulled his closed fist across his chest. "It is not something that requires an apology, Draleid. It simply *is*."

It was Calen's turn to frown. "I am still sorry. I should have thought. And please, call me Calen. I'm not sure how I feel about *Draleid*."

"As you wish," Vaeril said with a shrug.

Calen let out a sigh. At times, he forgot that the elves had sworn an oath to him. It wasn't something he was comfortable with. Ellisar had died honouring that oath. The images of the elf's headless body crashing to the floor still haunted Calen's dreams. He didn't want anyone following him out of obligation; he didn't want anyone else dying for him. There had been enough death already. "I'm going to practise my sword forms," Calen said, changing the subject. "I need to clear my mind. Would you like to join me?"

Vaeril shook his head. "Again, *Calen*," the name seemed to catch in Vaeril's throat, as though he had to force himself to say it, "I think it is best that while we are here, I keep my visibility low."

Calen could not help but allow a flicker of rage rise in chest. Vaeril had laid his life down more times than Calen could count. Calen would not leave him to sit in a freezing barn on his own. He would not allow the ignorance of fools to win the day. "Vaeril, practise with me."

"I—"

Calen fixed his gaze on Vaeril's, not allowing it to waver for even a moment. "Before the battle, Gaeleron was teaching me a new form. One used by the elves and later by The Order. Fellensír. I would like you to continue his teachings, please."

Calen thought he saw an acknowledgement in Vaeril's eyes as the elf gave a cautious nod. "Fellensír, the lonely mountain. It is a good balance to svidarya. I will do as you ask."

"Du haryn myia vrai." *You have my thanks.* That was one of the first pieces of the Old Tongue Therin had taught him.

Vaeril gave him a soft smile and laughed a little. "Din vrai é atuya sin'vala. You are coming along very well. Even among my people, the Old Tongue is not as prominent as it once was. The Common Tongue is simply more practical. I will teach you some more if you like."

Calen thought he recognised the phrase, but he wasn't sure. *Din vrai é atuya sin'vala.* It sounded like 'you are welcome', but the way Vaeril spoke the words was slightly different to Therin's pronunciation. "I would like that very much. But first?" Calen nodded to the open area of snow in front of the barn.

Vaeril nodded, snatching up his sword and bow.

Looking at the thick layer of snow that sat about a foot off the ground, Calen reached for the Spark. He took a look around him, making sure that nobody was near. It was early enough that most people would still be fast asleep in their beds, but it was still best to keep his use of the Spark to a minimum.

He pulled threads of Fire into himself. The heat of the Fire flowed through him from head to toe, seeping into every crack and crevice in his mind. In an instant, the chill that had buried itself into his bones was gone, cast away as though it had never existed. Calen pushed himself to focus. Of all the elemental strands, Fire always felt the most seductive. Calen knew that if he were not careful when drawing on threads of Fire, he would easily lose himself.

With a deep exhale, he pushed delicate threads of Fire into the snow before him. At the same time, he drew on threads of Water. He weaved the two threads together, using the Fire to melt the snow and the Water to funnel it outward. In moments, a large rectangle of grass was clearly visible just in front of Calen, the edges slightly frayed where the outgoing water had melted some of the surrounding snow. As soon as he released his hold on the threads of Fire, a shiver ran through Calen's body, the threads no longer holding the cold at bay.

He looked over the new practice space he had just created, not moving to stop the proud smile that touched his face. What's more, he had barely felt the drain at all. Therin was right, the Spark was like a muscle; the more Calen used it, the stronger he got.

"Very well done," Vaeril said, stepping out onto the newly exposed grass. "The primary limit to the Spark is your mind. Next time, try to use only threads of Fire. Push a little bit more in and turn the snow to vapour. It will rise into the air and drift away. Fire does not take as much strength from you as the other elements do – I can feel it. And weaving two elements together always takes more strength than one. You must always think, for in battle, the Spark can be the difference between life or death."

Calen nodded, stepping out onto the grass and pulling his sword from its scabbard, but he couldn't help but let a frown show on his face. "I will try as you say."

Vaeril pulled his green cloak from around his shoulders before removing his sword from its scabbard and placing both the cloak and scabbard down at the edge of the grass. "The fellensír," he said, moving to stand beside Calen, "is a defensive movement. It comprises fifteen major forms around which other minor forms can flow. The first major form is one you know well." Vaeril opened his stance, spreading his feet just over shoulder width apart, moving into the Crouching Bear. "It is a movement that requires the utmost discipline, and it takes a long time to truly master." Vaeril looked over at Calen, who watched him with unblinking focus. "Let us begin."

For a little over an hour, Vaeril and Calen moved through the fifteen major forms of the fellensír. Calen recognised some from the training with Gaeleron, Aeson, and his father, though their names seemed to vary depending on the teacher.

Even in the sharp morning air, sweat dripped down Calen's brow and tacked his shirt to his chest and back. But he didn't mind it, not even in the slightest. There was nothing that calmed his mind like practising sword forms. If he had closed his eyes, he would have imagined himself in The Glade, the sun cresting over Wolfpine Ridge, his fingers wrapped around the handle of his wooden practice sword, and Faenir sitting by the wall of the house, watching him. A melancholy sank into his heart. Those days were gone, and they would never return. He was no longer in The Glade. The sun still rose from the east, but it rose over a different mountain.

"Are you well?" Vaeril pulled himself to his full standing position, looking at Calen with an expression of concern.

"I'm all right," Calen said, letting out a deep sigh. He dropped himself to the ground, thankful for the release the soft grass provided his legs. "Just thinking of home."

"I, too, think of home."

"Do you miss it?"

"I do. But I know I am doing what is right. I follow my oath."

Calen shifted uneasily. "Why did you swear that oath, Vaeril? You did not know me. You did not know who I was. Even now, you still do not *truly* know me."

Vaeril gave Calen a look that he had seen his parents give him many a time. It was a look of amusement suggesting they believed Calen missed something that was apparently obvious. "Even if Therin Eiltris and Aeson Virandr had not stood by your side, I would have sworn that oath, and I would swear it again today."

"But *why*?" The question was one Calen had asked himself a thousand times.

"Why would I still have sworn it? Because my people needed hope, and you represented hope. Why would I swear it again? Because I now know the kind of man you are."

Calen brought his hand up, digging his nails into the skin at the back of his neck. His throat constricted, and he felt a weight compressing his chest. *He* didn't even know what kind of man he was. "So many have died because of me, *for* me. My family, Arthur, Ellisar, all the soldiers who died at Belduar. Men, dwarves, elves… their blood is on *my* hands."

"You would have died to save those men in the Wind Runner Courtyard," Vaeril cut across, leaning forward. "You almost did. Which would not have been smart, but it was admirable. I have watched you risk your life for others, time and time again. I have seen you lead when you would have rathered follow, just so others had a beacon to look to. This was coming. The empire has sat still for too long, growing fat on the spoils of the last war. They were never going to leave my people alone in the Aravell. They would have come eventually. Just as they are now coming back to the South in force. You might have been the trigger, Calen. But you are not the cause. I am proud to follow someone who would lay down their life for those who stand beside them."

Calen didn't respond. In truth, he didn't know what to say. Would they have come? It was impossible to know. All he knew was that they did come, and they came because of him.

Calen and Vaeril sat there for a while, the cool touch of the morning air prickling their skin. Calen was happy for the silence. He leaned back, propping himself up on his elbows and letting his head drop, then closed his eyes. Without even realising he had done it, he reached out to the Spark, pulling threads of Spirit and Air into himself. Just as he had done in the tunnels, he let the threads drift through the air, picking up the sounds and vibrations, before funneling them back towards his ears.

With his hearing amplified, Calen realised this was so very different from the silence in the caves. The soft susurration of the trees around him as they stood against the morning breeze, the chirps and tweets of the birds, the burbling of the nearby river, the murmur of conversation as the village began to wake – he heard all of it, and again, it sounded like home. How many mornings had he sat on the wall of the market square, listening to The Glade as the village woke? He would have sat there for hours if Vaeril had not spoken.

"You truly have a gift with the Spark."

Reluctantly, Calen released his hold on the threads and opened his eyes. "I have nothing. I can only touch the Spark because of my link with Valerys."

Calen could feel Valerys even then as the dragon sat curled up in the barn. The only time he could not feel Valerys was when he was asleep. But it was not an irritation, not at all. The touch of Valerys's consciousness was the most comforting sensation Calen could ever remember. It was as though Valerys had always been there. A piece of him that not only belonged, but was essential to the very essence of Calen's existence.

"That may be true," Vaeril said, plucking a blade of grass. "But that does not change that what you can do, for one who is so new to the Spark, is nothing short of incredible. Bringing down those buildings in Belduar was not a common strength."

"I failed, Vaeril. I failed and men died. I would not call that a strength." In his mind, Calen watched as the Lorian soldiers tore through the Kingsguard, slicing them to pieces as they fled. A knot coiled in his stomach, and the hairs on the back of his neck stood on end. Ever since he had been bound to Valerys, so many had looked to him as though he were a warrior of legend; as though he were truly a Draleid. Tarmon and Vaeril, warriors with far more experience than he, deferred to his word. But he didn't deserve that title. He had not earned it.

"I have seen galdrín train for years before they could work stone so it crumbled like that. And even then, they could not do it on a piece of rock any bigger than your head. Galdrín who can bring down entire buildings like you did are rare. In our learnings, it says there used to be entire regiments of galdrín who would man the walls of cities during a siege just to keep enemies from bringing them down. I think I saw some at the battle in Belduar, but I cannot be certain."

It had taken Calen a moment to place the word 'galdrín'. He thought he remembered it as being the rough translation for 'mage' in the Old Tongue, but then he remembered Therin going off on a tangent about the direct translation and how it wasn't precise – so he wasn't entirely sure. Either way, the topic of the warriors who died in Belduar was not one Calen wanted to continue with. "Vaeril, after the kerathlin attacked, you should not have been able to move the way you did with the injury you had. I could feel you drawing from the Spark, weaving threads of Spirit into yourself. What was that?"

Vaeril gave him a half-grin. "There are rules to using the Spark. But like anything, there are ways to bend what cannot be broken. It is true, a person cannot heal themselves. To even try often results in death, as the toll taken on the healer is twice what is given. Spirit is… *unique.* It is said that one of the greatest limits of the Spark, apart from a person's raw power, is that person's own mind. You cannot do what you believe you cannot do. You are limited by your own imagination. This is true even more so for Spirit. Spirit can be used not only for its own purposes, but also to amplify the power of other threads and to augment the galdrín who uses it. I used threads of Spirit to still my pain so I could push through, though even that has its own risks. If we had not found the Portal Heart, I most certainly would have died. It is an ancient practice that has mostly been lost to the human world in favour of more direct uses for the Spark. Your people often do not understand what they cannot see."

Calen just sat there, his head spinning. With each passing day he realised more and more that everything he thought he understood about the Spark paled in comparison to the vast ocean of what he did not. "Can you teach me?"

Vaeril fixed a serious stare on Calen. "You must learn to walk before you can fly. You are powerful, even now, but there are many things you must learn before you can wield the Spark in such a way. But yes, I will teach you, if only until we find Therin again. My knowledge in the Spark is that of a child's next to his."

Calen couldn't help but smile. "We have a deal."

"That we do, Draleid."

Calen gave Vaeril a flat look, the corner of his lips turning to a frown.

"Calen," he corrected himself.

Calen laughed, pushing himself to his feet. "Come, we need to find the others. They will most likely still be in their beds." He reached out his hand, pulling Vaeril to his feet.

"I believe you are right," Vaeril said, slinging his bow over his shoulder and clipping his sword belt around his waist. "In truth, I am surprised you rose this morning before the sun."

"I couldn't sleep, and I didn't want to miss the sunrise for another day. What of you?"

Vaeril shrugged. "Elves do not sleep very much. Three, perhaps four hours each night is more than enough."

Calen hadn't thought about it before, but that explained why Therin had always nominated himself for first watch yet never seemed to be tired. Except for the time they found him outside of Camylin, which Calen now knew was due to the Spark.

The common room of The Brazen Boar was empty when Calen and Vaeril pushed open the door. A strong smell of ale, soap, and some form of roasted vegetables hung in the air, while two serving girls ambled about, sweeping the floor and wiping down the long tables.

"How can I help you?" A heavy-set man with a thick beard and a grease-stained apron stepped out from a door behind the bar that must have led to the kitchen. He had a crooked nose and a reddish face marred by pockmarks. His deep belly and thick chest were covered with what looked like heavy muscle under a layer of fat. The man came out from behind the bar, rubbing his greasy hands in a thick cloth. His eyes narrowed as he approached Calen and Vaeril. "Your friend is gonna have to wait outside."

"Excuse me?" Calen couldn't hide the surprise in his voice.

"The elf. Outside. I can't be seen to be having dealings with his kind."

Even before Calen's hands clenched into fists by his side, he felt Valerys roaring through his mind. Though the dragon lay in the barn, he felt everything Calen felt – and Valerys's rage only amplified Calen's own. "I'm going to give you another chance to choose your words more carefully."

"It is all right, I will wait outside."

Calen took a step closer to the man, trying his utmost to calm his own anger and keep Valerys's burning rage to the back of his mind. "We're looking for some friends. They stayed here last night."

"I'll not be speaking to you while your little pet stands in my inn. Them pointy-eared bastards bring trouble with them wherever they go. The empire shoulda killed them all."

Calen stepped up to the innkeeper, so close he could smell the stench of day-old ale on the man's breath. He stared into the man's eyes, reaching out to the Spark. He didn't even think; the act was almost as natural as breathing. Calen wasn't sure what he intended to do, but he pulled on threads of Earth, feeling the rough grate scratch through the back of his mind. The sounds around him yielded to a low thrum that seemed to fill his ears, and he felt the thumping of his heart as it beat against his ribs. His anger, amplified by Valerys's, burned through him like a white-hot flame. This greasy innkeeper had no right to speak to Vaeril that way.

"Everything all right?"

Calen hadn't heard the door swing open. The sounds of the inn came rushing back as he let go of the Spark, startled at the sound of Alleron's voice.

"Lord Alleron, I was just telling this child here that his pet needs to wait outside."

"You will apologise, Ulfrik. These men are my guests and guests of my father here in Drifaien."

The heavy-set man's eyes darted between Calen, Vaeril, and Alleron. "But he's a fucking—"

"That's the last I'll hear of it, Ulfrik, or we will no longer be so lenient with your taxes." Alleron's voice had a hard edge to it, stern and unyielding. He glared at the innkeeper, daring him to continue his challenge. "Now, we would like a table and some food. If I remember right, their friends are in rooms six and ten. Could you send one of the girls to wake them, please?"

Calen could see the fury on the man's face as it twisted between irritation and disbelief. "I…" A large huff escaped the innkeeper's throat as he took a step back from Calen. "The drawing room is free. Close the curtains, and I'll bring you food."

Calen tried his best to calm himself, slowing his breathing and unclenching his fists as the innkeeper stormed off, muttering.

"I'm sorry about him," Alleron said, gesturing for Calen and Vaeril to follow him towards the drawing room.

The drawing room itself was set at the far side of the bar. A large doorless frame sat in the wall with a rail at its top lip that held a heavy green curtain. The room was about twenty feet across and thirty from side to side. A couch, upholstered with the same fabric as the curtain, was set into both the far wall and the wall that ran along the right side of the room, while the wall on the left-hand side held a lacquered bookcase that stretched from floor to ceiling. A sickly feeling set into Calen's stomach at the sight of the bookcase. He couldn't help it. Even the *smell* of the books reminded him of Rist.

"The empire has done a good job of sowing the hate for elves in these lands. Many believe it was the elves who cursed the weather here, that named it the Eversnow. Either way, the empire needed someone to blame for the hardship," Alleron said as he stood in the doorway, gesturing for Calen and Vaeril to step into the drawing room. He clasped his hand on Vaeril's shoulder as the elf passed. "It is easy to hate what is different. I am sorry."

"It is all right. There are many of my kind who feel the same way about humans. They do not speak for us all."

Alleron let out a sigh, a grim look sitting on his face.

They were not sitting there long before a short serving girl with wild brown hair dropped off a large teapot and three clay mugs. Calen recognised the smell immediately: Arlen root tea. He took a deep breath in through his nose and let out a laugh as he reached for the nearest mug.

"What is it?" Alleron said, grasping the teapot by the handle.

"Nothing." Calen watched, allowing a smile to creep across his face as Alleron filled his mug to the brim with the pungent brown liquid. "Just reminds me of home." Calen took a deep draught from the mug, as though it were filled with mead from The Gilded Dragon. He would be lying if he said it tasted any better than it had half a year ago, but it tasted familiar, and he needed familiar.

Erik and Tarmon were the first to step through the door frame. They both wore fresh shirts and trousers that Alleron must have left for them. It was more than a little strange to see Tarmon out of his plate armour. The man looked as alert as ever, his eyes searching every corner of the room as though a Fade might leap from the shadows. He never seemed to let himself rest.

Erik, on the other hand, had a dour look on his face and dark purple rings under his eyes. He held his hand at the back of his head as though he had been hit from behind with a hammer. It looked like he had celebrated their escape from the tunnels a little too hard.

"Calen," Tarmon said, nodding in Calen's direction before greeting Alleron and Vaeril.

Erik didn't speak. He threw a weak glance in Calen's direction, accompanied by a regretful sigh, then took a seat beside Vaeril.

The two dwarves weren't far behind, and neither Korik nor Lopir looked much better off than Erik. They hung their heads as they trudged into the drawing room, collapsing on the two chairs that sat in front of the bookcase.

Falmin was the last to arrive. His hair was slicked back over his head, and his fresh cotton shirt dangled from his gangly frame. "Really? I was hopin' to sleep for at least... ten more hours? What is it with you military types an' early mornins?"

"It wasn't me," Tarmon said, leaning back into the couch with a laugh.

"You?" Falmin asked, his eyes narrowing as he looked at Calen. "I didn't think you'd be awake till the sun set again. Though, tis good t'see ya up 'n about. How's the dragon?"

Tarmon and Alleron frowned at the same time.

"Probably best we don't talk about Valerys out in the open," Calen said, running his hand along the back of his neck.

"Oh, right. That'd make sense. Sorry." The sincerity of Falmin's words was cast into doubt by the languid shrug he gave as he spoke.

"It's all right," Calen said, taking another mouthful of the Arlen root tea, letting the horrible taste settle his mind. "Can you close the curtain?"

Falmin nodded before pulling the green curtain along its rail, covering the entrance. He moved to the side and leaned his shoulder against the wall, looking as unperturbed as ever. "So, what's this all 'bout?"

Calen glanced at Vaeril, who lifted his eyebrow as a question. "Can you cast a ward?"

The elf nodded, and immediately Calen felt him reach for the Spark, pulling on threads of Earth, Spirit, Air, and Fire. The complicated weaving of the strands together set a dizziness in Calen's head. No matter how much he thought he was learning, his understanding was nothing more than a seed in a great forest. He could feel the ward as soon as it was erected. It was the same sensation he had felt Therin cast one in the mountain pass, but he had not understood it then. It was a low thrum that resonated through the air, only slight, but enough that anyone who held the Spark would notice.

Without waiting any longer, Calen turned to look at Alleron, who nodded. "Alleron's father is Lothal Helmund."

"Lothal Helmund," Falmin spat, spraying Arlen root tea from his mouth. Calen had not even seen him take the cup, that should have been Vaeril's, from the table. "As in Lothal Helmund, High Lord of Drifaien? Lothal Helmund the Wyrm Slayer? The Wolf of the Eversnow?"

"The very same," Alleron said with an unreadable expression. "Though he is not the man he once was."

"What does that mean for us?" Tarmon asked, sitting forward, his eyebrows raised.

"It means Alleron can arrange a ship that can take us back to the Lodhar Mountains, back to the Freehold, and back to the Belduaran people." Calen bit his lip as he finished his sentence. "We need to leave tonight."

"Tonight?" A look of incredulity spread across Falmin's face. "Give us a break. Can we not stay at least one more day? I had planned on drinkin' a lot more o' that whiskey tonight."

Calen gave a slight shrug. "You don't have to come with us, Falmin. I'd like it if you did, but it's your choice. We can't stay here. Valerys can't stay in that barn, and if the wrong eyes see of him here, there's no telling how quickly the empire will catch wind of where we are. We need to be a lot more careful than we have been."

"I'm with you," Tarmon said, giving a slight nod towards Calen.

"You know I am too." Erik shrugged. "I'm just happy to be out of those tunnels, and the fresh air might knock this ache out of my head."

Calen smiled. He turned towards the two dwarves, who lay half-comatose in the chairs beside the bookshelf, raising his eyebrow.

"Aye, we are with you, Draleid. Home is where we are headed."

"Det være myia haydria," Vaeril said, tilting his head slightly. *It would be my honour.*

"What did he say?" Falmin leaned forward from the wall, sagging his shoulder back. "Aw, fuck it. It doesn't matter. Can I at least get some whiskey to bring with us?"

Rist sat with his back against the trunk of an enormous oak tree. One of many that provided shade to the embassy's gardens. The skies above were clear and blue, with the marigold sun hanging at its midway point. He had been reading there for hours while the other apprentices relaxed in the sun, embracing their reprieve from training.

Rist had stood in shock when Brother Garramon had taken him to the embassy's library a few days ago. Never in his life had he seen so many books amassed in one place. It had always taken Rist at least a month or so to work up the coin to simply buy a single book from a trader back in the villages. And now more knowledge than he could ever comprehend waited at the touch of his fingertips.

Neera and the others had to, quite literally, drag him from the library's candlelit halls. Not that he minded too much. He had gotten through two books by the time the sun had moved a quarter way through the sky – *The Sea of Stone, a Tale of Gods* and *The Rise of the Righteous*, a book on the rise of the empire and the fall of The Order. Both books were fascinating and shocking in equal measure. Rist found he had to take everything he read in their pages with a 'grain of salt', as his grandfather used to say. The differences in history that arose across the continent were incredible. Most of the people in the villages regaled the Draleid and The Order as heroes, the last line of defence against tyranny and death. In the North, it appeared that The Order themselves were the tyrants and the Draleid their puppets. Though, which tales to believe, he was not sure.

But what shocked Rist most was that in the North, Efialtír was not 'The Traitor', he was 'The Saviour'. The concept of religion had never particularly interested Rist. It did not matter which god oversaw which aspect of life, or which god was 'good' or 'evil'. He had not seen evidence that *any* god so much as lifted a finger to influence events in the tangible world. But what did interest him was the influence these gods had over *people*. He had made the mistake of mentioning Efialtír as 'The Traitor' when in conversation with Tommin the other morning, and the usually pleasant young man wound up on the cusp of a swelling rage that only subsided once Neera calmed him down.

Laughing, Rist licked the pad of his index finger, then turned the page of his current read – *Druids, a Magic Lost.* They had been told not to remove the books from the library, but he had not been given much choice. The others were adamant that he join them in the garden, and he was adamant that he was busy reading. Bringing the book outside had seemed the natural compromise. He would slip it back in its place later

Arching his back, Rist tilted his neck to the side and rolled it around, eliciting a cascade of cracks as he did. The half-trodden grass and the trunk of the oak tree were not as comfortable as the leather chairs in the library. He let out a sigh, shaking his head as he retraced his words back to the start of the page, as he had done several times in the past hour. The book was interesting enough, but his mind wasn't truly there.

Over the past few weeks, he had sent more than twenty letters addressed to Calen and Dann. Some went to The Glade, others to the guards' quarters at Camylin and Midhaven. He had heard nothing back. Not that he had truly thought he would, but he had hoped that maybe, with luck, he might have been able to reach them.

Reports had been flooding into the embassy of how the Dragonguard had reduced Belduar to nothing more than a charred tomb. Rist had to believe that Calen and Dann were all right. He had to.

"You're still reading that book, I see." Rist had been so lost in his own thoughts, he hadn't heard Neera approach, Tommin and Lena beside her.

"He's always reading," Tommin said, dropping himself down on the grass across from Rist. Tommin was a tall young man from the city of Khergan who had been sponsored by Sister Danwar of the Healers. He had seen about as many summers as Rist. His hair was raven-black, and his blue eyes were often accompanied by a broad, unrelenting smile. "What is it this time?" Tommin reached over, lifting the back of Rist's book so he could see the title. "*Druids, a Magic Lost.* I've not read that one, any good?"

"You've not read *any* of the books in the library, Tommin," Lena said, a mocking smile on her face. She picked up the edges of her brown robes as she sat down, careful not to dirty them. She had been sponsored by Brother Halmak of the Consuls. She frowned, raising her eyebrows as she looked at Tommin. "I doubt you've read any books at all."

"I have too."

"Letters from your mother don't count."

"What about letters from *your* mother?"

As Lena and Tommin exchanged smart remarks, Neera kept her eyes locked on Rist's as she sat down beside him, resting her arms on her knees and pushing her back up against the trunk of the tree.

Rist gulped. He wasn't sure what it was about Neera, but whenever she looked at him, she always seemed to be… *examining* him? He folded over the corner of his page and shoved the book into the cloth bag that rested on the grass at his side and gave a shrug, trying his best to seem unperturbed by Neera's fixed gaze. "I've never seen so many books in one place. It's hard not to get lost in them."

Neera didn't respond, but a grin spread across her face. Rist couldn't stop his pulse from quickening. He found Neera irritating beyond measure, but her mind was sharp, and her wit was quick – both qualities Rist had recently discovered he found attractive, despite his best efforts to the contrary.

"Have you heard any new reports?" Rist asked, attempting to change the subject.

Neera gave a shrug. "More Urak attacks. I overheard two of the couriers talking this morning. They said most of the villages along the base of Mar Dorul have been evacuated, and fewer than half of the caravans travelling past Dead Rocks Hold are arriving at Kerghan."

Rist nodded. "I'll be happy if I never see another Urak again as long as I live." A shiver ran up his spine as he thought back to that day in Ölm Forest. "What of the South?"

Suddenly, Neera's eyes seemed razor-sharp. She twisted, turning her body towards him with a sceptical look on her face. "*You* have seen an Urak? Aren't you from some little farming village?"

There you go again, ruining it. "I have, and it's not a farming village."

"Okay, okay. No need to get all defensive. I was only asking. I won't dig any deeper." Neera put both her hands up in the air as if she were attempting to prove her innocence, but Rist heard her whispering to herself, "Men are always so sensitive." He had a feeling she had said it just loud enough for him to hear on purpose.

He tried his best to ignore her. She always seemed to have news of what went on outside the walls of the embassy, so he decided it was best to keep her happy. "If you tell me what you know about the South, I'll tell you what happened with the Urak. Deal?"

Neera's face lit up. "Deal." She turned back towards him with one eyebrow raised. "I've heard rumours the Draleid set fire to Belduar's walls himself to cover his escape."

Chapter Twenty

No Place Untouched

he breeze drifted through the street outside The Dusty Cove, whipping up small clouds of dust and dried leaves as Ella ran her hand down the length of the horse's long snout, resting the palm of her hand on its muzzle.

"It's not easy, is it?" Ella said, resting her hand on the horse's bridle. "Having to tow that carriage behind you all day. Thank you."

The horse let out a soft neigh, pushing his muzzle into Ella's cheek. She leaned against it, feeling the warmth of the animal's appreciation.

"You have a way with animals."

Ella looked up to see the carriage driver, Loran, standing at the entrance to The Dusty Cove, tossing an old rag between his hands. By the look of him, Loran had seen at least fifty summers. His left eye wandered, and he walked with a barely noticeable limp. Loran didn't wait for a response. He simply smiled and carried on into the inn.

Ella let a smile touch her lips as she scratched at the hair on the side of the horse's neck.

There had been a bit of buzz in the town when Ella and Farda had arrived earlier that day. The dusty streets had been packed with traders and pedlars alike, flogging fresh fruit, fine linens, pots, pans, and everything else Ella could think of. It had reminded her of the markets at Milltown. But now, as dusk drew its hazy cloak over the streets of Farenmill, and the setting sun washed the houses in an orange glow, a peace descended. Up above, the outline of the moon was barely visible in the cold winter sky, like a chalk etching on a canvas of icy blue. Ella always loved that point of day – that time when she could see the sun and the moon in the sky at once.

Across the street, a mother hurried her child along, her hand wrapped in his as she half-led, half-dragged him off towards their home. Ella couldn't help but laugh at the stubborn look on the child's face. She could remember Calen putting up the same protest whenever their mother had tried to bring him somewhere he didn't want to go. Ella sighed, feeling her heart sink in her chest. Thoughts of home were often bittersweet. They wrapped her in a blanket of comfort, warming her heart. But at the same time, knowing how long it might be before she saw her mother's face once more filled her with a great sadness.

A low puff of air escaped Faenir, who lay curled up a few feet away, his head resting on his paws. The wolfpine had not had any trouble keeping up with the carriage as they travelled from Antiquar to Berona – not that she had expected him to. Though, she still wasn't sure how he had found her in Gisa in the first place or why he was not with her father and Calen. Whatever the reason, she was happy he was there. She wasn't sure how she would have coped without him. "Not long now."

The wolfpine lifted his head at the sound of her voice, cocking it to the side as if questioning her, an intelligence in his gleaming yellow eyes.

"Don't look at me like that."

With a huff, Faenir dropped his head back down, resting his snout on top of his paws.

"Oh, fine then. I'm not sure what we'll do when we get there. We'll go to Tanner, talk with him. Then maybe we'll—"

"Does he ever talk back?"

Ella looked up to see Farda standing at the side of the carriage. She had been so lost in her own thoughts she hadn't heard him coming. She wasn't sure if she would ever get used to the sight of him in that steel breastplate, with the black cloak draped over his shoulders. In truth, he had been better company on the journey than she had anticipated. He even told jokes from time to time. Not particularly good ones, but she could tell he was trying. He stared at her now with those deep green eyes, always searching.

Ella's throat constricted under the weight of Farda's gaze, and she could feel her pulse throbbing in her veins. Every time she began to let her guard down, she was reminded he was the enemy. *Don't show weakness.* She narrowed her eyes at him, furrowing her brow. "All the time," she said with a shrug. "He holds a better conversation than most men I know."

She thought she heard the beginnings of a chuckle in the man's throat, but he held it back. Her eyes fell to the sword strapped at his hip; it stripped her mind of what little calm it had left. *He is a soldier of the Lorian Empire. I cannot trust him.*

"I do not doubt that is true," Farda said. "Despite that, would you care to walk with me? I have a package to pick up from an inn on the other side of the town, and the company would be appreciated."

Ella paused for a moment, debating with herself as to what answer would arouse the least suspicion. She could say no, but she was not going to be doing anything else other than sit in the common room of their inn and drink ale until she could no longer stand the taste, and she had done that too much already. "Sure."

A grumble of disagreement came from Faenir, but it dissipated as she scratched behind his ear. Sometimes it seemed all the wolfpine wanted in life was a scratch. "Come on, you can come too."

Here and there people scurried through the streets, wearing nothing but thin linen shirts and trousers despite the season. That was perhaps one of the strangest things Ella had noticed about the North, at least along the edge of the Burnt Lands: even in winter, it just wasn't cold. At this time of year in The Glade, Ella would usually spend her time wrapped in a thick winter coat and gloves. But here, anything more than a thin summer dress would cause her brow to slicken with sweat.

The empty streets were a strange contrast to back home, where the villages gained a new lease of life once the sun retired for the night. Ella never thought she would long to hear the drunken songs and chants emanating from The

Gilded Dragon after dark, but she did. There was very little she wouldn't give to be sitting in that common room, a mead in hand, her family around her, and the scent of freshly baked bread filling the air.

She nearly stumbled over herself as a group of Lorian soldiers came marching out of a side street. Four of them, garbed in black and red leathers, each with a sword strapped to their hip. It was all she could do to fight her instinct to run. The men looked no different to the ones who had attacked them outside Gisa. The ones who had killed Rhett.

Ella's heart palpitated as the men turned their attention towards her. She clenched her jaw and balled her right hand into a fist.

"Evening, sir," one of the Lorian soldiers said, looking straight past Ella.

"Soldier," Farda replied with a brisk nod, his voice assuming an authoritative tone. Ella had never considered Farda to be a softly spoken man, but she heard the difference in his tone when he talked to the soldier compared to when he spoke to her. "All is well?"

"It is, sir. No signs of anything."

"Good. Carry on."

Each of the soldiers gave a slight nod as they turned away, noticeably picking up their pace.

"Why are there so many soldiers in the towns and villages?" Ella folded her arms across her chest as they walked.

"Not that I should be telling you this, but from the reports I've gotten at each stop, it seems there have been a high number of Urak attacks along the foothills of Mar Dorul and the edges of the Burnt Lands. Even Berona is on high alert. One of the local patrols apparently sighted more of the creatures to the south of the village. That's where we are heading now. I need to take a look over some of the reports and confirm what they saw."

Ella tried her best to not let her surprise show on her face. The Uraks Calen had found in Ölm Forest were one thing, but this was different. A shiver ran up her spine as images flashed through her mind of the last time Uraks had attacked The Glade, the night Haem died. As if he could sense the fear that was beginning to set into Ella's mind, Faenir nuzzled into the side of her hip, almost knocking her off balance. She smiled at him, ruffling the fur at the nape of his neck as they walked.

"Farda, what exactly *are* you?"

"What am I?" The man lifted an eyebrow, tilting his head slightly at the question.

"I mean, you are part of the Lorian army, but you've not told me what you do."

"I see," Farda said, hesitating for just a moment. "I am a Justicar."

Ella continued to stare at Farda, letting the silence fill the air between them.

"I serve the will of the emperor across the continent. It is my duty to hunt down traitors to the empire and to lead the line should we find ourselves in times of war. It is a role that has many duties, most of which are not clearly defined."

"I see," Ella said, narrowing in on the question she had truly intended to ask. "And what brought you to the South?"

A thin smile spread across Farda's mouth, turning at the corner into a reluctant half-frown. He turned and gave a nod ahead of them, ignoring the question. "We are here."

The building that stood in front of them was two storeys tall and easily three times the size of The Gilded Dragon. A large wooden sign reading 'The Saviour's Chest' hung from a pole that extended out from the second storey.

Ella dropped down to one knee and ran her hand through the fur on the side of Faenir's neck. "You're going to have to stay out here, all right?"

Faenir let out a low growl of disagreement, lowering his head as his nostrils flared.

"I don't have a choice. They won't let you in. Just wait for me by the porch. I'll bring you food when I'm done."

Another growl followed, but Faenir padded past her and folded himself into a heap by the door. *Good boy.* Ella would much rather have him inside the inn with her – she always felt safer when Faenir was there – but not one of the inns between there and Antiquar had allowed him in so far, and she didn't figure it would be any different with this one.

The warmth of the inn caressed Ella's face as she stepped through the doorway after Farda, followed quickly by a wave of sound: the drum of conversation, the clinking of tankards, and the overexcited shouts of drunken young men. The smell of beef stew, freshly baked bread, and smouldering charcoal only partially masked the bitter aroma of soaked-in ale that was so intense Ella had no doubt it had permeated the wood itself.

Except for the serving girls, the bard playing the flute in the corner of the room, and the slight woman who stood behind the bar with a dour look on her face, Ella didn't think there was a single person in the common room who wasn't either a town guard or a soldier.

"Weapons, please."

Ella had not noticed the gangly youth with long black hair who stood to the right of the doorway, a row of wooden weapon racks on the wall behind him. The youth wore a dark leather jacket over a linen shirt and his trousers were tucked into his boots.

"I am Farda Kyrana, Justi—"

"Don't care who you are, respectfully," the youth said, shrugging his shoulders and turning his mouth into a pout. Ella didn't think for a second there was an ounce of respect in his voice. "There's no weapons allowed in here. Drink and steel don't mix."

Out of the corner of her eye, Ella saw Farda reach to his trouser pocket, the pocket he kept his coin in. But just before he dipped his hand inside, his eye caught hers, and he pulled his hand back to his side. "No, I don't suppose they do," he said, letting out a sigh.

He unstrapped his sword belt and handed it to the young man. Before letting go of the scabbard, Farda pulled the youth in a little closer and looked him in the eye. "If I come back and that sword isn't here, I *will* kill you."

The young man gulped, giving a short nod in response.

The hairs on the back of Ella's neck stood on end. There was something about the way Farda spoke that made her believe he fully meant what he said. Farda's eyes caught hers once more as they moved away from the young man at the door. He didn't need to speak. The coldness in his stare said it all.

Nodding to someone on the opposite side of the room, Farda turned to Ella and produced a small coin pouch from his coat pocket. "Here, I will only be a few minutes. Why don't you get yourself a drink? I will be back shortly."

Ella raised her eyebrow, set her feet, and scowled. "I have my own coin, thank you very much," she said before storming away towards the bar. She stuffed her clenched fist into her coat pocket as she walked between the groups of drunken soldiers, glaring at any whose gaze lingered longer than it should have.

"Why don't you get yourself a drink..." she muttered as she lifted herself up onto a stool, resting her arms on the long, stained countertop that fronted the bar. Just as she relaxed into the stool, Ella let out an involuntary sigh, and her shoulders sagged. The problem with getting angry was that it let the other emotions in, and she couldn't deal with them, not yet. A slight tremble set into her hands, and her throat tightened as though the life was being squeezed from her. For a moment she was back on the Merchant's Road to Gisa, the wind whipping spirals of dust into the air, her heart torn in half as she looked down on the pile of stacked stones that marked Rhett's resting place. Ella's chest tightened, and she could feel tears beginning to burn at the corners of her eyes. She drew in a deep breath, clenching her jaw, holding the tears at bay. She couldn't afford to weep. She couldn't afford to give Farda reason to ask any more questions. Mourning was not a luxury she could afford. And so, she closed her eyes for a moment, buried her agony deep down in her heart, and exhaled. Opening her eyes and wiping the moisture from her right cheek as inconspicuously as possible, Ella called to the innkeeper. "Can I get an ale, please?"

The sour-looking innkeeper gave Ella a belligerent nod, narrowing her eyes. She looked as though she were going to ask a question, but proceeded to snatch a tankard from behind the bar and open the tap on one of the massive casks behind her. "Two coppers."

Ella glared at the woman, holding her gaze for a moment before producing two coppers from her purse. Reluctantly, she handed them over to the innkeeper before grasping the handle of the tankard and taking a deep draught of the yellowish liquid that sloshed around within. She was getting better. She barely grimaced at the taste of it anymore. Rhett would be proud.

"It's getting worse."

Ella shifted in her seat, turning just enough so she could see the group of soldiers hunched over a small wooden table, drinks in hand, listening to one man speak.

"My brother is the Battalion Commander at Fort Harken. He sent me a letter last week. Says the Uraks attack at least once a week, and more of 'em each time. Says it won't be long before they get over the walls."

"Load a shit!" one of the other soldiers shouted, sitting back and taking a deep mouthful of his drink. "Nothing's coming over the walls at Fort Harken. Those walls are a hundred feet high with more archers than you could shake a dog at."

"You callin' my brother a liar?" the first man said, slamming his tankard down on the table and leaning forward, his eyes level with the other. Ella could see precisely why the weapons were kept at the door. "Us Urnells ain't no liars!"

"And what if I am?"

"Then I'll—"

Ella turned a bit, trying to listen in on the argument. But the man had stopped and was now craning his head up in the air.

"You'll what?" the other soldier shouted, jumping to his feet. "What'll you do?"

"Shut up, you twit! Can't you hear that?"

"Don't change the subject!"

The argument descended into an indecipherable mess of roaring and slurred insults. But Ella could hear the shouts. They were difficult to make out over the noise of the common room, but she could definitely hear them. Something was happening outside. She looked over to Farda, who sat on the other side of the inn. He was deep in conversation with two men and a woman, all three of whom were dressed in the red and black leathers of the empire, and the woman had silver markings on her shoulder.

Downing the last quarter of her ale in one mouthful, Ella slid the tankard back towards the innkeeper. "Another, please." She made sure to give a wide grin and hold eye contact with the sour-faced woman as she slapped two more coppers down on the countertop. "I'll be back in a minute."

Whatever was happening outside – it was probably just drunken soldiers having an argument – she wanted to check on Faenir. She never liked leaving him on his own, and he was better company than anyone in that grotty inn.

She took one last glance towards Farda as she made her way across the inn. As she did, he looked up, his eye catching hers. He raised an eyebrow, but she ignored him and continued towards the door. He could follow her out when he was done.

The fresh night air greeted her as she pushed open the door and stepped outside, letting the noise of the inn fade away. She found Faenir just where she had left him, but he no longer lay folded in a heap. He stood at his full height, his ears pricked up, a deep rumble resonating from his chest as he stared out into the night.

"What is it?" Ella turned towards the street, trying to see whatever it was that had unsettled Faenir, but all she saw were shadows. The only light that touched the streets was the dim glow of the moon and the occasional candle that sat in a window here and there. In the distance, Ella could still hear the faint rumble of men shouting.

"It's just drunks arguing. It's all right..." A shiver ran down Ella's spine as the shouting in the distance stopped, abruptly cut from the world. She held her breath, hoping to hear anything but the eerie silence that drifted on the wind. But the night had suddenly grown unnaturally still. Moments passed where the only sounds Ella could hear were the thumping of her own heart and Faenir's growl resonating in his chest. A ripple of awareness swept through Ella's body as Faenir stepped up beside her, his hackles raised, nose creased, and his growl deepening.

The crunch of dirt beneath boots sounded to the right. Ella snapped her head around, her blood going cold in her veins and her stomach turning in anticipation. A wave of relief flooded through her as three guardsmen stepped out from the shadow of a side street and started walking in her direction. She let out a sigh, ruffling the hair at the back of Faenir's head. His hackles did not settle, and the low growl in his chest persisted. Resting her hand on the back of the wolfpine's neck, she could feel something… Something she couldn't quite put her finger on. It was as though Faenir's worry was wrapping itself around Ella's consciousness. "Faenir, it's all right. Look, it's only—"

Ella's heart dropped into her stomach as an enormous black spear sliced through the night. It caught one of the guards in the side, lifting him off his feet and sending him crashing to the ground, spraying gore through the dirt. The man didn't move.

Another spear followed immediately after, bursting through the side of the second guard's head, sending a plume of blood mist into the air. The guard's body went limp and crashed to the ground, whipping spirals of dust up into the wind. A third and fourth spear flew towards the last guardsman, but he tumbled out of the way and managed to shout, "Attack! We're under attack!" before a fifth spear sliced through his chest at such speed that it held him upright, its tip buried in the ground.

Before Ella could even think to move, massive hulking creatures with pale skin came barrelling from the shadows, howling and screaming. She recognised them from the night Haem died: Uraks. Each of them stood at least seven feet tall, their blood-red eyes shimmering in the darkness. Some wore various bits of battered steel and iron armour. Breastplates, greaves, helmets. But most were bare-chested, hefting blackened swords and spears.

Ella wanted to move. She wanted to run, but she couldn't. Her feet would not respond to any command she gave them. No matter how much she screamed within her mind, she was frozen.

Faenir leapt in front of her, snarling, his head lowered to the ground, his hackles sticking straight up into the air.

As the creatures got closer, soldiers and guards began charging out of side streets and doorways. But they were cut down just as fast as they appeared. Cries and shouts rang out into the night. "Uraks! Uraks! We're under attack!"

"What is going on out—" A soldier burst from the inn behind Ella just in time to take a massive spear through the rib cage, pinning him to the door frame.

Ella screamed at the sight of the man dangling there, blood streaming from his side, trickling down onto the wooden porch of the inn. His eyes were vacant, void of life. She stumbled backwards, tripping over a bucket as she did, which sent her tumbling onto the tight-packed dirt of the street. A sharp pain ran up her back as she hit the ground.

Grimacing, Ella looked up to see an Urak charging towards her, a long black sword in its hand and a guttural howl escaping its throat. The dirt and stones scraped against her skin, bedding under her nails as she frantically clawed her body backwards, unable to get enough purchase to lift herself to her feet. *No, no, no.*

A blur of grey flashed past Ella's face. With a ferocious growl, Faenir leapt at the creature, his powerful limbs lifting him into the air, his jaws clamping around the Urak's neck. The Urak swiped at Faenir, hammering the pommel of its blade into the wolfpine's back, but Faenir held on, clamping down harder. Ella watched as the Urak stumbled, blood streaming out around Faenir's jaws.

Faenir swung his head from side to side, his teeth sinking even deeper into the beast's neck, tearing at its flesh. Then, with a terrible ripping noise, Faenir came free and landed on all fours, snarling, blood dripping from his mouth.

The Urak followed Faenir to the ground, crashing to its knees, a fountain of blood rolling down over its chest from the gaping wound where its throat had been. As the Urak dropped, lifeless, to the dirt, Faenir tossed away the lump of flesh it had torn from the creature and turned to face what was coming, a deep growl rising in his chest.

Ella heaved at the sight of the dead Urak, its neck a knot of mangled flesh, blood soaking into the dirt around it. She dragged herself to her feet, pushing the nausea down. The streets were filled with Uraks now. All around her the beasts ripped the guards and soldiers apart, cleaving bone with single swipes of their blackened blades and rending flesh with claws and teeth. The soldiers didn't stand a chance.

Keep your head. You didn't come this far to die here. Reaching down, Ella snatched up a bloody sword that lay in the dirt near her feet. One of the soldiers must have dropped it. They wouldn't need it anymore. *Breathe... breathe.*

Ella wrapped both of her hands around the hilt of the sword, just as her father had shown her. The feel of the weapon in her hands was familiar. The smooth touch of the leather-wrapped handle, the weight of the steel. She swallowed, set her feet apart, and slowed her breathing.

"We'll get through this," Ella said, looking at Faenir, her voice trembling. The wolfpine backed up in front of Ella, his head darting from side to side as the fighting descended into chaos. The screams of dying soldiers melded with the primal war cries of the Uraks, echoing against the sound of colliding steel. Ella could do nothing to keep her heart from racing. It beat against her ribs, eliciting audible thumps, like her father's hammer crashing down on the anvil in the forge. *Thump, thump, thump.*

A roar erupted to Ella's left. She swung the sword without hesitation. A horrendous vibration shot down her arms as the blade collided with an Urak's, the force of the collision sending her sword clattering against the dirt. She stumbled backwards as the beast stepped towards her, death in its eyes.

As the creature loomed over Ella, Faenir let out a ferocious howl and leapt at the Urak, clamping his jaws around the beast's sword hand. Crying out, the creature let its sword drop to the ground. But it only took a moment for it to recover from its shock. Twisting its heel into the ground, it threw a punch into Faenir's ribs, eliciting a yelp from the wolfpine, then swung its arm in an arc, tossing Faenir to the dirt.

With a snarl, the Urak snatched its sword up from the ground and turned towards the wolfpine, blood dripping from its wrist.

Ella's pulse quickened, and a gut-wrenching feeling set into her stomach. *No.* She would not let anything happen to Faenir. With every hair on her body standing on end, she pushed back the panic and fear that threatened to swallow her whole, grabbed hold of the sword she had dropped, and ran towards the towering monster.

Screaming so hard she thought her lungs might burst, Ella swung the sword through the air, a solid *thump* vibrating through the steel as the blade lodged itself into the beast's back like an axe in the trunk of a tree. The Urak howled as the steel sank in, turning its head, its face contorted in fury.

In a frenzied panic, Ella tugged on the hilt of the sword, trying desperately to spring it free from the Urak's thick leathery hide. But before she could pull it loose, the creature swiped out with a backhand. A burst of pain shot through Ella's face, and the force of the blow sent stars spiralling across her vision as she crashed to the ground, her head slamming off something solid.

Ella reached her hand back, groaning as she felt a tacky dampness at the back of her head. Ignoring the pain, she shook her head from side to side, trying to clear her blurry vision. "Faenir..." she tried to call out, but her words were barely a whisper

Through the muddled haze that covered her eyes, Ella saw Faenir standing over the body of the Urak, smoke drifting from the creature's back. The pungent smell of charred flesh filled Ella's nostrils, causing her to gag. The acidic taste of vomit hit the back of her throat, and she emptied the contents of her stomach into the dirt.

Trembling, she pushed herself to her feet, stumbling towards Faenir, using her sleeve to wipe away the vomit at the edges of her mouth. The wolfpine bounded towards her. He pushed his side up against her legs, but kept his head facing outwards, a deep growl reverberating through his body.

"It's all right. Good boy." Ella turned, spitting a mixture of blood and saliva into the dirt. Pushing the smell of charred flesh to the back of her mind, she reached down, wrapping her hands around the hilt of the sword that was still buried in the creature's back. Placing the flat of her foot on the beast's shoulder for leverage, she pulled as hard as she could. At first, the weapon only gave the slightest of budges, eventually shifting, then sliding free entirely. With the sword in her hands, she looked down over the Urak's body, her eyes resting on the mess of charred, molten flesh on its lower back. *What did this?*

"Ella."

Ella hadn't even noticed Farda approach. She could barely see anything outside her direct line of sight. Everything else was still a blur. "I'm all right."

"Are you hurt?" Farda reached out his hand to touch the side of her face, but Ella batted it away.

"I've been worse."

Ella thought she heard Farda stifle a laugh, but in truth she wasn't sure.

"Get behind me." Farda stepped between Ella and five onrushing Uraks, not so much as a knife in his hands. His sword must still have been on the rack in The Saviour's Chest. *What is he doing? He's going to die.*

Four of the Uraks attacked together, swinging their swords in sweeping arcs. But the fifth ran straight past, heading for Ella and Faenir.

Ella set her feet as the Urak drew closer, its blood-red eyes fixed on her, its mouth drawn into a horrific grin, exposing its jagged yellow teeth. The creature's leathery grey skin rippled as it ran, its muscular arms swinging its sword above its head.

Before the beast could reach Ella, Faenir lunged. The wolfpine crashed into the Urak's chest, tearing at its skin and knocking it off balance.

As the Urak raised its arm to strike at Faenir, Ella shifted her weight onto her back foot and swung her sword, slicing through the creature's wrist. She felt a resistance at first as her blade met bone, but then the weight of her strike carried her through.

The Urak howled in pain as it reeled backwards, its face twisting in agony and rage. With its good hand, it grabbed Faenir by the scruff of his neck and slammed him into the ground, eliciting a snarling whimper from the wolfpine. Faenir pulled himself to his feet, then leapt at the Urak once more, sinking his teeth into the creature's leg.

Pulling her arm back, Ella lunged. She had learned from her earlier attempt, and instead of swinging the blade against its thick hide, she threw her weight into the strike and drove her sword up through the Urak's chin. Blood sprayed from the wound, the Urak's eyes rolling to the back of its head. Plumes of dirt and dust shot into the air as the creature fell backwards into the hard-packed dirt, the life draining from its bones.

Ella pulled her eyes from the creature's lifeless body, afraid to look towards Farda. When she did, she found the man held a blackened blade in his hands, and one of his attackers already lay lifeless on the ground, its blood spilling out into the dirt.

Farda swept aside the remaining Uraks's strikes, before driving the blade through one of the beasts' chests. The Urak stumbled backwards, then collapsed to the ground. Ducking beneath the sweeping blades of the two remaining Uraks, Farda stuck his hand out, as though he were snatching at thin air. Ella gasped as the blackened blade in the dead Urak's chest shook for half a second, then launched itself into Farda's grasp.

In one smooth motion, Farda caught the blade, swivelled, and severed the nearest Urak's sword arm at the elbow. The creature howled in pain, but its cries were cut short as Farda switched his grip on the sword and drove it back up through the beast's ribcage. The Urak slumped to the ground as Farda ripped the blade free.

A coil of dread twisted in Ella's stomach as the last remaining Urak grabbed Farda by the shoulder and slammed him to the ground.

"Faenir!"

Without so much as another word passing Ella's lips, the wolfpine charged, deftly avoiding the swing of the Urak's blackened blade, before leaping and closing his jaws around the creature's neck. The weight of the wolfpine's charge sent the Urak crashing down onto its back, frantically swiping at Faenir's side. But the wolfpine ripped his head from side to side, ignoring the Urak's desperate strikes. By the time Ella had reached Faenir, the Urak was dead, and its blood dripped from Faenir's open mouth.

"Thank you," Farda said, dusting himself off as he got to his feet. "You handled yourself well. We need to go. *Now.*"

Ella stared at the man, her heart still racing in her chest. "What... what are you? I saw what you did."

"Ella, please, we don't have time for this right now. I will explain, but we need to go." Farda took a step closer, but Faenir blocked his path, snarling as he lowered his head to the ground.

Ella looked around her. Even then, more Uraks filled the streets, charging and howling. The soldiers were being mowed down as though they were nothing but children.

"We *need* to go." Farda repeated, reaching out his hand, ignoring Faenir's snarls.

Ella looked around her once more. She watched as an Urak's axe sheared through a soldier's neck with a single swing. As it did, the gemstone set into its blade shimmered with red light. She pushed the questions down, looked back to Farda, and gave a short nod. "All right, but you're telling me everything."

"Agreed. First, I need to go back in and get my sword."

By the time Farda and Ella reached The Dusty Cove, the carriage driver, Loran, stood out front, the two horses tethered and ready.

"Master Farda, I heard the alarm and took the liberty of preparing the carriage. Your bags are already aboard."

Loran was an older man, at least fifty summers, with a lazy eye and a slight limp. Though the irony had not been lost on Farda of considering a man of fifty summers to be 'older', when he himself had seen ten times that. Despite the man's flaws, he was one of the few dependable men Farda had come across in quite a long time. "You have my thanks, Loran. Please help the lady aboard."

Nothing could have prepared Farda for the thunderstorm that came his way.

"Help me aboard?" Ella roared, ramming her hands into Farda's chest. "I am not some trophy made of glass for you to control. What happened back there? What did you do?" A fury burned in her eyes as she glared at him. The wolf stood at her side, its lips pulled back in a snarl, teeth bared. "What are you?"

"I am a mage," Farda replied, his voice flat and level. "The intricacies of which I am happy to explain to you, but can we please get out of here first? There are too many Uraks here, even for me."

The fury in Ella's eyes shifted, changing to shock and then back again. "You intend to leave the people here to die?"

"Would you prefer we die with them? Because that was not part of my plan. I cannot save them. We have lost here today. You can stay if you wish."

Farda reached out to the Spark, pulling on threads of Air and Spirit, just in case. If she chose to be stubborn, he would have to take her by force and put the wolf down. Though that may have been easier said than done.

He saw her hesitancy. She looked at the wolf, then back to Farda, then over towards Loran. "My bags are on board?"

The carriage man nodded. "They are, miss."

Ella knelt and whispered something in the wolf's ear. Farda watched as the animal growled before bounding into the night.

Throwing a sneer in Farda's direction, Ella stormed past him, then pulled herself up into the carriage.

Farda released his hold on the Spark. He let out a sigh, pushing his hand into his trouser pocket. He ran his fingers around the hard edges of the familiar coin. Pulling it out, he flipped the coin over, examining the insignias on each side. The Lion and the Crown. With a *clink*, he flicked the coin up into the air. On which side it landed did not matter. What mattered was the question: continue on this path, or bring the girl straight to the Inquisition where she could be broken and used?

He felt a strange sense of relief when he saw the Lion staring back up at him from his open palm. It was fate's choice – he should've had no stake in it – but he did.

Snow crunched under the horses' hooves as the group made their way through the night. Alleron had wasted no time in assembling a party that would see them safely to Arisfall. Hunters, trackers, soldiers, and some who simply wished to make the journey. They numbered nearly fifty now, twelve horses between them all, with the rest travelling by foot.

Calen could feel Valerys overhead. He could feel the wind as it rippled over his scales, see the forest as it spread out for miles in all directions in brush strokes of mottled green and glistening white, smell the fresh blood that dripped from a wounded stag over a mile away. He shook his head, pulling his mind back from Valerys's. At times, the separation between them was so thin he felt he might lose himself if he pushed too far.

"How long to Arisfall?" Calen asked, pulling his coat tight around himself and turning to Alleron, who rode beside him.

"About two weeks, maybe more. Travelling takes a bit longer down here than it does where you're from. The snow and the cold see to that. But there are a few villages along the way, and we have walked these lands since we were children. It's not the journey itself that we need worry about."

Calen raised an eyebrow.

"The Urak attacks have become ever more frequent in the last couple of weeks," Alleron said with a grim shrug. "And if that wasn't bad enough, all their activity seems to have irritated the wyrms."

"What?" Calen nearly fell from his saddle. He wasn't sure why. In the past few months, he had learned of true magic, dragons, Uraks, kerathlin – no fairy tale should have surprised him. "I thought wyrms were just… stories?"

"They might be where you're from. But *here*, they are very real, and they can tear a hole straight through a horse in a single strike. They usually hunt alone, but like I said, the Urak activity seems to have irritated them. We've heard reports recently of them attacking in packs. Nasty bastards."

"What do we do if they attack?"

"Well, we have some ways of dealing with them, but we usually only have to deal with one at a time. In this case, maybe you can pray to Achyron?"

Calen let out a sigh. "Great…" he muttered.

Alleron laughed. "With any luck, we won't run into them at all."

"Luck is not something we seem to have much of," Calen replied, the corners of his mouth twisting into a frown.

Chapter Twenty-One

You Are Home

Rist pulled the air into his lungs, feeling them expand as he did. He held it there, counting his heartbeats as they slowed. One. Two. Three. In his mind, he could see the Spark. See the separation of each strand. Power radiated from the strands, pulsating through the fabric of his mind.

Air.

Rist pulled on threads of Air, feeling their cool touch crash over his skin, causing every hair on his body to stand on end.

"Loose."

The snap of a bowstring being unleashed rippled through the air. Rist opened his eyes. He had only a fraction of a second to react. He wrapped the arrow in threads of Air, feeling it push against him as he slowed its momentum, bringing it to a full stop only inches in front of his face. Releasing his hold on the threads, he allowed the arrow to fall to the ground, its steel head clattering against the stone.

"Good," Brother Garramon said, his lips turned up into a mildly impressed pout.

"But?"

"There are a hundred ways to do anything with the Spark. A thousand, even. What separates a good Battlemage from a great one are their choices.

You need to be clever, not just talented. It takes a fraction of the energy to deflect an arrow using threads of Air than it does to bring it to a full stop. As you grow stronger, the drain will affect you less, but it *will* affect you. With increased power, the risks of overreaching grow more dangerous. Those small decisions seem like nothing now, but in battle, they will be the difference between life and death."

"Yes, Brother Garramon. I understand." Rist gave a slight tilt of his head.

"I will be the judge of that. For now, we break." Garramon waved away the soldier who had fired the arrow, leaving only the two of them in the courtyard.

The sun had already dipped out of Rist's view, and a slight chill had set into the air. The palace walls were far too high for most of the smaller courtyards to gather a breeze, but ever since winter's touch had arrived, the nights had become noticeably cooler.

This particular courtyard they stood in, along with four others within the palace grounds, was dedicated specifically to the embassy of the Circle of Magii. It was used for the sole purpose of training and also, from what Tommin and Neera had told him, sometimes for the trials as well. Rist knew that to earn the colours of his chosen acolyteship, he would have to pass trials. What those trials entailed was another matter altogether. The actual details of the trials seemed to be a closely guarded secret. Every book only referenced them as 'The Trials', and Rist could not find anyone who was willing to give any more information than that.

"How go your histories with Brother Pirnil?" Garramon asked, handing Rist a small cup. As he did, Rist felt the Exarch touch the Spark, channelling threads of Water into the air. Rist watched as small droplets of water coalesced from what seemed to be nothing, then joined together before dropping into the cup with a slosh.

"Good," Rist replied, taking a sip from the cup as Garramon repeated the trick for himself. "But now there are more scars on my back than hairs on my head."

Garramon let out a short laugh before emptying his cup and placing it on the ground. "You are lucky. When I first took my apprenticeship,

Brother Pirnil's practice was not just considered the standard, it was the preferred method of education." Garramon pulled the black cloak from around his shoulders, leaving only a fine linen shirt embroidered with the symbol of The Circle across the chest. With particular care, he folded the cloak over and lay it down beside his cup. "I was a slow learner," he continued as he lifted his linen shirt up over his head.

Rist tried his best to stifle the gasp that escaped his mouth. A shiver ran up his spine at the sight of Garramon's bare flesh. The man's chest and back were almost entirely covered in a motley array of scars and twisted flesh that ranged from one or two inches long to over a foot, and spread from his hip to the top of his shoulder blade. Rist recognised the scars immediately. He twitched, remembering the sensation of Brother Pirnil carving his lessons into his back. Across Garramon's back, layered over the markings of torn flesh, was a tattoo of black ink in the shape of The Circle insignia – two concentric circles, with six smaller solid circles set into them at evenly spaced intervals. The tattoo stretched from just below the nape of Garramon's neck, out to his shoulders, and over halfway down his back.

"Why... why did you not have them healed?"

The look on Garramon's face made Rist feel ashamed for even asking the question. "Because these scars built me. Each one is a reminder of the pain I endured and the pain I overcame. That is what yours are, as well. Cherish the pain. Let it bind to who you are. You will be the better for it."

Garramon pulled his linen shirt back on, letting it slide down over his torso, once again obscuring his scars from the world. "Come, walk with me. I have a meeting I must attend in the palace, but first we have things to discuss."

Rist's brown robes drifted lazily behind him as he and Garramon made their way through the palace gardens, the half-light of the fleeing sun casting languid shadows in their wake. The gardens of the imperial palace had given Rist a new appreciation for flora. Some were simple, holding nothing more than oak trees, grass patches, and benches. But the decorative gardens were a sight to behold. He had never before seen such a wide variety of plants and flowers in a single place. He was entirely confident he could have read every book on plants in the great library and still never have been able to name half of what the gardens held. There were flowers that shot ten feet into the air, with yellow petals that spread out like sunbursts, and massive plants that held broad green leaves and white tops shaped like cups, with dark purple flowers and long thin whiskers that draped all the way to the ground. One particular plant looked like the coral that fishermen from Salme got their nets caught in, but it shone with a luminescent purple light. He could have gone on for days just categorising the varying shades of reds, blues, and yellows that sprung up all around. He had even spotted some of the Purple Ember they had found in the cave during The Proving climbing up a wooden framework set into one of the garden walls.

Each of the gardens were divided into sections that followed predetermined shapes and patterns, and were bisected by stone pathways. It was along these pathways that Rist and Garramon walked, oil lamps atop pedestals providing a warm glow to dusk's embrace.

"I think you are almost ready for your trials," Garramon said, breaking the easy silence that had hung in the air as they walked.

Rist tried to hide the shock that hit him. His trials, already? Most apprentices trained for at least a year before they were allowed to take their trials. He knew those who were sponsored advanced more quickly, but he didn't think it would be *that* fast. A ball of nerves twisted in his stomach, making him feel physically ill.

"Don't be alarmed. Usually, it would not be this quick," Garramon said with a half-smile that let Rist know he had failed in his attempt to hide his shock. "But needs must. Reports of increased Urak attacks come in by the day. Some of the towns and villages closer to Mar Dorul and the Burnt Lands have already been abandoned, and even Fort Harken has called for additional garrison. Between the Uraks and the unrest in the South, more Battlemages are needed. In truth, more mages of every affinity will be needed, but none more so than ours."

Rist swallowed, attempting to add moisture to a throat that felt as though it had been rubbed with cotton. "I'm not ready. I know nothing of the trials."

"There will never be a point where you stop learning, young apprentice. That is a simple truth of life." Garramon stopped at a juncture between four paths, one of which led back towards the palace entrance behind them. "As for the trials, they will not be made clear to you until the day you undertake them. This is the way it has always been, for in life the most difficult challenges are the ones which you do not expect. For now, you may know this. Like each of the affinities, the trials of a Battlemage are set in two parts – a Trial of Will and a Trial of Faith. Your power is raw, but your potential is vast. I would not have sponsored you if that were not the case. All swords were once scraps of metal buried in the earth, waiting to be forged." Garramon smiled, momentarily tightening his grasp on Rist's shoulder. "I will see you here tomorrow for practice at first light, before your mathematics with Brother Audurn."

"Yes, Brother Garramon."

With that, Rist stood alone in the garden courtyard, the full moon now visible in the dark blue sky above. He held his hands at the back of his head, closed his eyes, and let out a sigh loud enough to scare the birds that had been perched at the corner of the garden wall. He could think about the trials tomorrow. He had received another letter from his parents that morning and had not had the chance to open it. It called to him now.

Rist was only five minutes from his chambers when he heard a second set of footsteps echo through the cold stone hallway, only slightly dampened by the black carpet that ran the length of the floor. He stopped in his tracks, as did the other set of footsteps. Instinctively, he reached out to the Spark, drawing threads of Earth into himself. He had found through training that Earth and Spirit seemed to drain him less than the other elements, Fire the most.

Just as he was about to spin around to face his night stalker, a pair of hands slapped down on his shoulders, and he strangled a yelp in his throat.

"Too easy."

Rist jumped forward, swatting away Neera's hands. "Get off me!"

"Oh, don't be such a baby." Neera shrugged, a smug look sitting on her face. "Running off to bed so early?"

Rist glared back at Neera, trying his best to ignore the turn at the corner of her mouth. Whenever she did something mischievous, she always smiled differently; he couldn't quite put his finger on it, but it *was* different.

Stop it. Stop it. Stop it. Tell her you're going to sleep and leave before you say something stupid. "It's been a long day – I was going to get some rest." *Good, now go.* Rist found that his feet seemed not to share the same inclination towards leaving that his head did. *Don't do it.* "Why?"

Idiot.

"No reason," Neera said with a shrug, that smile growing a little wider. "I was just going to go for a walk. There's a nice tavern out near the docks."

"The docks?" Rist's pulse quickened. Was she asking him to come with her? Did he want to go with her? It took a moment for his brain to stop spiralling and remember that the docks were very clearly outside the palace. "Neera, we're not allowed to leave the palace grounds. No apprentices are."

Neera just shrugged. "I'm not sure what you mean. I would never leave the palace grounds." Her smile widened. "I guess I'll see you tomorrow," she said, spinning on her heels.

She got about halfway down the corridor before Rist let out an audible sigh. "Wait."

Rist and Neera stood in a dimly lit nook, one of many meant for quiet reflection in the palace gardens. Rist had often used the nooks for reading when the inside of the library had become too stuffy. But now, as the pale light of the moon drifted into the hollowed-out recess in the wall, Rist shuffled his feet, fighting a semi-conscious urge to scratch the skin on the outside of his arm, as he always did when he felt uncomfortable.

"Give me that and put this on," Neera said, pulling a long, dark blue, hooded cloak from the leather bag at her feet and handing it to Rist, holding her other hand out for him to give her his brown robes in return.

Rist hesitated, clasping his hand at the back of his head and puffing out his cheeks. Neera just stared at him, her dark eyes fixed on his, one eyebrow raised. "I, eh…"

"Oh, come on," Neera said with a sigh, a hint of frustration in her voice. "You think I haven't seen a man in his smallclothes before?" Rolling her eyes, Neera shoved the cloak into Rist's chest and proceeded to let her own robes slip down over her shoulders, exposing her bare skin. Rist stifled a gasp, diverting his gaze towards a dark corner of the nook as he realised she wore nothing but her own body beneath her brown apprentice's robes.

Were all northern women this brazen? His heart beat so heavily he was all but certain Neera could hear it.

"Well?"

With a gulp, Rist raised his eyes. Neera stood in front of him wearing a long, flowy blue dress decorated with yellow and white flowers, her dark hair cascading over her shoulders. He had never seen her in anything but her brown robes before. She looked… beautiful.

"Would you like to draw a picture?"

"What?" Rist stumbled over his words, caught off guard by Neera's question.

"Would you like to draw a picture?" she repeated, leaning her head toward him and narrowing her eyes. "It would last longer."

"I, ehm—"

"Stop stuttering, take your robes off, and put on the damned cloak. We don't have all night."

Rist tried to take in a deep breath to calm himself, but it caught in his throat. "I don't have anything else to put on under the cloak."

"I have another dress in here," Neera said, shrugging. "Or you can go back and get a shirt, but I won't be waiting."

Rist narrowed his eyes and threw a glare back at her. He now understood what his father meant when he said that women were equal parts confusing, irritating, and completely unavoidable. Everything in him told him to just turn around, walk back to his chambers, and fall asleep reading the last few chapters of *Druids, a Magic Lost.* On any other night, he would have listened. He had been trying to finish the book for a while now, he was to meet Garramon in the practice yard at first light, and apprentices were not meant to roam the city streets. All three were convincing reasons why he should simply walk back to his room.

But he didn't walk back to his room. In fact, his feet seemed to have absolutely no intention of listening to his head whatsoever. They were far more intent on planting themselves where they were and forcing Rist to stand there with Neera mocking him. He knew what she was doing. Dann had done it to him every day in The Glade. She was trying to poke fun at him until he felt like he needed to prove her wrong. He could see it plainly, but it was still working.

With a sigh, he pulled his robes from his shoulders, letting them fall across his arm. Every hair on his body stood on end at the touch of the night's breeze as he stood there, bare-chested, in nothing but his smallclothes. Neera's grin was so wide that the corners of her mouth almost touched her ears.

"Shut up," Rist said, tossing his robes at Neera and throwing the dark blue hooded cloak over his shoulders.

"I didn't say anything." Neera chuckled as she stuffed Rist's brown robes into the bag with her own. Her laugh only grew louder when Rist glared at her. "Come on, we only have a few hours. Best make the most of it."

It only took a few minutes for them to reach the entrance to the palace grounds. A massive gatehouse framed by two enormous hexagonal towers rose about fifty feet higher still than the grey stone walls of the palace. The main entrance through the gatehouse was an archway about forty feet long and about the same in height at its highest point.

Four of the palace guard stood in pairs on either side of the gate. Even in the pale moonlight and the dim orange glow of the oil lamps, their black steel armour gave off a magnificent shimmer.

"How do we get past the guards?" Rist's throat was as dry as cotton, and a sickly feeling had set into his stomach. He knew it seemed childish, but breaking the rules had never been something he did. It wasn't so much the rule-breaking itself, it was more what would happen if something went wrong. Even the idea of having to talk his way out of a confrontation caused his stomach to lurch; that was Dann's area of expertise. The idea of having to explain to Garramon what he had done was not even worth contemplating. How long had he been there? Months? And he had never actually seen the city. Apprentices were not permitted to do so. The Circle were guests in the city. For all the training that occurred within the embassy, it was still only that: an embassy. They couldn't have untrained apprentices roaming about, causing havoc.

It was only then that Rist realised Neera had not answered him – she had simply continued walking. He cursed to himself, then picked up his pace to draw level with Neera.

"Just relax," Neera whispered. "Say nothing, keep your head down, and follow my lead."

Rist didn't get a chance to respond. As he and Neera approached the guard, a man in a long black cloak stepped out in front of them, seeming to come from almost nowhere. Silence hung in the air as the man stood there, his hood obscuring his face.

"And where might you be off to?" The man's accent was thick, but it wasn't one that Rist recognised. Reaching his hands up, the man drew down his hood, revealing a dark complexion that was synonymous with the people of Narvona. A gold ring hung from his nose, and his head was shaved smooth, with a short black beard covering most of his face.

"Nowhere, Brother Tharnum," Neera said, bowing her head.

"Nowhere indeed," replied the dark-skinned man. "Ensure that nothing of note happens nowhere, and that nobody is any the wiser."

"As always, Brother Tharnum."

The man took a step to the side.

"Come on," Neera whispered, tugging at Rist's cloak.

Rist couldn't help but look back at the man. Brother Tharnum, Neera had called him. He was a Battlemage. Even if Rist had not been able to feel the sheer power that radiated from him, the way he held himself would have been enough. He oozed self-certainty, and there was an undisguised arrogance in the way he moved. Even then, as Rist half-stumbled after Neera, with his head turned over his shoulders, the man stared at him, unblinking. Brother Garramon was exactly the same, as were all the Battlemages Rist had come across. How was Rist ever to become anything like that? He would be much better suited to the Scholars. Not that he could say as much to Brother Garramon.

The palace guard stared straight ahead as Neera and Rist walked past them, through the long, arched entrance. They acted as though they were not watching two apprentices walk straight out of the palace and into the city of Al'Nasla. Rist waited until they were halfway down the long staircase that descended into the city before he spoke.

"What in the gods was that?" He did nothing to mask the release of the breath he had been holding.

Neera shrugged. She seemed to do a lot of that. "Brother Tharnum lets us visit the city at night as long as we are not seen."

"What if we are seen?"

"Then he never saw us."

Rist grabbed Neera by the shoulders, stopping her in her tracks and spinning her towards him. "Why do you always speak in riddles?"

She raised one eyebrow but didn't complain. Rist was suddenly aware of how close her face was to his. "If we are discovered out here and The Circle finds out, then Tharnum will pretend he knew nothing of our trip. We will be brought before whichever High Mages currently reside in the embassy, and we will be judged." Neera must have seen the question on Rist's face – she took a step back, patting down her cloak as if removing invisible wrinkles. "We will either be put in a cell or have the Spark burned from our bones."

"They can… take it from us? I had heard rumours, but I thought it was just to scare us."

"They can," Neera said with a grim look on her face. "I have seen it done before." With that, she turned around and continued down the staircase. "I'm surprised you haven't already read about it in one of your books."

"Wait." Rist dashed down the stairs after Neera, ignoring her jibe about his books, stopping just in front of her. "We need to go back. How are a few drinks in a tavern worth having the Spark… *burned from our bones*?"

Neera moved her face so close to Rist's that he could feel her warm breath against his skin. She held her dark eyes level with his. Rist was now under absolutely no illusions that she could hear the racing beat of his heart. "Are you coming for the drinks?"

"I..."

A wide grin spread across Neera's face as she spun around, darting down the steps towards the city streets below. "Come on, keep up."

Rist let out a sigh, tilting his head back. Books were so much simpler than women.

Even at that time of night, while the moon stood in enmity against the dark sky, the streets of Al'Nasla were alive. Rist had never seen the likes of it before. It was as though someone had taken the Moon Market and placed it at every street corner, then decided that was not enough. With every few feet they walked, there was a new bard telling a different story or singing a different song, the buzz of the gathered crowds preventing each bard from overshadowing the next. Scantily clad men and women traipsed through the throngs of people, loudly offering themselves in exchange for coin, unashamed of their nakedness.

At one corner, Rist stopped for a moment to watch as a man blew fire from his mouth up into the air. The flames spiralled, twisting and turning as they moved, taking the shape of two serpents winding around each other. Rist could sense the threads of Fire and Air the man weaved through the flames. They were weak, barely capable of sustaining the spiralling flames, but they were definitely there. The man must have been an Alamant – one who was capable of touching the Spark but who had failed to pass the trials. Rist had learned about them in Brother Pirnil's lectures, but the Lector had not spent much time on them other than to voice his disdain for them in their entirety. *'Their very existence threatens to undermine The Circle and everything it stands for. To leave them alive is weakness, not mercy.'*

Alamants were another thing Rist had not been able to find much information on in the library. Rist was finding that more and more. Things that just seemed to be 'absent' from the library. He was sure someone would have chronicled the history of the Trials or written about Alamants. Until he found that information, though, he would just have to ask the right people.

"Come on," Neera said, tugging at Rist's robes. "Mixing with Alamants is not something we want to be doing down here. Wherever they go, trouble follows."

Rist made to argue, but Neera had already started off again. He looked over his shoulder at the man, snapping his eyes back around when he found him staring back.

He stayed close to Neera as they shuffled their way through the throngs of people. If he lost her, he would be wandering the streets for hours.

One thing that stood out to Rist more than anything else as they steered their way through the packed streets was the people. Pale skin, dark skin, copper skin. Hair tied up in braids, shaved at the side with top knots, knotted and twisted in all directions. Dresses, shirts, skirts, tunics, and robes – all in a wider variety of colours than Rist even knew existed.

Traders, pedlars, and bards passed through the villages frequently. Rhett Fjorn's family had come from Berona, and Marlo Egon claimed his grandparents had travelled from Arkalen, but for the most part, the people of The Glade were all similar. The villagers of Salme had a slightly more bronze hue to their skin, and they were fond of their brass nose rings and earrings. A man from Talin could sell water to fish, and everybody knew you couldn't trust anyone from Pirn as far as you could throw them. But again, there wasn't much difference between the villages, not truthfully. But here, it was almost difficult to find two people who looked even slightly similar.

"Will you stop gawking at everyone who walks by?" Neera snapped, a frown set into her face. "We're supposed to *not* be drawing attention to ourselves. You Southerners don't get out much, do you?"

"Sorry, it's just—" Rist stopped when he saw the look on Neera's face and realised it was a rhetorical question. He nodded for her to lead the way.

Even as they drew further and further out towards the edge of the city, the crowds barely seemed to dwindle at all. In fact, in some areas, they even grew larger, chanting and cheering drunkenly. Rist and Neera walked for what Rist figured was at least half an hour more, until the buildings started to peel away, and the smell of salt water and fish added their recognisable tinge to the air.

"Wait here," Neera said as they stepped out onto the wooden docks of the port.

"But I… And she's already gone," Rist whispered, letting out a sigh. It seemed there was nothing and no one that made him sigh more than Neera. He would be happy if he just got to finish a sentence every once in a while.

Neera returned within a few minutes, clutching what looked like a small waterskin.

Rist raised an eyebrow when she handed it to him. "I thought we were going to the tavern?" he said, eyeing the waterskin with more than an ounce of suspicion.

Neera shrugged again, apparently her favourite motion. "The sailors always have the best spirits, and besides, what tavern is better than the Tavern of the Sea?" She opened her arms towards the water as she spoke, a delighted grin on her face.

Rist frowned before unscrewing the lid from the waterskin. He recoiled, holding the nozzle away from his face as he coughed. "What in the gods is that stuff? It smells like death."

"Wyrm's Blood," Neera replied, snatching the waterskin from Rist and pressing the tip to her mouth. She shook her head side to side and puffed out her cheeks. "Well, he wasn't lying when he said it was strong. Come on, don't be a baby."

Don't do it. Rist took the waterskin from Neera. He could smell the spirit almost immediately. It had a harsh, botanical tinge to it, and something else as well. The best way he could think to describe it was as if fire itself was a smell.

Do not do it. He pressed the tip to his mouth and took a swig. It burned instantly and continued to burn as it made its way down his throat. He shoved the waterskin back into Neera's hands as he doubled over coughing.

"There, there. I remember my first drink." Neera's voice dripped with amusement as she patted him on the back.

"Oh, fuck off," he said, swatting her hand away, pulling himself back to full height. His throat still burned, and it was everything he could do to stop himself from coughing again.

"Now, now. No need for that kind of language," Neera said, grinning ear to ear. "You keep that up and I won't share."

"Oh no, whatever will I do," Rist replied, scrunching his nose and narrowing his eyes. "So where do we sit in this, 'Tavern of the Sea'?"

"In the prime location, of course." Neera walked over to the edge of the dock as she spoke, dropping her leather bag at her feet. She took off the dark blue hooded cloak, removed her sandals, and sat down, dangling her feet over the water.

Rist gulped involuntarily, trying his best to ignore the knot that twisted in his stomach. That blue floral dress clung to Neera's figure a lot more than her robes ever had; it was difficult to take his eyes off her. It irritated him that she put him off-kilter. Taking a deep breath, he strode over to her, dropping himself down by her side. He slid off his shoes, placing them on the dock, and let the tips of his toes dip into the cool water.

He wasn't going to admit it to her, but Rist was much happier sitting there than he would have been in any tavern. There, where the moonlight shimmered off the water, the gentle sea breeze rolled over his face, and the sounds of the waves crashing against the docks drifted through the night air. It wasn't home, not by any measure, but it was the closest he had been in a long time.

"Are you not cold?" Rist broke the silence, turning to see Neera's bare feet hanging just inches above the water.

She took another swig from the waterskin, then handed it to him. "The more I drink, the warmer I get."

Rist couldn't help but laugh as he took the waterskin. Again, the liquid burned as it went down, but he didn't cough, and it did, indeed, make him a bit warmer. "Has Sister Ardal chosen which affinity she wishes you to pursue?"

"Not yet," Neera answered without looking at him. He felt her reaching out to the Spark, drawing in threads of Water and weaving them into the water just below her feet. Rist watched as large strands of the sea water rose, coalescing into a floating sphere that encased both of Neera's feet. She turned to him, a wry smile on her face. He couldn't help but laugh.

"Either a Consul or a Battlemage. She has long deliberated over the two. Though she is a Consul, so I imagine that is where her final decision will rest."

"And you? What do you want?"

"It doesn't matter what I want."

"Of course it does," Rist scoffed.

"No," Neera said, a deep sadness glistening in her eyes as she stared out over the water. "It doesn't."

Rist let his gaze linger on Neera for a few moments, before turning to the ever-shifting surface of the water as the moonlight caught the breaking waves. Talking had never been his strong suit, especially not to women. He had never had a problem talking with Dann and Calen, but they were different. Talking to them had always felt as comfortable as talking in his own head. A hollow fluttering feeling ignited in Rist's chest at the thought of Dann and Calen. That had been the way ever since he had begun training with Garramon. The training would push the thoughts of home to the back of his mind, sometimes for hours, sometimes for days. But in the end, they always came back. And when they did, he always felt that same hollow feeling. He missed his parents and his home. Of course he did. But most of all, he missed his friends.

"Are you all right?"

Rist hadn't noticed Neera shuffle closer to him. She was barely a few inches away. She took another swig of the Wyrm's Blood, then handed it to Rist, who took it without hesitation.

"Yeah," he sighed, before lifting the waterskin to his lips and taking as deep a draught as he could handle in one go. He clenched his jaw and grimaced as the horrid spirit burned its way through him. "Just thinking of home."

"You *are* home."

Rist lifted his head from the waves and found himself looking into Neera's eyes. In the light of day, they were the darkest of brown, but now they shimmered like polished jet. Since he met Neera, he had always figured her for an unbreakable wall of steel, unbending and unyielding. Her mind was sharp, her tongue was that of a viper, and she carried herself with an air of unbridled confidence. But in that moment, with her eyes fixed on his, all he saw was vulnerability.

Rist held his breath, trying desperately to slow his heart. A nervous mixture of calm and untethered panic burned inside him. *What do I do? Please, don't do anything stupid.* Rist went to speak, but before he could, he felt Neera's fingertips tracing along his cheek, and the soft touch of her lips on his. They stayed like that for what felt like an eternity, but at the same time, nowhere near long enough.

"I—"

Neera gave him a wry smile and placed her finger on his lips. "Don't ruin it."

Rist didn't move to stop the smile from spreading across his face as he gave a soft laugh and leaned back in, his thumb resting on Neera's cheek. He thought about speaking again but decided against it. Instead, he pressed his lips against hers once more, losing himself in their soft touch. He felt Neera's lips move into a smile.

"Better," she said, pulling him in closer.

Dahlen and Ihvon sat in the corner of the common room of The Broken Stone, a dingy old tavern in the dwarven kingdom of Volkur. Most of the tavern's occupants were dwarves – the rough kind, by the looks of them. Like many of the dwarven buildings Dahlen had seen so far, the entire tavern looked as though it had been cut straight from the stone it was set into, even the furniture. He found it strange to think of wood as an exotic material, but that is precisely what it was here in the Dwarven Freehold. The methods they used to grow their crops obviously weren't capable of providing a steady flow of timber. The only place where wood had seemed commonplace was in the Heart of Durakdur. Though, he supposed, that was often the way. The wealthy always tended to flaunt whatever the common folk didn't have.

"I thought you said it was best to bide our time?" Dahlen took a draught of his ale, letting it sit at the back of his throat for a moment before swallowing; it wasn't the worst he'd ever had.

"We are," Ihvon replied, draining a small cup of a dark black liquid, before moving on to his ale. "But only a fool would simply sit and wait. Daymon is not in the right mind at the moment. He is fuelled by grief, a mistress I know all too well. He wants to charge headfirst into a nest of spiders, for that is what these dwarves are." Ihvon lowered his voice towards the end, half-leaning across the table in a whisper. "We need to tread carefully and gather as much information as we can. There is more going on here than meets the eye. Why would Queen Elenya try to assassinate Daymon? What purpose would it serve her? And why would she send an assassin who was clearly not up to the task?"

Dahlen nodded, taking another mouthful of his ale. He hadn't thought about it like that, but it made sense. Elenya would gain nothing from Daymon's death. "Who is it we are meeting here, anyway?"

"You are about to find out. Here she is now."

Dahlen turned his head to follow Ihvon's gaze. His eyes did not have to search for long to find the woman Ihvon was talking about. In a sea of gruff-looking dwarves, with thick, knotted, ring-laden beards, the tall woman in the long purple dress stood out like a signal fire. Her skin was dark, and she had short-cropped black hair. By the gods, she was beautiful. If Dahlen hadn't known better, he would have thought she was Elyara herself.

As the woman approached, Ihvon stood up from his seat and pulled her into a tight embrace. "Dahlen," he said, "this is Belina Louna."

Chapter Twenty-Two

The Rider

Dayne sat on the edge of the pier. His feet dipped in and out of the gelid water, bobbing with the ebb and flow of the waves. Alina had not told him precisely why she left or where she was going – not that Dayne had expected any less. It was clear she didn't trust him. But still, she had saved him. That had to count for something.

She had left him a 'personal guard' though, which he knew was just a platitude for armoured babysitters. Dayne turned his head to see the two guards standing behind him. Juna and Thuram.

Juna was a tall woman with dark brown hair tied in a braid that ran from the front of her head straight through and down into a ponytail. The sides of her head were shaved smooth, showing the black ink tattoos that spiralled from front to back – the markings of House Vakira. Her cuirass was enamelled with ornate spirals of white, and she held a long ash wood valyna in her fist and carried a short sword at her hip. She bore three black rings on her right arm and two on her left.

Her partner, Thuram, was slightly shorter and looked to have seen about fifty summers. He had fair hair, a thick chest, and eyes that never seemed to blink. The green and gold of his armoured skirts marked him as House Deringal, and the ring tattoos that ran along his left arm marked him as a blade master.

Alina had most certainly not taken any chances. Not that he blamed her. He was curious as to where she had gone, though. She could not have returned to Redstone, not after what she did for him – another thing he had taken from her. He had asked Juna and Thuram, but they weren't exactly a talkative pair. Their names had been all he had managed up to that point, and even that was like drawing blood from a stone, particularly with Juna. He still had not tried ale though. That often loosened lips. He would try it tonight.

Leaning forward, Dayne rested his elbows on his knees. He looked out over the harbour of Stormshold, sheltered within the mountain beneath the city from which it took its name. The fact that this makeshift group of rebels had managed to find enough Craftsmages to build such a stronghold was impressive enough on its own. But keeping it hidden was even more so.

Four boats were moored in the harbour along with a slightly larger ship like the one he had arrived in. Most carried crates of fruit, meat, vegetables, and clothes – supplies necessary for survival. But others carried piles of weapons and armour: arrows, swords, spears, shields.

The ships that carried the weapons and armour were almost always Koraklon ships. Even if it were not for the pale blue markings on the sails, the distinctive carvings of the Oranak Squid – the sigil of house Koraklon – that sat at the prow of the ships made it obvious. Those ships would be coming and going from Ironcreek.

The ships Dayne kept his eye on, though, were the ones that came bearing oranges. Not just any oranges, but oranges bigger than his fist with thick, dimpled skins.

One such ship had come in three hours ago, and the crew were now loosening the moorings to cast off on the return journey. Dayne flicked the hourglass in his head, noting the turnaround time from docking, to unloading, to setting sail once more. It varied slightly, but it was usually around two and a half hours, depending on the crew. The crews seemed to rotate journeys, each taking every second trip. This particular crew always took at least three hours between docking and setting off again. One of the women had a limp in her left leg, which slowed them down.

The reason he paid particular attention to the ships that carried the oranges was because only one place in Valtara grew oranges of that size: the Redstone orchards.

The fragrant aroma of those oranges permeated Dayne's entire childhood. When he was but five summers, one had fallen from a high branch and knocked him unconscious. Dayne let out a laugh as he remembered waking up to Marlin shaking him by the shoulders. It was probably the only time he remembered the steward uttering a curse. But more importantly than nostalgia, if the ship was carrying oranges from the Redstone orchards, that meant it was coming from Skyfell. Which in turn meant Dayne had found a way back to the city. He did not intend on trying to leave Stormshold before Alina returned. He had left her once, and he would not do it again. But old habits died hard, and knowledge was never a bad thing. So, he chalked it off in the ledger that he held in his mind. Charting and assessing each ship, each crewmember, their habits, their ailments, and their strengths. He noted the times the ships arrived, which ships carried what, and where those ships would be going.

As the ship that had brought the oranges pulled away from the harbour and made its way between the two platforms that jutted out into the water, a shadow flickered overhead, sweeping past Dayne, then moving out over the water. Dayne watched as the shadow moved across the undulating waves, changing direction and sweeping back. He lifted his head just in time to see a reddish blur flash past him, the beating of wings drumming in his ear.

The wingbeats slowed, and gasps rang out behind him. Dayne pulled himself to his feet, turning as he did. Before him, just past Juna and Thuram, its neck craned in the air, was a wyvern.

The creature was the size of a large war horse, its tail snaking out behind it. Its body was covered with overlapping red scales that dimmed to a cream colour on its underbelly. The muscles on the wyvern's neck rippled with each movement as it turned its head about. A pair of golden eyes, gleaming with intelligence, surveyed its surroundings. The creature's head and snout were short, with powerful jaws and razor-sharp teeth. A pair of thick forelimbs fanned out into leathery wings that stretched back, connecting with the creature's body.

Dayne stared in amazement. He had not seen a wyvern so close in over a decade, not since he had been exiled. And truthfully, he had never expected to see one again.

The woman who climbed down from the saddle atop the wyvern's back was garbed in black and orange leather armour and a blackened steel helmet in the typical Valtaran style, a sword strapped to her hip. She ran her palm along the creature's jaw, whispering something in its ear. With a gust of wind and beating of wings, the wyvern took off, lifting itself into the air, and up towards the alcoves set into the top of the enormous cavern.

"Dayne Ateres, I heard rumour you had returned." The woman's voice was familiar, a distant memory hazed by time. She strode past Juna and Thuram as though they were not there. The two guards did not even consider protesting. Instead, they gave the woman a slight bow before stepping out of her way, timid as mice. Dayne would have expected no less. She was, after all, a wyvern rider.

"Am I to know who I am talking to?" Dayne asked, raising one eyebrow, doing his best to hide the slight trepidation that sat in his stomach. Even if he had still been a respected member of House Ateres, he would have needed to watch his words around a wyvern rider.

"Have you been gone so long you forgot those you left behind?" The rider placed her hands on either side of her helmet as she spoke, lifting it from her head to reveal a face of bronzed skin, three claw marks running from her forehead, stopping just over her eyes before continuing down to her jawline. Her brown hair was tied back, shaved at the sides, and her eyes shimmered like two pools of blue.

Dayne's heart skipped a beat, a tangible shiver running along his skin. His chest constricted, as though something had hold of his lungs. "Mera..."

"So, you do remember me?" Mera continued to walk towards Dayne, her steps slowing as her eyes took him in.

"Of course I do." Dayne tilted his head, tracing every line on her face. The scars were new. They suited her. As were the small creases at the folds of her eyes. They suited her too. "I..."

"There is no need," Mera said, raising her hand, a soft smile touching her face. "You are alive. That is all that matters."

She walked past him, then removed her leather riding boots and socks before sitting down at the edge of the harbour and letting out a sigh of relief as she dipped her feet into the water. "Are you going to join me?"

Silence hung in the air as Dayne and Mera sat at the edge of the water. It wasn't an uneasy silence, but neither was it one of those effortless, comfortable silences between old friends who were simply content in each other's presence. There were things that needed to be said – a lot of things. Things Dayne didn't know how to say. He closed his eyes, listening to the repetitive swish of the waves as they moved back and forth, building up courage.

"So, you're a wyvern rider now?" he said, opening his eyes once more.

"Clearly."

Dayne smiled. If one thing had not changed, it was Mera's sense of humour. He turned towards her, pulling his feet out of the water and folding them in front of him. "Can I see?"

For a moment, Mera hesitated, her eyes locked on Dayne's, but then she nodded. With practised care, she pulled at the fingertips of the leather gloves that covered her hands, loosening them before sliding them off entirely.

Dayne took Mera's hands into his, a smile touching his face as he looked over the markings of the wyvern rider that had been tattooed onto her skin. Black ink covered each of her fingers, turning to thin lines at the second knuckles, before joining together at the bands of black that ran around each wrist.

"A lot has changed since you left." Mera's voice was soft, but there was a touch of venom in her words, whether she meant it or not.

"It was not my choice."

"You always have a choice."

Dayne held Mera's gaze, unblinking, unyielding. "Not this time."

"You could have told me." Mera lifted her gaze from the water, a chaotic blend of ferocity and sadness in her eyes. "I would have come with you."

"That's why I didn't tell you," Dayne said, pulling his eyes free of Mera's, staring vacantly out at the water. He remembered the night he left with more clarity than any other point in his life. It had been etched into his mind. He remembered standing outside Mera's chambers, his bag strapped across his back, tears welling in his eyes. He had thought about telling her what was happening. Asking her to come with him. But that would have been selfish. He knew well that she would have come with him, just as he would have gone with her if she were in his place. But he hadn't wanted to force that life on her. It wouldn't have been fair.

"Can I have those back?"

It took Dayne a moment longer than it should have to realise he still clasped Mera's hands in his, his thumb tracing the line of ink that ran around her wrist. He had missed the feel of her skin, the touch of her hands on his. "I'm sorry, I…"

A smile curled at the edge of Mera's mouth. "Don't be. This is strange for me too. I never thought I'd lay eyes on you again."

"Nor I, you." Dayne hesitated for a moment. He knew the question he wanted to ask, but he was unsure as to whether he should ask it. "Mera. Do you know where my sister has gone?"

The look on Mera's face changed. She pulled away from him, and her eyes darkened to a stony stare.

Gods dammit, why am I such an idiot?

"It was good to see you, Dayne," she said, replacing her gloves, boots, and socks before pulling herself to her feet. "But I have things that need doing."

Dayne leapt to his feet, catching Mera's arm as she turned to leave. "Mera, if there is something going on that could put Alina in danger, I need to know."

"She will be fine, Dayne. Alina can look after herself."

Dayne held Mera's gaze. "Mera, please."

Mera glanced over her shoulder towards Juna and Thuram, who were feigning disinterest but were clearly trying their best to eavesdrop. She pulled him into a hug, whispering in his ear. "Tonight, in Audin's Rest. I will mark it for you."

Dayne nodded. "I'll just need to get rid of my 'personal guard', first."

As it turned out, both Juna and Thuram were quite fond of ale. So fond, in fact, that while Dayne climbed the rock face of the cavern towards Audin's Rest, they lay face down at the inn table. All it had taken was a pair of silver pieces for the innkeeper to have them carried to a room. They would likely want Dayne's head on a spike when they woke up, but that was a problem for another day.

Gritting his teeth, Dayne swung his arm up, fingers clasping the edge of the rock. Sweat streamed from his brow and stung his eyes. The muscles in his shoulders bunched, screaming in pain. He dared not look down. Heights did not scare him, but only to a point. Any man who dangled on the edge of a two-hundred-foot drop without fear was a man with no sense at all. Resting his sweat-slicked forehead against the rock, Dayne laughed. Not a hearty laugh, or a laugh that built in his chest, but the kind of laugh that could only come from someone who had suddenly realised they were doing something utterly stupid.

"We could have just gone for a drink," Dayne muttered before taking a deep breath and heaving himself up over the ledge onto a narrow lip in the rock. He tilted his head back, exhaling, his breath misting in front of him. He rolled his shoulders, trying to loosen the muscles that had begun to knot. Taking another deep breath, he looked out over the cavern, searching for Mera's marking. Hundreds of Alcoves were set into the walls at the top of Stormshold, each acting as a wyvern's Rest, their home. Most of the alcoves emitted a soft orange light from within, meaning the riders were in the Rests with their wyvern.

It was incredibly dangerous for anyone to creep into a wyvern's Rest – even with permission. They were intelligent creatures but fiercely territorial. It was Dayne's guess that it was Mera's wyvern, Audin, who had given her that scar. Dayne had seen women take much worse wounds to become riders.

As his eyes scanned the rockface, he noticed a small marking in orange paint, a figure eight with three lines through the central axis. It was the symbol his father had used as a sign for the second rebellion, the rebellion that never was.

"All cycles can be broken, my boy," Dayne's father said, his hand tracing along a figure eight roughly drawn with chalk on the wall. "But they do not break on their own, not while good people stand by." His father drew three lines straight through the centre of the coiling shape. "Anything can be broken with enough force of will. Any chains, any bonds or ties—" Arkin Ateres thumped his son in the chest with the palm of his hand, then dropped to one knee. "You see this heart? It is the heart of House Ateres. It beats in you, it beats in me, in your mother, in your sister, and your brother. No matter what happens, you protect them, protect the heart of House Ateres, and together, you will break the chains. Valtara will be free. By blade and by blood."

Pulling himself from his thoughts Dayne looked for a path towards the alcove that sat below the marking. The alcove was on the opposite side of the cavern, a firelight emanating from within. It was too far to sling himself with threads of Air, and he could see only two ways across. Down and back up or skirt the whole way around. Why couldn't she have just pointed it out to him? He let out a sigh, muttering to himself. "I'm not climbing back up this thing."

Letting out a sigh, Dayne lowered himself back down off the ledge.

It took another half hour for Dayne to skirt his way around the cavern to Mera's alcove. He grimaced, pulling his hands free from the split in the rock. His fingertips were cracked and bleeding, as were the pads on his knuckles on the inside of his hands. His back was about two minutes from seizing, and a long gash ran along his shin from where he had lost his grip and cracked his leg on a sharp rock. But he was there.

With one final tensing of his muscles, Dayne swung himself down into the alcove that had been marked with the orange symbol. He pushed the impact of the landing through his bent legs, rolling forward onto his haunches.

Warm breath rolled over his head and face, the smell of saliva and the iron tang of fresh blood filling his nostrils. Dayne's heart pounded as he tilted his head up. It was all he could do to fight his natural reflex to reach for the Spark.

The wyvern, Audin, stood before him. His neck craned downward, his powerful body tensed and ready. The wyvern's red scales shimmered in the light of the fire that illuminated the cave. Dayne didn't dare take his eyes from the creature to see if Mera sat by the fire. The two slits at the end of the wyvern's nose flared, his lips pulling back to expose a row of gleaming white teeth, sharp as fragments of obsidian. The creature's eyes, pools of molten gold, watched Dayne's every move. Weighing him, measuring him.

Dayne didn't move, not even an inch. He kept his eyes fixed on Audin's, matching the tilt of the creature's head. Wyverns were intelligent, they were loyal, and their bonds ran deep. But they were also immensely powerful predators. And Dayne needed to make sure this one didn't see him as prey.

"Audin." Mera's voice rang out through the Rest, rising from beside the fire. "Friend."

The wyvern ignored Mera's call, his eyes narrowing, his snout moving closer to Dayne's face. Bits of torn meat sat wedged between the creature's teeth, blood dripping out over the edge of its lips. If he had already eaten, maybe he wouldn't want dessert.

Dayne swallowed hard as a deep growl began to resonate from the creature's chest. But then, as though finally making a decision, Audin exhaled through his nostrils, blowing warm breath over Dayne's face one more time before turning back towards the fire, his muscles rippling beneath his scaly armour. With one last look towards Dayne, a growl still emanating from his open mouth, Audin curled up by the fire, laying his head down on the rocky ground.

With the wyvern resting, Dayne finally risked a glance towards Mera. A smile crept across the woman's face as she sat there, her legs crossed, the orange firelight flickering shadows across her. "Come, sit."

The Rest was larger than Dayne had anticipated, stretching back over thirty feet into the rock and breaking out into four smaller alcoves. A small fire sat at its centre, a cookpot sitting over it incensing the air with the scent of burned wood and bone broth.

A small table sat against the wall on the right side. Three clay bowls, a ladle, two mugs, two spoons, a small wooden box, and a teapot rested on the table. Dayne wasn't surprised by how sparse and tidy the Rest was. Mera had always been fastidious when it came to those things.

"I trust the climb wasn't too difficult?" Mera stood up, grabbed two of the clay bowls, two spoons, and the ladle, then walked back towards the fire. Dayne could hear the mirth in her voice.

"Fantastic," he replied, sitting down by the fire. "I was only just telling Juna and Thuram that I didn't have enough cuts and bruises."

Mera laughed, setting everything down beside the fire. She reached her hand into her pocket, producing a small tin and tossing it to Dayne.

"What's this for?" he asked, sitting down beside Mera and screwing off the lid of the tin. An immediate waft of antiseptic hit his nostrils. *Brimlock sap.*

"That's for your hands," Mera responded, a knowing tone in her voice. "And for your leg."

A sudden sharp pain shot through Dayne's shin as he inspected the tin of brimlock sap. He jerked his leg back instinctively. "Gods dammit, Mera!"

"Hold still," Mera sniped, burying a thin needle back through the skin around his shin, a line of catgut tied to its end. "Stop being such a child."

"Agh." Dayne clamped his teeth together, gasping as Mera threaded the needle through the wound. "A little warning, no?"

He had not thought the wound that bad. She probably just wanted to see him wince.

"There, all done," she said with a grin on her face. "Now, you cover that with brimlock and I'll sort the food."

Dayne cursed as he rubbed a thick layer of brimlock sap along the neatly stitched wound on his shin before applying it to his hands and fingers. It stung like a scorpion and smelled worse. He knew he would have to apply more again tomorrow as well, and he didn't look forward to it. It didn't matter how many times he had been cut open and stitched back up, he would never get used to the sharp medicinal smell of brimlock sap. The pain? He felt it, but it was like the embrace of an old friend at this stage. The smell of brimlock sap, however, that sent his stomach spinning into cartwheels every time.

"You were sent by Elyara herself," Dayne said as Mera handed him a spoon and a clay bowl filled to the brim with bone broth.

Mera gave him a flat stare, then slapped the stitches in his shin.

"Fuck! Why?"

Mera shrugged. "Somebody needs to keep you in line."

"Alina has no trouble doing that." Dayne let out a sound not dissimilar to a purr as the warm broth touched his lips. It tasted like home. On cold winter nights, his mother had always made bone broth for Dayne and his siblings while they sat in front of the fire, his father telling old stories.

Mera shifted. "Alina knows what she is doing, Dayne. With you gone..." Mera paused for a moment, her eyes not meeting Dayne's. "With you gone and Baren's thoughts turned towards the empire, things got worse than they had ever been. We stand behind Alina because she is the one who rose to lead us."

Dayne stopped eating. He left the spoon in the bowl, the warmth of the broth heating his lap. "You stand behind Alina?"

Mera must have seen the surprise on Dayne's face, for he could see it now on hers. "She didn't tell you."

"She didn't."

Mera exhaled through her nose, staring into the fire. "Not long after Stormshold was built, the council nominated Alina as its leader. There were others who sought the position, but they did not go against the decision. At least, not openly. She is a strong leader, Dayne."

"Of that, I have no doubt." Dayne swirled the spoon around in his bowl of broth. It all made sense now. Why Alina had not wanted him to make himself known to the council. He was her elder. He would offer a threat to her seniority within House Ateres. "You said things were bad. How bad?"

"They take two-fifths of everything we produce. Many starve. And, as they have since the rebellion, they take all the first-born males from each family, feeding them into the Lorian army." Mera's eyes were wet with tears, glistening in the light from the fire. "All children are tested for their magic at ten summers, not like before." Her eyes held a knowing look as she spoke those words. When Dayne was younger, he had not told anyone of his ability to touch the Spark. His father had warned him not to, as the empire took children who could touch the Spark. He had told Alina and Baren, but they were the only ones. Though he had always suspected Mera had known. It was difficult to be so close to someone and hide such a large piece of yourself. "They are thorough now. Any child found between eleven and eighteen with the ability to use magic is hung in the main plaza of Skyfell, no exceptions."

Dayne's heart bled as Mera spoke, and his throat felt as though it had been rubbed dry.

"Even the wyverns… No more than five years after you left, the wyverns started to die. It was slow at first, but after a while, we would find ten, twelve, fifteen a day lying in pools of their own blood. The empire deny it was them. They blame it on a plague. But it was them, I'm sure of it. Had Alina and a few others not hidden a stash of eggs, and had they not had Stormshold built by Alamant Craftsmages… they would all be gone. All of them." Mera's gaze drifted to Audin, who lay curled up on the other side of the fire, his chest swelling slowly before falling again, moving in a methodical rhythm.

"Mera, I didn't… I couldn't… there was no choice." Dayne searched his mind desperately for the right words. But there were no right words. Some things could not be explained or fixed with words.

Mera pulled herself up on to her knees, bringing the outside of her hand up to rest against Dayne's cheek. "I don't care why you left. I know you well enough to know that there was good reason. All I care about is that you are back. You are *back*, aren't you?"

A tear burned at the corner of Dayne's eye. "There is nothing but death that will ever take me away again."

Dayne brought his hand up to his face, wrapping his fingers around Mera's. For a moment, everything else faded and there was only him and Mera. His mind drifted to their first kiss, on the cliffs of Ahgar. Mera always had the biggest heart Dayne had ever known. It was a large part of why he had loved her. She had been beautiful – still was – but it was not her beauty that drew him in. Beauty faded with age, yielding to the incessant abrasion of time. It was fleeting. The heart's capacity for love was the true gauge of one's soul. "Mera, I…"

Dayne's mind went blank at the feel of Mera's lips on his. Her fingers brushed the side of his face, reaching back, running through his hair. Dayne's heart beat so hard against his ribs he thought it might break free. He brought his hands up, cupping them to either side of Meera's face. For a brief moment, he pulled away. "Are you sure?"

"Shut up." Meera grabbed Dayne and pulled him in closer, kissing him.

The fire crackled and popped, casting an incandescent glow through the Rest as Dayne and Mera lay there, the warmth kissing their bare skin. Dayne traced his finger along the soft skin of Mera's arm, up towards her shoulder. He brought his hand back down, resting it on her hip as he placed a gentle kiss on her neck.

"Alina has gone to Skyfell," Mera said, a resignation in her voice as she stared into the fire, its flames dancing in the night.

Dayne propped himself up on his elbow, looking down at Mera. "Mera? What is she doing in Skyfell?"

"What do you think she's doing, Dayne? She's going to kill the Inquisitor, force the empire's hand. You wanted another rebellion. She is giving you one."

"Baren would never let her…" A sudden realisation crossed Dayne's mind. "She's going to kill Baren too. I have to stop her, Mera."

"You can't, Dayne."

"He's still my brother, Mera. I have to try."

CHAPTER TWENTY-THREE

WYRM'S BLOOD

espite the cold, sweat dripped from every inch of Calen's body as he moved through the forms of fellensír. He dipped under Tarmon's sweeping strike, moving into Eye of the Storm, bringing his sword up, just barely deflecting Erik's downward swing. A flash in the back of his mind from Valerys was the only thing that allowed him to catch Tarmon's backswing. The man hit like a hammer, each blow sending jarring vibrations through Calen's arms.

Even Valerys had not been able to warn him of the sweeping foot that took his legs from under him. Calen hit the ground like a stone dropped from a height. He lay there for a moment, ignoring the pain that ran through his back. *Just a few minutes' break.* Calen opened his eyes as he felt a set of fingers wrap around his hand. He sighed as Erik pulled him to his feet. "Thanks," he said, sarcasm oozing from his voice.

Erik let out a deep laugh. "Hey, don't give me that look. It's Vaeril who insists you spar with both of us at the same time."

"In battle," Vaeril said as he stepped up beside Calen, Erik, and Tarmon, "you will rarely fight against a single opponent at one time. Although practising alone is beneficial for developing technique, it is ultimately flawed. It does not teach you to be aware of your surroundings. Practising against multiple opponents is more practical."

"The elf speaks true," Tarmon said, leaning over the crossguard of his sword, the tip buried in the ground.

Calen let out a sigh and tightened his grip on his sword. "Again?"

"Again," Vaeril said with a nod.

Calen took a few steps backwards and dropped into Crouching Bear. He gave a nod to Erik and Tarmon. Both men charged at him without hesitation.

Calen took a deep breath, settling his heartbeat. He watched as the two men rushed him. Their fighting styles could not have been further apart. Erik was quicker; he struck like a two headed viper, always nipping and slicing, moving his blades in a whir of steel. Tarmon, on the other hand, was slower and more purposeful but not a fraction less deadly. He was always aware, he never overexposed himself, and he never let his guard slip. To make things worse, the man struck with the force of an avalanche.

Erik reached him first. Calen followed two quick blocks with a sweeping strike that forced Erik to leap backwards. But Tarmon wasn't far behind. His strike sent Calen stumbling backward, and he followed it up with a jab that Calen only just managed to evade.

They went at it like that for two or three minutes, exchanging blows back and forth as Calen moved into Rising Dawn, then Howling Wolf, before an unceremonious pommel to the side of the head sent him reeling.

"Fuck it!" Calen fell to his haunches, throwing his sword to the ground. He reached his hand to where the throbbing pain ached at the side of his head, pulling it away to find his fingers stained with blood. He stayed like that for a moment before closing his eyes and letting out a sigh. "Sorry," he said, snatching up his sword and rising to his feet. "That is enough for now. Thank you."

Tarmon slid his greatsword into its scabbard as he watched Calen walk away, the young man's frustration evident in his stride. Just as the young man reached the edge of the camp, the sound of wingbeats rang through the air, and the dragon dropped to the ground in front of him, sending spirals of snow pluming in all directions.

Tarmon couldn't help but think of Daymon when he looked at the Draleid. Such young men, to have lost so much, and to hold the expectation of so many on their shoulders. He could not be there for Daymon now, but he could be for Calen – and so he would be.

"He is coming along well, master elf," Tarmon said, turning to Vaeril who had stood silently by his side, also watching the Draleid.

"He is," Vaeril replied. "Though he does not see it himself. Anger and loss dominate him."

Tarmon bit the edge of his lip, pondering. He watched as Calen sat himself on a large stone beside the dragon, running his hand along the creature's neck with such tenderness you would think Valerys were made of glass. "They fuel him. I do not believe they dominate him."

"True enough. You would follow him?" The elf didn't turn to look at Tarmon as he spoke, he instead held his gaze on the Draleid.

"I already do."

"But would you follow him if you had the choice?"

"To the void," Tarmon replied without hesitation. And he spoke the truth. The Draleid alone would not win the coming war. The empire had the Dragonguard. Nine fully grown dragons, along with the warriors bound to them. Warriors who themselves were once known as Draleid. Warriors with centuries' more experience than Calen.

No, the Draleid would not win the coming war, not simply by existing. But the South was primed to explode. That much had been obvious long before Belduar had fallen. In the centuries since The Fall, there had been no fewer than seven rebellions – the Valtaran Rebellion being the largest. The empire had quashed each one without mercy. And with each rebellion buried under the imperial boot, the resentment had grown. But if the nations had something, or someone, to rally behind, to bring them together, then it might be different. Tarmon figured himself a good judge of character. And by his measure, Calen Bryer was a man worth following. Or at least, he had the makings of one. "Would you follow him, master elf, if you had a choice?"

"I made my choice already, Lord Captain."

Calen pulled the heavy fur coat tighter around himself, doing all he could to keep the heat in.

"We should camp soon, my lord," one of the soldiers, Alwen, said, addressing Alleron as he made his way through the snow. "The horses grow tired, and it is becoming difficult to see with the snow."

"Agreed, Alwen. As soon as you see somewhere suitable, make camp."

"Aye, my lord."

With that, the soldier strode off through the knee-high snow that was only getting higher. Calen wasn't sure how any of them had been able to see at all up to this point. Between the night and the implacable blanket of snow that drifted down all around them, he could barely see ten feet in front of his nose.

Calen grunted, shifting his weight side to side on the saddle. After all the weeks in the tunnels and the time spent in Belduar, he had forgotten just how hard riding was on the body. The insides of his thighs chafed, his back ached, and the muscles in his stomach burned from trying to keep himself stable. But even with the pain, he had to stifle a laugh as he looked down at Korik and Lopir. The two dwarves had refused horses and had instead chosen to trudge through the snow that came up to near their hips.

It wasn't that which made him laugh, though. The dwarves had been trying as best they could to follow in the trails that were left by the men ahead of them, making their journey a little less arduous. But for the past hour or so, Falmin had been using threads of Air to funnel more and more snow into Korik and Lopir's path, much to their confusion.

Calen raised an eyebrow at Falmin as he managed to catch the navigator's eye, trying his best to hold a stern expression. But Falmin just shrugged, throwing a sly smile back at Calen before wrapping a small ball of snow in threads of air and launching it at Tarmon Hoard's back. Calen couldn't help but laugh as the Lord Captain of the Kingsguard stopped in his tracks and glared straight at Falmin, who ducked, pretending he didn't see Tarmon glaring.

Calen had not spoken much to Tarmon Hoard before the battle of Belduar, but he saw why Daymon valued him so highly. The man was a behemoth, both in his stature and his skill with a blade. But he was more than that. He was a leader to his very core. In truth, Calen wasn't sure any of them would have made it out of the tunnels if it were not for Tarmon. He just knew how to handle the hearts and minds of men. Calen would be sad to see the back of him when they returned to Belduar.

A silence fell over the group as they marched. The further they pushed, the heavier the snow fell, as though it were trying its best to stop their advance. It had grown so fierce that Calen could no longer see anything past two feet, and even then, he saw mostly nothing but white. They could not keep going as they were. Sooner or later they would simply have to give in and stop for the night.

More than once, Calen had let his mind drift into Valerys's, just to reassure himself the dragon was all right. Each time, he was reminded that the Valacian Icelands were Valerys's home. Though he had not been born there, he knew it like it was a part of him. Even as winter's touch crept into Calen's bones, he wore a smile at the sense of unbridled joy that radiated from Valerys's mind as the dragon soared through the sea of snow that fell languidly from the sky.

A blood-chilling inhuman shriek pierced through the blanket of snow, drawing Calen from Valerys's mind. Even before he could ask the question, the answer echoed in the night.

"Wyrms!"

The emotion in Valerys's mind shifted in a heartbeat. The ferocity with which the dragon plummeted from the sky set fear into Calen's heart. Something in Valerys's mind knew these creatures, and the images he saw screamed only one thing: danger.

Calen ripped his sword from his scabbard, trying desperately to see anything through the never-ending snowfall. Other shrieks began to ring out through the night, harsh, piercing sounds that set the hairs on the back of Calen's neck on end.

"To me," Calen heard Alleron shouting. "Follow my voice. To me!"

Calen tapped his horse to move towards Alleron, but panic had already begun to set in. The animal shook its head from side to side, neighing wildly. Calen tried his best to calm it down, running his hand along the hair on its neck, but it paid no heed to him. Just as he thought it would throw him from its back, the world started to spin.

The snow broke Calen's fall, but it also surrounded him, almost encasing him. *Get up.* The howls and wails of men accompanied the wyrm's horrible shrieks as Calen tried to lift himself to his feet. He stumbled, losing his footing with every movement, his feet disappearing into the snow.

It didn't take him long to understand what had happened to the horse once the white snow around him shifted to a deep crimson. His stomach lurched as his hand rested on something warm. He didn't want to look, but he did.

The horse's body lay on its side, pressed into the snow, a gaping hole torn through its belly, steam drifting into the air from its shredded intestines. The wyrm had ripped straight through the creature with one strike. Had it hit a little to the left, it would have taken Calen's leg as well.

Calen's heart pounded the blood through his veins, fuelling the fear in his bones. With the blanket of snowfall obscuring his vision and the chill setting into his skin, he tightened his grip on the hilt of his sword and reached out to the Spark, drawing on threads of Fire, Spirit, and Air. The warmth of the Fire radiated through his body, calming him instantly. The snow was falling too heavily for him to try and use Air to clear it, but he hoped that if he weaved the threads of Air together with the threads of Spirit, then maybe he would be able to hear the wyrms coming before they struck – maybe. But before he could do anything, a piercing shriek rang through his ears, and he saw something move, just ahead of him, a shimmer of blue against a blanket of white.

Calen set his feet and clenched his jaw, readying himself, time passing with the beats of his heart. Then he saw it. Two gleaming yellow eyes, staring at him through the snowfall, set into a serpent-like head covered in armoured scales of deep blue. He couldn't tell how large it was, but its head was only a fraction smaller than Valerys's. Either way, it didn't matter how large it was; he saw what it did to that horse.

The creature held his gaze for a moment, its yellow eyes watching him as its head drifted slightly from side to side. Then, like a coiled spring, the wyrm launched itself towards Calen, opening its mouth mid-air to expose a set of razor-sharp fangs that made Calen understand how it had torn straight through the horse's body. Just as Calen braced himself for what was to come, Valerys plunged from the sky.

The dragon crashed straight into the pouncing wyrm, driving the talons on his hind legs through the serpent's scales and down into the soft flesh beneath. The ground around Calen shook, and snow erupted into the air as Valerys slammed the wyrm into the hard-packed dirt that lay beneath the snow. The wyrm shrieked, its cries laced with fury and pain.

Valerys's rage poured into Calen, seeping into every crack and crevice of his mind. As one, they tore through the wyrm's scales, ripping it in half with their jaws and tossing its limp body to the side. Calen didn't fight it. He pushed harder, letting his mind sink into Valerys's. He let his fear fall to the back of his consciousness, a distant memory. *Draleid n'aldryr.* The connection was like nothing he had ever felt before. Every movement was his own, and at the same time, it was not. He knew where his body ended and where Valerys's began, but he did not care for the distinction. He felt the ache in his own muscles and the power in Valerys's.

Another shriek sounded to Calen's left, and a flash of blue tore through the night, moving like a bolt of lightning, too fast for Calen's eyes. But not too fast for Valerys's. The dragon's gaze pierced through the falling snow, feeling the heat that radiated from the armoured serpent's body. Calen pulled on threads of Water, Fire, and Air. In one motion, he melted a length of snow, pulled it through the air, and forced it into the shape of a spear, using the threads of Fire to draw the heat into the air, freezing the spear into solid ice. Then, just as the creature erupted from the snowbank to Calen's left, he launched the spear of ice straight into its open jaws. The wyrm's blood sprayed across the snow in a fine mist as the ice spear burst through the back of the creature's head. With an audible thump, the wyrm's body crashed to the ground.

The others.

In a plume of snow, Valerys leapt into the air. Calen moved after him and with him, feeling every wingbeat as his own. He could see the others, feel their warmth. Fewer than thirty remained, and they were surrounded. Five wyrms weaved their way through the snow, lunging out at the surviving warriors, who had managed to gather themselves. Calen tried not to think about how many of those warriors were his own companions. It would do him no good.

Drawing on threads of Fire, he melted the snow that lay in his path, heating it until it turned to steam and drifted into the air. As he ran, his feet hammering against the earth and his pulse pounding, he felt a familiar pressure building in his mind.

Valerys had spotted two wyrms moving together to the left of the group. The dragon swooped down, the pressure building from deep within. A sudden surge of power burned in Calen. It seared through Calen's entire body. His legs felt stronger, the ache in his back subsided, and the drain from the Spark that had begun to seep into him faded. Then Valerys opened his jaws, and the night erupted in a blazing light as dragonfire crashed down on the two wyrms. Their shrieks rang through the dark as the flames washed over the creatures' hardened scales only to melt the soft flesh underneath.

Three more.

Calen could see the other three, feel their heat. They circled the group, weaving in and out. He watched as one of the armoured serpents lunged, snapping its jaws around a Drifaienin soldier and dragging him back down into the snow. The wyrm doubled back, again lunging towards the group. Pulling in threads of Fire, Water, and Air, Calen launched another spear of ice. But the creature twisted mid-air, and the side of the spear simply bounced off its scales.

"Now!"

At Alleron's call, two Drifaienin tossed a massive net up into the air, directly in the path of the lunging wyrm. The creature had no way to avoid it; it dove straight into the net, crashing to the ground in a plume of snow. Before it had a chance to move, the soldiers fell on it with swords and axes, and within seconds, the snow was stained crimson.

A wave of relief flooded through Calen as he spotted Erik, Vaeril, and Falmin huddled together at the edge of the group. Falmin was wreathed in threads of Air, while Vaeril and Erik were stained in blood from head to toe, but each of them seemed to move without any major injuries. Calen scanned the remaining survivors, but he couldn't make out any other faces through the snowfall.

"Korik, Lopir?" Calen called as he reached Erik.

"Don't know. These things don't stop."

"There's only two of them left," Calen said, following the two remaining heat sources with his eyes.

"How do you…" Erik tilted his head sideways but didn't finish his question as Valerys plunged from the sky and crashed down into the ground, sending a slight tremor through the earth. Only a second or two passed before a scaled serpent-like wyrm head, along with about two feet of its neck, flew through the air and landed in the snow just a foot or two in front of Erik. "One left," Erik said with a shrug.

Calen followed the last heat source as it weaved its way through the snow, drawing ever closer as it moved. "It's coming!" he shouted, ensuring everyone could hear. Snow plumed up into the air as the wyrm leapt from its depths. Two of the Drifaienin threw up a large net, but they were too late. The weights attached to the end of the net bounced harmlessly off the wyrm's scales. Ripping through the air, the creature crashed into one of the soldiers, tearing through the man's chest in a spray of blood and bone.

Three more times the creature leapt from beneath the snow, and three more times it took a man or a woman with it, howling and screaming. It was clever. It stayed close to the group, weaving in and out of the snow, making it difficult for Calen to distinguish its heat from the others.

It leapt again, but this time Calen caught it out of the corner of his eye. It was coming straight for him. Reaching out to the Spark, Calen pulled on threads of Fire, Air, and Water, launching two spears of ice straight at the creature that twisted and turned in the air. One spear bounced off its scaled hide before disappearing into the night, while the second spear crashed into its side, gouging a deep furrow that fountained blood. Shrieking, the creature reeled to the side, plunging itself back into the snow, but not before catching Calen clean in the chest with its tail.

The force of the blow knocked Calen off his feet, and before he could get his bearings, the wyrm leapt from the snow again. Coiling upwards like a snake, it stood over him, its fangs bared and its forked tongue flicking back and forth. But before it could strike, Tarmon lunged, swinging his enormous greatsword over his head. The blade sliced deep into the wyrm's side, splitting its scales and driving into the flesh beneath. The creature shrieked, writhing in pain as it reeled away, sending Tarmon crashing to the snow.

Calen heaved himself to his feet. Calls and shouts rang out through the night as the survivors surrounded the wounded wyrm. The creature hissed and shrieked, flailing its tail. One of the Drifaienin howled as the creature's tail whipped against the side of her leg, snapping the bone in two at the knee.

Calen reached for the Spark, but as he did, the drain hit him like a battering ram, and he stumbled, dropping to one knee. The sensation was terrifying. It was as though he could feel his soul being pulled from his body. He watched as the wyrm dove underneath one of the Drifaienin nets before tearing through two more men and plunging back into the snow.

Valerys. Calen pushed his mind further, letting it fall into Valerys's entirely. He could see the wyrm through a haze of snowfall, feel the heat that radiated from its body. Wind rippled as it crashed against his scales, but it did not slow him. Valerys dove from the sky, crashing into the wyrm. The world spun as Valerys and the wyrm tumbled through the snow, tearing at each other with fang and claw. As they came to a stop, Valerys sunk his jaws into the creature's back, feeling its scales crack, tasting the metallic warmth of the blood that pumped from the wound.

Lifting the wyrm into the air, Valerys slammed it back to the ground with incredible force. Then pressure flooded through Calen and Valerys's shared mind. It rippled through them like lightning unleashed from the void. With a surge of energy, Valerys kicked back his head before unleashing a column of roaring dragonfire down on top of the wounded wyrm. The creature hissed and shrieked as the flames consumed it. For a moment, a pang of guilt burst into Calen's mind as the creature wailed, but then Valerys's rage took over again. This creature had tried to harm his Draleid, had tried to harm those he travelled with, his family, and for that, it would die; it would burn in his fire.

Valerys's fire raged like a blazing inferno until the wyrm's shrieks faded to nothing, and even then, the flames poured forth from his jaws like a river unleashed.

It's gone. It's all right, it's gone.

Slowly, the pressure and the rage subsided from Calen's mind. With the energy seeping from his already tired body, he let his shoulders sag, his mind drifting back into itself. The air around him whipped up, crashing against his face as Valerys landed in front of him.

Concern flooded from Valerys's mind into his own as the dragon craned its neck down, nudging the side of Calen's head.

"It's all right. *I'm* all right," Calen said, reaching up and running his hand along the ridges of horns that framed Valerys's jaws.

Using Valerys's neck for leverage, Calen pulled himself to his feet and made his way over to where Vaeril knelt beside Tarmon in the snow. "How is he?"

Tarmon's face and arms were covered in cuts, and there was a deep gouge along his left leg.

"He will live," Vaeril said, running his fingers along the edge of the wound in Tarmon's leg. "It didn't cut any of the major blood vessels. I can heal him."

Erik stepped up beside Calen, blood dripping from the ends of his swords. "You've looked better," he said to Tarmon with a half-smile.

"I still look better than you," Tarmon replied, grunting as he lifted himself up to a seated position. "Though I could use some of that Drifaienin whiskey."

Calen knelt beside Vaeril. "Are you sure you're strong enough?"

"I am. I can get him on his feet at the least. Go check on the others."

Begrudgingly, Calen pulled himself to his feet, giving a slight nod to Tarmon as he did.

"Draleid."

Calen turned to see two figures standing in front of him, half obscured by the fading snowfall. But he didn't need to see their faces to know who they were – their short stature and their long beards gave them away. "Korik, Lopir, by the gods, I thought you were dead."

"We were close enough," Lopir said, stepping closer so that Calen could see his face. Blood seeped from an enormous gash that ran from his forehead to his upper lip, and his left eye was now just a knot of blood and torn flesh. "It's dead," the dwarf said when he saw the shocked expression on Calen's face. A twisted grin spread across Lopir's face. "I took its eye too." The dwarf held out his hand to show a gleaming yellow eye, dripping with blood, stringy bits of flesh dangling from its back. "An eye for an eye."

"Shit, Lopir, put that away!" The acidic taste of vomit hit the back of Calen's tongue once more.

The dwarf only laughed. "Humans are so squeamish. Do you not keep trophies?"

Lopir stopped as Korik threw him a disapproving look.

"My apologies, Draleid."

"I'm just glad you're all right," Calen said, resting his hand on Lopir's shoulder. "Go see if Vaeril or any of the others have bandages."

Calen's heart bled as he turned away from the dwarves and cast his eyes over the scene around him. As the snowfall finally began to abate, it only showed the depths of devastation the wyrms had wreaked.

Everywhere Calen looked, steam drifted languidly from mutilated corpses, and pools of blood melted the snow. *So many dead.* They had started out with nearly fifty, and now he counted no more than eleven. Calen trudged through the snow, scanning the faces of the survivors and the dead. He had been travelling with them all, yet he never even knew most of their names.

Calen knelt beside a body that lay prone in the snow, hesitating for a moment before turning it over. He turned away at the sight of the dead woman's mangled face, retching. He took a moment, taking a deep breath before turning back to look at the woman. Gently, he lay her back into the snow. "May Heraya take you in her arms."

Settling the tremble that had set into his legs, Calen pushed himself to his feet. He didn't think he would ever get used to death, no matter how much of it he saw. Growing up, he had always adored the stories of noble heroes going off to war and hearing of the incredible feats of heroism achieved by one man against all odds. Every time the bards told those stories, Calen had hung on every word they said. But now he knew there was a difference between hearing the stories and living them. When you heard the stories of war and heroes, you couldn't smell the death, the scent of crackling flesh, the stench of voided bowels. You couldn't see the utter devastation, taste the blood on your tongue, feel the fear and horror in your bones. Stories were beautiful. They were words that painted a canvas in your mind. But death could not be beautiful. He had come to that decision in Belduar, and it echoed again in his mind, here.

Chapter Twenty-Four

Things That Should Not Be

he smell of roasting boar drifted from the nearby cave as the meat crackled above the campfire. Calen pulled the warm scent into his nostrils. His stomach rumbled as he ran his hand along Valerys's neck, feeling the cool touch of the dragon's scales beneath his fingertips. He remembered the first time he touched those scales, his surprise at how soft they had felt. Valerys had seemed so vulnerable then. So small and fragile. His mind just a sensation in the back of Calen's mind. It was almost disconcerting to see how much he had grown. Even the time trapped in those tunnels had not slowed him. He was now easily larger than any horse Calen had seen, even the Varsundi horse that rode into The Glade three summers past – the Blackthorn, he thought it was called – and in time, he would be as large as the dragons that had razed Belduar to the ground. There would be no hiding him then; the Dragonguard would be able to find them wherever they went.

Valerys nuzzled his snout against Calen's arm, a feeling of comfort radiating from his mind. The dragon's pale lavender eyes drew level with Calen's before he arched his head forward and touched the flat of his head against Calen's forehead. Valerys's intention was clear.

"Draleid n'aldryr," Calen said, only loud enough to be considered a whisper. "Unira." *Always.*

A low rumble resonated from Valerys in acknowledgement.

Calen reached up and ran his hands along the ridges of horns that framed Valerys's jaw. "I'll ask Vaeril to take a look at your wounds after he has eaten. He is already tired from healing the others. Until then, get some rest."

Valerys puffed out air through his nostrils in a touch of defiance.

"Don't be such a baby. They're only small cuts." Calen held a smile on his face as he narrowed his eyes at Valerys. The dragon nudged Calen with his snout before nestling his head back on top of his forelimbs.

Even as he walked towards the cave, snow melting as it touched his skin, Calen could feel the sombre atmosphere that had settled over the camp like a dense fog. They had started out the journey with just under fifty souls. The wyrms had ravaged them. Were it not for Valerys, none of them might have survived at all.

Calen eyed Lopir sitting to the left of the fire beside Korik and Tarmon, absently fingering the mound of mottled flesh where his eye had been. He had been lucky.

A slight pang of guilt struck Calen as he looked out over the survivors. Most of the Drifaienin had not made it. Out of the eleven that were still left, the Drifaienin numbered only five. The guilt he felt was not about their deaths, though that was there too. It was guilt due to his relief that none of his friends had died in their places. It didn't feel right to place the lives of his own friends above the lives of the people who were helping them, but he did.

Calen sought out Alleron with his eyes and found him at the edge of the makeshift camp, leaning on top of his axe with the pommel buried in the snow and a thick coat of furs draped over his shoulders. Ignoring the hunger in his belly, Calen made his way over to the man, snow crunching under his feet with every step. They had gotten a brief reprieve from the snowfall, but the ground was still coated with a blanket of white, and the air still nipped at Calen's skin.

"All is well?" Alleron asked, without looking at Calen. The man kept his eyes fixed on the forest in front of him. Calen didn't think he would ever get over how bright it was at night here once the snowfall eased. It might have been something to do with the snow, but he wasn't sure. Rist would know. He always knew those sorts of things. *All three of us will find each other again, I promise you.*

"Aye," Calen replied, stepping up beside Alleron. "And you?"

"I'll live." The usual mirth that permeated Alleron's voice had vanished, replaced by a grim emptiness.

"I'm sorry for those you lost."

Alleron turned to Calen and stood to his full height. "Your apologies are not needed. Drifaien is a dangerous place, now more so than ever. Travelling these lands is perilous, yet those men and women would have made this journey at one time or another had you not shown up. I know the look in your eyes. You do not hold their deaths on your shoulders."

"I..."

"They died fighting. They died heroes' deaths. Don't take that away from them with your guilt. Let them celebrate in Achyron's halls."

Calen gave a nod. He wasn't sure he truly understood, but he didn't have to. Sometimes acceptance was all that mattered. "How have any of you survived with attacks like that? We barely did, and we had Valerys."

A look of genuine uncertainty painted Alleron's face. "I've never seen so many in one place. Like I said before, the wyrms usually hunt alone, and even then, they're hard to kill, but we manage. If they start attacking like this, in packs..." Alleron's shoulders dropped. "Truthfully, I don't know how my people will survive. But we will find a way."

Calen didn't know what to say, so he said nothing. Instead, he stood there beside Alleron, in silence, staring out into half-lit depths of the forest. It was Alleron who spoke. "What do you intend to do?"

"What do you mean?"

"When we get to Arisfall and you get on your ship." Alleron again turned to face Calen. The man's thick beard concealed most of his face, but there was a genuine curiosity in his eyes. "There is a war coming, Calen. The empire is using you as an excuse to increase their forces in the South. Reports come in every day of imperial ships landing at Gisa and

Falstide. By the time we arrive at Arisfall, the imperial mage will have already come and gone with his instructions to capture the Draleid, should he appear. Some of the High Lords will fall in line, but others will not. What do you think Castor Kai will do in Illyanara, or Syrene Linas of Arkalen? Do you think the Valtarans will lay down with a boot already on their neck?"

"I didn't mean to start this…"

Alleron sighed. "You didn't. It started centuries ago. But you will be a part of it, like it or not. So, what do you intend to do?"

Valerys rumbled in the back of Calen's mind, a bold defiance that thrummed through him. "We intend to fight."

"We?" Alleron raised an eyebrow. "Ah… I see," he said, his eyes falling on Valerys.

"And you?" Calen asked, keeping his eyes fixed on Alleron.

"Me?"

"Your father is High Lord of Drifaien. What will Drifaien do?"

Alleron let out a sigh, resting his back against the trunk of the tree. "My father is not the man he once was. In truth, I don't know what he will do. I can only be sure he will do whatever benefits him most. But I will fight. My people bleed for this land. I don't intend to let the empire take even more from us." Alleron pushed himself away from the trunk. "Go, eat some food. It will be a few days before we reach Kalingat and then another four days from there to Arisfall. With any luck, we won't see more wyrms." With that, Alleron hefted his axe up over his shoulder and set off on a slow walk around the camp's perimeter.

"There's that word again," Calen muttered. "Luck."

Almost as soon as Alleron started to walk away, Calen's stomach rumbled. It had been a while since he had eaten anything, and the smell of the boar meat hung heavy in the air.

Everyone was eating in silence as Calen walked into the cave and took a seat in the dirt between Vaeril and Alleron's lieutenant, Alwen.

"Just in time, Draleid," Alwen said, handing Calen a piece of half-stale bread and a cloth wrap stuffed with boar meat. "I saw the dwarves eyeing up the last of it." Alwen spoke just loud enough for Korik and Lopir to hear him. Calen found it difficult to tell if the man was joking or if he was trying to stir up trouble. Luckily, Lopir just threw Alwen a dirty look, and Korik ignored him. Calen didn't have the energy to deal with any of that. He nodded at Alwen as he took the bread and the meat, not wasting any time before he shovelled it into his mouth.

Calen couldn't help but look out at Valerys, curled up in the snow where he had left him. The dragon had flat out refused to come inside the cave. It was big enough to fit him comfortably, but that wasn't the issue. A deep wave of anxiety flooded through Valerys's mind at the thought of being inside anything that even remotely resembled the tunnels that ran under the mountains. What had happened still sat fresh in both of their minds. They had nearly brought the tunnel down on top of themselves and everyone else. In his panic, Valerys had lost control, and with that, so had Calen. That was how simple it was. If they lost control for even a moment, they could bring everything crashing down.

"How do you feel?" Vaeril asked Calen, breaking the silence that had sat comfortably in the air. The elf's shoulder-length blonde hair shimmered in the glow of the firelight as he stared absently at the ground.

"I'm all right. Just a few scratches. Could have been worse. How about you?"

"I don't mean physically." Vaeril lifted his head slightly. He shifted his gaze from the hard dirt of the cave floor to the ever-flickering flames of the fire. "You should have died out there."

A knot twisted in Calen's stomach. "What are you talking about?"

Vaeril turned to match Calen's stare. "You should not have been able to draw so heavily from the Spark. First in Belduar, now here. It might be because of your bond with Valerys. I have never seen someone be able to draw so heavily, so quickly. Just… be careful."

Calen didn't know either. He had felt the drain pulling his soul from his body both times, just as he had before. Yet each time, he felt stronger. Even then, as he sat by the fire, he felt stronger than he had before the wyrms attacked. His knees still felt weak, and a slight burn still worked its way through his spine, but he felt stronger. Was he truly stronger? Or was that simply the Spark's way of tempting him to take more? Urging him to dig deeper. "I will be."

Vaeril gave a slow nod, as though he only half-believed Calen. "Once we return to the Lodhar Mountains, perhaps Aeson Virandr will know more. I cannot keep you safe from the things I do not know."

Calen gave Vaeril a weak smile before standing up and grabbing his sleeping sack from the ground. "Wake me when we are ready to leave. I'm going to sleep with Valerys."

He could see the hesitation on Vaeril's face, but the elf didn't argue. "It will be done, Draleid."

Calen nodded his thanks at Vaeril before making his way out of the cave. The elf still hadn't truly taken to calling Calen by his name, and it seemed he specifically used the title 'Draleid' whenever he disagreed with Calen's choices.

Calen shook his head and sighed as he tossed his sleeping sack on the ground beside Valerys, who lifted his head slightly at Calen's arrival. Of all the problems in the world, Vaeril's word choice was among the smallest. First, he had to think about what exactly they were going to do once they reached Arisfall.

Calen pulled on threads of Fire, using them to clear the snow beside Valerys. In its place, he unfurled his sleeping sack. It was of Drifaienin design, made to withstand the cold and the harsh conditions. It was like two blanket rolls stitched together at the sides and lined with sheep's wool on the inside, while the outside was covered in worn leather. Most importantly, it made for a warm place to sleep, and sleep was something he desperately needed.

As Calen shuffled himself into the wool-lined sleeping sack, Valerys extended his wing, acting as a canopy in case of snowfall.

Thank you.

A low rumble of acknowledgement touched the back of Calen's mind and a comforting warmth filled him. There, with Valerys watching over him and the heat of the dragon's body banishing the chill in Calen's bones, he let himself drift off into the world of dreams.

Chapter Twenty-Five

The Shadow of War

rden stood at Brother-Captain Kallinvar's side as each of the nine captains surrounded the war table, the Grandmaster at their head. They had been there for hours.

"With each passing day the Urak attacks grow in number," one of the captains, Sister-Captain Valeian, leader of The Fourth, said. She was tall for a woman, closing on six feet. Her black hair was tied at the back of her head, and her sharp eyes were like those of a hawk. "We need to mobilise the full knighthood."

"Aye," Brother-Captain Armites of The Sixth called out. A powerful man with deep-set eyes, a thick beard, and long, matted hair. "We don't have time to play generals. The Shadow is not waiting, and neither can we."

"I understand your concerns, Valeian, Armites. But we cannot expose ourselves completely when we do not yet know the extent of what we fight." Grandmaster Verathin stood at the head of the table, his arms folded across his chest. As always, his voice commanded attention in the chamber, and his presence consumed the room. "We need to understand what the Shadow is doing. We must see the moves The Traitor is making, otherwise we will fall into his trap."

"But how long must we wait?" Brother-Captain Illarin asked, a little too curtly, in Arden's opinion. Though, if any had earned the right to speak out of turn, it was Brother-Captain Illarin. He was one of the seventeen knights who survived the battle of Ilnaen – the only survivor of The Seventh. Arden had heard tales of how he had taken on ten Bloodmarked single-handedly. Whether it was true or not, Arden could well believe it. He had watched Illarin and Kallinvar spar on five occasions, Illarin taking two victories, Kallinvar taking three. Until then, Arden had never seen another knight best Kallinvar. "You were there, Verathin. You felt our brothers and sisters die, as I did. Must we wait until the Shadow has once again reached that strength? Must we continue to stand idly by?"

"Illarin, you overstep!" Kallinvar growled, leaning over the war table, his eyes fixed on Brother-Captain Illarin.

But Illarin did not yield. "Do I, Kallinvar? Will we not see the Blood Moon in less than a year? What do you propose we do then?"

The chamber broke out into a cacophony of arguing. Many of the captains agreed with Grandmaster Verathin, but almost half saw the merits of what Illarin said. Even Arden saw truth in it. They could not wait like lambs to the slaughter, yet at the same time, running unknowingly into the darkness was the surest way to seal their fate.

Arden tuned out the arguing, instead focusing on the war table. It had been carved from solid stone aeons ago by the priests. Each river and lake, every hill and every mountain had been carved by hand. Since its first carving, adjustments had been made by commissioned Craftsmages as the land shifted, or so the texts said. According to those ancient texts, Epheria had once looked very different. It was said that at the height of The Order, rivers, lakes, and even mountains had been formed at the will of the mages. It was even said that the Sea of Stone itself had been forged by the mages' magic – the Spark.

On the table, all the known Lorian armies were marked by black lion carvings, with small white counters beside each carving to indicate the relative size of troops in their thousands. The same was done for each Southern army, though they were far fewer, and most remained at their capitals. Any knights currently outside the temple were marked with green counters. Where more than one knight travelled together, the counters were stacked. Black counters were placed wherever a major attack had occurred, while red counters were placed wherever a major attack had occurred and the knights had not arrived in time. There were a lot more red counters than black, and it had been days since they had received their last report.

"What do you think, Brother Arden?"

Grand Master Verathin's voice caught Arden so off guard that it took him a moment to realise that it had not simply been a figment of his imagination. It was accepted that each captain might bring a single member of their chapter to war meetings for counsel, but in the times Arden had accompanied Brother-Captain Kallinvar, he did not remember ever seeing any other captain exercise that right. Nor did he remember Brother-Captain Kallinvar ever asking him to speak. It was more an old tradition that only Brother-Captain Kallinvar seemed to adhere to and the other captains tolerated. Arden never truly expected to be addressed.

Arden looked up from the table to see each of the nine captains staring at him, some with expectant faces but most with looks of disinterest or outright irritation. None of them had brought a member of their chapter as counsel, and they clearly didn't see the value in whatever it was Arden might have to say.

Arden swallowed, trying to provide moisture to his rapidly drying throat. He examined the war table once more, scanning it from top to bottom. "There is merit in both approaches," he said, to mumbles of annoyance. "But neither is the correct one."

The mumbles turned to shouting within seconds.

"He is naught but a child, Kallinvar!" one of the captains called. "He bears the Sigil no more than two years."

"Aye," answered another in a lilted Drifaienin accent. Arden knew her: Sister-Captain Olyria. She stood no more than five and a half feet, but she was a fierce woman with a wit as sharp as her blade. For all that though, she was measured in her speech, and he knew her as a friend to Kallinvar. "I'm sorry, Brother Arden, but you do not yet know war."

"Let him speak." A chorus of 'Grandmaster' rang through the chamber as Grandmaster Verathin's voice boomed. The Grandmaster raised his hands to quieten the din before turning towards Arden. "Go ahead, Brother Knight."

Arden hesitated for a moment, looking to Brother-Captain Kallinvar, who gave him a nod. "We cannot overextend ourselves too quickly. Grandmaster Verathin is the only one who can summon the Rift, so we cannot rely on it for mobility. With each passing day, we place more and more red counters on the table because we simply cannot react fast enough. If we send all our knights into the field, then we lose our greatest advantage – our mobility. With the Rift, we can react immediately to the ever-changing landscape, cutting off the Shadow wherever it rears its head."

A slight rumble sounded through the gathered captains, some agreeing, some not. Arden ignored it, cleared his throat, and carried on. "Reports grow more frequent by the day, and with each report we are hearing of greater and greater numbers of Bloodspawn. Bloodmarked and Shamans are becoming commonplace. It will get to a point where we simply cannot hold back the tide alone, no matter what approach we take…" Arden let his words hang in the air as he glanced at Brother-Captain Kallinvar. The look on his captain's face told Arden that Kallinvar knew what Arden was about to say next. They had talked about it many a time, and Brother-Captain Kallinvar had argued with him every time. But surely he wanted Arden to say it now. He had called Arden to the table, after all. "We need to find allies. We need to reach out."

That was all it took for the chamber to break out in screaming and shouting, the captains jumping down one another's throats.

"We are warriors of Achyron," one of the captains called out. "We fight the Shadow. We do not involve ourselves in the politics of the continent."

"They are one and the same," Arden answered, his voice low and his hands trembling. "Just as it was at The Fall. The Shadow does not shy away from twisting the minds of men. It uses our absence to its advantage. We need to—"

"You know nothing of The Fall," one of the captains cried.

"The child speaks of what he does not understand!"

"Silence!" Once again, Grandmaster Verathin's voice boomed through the chamber, bringing all argument to an immediate standstill. A tense few moments passed as the din receded to nothing more than shuffling feet and hushed whispers. Grandmaster Verathin let out an irritated sigh before turning his gaze to Arden. "Brother Arden, I thank you for your input. You have given us much food for thought. Now, would you please leave me with the captains? There are some things that must be discussed."

"Yes, Grandmaster," Arden said through clenched teeth, before giving a slight bow at the waist. "Thank you for allowing my presence."

"Your presence is always welcome, Brother Knight."

Arden caught Brother-Captain Kallinvar's eye before turning. The man's mouth was an almost unreadable thin line, and his eyes were cold. He gave a slight nod, which Arden returned before making his exit from the chamber.

Arden was not five steps from the table when the arguing, once again, broke out. He kept walking. His frustrations would be better left to the sparring chamber.

Arden grimaced as Lyrin caught him with an uppercut, sending him stumbling backwards. His frustration from the war chamber was still yet to subside, and he always found unarmed sparring was a great way to burn away the anger. Rolling his head side to side, he lunged towards Lyrin, only shifting direction at the last minute. Lyrin didn't anticipate the shift, and his kick found nothing but air. Pushing on the ball of his foot, Arden swept in with an elbow, catching Lyrin square on the jaw. In the same motion, he pulled his knee up to his chest and caught Lyrin in the side with the flat of his foot.

Lyrin staggered backward from the force of the kick, but just about managed to keep his footing. "What's gotten under your skin?" his friend asked, cracking his jaw then clearing the distance between him and Arden in a single stride. A swift exchange followed before Lyrin hit Arden in the chin and the nose with two left jabs.

"Nothing," Arden replied, spitting blood onto the sand of the sparring pit. Bringing himself low, he charged at Lyrin, ducking under a swinging left leg. Just as Lyrin's foot landed, Arden lunged, catching Lyrin with a spear tackle before lifting him into the air and slamming him back down into the sand. Before Arden could even contemplate following up his tackle, a pair of legs wrapped around his waist, and two sharp bursts of pain hit him in the side. Sand filled the air as he was flipped onto the flat of his back after Lyrin somehow managed to reverse him.

"Don't..." Lyrin said, panting heavily and catching Arden with a quick jab to the face, "lie"—Arden pulled his hands up to protect his face while Lyrin switched to jabbing his ribs—"to me."

Arden kept his guard up, Lyrin raining down punches on top of him. He definitely had a weight advantage on Lyrin, but his friend's mind was sharp as a blade when it came to close quarters brawling. He also had Arden beaten for speed. *Be patient.*

Arden let the punches fall, waiting for an opening. Then, as if by chance, he saw one. Lyrin paused, only for a fraction of a second to take a half-breath, but that was all the time Arden needed. Pushing with everything he had, Arden head-butted Lyrin square on the chin. It wasn't the perfect place to catch someone with a head butt, but it was enough to knock some stars into Lyrin's head.

With Lyrin's guard down, Arden hit him in the cheek with a hook, then threw him to the ground. Leaping to his feet, Arden kicked Lyrin onto the flat of his back, then pressed his foot against Lyrin's chest. "Submit?"

"You fughin ashhole," Lyrin spat, his voice muffled.

Arden laughed, reaching his hand down to his friend. Lyrin took it, pulling himself to his feet.

"Yourh shtill an ashhole." Lyrin bent over double, spitting blood and saliva into the sand. "Buh guh figh."

Arden snatched his waterskin up from the side of the sparring pit, took a long swig, then tossed it to Lyrin, laughing as he did. The sparring did its job. His body ached and groaned, and he would wake up with a headache and more than a few new bruises in the morning, but the frustration had leached from his bones. "Drink some of that, and for the love of the gods, stop talking. You're hard enough to put up with when you don't have a swollen tongue."

"Vehy fuhnny."

Arden smiled as he put his hands behind his head and stretched out his back. Sweat dripped down his chest and back, shimmering as it passed over the Sigil fused with his chest. The Sigil that had given him a second chance.

"Arden."

Arden let out a deep sigh at the sound of Brother-Captain Kallinvar's voice. He would follow his captain to the void and back, but right now, he wasn't in the mood for a lecture on when best to speak and when not to, which was a lecture he knew was coming. He had clearly misread the situation in the war room.

A thrum rippled through Arden's Sigil as a blade of bright green light burst from Brother-Captain Kallinvar's hand.

Arden nodded at his captain. He did not need to speak. Taking a deep breath, he called to his Sigil. The power of the Spirit of Achyron burned through him in response. He could feel it in every fibre of who he was. It was with that power that he summoned his Soulblade. Within moments, the tendrils of green light that burst from his hand had bound together to forge a blade of shimmering green light. Its shape was identical in every visible way to the sword Arden usually wore at his hip. Arden's Soulblade was an extension of who he was. It was a manifestation of the bond he had made to the warrior god.

Releasing the breath he had been holding, Arden nodded, and the two knights charged at each other. They traded blows back and forth for a while, their Soulblades colliding in flashes of green light. It was more a formality than anything else. At this stage, they knew each other's fighting styles as well as they knew their own. It did not take long for the formalities to end.

Kallinvar attacked with lightning speed, twisting and turning around Arden's counterstrikes as if he knew where each one would land before

Arden had even thrown it. Frustration rekindled in Arden's mind, but it only had a moment to dwell there before he overstepped and Kallinvar caught him with a kick to the side of the knee. By the time Arden's knees hit the sand, the green glow of Kallinvar's Soulblade shimmered beside his head.

"Speak."

Arden clenched his jaw and kept his gaze fixed on the sand. He knew he was being stubborn, but his own stubbornness refused to let him admit it.

"Arden, I said speak." Kallinvar's voice held no frustration. It was calm and level, which only serve to irritate Arden even further.

"Why did you let me speak, Brother-Captain?" Arden fixed his head where it was, refusing to raise his chin. His words were met with silence. "You knew what I was going to say. Why did you let me speak?"

"Because it needed to be said."

Ignoring the Soulblade that shimmered beside his head, Arden pulled himself to his feet, keeping his eyes level with Kallinvar's. He didn't think he had ever looked at his Brother-Captain that way before – eye to eye, with anger. "So, you agree with me?"

"I do," Kallinvar replied, his Soulblade dissipating from his grasp.

Suddenly Arden didn't know what to say. He hadn't expected Kallinvar to back down so easily, and he most certainly hadn't expected Kallinvar to say he agreed. He released his Soulblade but kept his eyes fixed on Kallinvar's.

"Come." Kallinvar turned, gesturing for Arden and Lyrin to follow him.

"I feel like I've missed something," Lyrin said to Arden, spitting out another mouthful of blood, the swelling in his tongue clearly going down.

Arden and Lyrin followed Kallinvar from the chamber and through the corridors of the temple of Achyron. Unlike many great structures across Epheria, the temple was not adorned with gold or draped in tapestries and banners of fine silks and linens. No elaborate carpets ran the lengths of its halls, and no oil paintings decorated its walls. But what it lacked in indulgent beauty, it made up for in sheer awe. The corridors were so wide an army could walk forty abreast, and the sweeping ceilings rose for hundreds of feet. With each step Arden, Lyrin, and Kallinvar took, echoes resounded against the grey stone walls, only serving to reinforce one thing: they were nothing but specks of paint on a canvas for the gods.

As they walked, they passed the war room, the kitchens, the sleeping quarters, and the library, taking a left at the watcher's chamber. It did not take Arden long to realise Kallinvar was taking them out to Ardholm. It had been a while since Arden had visited the village. In his first year with the knighthood, he had spent a lot of time there. It felt nice to be around regular people. It felt like home. But as his responsibilities grew, he visited less and less.

Kallinvar stopped before the gargantuan wooden doors that marked the entrance to the temple. The doors rose almost as high as the ceilings, hundreds of feet, arching together at their highest point. According to the ancient texts, they had been built from the wood of the old trees of Lunwain, the first forest sung into existence by the Jotnar.

"You are both young," Kallinvar said, making his way over to where a small wicket gate was set into the great doors to allow easier access to both the temple and Ardholm. "Not simply in terms of how long you have borne the Sigil, but in the summers you have spent in the living world. That youth can bring a naivety with it. Yes, I agree with you, Arden, and so does the Grandmaster. The knighthood needs to look outside itself. What has always been done is not always what should be done."

A sliver of light streamed through the gap in the wicket gate as Kallinvar pushed it open and stepped through. Following Kallinvar, Arden stepped out onto the stone staircase that descended from the temple, bringing his hand up to his eyes to block out the harsh sun that sat overhead in the pale blue sky. His eyes adjusting, he smiled, looking down over the village of Ardholm.

The village itself was situated at the foot of the temple, built around a horseshoe shaped cliff nestled into the side of the mountain that rose at its back. How high up they were, Arden didn't know, but he knew that if he looked over the edge, he would see nothing but cloud.

Twenty-foot-high walls lined the cliff edge the entire way around the horseshoe, joining back into the mountain at either end. A gate was set into the wall on the eastern edge where it met the mountain, providing passage out to an enormous plateau that rose another forty or fifty feet. There was no view in the known world more beautiful than sitting on the edge of that plateau at sunset.

"Do you know the story of Ardholm?" Kallinvar asked as he moved down the steps towards the village.

Arden had heard stories from the elders of the village, but they had always seemed to change depending on who was telling them. "The village was built at the founding of the knighthood, was it not? The villagers are descendants of those who constructed the temple."

"Very good, Brother Arden." Kallinvar stopped at the bottom of the steps. He nodded towards the villagers who passed him, raising their fists to their foreheads, a mark of respect. "But that is not the entire story."

Arden smiled as three children passed him and raised their fists to their forehead. He imitated the gesture, earning wide-eyed looks of amazement as the kids charged off down the street.

Turning, he tilted his head back, looking up at the statues that framed the entrance to the temple. The two statues stood hundreds of feet tall, rising slightly higher than the great doors themselves. They were carved to depict knights of Achyron in their Sentinel armour, their Soulblades held with two hands, the tips resting at their feet. The first time Arden had laid eyes on the statues that watched over the village of Ardholm, he had simply stood there, awestruck by their sheer size and scale.

"It is true," Kallinvar continued. "The village was initially founded by those who constructed the temple. They made the sacrifice of not leaving, so as to never reveal the temple's location. But that is not where the story ends. Over two and a half thousand years ago, centuries after the temple was built, the Knights of Achyron fought a great horde of Bloodspawn in what was then known as the province of Lurïnel. After the battle, survivors from a nearby village asked the Grandmaster for refuge. In his compassion, seeing the devastation they had suffered, he acquiesced."

Gesturing for Arden and Lyrin to follow, Kallinvar set off eastward through the village, towards the plateau. As they walked, villagers made a point of coming out of their homes to pay their respects, each of them raising their fists.

The priests and the Watchers swelled their ranks from the population of Ardholm, as did the porters, cooks, and chambermaids who served in the temple. But besides that, Arden had never really thought much of where the villagers of Ardholm had come from. To him, they were just… *there.*

"What's wrong with that?" Lyrin said, ruffling the hair of a small, rosy-cheeked girl who passed by. "They are happy here."

"Are they?" Kallinvar's mouth turned into a half-frown, twisting at the edges. "They can never leave, Lyrin. Now, they do not know any different; they have been here for thousands of years, and even still, not all are satisfied by simply serving the will of Achyron."

Reaching the gate set into the eastern edge of the wall, Kallinvar led Lyrin and Arden through the giant archway and up towards the great plateau.

"No. They were not happy. At first, of course, they were thankful for the refuge. But after a while, when it became clear none of them would ever be allowed to leave, everything changed. Of course, they had been told the terms before they were brought here, but in their desperation, they had not taken them seriously. You will not read of it in any of the books in the library, but in the year five-twenty-one, After Doom, a rebellion broke out in Ardholm."

"What?" Arden stopped in his tracks, a shiver running through his body. "That's not true. Somebody would have recorded it somewhere."

"It is true, brother. Books are not a complete history. They are only the history people chose to record." Kallinvar rested his hand on Arden's shoulder, and Arden could see a melancholy in his eyes. Giving Arden a weak smile, Kallinvar continued towards the plateau. "Many innocent people died. It is one of the darkest days in the history of the knighthood, and one that has been scrubbed from all records. Ever since, we have kept to ourselves and refused to meddle in the affairs of the common people. Our task has been to drive back the Shadow, nothing else."

"But… how?" From his vantage point on the plateau, Arden looked down over the village, a knot in his stomach.

"Do you see now why the other captains might be hesitant to reach out? But despite their hesitation, if we do not build alliances with others who will fight the Shadow, then we will be pulled apart and shattered, just as we were at the fall of The Order at Ilnaen. We came too late that day, refusing to join the fold until we could feel the Taint of blood magic radiating from the city. We should have been there sooner. Our failure was in not seeing the binding of things, and it still is. It is not enough to simply hold up the sky as it falls, when we always knew it was going to collapse. We need to bring together those who would stand by our side."

Arden turned, fixing his stare on Kallinvar. "If you agreed with me, then why have you always argued with me? What did you not say this yourself in the chamber?"

Kallinvar shrugged. "I argued with you to test your conviction in the same way you might repeatedly heat a blade and temper it to bring out its true strength. As for why I did not speak up? Politics."

"Politics?" Arden scoffed, feeling an anger rise in his belly. "Politics has no place in this temple. We are the Knights of Achyron!"

Kallinvar laughed, his mouth twisting into a condescending smile that only served to further stoke Arden's fire.

"You mock me?"

Kallinvar's demeanour changed in an instant, the laughter vanishing from his face. "Remember who it is you speak to, Brother Knight. We are familiar, but I am still your Brother-Captain."

The fire in Arden's belly was quickly replaced with a sinking feeling. He had forgotten his place. "I am sorry, Brother-Captain."

"It is all right." Kallinvar sighed, a frown setting itself on his face. "I do not mock you. I simply admire your idealism. It is a trait that I once held, though sadly, the centuries have stripped it from me. Politics exists everywhere. That holds true in one way or another in every facet of life within our temple and beyond. Sometimes it is as subtle as who speaks first, sometimes it is as complex as what you witnessed today."

Arden looked over at Lyrin, who didn't speak but appeared to be listening as closely as he could. If there was one of them who understood politics and the way to talk to people, it was Lyrin.

"Do you think," Kallinvar continued, "that just because the men and women in that room are a part of the knighthood they do not still hold their own ambitions, their own pride, their own vanity?"

Arden started to speak, but Kallinvar beat him to it.

"Do you not hold your own ambitions, your own pride, your own vanity?"

"I do not," Arden replied. "I swore the oath to serve Achyron, to forget everything that held me to the man I once was."

"Then why the anger? Why were you here in the sparring pit with Lyrin? I watched you. You did not fight with your head, you fought like someone who was angry, frustrated."

"I was angry!" Arden yelled, losing control of his temper.

An awkward silence hung in the air as Kallinvar held Arden's gaze. Arden held his breath as he expected a chastisement that never came.

"Why were you angry?"

"Because I have given my life to this knighthood. To Achyron. Just as they have, and yet they treat me as though I am a child."

"Then you see."

Arden thought about arguing, but then it finally sank in. He let out a sigh and nodded his head. "I do. You couldn't suggest it because then, when Grandmaster Verathin supported you, it would harm the others' pride, just as their dismissal harmed mine. But if I planted the seed, then others might come to it eventually, as if it were their own idea."

A smile crept across Kallinvar's face as he grasped Arden's shoulder. "There is not a soul in this world who does not feel the push and pull of pride. Damage it, and you can make an enemy for life. Keep it intact, and you may find allies in the strangest of places."

"Can someone please explain what we are talking about? I think I understand what is going on here, but I also feel like I'm missing something."

Arden laughed, shaking his head – partly at Lyrin and partly at his own ignorance. "It's nothing, Lyrin, I was just being pig-headed."

"What's new?" Lyrin said with a shrug, pouting.

Arden threw a glare at his friend. "So, what do we do now?" he said, turning to Kallinvar.

"Well, firstly, we will wait and let the seed take hold. There are others who think along the same lines. If a Brother Knight not more than two years with the Sigil has the courage to challenge tradition, then maybe they too will find it within themselves. Secondly, there is a task that must be seen to."

"Whatever Achyron requires." Arden straightened his back, throwing a sideways glance at Lyrin.

"Whatever Achyron requires," Lyrin chorused, with slightly less enthusiasm.

"Good. Now that is settled. Grandmaster Verathin has sensed a convergence of the Taint along the base of Wolfpine Ridge. I will be taking you both, along with Ildris."

Arden nodded. "When do we leave?"

"As soon as we are finished here.

Chapter Twenty-Six

Hope

The heat of the water almost scalded Dann's feet as he lowered himself into the large brass tub. He didn't care; the relief it gave his joints and muscles far outweighed the pain it caused. All he wanted was to remove the thick layer of dirt and dust that had crusted onto his skin. Five days. Not four days. Five. That's how long it had taken to get back to Durakdur. Though, he couldn't entirely blame Nimara; were it not for the dwarf's quick thinking in the tunnels, those stone spiders would have eaten them for breakfast. Still, it was a mite quicker than it had been to find that wrecked Wind Runner in the first place.

If it were up to Dann, he would have soaked in that bath until the water turned cold, then he would have emptied it and filled it right back up. It was not up to him, though. Aeson made it clear he would give them all two hours, and then he would send for them. It's not like Dann had a right to complain. He couldn't right well argue that they all should have stayed to keep searching the tunnels and then tell them he couldn't meet to arrange the plan forward because he was busy refilling his bath. He laughed to himself at the idea of it and at how Aeson's and Therin's faces would look.

Absently, Dann fingered the scarred flesh that stretched up along his collarbone and over his left shoulder. He had told Calen, and Therin for that matter, that he had kept it to impress women, and honestly, that was a factor. But it was also a reminder. A reminder of how close he had come. A reminder of what they faced. He pondered it as he traced his finger over the mess of twisted skin. He turned his lip upwards and shrugged. "It will definitely impress the women, though."

Once the water had turned cold, Dann reluctantly lifted himself out of the tub, flinching as his blistered feet touched the cold stone. After drying himself, he tied the drawstring on his trousers and pulled on the fresh linen shirt that sat on the chair opposite the tub. If there was one thing he would never tire of in this place, it was the never-ending supply of fresh clothes.

It was not long before he heard a short knock on the door to his chambers. Well, at least he thought of them as *his*. It's where they had put him before the battle of Belduar – or the *second* battle of Belduar, whatever they called it. Nobody had come to remove him, so he figured the chambers were his.

He opened the door to find a young boy staring back at him, no more than sixteen summers, wide-eyed and golden-haired, with a firm jaw and a surprisingly strong chin. Dann recognised him as the porter who had shown Calen around in Belduar. He wore a tunic in the purple of Belduar with a yellow trim and a high collar; it looked a little big on the boy's slight frame, as though it had not been made expressly for him. Dann almost stumbled backward when the porter bowed to him.

"King Daymon summons you, m'lord. I am to take you to his meeting chamber at once."

Lord? I think I could get used to that. "At once, he says?"

The boy nodded, not noting Dann's sarcasm.

"Conal, isn't it?"

"Yes, m'lord. Conal Braker."

"Good to meet you properly, Conal. My name is Dann Pimm, and I'm ready to go when you are."

The knock on Aeson's door had come sooner than he had expected. Dropping the razor into the clay bowl that sat beside the tub, he splashed some water on his face and patted it dry with a cloth. He threw his shirt over his shoulders as he made his way to the door.

"I came as soon as I received your message."

Aeson was a little surprised to see Dahlen at the door. He had not expected to see him until they met Daymon to discuss everything, but it was a welcome surprise. He reached forward, pulling his son into a tight embrace.

"It's good to see you, son."

Dahlen was silent for a moment, but then Aeson felt him lean into the embrace. "It's good to see you, too. You didn't find them, then…"

"We didn't." Aeson couldn't hide the disappointment in his voice, as much as he tried. "But we are not stopping. We *will* find them. We found the wreckage of their Wind Runner – they weren't among the dead, thank Heraya. I'm going to reach out to the Wind Runners Guild. Now that everything has calmed down here, they might be able to spare someone. We head out again in the morning once we have gathered supplies." Aeson had prepared himself for some sort of reaction from Dahlen. A request to join them, but none came. "Come in," he said, stepping aside to let Dahlen into his chambers. The room was relatively small, comprising only a bed, two chairs, a desk, and very little else, though it did have its own washroom at the back. "How goes everything here?"

Dahlen dropped himself into one of the chairs by the desk. "There have been no more attempts on Daymon's life, but there is definitely something going on here. Something more than is plain to see. Ihvon and I have been looking into it."

"Just be careful, son." Aeson had known Ihvon long enough to know the man didn't shy away from trouble. Ihvon knew court politics, and he knew how to talk his way around most situations, but he also put himself in more danger than was ever necessary. And his history with the dwarves was worrisome, to say the least.

"What do you mean?" A frown sat on Dahlen's face as he pulled himself upright in his seat.

Aeson could tell by the stubborn look in Dahlen's eyes that he was going to have to be very careful with his words. "Ihvon is a good friend and an even better man. There are few people I would prefer at my side in times like these."

"But?"

Aeson sighed, running his fingers along his scalp. "But when it comes to the dwarves, he can't always see straight. His loss clouds his judgement."

"It's Daymon who can't see straight. All he sees is danger around every corner. His people are left wasting away while he—"

"Dahlen, that is a king you are talking about. Hold your tongue." Aeson let out a short sigh, pressing his fingers into his freshly shaved face.

Aeson could see the anger rising in Dahlen's face. Ever since Dahlen was a child, every time he got angry, his ears would turn red, and he would clench his fists at his sides – just as he was doing then. "What does it matter if Daymon is a king? Are kings not held responsible for their actions?"

"That's not what I'm trying to say, Dahlen."

"Then what *are* you trying to say? Because it sounds to me like you either don't trust my judgement, or you are telling me to put someone's title before their honour."

"Just listen to me!" Aeson roared, unable to hold his temper. Almost as soon as the words left his mouth, Aeson wanted to drag them back. He always tried to keep himself level, which was difficult enough with the gaping wound in his soul where Lyara should have been. But Dahlen had always known how to pull the right chords to provoke a reaction. "I'm sorry," Aeson said, bringing his voice down near a whisper. "Ihvon's history with the dwarves is not a friendly one, no matter how he acts on the outside. I'm just asking you to be careful, please."

Waiting for Aeson to finish, Dahlen rose to his feet, his jaw clenched. "I trust him. I just wish you would trust me. I will see you in the meeting chamber."

"Dahlen. Dahlen, please," Aeson called after Dahlen as he stormed out of the room. "Gods dammit!" Aeson slammed the door shut, sighing as he rested his elbows and head against the hard wood. "Naia, things would be a lot easier if you were here. You always knew what to say…"

Dahlen, Ihvon, and Daymon were already there when Aeson entered the king's meeting chamber, as were Dann, Therin, and the two elves, Alea and Lyrei. The dwarves had certainly not skimped when it had come to providing Daymon with whatever he needed. The meeting chamber alone was three times the size of Aeson's bedchambers, and the decoration was far more lavish. A rail of gold skirted the walls on both the top and the bottom, busts of old dwarven rulers stood on pedestals along the far wall, and large ornate lanterns of winding crystal filled with bunches of the luminescent blue flower hung from the ceilings. Two couches sat facing each other with a matching quartet of armchairs at either end, each made of the finest quality Arkalen leather. They must have paid a pretty penny for that; the Arkalen were not known to drive an easy bargain.

"That is all of us, then," Daymon announced as Aeson stepped into the room. "Please, please, take a seat. Would you like anything? Food, water, ale?"

"I'm all right, thank you, Your Majesty." Aeson took a seat in the empty leather armchair closest to the door, Dann occupying the one beside him. "Let's get started."

They sat for three or four hours, going back and forth over everything that had happened in the past few weeks. The situation in the Freehold was worse than Aeson had anticipated, and as much as he hated to admit it, Dahlen was right. Daymon was not seeing straight. The boy seemed more concerned about more potential assassination attempts and about trying to retake Belduar than he did the plight of his people. From what Aeson could gather, the Belduaran refugees had been split up and spread across several camps in each of the four kingdoms of the Freehold, and most of them were not living like their king. There was not much Aeson could do, but he would try and broach it with Daymon once they had found Erik and Calen.

"I will talk to the Wind Runners Guild once we are finished here," Ihvon said, stroking his long beard. "You wish to leave in the morning? All right. I will see to it that supplies are arranged. We should be able to muster enough for two weeks, but after that we won't have the resources to send you down there again, Aeson. We simply don't have them. I wish there was more we could do, old friend."

"Thank you, Ihvon. I understand." Aeson nodded absently, pursing his lips. He had known that already. The Belduarans were stretched thin as it was, and supporting a kingdom's worth of people while you yourself were a refugee was not a task Aeson envied. If they were not successful on this trip, he would have to plead with the dwarves. Nimara and the others who had accompanied them to the tunnels were evidence enough that the dwarven people still held the Draleid in high regard.

"What will you do if you cannot find them within the tunnels?" Daymon asked, producing a crystal flask filled with a brown liquid from behind his heavy wooden desk. As soon as the king removed the plug from the flask, the scent hit Aeson's nose: Drifaienin whiskey. There was always the chance it had been given to him as a gift, but this far from Drifaien, buried beneath a mountain, it was unlikely. The only place Drifaienin whiskey was cheap was in Drifaien. He had once seen an old widower trade three cows for a single bottle. He would have to keep an eye on his old friend's son. Times like these could make a shadow of even the greatest men, and someone as young as Daymon needed guidance; twenty summers was not enough to carry the weight of a kingdom on his shoulders.

Were dwarves not involved, he would have believed Ihvon to be the ideal person to provide that guidance. But when Alyana and Khris were killed, Ihvon's judgement was forever clouded. Aeson knew Ihvon blamed the dwarves for leaving them behind. But the dwarves had no choice. They couldn't have gone back for them; if they had, they all would have died. Ihvon was only alive *because* of the dwarves, but the man didn't see it that way, and in truth Aeson understood him. Had he been in Ihvon's place, had it been Naia, Erik, and Dahlen instead of Alyana and Khris, he would have felt the same way Ihvon did.

"Perhaps," said a wispy voice, "I can help."

Aeson reached out to the Spark, but it did not respond. It hovered just out of reach, as it had many times since Lyara's death. He leapt to his feet, ripping his swords from their scabbards, swivelling to face whomever the voice belonged to. The others around him did the same, though not all had brought their weapons.

"Who goes there?" Ihvon yelled, not the slightest sign of a quiver in his voice. "And how did you get past the guards?"

What stepped out of the shadows at the edge of the room took Aeson by surprise. It stood like a man, just over six and a half feet tall, with long, willowy limbs. But it did not look like a man. Its body was covered head to toe in a harsh, grey fur. Its feet were more like claws, while even its fingernails looked as hard as steel. Only its face seemed relatively human, and even at that, its eyes shimmered golden – like Alea and Lyrei's. Aeson had met its kind before, although that had been a long time ago. This was an Angan. *Shapeshifter.*

"Baldon, may the spirits of the gods guide your light," Therin said, ignoring the shocked faces of everyone around him. Of course, the elf knew what was going on. Aeson wasn't sure he had ever seen Therin any other way. "You received my message through Asius, then?"

"We did, and clan Fenryr thanks you, Silver Fang. Asius sent me to tell you that we have found the son of the Chainbreaker. Though our people weep for the death of the Chainbreaker himself. How did he die?"

Therin stepped towards the Angan, a deep sadness etched into his face. "Not in the way he should have, Baldon. At the tip of an Inquisitor's blade, defending his son."

"May the spirits curse the man who held the blade." A deep growl crept into the Angan's voice when he spoke. More animal than anything else.

"He will pay the price of blood." Therin's voice did not waiver as he spoke. His eyes remained fixed on the Angan's. "Vars Bryer deserved better…" Therin looked as though lost in thought, his jaw clenched.

"Vars Bryer? Therin, does that mean he knows where Calen is?" Dann interrupted. "And…" Dann looked towards the Angan, tilting his head sideways, "what *are* you?"

Both Aeson and Therin glared at Dann. The boy had a habit of never knowing when to be quiet.

"Sorry," Dann said, holding his hands up. "I'll ask them what you are later," he continued, nodding at Aeson and Therin in turn. The boy simply had no concept of what he should and should not say. "Carry on."

"Shut up," Dahlen whispered, just loud enough for Aeson to hear.

Therin gave Dann a sidelong look, a flicker of irritation on his face, but then he turned to the Angan. "Baldon, I need you to tell me if you can lead us to his son."

"I can, Silver Fang," the Angan replied, the growl still resonating through its voice. "He has been seen by our eyes in Drifaien."

"Well, then, to Drifaien we go."

"Surely they could not be in Drifaien, Therin," Aeson said, his face twisting into a frown. "It would have taken them months to get to Drifaien. Your eyes are mistaken, Angan."

The Angan smiled. At least, Aeson thought it was a smile. Its lips peeled back to reveal a set of sharpened teeth that looked more like fangs. "They are not mistaken. The son of the Chainbreaker is in Drifaien."

"You are sure?" Aeson said, fixing his gaze on the Angan. *The son of the Chainbreaker?* "You are absolutely certain they are in Drifaien?"

"Aeson, he would not—"

Anger bubbled in the pit of Aeson's stomach. "My son is with him, Therin. We must be sure!"

"I am certain, Broken One. He travels with a party across the Eversnow, humans, dwarves, an elf, and the young dragon among them."

A shiver ran down Aeson's spine as the Angan spoke. *Broken One.* He knew the creature only meant to show him respect, but its words were a reminder of what he had lost. The feeling was not something he could easily explain to anyone who had not experienced it. A constant emptiness sat in the back of his mind where he knew Lyara should have been. It was like missing a limb, but more than that. The elves called him 'Rakina' out of respect – 'One who survived'. But what the Angan had said rang truer to how he felt. Broken. He had survived by simply existing, but surviving was not living.

"Thank you, Baldon." Therin moved closer to the Angan. They placed their hands on the one another's shoulders, palms facing down, and then rested their foreheads against each other.

"May the gods watch over your journey, Baldon," Therin said.

"And yours, Therin Silver Fang," the Angan answered. "When you are ready, I will meet you by the Southern Fold Gate that opens to the mountain pass. The dwarves will show you the way." With that, the creature stepped from the room, eliciting not even a whisper from the stone floor.

With the Angan gone, the room broke into a furore.

Aeson looked out the window at the streets below as the room began to empty. The decision had been made. They would follow the Angan. It was their best option by far. They could have spent months – years, even – searching through the tunnels that ran through the mountain. And that was time they simply did not have. If Therin trusted the creature, then so would he. His old friend had earned that twice over.

"Father?"

Dahlen's voice pulled Aeson out of his own thoughts. "Dahlen. What is on your mind?"

"I'm not coming with you."

It took Aeson a moment to realise what Dahlen meant. And even then, he still did not truly understand. When Aeson had left him in Durakdur the first time, he had been furious, and now he didn't wish to come? "What do you mean you're not coming with us? We know where Erik is now, Dahlen. We must go and get him."

Aeson saw a flash of hesitation on his son's face, but it was quickly replaced with an expression he had seen many times over – gritty determination. "I know. But I truly think there is more happening here. Ihvon and Daymon need me. You go and find Erik. I will make sure there is a safe place for you both when you return."

"Are you sure about this?" Aeson rested his hand on his son's shoulder.

"My gut is telling me that what is happening here is important. I need to stay."

Aeson nodded, letting out a sigh of resignation. He could not argue any further, nor would he wish to. If Dahlen truly believed he was needed in Durakdur, then Aeson believed him. "All right. But I expect a hawk sent out to Arem's waypoint in Argona. We should be there in two weeks' time."

"It will be there, waiting for you," Dahlen said with a nod. "And… I'm sorry. I know you were only trying to help, but Ihvon is a good man. I trust him. I shouldn't have lost my temper, and for that, I am sorry."

"It's all right." A half-smile formed at the corner of Aeson's mouth as he looked at the man his son had become. Both Dahlen and Erik had truly grown into good men. Aeson remembered when they had been small enough for him to hold one in each hand. What he would have given for Naia to be able to see them now. "Be careful."

There was something familiar about the jolt that ran up Ella's spine as the carriage wheel cracked against a large stone. She did her best to hold her composure, though; she didn't want Farda to see any signs of weakness. Everything had been dangerous enough before she had learned he was a *mage*. Even the word itself sounded strange in her head. Calen had always been the one who loved the stories of the old times, when 'noble warriors rode astride dragons, and magic shaped the world'. That was how her dad always said it when Calen was little.

If Ella was being honest with herself, she had always liked the stories too, particularly Therin's. But magic? *Real* magic. An uneasy feeling twisted in her stomach at the thought of it. Men were dangerous enough with a bottle in their hands, never mind a sword. But magic changed everything. She could talk her way around a man with a bottle, and she could fight her way past a man with a sword – at least, she could with Faenir by her side. But what could she do against a man who could wield magic?

Ella let out an irritated sigh as she stared out the carriage window at the gleaming sunlight and passing farms. That was all she had been able to see for hours. Farm after farm and the occasional inn. Now and then, she thought she could see Faenir running between the fields. It was hard to be sure, but something in the back of her mind told her she was right.

"You're going to have to speak full sentences to me at some stage, you know?"

Ella took a deep breath and then held it to emphasise that she was annoyed. After holding it for three or four seconds longer than was normal, she let it out, shifting in her seat, moving to face Farda. "You can use magic," she said, leaning forward, raising her eyebrow. "But clearly you can't read a woman's mind. Which of the two skills would you think is more valuable?"

Farda's laughter was not what she had expected. She had expected an awkward silence or, at the very least, an irritated frown. Nobody enjoyed being made fun of, particularly men. Calen *hated* it. If she ever wanted him to lose his temper when they were younger, all she ever had to do was tell him he was short. But she had never received laughter as a reaction. "What's so funny?"

"Nothing," Farda said, a grin spreading across his stubbled face. "Are you always this obvious?"

"I beg your pardon?" Ella twisted her tongue in her mouth, clenching her jaw.

"Are you always this obvious when you're clearly trying to make somebody angry?"

Ella glared at Farda but refused to give him the satisfaction of an answer.

"This is a long carriage ride, Ella Fjorn. The silent treatment will get old quickly."

Ella's veins turned to ice, and her stomach lurched. Ella Fjorn. She had forgotten she had given Farda that name.

It was her true name that had started all of this: Ella Bryer. That name had killed Rhett. Ella Fjorn was the name she had been robbed of. Why shouldn't she have it now?

Chapter Twenty-Seven

Hearts and Minds

Calen took a swig from his waterskin, panting as he sat in the clearing of grass he had created so that he and Vaeril could practise unimpeded.

The fellensír was as different to the svidarya as water was to stone. He was getting the hang of it, though. But it was more than just knowing the sword forms. It was understanding the movement between them, feeling the essence of how each form flowed into the next.

His neck clicked as he shifted his head from side to side, trying to relieve some of the stiffness that had set in. He felt as though he was once again travelling from The Glade to Belduar. Ride, train, eat, sleep, repeat. The riding was the worst part. No matter how much riding he did, he never seemed to get used to it. His back was sore, his stomach muscles were in tatters, and the insides of his legs were raw and tender. The snow didn't help one bit. Even then, as he and Vaeril sat in the small clearing in the forest, tiny flakes of snow drifted through the canopy, tingling slightly as they landed on his skin, melting in an instant.

The others were in the village of Kallingat, but Calen, Vaeril, and Valerys had stayed in the forest. It was easier to practise with a bit of peace and quiet. Besides, they couldn't bring Valerys into the village; the fewer people who saw him, the better.

"What do you feel when you call to the Spark?" Vaeril asked, breaking the silence as he picked a few blades of grass, his legs folded and his sword resting by his side. The elf never seemed to sweat; at least, not often. Calen couldn't help but notice it as he looked at Vaeril, his blonde hair resting on his leather pauldrons. Whenever Calen sparred in his full leathers, like now, he sweated as though the sun was blistering overhead, and he smelled as though he hadn't washed for days. But sitting in front of him, in the full leather armour that all the elves of the Aravell wore, Vaeril looked as though he had merely been enjoying a casual stroll. Not a single bead of sweat adorned his brow.

Calen shifted where he sat, tilting his head to the side, thinking. "It's hard to describe. When I reach out to it, I feel… a warmth? But the longer I hold on to it, the more I draw…"

"You feel the drain."

Calen nodded. "It feels as though my soul is being pulled from my body, dragged kicking and screaming. Sometimes it hurts, like a sharp burning pain. It's so intense I feel like screaming."

Calen felt Vaeril reach out to the Spark, drawing on threads of Air. The elf tossed the blades of grass he had been playing with, wrapping them in the threads. They hung there as though suspended in time. "When you reach out to the Spark, you open a door. This door lets you reach through and lets the Spark flow back the other way. The longer that door stays open, the more of the Spark can flow through. Leave it open too long…" Calen felt Vaeril draw on threads of Fire, and the blades of grass flared, glowed a bright orange, then disintegrated to charred dust. "If you are new to the Spark, you will often simply lose consciousness before you can get to that point. But once you are strong enough to hold more of it, the danger increases. As the drain affects you less and less, the risk of burning out rises. I have seen what happens when a powerful mage takes too much." Vaeril turned to Calen, a severe look in his eyes. "You need to be careful. With each day, I see you push your limits. You draw deeper from the Spark, you push harder. I saw what you did in Belduar, in that ruined dwarven city, and to the wyrms.

You are already a powerful mage, if untrained. But that training is important: it teaches you where your limits lie, and it teaches you control. Draleid or not, you need to know those limits. Because the Spark will not hesitate to consume your soul."

The hairs on the back of Calen's neck stood on end and his throat tightened. How close had he already come to the Spark being burned from him without knowing it? How close had he come to his soul being consumed and Valerys's with it? He shuddered at the thought, fear snaking its tendrils around his heart. In response, a feeling of warmth and comfort flooded through Calen's mind, seeking to calm his fear. Valerys emerged from a thicket about twenty feet away, the body of a limp deer in his jaws. Dropping the dead animal to the ground, Valerys moved towards Calen, lowering his neck and touching the tip of his snout against Calen's forehead.

Images flashed across Calen's eyes as their minds embraced. Images of Valerys's egg, the Fade in Belduar, the kerathlin, the tunnels, the wyrms. Every moment they had spent together, every adversity they had faced, rippled through Calen's mind in fractions of a second, and his fear was gone. Calen reached up, running his hands along the cool scales of Valerys's neck. The dragon's message was clear: Calen was not alone. No matter what foe they faced or what darkness threatened to swallow them whole, they would stand together. "Myia nithír til diar, Valerys. I denír viël ar altinua." *My soul to yours, Valerys. In this life and always.*

A soft grumble escaped Valerys's throat, and the dragon curled up on the ground beside Calen, his head resting against Calen's leg.

"The words you chose were beautiful," Vaeril said, a smile touching his lips as he watched over Valerys. "What is it like to be bonded?"

Even the notion of it made Calen smile. But how could he ever describe that feeling? "It's like your own mind is not yours, but at the same time, it is. Like every thought belongs to you, but it belongs to him. Mostly, I can tell the difference. We're not always completely blended. I can feel a separation. But there are times, when I let go, that it becomes…" He let out a sigh. It was hard to grasp the essence of that feeling. "I see through his eyes, I feel through his body, and I breathe through his lungs. We are one and the same. I am my own, but I belong to him, and he belongs to me."

"Incredible," Vaeril whispered, more to himself than anything else, his eyes never leaving Valerys.

"It is," Calen agreed, his mind lingering on the feeling. "Come on," he said, getting to his feet. "Let's join the others and get some food in our bellies. I'm starved."

Vaeril's expression changed in a flash. "I think it's best if I stay here. I can hunt something. It will be easier."

It took Calen a moment to realise why Vaeril's mood had changed at the drop of a hat, and it was not something he was going to allow to continue. He would not have someone who stood by his side be left to sit alone in a forest just to satisfy the whims of idiots. "You're coming."

"I—"

"Vaeril, I'm not having you sit in a forest in the cold, cooking rabbit on a spit while I eat stew in a warm inn. Either you come, or I stay. I'm happy with either."

Taking a few moments, Vaeril nodded, pulling his hood up over his head, covering his ears. "Let's go."

Kallingat was no bigger than the village where they had stayed at the base of Mount Helmund. The houses were built from the same thick wooden logs with heavy glass windows set into them and smoke streaming from their chimneys. There was a bit more of a buzz about Kallingat, though. Hawkers and pedlars filled the streets. Some stood behind stalls of thick wood that seemed as though they were permanent fixtures built to withstand the weather, others flogged their wares from the backs of carts, and some stood beside stacked crates and boxes.

A small woman with a soft, pale face and straw-blonde hair stood behind one of the heavy wooden stalls, dressed in a flowy brown dress with a thick wolf fur draped over her shoulders. A child stood beside her, dressed much the same way, but her cheeks were rosier, and her hair was closer to light brown. It wasn't until Calen heard the young girl calling out that he realised what they were selling. Rows upon rows of knives, all shapes and sizes. Some with big broad blades with small notches cut into their length, some with short slightly curved blades and a stout handle – good for skinning. Others had long flat blades and thick wooden handles, and there were even a few throwing daggers, weighted blades with small necks that fed into finger loops. Calen couldn't help but admire the craftsmanship. He had never been gifted when it came to blacksmithing, not even close, not compared to his father. But he knew good work when he saw it, and those knives were good work. His hand fell to the pommel of his own sword, the last thing his father had given him, hanging in its scabbard from the loop on his belt. For the most part, Calen tried to keep the thoughts of his family at the back of his mind. Not because he didn't want to think of them, but because every time he did, it consumed him. Swallowing hard, he pushed the thought down, sweeping his coat over his sword, obscuring it from view as much as he could.

"Fruit, sir?" a little voice to Calen's left said. He looked down to see two small children, no more than seven or eight summers, a boy and a girl. Both with large dark eyes and rose-coloured cheeks with fur coats that were much too big for them, draped over their shoulders. The little girl was the one who had spoken; she held both of her hands up in the air, a shiny green apple clutched in each one. "One copper for the pair," she said, before adding, "sir."

"That sounds a bit cheap. Are you sure I only have to pay that much?" Calen asked, leaning a bit closer as though he were inspecting the apples closely. A copper should have bought him four or five apples, but he wasn't going to argue.

"Yes, sir. Ours are the cheapest in Kallingat."

Calen pulled a copper from the purse in his coat pocket, took the two apples and then dropped the copper in the girl's hand. The two kids thanked him gleefully before running off into the rambling crowd.

"You know they bought them from the fruit cart across the street," Vaeril said, nodding to the fruit seller as Calen tossed him one of the apples.

"I know," Calen said with a laugh, biting into the apple, the juices rolling down his chin. It was just what he wanted, crisp and sweet with just a little bit of tartness at the end.

"I'll never understand humans," Vaeril whispered. Calen wasn't entirely sure if he was meant to hear that or not.

Calen stopped as they passed a heavy-set man with a thick knotted beard to match his hair, a broad swollen chest, and a leathered face standing behind a stall lined with winter clothes: fur coats, fur hats, fleece-lined boots, and deerskin gloves that looked as though they had been made by a craftsman with the skill to rival Tharn Pimm.

"Come, take a gander, the finest of leathers and the thickest of furs, caught and crafted right here in Kallingat," the hefty man bellowed. The lilt in his Drifaienin accent made his voice seem hearty and full, almost inviting. Even if Calen had not wanted to buy a new pair of boots and gloves, he still might have gone over simply from the man's voice. But his rumbling stomach told him new shoes could wait.

The Frozen Goat seemed like an odd name for an inn, but then again, Calen had heard even stranger names. Warmth hit him as soon as he stepped inside the inn, sending a shiver up his spine as it brushed the cold from his skin. It was busier than Calen had expected. Most of the patrons seemed to be Drifaienin, with their thick beards, and in the women's case, their tough stares, giving them away. There were a few patrons scattered around who looked as though they had come from afar. A man sitting in the corner, dressed in flamboyant red breeches and a brazen yellow doublet, looked as out of place as any of them. Calen could not place him anywhere; maybe Arkalen? He had heard people from Arkalen were as audacious with their clothing choices as they were loose with their purses, and they cared little for what people thought of either. The man certainly fit that bill, sitting like a peacock among pigeons.

A pair of women in the corner had the coppery skin of Valtarans, and the tattoos of black ink that lined their arms only confirmed that further. Calen had never met a Valtaran, but he had heard many stories of the rebellion, of how Valtaran men and women fought side by side, and how one Valtaran was worth ten of any other in combat. Some of the bards who visited The Glade were clearly biased towards the empire, but even they often admitted that the Dragonguard were the only reason the rebellion failed. Skill with a spear and a shield meant little when faced with dragonfire.

His eyes lingered on the two Valtarans only a moment before he spotted Falmin, Tarmon, and the two dwarves sitting at a booth over in the corner of the inn. He recognised the man and two women who sat at the table next to the booth as well, Heldin, Sigrid, and Gudrun, the other Drifaienin, besides Alleron and Alwen, who had survived the wyrm attack. He nodded to them as he took a seat beside Korik.

"Where are the others?" Calen asked as he snatched a piece of bread off the table from under Falmin's fork, receiving a glare from the navigator.

"Erik and Alleron have gone to source more horses," Tarmon answered, taking a swig of tea from a broad-bottomed wooden mug. "Alwen, in his own words, has gone to get us a bottle of 'liquid happiness'. How goes the practice?" Tarmon didn't direct the question at Calen; instead, he turned to Vaeril.

The elf gave a pout, pulling back his hood and giving a slight shrug of his shoulders. "He learns quickly, though his patience wears thin at the same pace."

"He will learn that, too," Tarmon said with a satisfied nod, gripping both hands around the mug of tea.

Calen's gaze moved between Vaeril and Tarmon. "You know *he* is sitting right here?"

"Aye," Falmin said with a laugh, his mouth still half full of stew. "The two of 'em do that sometimes. Two peas in a pod so they are. I—"

Falmin stopped mid-sentence, his eyes narrowing as a man walked up to the booth. He was big, with a nose twisted like the roots of a tree and short hair curved into a widow's peak at the top. "You all right?" Falmin said, swallowing the food in his mouth.

"I would be, if it weren't so tough to stomach my food." The man's words would have made no sense to Calen if he had not been glaring at Vaeril while he spoke.

"Not this shit again…" Calen whispered to himself, his jaw clenching involuntarily.

"Look, you're welcome to eat outside. But your kind can't come in here. I'll give ya till a count of ten." The man didn't move. He stood right at the end of the booth, feet planted, his eyes fixed on Vaeril. "Ten…"

Calen clenched his hand into a fist and moved to stand, but before he could do anything, someone grabbed the man by the back of the head and slammed his face on the wooden beam that fronted the joining wall between their booth and the next. The man's already mangled nose burst open as it cracked against the wood, spraying blood across the floor and the table, a few drops landing in Lopir's soup. Four more times the man's head bounced off the wooden beam, blood spraying like a fountain each time. The fifth time, the man dropped to the floor like a sack of potatoes, limp but still breathing.

It was Gudrun that stood over him, one of the Drifaienin women, her blonde hair tied in a knot, her face frozen in a cold stare. She leaned over the man, blood dripping from her right hand, then spat on his back. "Filth," she said, her lips curling into a snarl. "I apologise, master elf, on behalf of my people. He is sorry, too," she said with a nod towards the prone man whose chest rose and fell slowly. "He will tell you so when he wakes." Gudrun bowed slightly at the waist, then gave a nod to Calen before returning to her seat, leaving the man on the floor unconscious but still groaning. Everyone else in the inn carried on as if nothing had happened, with the exception of the Arkalen man, who looked about as horrified as Calen would have expected.

"I like 'er," Falmin said with a shrug. "I wonder if she's spoken for?" The navigator scrunched up his face and ran his hand through his slicked back hair as he pondered the answer to his own question.

"That," Tarmon said, nodding towards the unconscious man on the floor lying in an ever-growing pool of his own blood, "is what you look for in a woman?"

Falmin shrugged again, shovelling another mouthful of stew into his mouth. "I like a woman who can look after 'erself."

Calen looked down again at the bloody mess of a man then over to Tarmon, who just shook his head and gave a slight shrug.

"Is someone going to pick him up?" Calen asked nobody in particular as one of the serving girls stepped over the man with a half-irritated look on her face.

"I don't believe so." Vaeril answered, looking down at the man, an unreadable expression on his face.

Calen gave Vaeril a slight nod that was acknowledged with the closest thing to a smile the elf could muster. As happy as he was to see the man feel the pain he so rightly deserved, it was still a bittersweet happiness knowing that so many of the Drifaienin likely shared his beliefs.

"How's the eye?" Calen asked Lopir, trying to move on from the incident.

"Good," the dwarf replied, picking a piece of meat from his teeth with a small wooden splinter. "Thanks to *master elf.*" Lopir aimed a cheeky grin at Vaeril.

"And how are you faring, being outside of Lodhar?"

"In truth?" Lopir said with a sigh. "I yearn for home. It's an honour to follow you, Draleid, don't mistake my words. But my heart bleeds for my wife's touch, and I long for the warmth of the mountain."

"We'll get you home, Lopir, both of you." Calen gave a weak smile to Korik as he spoke. "I promise."

"I will introduce you to my son," Lopir said. "He would love to meet you."

"And I him."

"Speaking of home, what exactly is our plan when we get to Arisfall?" Tarmon leaned his two elbows on the table, his hands cupped under his chin, a serious look on his face. "If an emissary from the empire has already been to see Lothal Helmund, how can we trust him?"

"We can't," Calen said, pursing his lips. "Alleron said there is a small fishing village just south of Arisfall. We will wait for him there while he sources a captain. When he's back, we will take a riverboat down to the coast, and from there we sail back up to the Lodhar Mountains. It should take at least a month off our journey, maybe more."

"A sound plan." Tarmon leaned in a little closer, dropping his voice to a whisper so the Drifaienin couldn't hear. "Can we trust him? Alleron."

"We can. He's brought us this far."

Tarmon nodded, refraining from saying much more, though Calen could tell by his eyes that he wasn't convinced of Alleron's trustworthiness.

Erik and Alleron had returned by the time the sun began to recede over the mountains to the west. Four horses had survived the wyrm attack, and they had been able to secure five more. Alwen returned a while later brandishing a bottle of Drifaienin whiskey that burned as though it were liquid fire. The innkeeper was not particularly happy, but her sour face changed once Alleron produced his coin purse. At one point during the night, they even got to play a few rounds of axes. It felt good, warm. It had been a while since Calen had been able to smile so freely.

But in the back of his mind, he was always aware that Valerys was alone, waiting in the forest. He could feel the dragon's consciousness pressing against his own, constantly searching for the reassurance that Calen had come to no harm. *I'm coming,*

"All right." Calen winced, draining the last of his whiskey then dropping the cup on the table, puffing out his cheeks as he did. "I will see you all in the morning."

It was only when he reached the door to the inn that Calen realised Vaeril was walking with him. He had long since accepted the elf was not going to stay any more than twenty feet from him. "Come on," he said, gesturing for Vaeril to hurry up.

They found Valerys no more than fifteen minutes through the forest. Although, even at the dragon's size, if Calen had not been able to sense him, they might just as easily have walked past. When he was crouched into the snow, with his wings fanned around him, the dragon was all but invisible, especially in the dark. Calen pulled his coat tighter around him, his breath pluming out and up towards the sky.

"I will take first watch."

Calen didn't even have time to argue. Vaeril was gone as soon as he turned around. The elf could have crept up on his own shadow.

Tarmon rubbed his hands together, eliciting a crack as he rolled his shoulders. The cold itself was fine for the most part, though he preferred a warm Belduaran summer, but he had recently come to the decision that he didn't much care for the snow.

Though, it wasn't all bad. He had a thick, fur-lined coat draped over his shoulders, one of those Drifaienin sleeping sacks across his back, and a flask of whiskey in his pocket. Those three things together would be enough to keep him warm for the night, at least.

An eerie shiver ran up the back of Tarmon's neck as he walked. The snow crunched beneath his boots, the odd rustle of dried leaves drifted on the wind, and the sound of his breathing filled the air around him. But besides that, he heard nothing. Nothing was never a sound he enjoyed. Nothing always meant something. He carried on walking, though, following Calen and Vaeril's footprints through the snow. Maybe he was being paranoid, maybe he wasn't. But there was something in the back of his mind, a gut feeling, and his gut hadn't steered him too far wrong before. Either way, he would rather be wrong and prepared than right and caught napping.

Snap.

Tarmon slid the short sword free from the loop on his belt and grasped a knife with his other hand. His heart beat methodically as he spun on his heels. Nothing. He held his breath for a few more moments, waiting. He had definitely heard that branch snap; he was sure of it.

Standing straight, he slid his short sword back into its scabbard but kept his knife gripped firmly in his hand. Turning back in the direction he was originally walking, Tarmon stopped dead.

Standing in front of him, hackles raised and lips pulled back into a snarl, was the single largest wolf he had ever seen. The thing was as big as a horse, with black and grey fur and razor-sharp teeth of alabaster.

"Whoa now." Tarmon swallowed hard, wriggling his fingers on the handle of his knife. He didn't dare reach for either his sword strapped to his hip or his back. He held one hand out in front of himself, palm up, with his knife hand to the side. "Easy, easy…"

The wolf's eyes followed him as he tried to slowly shuffle his way around it, but it didn't attack, it just watched. How in the gods was it so big? He had never seen one that size before, not even close. He clenched his jaw as the wolf started to move, circling him, sniffing the air. Suddenly, it stopped snarling, held his gaze for a moment, then bounded off into the night, clearing huge distances in single leaps.

Tarmon let out a sigh of relief, then collapsed against a tree, sliding to the ground. Cold sweat slicked his brow, and his heart thumped at a steady pace, each beat like a battering ram against his chest. "What in the gods was that?"

Rist flicked his tongue across the bottom of his teeth as he sat with the letter in his hands. He had intended to read it almost a week ago, before he had run into Neera. The thought of Neera sent a shiver across his shoulders and down his back. *Focus.*

He sat in one of the nooks in the palace garden, the soft light from the afternoon sun providing just enough light to read by. Holding out the letter in front of his face, he cast his eyes over it once more.

My dearest son,

I'm sorry I haven't written sooner. Things haven't been easy recently. The Lorian soldiers left a few days ago. They didn't say why, but Erdhardt Hammersmith said that he heard there had been riots in Camylin. Whatever the reason, since they have been gone, Uraks have started to raid.

We've been lucky here in The Glade. The new palisade wall has kept them out for the most part. Orm Matin's son Jon suffered a broken arm in the last raid, but we haven't lost anyone. Erith hasn't been so lucky.

We had hoped Castor Kai would send soldiers, but all the pedlars that pass through are saying the same thing. They're saying that the South is in chaos, and that the Illyanaran army is already spread thin across the region.

There is a meeting of the council tomorrow, so hopefully something can be done. Don't worry too much about your mother and I, we are well, as are Tharn and Ylinda. You just look after yourself. That is what's important. How is your training? What is it like? Are they treating you well? Tell us everything.

Missing you with all our hearts,
Mam and Dad.

Rist folded the letter over four times, taking care not to wrinkle it any more than was necessary, and placed it into the pocket on the inside of his brown robes. He buried his fingers into the hair at the back of his head, pushing into his scalp until each of his fingers was pressing so tightly that it hurt. Tears burned at the corner of his eyes, but he held them back. They would do him no good.

Chapter Twenty-Eight

Broken Bones and Shattered Hearts

et behind me!" Erdhardt roared. "Aela, behind me now!" He swung his warhammer through the air, feeling a crunch vibrate through the shaft as it crashed into the Urak's chest. Blood sprayed from the creature's mouth, and its eyes rolled to the back of its head. He hit it again for good measure, caving in its skull.

Flames raged all around as the entire village was consumed. "Stay behind me," he said, turning to his wife, his hard, calloused hand resting against her soft cheek. "It will be all right."

"Don't be an idiot," she said, snatching a knife, so big it looked like a sword in her hand, from the dead Urak's belt. "Come on."

I love you, woman.

A scream rippled through the night, sending a shiver racing down Erdhardt's spine. Rolling his shoulders out, he clenched his jaw and tightened his grip on the hammer. It had been a few years since he'd held it in his hands. It shouldn't have been that long. He should have picked it up when the empire killed the man who had crafted it. Vars Bryer was a man who deserved more. A lot more. Erdhardt shook the thoughts from his head. There were people who needed him now; he didn't have to time to pine over the people he had failed.

He caught sight of Mara Styr, her dress covered in dirt, blood running down the side of her head. Young Lina was clutching her mother's hand. The two of them were cowering behind old Guna Lindon's house.

"Mara!" Erdhardt was halfway to her when two Uraks stepped out in front of him, their eyes set on Mara and Lina. His hammer crushed a knee before the Uraks even knew he was there. He heaved the hammer back, caving in the beast's skull with a second strike. Erdhardt twisted to avoid the thrusting spear of the second Urak, but he wasn't quick enough to evade it entirely. He roared in pain as the blackened tip of the spear scored his side. The beast pulled back its spear for a second strike, only to howl as Aela thrust her knife into its ribs. The creature snarled, unleashing a guttural roar as it pulled its spear back again, this time directing it at her.

But the beast coughed and spluttered as an arrow burst through its throat from the back, a spray of blood following the steel arrowhead.

"Hammersmith, to me!" Erdhardt could see Tharn Pimm standing beside Mara and Lina Styr, his long yew bow clutched in his hands. Erdhardt didn't think he had ever been happier to see the man.

"Are you all right?" Erdhardt asked, turning to Aela, checking her over.

"Me? You bumbling fool, it's you who's bleeding!" She furrowed her brow and rested a tender touch on his cheek. "I'm fine," she said with a soft breath.

"The guard?" Erdhardt asked as he reached Tharn, casting a glance over Mara and Lina. The young girl was fine, if a little terrified. Mara, however, looked worse for wear. The cut on the side of her head wasn't too deep, but a worrisome blood stain was beginning to seep through her dress.

"Ferrin has a few of them at The Gilded Dragon. We're trying to get everyone there now."

"We need to get to them, and then we need to go."

"What? Abandon the village?" Incredulity permeated Tharn's voice.

"Look around you, Tharn. What village? The only thing worth saving now are the people, and if we pile them into The Gilded Dragon then these beasts will just burn it down with them inside."

Tharn swallowed, nodding, half to himself and half to Erdhardt. "All right. Let's go."

Erdhardt's heart stopped in his chest as they turned the corner to The Gilded Dragon. "By the gods…"

Fewer than twenty of the town guard were still fighting, swarmed by thick leathery beasts swinging blackened blades. The rest lay strewn about the street, mangled, misshapen, missing limbs, their blood seeping into the dirt.

Mara and Aela both shrieked, tears streaming down their faces. It was not just the town guard who lay in the dust. Men, women, children. Marlo Egon, half his face missing; what was left was barely recognisable. Denet Hildom, his neck twisted halfway round, bones piercing the skin.

Erdhardt's chest twisted as his eyes fell on the misshapen body of Verna Gritten, her limbs twisted and broken, her skin pale and blue, her eyes empty. He had known her since they were pups; she had a pure heart. But nothing prepared him for the sight of young Aren Ehrnin's head laying in the dirt more than five feet from his body. The boy had not seen five summers.

But in the middle of it all, it was the burning creatures that set stones in his stomach. Standing amidst the smaller creatures – though it felt strange to use that word for an Urak – were four hulking masses of muscles, at least ten feet tall, their bodies covered in thick, carved runes that gave off a red glow and streamed smoke. They looked as though the traitor god himself had risen.

"Tharn, we need to help them." Erdhardt's mouth went dry as he spoke the words. What help could they be? But Tharn simply gritted his teeth and gave a short nod. "Aela, I need you to take the others and make for the northern edge of the village. Head for Talin, it's the closest."

"I'm not leaving y—"

"For the love of the gods, woman! Will you not listen to a single word I say?" Erdhardt regretted the anger in his voice, but he could find no other emotion to fuel his tongue. "No matter what happens here, I will not see another sunrise if you are not by my side. Now take Mara and Lina and anyone you find along the way. Head for Talin, and tell them what has happened. I will follow as soon as I can." Erdhardt's last words felt hollow, even to himself. He would die this night, and he knew it. Aela was cleverer than he could ever have hoped to be – the woman was a fox – which meant she knew it, too. But maybe, if he could hold the Uraks there, he could buy her some time. Tears welled in the corners of his eyes as he once more brought his hands up to touch her tender cheek. "For all the stars in the sky, I would not trade a single day. Now, go."

He savoured the soft touch of her lips on his, the sweetness of it. He had been a man beyond his luck when she had kissed him for the first time over thirty summers gone, and he was a man beyond his luck still. He let his gaze linger for a moment before setting himself to what must be done.

Reluctantly, Erdhardt pulled his eyes from Aela's back as she and the others disappeared into the night. He charged into the chaos of man and beast. He didn't look back. The tang of iron and voided bowels filled the air, mingling with the harsh smell of burning wood. Clenching his jaw, he swung his hammer, feeling the crunch of bone vibrate through its shaft as he connected with an Urak's hip. The beast stumbled, howling as it dropped to one knee, one of Tharn's arrows plunging into the back of its head.

Erdhardt's blood shivered through his veins, pumping in his head. The screams of men and the howls of Uraks, the shrieking clash of steel colliding, the crackling of homes as fire consumed them, all of it faded, muffling together. Even his own voice was nothing but a muted roar as he shouted at Tharn, pointing towards Ferrin Kolm and the other guards who stood in a fragmented semi-circle before the steps of The Gilded Dragon. Only a handful of them still stood, spears and sword grasped in their fists, fear etched on their faces. They were right to be scared. Erdhardt was terrified, yet he pushed forward.

Again he swung his hammer, catching an Urak in the side. He saw its ribs break, the bones splinter, the blood spray. He pulled his hammer free and let the beast fall.

Erdhardt called to Ferrin, saw the whites of the young man's eyes as he heard the call, then watched as a charcoal axe caught Ferrin in the side of the neck. It wasn't a clean strike; Ferrin still clung to life as the blood cascaded down. He dropped as the axe was yanked free, then Erdhardt lost him to the chaos.

Erdhardt's fear gave way to anger, and anger yielded to a white-hot rage. He leapt headfirst into the fray, swinging his hammer about him. Bones broke beneath its weight and blood stained its surface. More than once, a searing pain screamed in his arms and legs where an Urak blade sliced his flesh, but they were not mortal wounds, so he pushed on. The constant spray of arrows from behind let him know that Tharn still stood; the man was only half as good as his son, but that was better than most.

A blinding white flash burst across Erdhardt's eyes, and the ground rose to meet him as he crashed. The battle rush flooded from his mind, and the sounds rushed in. The snarls, the harsh rasping of blades, the screams. He tightened his fingers. *Good.* He could still feel the leather-wrapped handle of his hammer, which meant he hadn't dropped it. With a grunt, he made to heave himself to his feet, but a weight crashed into his ribs, sending him spinning back to the dirt. Blood tickled his throat, and his side throbbed. Shaking his head, he spat blood onto the dirt and peeled open one eye to find an Urak staring back at him, its lips pulled back, jagged yellow teeth on display and a snarl in its throat.

The Urak loomed over him, a thick-shafted black spear clutched in its fists. A fierce red glow emanated from a smooth gemstone set into the blade of the spear, glittering a red light across the weapon's surface.

Not yet. I won't die yet.

Erdhardt snatched at the spear with his free hand, grasping it just below the blade. He pulled with all his strength, careful not to bring it down on top of himself. The Urak stumbled forward, caught off guard. Just as it did, Erdhardt let go of his hammer – it was too heavy to swing with one hand – and wrapped his fingers around the back of the beast's head. Roaring, he rammed the Urak's head into the ground with every drop of strength he had. Feeling his opportunity, he swivelled onto his knees, grabbed the beast's head with both hands, and slammed it down repeatedly. When it stopped moving, he pulled himself to his feet, wrapping his fingers around the shaft of his hammer. He now stood shoulder to shoulder with the remaining guards.

Joran Brock, Dana Holmir, Allan Dornin. All good souls. He couldn't catch sight of the others' faces, but no doubt they were men and women he would be proud to die beside. He had known most of them since they were nothing but pups at their mothers' tits. It was fitting that he should be there at their end.

A piercing pain flashed through Erdhardt's right thigh. He ignored it. He could feel the blood trickle down the inside of his leg. It was a shallow cut. "Hold fast!" he yelled, swallowing hard and clenching his jaw. They wouldn't last long. Not against these monstrosities.

A din of howls erupted to his left. One of the larger beasts with the runes carved into its skin had sent some form of shock wave rippling through the men, collapsing the left side of The Gilded Dragon's porch. Another of the beasts ripped a man's arm clean off with its bare hands, roaring into the night as it did.

How were men meant to fight against such things? He had seen war, and he had fought Uraks before, but not like this, not with these numbers, and not with these monstrosities by their side.

Fewer than ten of the guard remained.

"To me!" Erdhardt shouted as he shifted his weight onto his back foot, swinging his hammer, feeling bone crumble beneath its weight. He let himself back slowly towards the stairs of the inn. After a few moments, some of the surviving guards stood by his side, beaten, bloody, half-broken. He counted only six. "If you die, take two with you!"

A chorus of roars answered him. They would not go quietly into the void, not men and women of The Glade.

Joran Brock was the first of the six to fall, his guts spilling out in front of him, steam drifting through the cold air as his body lay lifeless. Olina Marken went next, her chest opened by one of the rune-marked beasts.

Run, Aela, please. Run as fast as your legs can carry you.

A roar trapped itself in Erdhardt's throat as a spear tip tore a gash through his side. He choked a rasping breath, his chest heaving. With an almighty swing, he caught one of the rune-marked in the leg, only to feel a tremor reverberate back up the hammer, jarring his arms. The creature snarled, red light drifting through the smoky mist that rose from its runes. It cracked him in the chest with a backhand. He hit the ground hard, tasting dirt and blood in his mouth. He dragged himself to his feet, swaying side to side, bile rising in his throat. Two more of the guard fell before his eyes. One was cleaved in half by an axe swing, another's neck broken.

Erdhardt's fear melted away as he watched the Uraks push forward. The knot in his stomach untied itself, and acceptance took its place. He grunted as he took a deep breath, shifting his weight from his right leg. It hurt to breathe, but he wouldn't have to breathe for much longer.

Roaring so loud his lungs felt as though they would burst, he charged. Three of the Uraks fell under his hammer, taken aback by his sudden rush. A sword cut deep into his shoulder. He felt the grip on his hammer loosen. He let it fall. He tackled one of the beasts to the ground, a snarl escaping his throat. It unleashed a guttural howl as the two of them fell. Erdhardt grabbed hold of its wrist, slamming it against the dirt until the black blade fell from its grasp. Snatching the blade up, he wrapped both hands around its hilt, then drove the sword down into the beast's chest. For a moment it gazed at him, shock on its face, then the life drained from its eyes and the gemstone set into the black blade glowed red with a renewed vigour.

As he knelt in the dirt, fear shot through Erdhardt's body, and he threw the Urak's blade to the ground, wanting it nowhere near him. He felt something as the beast died, a shiver that rippled through him. It made him want to vomit.

A series of shrieks broke him from his thoughts. They weren't the shrieks of men, but the guttural howls of Uraks. *What is happening?* He dragged himself to his feet, leaving his hammer where it lay; he didn't have the strength to wield it. An Urak crashed into his side, sending him spiralling; he caught himself before he hit the ground, just keeping his balance. He turned to brace himself, but before the beast struck, a green light flashed through the air, separating its head from its shoulders.

"What in the gods…" Erdhardt stumbled backwards, tripping over something that lay lifeless on the ground. All around him, flashes of green rippled, illuminating the night. Wherever the light shimmered, Uraks fell. Then he saw the source of the light. It was a man. At least, he thought it was a man. Plate armour of smooth green metal covered him from head to toe, an insignia of snow white emblazoned across the breast. The man held a sword in his fist, a sword that looked as though it was wrought from pure green light. Erdhardt would not have believed it if he hadn't seen it for himself. He watched, stunned, as the man's blade cut straight through one of the rune-marked's legs, then took its head from its shoulders.

Erdhardt struggled as a pair of hands clamped down on his shoulders.

"It's all right, Erdhardt, it's me!" Aela's voice gave him both warmth and despair.

"What are you doing here?" Panic clung to his voice as he turned to look his sweet wife in the eyes. She clutched a spear in her fist, blood dappled her face – not her own blood – and dirt crusted the edges of her dress. "You should be long gone."

"I left the others at the edge of the village, outside the Palisade. They went with a group to Talin. Ylinda Pimm and Anya Gritten led them. I wasn't leaving you."

"Gods damn you, woman. Gods damn you!" His chest heaving from exhaustion, Erdhardt lowered his weary legs and snatched a bloody sword from the ground, one of the guard's swords. He would not touch an Urak blade again.

Green light continued to flash, tearing through the Uraks like a maelstrom of death. There was not one man in green plate, but four. They moved as though the wind itself obeyed them, splitting bone and opening hides. Erdhardt swung his head, looking for any more survivors. His eyes fell on Dana Holmir and Allan Dornin. Allan lay in a crumpled heap on the ground, his hand clutched to his chest, blood staining his blue tabard. Dana stood over him, limping on her left leg, a spear and shield clutched tightly. Uraks surrounded them.

"Come," he shouted to Aela, still furious at her for returning. She gave a short nod, her mouth a grim line.

Erdhardt drew his blade across an Urak's legs, hamstringing it. The creature bellowed as it collapsed to its knees, its cries cut short by Erdhardt's sword punching through the back of its head. They were big, and they were quick, but they held little awareness. He took two more from behind, pushing his way through to Allan and Dana. Fresh cuts raked Dana's side, and blood seeped out through a gash in her breastplate. Erdhardt glanced over his shoulder and saw that Aela still held tight to him, her knuckles pale as she grasped the spear.

"Can he stand?" Erdhardt asked as they reached Dana, nodding at Allan.

"I don't know," she said, panting. "I don't know if he's even…"

Erdhardt went to reassure the woman, but a hammer blow caught him in the back, knocking him to his knees. Pain flared through the gash in his thigh as his muscle flexed, trying to keep him upright.

One of the rune-marked crashed in between him and Dana, raking its clawed hands across her chest, rending her breastplate in a stroke of blood and steel. Dana collapsed to the ground, gasping for air as she clutched at her chest.

Erdhardt fought through the pain, biting his lip as he pulled himself to his feet, lunging towards the beast. He threw all his weight behind the blow as he drove his sword up through the creature's ribs, burying it to the hilt. The rune-marked beast howled. Spinning, it grasped Erdhardt by the neck and lifted him off his feet.

He choked, dragging ragged breaths into his closing windpipe, gasping for air as he floated. The rune-marked lifted him until its eyes, glowing with a crimson fury, drew level with his own. He saw nothing as he stared into those incandescent hollows of red. The beast's grasp tightened, thick fingers closing around Erdhardt's throat. It held him there as he floundered like a rag doll.

Erdhardt felt his grip on consciousness slipping, stars flitting across his eyes. His vision faded to black, then blurred before seeing flashes of light, then returned to black. His lungs gasped for air, burning, but found nothing. He kicked, clawing at the beast's arm, flesh coming away under his fingernails, but it didn't so much as flinch.

Then he was free, his body hitting the ground like a hammer on steel. He gasped, dragging air into his screaming lungs, the iron tang of blood on his tongue. Coughing, he lifted his head, only for his heart to rend when he saw why the beast had let him go.

Aela stood between Erdhardt and the monster, her spear buried beneath the pit of its arm.

Erdhardt scrambled to his feet, digging dirt into his fingernails as he stumbled, his vision still a half-blurred haze. His blood pounded through his veins, panic shivering through his skin. He snatched up a fallen spear, launching it at the beast. It roared as the spear plunged into its shoulder. Swinging its hand down, it shattered the shaft of Aela's spear before catching her with a horrifying backhand that left her in a crumpled heap.

No, no, no.

Erdhardt crashed to the dirt beside his wife, ignoring the explosion of pain in his knees. Blood covered her face, tacking her fine hair to her head. "Aela, Aela!" Erdhardt tried to breathe, but the air just caught in his throat, an emptiness in his chest. "Aela! God damn you, woman. Open your fucking eyes!" *I can't feel her breathing.* Erdhardt's throat went as dry as sand, his voice splitting and cracking as he tried to shout. "No, no, no… gods dammit, no!"

Kallinvar swivelled, slicing his Soulblade through the Urak's arm before ripping it across the creature's gut, opening the contents of its stomach onto the dirt. The Urak cried out, the sound cut short as it choked on its own blood.

He paused a moment to take in the battle. Around him, his knights tore through the Bloodspawn mercilessly. Arden and Lyrin had each claimed a Bloodmarked, and Ildris held his own against a clutch of Uraks. But where was the Shaman? Four Bloodmarked in one place. Where was the Shaman that had carved the runes?

It was a question he would have to answer when the fighting was done. His eyes fell on the last of the Bloodmarked, two spears protruding from its thick hide, one with a shattered shaft. It stood over a crumpled man who held a body in his arms. Kallinvar took in a breath, then charged, the power of the Sentinel armour surging through him. He cleaved through two more Bloodspawn as he moved, arcing his Soulblade about him before he bent at the knees and leapt into the air, his armour-enhanced legs lifting him.

He buried the Soulblade into the Bloodmarked's back, eliciting a blood-curdling howl from the creature. As the beast spun, Kallinvar released his Soulblade, summoning it once more as he hit the ground, shearing the beast's leg at the knee. It collapsed, no longer supported by its right leg. Kallinvar followed it to the ground, staring into its eyes as he drove his Soulblade through its chest, where its heart should have been. The runes on its skin glowed furiously as they tried to keep the Bloodmarked alive, but even that dark magic could do nothing for the beast now. Kallinvar dropped his weight, driving the blade through the creature and down into the dirt. He watched as the light in its eyes died out. "For Achyron."

Kallinvar stood there, his foot on the beast's chest, heaving air into his lungs. The fighting around him was beginning to fade, and what was left of the Bloodspawn were fleeing into the night. He still saw no sign of their Shaman.

Releasing his Soulblade, he cast his eyes around. The man to his right was a sobbing, convulsing mess holding a woman's body in his arms – his wife, most likely. Kallinvar left him to feel his pain, to grieve. He had felt that pain before. There was no other thing in the world that compared to it. To lose the other half of you was to have the skin peeled from your living bones, to have your heart pulled from your chest and your eyes burned out.

"That is the last of them, Brother-Captain," Arden said, stepping up beside Kallinvar, his voice holding an uncharacteristic tremble as his gaze fixed on the sobbing man.

"See that it is. Secure the village and bring any survivors here."

"As you say…" Arden hesitated for a moment, his gaze never leaving the sobbing man. "Brother-Captain."

"Are you all right, Arden?" Kallinvar called out to the Sigil, commanding his helmet to recede, allowing him to look at Arden with his own eyes. The young man did not do the same.

"I am, I just… I'm fine," Arden said, turning away. "I will continue to search for survivors, Brother-Captain." Arden strode into the night with not so much as a glance over his shoulders. Something did not sit right, and Kallinvar would find out what it was, but for now it could wait.

Once they were back in the temple, Kallinvar found Arden exactly where he expected him to be: sitting beneath a Hallow tree in the Tranquil Garden. Ever since the young man had received the Sigil, this was where he seemed to spend most of his downtime. Kallinvar understood the desire. He had spent many days alone in the Tranquil Garden after the battle of Ilnaen, until duty called him to rise – many of the knights had. To be one of Achyron's chosen was not an easy burden to bear. The Tranquil Garden was a symbol of Heraya's gratitude.

The moss underfoot yielded to the weight of Kallinvar in his full Sentinel armour, receding with each step of his plate boots. The armour was such a part of him that he often forgot he wore it.

Calling to the Sigil, Kallinvar released his Sentinel armour, feeling the cool sensation wash over his skin as the dark green plate turned to liquid metal before returning to its home within the Sigil. With a sigh, he rolled his shoulders back, feeling his muscles bunch as he did. Sentinel armour kept the weariness at bay. It helped carry the burden.

"What is on your mind?" Kallinvar said as he approached Arden, though he knew well what troubled the young man's mind.

Arden sat on the ground, his back resting against the trunk of a Hallow tree, the tree's luminescent purple flowers dangling around him. A vacant look filled his eyes as he stared off towards the other side of the garden.

"My mother loved flowers." Arden smiled absently, holding a small purple leaf between his thumb and forefinger. "She was a healer. She saved people."

Kallinvar let his gaze linger on Arden for a moment before dropping himself down onto the ground beside the man, resting his back against the same tree trunk. "When we take the Sigil, we forego our past lives, Arden."

"I know, Brother-Captain. But must we forget? Because I can't. It is my family that I fight for. It is to protect them that I serve Achyron."

"No, brother, you need not forget them. To be a Knight of Achyron is not an easy charge. Sometimes it is easy to forget what it is we fight for." Images flashed across Kallinvar's mind as he spoke, images of the battle of Ilnaen – of The Fall. His blood shivered through his veins as the images flooded him. Blood, fire, death. They were no strangers to him. They plagued his dreams every time he closed his eyes, as vivid as the night they happened. Even now, sitting at the base of the Hallow tree, they were clear in his mind. Eltoar Daethana's shimmering blue níthral bursting through Brother Ohren's chest. The scream of Ohren's soul as the weapon ripped it from the world. "Those villagers will be safe with their neighbours. The village where we brought them is too far from the mountain for Uraks to bother them again for a while yet."

"Why could we not have brought them to Ardholm? They would have been safe there."

"You know we could not do that. Not yet. The others must be convinced."

Arden nodded half-heartedly at Kallinvar's words, twirling the purple petal across his fingers, only a momentary pause betraying him. "What is it you fight for, Brother-Captain?"

Kallinvar sighed, letting the back of his head rest against the rough trunk of the Hallow tree. "I fight for all who would be consumed by the Shadow if I stood back. I fight for those who cannot. I was there at Ilnaen, at The Fall. I saw what the Shadow will do when good people stand back. Bloodspawn kill without prejudice. We should have stood against it sooner on that day, and I will not allow us to make the same mistake again. We are Achyron's chosen, Arden." Kallinvar reached out his hand as he spoke, holding it in front of Arden. "Had he not sent the Grandmaster to us, we would both be dead. We were saved for a purpose. But that does not mean our path will be easy. We must be strong."

Arden reached out, grasping Kallinvar's hand. He let out a short sigh, then Kallinvar saw a steeliness set into the young man's eyes. "Pain is the path to strength."

Chapter Twenty-Nine

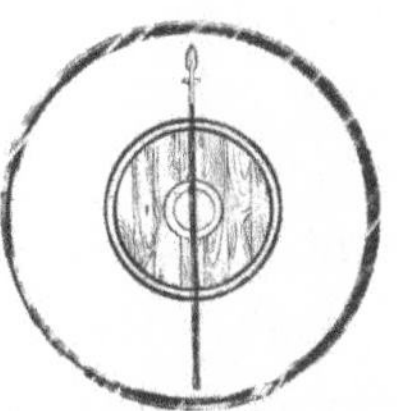

Plans Within Plans

Alleron sighed as he stepped out into the street, feeling the crunch of the frost-crusted snow beneath his feet. What he would have given for a few more nights of drinking and singing! He could still hear the muffled sounds of revelry through the door of The Hanged Maiden behind him. But his task was done, and Calen and the others would no doubt be drawing close to Liga by now. He needed to be in the saddle by dawn's light to meet them in time. Calen would have his ships, and Alleron would be aboard them when they left.

He loved Drifaien with all his heart; it was his home, and it always would be. But the empire's hold was too strong, they took too much, and his father was all too content to live under their steel boot. 'The Wyrm Slayer'. That was a man Alleron had never known; those days had passed while he was still but a child. Now, Lothal Helmund was a brooding drunk who cared more about holding his power than he did protecting his people. He feasted while those in the outer villages starved, he hoarded the Drifaienin army in Arisfall while the wyrms and Uraks made the roads all but untravellable, and he sent boatloads of Drifaienin furs to the North with little coin coming back the other way. Anything to keep the torc around his neck. To him, it was a sign of power; to Alleron, it was a collar fit for a slave. Alleron had no doubts his father would have turned Calen over to the empire the moment he discovered who he was.

Calen still had a lot to prove. Only time would tell if he was someone worth following. But if he could bring the empire to its knees, then Alleron would follow him to the void and back. And if Alleron died doing so, all the better. A beautiful death it would be. The bards would sing songs about the Draleid, of that much he was sure, and he would be a part of those songs.

Snow fell heavy as Alleron walked the city, glistening flakes drifting through the pale light of the moon, coating the slate rooves and carpeting the wide streets. A weight sat in his heart at the number of souls that lay huddled beneath awnings, curled up in porches, and crammed together in the small alcoves that nestled into the sides of buildings, the orange glow of small fires glittering against the snow. They were not all simply drunks or beggars, people who had gambled their livelihoods away. These were families: men, women, children with barely a blanket between them. Since the wyrm attacks had become more frequent and the Uraks had raided in larger numbers, people had begun to flock to Arisfall from the outer villages. It was difficult enough to live outside of a city in the Eversnow, but with travel being so dangerous and the constant fear of attack, many families had abandoned their homes for the chance of protection. But *this* was the protection they found. Many of them would not even last the night; the cold would carry them silently to the void while they slept. Alleron had seen enough frozen bodies to know this.

There was simply not enough space or work within the city's walls to accommodate the number of refugees that flooded in every day from the outer villages. And his father was more than content to let them freeze to death in the streets – fewer mouths to feed. Alleron allowed his gaze to linger on the refugees, letting the shame fill him. They were his people. They deserved better than this, and he would see that they got it.

The castle of Arisfall was an immense thing, set upon a rise at the rear of the city and backed up against the sheer mountain walls. Its slate-grey towers stretched high into the sky, their conical rooves built to prevent collapse beneath heavy snow. Torches flickered all along the battlements, which were manned day and night as though the Uraks could breach the city at any moment. Alleron couldn't keep the anger from bubbling in his stomach as he thought of all the good that could be done if those soldiers were sent to keep the villages safe or to guard the caravans of food that were raided day and night. What good were the soldiers manning the walls of a castle that already stood behind walls? He shook his head, his breath misting out in front of him.

"Who goes there?" A voice called as Alleron reached the main gates of the castle.

"Alleron Lothalson, of Helmund."

There were a few moments of silence as Alleron awaited a response, the sound of footsteps crunching against snow. A tall man with blonde shoulder-length hair and a thick knotted beard of gold and brown stepped out from the stairwell of the gatehouse, a coat of mail tied at his waist by a leather belt, fur draped over his shoulders, a spear clutched in one hand, and a wooden shield strapped to his back. "Alleron, by the gods it is good to see you back."

"Leif, it is good to be back. How goes it here?"

The two men pulled each other into a tight embrace. It had been weeks since Alleron had left Arisfall, furious with his father's decision to leave the outer villages to fend for themselves. Weeks could be a long time when wyrms and Uraks roamed the lands.

"Aye, it is quiet," Leif said, a grim look on his face. "Your father has been in a rage since you left."

Alleron nodded, furrowing his brow. His father seemed to be perpetually in a rage, so that was not news. But if he was in enough of a fury for Leif to think it worth mentioning, then Alleron would be smart to tread carefully.

"Come," Leif said, turning back towards the courtyard that lay between the main gates and the castle's entrance hall. "My shift is nearly over, and it's not as if there is much point in me standing on that wall freezing my balls off anyway." Alleron could see the grin beneath Leif's knotted beard. "So tell me, how went the patrol?"

Alleron's throat tightened as he and Leif walked through the main courtyard. "Not well..." he said, exhaling through his nose, a sickly feeling in his stomach. "Only myself, Alwen, Gudrun, Sigrid, and Heldin returned."

"I am sorry, my friend. May Achyron guide them to his halls and may Heraya bless their souls. Did they die good deaths?"

"Aye, with swords in their hands and courage in their hearts."

"There is not much more a warrior could ask."

"There is not."

The warmth of the castle's entrance hall washed over Alleron as he and Leif stepped through the doorway. The warmth sent a tingling sensation over his skin, eliciting an involuntary sigh of relief. No matter how used to the snow a man was, the warmth of a hearth fire always felt like home.

An enormous red carpet stretched the length and breadth of the entrance hall, a white spear in front of a wooden shield with a steel boss woven into its centre – the symbol of Drifaien. Two staircases ran against the walls on either side of the entrance, jutting out to the side and then upwards to the second floor. Along the walls, arch-shaped alcoves holding brass lanterns alternated with crimson tapestries that fell from ceiling to floor, depicting battles of times long past. Here and there servants darted about in white and red tunics, some carrying baskets of food, some blankets and bedclothes, some simply trying to appear busy.

The castle had been Alleron's home since he was a small child. He had known many warm moments within its walls, mostly thanks to his mother, and many dark nights, mostly thanks to his father.

"I will go to see my mother. Walk with me?" Alleron asked. Leif nodded, following Alleron up the stone staircase to the right.

"I am sorry," Leif said as they turned down the long corridor that led towards the gardens. Alleron's mother always spent her late nights in the gardens – she had since he was a child. "I would have gone with you if I could have."

"There is nothing to be sorry for, my friend. The choice was not yours, and in truth I am glad you were not there."

Leif grabbed Alleron by the shoulder. "Why do you shame me so? You do not wish me by your side, staring down the beast?"

"I do not shame you," Alleron said. "You could not come, as my father decided. And now that I know the fate of our journey, I am glad you were not there. You are like a brother, and I would not see you dining in Achyron's halls just yet."

Leif gave a short nod. "Forgive me. Being chosen as a guard captain does not suit me. The longer I stand on those walls, the more I see things that are not there."

"You were forgiven before you asked, my friend. But my mind has deserted me. The others, have they returned from their patrols to the other villages yet?"

"Audun and Destin returned from Kolnsfjord about a week past with a few scrapes and bruises, but they are all right." Leif's tone took a sombre note. "We have not heard from Fell, Kettil, and Baird."

"Don't lose hope," Alleron said. "They drew the shortest stick. Harling and The Hearth are over a month's journey from here. Were their party back already, I would be worried."

"Will I see you before the rise to break the fast?" Leif asked as they reached the doors to the guards' quarters.

"Aye, though I will be gone shortly after." He reached into his pocket, pulling out a tightly wrapped scroll secured with a piece of twine. "Open this when the sun sets tomorrow, not before. Understood?"

Leif nodded, taking the scroll, running his hand over its surface. He slipped it into his coat pocket and pulled Alleron into another embrace. "What are you planning?" he whispered in Alleron's ear.

"You will see, my friend."

"And why can I not just simply open it now?"

"Do you trust me?" Alleron asked, pulling back to look Leif in the eyes.

"Like my own flesh and blood."

"Then wait."

With that, they said one last goodnight before Leif stepped through the door into the guards' quarters. Alleron continued down the hallway, through the main hall where his father kept his 'throne', and out into his mother's garden at the back.

Growing anything in Drifaien required skill. Many of the crops that filled the farms had been cultivated over generations to withstand the extreme cold and snowfall, but almost nothing grew that wasn't green or brown. Alleron's mother's garden was the only place he remembered truly seeing colour within the boundaries of Drifaien. Even when he and his company travelled all the way to Illyanara, he rarely saw flowers as beautiful as those his mother grew in her garden. Orlana Helmund's garden was filled to the brim with blooms of all shapes, sizes, and colours. The plants ranged from knee-high to towering stalks that swept overhead with flowers of pink, blue, orange, purple, red, and every other colour he could imagine.

The garden was bounded by two long stone walls that ran almost a hundred feet, with thick panes of glass set into them at precise intervals. The roof was built at an angle, in the same way as the tower tops – slanted to prevent snow build-up. Long panes of glass were set into the roof, each about four feet wide and ten feet long. '*To allow sunlight,*' his mother told him when he was a child. '*Nothing grows without the light of the sun, my dear Alleron.*'

Cast iron chandeliers hung from the midline of the roof, though Alleron did not remember the last time he had seen a single candle alight in their grasp. Changing them was just too difficult. Most of the light and warmth in the room came from the cast iron sconces that lined the walls and the oil lamps that stood atop pedestals throughout the long room.

He found his mother at the centre of the garden, nestled into a long, brown leather couch, book in hand. Her black hair flowed down over the fox fur that adorned her shoulders. His mother was a beautiful woman; Alleron held no uncertainty in that regard. But what was more, she was kind and intelligent. It was she who taught him to read, write, and count numbers. The entire design of her garden was of her own mind. Somewhere to keep the heat in and protect the flowers from the elements, but allow them to drink in the light from the sun at the same time.

"It is the stag who waits to drink last," Alleron said, his mouth drawing into a smile as he approached his mother.

"That avoids the waiting wolf," Orlana replied. She beamed as she slid a thin strip of wood-backed leather into her book, dropped it on the couch, then pulled her son into a warm embrace. "Don't you do that again." Orlana leaned away from Alleron, drawing her eyes level with his. "Do you understand me?"

"You know I cannot make that promise, Mother. The people need protection, and I will not let them fight alone."

Orlana frowned, running her thumb down her son's cheek. Her frown softened. "You remind me of your father when he was young."

Alleron grunted, pulling his cheek away from his mother's hand. He knew her words were meant as a kindness, but comparisons to his father were not the ones he wanted to draw. "Your garden still thrives, then?" Alleron said, moving away, rubbing the vibrant red petal of a shoulder-high flower.

"He was a good man, Alleron." Orlana never did play games. It was not her way. She was always straight to the point, like an arrow to the heart. Alleron liked to think that he got that same quality from her.

"I'm sure he was," Alleron said with a sigh. "But seasons change, leaves fall, their colours fade, and they crumble."

"He is still your father." Orlana rested her hand on Alleron's shoulder, her voice dropping to a whisper. "And his eyes see far."

Alleron turned towards his mother, once more pulling her close, feeling the same comfort she had always given him as a child. "The winds are changing," he whispered. "I do not know how long I will be gone."

"Where do you go?" Orlana asked in a hushed voice.

"To fight."

Orlana leaned back, a glint in her eye from the light of the oil lamps. A smile touched her lips before she pulled Alleron into another tight hug. "If Achyron takes you to his halls, let it be while you fight for what you believe in."

A warmth filled Alleron's chest at his mother's words. "I will come back."

"I know you will. Now, go. I have more reading to do." Orlana pulled her hand up to Alleron's cheek once more, letting it linger there for a moment before she once again took her seat on the leather couch, book in hand, reading away as if he weren't there.

Alleron thought to speak, to tell her how much he loved her. But instead, he strode from the room at the sight of the solitary tear rolling down his mother's cheek. His mother was a proud woman, and he would not do her the disservice of watching her cry. All he could do was make sure he came back to her.

Alleron's footsteps echoed through the main hall as he left his mother's garden. Dark red tapestries hung the length of the walls, two on each side of the hall. Each of the tapestries held embroidered depictions of animals in brilliant whites and blues: a wolf, a stag, a bear, and a frostkat. All four of the animals were native to Drifaien. The hall was lit by two blazing hearths set into the wall on either side, in between the tapestries.

"You have returned."

A shiver ran down Alleron's back at the sound of his father's voice. He turned to see the brooding figure of Lothal Helmund sitting on his throne, a tankard in his left hand. His father hadn't been there when Alleron had first walked through the main hall – he was sure of it. Had he been listening to Alleron and Orlana talking? Surely not. One of them would have seen him.

"I have," Alleron said, turning to face the throne, a twist in his gut. He had hoped to not see his father on his short visit home.

"And how went it?" His father stood from his throne, the contents in his cup sloshing as he approached Alleron. "How was your little *adventure*?"

"The villages at the base of Mount Helmund are safe – for now." Alleron made to leave, but felt the firm grip of his father's hand wrap around his forearm.

"And what of the soldiers who went with you? I heard word that you entered the city alone. Hours ago, no less. Were you not planning to come and see your father? Or was it just that mother of yours? Will I have to teach her some respect?"

Alleron's voice lowered to a growl as he drew his eyes level to his father's. "If you touch a hair on her head, I will break your bones."

"Strong words," Lothal said, a deep rasp in his throat. "For a child who leads men to their deaths just to prove his father wrong."

Rage burned through Alleron as his heart thumped and the blood shivered through his veins. A cold silence hung between them, neither willing to break eye contact. Gritting his teeth, Alleron again turned to leave, only to feel his father's hand wrap around his wrist a second time.

"Be careful, my son." Lothal's words were weighed and measured, his eyes fixed on Alleron's. "I cannot protect you if you stay on this path. And you are incapable of protecting anyone."

Alleron held his father's gaze for a few moments, then shook his arm free and stormed from the hall.

Chapter Thirty

The Darkest Night

Languid flakes of snow drifted to and fro in the gentle breeze as the fire snapped and crackled, bits of charred branches collapsing in on themselves and spewing sparks into the air. The snowfall had been fierce most of the day but had calmed in the last hour or so. Calen had no idea how the people of Drifaien went through this year-round. It snowed in the villages and across Illyanara, but only really in winter and never with the relentless ferocity it did here. Drifaien: the land of the Eversnow.

Calen pulled the fur blanket tighter around his shoulders as he bit into the flaky white flesh of the fish he held, skewered by a small twig, in his hands. It didn't taste of much past the blackened char that coated it, but he was glad of the food in his stomach. Steam wafted from his lips as he blew outward, trying to cool his mouth.

"Hungry?" Falmin asked, laughing.

Calen grunted, choking from the steaming hot fish as it burned its way down his throat, which only caused Falmin to laugh more.

They had been there for a few hours. Just east of the fishing village, Liga. Alleron said he would meet them as the sun began to set across the horizon, but that had been and gone. Calen still held faith in the man, but he would be lying to himself if he said worry had not begun to creep its way into his bones. Without Alleron, there was no ship. And no ship meant months of travelling across the mainland. Keeping Valerys hidden would be almost impossible; he grew larger by the day.

Calen looked out over the makeshift camp at those who had followed him this long way.

Falmin sat to his left, his black hair slicked back, picking through the fish he held in a piece of parchment, removing every single bone with meticulous precision. On his right, Erik leaned against a tree, smoothing a light coat of anseed oil along the blades of his swords.

Tarmon, Korik, and Lopir sat across the way, at the other side of the fire, their faces partly obscured by the flames.

Gudrun turned the spit that sat over the flames, though judging by the taste of char in Calen's mouth, it was not her usual task. Sigrid, Alwen, and Heldin sat to the fire's left, deep in discussion about the wyrm attack. Vaeril was over at the horses, settling them down for the night.

All of them had followed him, some all the way from Belduar, through battle, collapsing tunnels, kerathlin, Uraks, and wyrms. He would see them safely home. That much he owed them.

In the back of Calen's mind, he could feel Valerys soaring just above the tree line a few miles away, watching as two stags darted their way through the forest below.

Calen yawned, bringing the back of his hand to his mouth in a futile attempt to hide his exhaustion. He probably could have slept as soon as they had set up the camp, but sleep was no longer a safe haven for him. Not a single night had passed without his mind thrusting him into nightmares. They were not always the same ones, but they always held a common theme: pain and loss. Haem dying. His father bleeding out on the ground. His mother burning alive. The Lorians slicing through the Kingsguard. The kerathlin swarming over the dwarves. Sleep was no longer his ally, not when the souls of so many weighed heavy on his shoulders.

The sound of frosted grass crunching under the metal of horseshoes, followed by a soft neigh, pulled Calen from his thoughts. He leapt to his feet, pulling in threads of Fire, Spirit, and Air as he did, forming a baldír, illuminating the space in front of him in a blinding light.

"It's me!" Alleron yelled, pulling one hand from the reins of his horse to protect his eyes.

Relief flooded through Calen at the sound of Alleron's voice. He pulled the energy back from the baldír, leaving only a dim light as the orb floated in the space between him and Alleron before allowing it to dissipate entirely.

"What are you trying to do, blind me?" Alleron asked as he dismounted, clasping his hand around Calen's forearm.

"It's good to see you," Calen replied. "You're late."

"The snowfall was heavier than I had expected."

Alleron greeted the others, pulling Sigrid, Gudrun, Alwen, and Heldin into particularly tight embraces. "I spoke to a captain who is docked at the port in Straga," Alleron said, settling down beside the fire, taking a spitted fish from Gudrun as he did. "You will have your ship. He went on ahead yesterday to ensure everything was ready."

Alleron's eyes met Calen's, lingering for a moment. Calen raised his eyebrow, and the man gave a short nod in response. An answer to a question Calen had asked that night in the barn, something he would push to the back of his mind until it came time.

"When do we leave?" Erik asked, the light of the fire glinting off his blades.

"Captain Kiron is to set sail by midday tomorrow, and Straga is about an hour or so downriver. If we charter a riverboat from Liga just after sunrise, we should give ourselves plenty of time."

A groan resonated from Falmin's throat as the gangly navigator threw his head back, steam wafting from his mouth. "What is it with you people an' gettin' up when the sun rises? It ain't natural, I can tell ya that much."

Calen couldn't help but laugh at Falmin's outburst. Aeson had made getting up before sunrise almost ritualistic. Even on mornings when Calen didn't need to be up before the sun crested the horizon, his eyes still opened to darkness. Once that happened, he found it very difficult to get back to sleep.

"What of Valerys?" Tarmon asked, ignoring Falmin. "I'm assuming there is a plan?"

"Valerys will fly with us, resting on the coast as we make our way towards Belduar," Calen answered, looking towards Alleron, who nodded. "He can fly a lot faster than the ship will be able to sail. Keeping up won't be a problem for him."

Tarmon nodded as he cast a pensive gaze into the fire. The man always seemed to be thinking, planning. Were it not for him and his calm mind, Calen was certain they would never have made it out of the tunnels beneath the Lodhar Mountains.

Just as Calen went to retake his seat beside Falmin, a tickling sensation pricked his mind, but before he had any idea what it was, threads of Air wrapped around his body, pinning his hands against his side where he stood. He looked to Falmin, but threads of Air were wrapped around the navigator as well.

"Thank you, Alleron," a voice called. It had a deep Drifaienin lilt to it. "You see, Exarch, I told you he would lead us to your Draleid. Well done, my son."

Panic set into Calen as he tried to break free of the threads of Air that held him in place. His eyes shot to Alleron, who had a stunned look on his face. Had he betrayed them? *Focus, break free.* He couldn't move even a finger. His heart pounded. He tried to reach out to the Spark, but again, nothing. There was something in his way, blocking him. Threads of Spirit wound around him, interlaced with the threads of Air. Fear and rage surged into his mind from Valerys and for a moment, their minds were one. The dragon's wings cracked against the air, lifting him off the ground, blood dripping from his open jaws, a dead boar lying in a heap of blood-red snow at his feet.

Rasps of steel rang out around the camp at the sound of the man's voice. It took Calen a moment to realise the others couldn't see the threads of Air wrapped around him and Falmin. Those who couldn't touch the Spark couldn't see its threads either. The only other person was… Vaeril. A sudden jolt of panic shot through Calen's mind when he looked over towards the horses and could no longer see Vaeril. *Please, be all right.*

"Step into the light, *Father,*" Alleron growled. Fury was etched into his face as he glared into the darkness where the voice had come from.

Alleron, please say you didn't... please... Calen continued to struggle, trying desperately to free his limbs from their invisible prison, constantly reaching out to the Spark, finding nothing. *What is happening?* He felt the wind ripple over Valerys's scales as the dragon tore through the sky, the fury burning in his chest like nothing Calen had ever felt.

A figure took shape, stepping from the night's grasp into the light of the fire. The man was as big as Tarmon, with a deep chest covered in chainmail, a thick knotted beard, and long black hair streaked with grey that fell around his shoulders. He wore a coat of bear fur, and two bearded axes hung from loops on his belt on both hips. "I cannot thank you enough, son. Were it not for you, we would never have found this *Draleid.*"

"I would never have brought you here," Alleron said, spitting in the snow at his father's feet.

Lothal's upper lip twisted in irritation. "No," he replied, reaching his hand out. Two Drifaienin soldiers, furs draped over their shimmering coats of mail, emerged beside Lothal, one of them passing him a leather sack. "But like I said in the castle, *you* are incapable of protecting *anyone.*"

Lothal pulled the drawstrings on the bag, opening it and emptying its contents. A gasp escaped Alleron's throat as a severed head dropped into the snow, dappling the white blanket of compacted flakes with blood. Calen thought he recognised the man's face, a head of blonde hair with a thick knotted beard of gold and brown. One of the men who had been with Alleron in The Two Barges in Milltown?

"No," Alleron whispered, just barely audible. "No," he said again, his voice turning into a growl. He leapt to his feet, drawing his face level with his father's, snarling. "Why?" Pure hatred seeped from Alleron's voice.

"I cannot let those who are disloyal survive. I must protect Drifaien." Even with his forehead pressed against his son's and Alleron's fingers gripped tightly around the hilt of his axe, Lothal sneered.

"You protect nothing but yourself!" Alleron roared, lunging forward.

In a flash of movement, Lothal caught Alleron on the jaw with a swift elbow, punching him in the gut as he recoiled. A knee to the face sent blood splattering across the snow, and Lothal shoved his son to the ground. "Me? You cannot even protect yourself, never mind your *friends.*" Lothal rested his foot against the severed head that lay in the snow, before kicking it with the side of his foot, rolling it over beside Alleron, who lay groaning in the snow. "Stay down. I will not lose another child."

"What do you want?" Erik yelled, clutching a blade in each hand, stepping closer to Alleron's father, who still loomed over his son.

"You are not the one asking questions here," a second voice said firmly, with a purposeful tone that spoke of wealth and power. "Now that the drama is out of the way, lower your weapons, all of you, or I will have my men loose their arrows." A man stepped out of the night-obscured darkness, a black robe with a trim of silver draped around his shoulders. His hood was drawn down, exposing a bronzed complexion, a short blonde beard, and cropped hair.

Four soldiers stood on either side of the robed man, swords drawn, armoured in smooth black plate from head to toe over coats of mail that glittered in the firelight.

"I am High Mage Artim Valdock, Exarch of the Imperial Battlemages of the Circle of Magii. And I am here for the Draleid." The High Mage glanced at Calen, a grin spreading across his face. He extended a finger. "That is him."

Calen watched as the others took up a defensive position in front of him. Tarmon stood at the front, his armour gleaming, greatsword grasped with both hands. Even the word 'mage' seemed not to set fear into his heart. Korik and Lopir stood by his side, axes drawn. While Gudrun, Alwen, Sigrid, Heldin stood to his left; Erik was to his right, closer to Calen.

"No one need die this night," the High Mage said, his black robes striking a stark contrast with the snow as he took a step forward. The man's eyes held a sharp glint as they glanced towards Calen. As quickly as the threads of Air had pinned him, they vanished, their firm grasp drifting into the wind, but that wall of Spirit still stood between him and the Spark. A shiver ran the length of Calen's body and panic scratched at the corners of his mind. He had not thought it possible, and yet the mage had blocked him from the Spark as though it were nothing. Even with all the power he had gained since his parents were taken from him, this man had reduced him to nothing in an instant. That familiar feeling of helplessness crept into his mind.

"It's a warding of Spirit," Falmin whispered to Calen, rubbing his wrists as though he had been chained. "I've only seen it a few times before."

"A gesture of good will," the High Mage said, turning towards Calen, a knowing look in his eyes. "Now, I'm going to make this very simple." The man reached into the inside pocket of his robes, producing a pair of thick manacles engraved with sets of runes that glowed with a dim blue light. "Put these on and come with us." His eyes were fixed on Calen. "You have my word you will not be harmed. We are to bring you to Al'Nasla. Do this, and we will let your companions leave this place with their lives. It is your choice. How many of their lives are worth yours?"

As the High Mage's words hung in the air, the sound of grating steel and the crunch of snow beneath boots sounded all around them as more warriors stepped into the light of the fire. Men and women in the red and black leather of the Lorian Empire, steel breastplates strapped across their chests. Easily fifty, probably more. The clink of steel sounded out past those Calen could see.

"Don't even consider it," Erik said, stepping closer to Calen. "We haven't come this far to just stand down. They'll kill us all anyway."

Images flashed across Calen's mind. Air rushing. Wings beating. Fire screaming. He looked around at his companions. How many of them would die if they fought? How many would die if they didn't? He had no way of knowing what the High Mage would do if he put those manacles on. Or what those manacles would do to him. He had never seen anything like them. The runes etched into their surface radiated a dim blue light that shimmered across the smooth steel. The last time he had handed himself over to the empire, the people he was trying to save died anyway. Once more, Calen found himself with a choice that was not truly a choice. No matter what he did, more people would die, and they would die because of him. A coil of dread twisted in his stomach. He had led them to their deaths.

Ignoring the icy chill of his blood as it ran through his veins, Calen looked over towards Tarmon, who held his gaze.

"We're with you, Draleid."

"We all die and are reforged by Hafaesir's hammer," Korik added, shifting his axe in his hands.

"I'm with ya too," Falmin chimed in, shrugging. "Though, I'd prefer not ta die, if we could manage it."

"A good death it will be," Gudrun said with a nod.

More Lorian soldiers came into sight, the shadows cast by the campfire flickering across their faces. Calen set himself, drawing in a deep breath. He let the realisation sink in: if they died this night, they would die fighting.

He reached out to Valerys, seeing through his eyes, hearing through his ears. *Thump.* Their wings beat against the sky, picking up speed. A small fire illuminated a patch of snow just ahead, casting shadows across the ground.

Calen pulled himself back into his own mind.

"Draleid n'aldryr," he whispered to himself. *Stay in the air, coming to the ground isn't worth the risk.*

A rumble of acknowledgement from Valerys was followed by that familiar sensation surging through the back of his mind, that build of pressure, then a flicker caught his eye in the sky above. He would need to clear the ground between them as fast as he could.

Three.

Was he making the right decision? Calen cast his eyes around, taking in his friends one more time. *Handing myself over means nothing.* His grip tightened on the hilt of his sword. The leather wrap of the handle felt like home. His father's lifeless body, lying in the dirt, flashed across his mind as his eyes fell on the swirls and spirals that ran the length of the slightly curved blade. *Not again.*

Two.

Calen's heart battered against his chest, blood shivered through his veins, the muscles in his jaw twitched. He set his eyes on the High Mage, the man's black robes flapping in the breeze. His threads of Spirit still surrounded Calen, still cut him off from the Spark. But he was not helpless. He was not the same person he had been when the empire came to his village. He was more than that now. He would not be helpless again. He would stand and fight.

One.

A deafening roar tore through the sky, followed by a pillar of dragonfire that streamed from Valerys's jaws, momentarily turning night to day, revealing the true number of soldiers Lothal Helmund and the High Mage had brought with them. Over a hundred, at least. Just as dread coiled in Calen's stomach, chunks of clay and earth were lifted into the air, dragonfire ripping a path through the soldiers who stood behind the High Mage, melting steel as easily as the snow. Screams and howls rang out, mingling with the almost instant smell of charred earth and flesh.

Calen felt a faltering in the bonds of Spirit that held his ward. The dragonfire had distracted the High Mage. He charged. "For Achyron!"

He wasn't entirely sure why he chose those words. It was the chant the Drifaienin had used in The Two Barges, and if there was any god they needed to watch over them right now, it was The Warrior.

"For The Warrior!" he heard the others call back.

He was less than two strides from the High Mage when the soldiers in black steel plate stepped in his path. Eight of them. A flicker of hesitation flashed across his mind. He still couldn't touch the Spark. He pushed the fear down, pressing into the far depths of his mind, bringing his hands into the first position of svidarya.

A tremor ran through his blade as it collided with the first soldier's sword, but he held firm, deflecting the second and third strikes. He needed to keep them in front of him. If they got behind him, he wouldn't stand a chance.

Calen stumbled backwards as a massive blade burst through the chest of the soldier before him, only for it to be pulled free, swinging, separating another soldier's head from his shoulders. The hulking frame of Tarmon Hoard stood over the two bodies, chest heaving, fire in his eyes. The man was a force of nature.

A quick nod, and they both charged at the six remaining soldiers in black plate. Good odds.

Calen slowed his breathing as he charged. His legs felt like lead as he heaved them in and out of the snow. Another rise of pressure in the back of his mind was followed by another river of dragonfire from Valerys, peeling through the Lorian and Drifaienin soldiers. The wails sent shivers down Calen's spine – the sound of men being burned alive. He wrapped his guilt around his fear, pushing them both aside. They would do him no good if he died.

Four of the soldiers in black plate swarmed around Tarmon, leaving two for Calen.

One, two. He met the strikes, plunging his blade into the leg of the soldier to his left, slicing through the rivets of his mail. The man screamed before Calen pulled his blade free and drove it up through the soldier's jaw, just under the rim of the helmet.

Calen howled as a searing pain cut through his side. The cut wasn't deep, just enough to slice through the leather, but it burned. He brought his blade around to meet the second strike, then a third. His foot hit something solid, and he stumbled, crashing down into the bloodstained snow.

The soldier stood over him, sword raised, a cold stare in his eyes. But before he could bring the sword down, an arrow plunged into his exposed armpit, causing him to howl in pain, reeling back before a second arrow took him in the eye, and he collapsed to the ground, body limp.

Calen scrambled to his feet, his throat dry and a tremble in his chest. In the madness, he couldn't see who had loosed the arrows, but he was sure Vaeril stood somewhere in the chaos. He looked to his left. Only two of the four soldiers who had swarmed Tarmon still stood.

"Go!" Tarmon glanced in the direction of the High Mage before bringing his greatsword down into the neck of the soldier before him, spraying the air with blood.

Another pillar of dragonfire ripped through the night as Valerys swooped low, again followed by screams and wails. *Be careful.*

Fury was the only thought that radiated from the dragon's mind, searing into Calen, burning through him. An all-consuming rage rippled through them both. Valerys would rather die than see harm come to his Draleid, and the dragon's wrath ignited every fibre in Calen's body.

The High Mage stood staring at Calen, threads of Spirit seeping from him, holding Calen's warding in place.

"Let's take the bastard together." Falmin stepped up beside Calen, blood trickling down the side of his head and a long gash in his arm.

Both Calen and Falmin dove to the ground as the High Mage sent a pillar of fire pluming towards them. A mist of snow sprayed up around Calen as he landed, tickling his face and setting a chill in his hands. He dug his fingers into the hard-packed snow, dragging himself to his feet. As he stood, an arrow plunged into the High Mage's shoulder. Suddenly, the Spark was there. He could feel it.

Calen reached out, desperately snatching at threads of Fire, Water, and Air. He melted the snow around him, forming it into short spears of ice, just as he had with the wyrms. He charged, Valerys's anger surging through him. With an almighty roar, he launched the spears towards the High Mage. One spear soared past the man's head and two others evaporated into the air, touched by threads of Fire. Roaring, Calen drew in threads of Air, letting their cool touch wrap around his bones before catapulting them towards the High Mage. The man, his black robes billowing out behind him, split Calen's threads down the middle with threads of Spirit, standing untouched between them.

Stunned, Calen tried his best to still the fear in his stomach. *How?*

With a wave of the High Mage's hand, two arrows burst into flames in mid-air, consumed by threads of Fire before they reached their target. Turning his attention back to Calen, the High Mage lashed out with a whip of Air, sending him crashing to the ground.

Pulling himself back to his feet, Calen watched as Falmin charged towards the High Mage. The navigator sidestepped a column of fire that erupted from the High Mage's hand, then sent the man hurtling to the ground with a whip of Air.

Just as it looked as though Falmin had the upper hand, the High Mage dragged himself to his feet, drawing in threads of Water, Fire, and Air, mimicking Calen's ice spears.

Calen's heart fell into the pit of his stomach as one spear burst through Falmin's abdomen, a second went through his leg, and a third sliced through his right shoulder, plumes of blood mist erupting from each wound. The navigator dropped to his knees, blood spilling over his body.

"No!" Calen roared as he ran. Two Lorian soldiers stepped in his path. He cut them down, swallowing three others in a column of fire. *No, no, no.* The only sound in Calen's ears was the pounding of blood as it rushed through his veins. He cast a glance at Falmin's body. His chest trembled and throat went dry. He let his mind slip into Valerys's, feeding on the dragon's rage, using it to push down his grief, his loss.

Calen cleared the distance to the High Mage in a matter of moments, swinging his blade. The man met the swing with ease, his sword moving in a blur of steel.

Pure hatred surged through Calen as he struck again and again. He felt the bite of steel more than once as the High Mage raked his blade across Calen's arm, then his ribs.

Drawing in threads of Air, Calen slammed them down on the High Mage's shoulders, dropping him to his knees.

"You have no idea what you face, do you?" the High Mage said, producing a gemstone from within his robes, his voice battered by the screams around them, the thump of Valerys's wings against the air, and the ringing of steel on steel.

Calen didn't answer. He tightened his grip on the hilt of his sword, setting his jaw. The cut in his side burned, his heart pounded, and a mixture of sweat and the blood of other men felt tacky against his skin. He levelled his blade against the man's neck. What he was about to do went against everything his parents had ever taught him. To take someone's life while they knelt before him; it was not something he could do on his own. He let his mind drift deeper into Valerys's. Let the dragon's fury consume him. He pulled back his arm and drove his blade towards the High Mage's black heart.

Calen's blood turned to ice in his veins as a red glow pulsated from the small gemstone in the High Mage's hand. He moved to plunge his sword into the man's chest, but his arm didn't respond. Neither did his legs nor his head. It was as though someone had tethered his body in place, but he felt no threads except for the threads of Spirit that encased him once more, blocking him off from the Spark. Calen's eyes moved to the shimmering red gemstone, panic crawling along his skin. *How?*

The High Mage got to his feet, dusting the snow off the collar of his robes.

A glint of steel flashed to the left, illuminated by the raging flames from Valerys's dragonfire. Calen watched as Lopir leapt from the swell of men around them, hefting his axe overhead, but then the dwarf stopped dead, suspended in mid-air. Again, Calen felt nothing holding Lopir in place. No threads of Air or Spirit. How was he doing it?

Calen could see the fear in Lopir's face as he hung in the air as though held by chains.

"I have no need for you." The High Mage glared at Lopir, reaching out his hand and snapping his fingers closed.

Calen shuddered as Lopir's neck snapped to the right, and the life disappeared from the dwarf's eye. The fury that had seeped into Calen's mind from Valerys's was swallowed whole by a wave of anguish that swept through him from head to toe.

Letting Lopir's body drop into the snow, the High Mage walked towards Calen. Even with the fighting raging around them and men screaming as dragonfire burned the skin from their bones, the mage's steps were slow and purposeful. The steps of a someone who thought themselves so far above everything else, worry did not so much as touch the edges of their mind.

"Did you think this would end any other way?" he hissed, drawing his eyes level with Calen's, the glowing red gemstone clutched in his hand. Calen tugged at his invisible bonds, willing his fingers to wrap around the man's throat. But no matter how fiercely he thrashed, his body didn't respond. "The power of the Spark pales in comparison to the strength Efialtír provides. Your people have denied him for too long."

An audible gasp escaped Calen's throat as an arrow stopped just inches from the side of the High Mage's head, holding there before dropping harmlessly into the snow. Threads of Earth followed, burying into the ground. Pillars of clay and stone erupted from beneath the snow, forming into spikes, launching straight towards the High Mage. Again, Calen did not feel the tingling sensation at the back of his neck when the spikes of stone and clay crumbled, falling into the snow. Nor did he feel them when Vaeril leapt from the mass of bodies, only to be slammed into the ground by an unseen force.

"An elf?" The High Mage pouted, an amused curiosity in his voice. "One of old blood, no less. Not the broken ones that work the mines at Dead Rocks Hold. The Inquisition will have questions for you, no doubt. Now—"

An earth-shattering roar peeled through the skies, drowning out the sounds of battle and the screams of dying men. Soldiers all around stopped, their eyes glassing over in fear as they looked to the sky.

With a gust of wind that could have uprooted trees, Valerys crashed to the ground, his claws rending steel and his wingbeats sending spirals of snow and blood pluming through the air. One swipe of his spear-tip tail sent two Drifaienin soldiers careening into a tree. He caught a third in his jaws, tearing through the man's chest.

Another deafening roar was followed by a column of dragonfire that scorched its way through the ranks of Lorian and Drifaienin soldiers. Men wailed as flesh and leather burned, incensing the air with an acrid tang.

Then a sharp pain shot through Calen's mind as a spear was thrust into Valerys's shoulder and a second into his hind leg. The dragon let out another ear-splitting roar as he spun again, his tail cleaving into the side of a Drifaienin woman's neck, his claws sundering the breastplate of a Lorian soldier. But still, pain burned through him.

A knot of dread coiled in Calen's stomach as he watched more men pick up spears. *Go! Take to the sky, now!*

Valerys roared once more, tearing a man's arm off in one bite, blood incarnadining the snow. Another sharp pain, another spear.

"Valerys, fly!" Calen screamed so loudly that it felt as though his throat might bleed and rip apart from the force of his voice. "Go, now!"

A crack of Valerys's wings whipped snow into the air, reflecting the light of the blazing fires all around. Another thump, and the dragon was in the air. The *whoosh* of arrows sliced through the night. Most bounced off Valerys's scaled hide, but one or two sliced through his leathery wings, sending sharp bursts of pain through Calen.

Calen pushed with everything he had, reaching out to the Spark with every ounce of strength in his body. He had to break through this barrier of Spirit. He had to help Valerys.

Then, within moments, he found what he was looking for. A gap, a split in the barrier of Spirit. As though believing it some sort of trick, he glanced over at the High Mage. The gemstone in the man's hand glowed with a violent fury. His attention was focused on Valerys. He had let his guard down.

Calen pushed again, focusing his mind on that gap. He screamed as his thoughts crashed into the barrier of Spirit. A look of surprise flashed across the High Mage's face as Calen burst through the barrier. Something still held him in place, unable to do so much as lift his finger. But he could touch the Spark, and that was all he needed.

He would only have moments – he needed to be quick. He needed to give Valerys time. Calen drew in threads of Fire, feeling their warmth sweep through him, pulling harder and harder until he could barely contain the force. The air rippled as the threads burst outward, a roaring plume of flames searing through air. The flames swept over the High Mage, consuming the Lorian soldiers who stood in its path. Calen pulled harder, feeling the Spark call to him, urging him to draw deeper. Reluctantly, he let go, his muscles sagging, his heartbeat weak. Even still, a weary smile crept onto his face as he felt the touch of Valerys's mind.

But the smile quickly faded as the flames before him flickered from existence, and High Mage Artim Valdock stood, untouched, amongst the crumpled, charred husks of the Lorian soldiers who had been caught by the blast, his face contorted in fury. "Insolent child!"

Calen howled as the threads of Air that held him in place pulled tighter, crushing him in their grasp.

"Call your dragon off," the High Mage hissed, drawing level with Calen. "Or I will kill this elf and all the others. They have no worth to me."

"You will kill them anyway," Calen spat, fury seeping into his mind again. He could feel Valerys swooping overhead. The dragon wanted to crash back down right on top of the High Mage.

Don't do it. I can't lose you.

A deep growl resonated back through Calen's mind. Images of loss and grief.

"I will not. You have my word."

"Your word means nothing."

"My word means everything. But it does not matter. Look around. Your companions will die anyway. And your dragon is far from fully grown. It will die trying to save you. I will take great pleasure in crushing its bones. Be smart, live to die another day."

Swallowing hard, Calen cast his gaze around him. Most of the trees within twenty feet of the fighting were on fire, blazing from Valerys's dragonfire, illuminating the campsite that had become a battleground.

Bodies lay everywhere. Draped in Drifaienin furs, plated in Lorian leather and steel. But more than that, his eyes fell on the lifeless bodies of Lopir and Falmin. Both had followed him from Belduar. They had stood by him, and he had failed them. Vaeril lay face down in the snow, held there by whatever magic that gemstone possessed. He saw Erik, Tarmon, and Korik grouped together just behind him, surrounded. Tarmon carried a heavy limp and blood seeped from wounds along Korik's arms and back. Even as Erik weaved in and out of his attackers, Calen could see the heaviness in his arms, the weariness in his eyes. They would die if he did nothing. But he could give them a chance.

Valerys, I need you to fall back. If we keep fighting, they will kill me and all the others. We need to survive.

Images flashed across Calen's mind from Valerys. A man dying, blood, his dragon howling, consumed by grief.

If you land, he will kill us both.

A roar erupted from the dragon's jaws, a roar of resignation and sorrow.

"Call off your men," Calen said, releasing a heavy sigh.

"You have made a wise choice."

Emptiness. A dark black pool of nothing set itself in Calen's chest and rooted itself in his heart. A loneliness echoed through him as he reached out to Valerys. He could sense the dragon, just faintly in the back of his mind, but he couldn't *feel* him. It was as though half of his soul lay just out of reach. There, but at the same time, not. An insurmountable sadness had hollowed out his bones.

It was everything Calen could do to hold back the voice in his head that told him life was not worth living. It was his voice. It echoed through the empty chambers of his mind. Even breathing felt as though it were not worth the strain it put on his lungs. Simply existing was not worth the pain.

The chains connecting Calen's manacle-clad hands clinked as he lifted them up in front of his face, only vaguely aware of the cold stone wall pressing against his back. The runes carved into the surface of the manacles cast a dim blue glow into the otherwise dark cell. They were light. Lighter than he expected, at least. The runes ran along the outside of each manacle, around the entire circumference. The Spark was used to create them, of that much Calen was sure. A constant thrum resonated from them into his wrists and through his body, culminating in a droning buzz that bored into the back of his mind.

Those manacles were the reason he was alone. They were the reason he could not feel the other half of his soul.

The void in Calen's body swelled, filling with fury. Lifting his hands up over his head, he smashed the manacles against the stone floor. The force of the strike reverberated through his arms, the steel of the manacles cutting into his wrists. But he didn't care. Again he lifted his hands, and again he struck them down against the stone. He beat the manacles against the ground until his blood coated the floor and his wrists felt like they would snap.

Calen dropped his head to the floor, holding his wrists out in front of him, his shoulders convulsing as he sobbed into the stone. Images of Falmin's lifeless body filled his mind. Blood seeping from the gaping wounds in his stomach, shoulder, and leg, staining the snow a deep crimson. Would Falmin still be alive if Calen had just given himself over? Would Lopir?

Lopir. A shiver ran through Calen's body as he remembered the fear in the dwarf's eye. The sheer terror of being completely helpless. It was a feeling Calen was all too familiar with.

His body still convulsing, Calen dropped to his side, lying in a mixture of his own tears and blood. He was alone. Truly alone. At times, he had yearned for sleep so as to have his mind to himself, to not have to feel everything Valerys felt. But now he yearned for the constant touch of Valerys's mind. Without it, he was not even half of who he had been; he was a shell.

The sliding of an iron bar and the clink of metal on metal reverberated through the cold, dark cell. Then, with an aching creak, the wooden door that guarded the cell's room swung open and the crack of leathered heels on stone echoed through the room.

"You put up a fight, I'll give you that much." Calen didn't have to lift his head to know the High Mage stood on the other side of the cell, looming over him.

Calen swallowed hard, fighting back a groan of pain as he adjusted his position, pulling himself up against the iron bars so he could stare directly into the man's soul. The High Mage's eyes were colder than ice, so dark they were almost black. Calen grunted as the throbbing wound in his side pulsed with pain. He knew his face was marred with a mixture of dirt, blood, and tears. He didn't care. Not one shred of his shattered soul cared. He wanted to look into Artim Valdock's eyes. He wanted to tear the man's head from his shoulders.

"Incredible, aren't they?" the High Mage said, gesturing towards the manacles secured around Calen's wrists. "Created by Fane Mortem himself. The only human to ever truly master the Jotnar art of rune crafting. What does it feel like to be completely cut off from the Spark? I have often wondered. Though I suppose, in your case, that is the least of your concerns. I've watched Draleid go completely insane when cut off from their dragons." The High Mage leaned in a little closer to the bars, lowering his voice to a whisper. "One elf peeled her own fingernails off from scratching at the walls."

Calen fought off a grimace as he lifted himself to his feet, his legs wobbling, his breath catching in his throat. "I… will… not… break."

Even to Calen, the words sounded weak. Hollow.

"I don't think you understand how this works." The High Mage's eyes grew even colder before something invisible crashed into Calen's body, slamming him into the cell wall. A shockwave of pain rippled through Calen's bones, but he clenched his jaw and gritted his teeth. The mage had already taken half of Calen's soul – Calen would not give him the pleasure of hearing him scream.

Reaching into the pocket of his robes, the man produced a thick iron key, slotting it into the lock on the barred iron door of the cell. He turned it left until it elicited a distinct *click*, and the door opened with a slow creak.

"You see," the High Mage said, stepping into the cell. "You think you understand this world, but you know nothing."

Calen couldn't sense the threads of Air, but he felt them pulling at him, dragging him closer to the High Mage, pulling his hands up into the air as though his manacles were suspended from the ceiling. A swift punch to the ribs took the air from his lungs, followed by a second punch to his gut. Calen coughed and spluttered, trying desperately to breathe before a third blow crashed into his gut again.

"You took sides in a war of which you do not have even the slightest comprehension."

Pain exploded at the side of Calen's head, stars flitting across his eyes. His head drooped and his arms went limp as his legs gave way underneath him. He hung there, suspended only by the threads of air that held his manacles above his head.

Fingers tugged at Calen's hair, pulling his head up so his eyes were level with the High Mage's. "You are nothing but a child who was told he could be a hero." The High Mage let go of Calen's hair. He pulled his black robes from over his shoulders, revealing a deceptively muscular physique beneath a pale linen shirt, ridges of innumerable scars visible through the thin fabric. "There are no such things as heroes, boy. A hero in one person's eyes is a villain in another's." The High Mage stepped forward, his right hand closing around Calen's neck.

Calen just hung there as the pressure closed in around his throat. At any other time, he would have thrashed around, clawing at any last gasp of life he could drag into his lungs. But that instinct was not there. It had been taken from him with Valerys. Now, the voice in his head told him to lean into the man's grip. To embrace death.

The High Mage raised an eyebrow. "Curious." Pulling his hand away, he let Calen's neck fall, limp. "I could kill you right now, but the emperor does not want you dead. It is a pity. Death would be cleaner. However, he does not need to know I have you. Not yet." The High Mage turned away from Calen, rolling the sleeves of his shirt up to his elbows. "You will tell me where to find Aeson Virandr, and you will tell me where to find the other leaders of your little *rebellion.*" A dark stare had set into the man's eyes when he turned back to face Calen. "Four hundred years they have fought this war in the shadows. No more."

Another swift punch landed in his gut, and Calen dappled the floor with blood.

A grunt escaped Calen's throat as the High Mage buried his thumb into a wound that scored Calen's chest. Calen screamed as the man dug his thumb in deeper, the pain blinding him.

"You think this is pain? This is nothing. If you do not speak, you will experience pain the likes of which you could not even have dreamt of in your darkest nightmares. I will burn through your mind like a wildfire."

The muscles in Calen's jaw twitched, his vision fading in and out of blackness.

"So be it."

Searing agony burned through Calen from head to toe. It sank into his bones until they felt as though they would crumble. It swept across his skin like a wave of fire. Calen's screams echoed through the room, crashing off the stone.

He reached out to Valerys and felt nothing.

He was alone.

The vibrations shook Dann's back as the horse trotted along the beaten path. The chill of the winter breeze nipped at his skin, while the deceptive warmth of the afternoon sun kissed the back of his neck. It had been a week since they left the Southern Fold Gate in the Lodhar Mountains. They had passed Midhaven only the night before last.

If there was something he had grown to love, it was riding a horse. The feel of the powerful animal beneath him, the ripple of its muscles as it broke into a gallop, the trust they placed in one another. There wasn't a feeling quite like it. He leaned down, running his hand along his horse's neck, feeling the soft touch of the animal's black hair along his fingers. "We're going to have to give you a name."

Dann looked down at Alea and Lyrei loping along the ground to his left. Both had refused horses. Dann wasn't quite sure why. They had done the same when they joined the group in the Darkwood, yet he distinctly remembered seeing the other elf riding that stag in the Darkwood. Though, if that animal could truly be called a stag, then a wolfpine was a dog.

Neither Alea nor Lyrei had spoken to him since his outburst in the caves. He knew he had been in the wrong. He had let his anger get the better of him, and he had taken it out on Alea. The only problem was he didn't know how to admit it. But he would have to start somewhere. "How do you name horses in the elf tongue?"

Alea turned her head, raising an uncertain eyebrow. She let out a sigh. The same kind of sigh Dann's mother always gave him when he asked questions that irritated her, which, to his knowledge, was often. "When we are children, we are taught both the Common Tongue and the Old Tongue. There is no *elf tongue*." With that said, she turned her attention back to the path ahead. Dann could see the snigger on Lyrei's face, but she didn't speak.

Dann did his best to ignore Alea's attitude; he knew right well what she was doing. Rist did it all the time. He would always give Dann *an* answer, but never the answer to the question he asked. Rist did it to annoy him, just as Alea was doing now. "Well, how do you name horses in the *Old* Tongue then?"

Alea turned her head once more, a touch of irritation plain on her face. "What do you care? You ride on that horse's back without any bond. He does not carry you because he wishes to. He does it because he is forced to."

Dann went to reply, but held his tongue. There was more sting in Alea's words than was born simply from annoyance. He saw his way back into her good books. "There are clearly things I don't know."

"Clearly," Alea replied, not even turning her head.

"Teach me, then."

Alea stopped at Dann's words.

"Whoa, boy. Steady." Dann gave a slight pat on the horse's neck, stopping himself beside Alea.

Lyrei eyed them both askance but continued, moving to catch up with Therin and Aeson, who rode further ahead.

"I care for him, too." Alea's chest rose and fell in heavy sweeps, and Dann could see the anger in her golden eyes. It was clear this was not about the horse – it was about Calen.

"I know you do," Dann said. "And I'm sorry."

"My people live in the Aravell not because we choose to, but because the choice was taken from us. My people were slaughtered after the fall of The Order. Driven from our homes, murdered in the streets. And still, we did not lose faith. Even when it cost us the unity of our people. Even when those in Lynalion blamed the other races for what happened, we held the faith, we stayed true. My parents, and their parents before them, were raised beneath the forest canopy of the Aravell, as I was. We never got the chance to see the sweeping cities of old, but I hold out hope. That is why I am here. That is why I swore an oath to protect the Draleid with my life. I am not here to garner fame and renown. I am here to fight for a better future, and Calen is the best chance of that."

Dann drew in a deep breath, waiting for the hairs on the back of his neck to lie down. A tremble ran through him, across his shoulders and chest. "Calen and Rist are the closest thing I've ever had to brothers. I've never not had them around me. They have always been the better parts of me, always made the right decisions when I made the wrong ones. Without them… I'm not sure who I am. I didn't mean to lose my temper in the tunnels. I'm just scared."

Without saying a word, Alea walked closer to Dann, laying a hand on the horse's flank. "Drunir."

"What?"

"It is your horse's name. It means Companion."

Chapter Thirty-One

A Darkness

alen grunted as he lay on his back, the cold stone of the cell floor providing some reprieve from the pain that burned across his back. Artim Valdock had been true to his word. The agony Calen felt was like nothing he had ever imagined. New cuts and welts littered his back, chest, and legs, some scabbed over, some still seeping pus and blood. He no longer had nails on his feet or hands, and he was sure some of his ribs were broken. A healer would be along soon to apply salve to his wounds, as they had each of the last eight nights. The better he healed, the more he could be tortured.

A pang twisted in his stomach, his body screaming for even the smallest morsel of food. Calen pushed his hunger to the back of his mind; it would do him no good to listen to it now. Gritting his teeth, Calen stretched his arm, snatching the loop of the waterskin with his finger, hearing only the slightest of sloshing noises from within. He gasped, a sharp pain shooting through his side as he pulled the stopper from the waterskin and lifted the nozzle to his mouth. Only a dribble remained at the bottom of the skin, just enough to wet his lips and tongue.

The voice in the back of his mind told him to empty the waterskin's contents onto the ground. He would not survive long without water. But alongside that dark, all-consuming voice, rang his father's words. *"The sun will set, and it will rise again, and it will do so the next day and the next. The gods are in charge of such things, but it is by our own will that we pick ourselves up when we fall."*

Dropping the empty waterskin to the floor, Calen closed his eyes. The High Mage had not lied, but he had failed to understand something crucial. No matter how much torture or pain he put Calen through, it paled in comparison to the absence of Valerys from his soul. It was a tangible emptiness. Half of him was gone, and his entire consciousness cried out for what was lost.

He still heard Valerys at night. The dragon's roars bellowed like thunder through the dark, sometimes even shaking the walls of the cell. He had urged the dragon to stay away, but he knew Valerys could no more hear him than he could hear Valerys.

"Just stay alive..."

The bread was hard and difficult to chew, gone stale maybe two days past. Soaked in the juices of the pork, however, it was edible. Dann choked it down hungrily.

He shuffled closer to the fire as it crackled and snapped, spitting plumes of embers into the night. As the days moved deeper into winter's grasp, the cold grew more ravenous and was forever nipping at his skin. The group had set up camp only an hour ago, three or so hours after the sun had set along the horizon. Riding in the dark didn't seem to bother anyone; they didn't have time to waste on the whims of the sun and moon.

He wasn't quite sure where they were. He had seen the Marin Mountains not too far in the distance that morning. At least, Therin had said they were the Marin Mountains. Dann did not know well enough himself. It had not been that long ago that he had not even laid eyes on Camylin, never mind the mountains that shaded the Illyanara capital, Argona. The Glade was far enough to the west that Argona was rarely ever mentioned, though traders and bards who passed through often told of its splendour and riches. That's all bards ever seemed to talk about: splendour and riches, the beauty of battle, and the honour of warriors. *I'd wager every one of those bards would shit themselves if they ever saw the pointy end of a sword.* The only bard who had ever truly captured Dann's attention was the one who currently sat to Dann's left, legs folded beneath himself, a tin of charcoal sticks balancing on his knee and a small sketchbook in his hand. "What's that?"

Therin raised an eyebrow. "This?" he asked, glancing towards the sketchbook. "Nothing interesting. Just my *valúr*."

Dann pursed his lips inwards, holding Therin's gaze, giving a slight questioning shrug. Getting straight answers from the elf was like drawing blood from a stone.

Therin smiled as though reading Dann's mind. "It is elven custom that any elf who wishes to hold an instrument designed to take life must also learn to create. A valúr is your gift to the world. This," he said, gesturing to the sketchbook, "is mine."

More than one smart remark crossed Dann's mind – he thoroughly enjoyed irritating Therin – but the idea of the valúr was something he genuinely understood. And so, he bit his tongue, reluctantly, and watched as Therin's hand moved the charcoal swiftly over the paper, the form of a wolfpine taking shape beneath his fingertips.

Aeson stood against a tree on the other side of the fire, barely visible through the flames. He always took first watch any time they made camp, and often last watch as well. Aela and Lyrei sat together to the right of the fire, conversing in low voices, their golden eyes gleaming. For a moment, Alea's eyes met his, lingering, then she looked away.

The Angan, Baldon, had not yet joined them that night. That was normal, though; he usually appeared long after the sun had set and was gone by sunrise. That was the only rhythm to his comings and goings.

Dann leaned back, resting his palms on the grass where the fire had melted away the thin layer of frost that clung to the forest. He never liked silence. Some people loved it, even craved it. Not him. Silence gave him too much time in his own head, and he didn't like his own head. With a sigh, Dann plucked a long blade of grass from behind him and placed it between his teeth to chew. It had seemed strange to him at first, all those years ago, but Dann still found that chewing on something like a long blade of grass often distracted him from his own thoughts while hunting. "Therin?"

The elf let out a sigh, dropping a piece of charcoal into the tin that rested on his knee and turning his attention towards Dann. He raised an eyebrow, a look in his eyes that said, 'What is it this time?'.

"Back in Durakdur, the shapeshifter, the Angan. He said Calen was the son of the Chainbreaker. What does that mean? Vars was the Chainbreaker?"

With an outward sigh, Therin closed over the lid of the charcoal tin, then placed the tin and the sketchbook into his leather satchel. Dann felt a twinge of regret as he saw the forlorn look in Therin's eyes.

"That is a story for another time, I'm afraid."

"But—"

"Another time, Dann." Therin's voice flashed from angry to melancholy, the firelight glittering in his eyes. "Vars was a dear friend, and Calen should be here when I tell that story."

Dann nodded. It was a story he desperately wanted to hear. How did Therin know so much about Calen's father? What was the Chainbreaker? But the look in Therin's eyes told Dann not to push it, and so for once, he didn't. "Can you tell us a different story, then? Like the ones you used to tell in The Glade?"

Therin gave a weak smile, clearly happy to change the subject. "Any one in particular?"

"I've always wondered what happened, you know, after The Fall."

"I see," Therin said, sadness evident in his voice. A forced smile touched the corner of his mouth, but then faded as though the elf had a fleeting memory of fondness that had been tarnished. He glanced towards Aeson. Dann wasn't sure how the man had heard a word that had been said, but Aeson's head turned, his eyes fixed in Therin and Dann's direction. "Aeson? It has been a long time. Would you care to listen?"

Aeson didn't respond. If sadness had been evident in Therin's voice, it flooded from Aeson's body like water through a broken dam.

"Very well," Therin whispered, only loud enough for Dann to hear. "Alea, Lyrei, do the Bralgír tell these tales in the Aravell?"

For a long moment, only the crackling of the fire and the sounds of the forest could be heard in the campsite, Alea's gaze shifting between Lyrei and Therin. Up until that point, Dann had forgotten about the uneasiness that passed between Therin and the elves from the Darkwood.

"Not often," Alea finally replied, much to Lyrei's apparent irritation. "But it would bring honour to my heart if I were to hear it from your lips, Therin Eiltris."

Dann didn't think he had ever seen Therin smile as widely as he did then. "Then it would bring honour to my heart to tell you."

With a languid grace, Therin rose to his feet, his mottled-green cloak sweeping around him as he did. A shiver ran down the length of Dann's spine as the elf spoke. "The time after the fall of The Order is one of the darkest times in Epherian history, second only to the great Blödvar – the blood war between the elves and the Jotnar that raged thousands of years ago.

"In the year two-six-eight-two After Doom, as the city of Ilnaen burned—" Therin raised his hand in the air as he spoke, the fire erupting in a blaze streaking towards the sky, spiralling around itself. Dann couldn't be sure, but he thought he saw a city within the fire. A city consumed *by* the fire, massive, winged creatures soaring through the sky – dragons. Dann rubbed the heels of his hands into the corners of his eyes. Though he had no doubt Therin was creating the images with his magic, it took nothing away from the wonder. "The Order was broken, and the agents of Fane Mortem and his fledgling empire went about their work. Ilnaen was not the only place Fane's soldiers struck that night – it was simply the most significant. All across Epheria, cities fell, and their rulers entered the void. Still, many mages and Draleid survived. But they were scattered—"

Again, the flames erupted in a plume of sparks and embers, and the darkness seemed to sink in around the camp. The firelight illuminated the sharp angles of Therin's face, coruscating off his silver hair.

"—Lost." Therin's voice sank to a slow requiem. "In one night, an entire continent was shattered, races were broken, and everything changed. Lost, alone, and fighting for their own survival, many Draleid and mages were slaughtered in the first weeks after The Fall. Many Draleid whose dragons had perished were taken alive, locked in chains forged with rune magic, a magic long thought lost in the annals of time. Those Draleid were tortured, hung in the streets, burned alive, stripped of their flesh in public plazas – a lesson to those who thought the Draleid could not be defeated.

"In a matter of months, the dwarves were driven back to their underground kingdoms. Without the Spark or dragons, they stood little chance. The elves broke after that, choosing to consolidate and survive. Though we did not all think the same way." Therin glanced towards Alea and Lyrei, a warm smile on his face. "Some chose to occupy the Aravell, to disrupt the empire's ability to communicate and send supplies. Others—"

"Chose to cower, to betray the ways of old," Alea cut across, a look of surprise on her face at her own words.

"It was not that simple, my dear Alea—"

"Not for you," Lyrei snapped, her eyes narrowing. "Not for the one who should have sat on the council, should have been a leader, but instead chose to abandon his people. You are no better than the *Astyrlína!*"

"Enough!" The darkness scattered, and even the insects seemed to quiet their chatter as Aeson's voice echoed through the forest. Dann had not heard Aeson rise, but now he stood in front of the flames, shadows dancing across his face, his eyes blazing with a fury Dann had never before seen in the man.

"You are nothing but a child," Aeson growled, his eyes burning into Lyrei, seething. "How *dare* you have the arrogance to believe your honour is enough to question that of Therin Eiltris. No better than the Faithless? You were not there. You did not watch the ones you loved skinned alive before a crowd. You did not stand and watch as they were kept alive with the Spark while the flesh was stripped from their bones. And you certainly did not drive daggers through their hearts so as to lessen their suffering. You have no idea about that which you speak. Do you know how many of your people Therin saved? Do you know *anything* of what he sacrificed?" Aeson moved closer to Lyrei as he spoke, staring down at her. The sudden flatness of his tone sent a shiver down Dann's neck. Then he spoke words that Dann did not understand. "Din haydria er fyrir."

Both Alea and Lyrei gasped at Aeson's words as the man stormed off into the dark of the forest. Tears streamed from Lyrei's eyes as Alea comforted her, and Therin ran into the forest after Aeson.

Aeson roared, reaching for the Spark, drawing in threads of Earth and Spirit. He dropped to his knees, slamming his fists into the frost-covered grass, cracking the frozen earth beneath. His heart hammered against his ribs, his blood raging through his veins, dimming all sounds to a dull drone. He filled the emptiness in his soul with anger, letting it flow through him like wildfire. Tears burned his eyes, and rage rent his heart.

He had not meant to lose his temper. The young elf was only a child, raised on the thoughts of others. In truth, her words were simply the spark that lit the fire, nothing more. The true cause of his rage was the spiralling absence that consumed his heart and soul. Over the past four hundred years, he had learned to bury most of the pain from Lyara's death. But that was all he did – bury it. It was never gone, not truly. A man could not overcome the loss of a dragon. How would that even be possible? How do you overcome the sundering of your soul?

Finding Naia had come some way to it. The feeling of her lips against his was the closest he had felt to being whole since Lyara had fallen from the sky. But now she, too, was gone, leaving him alone to raise two sons in a world that sought nothing but death. And he had not even managed to keep *them* safe.

The sound of frost-covered grass crunching under footsteps broke the half-silence that filled the air around Aeson.

"Those words will haunt that young girl." There was no anger in Therin's voice, just simple fact.

"She should not speak of what she does not know." Aeson closed his eyes. He clenched his jaw, taking a deep breath through his nose, letting his chest swell, trying his best to calm himself.

"Your honour is forfeit? Aeson, you know what that means to her. She respects you. If you say her honour is forfeit, then it is."

"I will speak to her. She *does* have an honour debt to pay. That is your way."

"We were young once too, my friend. We did not always see things as we do now."

The anger that had so quickly overcome Aeson ebbed away. The tangible feeling of loss returning. Aeson opened his eyes and pulled himself to his feet. "I am sorry. I… I lost control. Lyara, she calls to me… Sometimes I feel as though I am going mad, as though my mind is not my own…" His voice trembling, Aeson lifted his gaze to meet Therin's, doing nothing to stay the tears that rolled down his cheeks. "I can't *feel* her, Therin. Sometimes I dream, and her heart beats with mine, her mind calls to me, her scales feel warm beneath my hands… Then I wake… and I'm alone."

Therin grabbed Aeson by the shoulders, pulling him into a tight embrace. Feeling his old friend's arms wrap around him, Aeson let his tears fall free.

Therin clasped Aeson's head in both hands and touched their foreheads together. "To be Rakina is a burden many cannot hold – never think that I do not know that, my friend. But you *are* not, nor will you *ever* be, alone. I have fought by your side for centuries, and I will die by your side if the gods grant me that honour. You will feel the touch of Lyara's mind again one day. But not *this* day."

"Silver Fang, Broken One. I bring news from my kin in Drifaien."

The hair on the back of Aeson's neck stood on end as the Angan stepped from the shadows of the forest, not so much as the crunch of frost-covered grass betraying its approach. He brought his hand up, wiping the tears from his cheeks. "What is it, Baldon?"

"The empire has taken the Draleid captive. They hold him in a tower in the keep of Arisfall."

Chapter Thirty-Two

Family

Ella rubbed her hands together, her breath misting out in front of her before streaming up towards the crisp morning sky. It reminded her of the smoke pluming from the chimneys of The Glade as the sun crested Wolfpine Ridge. Strangely, the comparison gave her a comfort, of sorts. Though, all it took was a moment to remind her that she was nowhere near The Glade.

The morning was full of the constant sounds of axles squeaking, horseshoes clapping against stone, and the general hubbub that Ella had come to associate with people on the road. An unbroken stream of people stretched down the long, paved road from the enormous gates of Berona, past the carriage beside which Ella and Farda walked and onward into the horizon, where the people looked as small as ants.

"So many," Ella said, a soft sigh leaving her throat.

"They seek safety." Farda's black cloak streamed behind him as he walked, his mouth turned down at the corners. He was clearly still irritated at Ella for insisting they walk instead of riding in the carriage. It's not as if she had a choice, though. As Berona had drawn closer and the number of people on the road had continued to grow more and more by the day, Faenir had begun to stay closer and closer to the carriage. Between the wide berth the other travellers gave him, the narrowed eyes, and the muttering, she wasn't about to leave Faenir to walk on his own.

Reaching down as she walked, Ella ran her fingers through the coarse fur at the back of Faenir's neck, receiving a low rumble of recognition in return. The wolfpine strode beside her with a languid gait that suggested he cared little for the wayward glances of strangers.

"If there are this many on the roads, then what happened in Farrenmill was not an isolated occurrence." Farda's lips puckered. "It is worse than I thought."

Farrenmill. What happened in that village had plagued Ella's dreams every night since. And to call them dreams would be lying. They were nightmares through and through. Even now she could see them in the back of her mind – the Uraks. Their thick leathery hides, eyes like blood, their blackened blades cleaving through bone. The blood. So much blood. More than once, Ella had awoken in a cold sweat with the cries of dying men shrieking through her head. She pushed those thoughts to the back of her mind, placing them in a small box. Something far more important lay up ahead.

The sight of Berona's snow-white walls glistening in the light of the sun sent shivers down the length of Ella's back. Camylin had astounded her, and Midhaven had taken her breath away. But they were nothing compared to Berona. The city was cast in the same white stone she had fawned over in Midhaven, but the beauty of the buildings held no comparison.

The city swept across the landscape, stretching off into the distance until the walls became nothing but a blur at the end of Ella's vision. The walls stood so high that Ella was fairly sure if she were to climb to the top, she would undoubtably get a nosebleed.

Enormous, rectangular towers with open tops jutted above sections of the wall, climbing higher and higher into the sky as though attempting to scrape the clouds. Red banners emblazoned with the image of a roaring, black lion hung from every second tower. The banners stretched over at least fifty feet in length and covered nearly a third of each tower's width. Their ends must have been pinned to the stone, else they would have folded up over themselves in the morning breeze. As it was, they simply rippled majestically, a striking contrast with the white stone behind them. It was truly beautiful.

Reluctantly, Ella dragged her gaze from the pristine white walls of the city, turning it instead to those who travelled along the road beside her.

There were men and women in torn clothes, marred with dirt and blood, trudging on foot, cradling children in their arms, or dragging them along by the hand. But there were also women in silk dresses and men in linen shirts, their shoulders wrapped in expensive looking furs, sitting at the front of horse-drawn carts.

But regardless of what clothes they wore on their backs, their eyes held the same despondency, the same scars adorned their skin. It seemed to Ella the Uraks cared little for how much gold lay in the coffers of the wealthy. Death and loss did not reserve itself for those with coin.

"What about Faenir?" Ella asked, turning back towards Farda.

A frown still clung to the man's face as he replied. "What about him?"

"I'm not going into the city without him."

"Well, then, you're not going into the city," Farda said with a shrug. "They're not going to let a wolf—"

"Wolfpine," Ella corrected, not letting Farda finish his sentence.

Farda glared at her, an irritated look in his eyes. "What is the difference?"

"Have you ever seen a wolf his size?"

"I have not," he admitted, sighing out his nostrils. *He doesn't mind being made fun of, but he hates being wrong*. "Either way. They are not going to let him into the city."

"They will if *you* tell them to."

Ella saw a twist of frustration on Farda's face as he dropped his hand to his trouser pocket, where he kept his coin. It wasn't even a conscious movement. She had seen him do it many times. What was it with him and that coin?

"Fine," he said, holding his hand on the outside of his pocket. "But I can make no promises."

They walked the next while in silence, trudging along the paved road that led to the great Lorian city of Berona. It had been an elven city once. Many of the northern cities had belonged to the elves, as had some in the South. But that was before The Fall. At least, that is what Therin had proclaimed in his stories.

Ella's chest tightened at the sight of the great white walls up close, stretching towards the sky, red and black banners rippling in the wind. Her throat constricted and tears burned at the corners of her eyes. How many months had it been since she left The Glade with Rhett? She truly was not sure, but it felt like a lifetime ago. So much had happened; so much had changed. It didn't feel real.

I did it, Rhett. I'm finally here. I finally made it to Berona.

Ella tried her best not to cry in front of Farda – she did not want to give him the satisfaction of seeing her weakness – but despite her best efforts, a single tear rolled down the side of her left cheek, escaping the armour she wore around her heart. Ella wiped away the tear with the pad of her thumb, moving as though she were rubbing a blemish from her cheek. Farda gave her a sideways glance, his eyes narrowing a little, but he did not question her. He turned his gaze away, pretending as though something caught his attention in the distance. She knew he was pretending. The man never missed anything – he was like a hawk. And still, he had chosen not to comment. Maybe he had more decency than she had given him credit for.

Shouting pulled Ella's eyes to the road ahead.

"Oi, is that a wolf?" The man who shouted had a deep, gruff voice. It seemed almost too deep to be natural.

"That's a fucking wolf," another man answered back, more than a hint of trepidation in his voice.

"It appears," Farda said with a sigh, "the city guards have spotted your '*wolfpine*'. Shall we go and correct them?"

Five soldiers in the red and black leathers of the Lorian army pushed their way through the ever-moving crowd. The man at their head looked to have seen at least fifty summers. He was a tall man with a strong build and a receding hairline that curved into a slight peak. What little hair he did have was flecked with grey. Deep wrinkles furrowed his face, which looked as though a permanent scowl had been carved onto it at birth.

"You there," he growled, pointing a finger towards Farda. "This animal yours?"

"It is," Farda said, letting out an exhausted sigh as though he were already fed up with what was about to happen.

"You can't bring that beast inside the city. Get lost."

Ella thought she saw Farda smirk, but the expression was gone almost as quickly as it had appeared.

"I am—"

"I don't care who you are. Fuck off. Haven't you looked around? There are enough people on this road to fill the city twice over. I—"

Just as the words were about to leave the man's mouth, they stopped, leaving the sentence hanging in the air. Ella wasn't sure what had happened until she saw the man grasping at his throat, his eyes bulging, veins popping in his neck.

"Stop it!" She glared at Farda, fury in her voice. He didn't answer her, but the look he gave her turned her blood to ice.

"I," Farda said, his voice slow and purposeful as he strode over to the man, who had now fallen to his knees with his hands around his throat, "am Farda Kyrana, Justicar of the Lorian Empire and member of Imperial Battlemages. And you will show me some respect."

A small crowd of onlookers had gathered around, gasping, mouths open and fingers pointing. The other soldiers had drawn their weapons from their scabbards before Farda had spoken, but now they looked as though the fear of the gods had set itself in their bones.

With a gasp, the choking man fell forward, his hands catching his weight before he crashed, face first, into the paved road. Ella shivered at the sounds he made, dragging air into his lungs like a dying animal. His hands trembled, and his chest shook.

"Fifteen lashings," Farda said, directing the instruction towards one of the other soldiers. "In the guard barracks, tonight. I will be there personally to ensure it is carried out. Am I understood?"

The soldier cleared his throat and wet his lips. Despite his best efforts to appear composed, Ella could see his arms, pressed down at his sides, were trembling. "Yes, Justicar Kyrana. It will be done." The soldier barked orders at his companions, and they dragged the half-conscious man to his feet, carrying him off through the crowds, back towards the city gates.

"You wanted the wolf in the city." Farda's eyes were cold and hard as he spoke. It was not a question or the beginning of a conversation. It was the end of one.

Ella did not move as the Farda walked over to say something to Loran, the carriage driver. Her hands shook with an odd mixture of fear and anger.

Most of the time, Farda was fine – good company, even – but there were moments when the façade slipped, and she saw pieces of what he was hiding. Moments like this one, which reminded Ella that he was Lorian. That he fought for the empire that had taken Rhett from her – the empire that wanted *her* by name. One slip up, and she had no doubt he would drag her off to a cell somewhere, or even just pull the air from her lungs where she stood.

But more than that, there was something else. A nagging feeling at the back of her mind. He always seemed as though he were holding something back, keeping something hidden that he did not want her to see. She *would* find out what he was hiding.

"Loran is going to carry on and bring the cart to the keep. I will take you to see Tanner. Are you ready?"

With a touch of reluctance, Ella nodded.

The gateway into Berona formed a huge archway that rose so high Ella could have stood on her own shoulders fifteen times before she could touch the ceiling. In awe, she tilted her head back as they walked through, trying her best to keep her jaw from scraping the floor.

Soldiers in the red and black of Loria waved them through. Each of them eyed Faenir askance, but they did not open their mouths. They simply straightened their backs and gave Farda a short nod when he passed. They had clearly been told what had happened.

If the road into Berona had been teeming with people, Berona itself seemed on the verge of overflowing. All around, men and women charged about the streets as though each one of them was late for something, but none of them knew what.

Enormous white stone buildings rose into the sky on either side of the main thoroughfare, taller than any Ella had ever seen, with rows upon rows of windows, semi-circular balconies, and great awnings of cream and red canvas.

The cries and calls of hawkers and pedlars rose above the din of chatter and footsteps, adding an even greater sense of urgency to the already busy city.

More scents drifted on the breeze than Ella even knew existed, creating a mishmash of almost indistinguishable smells. She could pick out a few. Fresh baked bread from the bakery at the corner of the street. The unmistakable tang of smoked fish. The sweetness of cinnamon pastries. Candles, or possibly soap – something that required lavender, among other things; she was certain of that much. Lavender was not a scent Ella could ever mistake. It was the smell of home, the scent that drifted in her window every morning from the bush her mam kept in the garden. It was a key ingredient in quite a few salves that were used to soothe raw skin.

"Are you coming?" Farda's voice broke Ella out of the trance-like state she had not even noticed she was in.

The advantage of having Faenir by their side was that the crowd parted before them, eager to get out of the wolfpine's way. Faenir, for his part, loped along by Ella's side, glaring at anyone who even thought about getting too close.

More than one soldier cast a suspicious glance towards them at the sight of Faenir but averted their gaze once their eyes fell on Farda, his sword strapped to his hip, black cloak billowing behind him, a cold stare in his eyes. What had gotten him so angry? Rhett was the only man Ella had truly ever understood. His moods always made sense. Nobody was like Rhett. He did have his flaws; everyone did. He could be pig-headed, arrogant, and just downright irritating at times, but he had been hers, completely, warts and all.

A pang flared in Ella's heart at the thought of Rhett, and that unsettling weightlessness took hold of her stomach. She swallowed hard, clenching her jaw. She would have taken a broken bone over the relentless pain in her heart.

Farda and Ella walked in silence for at least half an hour, Faenir padding along by Ella's side. There had often been long silences as they rode in the cart from Antiquar, but those silences were usually of the absent-minded kind. The ones that existed simply because neither party felt the need to speak. This was different. The air between them was thick with tension.

Ella stopped dead, folding her arms across her chest and twisting her tongue in her mouth as her mother had taught her. It took a few paces for Farda to realise she was no longer walking beside him. He raised his eyebrow, an unamused look in his eyes. And, just as her mother had taught her, Ella held her tongue for five seconds and then said what needed to be said. "You didn't have to do that."

Her words didn't require any further explanation. Men's moods might swing like a pendulum, but the root of them tended to be the same. He was angry at her for making him feel guilty about using his magic to choke the soldier. Now she just needed to get him to admit it.

"I did what I had to do," he replied, his eyes narrowing.

"No, you did what made you feel like a bigger man." Part of Ella wanted to claw those words back into her mouth even as they left her lips. She had overstepped, and she knew it. She was not talking to Calen or her father. She was talking to a Lorian mage – a powerful one, judging by the way people reacted to his title. Next time, she would hold her tongue for ten seconds instead of five.

Tilting his head to the side, Farda's gaze was unblinking as he studied Ella. With a turn at the corner of his mouth, he walked closer, until he was less than an arm's length away. "You wanted your wolf*pine* in the city. I did what needed to be done so that could happen. Are you always so ungrateful?"

"Are you always so pig-headed?" Again, the words just slipped out.

The tone in Farda's voice changed, becoming even firmer than before. "You are not from the North. You do not understand our ways. Yet you are so full of pride that you think you can judge me?"

It wasn't really a question, Ella knew that. She also knew he was right, but she would be damned if she would admit it. "Take me to Tanner, and then we will be done. All right?"

Berona's keep lay in the centre of the city. It had taken Ella and Farda almost a full hour of walking before they stood before the white walls of its outer gate. Had Faenir not cleared the path around them simply by his presence, it would have taken twice as long.

If Ella had thought the city walls to be the largest she would ever see, the walls that surrounded the keep proved her wrong. They were almost half again taller, with open top towers along their length set at regular intervals – towers so absolutely enormous that Ella just could not seem to wrap her head around them. Her first instinct was to ask Farda what purpose they served. Surely there was a reason to construct such monstrosities. But one glance at his stony face tempered that thought.

The gateway into the keep was again at least one and a half times as big as the one that led into the main city, with a latticed iron portcullis lowered halfway down.

Two soldiers in gleaming plate mail stood on either side of the archway, long, butt-ended spears in their fists and heavy swords belted at their hips. They gave each other a sidelong look at the sight of Faenir by Ella's side.

"Farda Kyrana, Justicar of the Lorian empire. I seek an audience with Tanner Fjorn."

"It is an honour, Justicar Kyrana." The guard on the left straightened his posture at Farda's words, dragging his eyes from Faenir. "The High Captain is in his quarters. Do you require an escort?"

"We do not. My thanks."

The man gave another short nod before returning to his station, his eyes focusing on the streams of people who walked along the street in the shade of the keep's walls.

The walk from the gateway to the keep was not a short one. Sweat glistened on Ella's brow as they marched along the paved path that ran through multiple courtyards, each bounded by yet another gateway and more guards. The pathway's incline was deceptive. It didn't look as though they were going upwards, but Ella felt it with each step, the path winding left and right, through stable areas, training yards, and gardens.

Servants in black and red livery darted around, carrying piles of fine linens, baskets of food, pails of milk and honey, and anything else Ella could think of. Each one of them seemed as though they did not have enough time left in the day to fulfil the tasks they had been assigned.

Up ahead, rising past the walls, Ella could see the central keep itself, massive white towers jutting upwards, some with enormous flat tops, others with pointed caps of dark orange slate.

Ella did not know the slightest thing about warfare. But she could not, in her wildest dreams, imagine how anyone could hope to take this city, never mind the keep. A few months ago, she would not even have been able to dream of cities like Camylin and Midhaven. But this? No, nothing could ever have prepared her for Berona. Every person in all the villages back home could have fit inside the city a hundred times over and still not been able to come close to filling it. It was everything she had ever imagined it would be, and more.

Even as Ella looked around her at the sweeping white walls, enormous towers, and sprawling gardens of the keep, a coil of anguish twisted in her stomach. Without Rhett to share it with, it felt… hollow.

She had always loved the way he smiled when she got excited. The way his lips would spread so wide that small creases would appear at the corner of his eyes. It was that smile that Ella needed right now. But instead, all she had was the unabating Beronan sun and a stone-faced Lorian mage.

Faenir let out a soft whimper, as though he knew exactly what Ella was thinking at that moment, nuzzling his head into her side.

"I know I have you," Ella said, scratching the top of the Wolfpine's head as she walked, receiving a low rumble in return. "And you have me."

Two more guards stood at the entrance to the main keep, garbed in the same gleaming plate as the others, the same spears gripped in their fists and swords strapped at their hips. Farda repeated the same greeting he had given to the soldiers who stood at the main gate, receiving much the same reply.

"Though I'm not sure we can allow the wolf inside," one of the guards added, giving an uncertain look to his companion.

"The wolf comes. If you have an issue with that, speak to the Grand Consul."

Ella wasn't sure who the Grand Consul was, but the soldiers' backs stiffened. "Carry on, Justicar Kyrana."

Farda nodded, gesturing for Ella to follow him inside.

The interior of the keep was just as breathtaking as the exterior. White stone staircases carpeted in a deep red swept up either side of the entrance, rising to a second-floor balcony that looked down over the main hall. Rows of pedestals stretched the length of the entrance hall, supporting intricately carved busts of men and women Ella didn't recognise. Enormous tapestries woven with fine threads of every colour imaginable hung on the walls, each one depicting scenes of past battles and coronations in astonishing detail. Everywhere Ella looked, people darted about: servants, chambermaids, cooks, kitchen staff. Nobody in Berona seemed to have the time to stop and take a breath.

Pulling her eyes from her surroundings, Ella realised that while she had stopped to gawk at the main hall of the keep, Farda had continued, his long strides carrying him quite a way down the hall. She caught up with him just as he reached the foot of the staircase at the far end of the hall, more white stone with red carpet gliding effortlessly upward.

"Tanner's office is just down that hall," Farda said, gesturing to a long hallway at the top of the staircase that veered off to the right. "I won't be able to stay long."

Ella cast her eyes over Farda. Something had changed in him, and she wasn't sure what. He stood a little straighter than usual, his entire body seeming tense, on edge. But what truly struck out at Ella was that he refused to meet her gaze. In all the time they had travelled together, that was never something he had shied away from. "Farda, is everything all right?"

The corners of Farda's mouth turned down at Ella's question, but he didn't answer. He simply continue to walk down the elaborately decorated hallway, his pace increasing slightly. He stopped at the third door down on the left, giving the hard wood a rap with his knuckles.

"Come in."

A lump caught in Ella's throat. This was Tanner's office. She was finally here, and she had no idea what she was going to say or how he was going to react when she lied and said she was his niece. Suddenly, this felt like a terrible idea. How had she gotten herself into this mess? Was that why Farda was on edge? Did he know she was lying? Ella's stomach turned, but before she could change her mind, Farda twisted the handle and pushed the door inward.

The room was large, but austere. No tapestries hung on the wall; there were no busts, or statues, or paintings. A small fireplace sat on the left-hand side of the room, adorned with a simple frame of white stone. Two bookcases stood side by side, backed up against the wall into which the door was set, each book neatly arranged in its particular place.

A heavy oak table sat facing the door, its corners banded in brass. A man sat behind the table, his head buried in a ledger of some sort, a pen in hand.

He looked as though he had seen just over forty summers. His hair was the same raven-black as Rhett's, with only a barely visible dappling of grey. Soft wrinkles creased at the corner of his eyes, giving his face a friendly look. A long white cloak was draped over his broad shoulders, and he wore a well-fitted suit of black half-plate armour – a solid breastplate of black steel, pauldrons with the image of a lion embossed across their face, and a pair of black steel greaves enamelled with white along the edges.

"High Captain Tanner, I bring you your niece, Ella Fjorn."

The hair on the back of Ella's neck stood on end as Tanner's brow furrowed absently, his head still buried in the ledger, his pen moving quickly across the paper. "My niece? I don't—"

Tanner's words caught in his mouth as he looked up from the pages of the ledger, his eyes settling on Ella for the first time. Ella saw a glint in his eyes, a recognition setting in. He went to speak, but nothing seemed to come from his mouth.

"Uncle." Ella felt a tremble in her voice that she hoped Farda didn't notice.

Without saying a word, Tanner got to his feet – he was just as tall as Rhett. In truth, they could have been father and son, not uncle and nephew. His eyes flickered between Farda and Ella, his jaw tight.

The man stopped in front of Ella. Her stomach twisted, a tense silence hanging in the air. But then Tanner leaned forward, wrapping his arms around Ella, pulling her in to the warmest embrace she had felt in a long time. A weightlessness peeled through Ella's body, and the tension drained from her muscles as she let herself slip into Tanner's embrace. She had never been so happy to receive a hug from a man she didn't know.

"It's good to see you," he said, the warmth in his voice indicating his sincerity.

"I will leave you both to catch up," Farda said, after what felt like several minutes. "I have some things to discuss with the Grand Consul."

"Thank you for bringing her to me, Farda," Tanner replied, relinquishing his almost vice-like grip on Ella. "We shall see you later for a glass of wine, maybe?"

"I will see what I can do."

There was a tense silence once Farda left the room, Tanner slowly closing the door behind him. Once the latch clicked into place, Tanner rested the flat of his forearms on the wooden door, not turning to Ella, and he remained like that for quite a while.

Just when Ella went to speak, he stirred. He turned towards Ella, his voice dark and sombre. "I'm assuming," he said, "seeing as you are here alone, that Rhett did not survive the journey."

And just like that, tears streamed down Ella's cheeks, her stomach twisted, her chest and shoulders convulsed, and her heart wrenched. Ella's legs gave way beneath her, but Tanner caught her just before her knees hit the ground.

"It's all right," he said, wrapping his arms around her. The man's voice held a tremble, and the side of his cheek was wet from tears, but he held her firmly, like her father would have. "It's all right."

Farda's fingers clenched into fists as he made his way through the white stone hallways of the keep, down the stairs, and out into the courtyards. He had known it would eventually come to this. He had taken it too far. What was he thinking, bringing her all the way to Berona?

He unclenched the fingers on his right hand, stretching them out to remove the stiffness that had set into them. He reached into his trouser pocket, stopping dead as he pulled out the golden coin, running his fingers over its familiar marks and scratches.

His blood rushed through his veins, and cold sweat slicked his brow. What was happening to him? Why was he so angry? *How* was he angry? He stood there for a moment, his chest rising and falling in heavy sweeps. Then he opened his palm, staring down at the coin that sat at its centre.

He flicked it, hearing the metallic whir as it moved through the air. All other sounds yielded to that metallic spinning. He had asked the same question each day: should he do what he had gone to the South to do? Should he take Ella to the Inquisition to be broken and used against the Draleid? And each day, the coin had landed the same. Each day, he had felt a sense of relief. Why had he felt relief? Why did this girl matter to him? She was nothing. A pawn on a board.

Only she wasn't.

The coin landed in his outstretched palm with a subdued *thump.* Taking a deep breath in, he looked down at the result of the toss. Twenty-two times he had asked that question, and twenty-two times he had seen the lion staring back at him.

He closed his fist around the coin, then closed his eyes, letting the cool air tickle his face and ripple through his cloak, providing some reprieve from the Beronan sun.

Ever since Shinyara had died two years after the battle of Ilnaen, Farda had been broken. He had been Rakina. A soul, once bound to another, could never be whole again. Farda understood that, viscerally. There was not a waking moment where his mind did not battle with the swirling black void that threatened to swallow him whole. When a Draleid's dragon dies, they always take an uncountable number of things with them: emotions, feelings, beliefs, personality, the Spark, sanity. Shinyara had taken more than most with her to the void, for she encompassed everything that was good about Farda. But for the first time in four hundred years, he felt something when he tossed that coin. He felt a yearning.

He cared for Ella. It should not have been possible. He had been stripped of the ability to care. Yet there it was, burning in him. He could not deny it.

But now he asked himself a new question. *What do I do?*

Chapter Thirty-Three

Revelations

rand Consul Karsen Craine stared silently out the iron slatted window, his bony, liver-spotted hands clasped together at his back, pulling at the fabric of his green robes. Karsen Craine was a dangerous man. A man of unshakable conviction. He had been there, at The Fall, and had lived many centuries before that. He was old blood, even then.

But as Farda stood, awaiting Karsen Craine's reply, he felt something that had not stirred in him for as long as he could remember: fear. A deep, tangible fear. It was not fear for his own life; death would have been a welcome relief. It was fear for Ella.

"She is here?" The words left the Grand Consul's throat like rusty nails dragged across iron. The man's eyes narrowed as he turned. "In this keep?"

"She is." Farda could have lied, and it would have given Ella some time. But he had sent letters, so the Grand Consul knew Farda had been chasing her, and he knew that she had arrived in Antiquar only a few weeks earlier. The empire would not willingly let go of the sister of the Draleid. She was too valuable a tool.

But most of all, Karsen Craine would not have believed him. The Grand Consul was not a trusting man. And he was well known for torturing those who lied to him. Farda didn't fear torture. It was a difficult thing to fear when he hadn't felt the sting of pain in centuries. But Craine knew of the things Farda had lost when he became Broken. The Grand Consul would not bother to flay him or burn him. He would leave Farda to rot in a cell, chained so he could not take his own life, where the centuries would eat away at his mind. That was the kind of man Karsen Craine was.

"Where, precisely?"

Farda hesitated, only for a moment, but it was enough for Craine's expression to change. "She is with Tanner Fjorn."

"The High Captain of the Beronan guard? Interesting indeed. We will take her tonight while she sleeps. There is no reason to make a scene in daylight."

"It will be done, Grand Consul."

The old man laughed, a deep cackling laugh, phlegm catching in his throat. "Not at all, Farda. You cannot be trusted."

"I have served this empire since the—"

"I know damn well how long," Craine roared, threads of Spirit and Air amplifying his voice. The old man was powerful. It was a wonder he was not chosen to be a Battlemage, though the bloodlines were stronger in his time. "I was there when you were selected to train with The Order. I was there when your *dragon* hatched. And I was there when Aeson Virandr drove a sword through that beast's skull. I know every inch of your broken little mind."

Farda did everything he could to force back a snarl. The old man had intended to anger him, and Farda would not give him the satisfaction of knowing he succeeded. There were very few things that elicited any true emotions from him anymore, but Shinyara was his heart. She had been everything that was good in him.

Farda dipped his hand into his pocket, running his fingers around the edge of the gold coin, feeling the embossed symbols on each side. Keeping his eyes fixed on Craine, Farda removed the coin from his pocket, immediately flicking it into the air.

"That infernal coin," Craine snarled.

Farda ignored the old man as the coin thumped into the hardened skin on the palm of his hand. He glanced down. *Crowns. Not today, then.*

"You are to leave with the Fourth Army."

The old man's words grabbed Farda's attention. If the Fourth army was mobilising, then the situation was far worse than he had anticipated. "The Fourth Army? To where?"

"You march for Fort Harken before sundown."

"Through the night? Can it not wait until we have the light of the sun at our backs?"

"No." Craine turned back towards his desk, snatching a piece of folded parchment that he then stuffed into Farda's hand. "It seems it cannot."

Farda peeled open the worn parchment.

Grand Consul Karsen Craine,

We require urgent reinforcements. One night past, the Uraks burned all the land that surrounded the fort, slaughtering all who inhabited it. Since then, they have held a blockade of sorts. Each night, they assault the walls, testing our strength. I fear it will not be long before they throw their full might against us. The scouts have reported the Uraks number near twenty thousand strong, and there have been sightings of larger beasts that glow with a red light – monsters, is how they've been described. Though I'm not sure I believe them, I have seen stranger things of late.

No matter, we will hold. For the people.

Battalion Commander Furst Urnell, Fort Harken

"Bloodmarked," Farda hissed, folding the paper back up and handing it to Craine, who was watching him with calculating eyes.

"Indeed. Do you not wish to extract a blood debt for what the creatures did to the dragon eggs at Ilnaen?"

"That debt has been paid," Farda snarled.

"Has it?"

"No." Anger peeled through Farda at the mention of the dragon eggs. Fane and Eltoar had said the dragon eggs would not be harmed in the sacking of Ilnaen. That it was part of the alliance with the Uraks. But the beasts broke that alliance, and so Fane had burned them with the city. But the debt those creatures owed was not something that could ever be erased. "I thought I could not be trusted?"

"With the girl," Craine croaked, the corner of his lip pulling upward. "Being a Justicar grants you certain *liberties* to do things your own way. But that does not include traipsing around like a lovesick puppy. The girl should have been hauled here in shackles, screaming for relief. What were you thinking? You *cannot* be trusted."

Farda gritted his teeth. The Grand Consul was right. There was more to it than that, but at the heart of it, he was right. Ella was a weakness, and weakness was something he could not afford. Weakness needed to be burned out like an infection before it could take hold. "The Fourth Army will be outside the city walls within the hour."

Faenir shifted at Ella's feet, the fur on his back prickling against her leg. Ella barely noticed, her raw red eyes lost in the flames of Tanner's fireplace. She tugged at the heavy blanket that hung around her shoulders, pulling it in to her chest. She wasn't cold, but the weight of it comforted her.

When Tanner had said Rhett's name out loud, something in her just gave way, like a rotten beam holding up a house. Nobody had said Rhett's name out loud since he had died. Again, tears burned at the corner of Ella's eyes, accompanied by the dull, throbbing headache that always accompanied tears.

"Drink this," Tanner said with a soft sigh, handing Ella a small crystal glass that held a mellow brown liquid. "It's brandy, the best Berona has to offer."

Ella held the glass to her nose. It didn't smell as potent as the spirits Lasch Havel sold at The Gilded Dragon.

"It won't bite you." Tanner laughed, sitting in a padded leather chair across from her, beside the fire. He pulled his own glass to his lips, inhaling deeply, a smile spreading across his face, then took a sip of the brandy. "Aged for twenty years in oak barrels. Any longer is just a waste in my opinion."

Ella lifted the glass to her lips; they were chapped, as though she had weathered the harshest of winds. The brown liquid soothed her senses as it hit her tongue. It burned a little, but mostly it tasted of dried fruits and of how cherry blossoms smelled. She wasn't sure if that made sense, but it did in her head. Either way, it was a far cry from the Wyrm's Blood she had bought from the sailors in Antiquar.

"You like it then?"

"I do, thank you."

An easy silence hung in the room as they sipped at the brandy, letting the crackling fire warm their skin.

"How did my nephew die?"

The sudden question caught Ella off guard, and she could see that even Tanner himself was a little surprised by his bluntness.

"I'm sorry," he said. "I didn't mean it to upset you."

"It's all right," Ella replied, wiping away a budding tear with her index finger. "He was killed… on the road to Gisa, by empire soldiers."

"He was what?" Tanner's eyes widened in shock. "Why would Lorian soldiers want to kill Rhett? Was he in some kind of trouble? He should have told me – I could have done something."

"No, he was not in any kind of trouble. Rhett was not that kind of man. He was sweet and kind, and he helped anyone who needed it…"

"That does sound like him." Tanner smiled, gazing into the fire. "But then, what happened?"

Ella's throat felt as though it were about to close, and an aching pain thrummed in her head. She held the glass of brandy in both hands, attempting to still the tremble that shook through her.

Tanner's expression turned from a look of sadness into a narrowed gaze, his eyes fixing on Ella. "Ella, my dear, what are you not telling me?"

"They wanted *me.* Not him. They knew me by name. They… they…" Ella's shoulders convulsed as tears burned her eyes. She wanted them to stop, she wanted to talk to Tanner, but she had no control.

Tanner lifted himself out of his chair, his hands coming to rest on Ella's shoulders. "It's all right. You're safe. It's all right." Leaning in, he wrapped his arms around her, his voice calm and level in her ear. "Ella, I need you to tell me what happened *exactly* as it happened. I need to know what we are dealing with."

It took a few minutes before Ella was able to regain any sort of composure. But eventually her shoulders stopped shaking, and she was able to stem the flow of tears, though her eyes continued to sting, and the pounding headache redoubled its efforts to bore a hole through her skull. Taking her time, stopping whenever agony or sorrow threatened to overcome her, Ella told Tanner everything that had happened on the road to Gisa and how she had marked Rhett's grave.

Tanner didn't interrupt her; he simply stayed silent and listened. When she was finished, he let out a long breath. "Ella, I must ask you a question." The sombre tone in the man's voice set a knot in Ella's stomach. "Why were you travelling with Farda Kyrana?"

"He is the only reason I am here. They wouldn't let Faenir onto the ship from Gisa—" A sudden realisation swept across Ella's mind. "Gisa, the tickets! I promise I will pay you back. I can't right now, but I will find a way, I'll—"

Tanner held his hand up in the air. "The money is not important anymore. Farda Kyrana is one of the most dangerous men you will ever have the misfortune of knowing, and he cares about nothing but his own whims. I need to know what he said to you, Ella."

"I… Why?"

"Because if that man has taken an interest in you, it is for a reason. And I have never seen a person come out on the good side of things once Farda has taken an interest in them. I believe he knows precisely who you are. I'm just not sure why he would care or why anyone would be looking for a girl from the villages in the South. It doesn't make any sense."

"He saved my life."

Tanner raised an eyebrow at that, leaning backward.

"In a town southwest of here, Farrenmill. It was overrun. The Uraks... if Farda had not been there, we would not have gotten out alive." Ella's hand fell to Faenir, who shook his head, a low rumble emanating from his chest.

"I see." The look of concern on Tanner's face was clear as he rose to his feet. "All right. For now, I will show you to a room. You try and get some rest. I'll ask around. I have a few friends who might be able to shed some light on why the soldiers were looking for you in the first place."

Tanner let out a sigh of exhaustion as he leaned back in his chair, the leather squeaking as it accommodated his frame. Reaching for the crystal flask of brandy, he poured himself another glass, then drained it in one mouthful before pouring another.

The girl had been through a lot. His heart bled for her, but ached at the same time. His nephew was dead. Rhett was dead. The last time he had seen Rhett, the boy was no more than fifteen summers. He had been a strong lad, even then. He had a tender sweetness to him. What was Tanner going to tell his brother? It was he who had given Rhett those tickets. He took another mouthful of brandy, running his free hand through his hair, digging his fingers into his scalp.

As much as it pained him, he could deal with his guilt later; the girl needed him *now*.

He could think of a handful of people off the top of his head who might know why the soldiers had been looking for Ella by name. But if Farda was involved, that narrowed the list quite a bit – there were few who held sway over the Justicars. Lifting the glass of brandy to his lips, Tanner closed his eyes, letting the sweet flavours sit on his tongue for a moment before swallowing.

With a sigh, he set the glass on his desk and stuffed his hand into his pocket, feeling the rough surface of the parchment he had been looking for. Removing the letter from his pocket, Tanner held it out in front of him, pausing for a moment before unfolding it.

T,

I trust you are well. It has been some time since we last spoke, but I hold fast that your convictions remain the same. There is a new dawn on the horizon, and mountains must be moved so that we may see its light. And with the dawn comes the birth of a new sun. One that was hoped for, but not expected. Should you wish to see this new sun, then burn the candle and let the birds sing.

A

Tanner ran his tongue across the front of his teeth as he read the letter over three times. With particular care, he folded the letter and slipped it back into his pocket – he didn't trust leaving it anywhere else, and he couldn't burn it there. Leaning forward, he rested his elbows on the table and held his face in his hands, cupping his fingers over his nose, then pressing them into his skin as he dragged them down to his chin.

He drained the last of the brandy in his glass, then poured another, larger this time.

Part of him had never expected to receive that letter. But if he was honest with himself, he always knew it would come. Tanner remembered the night he first met Aeson Virandr. The man had stood before him, surrounded by the bodies of imperial soldiers, wreathed in spirals of flame.

On that night, Tanner had been sent to a village just north of Copperstille, along with about thirty men. He'd been given orders to burn the village to the ground for refusing to pay its tithes. When he got there and refused to comply with his orders, his commander had chained him to a post, to watch 'what real soldiers did'.

That was the night he decided he did not want to be a 'real soldier'.

Chapter Thirty-Four

Run

lla peeled one eye open, tossing and turning in the bed. The light from the moon drifted through the window behind her, just bright enough to make out the shape of Faenir's snout sticking out past the end of the bed. The slow draw and release of the Wolfpine's breaths signalled that he was not having as much trouble sleeping as she was.

It was all the crying. The crying in of itself wasn't the problem; it was the stinging eyes, the sore throat, and the pounding headache that came with tears. Whichever one of the gods decided such sorrow wasn't enough pain to bear on its own was a god Ella would like to have a few words with.

She let out a soft sigh as she rolled onto her back, staring up at the ceiling which was ornately decorated with square inlays of wood-carved floral patterns. It seemed a waste to have such beautiful craftsmanship displayed on the ceiling of a room that was designed solely for sleeping. She shook her head at the notion, running her fingers through her sleep-deprivation tousled hair. As she lay awake, it felt like she could hear even the slightest of sounds that would not usually even register: the nightsong of the crickets who made revelry outside, the rushing of the wind as it swept over the walls of the keep, the rapid beating of her heart in her chest.

A creaking floorboard gave Ella a jolt, and she shot upright in the bed. Down by her feet, Faenir was now awake, his head tilted to the side as he stared at the door.

"What is it, Faenir?"

The hackles on the back of the wolfpine's neck stood on end and a low rumble began to resonate from his chest, starting off quiet but building until it sounded more like a growl.

Ella pulled the sheets off her as quietly as she could. She wore nothing but the nightdress one of the chambermaids had left out for her. Her clothes lay folded atop the desk on the other side of the room, but she left them there for now.

"Faenir," she whispered again, her feet touching the floor. "What is it, boy?"

A small rattle came from the door, as though someone had placed their hands on the handle on the other side but had yet to turn it.

Ella held her breath, trying desperately to calm herself. Her eyes fell on a long brass candlestick that sat beside her folded clothes on the desk. She grabbed it in both hands, then moved towards the door as quietly as she could, walking with her shoulder pressed against the wall.

Faenir had raised himself to his feet, his head held low, pointed at the door, his lips drawn back in a snarl.

Another rattle, and the door burst open. Faenir lunged. Ella couldn't see who came through first, but they hit the ground fast, the sound of ripping flesh making her retch.

The second man through the door shouted something unintelligible as he charged at Faenir. Ella caught a glint of steel in the moonlight as the man raised his sword. Without thinking, she leapt forward, a surge of panic blended with fury pulsing through her veins. A deep thrum vibrated through her arm as the candlestick connected with the man's skull. He went limp, crashing to the floor like a stone.

Ella's stomach lurched. She had just killed someone. Not an Urak, but a man. He was dead, she was sure of it.

An explosion of stars flitted across Ella's eyes as something hit her in the side of the head, knocking her to the ground, causing her fingers to lose their grasp on the candlestick.

"Get on your feet, you little wretch," a man's voice growled, fingers wrapping through Ella's hair. "He said he wanted you alive, he didn't say I couldn't—" The man wailed, and his fingers let go of Ella's hair. Screaming, he swung his arms at Faenir as the wolfpine clamped his jaws around the man's leg.

Catching a glimmer of steel on the floor beside her, Ella snatched up a sword that had belonged to one of the dead men and dragged herself to her feet. She swung the blade through the air, a vibration running through her arms as it sliced into the man's neck and connected with bone. A knot twisting in her stomach, Ella pulled the blade free, and the man dropped to the floor, blood spurting from the wound.

Faenir stood over the three attackers, snarling, as though warning their ghosts not to try a second time.

For a moment, Ella's fingers loosened on the hilt of the sword, but she forced her grip tighter, the edge of the brass cutting into her hand.

"Come on," she said to Faenir through rasped breaths. "We need to find Tanner."

The sound of Ella's pounding footsteps echoed down the white stone hallway. Faenir loped ahead, his claws clicking off the floor, a trail of blood dripping from his mouth as he ran. It was only then, with a shiver running down her spine, that Ella realised what a sight she must have been. Running through the hallways of the keep, a wolfpine by her side, a sword in her hand, and her nightdress blotched with crimson stains. She prayed to The Maiden that she would not run into any guards.

Ella thought she remembered how to get to Tanner's office, but Faenir had taken off ahead of her, never hesitating at any turns. He knew where she needed to go. She just hoped that Tanner was the kind of man she thought he was: a man like her father, who stayed up late when he had things to think upon. Because if he had already gone to his chambers, she would never find him.

When she reached the doors to Tanner's office, Ella didn't stand on ceremony – she burst straight through. Tanner was sitting behind his desk, scribbling something on a piece of paper.

"Ella?" Tanner pushed his chair back, slipped the piece of paper into his pocket, and got to his feet, his eyes widening in surprise as he took in the sight of her. "What in the gods has happened? Are you all right?"

"It's not my blood," Ella said, looking down at the marks on her dress and the half-dry blood that stained the surface of the sword.

"Come with me." Tanner lead Ella and Faenir through a labyrinth of corridors and stairwells, moving as quickly as they could. To Ella, each corridor they passed through looked almost identical to the one before it. White walls, heavy oak doors, red carpets, tapestries. With her lungs struggling to draw in full breaths and her blood trembling through her veins, the corridors all blurred together.

As she passed a particularly large window, Ella could see thousands of flickering flames marching away from the city in a long column, their orange light carving a path through the darkness.

"What's that?" she asked, coming to a dead stop.

"Ella, we need to keep moving."

Ella didn't look at Tanner, but she could hear the irritation in his voice.

"It's the Fourth Army," Tanner said once he realised Ella wasn't going to move. "They head for Fort Harken. The Grand Consul assigned Farda to lead their mages. At least that's him gone. Now, come on."

Ella's gaze lingered on the column of marching torches as Tanner tugged at her arm, pulling her down the corridor. She wasn't sure why, but she felt a sadness at the idea of Farda being gone. The man was the most arrogant person she had ever met, and he was an imperial mage. Deep down she knew it was a good thing that he was gone, but a small part of her hoped it wouldn't be the last time she would see him.

The corridors of the keep seemed to go on forever. With each turn came another long hallway, at the end of which was *another* long hallway. Ella cast her gaze over her shoulder every now and again to see if they were being followed, but she never saw anything. After what felt like an eternity, Tanner came to a halt before a plain wooden door, tapping his knuckles against it.

"Yana?" he whispered, looking back down the corridor before saying the name again. "Yana?"

Footsteps sounded on the other side of the door, and then it creaked open just a crack, revealing a woman who had seen no more than thirty summers, with hair as black as coal and eyes to match.

"High Captain Fjorn?" The woman rubbed sleep from her eyes, seeming as though she weren't entirely sure whether she was dreaming or not. "Is everything all right? What can I do for you?"

"Yana, I need you to take this woman to Farwen."

"Tanner," she said, opening the door another crack and dropping all formality. "We cannot use that name here." The woman's eyes narrowed as she spotted Ella standing beside Faenir. Then they flickered between Ella and Tanner. She opened the door a bit further. "What have you done?"

"Yana, focus. I need you to take Ella to Farwen, and I need you to do it *now*."

Yana and Tanner held each other's gaze for a long moment. Then Yana took in a deep breath, biting the corner of her lip. As she exhaled, she nodded. "Give me a moment."

Yana went to close the door, but Tanner caught it with his open hand. "Yana, *now*."

Yana glared at Tanner, her eyes widening. "She's covered in blood, Tanner. Give me a damn moment."

Not waiting for Tanner's answer, Yana disappeared into the room, returning a few moments later with a bag on her back and some clothes in her hands.

"Put these on," she said to Ella, thrusting the clothes into her arms.

"What, here?"

"You can kill a man, but you're worried about your modesty? Put them on and be quick about it."

Ella looked to Tanner for support, but the man simply looked away. Sighing, she snatched the clothes from Yana and pulled them on as quickly as he could.

"What about you?" Yana said, turning to Tanner.

Ella could see genuine concern in the woman's eyes as she studied Tanner. She looked at him the way Rhett had looked at Ella – as though it was her and only her who made the sun rise each morning. Tears stung the corner of Ella's eyes, and she felt a pang in her heart as she remembered Rhett, knowing she would never see that face again.

"I'll be all right," Tanner said, a weak smile touching the corner of his mouth. "There is something I must do first. You two go now. And, Yana, when you bring her to Farwen, I think it's best you stay with them."

Yana went to argue, but Tanner just shook his head. "Go." Before either Yana or Ella could reply, Tanner had turned around and strode back down the hallway.

A shiver ran down the back of Ella's neck as Yana turned to her, eyes narrowed like a hawk's. The woman looked her over from head to toe, her jaw tight and her tongue twisting in her mouth. Then, calmly, she leaned in close, her nose only inches from Ella's, and whispered. "If that man is harmed because of you, I will kill you myself. Do you understand?"

"I didn—"

"*Do you understand*?"

Ella nodded.

"All right then, let's go." Yana's eyes fell to Faenir once more, and Ella could have sworn she saw the woman snarl at the wolfpine before flitting off down the hallway and gesturing for Ella to follow.

An uncountable number of long corridors and spiral stairwells later, Ella found herself staring at the back of Yana's head. A tall bookcase covered the wall in front of her, at the end of a dimly lit corridor. It was a dead end. A knot of fear twisted in Ella's chest, and the hairs on her arms stood on end. Where had the woman taken her?

Ella reached down, resting her hand on the back of Faenir's neck. The wolfpine pressed closer to her, his eyes fixed on Yana, his lip drawing back as a snarl formed in his throat.

The woman's head shot around. "Can you please tell that damn wolfpine to shut up?"

To Ella's surprise, Faenir stopped snarling, instead giving a slight whimper of apology.

Yana stepped closer to the bookcase, reached her hand down to a thick red book on the bottom shelf, then tilted it forward. The sharp click of a latch echoed through the hallway, followed by a low creaking noise as the bookcase slid backward, revealing a passage hidden behind it.

"Come on," Yana said, waving Ella forward, pushing the bookcase open a little more. "Stop gawking at me and come on, we don't have time."

Ella stumbled down the dark passage after Yana, her hands running against the walls, desperately trying to find some sense of bearing. She had never been scared of the dark, not in the way the other children had been growing up, but this passage was completely devoid of light. It was as close to absolute darkness as Ella thought she had ever seen; it felt endless.

"Come on, keep up," Yana whispered ahead of her. "It's not much further now."

Ella couldn't be sure, but it felt as though the passage began to slope downwards. It was the strangest sensation. Her eyes saw nothing but black, and her feet told her she was walking in a straight line, but she could feel the change in orientation. The further they walked, the more drastic the slope became, until she was worried she might tumble forwards at the slightest misstep. It was more than a little disconcerting.

After what Ella gauged was about twenty minutes of walking, the passage began to level out once more.

"We're here. You go first."

Ella couldn't see the woman, but she felt Yana's hand rest on her shoulder, gently willing her forward.

"What do you—" Ella stopped, her question answered as her extended hands felt the cool touch of an iron rung. She reached her left hand up a bit further, feeling another rung. It was a ladder.

"Climb to the top," Yana whispered. "Once you're there, just push up with your arm. It's only a wooden hatch, it should come open without much effort."

"What about Faenir?"

Yana let out a sigh of frustration. "Right, I'll go first. I'll get help, and we'll throw down a rope."

"All right," Ella said with a nod. The nod was more force of habit than anything else. She knew Yana couldn't see her.

"Why is it never easy?" Yana muttered to herself as she pushed past Ella, her hands eliciting a clang from the iron rungs as she pulled herself up towards the top. Ella could tell Yana had reached the hatch at the top when a sliver of moonlight pierced through the dark. As Yana pushed the hatch open fully, moonlight poured down into the tunnel, bathing every stone in its silvery light, revealing a black sky dotted with shimmering stars.

"I'll be back," Yana called down, pulling herself out over the top of the hatch before disappearing from view entirely.

Suddenly, Ella felt completely exposed. She was now at the bottom of a ladder in a dark passageway with nowhere to go if somebody found her. She couldn't run back towards the keep, and she couldn't climb up the ladder and leave Faenir there on his own.

The wolfpine let out a low whimper as he pushed his side up against Ella's hip. With all Faenir's strength and ferocity, it was easy for Ella to forget that sometimes he got scared as well. "It's all right," she said, running her hand through the prickly fur on Faenir's back. "Yana will be back in a moment, and we'll lift you out of here. Don't worry."

As though he understood her, Faenir's whimpering stopped, but his side remained pressed against Ella's hip.

A few minutes passed before something hard hit Ella in the shoulder and she yelped, nearly jumping out of her skin.

"Shh," Yana called down from the top of the ladder. "Will you keep quiet? Put the wolfpine's legs into the loops."

Ella reached out for the length of rope that had struck her in the shoulder. Two elaborate pairs of loops were knotted together, each pair bridged by a length of cord, a third length of cord then connected the two pairs. A length of rope from each loop fed back up to Yana. It was incredibly intricate knot-work, and Ella couldn't help but be impressed not only by the knots themselves but also by the speed at which Yana had put the harness together.

It was difficult to see in the sparse moonlight that drifted down from above, but Ella quickly went about slotting each of Faenir's front legs through one of the loops, checking that the bridging cord held tight against his chest. Wiping the slowly forming sweat from her brow, she then slid Faenir's hind legs through the second pair of loops, giving a firm tug on the length of cord that now ran across his belly from his front to his hind legs.

Faenir let out a low whimper as Ella tugged on the chord, nuzzling his snout into her cheek.

"It's all right, boy," she said, running her hand through his fur, casting a glance back down the passageway they had come from – not that she would have seen anything anyway.

"It's on," Ella called up, still holding her voice to a whisper. She could feel her heart thumping as she stood there, one hand on the back of Faenir's neck, waiting for a response.

"You're going to need to climb the ladder as we hoist him up. Try to keep him calm. If he struggles too much, we mightn't be able to hold him."

Ella let out a deep sigh, resting her hand on an iron ladder rung. "It's all right," she said, turning to Faenir, who let out another low whimper. "Just a few minutes and you're going to be out of here."

With Ella's words, the whimpering stopped. Though Ella's thought remained: how in the gods was Yana going to be able to hoist Faenir's weight up to the open hatch?

"I'm coming up," Ella called out. It only took a moment before the ropes that fed upwards tightened, pulling close around Faenir's shoulders and hind legs.

As Faenir was lifted up the short shaft one tug at a time, Ella stayed with him, slowly moving up the ladder, rung after rung. Once or twice, he let out a whine, but a hushed whisper from Ella settled him down. It was only a few minutes before they reached the top of the shaft and Faenir gripped the edge with his front paws, heaving himself up and over.

Ella stumbled, dropping to her knees as she pulled herself out through the hatch. Her brow was slicked with sweat, and her blood rushed through her veins in fierce pumps. She now knelt at the side of a broad cobbled street, dimly lit by the moon's light. Beside her, Yana was pulling the ropes free from a slightly dazed Faenir.

"Take my hand."

Slightly panicked at the unexpected voice, Ella fell backwards, catching herself with the palms of her hands. Before her stood a tall woman, three long scars running from her jaw down into the folds of her dark mantle, her white-streaked auburn hair tied back. But it was the way her ears tapered into a point that stood out to Ella. The woman was an elf.

"Well?"

Ella hadn't realised that she was so startled she hadn't reached for the elf's hand. Skittishly, she reached up and let the elf pull her to her feet. *An elf. In the streets of Berona of all places?*

"My name is Farwen." The elf's eyes looked as cold as Farda's, and they, too, held a deep sadness. "Come, we need to leave this city. Tonight."

CHAPTER THIRTY-FIVE

AN OLD PACT

rtim Valdock considered himself a practical man, and he was right. Which was why, as he looked down over the crumpled heap that lay in the cell before him, he decided it was time to give up on extracting any useful information from this 'Draleid'. It was time for him to send a message to the Dragonguard, as he had been instructed.

Reaching out to the Spark, he pulled in threads of Earth and Air – the two elements with which he was strongest. He didn't think the young man had enough left in him to attempt an escape, but it was always better to be prepared. Risks should always be taken, for nothing is gained when nothing is risked, and preparedness was the key to a successfully taken risk.

The young man's chest rose and fell slowly, a hoarse rattling coming from his lungs. Artim would have expected no less. The cell was borderline freezing, and he had been starving the young man for almost three weeks. It was not something he took pleasure in, but it was effective. Usually.

However, this situation was… *unique.* The manacles made it possible to control the Draleid, and crucially, they also stopped the dragon from finding him. The beast had killed more than its fair share of men since Artim had taken the Draleid, but it had been smart enough not to attack the city. Had it known that its Draleid was here, Artim doubted very much it would have exercised the same caution. But the problem the manacles created was that once the Draleid's mind had been separated from the dragon, he had become unresponsive. No matter the beatings, or the pulled nails, or the starvation. He hadn't spoken since that first night.

Tilting his head, Artim looked down at the Draleid, the blue glow from the manacles shining across the stone floor of the cell. He could kill him right now and end the problem before it even truly began. But the Primarch had been explicit in his instructions to the Battlemages. *'Beat him, break him, reduce him to a snivelling wretch for all I care. Just capture him alive.'*

It did not matter. It would take only a few days or so for the message to reach the Dragonguard camped in Illyanara. While he waited, he would start working on the Draleid's companions. He did not have to inform anyone of *their* capture. Knowledge was power, and he must glean as much knowledge from these prisoners as he could.

Alleron stood on the battlements of Arisfall castle, looking out at the lights of the city as they glimmered in the languid snowfall. His nose still throbbed from where his father had broken it, and a sharp pain shot through his ribs with every breath he took. But both wounds paled in comparison to the strips of scabbed flesh that raked his back from where Lothal Helmund had flogged him. With each movement, the scabs cracked and bled, only to scab over once more. Even as he stood there, he could feel the blood trickling down his back.

The wind bit at Alleron's skin, so harsh and bitter the tear streaming down his right cheek began to freeze. He pushed it away with his hands and pulled his fur hood over his head. It was dangerous to be out on the battlements in these conditions. Men had died from exposure on more than a few occasions, but he always thought better when he was outside. And seeing as his father had forbidden him from leaving the castle, the battlements were the only place for him.

It had been his fault. It was he who had given that letter to Leif. It was he who had led his father and the High Mage to Calen. It had been weeks and Alleron still couldn't shake the image of Leif's bloodied head lying in the snow, devoid of life.

"You'll catch your death out here."

Alleron turned to see two men standing on the battlements to his right, both garbed in long coats of mail that peeked out under coats of heavy fur. He couldn't make out either of their faces in the darkness, but he recognised the voice. "Baird?"

The man on the right stepped forward, drawing back his hood to reveal a head of thick black hair and a scraggly beard. A bloodstained bandage stretched over his left eye.

"What happened to you?" Alleron stepped closer to his friend, ignoring the wind's icy touch as it blew his hood down over his shoulders.

"Your father's men, two days' march from here. They were waiting for us. Fell and Kettil are dead."

Fury bubbled in Alleron's chest, fuelled by a deep, visceral hatred. His father had not always been the cruel, twisted bastard he was now, but he had taken to it like a fish to water. "Leif…"

"I know. His head is on a spike outside the city walls."

Blood trickled through Alleron's closed fist, his nails slicing into the flesh of his palm.

"Do you know where the mage is keeping the Draleid?" It was the man beside Baird who spoke. His accent was like none Alleron had heard before, as though the words were foreign to his tongue.

"I do," Alleron answered. "Baird, who is this?"

"She is a friend."

Alleron was sure neither Baird nor his friend could see the perplexed expression on his face, but he tried his best to hide it either way. He had simply assumed the other hooded figure was a man, both because of their height and the harsh sound of their voice.

"Alleron," Baird continued. "We need your help, and you need ours."

"We do not have time for this," the woman said, stepping past Baird and dropping her hood.

Alleron gasped, stumbling backwards. The woman was not a woman at all. Or maybe she was, but she was not human. She stood just over six feet, and where Alleron should have seen skin, there was fur, like that of a wolf. It covered her arms, legs, and neck. Even her face had fur, though it was a lot shorter. Her eyes were a shimmering gold, gleaming in the moonlight. Alleron's hand dropped to the axe that hung from his belt, but Baird stepped towards him, arms outstretched.

"No. Aneera is a friend, Alleron."

Before Alleron could respond, the wolf-like creature stepped closer, its eyes fixed on him. "We intend to free the Draleid."

"Wait," Alleron said, raising his hands in the air. "Baird, how do you even know about the Draleid? What is going on?"

Baird put his hands on Alleron's shoulder, looking him straight in the eye. "I will answer any questions you have. For now, I need you to trust me. We are going to free the Draleid, but we need you to help get him and the others out of here and onto a ship. Once we are done…" Baird paused, taking in a deep breath. "Once we are done, we are going to free Drifaien."

Chapter Thirty-Six

The Ties That Bind

Dayne kept still as the boat came to a stop, bobbing in the waves. The residual, bittersweet smell of orange peel from the empty crates stacked beside him filled his nostrils, reminding him of home. He wrapped his arms across his chest, knotting his fingers in the sleeves of his soaked shirt. He wanted, desperately, to create heat for himself, but he dared not move any more than he had to for fear the tarp covering him might shift unnaturally.

It had not been too difficult to get out of Stormshold. He had waited six days. Three for the next orange shipment to arrive and then another three as he waited for the crew with the woman who had damaged her leg. Once Mera had distracted the crew, he had swum through the water and scaled the outer hull of the ship, sliding beneath a tarp that covered some of the empty orange crates. The only flaw in the plan was that his clothes had been soaked through for the entire journey, and the harsh winds had set a shiver in his bones.

The hustle and bustle of the port filled the air and the deck of the ship creaked and groaned as the crew set about fastening its moorings. But still, Dayne waited for Mera's signal.

A few moments passed, then he heard her.

"Many thanks, Olem. The passage was most appreciated. Sometimes you just need to get back ashore without everyone knowing. May The Warrior and The Sailor both, watch over you."

"It honours me, *Wyndarii,* to have you aboard my vessel. We set sail again in three days' time. Will you be honouring us once more?"

Wyndarii, the old title of the Wyvern riders. That word had not been common since before Dayne's father's time.

"I believe so, Olem. Now is the time…"

Now is the time. Dayne clenched his jaw, fighting back the cramp that had begun to set into his muscles, and readied himself. He didn't hear anything else Mera said as he cleared his mind. Three, two, one.

Slipping under the tarp where it connected to the side rail of the ship, Dayne threw himself over the edge. The light from the morning sun was like fire in his eyes as he caught sight of the crate Mera had 'accidentally' knocked overboard to conceal his landing. Less than a second, then *splash.*

He let out an involuntary gasp as the water engulfed him, its icy touch sliding over his skin, knocking the air from his lungs.

Filling his lungs once again, Dayne plunged back into the water, sweeping his arms and kicking his legs, creating as much distance between himself and the ship as he could. When he was far enough away, he removed his clothes, leaving them to float, then set off for an empty section of the port to his left, where the docks gave way to the sandy beach. It was easier to swim without the drag of clothes, and Mera had dry ones for him anyway. Before they had left, they had decided the least conspicuous thing would be for it to seem as though Dayne was simply an overly enthusiastic winter swimmer. It wasn't his favourite plan, but it served its purpose.

Reaching the wooden jetty that protruded from the port, Dayne heaved himself out of the water, his teeth chattering as the bitter coastal wind swept over him. Even in winter, Valtara tended to be rather warm, but the winds were anything but.

The jetty was empty for the most part, but Dayne received more than a few side-eyed looks from the dockworkers that were going about their morning routines.

"You know there're easier ways to kill yourself than freezing to death, young man?" The man who called to him sat in a shoddy chair, a pipe wedged between his lips and one leg crossed over the other. He looked as though he had seen the better half of eighty summers. His skin was wrinkled and leathery, covered in all variety of Valtaran tattoos, some of which Dayne did not even recognise.

"You speak the truth," Dayne replied, standing in nothing but the skin he was born in. "But nothing easy was ever worth having."

Dayne thought he saw a crooked smile spread across the man's wrinkle-laden face. "Wise words for one so young." As he finished his sentence, his eyes narrowed, and one eyebrow raised. "The Warrior and The Sailor. By blade and by blood, I am yours, son of House Ateres."

It was only as the man spoke his last words that Dayne realised he was staring at the sigil of House Ateres tattooed across the left side of Dayne's chest. Only the direct line of each house bore the marking across their heart. Immediately, Dayne brought his free hand up to his chest, covering the sigil.

Eliciting a creak from the wooden chair, and possibly from his own bones, the man lifted himself to his feet. He was taller than Dayne had expected. "Do not cover that sigil, Dayne of House Ateres."

Dayne's heart stopped for just a moment, a weightlessness setting into his stomach. "How?"

The old man coughed, pulling his hand to his chest. "Well, you are certainly not Baren. Owain was taken too young to have been given the marking. You are not Alina. And your father, Heraya harbour his soul, no longer walks the mortal plains. That leaves only you."

"There you are."

Dayne was both relieved and uneasy at the sound of Mera's voice. The old man's eyes stayed locked on his, unwavering.

"Making friends already, I see," Mera said, drawing up beside Dayne and the old man, a satchel in her hand. As Mera stared at Dayne, a wide grin crept across her face, seeming to reach all the way to her eyebrows. "The water was cold, then?"

Dayne dropped his hand from his chest and instead cupped it around his privates, snatching the satchel from her hand and glaring at her all the while. Wasting no time, he pulled the smallclothes, tunic, trousers, and sandals from the satchel and put them on.

"How long?" the old man asked, turning to Mera as Dayne dressed himself.

"How long what?" Mera raised an eyebrow in curiosity, and Dayne himself stopped with his shirt only half over his shoulders.

"Those scars on your face. I know wyvern scars when I see them. My wife was a Wyndarii."

At the man's words, Mera raised her hand, cupping her fingers over the three claw marks that raked down her face. For the first time since Dayne and Mera had been reunited, he saw a crack in her confidence – and felt a fury towards the old man for putting it there.

"You are like him," the man said, nodding towards Dayne. He reached up with his wrinkled, bony fingers and softly pulled Mera's hand from her face. "You both hide what you should not. You need not smile, nor frown. Those are the whims of emotions, usually born to satisfy the expectations of others. But wear your markings with pride. You have earned them."

It was then that Dayne caught sight of the tattoo on the man's left arm that had previously been hidden by his sleeve. Two wyverns coiled around each other, a spear between them: the symbol of the Valtaran Rebellion.

When Dayne was but a boy, his father had told him of how each soldier who fought for Valtara in the rebellion had gotten that marking on their wrist. It was to be the new emblem of a free Valtara. The man was older than he looked. The original rebellion was over eighty years past. He must have only been a child.

"Come," Mera said, pulling the old man's hand from her face, still clearly rattled by his comments. "We must be on our way."

Dayne nodded, tossing the now empty satchel over his shoulder. He paused for a moment, his gaze meeting the old man's. "Do you regret it?"

A flicker of a smile touched the old man's face. "Not for a second. It is better to die with a sword in your hand than to kneel with a chain around your neck. Go, do what we could not."

Dayne's eyes narrowed. "How do you know what I am going to do?"

"Because you are your father's son." With that, the man turned away, dropped himself back into his chair, put the pipe between his lips, and stared out at the ocean as though Dayne was no longer even there.

"Are you all right?" Dayne asked as he caught up to Mera.

"I'm fine," Mera said, nodding at something ahead of them.

Dayne looked ahead to where the jetty met the port. Lorian soldiers, scores of them. They paraded up and down the port, some garbed in black and red leathers, others in the full ruby-red plate of the Inquisition. "So many…"

"Something tells me there are a lot more we can't see."

As they made their way through the port and out further into the city streets of Skyfell, it was clear that Mera was right. Lorian soldiers marched down every street in groups of four and five, spears in their fists and swords strapped to their belts.

"Alina is going to move today," Mera said, leaning in towards Dayne as they made their way down a particularly busy street.

Dayne stopped, grabbing Mera's shoulder. "Today? I thought we had time?"

"I received a message from some of our people in the city," Mera whispered. "Just after you boarded the ship. Consul Rinda left for Ironcreek last night, and then on towards the Hot Gates. We have reports the empire is sending Battlemages to join the Inquisitor. Consul Rinda and High Lord Loren are gone to welcome them. Alina wants the Inquisitor dead and Skyfell in our hands before that happens."

"Then we need to move faster."

Dayne and Mera weaved through the streets as fast as they could without drawing any unwanted attention to themselves. They were aided by the fact that the streets were jam-packed with people going about their morning routines, buying fresh fish, bread, meat, and cheese for their breakfasts.

After about a half hour of pushing through crowds, they passed the temples of Achyron and Neron, the enormous statues of each god casting long shadows over the street.

"By The Warrior and by The Sailor," Dayne whispered to himself as they passed the temples.

"By blade and by blood," Mera continued.

"I am yours."

A smile spread across Mera's face before she knocked her shoulder into Dayne. "I know you are, Dayne Ateres. You're just lucky that Audin kept my attention all these years."

"Lucky?"

Mera glared at Dayne in response, but he could see the cheeky smile beginning to form at the corner of her mouth.

Once past the temples, it was not long before Dayne and Mera approached the edge of the city, where the keep of Redstone looked out over the Antigan Ocean.

"Perfect," Mera said, the sarcasm evident in her voice. Just as before, two guards flanked the gates of Redstone, surcoats of orange and white draped over their armour. But unlike before, the two guards were accompanied by four men in ruby-red steel plate – Inquisition Praetorians. Aside from the Praetorians who stood by the gate, the plaza in front of Redstone was flooded with imperial soldiers.

"We're not going in this way."

Dayne's sandal scraped off the ground beneath him, sending bits of sandy stone plummeting over the narrow ledge that ran along the back of Redstone and down into the ocean below. "Try not to look down."

"I'm a Wyvern Rider," Mera called from behind him. "A fear of heights doesn't last long."

Dayne laughed as he shimmied along the ledge. He, Baren, and Alina had used the old hidden passage many a time when they were children. It was always helpful when trying to escape whatever chores Marlin had tried to assign them. None outside of House Ateres knew of its existence. The ledge that led to the passage was little more than a few handspans wide, with just enough room for someone to move along with their back pressed against the stone. If you didn't know it was there, it was near impossible to see as it ran along the edge of the cliff, facing out towards the Antigan Ocean.

"How much longer?" Mera called out, exhaustion permeating her voice.

Dayne lifted his hand, wiping the sweat from his brow. Even in the height of winter, Valtara was warmer than most nations in Epheria, especially there at the side of the cliff, the sun beaming down over them. "Not much further."

It took no more than five minutes before the familiar cave mouth came into view. From the ocean, it looked like nothing more than a small alcove born naturally into the rock. But Dayne knew better than that.

He let out a large breath as he stepped into the considerably wider space of the alcove, throwing his hands behind his head in an attempt to let more air into his lungs. "You see?" he said, panting as Mera stepped from the ledge. "I told you it wasn't much further."

"Where does this lead?" Mera asked, reaching into her satchel to produce a steel water bottle wrapped in a leather skin. She drank deeply from it, then passed it to Dayne.

"It leads up to a passage that sits behind a bookcase in my father's old study."

"Baren's study."

Dayne nodded, wiping the excess water from his lip and passing the bottle back to Mera. "We need to move. Alina will already be inside. I hope we're not too late."

Breathing deep, Dayne drew himself to his full height and pressed on, Mera following close behind. The roof of the cave drew lower as they stepped further into it, as though it were closing off into the ground. Dayne bent over double as he walked, getting lower and lower until eventually he lay on the flat of his stomach, the loose rocks scraping him through his thin shirt.

"You couldn't have made it a little bigger?" Mera asked, sliding along on her belly behind him.

Dayne laughed, coughing as he swallowed a bit of rock dust. "It opens up ahead."

Just as he spoke, Dayne could hear the whistle in the air as it filtered through the tight space ahead of him. It was near impossible to see, as his and Mera's bodies blocked out the light from the sun, but he pulled himself along the ground, sliding until he felt the roof begin to lift. In a matter of moments, the roof had pulled up enough for Dayne to get to his knees, then to his feet, until eventually he was standing upright.

The chamber was bathed in darkness, but he knew it well. Every groove, every inch of rock. Walking over to one of the far walls, he reached out, feeling the touch of wood as he picked a torch up from the sconce in which it sat. He could smell the stench of the cloth wrapped around the torch's head, soaked in rendered cow fat.

"Mera, firestarter?"

He couldn't see her, but Dayne heard Mera drag herself to her feet and pat the dust down from her chest before placing something into his hand: a long piece of flint and a sharp strip of steel specially quenched to produce sparks. He could have used the Spark, pulled on threads of Fire. But with the Inquisitor so close within the keep, it was not worth the risk of detection.

Stepping back, he struck the steel at an angle against the flint, sending a burst of sparks towards the fat-soaked cloth at the end of the torch. The torch erupted in a burst of flames, illuminating the chamber.

"Are you all right?" Dayne asked, turning to Mera; scrapes and cuts from crawling along the rocks decorated her arms.

She raised one eyebrow, as though amused, her eyes moving between Dayne and the cuts on her arms. "Have you even looked at my face?"

Dayne tried not to laugh, but he was powerless. When he stopped laughing, he reached out his hand, resting his thumb on the raised line of scarred flesh that ran over her chin. Scars or no scars, she was still the most breathtaking woman he had ever laid eyes on. "Not for twelve years, and for that, I am sorry."

Mera rested her hand on top of Dayne's and, for a brief moment, he felt at peace.

"Come on," Mera said, pushing Dayne forward, a weak smile flitting across her face. "Or I will tell everyone that Dayne Ateres is nothing but a lovesick puppy."

Reluctantly, Dayne acquiesced. At that moment, the most important thing was reaching Alina before she did anything she would regret.

A single tunnel led from the chamber, bearing upwards at a sharp incline, the ground beneath their feet cut into rough steps. Dayne had forgotten just a how long the tunnel was and how many steps it held. His entire body was dripping with sweat by the time he could see the top, his shirt stuck against his back and chest, and his hair slicked to his head. With a sigh, he stopped, staring towards the top of the staircase.

"Why did you stop?" Mera asked.

"The doorway is open," Dayne replied, his voice a whisper. *Alina must have come this way. Please, don't let me be too late.* "Extinguish the flame, will you?"

Without a word, Mera reached into her satchel and pulled out a heavy cloth, quickly draping it over the torch to completely engulf the flame in one motion. In an instant, the tunnel went dark, the only light emanating from the open door at the top.

"Are you ready for this?" Mera's hand rested on Dayne's shoulder as she whispered in his ear.

Dayne simply gave a short nod, unsure as to what words would fit the occasion. What did someone say when trying to stop their sister from murdering their brother?

Dayne reached down, removing his sandals – he couldn't risk the sound of his footsteps echoing up the staircase. Mera did the same. Then, slowly, they made their way towards the open door.

Reaching the top of the staircase, Dayne recognised Alina's voice immediately.

"Did you not think this day would come, brother? Did you not think I knew?"

He's alive.

Dayne heard someone spitting, then Baren spoke. "I'm sorry, Alina. I did what I had to do. For you, for the House – for Valtara."

Dayne stepped through the open doorway into Baren's study, his heart racing, his stomach bunched into a ball.

At the other side of the room, Alina stood with her back to Dayne, garbed in dark leather armour enamelled with orange swirls, a short sword strapped to her hip. She loomed over Baren, who was tied to a chair in front of the far wall, upon which he had hung the old Valtaran weapons. Baren's left eye was swollen, his lip was cut in multiple places, and two patches of dried blood ran from his nostrils.

The main door to the study was closed. There was no way for Dayne to tell if anybody outside had any idea what was going on. Dayne reached back, pressing his hands against the top of Mera's chest, mouthing the word 'stay'.

"You did it for me?" Alina hissed, contempt seeping through her voice. "You murdered the father of my child for me? You handed my son, your own nephew, to the empire, to be trained to pull the chains around our neck – for me?" Alina knelt on one knee in front of Baren. "I am your little sister. Does that mean nothing to you? You are meant to *protect* your family."

"I'm sorry," Baren said, tears streaming down his face. "I made the hard choices, Alina. House Ateres is not what it once was. Loren could swat us like—"

Dayne heard the crunch as the back of Alina's hand cracked Baren in the cheek, spraying blood across the stone floor.

"Enough," Alina said, rising to her feet and pulling her sword free from its scabbard.

"Alina, no."

Alina jerked her head around, her eyes piercing through Dayne. "So, you did come."

"Please," Dayne said, reaching his hands out. "Don't do this. Don't become the monster you despise."

Dayne could see the hesitation, the welling of a tear at the corners of Alina's eyes. "I will become what I have to!"

"Not this way, Alina." Dayne said, stepping closer to Alina. "Never this way."

"He doesn't deserve to bear the name of our House," Alina whispered, a slight shudder in her voice. "He doesn't deserve to sit in our father's chair!"

"You're right," Dayne said, wetting his lips. "He does not deserve to bear the name of House Ateres. But neither do I. Will you kill me too?"

A look of shock spread across Alina's face, a flash of uncertainty. "I..."

Reaching out, Dayne stretched his arms past Alina's sword and placed his hands on her shoulders. "His death will not bring Kal back. It will only add more weight to your already heavy heart. I have not been here for you when you needed me, but let me be here now."

Alina lifted her head, her eyes meeting Dayne's.

"I have killed more people than I would ever dare count. I have killed for money, for purpose, for revenge. Trust me when I say there has not been a life I have taken that has brought me even the slightest shred of happiness. And to kill in this way, with your blood cold in your veins – that stays with you, Alina. It haunts your dreams."

"He killed Kal," Alina whispered, almost to herself, leaning in closer to Dayne. "He might not have been the one who held the blade. But he killed him, Dayne. He took my love from me..."

"I know." Dayne pulled Alina in, wrapping his arms around her. "And he will hold that in his heart until his dying day." After a few moments, Dayne leaned back, looking Alina in the eyes. "The Inquisitor?"

Alina shook her head. "Not yet. He is in a chamber down the hall, guarded by Praetorians."

"Go. The Inquisitor is what's important. And before you argue with me, I know I have no right to tell you what to do. But please, leave Baren to me. My dreams are already haunted."

"He needs to pay for what he's done, Dayne."

"And he will. But right now, you need to do what you came here to do. It is time to set the wheels in motion. It is time for Valtara to be free."

Alina drew in a deep breath then exhaled through her nose, her eyes flitting from Dayne to Baren and back again. Finally, her gaze settling on Dayne, she nodded. "For Valtara."

"For Valtara." Dayne gave a weak smile. It was all he could muster. For as happy as he was to hear those words leave Alina's mouth, he did not look forward to being left alone in the room with his brother.

Turning, Alina knelt in front of Baren, her gaze locked on his. Swifter than Dayne's eyes could follow, she pulled a knife from her belt and drove it down into Baren's leg, plunging the blade to the hilt. Baren screamed as Alina gripped the hilt of the knife and leveraged it to pull herself closer. "You are not my brother. You are not a member of this House. You are not Valtaran. You will walk the emptiness of the void until time itself breaks."

Alina twisted the blade in Baren's leg one more time as she rose to her feet, turning to Dayne. "Do *not* make me regret this." Alina stared at Dayne with cold eyes, holding his gaze for a few moments before she strode from the room without looking back.

Dayne turned to Mera, who hadn't said a word as she stood at the mouth of the hidden passage. "Mera, go with her, please. I'm sure there will be more guards in the corridors."

Mera reached up, grasping the back of Dayne's head. She placed a kiss on his cheek, then touched her forehead against his. "Be strong."

And then Dayne and Baren were alone.

For what seemed like an eternity, silence hung in the air, thick and dense.

"Do you think you are better than me?" Baren's words rang hollow in Dayne's ears.

Dayne turned, clearing the distance to Baren in two strides, then drove his fist into his brother's face as hard as he could. A sharp pain erupted in his knuckles as they connected with Baren's cheek. Blood splattered over the floor.

His chest trembling with anger, Dayne dragged one of the wooden chairs from beside Baren's desk, placed it in front of his brother, and took a seat. Then, reaching across, he wrapped his fingers around the hilt of the knife Alina had left buried in Baren's leg, and yanked it free. "No. I know I am not better than you."

"Ah, fuck!"

"Keep pressure on it," Dayne said, ripping a strip off his tunic. Lifting Baren's hand, he wrapped the strip around where the knife had been lodged, pulled tight, and tied it in a knot. "That should hold for now."

Baren's lips moved as though he were going to say something, but his voice seemed to catch in his throat.

"You better speak, and you better speak now."

Baren hesitated for a moment, grimacing as he shifted in the chair. "You weren't here, Dayne. We were alone. With you gone and Father dead, the wolves were at our door. I kept them at bay the best I could, and Marlin was always there for us, but eventually I had no choice. I had to play by their rules. I didn't have Kal killed because it gave me pleasure. And I certainly didn't hand over my nephew for that reason either. High Lord Loren told me that if I didn't do those things, he would string Alina up in the street and have her flogged. Then he would kill her." Dayne could hear the tremble in Baren's voice. "I've seen what happens to the people Loren has flogged. The soldiers strip them naked, then compete to see how much skin they can remove from their backs without killing them. I… I couldn't let that happen to her, Dayne. I couldn't let it happen to this House."

"Why didn't you tell her?"

"I tried. I did, but she didn't have ears for it." Baren let out a sigh, then lifted his chin, looking into Dayne's eyes. "Valtara can't survive another failed rebellion, Dayne. We are still broken from the first one. You saw what happened the last time Aeson Virandr asked our family to lead a rebellion." Baren's eyes began to narrow as he pulled his chair forward, his hands still bound. "Look at us. Look at what they did to the 'Great House Ateres'. Our father is dead. Our mother is dead. We are broken. They made me murder my sister's love." As Baren spoke, his lip trembled, and tears muddied by blood and sweat streamed down his face. "They made me give away my own nephew!"

It was at that moment Dayne saw Baren for what he was: a broken man. The empire had done to him what they had done to Dayne. They'd forced him to choose between his own honour and his family. *I let this happen.* "I should never have left, Baren. I'm sorry. They gave me as much choice as they did you."

"No, you shouldn't have." Baren shook his head. A bead of blood, sweat, and dirt dripped from his nose. He let out a sigh. "But I understand. I know Alina will never let me live. I don't blame her." Baren's eyes were red and raw as he met Dayne's gaze. "I hate what I've become. I tell myself every day that it is for the greater good. That if I can just keep this House alive… Please, just make it quick."

Tears stung Dayne's eyes as he looked at his brother and saw the broken mess he had become. The simple idea that Baren thought Dayne would even consider taking his own brother's life tore at Dayne's heart, burning like hot coals through his veins. "I'm not going to kill you, Baren. But I will drive a knife through High Lord Loren's heart, after I burn out his eyes." Dayne rose to his feet, his blood boiling, his jaw clenched so hard it burned. "I will kill them all for what they have done. I will drive them from our lands, and I will burn their cities to the ground."

Reaching out to the spark, Dayne drew in threads of Air. It did not matter if the Inquisitor or any other mages he brought with him could sense it. *Let them come.*

Dayne weaved the threads of Air through the ropes that bound Baren to his chair, pulling them apart. Shakily, Baren rose to his feet, rubbing the raw skin on his wrists.

Dayne ignored his brother. "Do not think that I have forgiven you. Just as I am sure you have not forgiven me," Dayne said, his eyes boring into Baren's. "Neither of us can take back what we have done. But we can atone through our actions. Go. Take the passageway. The farm west of Myrefall. Is it still there?"

Baren nodded.

"Go there. Do not be seen. I will come for you, Baren. And when I do, you will answer my call."

Barren nodded again, holding Dayne's gaze. "What will you do?"

"What you should have done."

Dayne's feet pounded against the floor just as his heart pounded against his ribs. He was not sure if he had made the right decision, letting Baren go, but it was the only decision he could live with.

The sound of horns bellowed through the corridor, joined by the crashing of armoured feet on stone. *What has Alina done now?*

Within moments, four Lorian soldiers turned the corner to Dayne's left, armed with swords and long, rectangular shields. "You! Stop!"

The men charged down the corridor towards him. They were clearly fresh recruits. They held the swords above their heads, despite the corridor being narrow. They broke rank, lessening their advantage. And they paid no heed to self-preservation. Dayne sighed. He took no pleasure in killing young men. But if he was going to start a war, he was going to have to live with doing horrible things.

"I'm sorry," he whispered, only loud enough for himself to hear. He reached for the Spark, pulling in threads of Fire. But then he released them. The least he could do was give these young men the honour of knowing how they died. He took in a deep breath, then flipped the knife he had taken from Baren's leg into reverse grip.

The first soldier swung his blade, arcing it towards Dayne's head. Lunging forward, Dayne slammed his forearm against the flat of the blade, pinning it to the wall, then drove his knife up through the young man's neck. As the man spluttered and coughed, Dayne kicked him square in the chest, knocking him backward into the soldier behind him.

Pivoting, Dayne turned towards the two other Lorians. The soldier closest to him was still moving and hadn't planted his feet. Throwing all his weight into it, Dayne rammed his shoulder into the soldier's shield. The man slammed against the wall, his head bouncing off the stone with an almighty *thump*. His eyes rolled to the back of his head, and he fell to the floor.

Dayne pushed off his back foot, charging towards the two remaining Lorians. The one nearest to him stumbled backwards. Dayne leapt towards him, seeing the opening. He drove his knife into the man's neck, pulled it back, then rammed it in again. He pushed forward as the soldier fell.

He exchanged blows with the last soldier for a moment or two before driving his knife into the man's sword arm. The soldier cried out, letting his sword drop. Dayne plunged his knife into the side of the man's head.

His chest heaving, Dayne turned. *Such arrogance to send young men to war without ever teaching them how to fight.* Casting one last glance over the four Lorian soldiers who lay lifeless on the floor, he carried on.

The limp bodies of six Praetorians, blood seeping into the cracks of the floor, marked the chambers of the imperial Inquisitor. Dayne reached out to the Spark before he made for the door, snatching up one of the Praetorian's swords. It was a little unbalanced, too heavy at the pommel. But Dayne wasn't surprised. What did the empire expect when they paid only half a weapon's value to Southern smiths?

The chambers given to the Inquisitor were among the finest Redstone had to offer. Not quite as large as he remembered his father's being, but still lavishly decorated and five times the size of any room Dayne had slept in since he had left the city. An enormous four-poster bed sat against the eastern wall, with a lace curtain hanging from its frame that provided little to no privacy for whoever slept in the bed.

The room was filled with fine art: tapestries, mosaics, oil paintings. But none of those things were what caught Dayne's attention. A body lay on the floor at the foot of the bed, eyes open, lifeless, soaking in its own blood. Thick, ichor-like blood matted the man's blonde hair, soaking into his already red robes.

Beyond the man, standing on the balcony through the archway at the far wall, was Mera, looking out at something over the city.

Dayne's mouth curled into a frown as he looked down at the mage's lifeless body. *Would that have been me if they had taken me as a child? Would I have become such a despicable wretch?* Pushing the thoughts to the back of his mind, Dayne stepped over the body, careful not to plant his bare feet in the blood.

"Where's Alina?" Dayne asked, stepping out onto the balcony. "Mera? Where's…"

Dayne's voice trailed off as he looked out over the city, every hair on his body standing on end as though he had been struck by lightning.

Wyverns. Hundreds of wyverns. So many they almost cast the entire city in shade. Dayne watched as the powerful creatures swooped down, ripping Lorian soldiers from the streets, tearing them from the city walls. As the wyverns swooped, their riders launched spears from their backs, impaling any who thought to stand and fight.

Before Dayne could speak again, a flash of orange swept past the balcony, followed by an enormous gust of wind that rippled through Dayne's hair. Stepping backward, Dayne looked to the sky, his eyes following the orange wyvern as it soared, its rider pressed down against its back. The creature was almost a half again bigger than Mera's wyvern, Audin. Scales of a deep orange, trimmed with black, covered its body. The creature banked left, tearing through the sky at a fierce speed, turning back towards the balcony upon which Dayne and Mera stood.

Dayne turned to Mera as the wyvern approached. She didn't speak, but a broad smile swept across her face.

A flurry of wind rushed over Dayne as the wyvern alighted on the edge of the balcony, its powerful legs holding it in place. The creature stared at him with eyes so blue they could have been sapphires.

"Witness the freedom of Valtara, brother."

As the wyvern craned its neck down, Dayne got a better look at the rider. His heart stopped. "Alina..."

It was at that moment, as he looked up at his sister garbed in her dark leather armour, orange swirls enamelled along the breastplate, Dayne realised the young girl he so fondly remembered, was gone. She was a warrior now – she was a *Wyndarii.*

Smiling, Alina unbuckled herself from the harness that strapped her to the wyvern's back, then slid gracefully to the balcony. She rested her hand on the wyvern's neck, whispering something to the creature. Lifting its head into the air, the wyvern let out a monstrous roar, then spread its wings and dove from the balcony.

Dayne took a step towards his sister. "Alina... when did you..."

"You have been gone a long time, brother," Alina said, plucking at the fingers of the gloves that adorned her hands. She pulled each finger out, just a touch, before removing the glove entirely, revealing the black ink that covered each of her fingers, trailing in thin lines to circles that ringed her wrists. "For the first time since our mother, an Ateres leads the wyvern riders of Valtara to battle. Will you fight by my side? Will you bear the colours of our people? Will you lead the armies of Valtara on the ground as we retake our homeland?"

Dayne's throat went dry, and his pulse slowed to a hammering beat, thumping his blood through his veins. Lead the armies of Valtara? That was an honour he did not deserve. But it was not one he would turn away now his sister had asked it of him. "I…" He took a deep breath, trying to calm himself. "What about the others? The council?"

"I will deal with them. What say you?"

"I will stand by your side until my lungs take their last breath and my heart ceases to beat. In darkness, and in light, by blade and by blood, I am yours. Let me be your sword."

Chapter Thirty-Seven

Chains

Tarmon took a deep breath, grunting as a bolt of pain shot through his ribs. The cold cell wall felt like ice against his bare back as he propped himself up against the stone. He ran his fingers over the partially healed wound along his left side, where the High Mage had raked the hot poker. It had blistered and burst, but one of the High Mage's servants had applied a salve that smelled like brimlock sap, which held any infection at bay. It still stung, but he knew it pained him half as much as it would have were it not for the salve.

Erik Virandr lay unconscious in the cell across from him, and the elf, Vaeril, lay on his back in the cell beside him. A pair of glowing blue manacles were secured around the elf's wrists to stop him from using his magic. Tarmon had no idea how they worked, but he found understanding something often did not matter. You did not have to understand an arrow for it to tear through your flesh.

The High Mage had taken the dwarf, Korik, three days before. He hadn't returned. They must have been holding Calen in a different room, because Tarmon hadn't seen him since they entered the castle.

Every night, the dragon's roars rippled through the sky like thunder. The creature was no beast; Tarmon had seen the intelligence in its eyes. It knew it could not siege the castle on its own, and even if it did, they would just kill Calen.

"Agh." Tarmon shifted his weight, turning to face Vaeril's cell. The wound on his side was far from the only part of his body that was in pain.

"Vaeril, are you awake?"

"Unfortunately," the elf said through gritted teeth. The High Mage had taken Vaeril for questioning more than any of them. Twice a day. Tarmon knew little of elves. And what he did know came from bards' stories. The travelling bards had often spun tales of the *old* elves. The ones who ruled the skies from dragonback. The ones who, along with the Jotnar, founded The Order. Of course, the recounting of history was a fickle thing. It depended on the bard as to whether the elves were heroes or villains of the story. What Tarmon did know was that the elf in the cell beside him was one he had grown to trust.

"We need to do something," Tarmon said between short breaths. "Korik has not returned."

"He is dead," Vaeril responded plainly, though Tarmon could hear the regret in the elf's voice. "I saw his body when they took me in this evening. They flayed him alive. He was strong, though. I do not believe he would have told them of the Portal Hearts."

Tarmon's head sank into his hands. "By the gods. May Hafaesir guide him."

"I fear it will not be long before we face the same fate."

With all the strength he could muster, Tarmon lifted himself forward onto his knees, wrapping his fingers around the iron bars that separated his and Vaeril's cells. "We cannot simply sit around and wait to die."

"Agreed," Vaeril said, propping himself up on his elbows.

"The next time they come for either one of us, we try to take them. They have grown lax in the past week. One always stays outside the room while the other opens the cell."

"We will most likely die."

Tarmon couldn't help but choke a laugh at the elf's candour. "Yes, we most likely will."

"What about him?" Vaeril nodded towards Erik, who still lay unconscious on the floor of his cell.

"I can carry him."

Vaeril nodded slowly, as though ruminating on the idea. "Then we find the Draleid."

"Then we find Calen."

The click of the key turning in the lock woke Tarmon from his slumber. It was followed by the rasping, scraping sound of the iron bar being slid free from the outside of the room's door. Grimacing, Tarmon pulled himself upright. He took in long, deep breaths, readying himself. He whispered, "Vaeril, they are coming."

Before Vaeril had a chance to respond, the door burst open, clattering against the wall. Only fractions of a second passed before two men rushed into the room, black mantles pulled about them, swords drawn and dripping blood.

"Keys," one of the men called, snatching a bundle of keys from the air as the other man threw them to him. He fiddled with the keys for a few moments before deciding on one and slotting it into the lock on Tarmon's cell door. A turn and a click, then the iron-barred door creaked open. The man drew back his hood, and Tarmon stumbled backwards in surprise. It was Alleron.

Alleron tossed the keys back to his companion, who proceeded to open Erik's cell.

"Can you stand?" Alleron asked, reaching his hand out to Tarmon.

"I can." Tarmon clasped Alleron's hand, heaving himself to his feet.

"Take the guard's shoes, clothes, and weapons," Alleron said, resting his hand on Tarmon's shoulder. "You won't get far in the snow if you're shirtless and shoeless."

While Alleron and his companion set about freeing Vaeril and Erik, Tarmon made his way to the room's door. Two guards in the red and black leather of the Lorian empire lay still on the ground, both leaking blood from knife wounds in their necks. Tarmon sized them up with his eyes. They were too small. Their clothes and shoes would suit Vaeril and Erik well, but his own foot would not even come close to fitting in those shoes, and there was not a chance he would be able to squeeze into that armour. As quickly as he could, fighting the creaking pains in his body, Tarmon stripped the men and brought their clothes back into the cells. He handed one pile to Vaeril, receiving a weak nod from the elf. How Vaeril was going to put the shirt or armour on while his hands were still bound by those manacles was another thing altogether.

Alleron, who now knelt by Erik's side, gave Tarmon a questioning glance at the sight of him still in nothing but his smallclothes.

"Those damned Lorians are too small," he said with a shrug. "I'll find more clothes. How is he?"

"Conscious, but barely. We won't be able to—"

"I'm all right." Both Alleron and Tarmon jerked their heads around at the sound of Erik's voice. The young man's eyes were open, his lips cracked and raw. "I can walk. Just help me to my feet."

"I'll carry you," Alleron said, setting his jaw.

"*I can walk*. Now, help me to my feet."

Alleron pursed his lips, then nodded, reaching out his hand and helping Erik to his feet. He then turned to his companion, tilting his head in Vaeril's direction. "Baird, the manacles."

Reaching into his pocket, Alleron's companion, Baird, produced a small steel rod etched with glowing blue runes that seemed to match the ones carved into Vaeril's manacles. "Elf, your hands."

Without hesitation, Vaeril held out his hands, chains clinking.

Baird reached out, touching the steel rod to the surface of the manacle on Vaeril's right arm, producing an audible click before both manacles opened and fell to the floor with a clang.

Vaeril let out a short, almost euphoric, breath, his eyes closing, a warm smile touching his lips. "We must find the Draleid."

It took a few minutes for Erik and Vaeril to dress themselves, but then they were moving through the corridors of the castle as quickly as they could.

Tarmon's lungs burned, straining to keep up with his urgency. He carried one of the soldier's swords in his right hand and Vaeril's former manacles in his left. Never leave anything behind that could be useful later. That was something his father had told him, and his father was often right.

"Where is Calen?" Vaeril called as they hurried down the stone corridor.

"He's being held in a cell on the other side of the castle," Alleron's companion, Baird, replied. He was a tall man with black hair and a long unkempt beard, a fresh white bandage drawn over his left eye. "He'll be under guard."

"And the mage?" Erik asked, panting.

"We're not sure," Alleron called back. "He might be in his chambers, he might..."

"He might be with Calen," Erik finished.

Alleron didn't respond, but Tarmon could see him give a grim nod.

A door burst open to the right, and a heavy weight crashed into Tarmon's side, knocking him sidelong into the wall of the corridor. A mountain of a man stood beside him, his fingers gripped around the haft of a short axe. The man was easily as tall and as broad as Tarmon, if not a little more so. He had a coat of mail tied at the waist with a leather belt and a wolf-fur cloak draped around his shoulders. His clothes would fit Tarmon perfectly.

Ducking below the swing of the axe, Tarmon brought his elbow up, crunching into the man's cheekbone. He followed the elbow with the pommel of his sword, slamming it into the side of the man's head. The man stumbled, howling as he touched his shattered cheekbone. Tarmon pressed, swinging the manacles in his left hand. The man screamed, tilting his head back as the heavy steel manacles cracked into his mouth, sending broken teeth into the air. Seeing the opening, Tarmon shifted his weight onto his back foot, then drove the tip of his sword through the man's exposed neck, blood fountaining from the wound.

As Tarmon slid the blade free, the man's body collapsed to the ground, blood still spilling out over the floor.

Vaeril was the first to reach Tarmon. "Are you all right?"

"I'll live," Tarmon said, reaching down and pulling the man's boots free, followed by his trousers, wolf-fur cloak, and coat of mail. They fit him well, better than he would have hoped. "Let's get Calen."

Baird and Alleron led the group down corridor after corridor as they made their way towards the cell where Calen was being kept. Tarmon tried not to think of what they might find when they got there. Calen was a strong-willed man. Tarmon had seen what torturers did to strong-willed men.

They ran into a few Lorian and Drifaienin guards along the way, but none of them posed much of an obstacle. Some of the Drifaienin even stopped once they saw Alleron's face, twisting their hands into fists and raising them across their chests.

Alleron finally stopped at a corner where their corridor intersected another, taking only the slightest of glances around its edge. "Down at the end," he said, gesturing around the corner. "Five guards. Possibly more inside."

"The High Mage is inside." Vaeril's eyes were closed as he spoke. "I can feel him drawing on the Spark."

Alleron bit his lip, pondering something. "Any chance you can use that Spark of yours to take out the guards?"

Vaeril shook his head. "I'm too weak. I would just harm myself."

Alleron nodded, the look on his face showing that he had received the answer he expected. "It's a narrow corridor. They can't stand any more than two abreast. I say we rush them."

"I can walk," Erik said, his hands resting on his knees, his breathing laboured as he leaned against the wall. "But there is no way I'll be able to fight."

Tarmon turned to Alleron, Baird, and Vaeril. "We can't charge them. The High Mage will hear the fighting."

"What do we do, then?" Erik asked, his head tilted to the side.

"We need to get them away from the door." Alleron's gaze fell on Erik, who was leaning against the wall, garbed head to toe in Lorian armour. "You're going to need to get their attention. You're the only one who might pass as Lorian."

Erik let out a strained laugh, his face twisting in a grimace. "I knew I wasn't going to get away that easily."

Tarmon gave an amused smile. "Nothing is ever easy, is it, young Virandr?"

"All right, what's the plan?" Baird asked, cutting through the chatter. "We don't have much time. It won't be long until someone finds the bodies we left."

Tarmon nodded, agreeing. "Erik, you step into the corridor and call for help. Make sure you're convincing enough for all of them to follow. When they pass by, we'll take them down as quietly as we can. Then, we move for Calen. Anybody disagree?"

Tarmon looked around to see hesitant but approving faces. It wasn't the most complex plan in the world, but it was always wiser to bring your enemy to you rather than the other way around.

As Erik stepped out into the hallway, Tarmon readied himself, rolling his shoulders and cracking his neck. His body was stiff. Weeks cramped in a cell would do that. He left the manacles on the ground by the wall, allowing him the use of both hands. He pressed his back up against the wall to keep himself unseen by the soldiers for as long as possible. Alleron, Baird, and Vaeril stood beside him, similarly pressed against the wall.

"Quick," Erik called down the corridor. "Come with me, the prisoners have escaped!"

"Who goes there?" a voice called back. "By order of—"

"Shut up and come on, all of you! If they escape, the High Mage will have all our heads." Without waiting for a response, Erik turned and began to run back down the long corridor, throwing a sideways glance towards Tarmon as he did.

The heavy clink of plate boots signalled that the soldiers had taken the bait. Tarmon took a deep breath, letting it swell in his chest as the footsteps got closer. He tightened his grip on the hilt of his sword, feeling the pressure in his knuckles.

Two guards passed in front of him, following Erik. Then two more. Tarmon's heart felt as though it had stopped beating as he waited for the fifth guard. Then he saw the glint of silver mail and swung. The blade sliced through the soldier's neck, between his breastplate and his helmet, sliding out the other side in one clean stroke of blood and gore. As the soldier's head lifted, separating from the neck, the body remained upright for a moment as though by strength of will alone.

Letting go of his sword with his right hand, Tarmon reached down, snatched a knife that hung from the falling soldier's belt, and drove it through the back of the skull of the soldier in front. Tarmon yanked the knife free, and the second soldier collapsed to the ground, lifeless.

Flipping the knife to a throwing position, he launched it through the air at the third soldier who stood across from him. The man wailed as the knife buried itself to the hilt in his eye, blood and clear fluid spilling out through his fingers as he tried to pull the knife free, screaming all the while. Lunging forward, Tarmon struck the pommel of the knife with the flat of his hand. The soldier's body went limp, dropping to the ground like a sack of stones.

Tarmon stood over the three dead soldiers, his chest heaving, sweat pumping.

"Remind me not to get on your bad side," Erik said as he walked over to Tarmon, grimacing as he surveyed the scene. Behind him, Alleron, Baird, and Vaeril had dealt with the other two soldiers, leaving them in crumpled heaps on the ground. "So much for being quiet. Let's get Calen."

Chapter Thirty-Eight

Pieces on a Board

alen groaned. Not at one thing in particular, but at everything. A drum pounded on the inside of his skull, his throat was raw and dry, and his lips were so cracked and broken that the coppery taste of blood was a permanent fixture in his mouth. Bruises and cuts marked his wrists where the manacles dug into his skin. Even opening his eyes for longer than five or six seconds at a time felt as though it took every ounce of his energy. He had no idea how long he'd been in that cell. He wasn't even sure when he'd last eaten. He knew it had been so long that his stomach no longer rumbled – it just hurt. Yet still, in all that pain, he was hollow. Numb. Without the touch of Valerys's mind, Calen was alone. Truly alone.

"You're awake."

Calen had grown to hate High Mage Artim Valdock's insidious voice; it slithered, and crawled from the man's mouth, trying desperately to drag the thoughts from Calen's head. He was a parasite.

Wincing, Calen curled up in a fit of coughs, shivering.

"You really are a wretch, aren't you? You will soon be gone from this place, and at the very least, I shall reap the rewards of your capture. I have only come to ask you one question. Why?"

With his lungs feeling as though they were on the verge of collapse, Calen pushed through the pain and emptiness, dragging himself to a semi-upright position, resting his shoulder on the solid stone wall of the cell, his eyes meeting Artim Valdock's inquisitive stare.

In the villages, the High Mage probably would have been considered a handsome man, with his sharp face, tanned skin, and blonde hair. But as he stood there outside the cell, looming over Calen, his black, silver-trimmed robes draped around his shoulders, he looked like nothing more than a viper.

"Let me clarify," Artim said. "Why do you put yourself through this for people who only seek to control you?" The High Mage lowered his head, ensuring his eyes were locked on Calen's. "The men and women you protect would see this continent burn, so long as they have their revenge. And they would use you as a puppet to achieve this. They are not your allies or your kin. They are your puppet masters. The Dragonguard are your only *true* kin."

Calen gritted his teeth as he stared at the man. He knew what the High Mage was doing. He was trying to get inside Calen's head again. Trying to plant the seeds of doubt. The only problem was that some of his words rang true. It had been Aeson Virandr who brought the empire to the villages. It was Aeson Virandr who brought the men who killed Calen's family and likely many others in The Glade. Faces flashed through Calen's mind: Tach Edwin, Jorvil Ehrnin, Mara Styr… Anya. Aeson Virandr would not know any of their names, yet he might have caused their deaths. And it was Aeson Virandr and Therin who brought Calen to Belduar, where the empire followed them. So many dead. Calen's heart would have sunk into the depths of his stomach if it had not already been swallowed whole by the void left by Valerys's consciousness.

But even considering everything, Aeson Virandr was the person who had brought Valerys to Epheria. And as Calen lay in that cell, the only thing he cared about was getting those manacles off and feeling the touch of Valerys's mind once more. Without it, everything was meaningless. It was not a feeling Calen thought he could ever explain to another person. It gave him great sympathy for Aeson, and an understanding as to what it meant to be Rakina. To be Broken.

Calen could still feel the slightest lingering of Valerys in his mind, just a sensation, an inexplicable spark that let him know Valerys was still alive. It was all that kept him sane. Aeson's dragon, Lyara, had died centuries ago. Yet still the man persevered. Pushing through all the pain, the loss, the anguish. What Calen was experiencing barely scratched the tip of what it was to be Rakina.

Artim Valdock stood completely still, the silver trim on his robes glimmering in the light of the sconces set into the walls. His eyes were fixed on Calen as though expecting an answer.

Calen did his best to hold the man's gaze, straining to keep his eyes open.

"Just something to think on." A slow grin spread across the man's face, his eyes unyielding. "When they come for y—"

The door to the room burst open, followed by a blur of motion that Calen could barely comprehend. Shadows flickered around the room, men charging. The High Mage screamed.

Calen grunted, pulling himself forward, clasping his hand around the iron bar of the cell door, dragging himself so he could better see what was going on. Calen's eyes strained in the dim light as he tried to make out faces, but he could feel his consciousness slipping, his vision growing darker.

Tarmon drew in a deep breath, his heart thumping as he stood beside the heavy wooden door, readying himself. He squeezed his fingers on the hilt of his sword and lifted his left hand up, gauging the weight of the heavy, rune-crafted manacles. Exhaling, he turned to the others, who all nodded.

With one last deep breath, Tarmon dropped his shoulder and slammed it into the door, flinging it open with brute force. The door crashed off the wall as Tarmon bounded across the threshold.

Tarmon knew he needed to close the distance between himself and the High Mage as quickly as he could. It was his only chance. The High Mage stood only a few feet away, staring at something in one of the cells, his black robes rippling in the back flow of air that had flushed through the room when Tarmon had opened the door.

By the time Tarmon was within striking distance, the man had only just begun to turn his head. *I need to take him down before he has a chance to think. Before he can use his magic.* Reaching deep into the pit of his stomach, Tarmon summoned all the strength he could find, channelling it into an almighty swing of his left arm. The heavy steel manacles in his left hand crashed into the High Mage's face. Tarmon could hear the crunch of bone as the man's nose gave way in a thick spray of blood. Before the High Mage could react, Tarmon drove down with his right hand, plunging his sword into the man's torso, just below his ribs.

The High Mage screamed, howling in pain. Tarmon pressed. He left his sword buried in the mage's torso, pulled his fingers into a fist and punched the High Mage square in the face, sending him stumbling backwards, collapsing to the ground. Diving after him, Tarmon grabbed hold of the manacles and clicked them into place around the man's wrists.

As soon as the manacles locked, the High Mage's eyes widened, bulging. "No, no, no—"

Tarmon punched the man again, blood spraying from his already shattered nose, his head bouncing off the stone floor. Waiting for a moment to see if he was still conscious, Tarmon punched the High Mage once more for good measure. If he died, he died.

Once he was sure the High Mage was unconscious, Tarmon pulled himself to his feet, his muscles screaming in protest. The torture and the weeks in the cell had left his body in a constant state of aching and groaning. But there was nothing he could do about it now but grit his teeth and keep going.

"Is he alive?" Alleron asked, walking through the doorway, Baird and Vaeril at his side.

Tarmon nodded. "For now. If he doesn't get a healer, he will die from blood loss. The manacles should keep him subdued until then."

"Move," Baird said, pushing past Tarmon, standing over the unconscious mage. "No sense in leaving him alive. He needs to die."

"There is no honour in that." Vaeril's tone was flat and straightforward as he spoke, as though it were a simple fact of life.

Baird raised an eyebrow, the one over his good eye, half chuckling. "Honour? We're going to war here, elf. Honour is not on my mind."

"It is a hollow victory if you win a war but lose who you are."

"Does he always speak like this?" Baird asked, his mouth drawn up in a disbelieving smile.

"Most of the time," Erik answered, half hobbling into the room, a weak smile on his face. He turned to Tarmon. "I say we kill him. He would do the same to us."

"But we are not him," Tarmon said, turning to Erik. "Leave him be. If he dies, good. If he doesn't, he'll wish he had. I've heard the Circle aren't very tolerant of failures."

"I'd rather kill him now and be done with—"

"By the gods, is that Calen?" Erik gasped, cutting across Baird. He dropped to his knees beside the cell the High Mage had been staring into.

The crumpled heap in the cell truly was Calen, stripped down to nothing but his smallclothes and those glowing manacles. He looked fragile, as though he might break at the slightest touch. He had not lost all his muscle, but he was certainly a lot skinnier than when Tarmon had seen him last. His ribs were only just visible, and his cheeks were sunken and gaunt. His body was covered from head to toe in welts, cuts, and bruises, a blend of all the colours one's skin should never be.

"Keys," Baird called, tossing a set of iron keys bound to a ring towards Tarmon.

Tarmon snatched the keys out of the air, taking a moment to select the correct one before slotting it into the lock and clicking it into place. The iron slatted door creaked open at Tarmon's push, and Erik hobbled over to Calen.

"Calen, Calen." Erik shook the young man, not too strongly, but enough that it should have woken him. Erik turned back to the others, one hand behind Calen's head and the other on his chest. "He's still breathing, but his heartbeat is weak."

"We need to get the Draleid out of here. Now." Vaeril stood at the door to the room, his ear facing outward as though he were listening to the wind. "There's more coming. They must have found the bodies."

"How many?" Baird asked.

"Too many, but if we move now, we can go around them. They don't know where we are, yet."

Tarmon knelt beside Calen. "I'll carry him."

"Are you sure you have the strength?" Baird asked, more than a touch of scepticism in his voice.

"If I can't carry him, I'll die with him. Do you know where we're going?"

Baird gave Tarmon a gruff nod. "I do. There's a sally port not far from here. If we go that way, we'll have a free run to the city gates, which will hopefully be open."

"Hopefully?" Erik's eyes widened.

"There is more than one piece moving on this board," Baird replied. "We just need to hope the other pieces complete their moves."

"Enough talk." Tarmon lifted himself to his feet, then pulled the black cloak from around the High Mage's shoulders. He draped the cloak around Calen, tying the drawstring, then, his muscles aching, he lifted Calen upright before draping the young man over his shoulder. Even in his half-starved state, Calen was not light. Tarmon wasn't sure how long he could carry him, but he would carry him as far as he could. He gritted his teeth. "Lead the way."

Tarmon followed the others as they made their way through the corridors of the castle, shifting Calen on his shoulder as he moved, his muscles groaning. Two left turns, a flight of stairs down, a long corridor, then another flight of stairs back up. His shoulder burned with a fury, his back ached, and his legs were near collapse.

A woman's voice echoed down the hall. "Alleron?"

Alleron, who was running just behind Baird, stopped in his tracks, turning to look down another corridor that ran perpendicular to their own. A woman stood in a long, red velvet dress; raven hair cascading over her shoulders. "Mother."

"Alleron, we don't have time for this," Baird said, grabbing Alleron by the shoulder.

Alleron shrugged him off. "Mother, I—"

"Go," the woman said, nodding slightly. "Get him to safety. I will create a distraction."

Before Alleron could respond, his mother was gone, flitting back down the corridor she had been standing in.

"Let's go," Baird called, tugging Alleron into motion by the shoulder.

Alleron hesitated a moment, but acquiesced, his face twisting into a frown.

Within minutes, the smell of smoke and char began to drift through the hallways, light at first, but growing heavier. Shouts and cries followed the smoke, echoing through the night. Tarmon saw Vaeril tilt his head slightly, as though listening for something.

"The gardens are on fire?" Vaeril said, more a question than a statement, as though he weren't entirely sure what that meant.

"My mother's gardens," Alleron whispered. "She must have done it."

"We can thank her later," Baird called back, ducking down another stairwell. "We're almost there."

Tarmon let out an audible groan at the idea of climbing down another stairwell with Calen on his back. He grunted, shifting Calen to a better position as he took the stairs one step at a time. It was a long, winding staircase that seemed to go on for eternity. At the bottom, Tarmon emerged into a dimly lit room that looked like a completely undecorated antechamber. It was large and rectangular, smooth stone on all sides, lit only by a single oil lamp set into the wall on the right-hand side. A large door of latticed iron was set into the far wall, leading into another corridor.

Tarmon dropped to one knee, lowering Calen to the ground, sighing in relief as he did. The muscles in his back and shoulders knotted and bunched, burning from over-exertion. "What's the plan from here?"

"At the end of this corridor," Baird said, "is another door, one that leads to the outer walls of the castle. Once we're out there, we're going to have to move quickly to get to the gates. There are horses tied up about two hundred paces from the gates. Any closer would have been suspicious. If we can get to the horses, we will get a riverboat to Straga and take a ship from there."

"There is a lot that can go wrong with that plan," Tarmon said, grimacing as he pulled himself to his feet.

"Do you have a better one?"

"I don't," Tarmon admitted.

"Well, then, onward we go."

"Wait," Erik said, an urgency in his voice.

"What is it?" Alleron turned to Erik, looking him over. "Are you hurt?"

"My swords. I can't leave here without them."

"For fuck's sake!" Baird barely held his voice to a whisper. "Steel is steel. We don't have time for this. We'll get you more swords."

"My mother forged those swords. I'm not leaving them here."

"They are safe and waiting for you," Alleron said, stepping between Baird and Alleron. "I had your things taken from the keep this morning. You are lucky the armoury guards are loyal to me, not my father. Now, can we go?"

After a moment's hesitation, Erik nodded.

Tarmon let out a sigh, dropped to one knee, and once again tossed Calen's dead weight over his shoulder.

Once through the long corridor, the group emerged through the outer door of the sally port. As the castle itself was already situated within the city walls, there was not much rough terrain to navigate before they found themselves stepping onto the city streets, for which Tarmon was very thankful.

Their pace did not slow as they moved through the streets, a thin blanket of snow falling around them. The ragtag group got a few sideways looks, but they ignored them and just kept moving. There had been no sight of any soldiers yet, but they were not going to wait around for them to show up.

"Are you all right?" Vaeril's face looked almost as gaunt as Calen's as the elf strode beside Tarmon, his eyes flitting between Tarmon and the unconscious man draped over his shoulder.

"I'm fine," Tarmon grunted, lying. "Keep moving."

Barely a handful of minutes had passed before the sonorous bellow of horns droned through the night, repeating itself, louder and louder.

"Pick it up," Baird called back, not even caring to hide his sword as he ran.

Each step sent vibrations shuddering up Tarmon's legs. The layer of snow that coated the ground softened the impact of each footstep, but it also sapped the energy from Tarmon's legs as he heaved his feet in and out, up and down. Even in the bitter cold, sweat dripped from his skin, and his chest burned.

"Almost there," Alleron shouted, before turning the corner ahead to Tarmon's left.

Stumbling over something hard hidden beneath the snow, Tarmon dropped to one knee, only just managing to keep from dropping Calen to the ground. *Keep going.* Clenching the muscles in his jaw, Tarmon pushed himself to his feet, the muscles in his leg feeling as though they were on the verge of catching fire. *Just put one foot in front of the next. Left, right, left, right.*

A chorus of shouts erupted from a side street, and three soldiers in Lorian leathers came charging at them. Vaeril split one of them across the navel, the man's guts spilling into the snow, steam wafting into the air. Alleron caught the second one with a strike through the neck, blood spilling down over the man's chest. The third soldier, however, passed through the others, heading straight for Tarmon.

"Fuck it," Tarmon muttered. Grinding his teeth, he pulled on his last vestiges of strength and swung his leg up, catching the charging soldier square in the jaw with a vicious *thump.* The man dropped to the ground in a heap, his helmet knocked clean from his head.

Tarmon stumbled, the momentum of the kick carrying him forward. The man groaned, pulling himself to his feet as he shook his head from side to side.

"Sorry, Calen," Tarmon said to the unconscious young man on his shoulder before dumping him unceremoniously in the snow. Moving with a speed his muscles made him regret, Tarmon snatched up the man's fallen helmet, gripping it as tightly as he could, then slammed it full force into the rising soldier's face. The blow produced an audible *crack* from the man's eye socket, and the soldier fell back down into the snow. Tarmon dropped his knees onto the soldier's chest and beat him across the face with the helmet until he stopped moving, blood and bits of skin dappling the snow around them.

When he was satisfied the man would not be moving again, Tarmon, chest heaving and heart thumping, dropped the helmet in the snow and dragged himself to his feet. With a sigh, he grabbed Calen and tossed him over his shoulder once more, grimacing as the young man's full weight came down on him.

By the time the group reached the city gates, Tarmon was all but certain his legs and back were on the verge of giving way.

"The gates," Alleron said, turning to Baird. "They're still closed."

"Patience," Baird whispered, his eyes fixed on the gatehouse. Moments later, a scream rang out from the battlements above the gate and a body plummeted to the ground. The blanket of snow did little to soften the soldier's fall, his body shattering in a burst of blood and bone. Then a creaking noise resounded from the gates, and they began to shudder open. "Move!"

As the group drew nearer to the gates, a group of Lorian soldiers formed a line across the threshold – six wide, two deep, spaced about a foot and a half apart and covering the entire gateway.

"There are too many," Vaeril called out, panting.

"We don't have any other options," Alleron shouted back.

Tarmon winced, his leg trembling slightly. There was no way they would be able to fight their way through that many armed men, especially not in the state most of them were in. Alleron and his companion, Baird, were all right, but Tarmon, Vaeril, and Erik were all barely managing to keep up, and Calen was unconscious. If Calen had been conscious, that would have been a different story entirely. Tarmon had seen what the young man could do – it was incredible. But Calen wasn't conscious, and this snow-covered shithole was where they would all likely die.

Either way, Alleron was right. They didn't have any other options. So Tarmon rolled his shoulders and marched forward. He would put Calen on the ground before he charged, but he would try his best to keep him close.

"If it comes to it," Vaeril said, stepping closer to Tarmon. "Take him and run. I'll do what I can."

Tarmon sighed, but gave a nod. The thought of running while those around him stayed and fought didn't sit well with him, but the elf was right; with the dragon behind him, Calen was worth more than a hundred of any of them.

The sounds of screaming, snarling, and crashing steel pulled Tarmon's attention back towards the soldiers at the gate. Where the soldiers had stood, all that remained was a mound of shredded, bloody armour and flesh. In the place of the soldiers stood the wolf Tarmon had seen in the forest outside Kallingat, its black-grey fur matted with dark blood, its lips pulled back in a snarl. The thing was enormous.

A shiver ran the length of Tarmon's spine. That wolf had just torn through twelve armoured men as if they were nothing but rag dolls, and now its eyes were fixed on his group.

"Go, now!" Baird roared.

"I'm not going anywhere near that thing, not while I can barely walk," Erik called back. "Did you see what it just did to those soldiers? We need to find a way around."

"Aneera is a friend." Baird turned to look at Erik, Tarmon, and Vaeril. "I don't have time to explain right now, but she is on our side. Now, I need you to move."

"She is an Angan," Vaeril whispered, just loud enough for everyone to hear. Tarmon might have been mistaken, but he thought he heard a touch of reverence in the elf's voice. "Of clan Fenryr."

"That she is, elf. We need to go." Baird didn't wait for a response from the others, turning on his heels and darting towards the gates, straight towards the enormous wolf, Alleron hot on his heels.

Both Tarmon and Erik looked to Vaeril, who pulled himself from his sense of awe to give a slight nod. And with that, they ran.

As Tarmon neared the gates, the wolf turned its head, staring straight at him, recognition in its eyes. Then it did one of the most unexpected things Tarmon could have imagined. It reached its right paw forward, stretching it out, and gave a slight bow of its head as though recognising a familiar.

With a slight, almost subconscious nod, Tarmon passed the wolf, eyeing it askance as he did. Then they were through the gates, the bellow of the horns still ringing through the night.

"The horses are just up ahead," Baird shouted back, his outline only visible thanks to the moonlight reflected by the blanket of snow that covered the ground and coated the trees.

Behind them, the sound of screams and ringing steel rose from the city. Tarmon looked back through the gate to see flashes of bright red light arcing through the air, cleaving soldiers in half. The other 'pieces on the board' that Baird had mentioned.

"Just stay with us," Tarmon whispered to Calen, who still hung motionless across his shoulders. If they didn't reach the horses soon, Tarmon knew he would collapse. His legs shook with each step, and a fire burned through the muscles in his back; it would not be long before he gave way. But he could hear the horses whinnying; they couldn't be far.

But something seemed strange. The sound of the horses was growing closer far too fast, and it was coming from the wrong direction, from the city. Tarmon turned his head once more, just in time to see a group of riders dashing through the city gates, throwing up clumps of snow and sod in their wake, horses snorting and neighing. Another flash of red light cut some of the horses' legs from under them, but even more kept coming.

"Riders!" Tarmon called out, pushing himself forward as fast as his legs could carry him, but he knew it wouldn't be fast enough. There was no way he was going to outrun those horses, especially not in the snow with Calen draped over his shoulders. His heart pounded, shivering the blood through his veins, urging him forward. But it was not enough. A cramp set into Tarmon's left thigh and his leg gave way. He crashed into the snow, dropping Calen.

"Ahh!" He tried to force himself to his feet, but the pain in his leg was excruciating, and his muscle spasmed out of control.

"Baird!" Vaeril shouted, only just rising above the drumming pain in Tarmon's head. "The key. We need to unlock the manacles. We're not going to make it!"

Tarmon looked up to see the uncertainty on Baird's face. He and Alleron could probably make it if they took off into the forest on their own, and the man was considering it.

With a deep frown, Baird stopped running, then turned and started sprinting back towards Tarmon and Calen, Vaeril and Erik now at their side. Rummaging in his pocket, Baird produced the small, rune-marked steel rod and flung it to Vaeril.

The elf snatched the rod from the air.

"Come on, come on!" Erik shouted, dragging Vaeril by the shirtsleeve. The man and the elf scrambled to the ground beside Tarmon and Calen. Tarmon risked a glance over his shoulder. The riders weren't far. They would be on them in moments.

Just as Baird had done for him earlier in the night, Vaeril held up Calen's hands and touched the steel rod to the glowing manacles, eliciting a click. As soon as the manacles opened, a gasp escaped Calen's throat, and his eyes shot open, glowing with a deep purple light.

Tarmon stumbled backward into the snow, his eyes wide, fear in his chest. "What is—"

A monstrous roar ripped through the night, tearing across the sky like rolling thunder.

CHAPTER THIRTY-NINE

FURY UNLEASHED

alen's eyes shot open, burning with a light so bright he could see nothing but a blank canvas of white. Anger. Pure, untamed rage filled him, searing his veins, filling the emptiness that had hollowed out his bones.

He thought he could hear voices calling to him, but they were nothing but a muted buzz at the back of his consciousness, drowned out by the heavy sound of wingbeats thumping in his ears. The wind rippled over his body, tearing past him as he moved. He could feel *something* again, something that had been taken from him, something he had yearned for. But now, rage filled him, boiling his blood. He would kill those who had taken from him, rip them from the world, shred their souls.

As the white light peeled back, images flashed across Calen's mind. A wide-open canvas of green, white, and black: a forest covered in snow. In the distance, city walls. A blazing inferno that rose as high as the castle beside it. But those images faded to the back of his mind, his eyes focusing on something else. A group huddled together in the snow, and riders heading towards them from the city.

A pressure began to build within him. Those riders would burn. As would all those who had harmed the bond. Harmed his soulkin. They would all burn.

Gathering his thoughts, Tarmon cast his eyes to the sky. A white shape dropped from the blanket of clouds above, ripping through the air at immense speed. The closer it got, the larger it appeared, its wings spreading wide against the dark night.

Its jaws opening, the dragon unleashed a roar so visceral and primal the air itself seemed to shudder. Birds jettisoned from the trees around them, swirling up into the night in plumes of black, and the hair on the back of Tarmon's neck stood on end.

The dragon soared over Tarmon's head, moving straight for the riders that charged towards them. Then, as though a signal fire the size of an inn had been lit, the darkness retreated, cowering from the column of dragonfire that poured forth from Valerys's jaws. The riders at the centre of the group didn't even have time to scream.

Once the light from the dragonfire died out, shadows returned, accompanied by the whimpering of the horses that had been on the edge of the pack and the wailing of their riders, whose bodies were blackened and blistered.

Some of the riders at the very edges of the group had escaped relatively unscathed. No more than five or six, though it was difficult to tell in the darkness renewed. With fear in their bones, their horses galloped even faster, their heads bobbing up and down as they charged feverishly. Then the dragon wheeled back around.

A fine mist of snow sprayed into the air as the dragon swooped down, catching one of the riders in its jaws, tearing him clean in half. Another beat of the dragon's wings and it lifted back into the sky.

Tarmon turned to look back at Calen; the young man was awake, but barely. His eyes still glowed with a pale purple light. Tarmon had no idea whether that was a good or bad thing, but at least Calen was alive.

Another spine-tingling roar echoed through the skies as the dragon dropped back down, crashing to the ground, a swing of its spearhead tail whipping two riders from their horses, killing their mounts instantly. Then, as the last three riders drew closer to Tarmon and the others, they were engulfed by a river of flame; they died howling and screaming in agony.

Moments passed, and the smell of charred flesh and burnt leather tainted the air. Then the crack of wingbeats sounded, and the dragon dropped to the ground right in front of Tarmon and the others, its lips pulled back, rows of alabaster teeth bared, sharp as swords. Valerys's eyes held nothing but wrath as the dragon loomed over the group. In the month they had been imprisoned, the dragon had grown even further. It now stood at least thirty feet from snout to tail, its wings longer still. Its jaw had widened, and its entire body looked fuller, more powerful. As it stood there, the dragon craned its neck forward, reaching its snout in to touch Calen, nudging him in the side, a low rumbling whimper escaping its throat. It was then, as Tarmon looked into the dragon's pale lavender eyes, gleaming with intelligence, that he realised where he had seen the glowing colour of Calen's eyes before.

That moment of relative calm was broken as the horn rang out from the city once more, shouts sounding from the city gates. More men were coming.

"We need to keep moving." Baird's voice trembled as he spoke, his eyes still fixed on the dragon that now stood in front of them.

"I can't outrun them," Tarmon said, his voice flat and plain. "Not while I have to carry Calen. My legs will give way."

Snarling with fury, the dragon swung its head around and let out a vicious roar before turning back towards Tarmon and the others. Reaching one of its front limbs forward, the dragon bowed its head and neck close to the ground, a deep, rumbling growl resonating from its throat.

"What's it doing?" Baird asked, his voice still shuddering.

"Put Calen on Valerys's back." Vaeril jumped to his feet, an urgency permeating his voice.

Erik grimaced as he pulled himself to a standing position. "On his back? But he'll just fall—"

"Erik, we don't have time." Tarmon grunted, forcing his legs to straighten. "We need to do what the elf says, or we'll all die. Alleron, Baird, can you help me lift him?"

The two men nodded, helping Tarmon lift Calen to his feet.

"N'aldryr…" Calen muttered, only half conscious.

"Is he all right?" There was a look of concern on Alleron's face as he pulled Calen's arm around his shoulder.

"No," Tarmon answered, taking Calen's other arm. "But he's alive, and we need to keep him that way."

Every fibre of Tarmon's being groaned in complaint as he, Baird, and Alleron heaved Calen up on the dragon's back, tossing his right leg over the other side and resting his arms against Valerys's scales.

"Our bralgír tell stories of how dragons hold an intrinsic magic, one that is tied to their Draleid," Vaeril said, placing his hand on Valerys's neck. "Once the dragon is large enough to mount, their scales mould to the Draleid, holding them in place."

"Is Valerys large enough to mount?" Erik asked.

"We'll see." Vaeril shook at Calen's leg. The young man was slipping in and out of consciousness, the lavender light in his eyes flickering. "Straga. We are taking a boat from Straga. I will light a signal fire."

It was impossible to tell if Calen had understood, or even heard, what the elf said. But it was all that could be done. Shifting its body weight, the dragon pulled itself back to full height, its muscular neck moving from side to side. With a roar, it cracked its wings, spraying clouds of fine snow up into the air. Taking a few more steps forward, its wings beat again, lifting it slightly off the ground, then again, and again. Within moments the dragon was shooting into the sky, rising higher and higher. Tarmon just prayed the elf was right, otherwise they had sent Calen to his death.

The sound of beating wings thrummed through Calen's entire body. He groaned, peeling his eyes open, forcing his body to yield to his mind. His hands and fingers traced over the coarse, almost stone-like scales that armoured Valerys's neck. They were cool to the touch but somehow provided him with a sense of warmth.

Calen knew he had no right to even be conscious. His body screamed in agony: every muscle, every bone, every inch of skin. But strength flowed from Valerys, seeping into the cracks and crevices of Calen's mind. He could see, feel, hear – everything. There was not a point where Valerys's body stopped and Calen's started. They were one. The light that had obstructed Calen's eyes had peeled back now, but everything was not as it had been before. It was sharper.

The sensation was a bit unsettling at first – seeing everything through Valerys's eyes and his own at the same time – but it quickly became natural. Hundreds of feet below, he could see the torches of the riders and soldiers that had taken up chase after his companions. He could see the glimmer of their steel, the fur on their cloaks, the heat radiating from their bodies. Then he felt a fury unlike anything that had ever touched his mind, a blazing wrath that all but consumed him.

A deep, primal roar erupted from Valerys's jaws, the vibrations resonating through Calen's body. Valerys wheeled around, diving, plummeting straight for the riders. Calen's instinct was to panic, to grab for something to hold on to as the dragon dove almost vertically downward. But another feeling in the back of his mind told him there was no need. He could feel Valerys's scales holding him firmly, an unseen force keeping him securely on dragonback. Every hair on Calen's body tingled as he closed his eyes and spread out his hands, feeling the air ripple over him as Valerys dove. His soul was complete once more.

Even with his eyes closed, Calen could still see everything through Valerys's eyes. He took a deep breath through his nostrils, letting it fill his lungs, then exhaled before leaning down, pressing his chest against Valerys's scales. "Draleid n'aldryr, Valerys. Myia nithír til diar." *Dragonbound by fire, Valerys. My soul to yours.*

With those words, a deep vibration thrummed through Valerys's body, resonating in Calen's. He felt the pressure building in the back of his mind before Valerys opened his jaws and bathed the riders in a river of dragonfire.

The flames washed over the soldiers, sweeping across their ranks from left to right as Valerys dove, devastating them. The force of the flames knocked men from horses and tore sod from the ground, incinerating everything it touched. Guilt crept into the corners of Calen's mind at the loss of life, but Valerys's fury held it at bay. Valerys's fury was Calen's fury; they were one and the same. And if those riders were left to carry on, they would run down Erik and the others. Calen could not let that happen.

Sweeping back down, Valerys snared a horse and rider in his claws, lifting them from the ground before rending them, bits of blood and gore staining the snow.

With that, the remaining riders and soldiers scattered, their morale broken. They fled in all directions, disappearing into the cover of the snow-capped forest. But Valerys's rage did not subside; it blazed like an inferno. The dragon wanted to kill them all for what they had done.

Soaring high into the sky, Valerys broke through a bank of clouds, the wind whipping past Calen's face, then he dove. As the clouds peeled away, Calen could see Valerys was diving towards Arisfall, and the familiar pressure was building at the back of his mind.

No.

Valerys let out an almighty roar, and for a moment Calen felt a deep loneliness flooding through him, washing over from Valerys. It was the same all-consuming loneliness Calen had felt in the cell. His heart bled at the thought of Valerys feeling so alone and helpless.

"I'm so sorry…" Calen ran his hand along Valerys's scaled neck, a deep rumble resonating from the dragon. "I'm sorry I let us be separated. I didn't know what those manacles would do."

The rumble in the dragon's chest intensified as more of Valerys's emotions spilled over into Calen's mind: grief, agony, fear. Valerys had felt the same emptiness Calen had. The same abject sorrow.

"I'm here now," Calen whispered, his head pressed to the back of Valerys's neck as the dragon dove through the sky. "But if we attack this city, the people of Drifaien will never trust us. We can't be like the empire. We can't be like the Dragonguard. We need to be better."

A long moment passed where Calen wasn't sure what Valerys would do, but then the dragon let out another monstrous roar, the vibration resonating through Calen's body. Arching his flight back upward, the dragon swooped away from the city.

As Valerys rose higher and higher, Calen let his eyes close, his body pressed against Valerys's scales.

CHAPTER FORTY

WIND IN THE SAILS

alen pulled the black cloak tighter around himself, the icy touch of the rushing wind probing at his bruised and battered skin. At first, he hadn't realised that all he was wearing were his smallclothes and the black cloak that one of the others must have put around his shoulders. Although he was glad for the cloak, the fabric felt like fire against his raw skin and offered little protection against the bitter winter winds that nipped at him as he rode on Valerys's back. The warmth that emanated from the dragon helped, but it was not enough to keep his teeth from chattering. Every fibre of his body ached and groaned: His lungs heaved as they attempted to drag in air, his muscles spasmed as he held himself upright, and his head pounded as though it were filled with galloping horses.

Down below, nestled into the landscape of white, he saw the port town of what he figured must have been Straga, torches flickering and smoke drifting lazily from chimneys.

"There." Calen's shoulder burned as he extended out his hand, his finger pointing to a small signal fire that sat atop a smooth patch of rock beside the port, devoid of snow. Vaeril.

With a rumble of recognition, Valerys plummeted. The change in direction was so sudden Calen felt a strange weightlessness in his stomach. As they dropped towards the ground, a rapid change of speed jerked Calen's head back as Valerys cracked his wings against the air, alighting on the patch of rock. Just as Valerys's claws clicked against the rock, Calen heard shouts coming closer.

Tarmon, Erik, Vaeril, Alleron, and another man, who looked vaguely familiar, were running towards them, looks of concern on their faces. They must have arrived not long before.

"Calen, are you all right?" Erik was the first to the rock, his face covered in cuts, his skin painted in black and yellow bruises. He seemed to be carrying a slight limp as well.

Behind him, Vaeril and Tarmon looked in much the same condition, their eyes sunken and their cheeks devoid of colour. Tarmon, in particular, was moving as though every muscle in his body was in spasm.

"I'm all right," Calen said, trying his best to muster even the weakest of smiles. He didn't feel all right. Calen couldn't remember another time in his life when his body had simply felt so helpless. The skin where his fingernails and toenails should have been had hardened over, feeling more like callouses to the touch, small nubs of nails starting to form at the base. His legs felt as though they would crumble beneath him if he put any weight on them at all, his stomach simply hurt, and he faced a constant fight to keep his eyelids from shutting against his will. "I might need a hand getting down, though. I had enough trouble learning how to get off the back of a horse."

Just as Calen spoke, Valerys dipped his neck down, lowering his back so Calen could almost touch the ground with his feet. Calen couldn't help but wonder how he would ever be able to get down from Valerys's back when the dragon was fully grown.

Erik laughed, reaching his hand up to take some of Calen's weight.

Grunting, Calen swung his leg over Valerys's back, lowering himself. Erik's hand caught him under the armpits, helping take Calen's weight those last few inches. He let out a sharp hiss as his bare, bruised feet touched the cold ground. Erik caught Calen as he stumbled, wrapping his arm around Calen's back.

"Thank you," Calen said with a grimace, pain shooting through his legs, up around his knees, and burning through his back.

"I'm just happy to see you alive. And your eyes are back to normal as well."

"My eyes?"

"When we took the manacles off, your eyes glowed a bright purple." Tarmon let out a small grumble as he stepped onto the smooth patch of rock. "The same colour as the dragon's."

"It is not something I have seen before," Vaeril added as he walked over to Calen, his eyes bloodshot and his blonde hair tied back. The elf reached out his hand, clasping Calen's forearm. "Det er aldin na vëna dir, Draleid." *It is good to see you.*

"Det er aldin na vëna dir osa, Vaeril."

Vaeril tilted his head in recognition, a warm smile spreading across his face at Calen's words.

Calen nodded at Alleron. "Thank you for what you did. I'm so sorry about Leif."

"And I'm sorry for what happened. My father is not the man he once was." A silence held between the two men for a moment before Alleron gestured to his companion. The man had thick black hair, a long, knotted beard, and a weathered bandage across his left eye. "I'm not sure if you remember Baird."

"I had two eyes when last we met, and you weren't a Draleid. I'm assuming Aeson had something to do with that."

"You know my father?" Erik asked, his eyebrows raised.

Baird nodded, producing a folded-over piece of paper from his pocket. "This letter is the reason you are all standing here right now. But look, we can go over it all some other time. For now, we need to get you on that ship. People are already starting to gawk at the dragon, and I'm sure Lothal's men won't be far behind us. Aneera and Asius will only have been able to hold them off for so long."

"Asius?" A surge of urgency swept through Calen. "Asius is here? We need to go back for him!"

"Easy," Baird said, reaching out his hand. "We are in no condition to go back for anyone. Asius and Aneera can look after themselves. But when you do see Asius, you and the elf might want to thank him for forging the key to your chains. They'd still be around your wrists without him."

Calen grimaced, shifting his weight under Erik's arm. Reluctantly, he accepted Baird's words as true; they couldn't go back for Asius. "I hope I get the chance."

Baird nodded. "Alleron, is the captain ready to set sail?"

"Where's Korik?" Calen asked before Alleron could answer Baird. A sinking feeling set into his stomach as his eyes scanned the surroundings for any sign of the dwarf.

Tarmon shook his head, the look on the others' faces telling Calen all he needed to know. Falmin, Korik, and Lopir. Three more good people who had lost their lives following him.

"Do not hold the weight of it on your shoulders," Tarmon said, as though reading Calen's mind. "More men, women, elves, and dwarves will die in what is to come. It is the way of things. We are born, we live, and we die. Those three things cannot be changed. The only thing within our control is what we choose to do with the short time we have – the things we fight for, the people we love, the things we hold dear. Good men stand even when it is against all odds. They were, each of them, good men."

Calen sighed, feeling the frustration swell within him. "That doesn't make it any easier."

"It wasn't meant to," Tarmon said, shrugging slightly. "Things that matter are rarely easy."

Calen dropped his head, nodding slightly. He pulled the cloak tighter, his hands trembling from the cold. Without warning, his right leg shook and collapsed beneath him. Were it not for Erik's quick hands, he would have crumpled in a heap.

"Come on," Erik said, wrapping his hand around Calen's back. "We need to get you aboard that ship before the cold seeps into your bones. You need rest. We all do."

"Thank you." Calen lifted his head and looked to Alleron, raising an eyebrow. Alleron responded with a nod, and Calen knew it was finally time to let everyone know about his true plan. "I'm not going with you."

In truth, he had expected more shock on his friends' faces, but he was simply met with blank stares. "I'm going to get Rist. You can take the ship around the western coast to the Freehold. Alleron has arranged transport to take me North."

"We know," Erik said after a long pause, a thin smile on his face. "And we're coming with you."

"What? How do you know?"

"I told them." Alleron's eyes tracking the ground, guilt ridden. Calen had told the man about his plans that night in the barn. "On the way here. I had to, Calen. You're in no shape to go anywhere alone."

"I'm going to assume you were not going to force me to break my oath for a second time," Vaeril said, an eyebrow raised.

"I…" Calen could only assume the same look of guilt sat on his face as it did Alleron's.

"We have come all this way," Tarmon said. "What is a little further?"

"What about Daymon and Belduar?"

"They will both be better off if I return with a Draleid by my side," Tarmon said, his expression flat.

His throat dry and his body aching, Calen looked out over those who stood around him. After the battle at Belduar, the tunnels, the kerathlin, and the Uraks, Calen had wanted to spare the others more hardship. He had not wanted to ask them to choose between going home and helping him – most of all, he had not wanted them to share the same fate as Korik, Lopir, and Falmin. But he would only be lying to himself if he said he didn't feel a weight lift right there and then. "Thank you."

"This is touching," Baird said, stepping into the middle of the group. "But you really do need to go. What about the dragon? He won't fit on the ship."

"Valerys will fly overhead and sleep along the coastline," Calen answered. "He can fly faster than any ship can sail, so he won't have a problem catching up with us each day."

At Calen's words, Valerys lifted his head, his lavender eyes searching across the group, a low rumble resonating from his chest.

"What will you do now?" Calen asked, turning to Alleron. "Are you still to come with us?"

Alleron sighed, shaking his head. "I will stay here and fight," he said, turning slightly towards Baird. "We will take back Drifaien. Starting with Arisfall."

"What of your father?"

"We will do what needs to be done," Alleron said, his mouth a thin line. "He does not deserve the title of High Lord. You will always have friends here, Calen."

"As will you," Calen replied.

"Come on, then," Baird said, cutting across Calen and Alleron. "We're all friends. Now let's get you on that ship, and us far away from this port."

Both Alleron and Calen nodded.

The ship was one of the largest Calen had ever seen, not that he had seen many, in fairness. It had to have been at least a hundred feet in length, with three enormous masts that jutted out from its deck. A large gangplank was extended out from the deck of the ship down onto the dock, framed with thick lengths of rope to act as guides so that whoever was walking the plank wouldn't fall off the edge.

Calen looked to the sky as he stepped onto the plank; there were so many clouds that his eyes couldn't catch sight of Valerys dipping and weaving among them, but he could feel the dragon watching.

"It's all right, not much further," Erik said, his hand resting on Calen's shoulder as they walked the length of the plank, Baird and Alleron leading the way.

On any other day, Calen would have been irritated with the all the fuss he was receiving. But considering he still felt as though he was only one moment of over-exertion away from collapsing, he was all right with it.

His fingers firmly gripping the two lengths of rope on either side of the plank, Calen stumbled his way onto the deck of the ship, closely followed by Erik, Vaeril, and Tarmon. Of all of them, it was the elf who seemed completely out of place. Vaeril had only been on the deck of the ship for all of five seconds when his pale complexion took on a slightly green tint.

"Calen, I would like you to meet Captain Kiron."

Calen pulled his eyes from the almost unnaturally seasick elf to find the man Alleron had introduced, Captain Kiron, staring directly into his eyes.

Captain Kiron was not exactly what Calen had expected. In truth, most of what Calen knew about sailors came from the people of Salme and the few traders he had seen pull into port in Milltown. Most of them were rugged-looking men with more scars, piercings, and tattoos than stitches in their clothing.

But Captain Kiron was nothing of the sort. The man was clean shaven with wavy blonde locks held down by a short, triangular black hat. He wore a finely fitted blue doublet with a white lace trim, dark padded trousers, and a pair of thick-soled sailors' boots. Most strikingly, though, he had all his teeth, and not a speck of dirt could be seen under his fingernails.

The captain took two steps closer to Calen, eyeing him from head to toe. He turned up his bottom lip with a slight shrug and a tilt of his head. "A little scraggier than I expected. But welcome aboard *The Enchantress*, Draleid. Your companion certainly piqued my interest with your story. And his gold."

"We need to—"

The captain raised a hand, cutting Baird off. "I do understand the situation, thank you very much. But, given my line of work, it is pertinent to know who I have on my ship. Especially when you bring aboard an elf, a wolf dressed in the skin of a young man, a soldier who looks as though he was bred from Jotnar stock, and a second young man you claim is the first Draleid free of imperial control in four centuries. I trust you may understand my need for certainty?"

Calen couldn't help but choke out a muted laugh at the man's candour. There was something about it that reminded him of Dann. It was refreshing.

"Is there something funny, Master *Draleid?*"

"Not at all," Calen said with a cough, still half smiling.

The captain raised an unimpressed eyebrow. "Right, let's be on our way then."

"That's it?" Calen asked, expecting the man to ask more questions.

Captain Kiron let out a laugh. "For now. Do you think I did not see you descend from the sky astride that magnificent creature? Yes, I do believe you are who you say you are. Though, that does not mean there will not be more questions. For now, we need to leave. I will have one of my men show you to your cabin. You need sleep."

The captain turned on his heels, clapping his hands together and calling orders to the crew, who began scuttering about, preparing the ship to cast off.

Calen felt a hand on his shoulder.

"I left your possessions in the cabin for you. I had them taken from the city this morning – I thought you might need them. I also left you some fresh clothes. Be safe, Calen." Alleron extended his hand out, wrapping his fingers around Calen's forearm. "This war is only beginning."

"Thank you," Calen said, returning Alleron's grasp. "For everything. If not for you, I would be on my way to the Dragonguard right now."

"Make sure it wasn't for nothing."

Calen nodded, wincing as a pain ignited in his ribs. He lifted his eyes, meeting Alleron's gaze. "Sigrid, Gudrun, Alwen, Heldin?"

"Gudrun and Sigrid live. Heldin and Alwen dine in Achyron's halls."

Calen swallowed hard, his throat throbbing as he did. *Two more.* "May they dine well."

"How do you feel?" Erik asked, helping Calen down onto the bottom cot of the bunk that sat fixed to the wall of the cabin. The cabin held four sets of bunks, two on each side, with large, banded chests at the bottom of each bunk.

Small pyramid-shaped prisms made of glass were slotted into the ceiling. The prisms filtered moonlight into the cabin from above, providing barely enough light for Calen to see in front of his own face, but he was happy for any light at all.

"I've been better," Calen said, dropping down onto the rigid cot. He tried his best to still the involuntary shivers that ran through his body, but it was an exercise in futility.

"That you have," Erik said with a laugh, his hand resting on Calen's shoulder. "I'll go see if the captain has any more blankets. You're freezing. I'll only be a minute."

Calen grunted in response as Erik left the cabin.

Grimacing, Calen shifted himself to the edge of the cot, then dropped down to his knees, his eyes fixed on the banded chest that sat at the end of the bunk, bolted into the wall. Hoping beyond hope, he removed the open lock that sat dangling through an iron loop and lifted the latch. Then, summoning more strength than he was sure he had, he heaved open the lid.

The chest was full to the brim. Fresh clothes sat at the top: some boots, a shirt, trousers, socks, a tunic, and a long fur cloak. One at a time, Calen removed each item of clothing and placed it onto his cot, letting the soft touch of the fabric linger on his fingers for longer than he ever would have before. It would be a pleasure all unto itself to put those clothes on.

The next things his eyes fell upon, sitting atop his leather armour, were the pendant and the letter he had found in Vindakur. Calen ran his thumb over the surface of the obsidian pendant, his eyes lingering on the symbol of The Order set in its centre. He placed the pendant and the letter down on the bed next to the fresh clothes.

With the clothes, the letter, and the pendant removed, Calen found himself staring down at his leather armour, still bloody and battered. It was far from the sturdiest armour in the world, but it was home. Then, moving the armour aside, Calen's eyes fell on precisely what he had been looking for.

Nestled firmly in its brown and green leather scabbard, its thick, silver, coin-like pommel glinting in the dim light from the prisms, was his sword.

A tear burned at the corner of Calen's eye, accompanied by the most genuine smile that had touched his face in as long as he could remember. Calen's hands trembled as he reached down and lifted the sword and scabbard from the chest, the touch of the leather feeling achingly familiar to his worn hands. The autumn red scarf he had bought his mother still hung tightly from the loops on the belt Tharn Pimm had given him. Calen tilted slightly as the ship battled the waves, his knees straining against the wooden floor, but he didn't care. His attention was on the sword.

Wrapping his finger around the ornately etched green leather hilt, Calen slid the sword out a few inches from the scabbard. The steel of the blade shimmered even more brightly than the pommel, the light catching on the beautiful swirling patterns that rose into the blade from the crossguard. In truth, the sword had not crossed his mind until he had boarded the ship, and even then, he had accepted its loss. But now, pulling the sword and scabbard into his chest, tears rolled down his cheeks, and he collapsed against the bed frame.

Hours later, Calen stood on the deck of the ship; one hand gripped tightly around the wooden rail that ran along the ship's edge, while the other rested on the pommel of his sword, which hung from his hip. If he loosened his grip on the rail even slightly, the crashing waves would likely send him sprawling to the deck, but he couldn't bring himself to take his hand from the sword.

As he stared into the night sky at Valerys, Calen curled his toes in and out, feeling the comforting touch of the sheep's wool socks Alleron had left in the chest. Along with the socks, Alleron had left him a full set of new clothes. A pair of sturdy leather boots that fit him a whole lot better than his old ones ever had. Two pairs of linen trousers, one thicker than the other, which Calen wore layered over each other, thicker over thinner. An undershirt, a tunic of cream linen embroidered with threads of purple, and a heavy bear fur coat. It was the most comfortable Calen had felt in a very long time.

Calen allowed a soft smile to touch the corners of his mouth, his eyes tracing over Valerys's white scales as the dragon soared along beside the ship, his tail hovering just above the water's surface. His muscles rippled with each beat of his massive, leathery wings, his long spearhead tail whipping through the air behind him.

Calen yearned to be up there with Valerys, his chest pressed against the scales on the back of Valerys's neck, the wind rushing through his hair. Even in the state he had been in, riding on Valerys's back had been nothing short of incredible. All Calen wanted was to feel that again, to feel his and Valerys's minds blend so completely that it was impossible to tell them apart. But he knew he didn't have the strength for it. He shouldn't have even been up on the deck. Closing his eyes, Calen let his mind sink into Valerys's, and for a moment the world was consumed by an empty blackness. But then everything burst to life.

The icy wind shivered over his scales, breaking across the tip of his snout, threading neatly between the horns that framed his face. Power thrummed through his body with every beat of his wings. In the distance, even in the dark of night, he could see waves breaking against the coastline, crashing against the stone, erupting in a mist of white foam. Calen stayed like that for what felt like hours, his hand gripped firmly on the rail of the ship, but his mind moving with Valerys's.

"Should you not be resting?"

Calen let out a soft sigh, allowing his mind to pull back a little from Valerys's, and opened his eyes. Erik stood beside him at the side of the ship, looking out over the dark water, his arms resting across the rail.

"I couldn't sleep," Calen said, grimacing as he shifted his weight. He had tried to sleep. He truly had. But as soon as his mind had drifted off, the nightmares ripped him back to the waking world. Artim Valdock had tortured him for days at a time in that cell. He had used the Spark to keep Calen conscious while he worked; pulling, slicing, peeling. Just the thought of the pain sent an involuntary spasm across Calen's shoulders. "You?"

"Me neither. How is Valerys?"

Calen smiled at the mention of Valerys's name, the dark thoughts fading, for now. He could still feel the dragon in the back of his mind, sweeping through the banks of clouds, rising and falling with the currents of air. "He's all right. I can still feel his anger, though, bubbling below the surface."

Silence held for a long moment as both Calen and Erik stared out at the dark waters. "How are *you*, Calen? Truly?"

Calen swallowed hard, his eyes never leaving the crashing waves. "I'm glad you didn't kill the High Mage." Calen's grip tightened on the wooden rail until the coarse wood grated at his palms. "Only so that I can be the one who takes his life."

"That's not who you are, Calen."

Calen narrowed his eyes, turning them towards Erik. "Not who I am? How many have I killed now? How many souls have Valerys and I sent to the void? People who did nothing but follow the orders of those above them. But Farda, Inquisitor Rendall, Artim Valdock – those are three people whose deaths would be for a reason."

Calen reached his hand down, tightening it around the pommel of his sword. His fingers traced the edge of the thick silver coin, feeling the smooth steel, then down onto the green leather wrapped around the sword's hilt. Finally, he felt the silk of his mother's scarf between his fingertips: smooth, almost waxy. He had seen so much death already. There was no possible way he could have kept count of the number of souls he and Valerys had taken from this world. The thought of it weighed heavy on him. But those three had taken everything from him, and he would take something back.

Swallowing and clenching his jaw, Calen turned back towards the open water, losing his concentration in the constant ebb and flow of the dark waves.

Rist pulled the air into his lungs through his nostrils, feeling its cold touch snake its way through his body. He pulled threads of Earth and Water into himself, feeling the contrasting sensations of rough iron and cool ice wash over his body. He pushed the threads into the ground in front of him, permeating the earthen clay.

Using the threads, he pulled a strand of smooth, cylindrical clay, about an inch thick, from the ground. He wound the strand of clay in a helical pattern until it was over two feet in height. Then, he used the threads of water to drag moisture from the earth around his strand of clay, funnelling the water upwards into a strand that ran in the opposite direction, forming a double helix of clay and water. Once the water was perfectly in place, Rist drew on threads of Fire, pulling the heat from the water, freezing it solid.

In the back of his mind, Rist could feel Neera watching him. Casting a judging glance over his work. He opened his eyes. The double helix of clay and ice stood exactly as he had pictured it in his mind's eye: two feet from the ground, less than half an inch distance between the strands, smooth, perfect. It was just like the drawing in *A Study of Control* by Primarch Andelar Touran.

Andelar Touran had been, and still was, the Primarch of the Imperial Battlemages ever since the dawn of the empire. Rist supposed it was not a common thing for the head of any affinity to change, given the life expectancy of most mages was at least five or six centuries, even longer for some. There were rumours that Grand Lector Aneese Linel was almost nine hundred years old. Apparently, she had served as a professor of The Order in the old times. Rist was sure he would be able to find some records in the library that either confirmed or denied those rumours. But in truth, they were of little import at the moment.

"Not bad," Neera said, rising from where she had been sitting, her legs crossed. "Though it took you long enough."

Rist could see the smirk forming at the corner of her mouth. It was as difficult to get a compliment from Neera as it was to wring blood from a stone. "I would like to see you do better."

"I would," she said with a shrug, the corner of her lips turning down. "But I have some practice of my own to attend to. Sister Ardal thinks my control of Fire is too weak. She intends to improve it."

Neera bent over, placing a kiss on the top of Rist's head. Rist raised one eyebrow, unsure as to what had just happened. He and Neera had been spending a lot of time together since that night at the docks, but her displays of affection were never so public.

Then, as though she were able to see into his mind, she kicked out, shattering his structure of ice and clay with the tip of her boot, before winking at him and striding from the garden. That was more like her.

Sighing, Rist lay back in the grass, opening the latch on the leather bag by his side and slipping out his copy of *Druids, a Magic Lost*. Holding the book up in the air at just the right angle to take the afternoon sun from his eyes, Rist picked up where he had left off.

Duran Linold, Ark-Mage, year 1798 After Doom.

The Druids of old came with the first humans to Epheria in the year 300 After Doom. Precisely what led them to flee their homeland of Terroncia, I am not sure, nor have I been able to find an accurate account in any of the histories I have researched. But either way, I diverge.
In my studies, I have so far noted there to be three strains of Druid, and I have classified them as follows:

Skydruids: Capable of manipulating weather on a large scale. These seem to be the rarest of the three strains. In all two hundred and forty-seven accounts, only two Skydruids are ever mentioned. With any luck, the bloodlines of the Skydruids are long past. Individuals with the power to manipulate entire weather systems are not ones to be trifled with.

Seerdruids: Capable of glimpsing potential future events, past events at which they were not present, and events happening at that current point in time. It appears that each of these talents is mutually exclusive. Each of the three talents has the potential to be immensely powerful if used correctly.

Aldruids: Aldruids, in my opinion, are perhaps the most interesting. According to the personal account of Angmiran Skarsden, Grand Historian of the first Lorian Kingdom, Aldruids were capable of innate communication with animals as well as the rarer gift of direct control. In his account marked on the year 542 After Doom, Angmiran states that a single Aldruid held sway over some fifty wyverns at a single time, using them to raid the villages along the western coast by the province of Valtara, near the Rolling Mountains. Though I remain sceptical as

> *to the merit of this claim, I have seen enough secondary and primary sources to believe there is at least some truth in this.*

The sound of footsteps rang off the stone pathways of the garden, drawing closer to Rist until they stopped by his side. "*Druids, a Magic Lost*, a fine read. Though I do fear that old Duran had reached his mind's limits by the time he was halfway finished writing that one. His writing lost all structure and became little more than babble."

"So far, it is an interesting read," Rist replied. "Brother Garramon, I am still yet to find a book in the library that you have not already read."

Rist turned over the corner of the page, marking his position, then closed the book, bringing it down to his chest. The broad frame of Brother Garramon stood over him, black cloak flapping lightly in the breeze. The man's face had been recently shaved and his black hair slicked back with an oil of some sort. A strange silence hung in the air. Rist lifted himself up to a seated position, his eyebrow raised. Something seemed off. "Is everything all right?"

Brother Garramon's brow furrowed. "It is time, my apprentice. Your trial of Will is to begin today."

Chapter Forty-One

A Magic Lost

The sound of horses whinnying echoed through the night as the fire crackled and popped, pluming sparks into the air.

Ella sat cross-legged in front of the fire, running her hand along Faenir's back as the wolfpine lay splayed out beside her, his head propped on her knee.

Yana lay unconscious to Ella's left, a woollen blanket pulled up over her shoulders, her fingers wrapped around a small pendant that hung from her neck.

The elf, Farwen, sat to Ella's right, holding her hands so close to the dancing flames it set a knot in Ella's stomach.

"Does that not hurt?"

"It used to," Farwen replied, without turning her head. "A long time ago. But no, not now. Not anymore."

Ella waited a moment, expecting the elf to elaborate, but nothing came. Farwen just sat, her eyes lost to the fire.

"Yana and Tanner," Ella said, looking over towards the sleeping woman. "They are married?"

To Ella's surprise, the elf let out a soft laugh. "No, they are not. Though I never truly understood the concept myself. Everything must be a grand gesture with you humans." A silence hung in the air for a few moments before Farwen spoke again. "Yana and Tanner are not 'married,' but they are what my people would call *Ayar Elwyn*. One Heart."

"Ayar Elwyn," Ella whispered to herself as she looked over towards Yana. "It's beautiful."

"That it is," Farwen said, with a slight nod of agreement.

Both Farwen and Ella sat for a while, letting the crackling of the fire fill the silence. "Farwen, where are we going?"

"We are going to Tarhelm, in the Firnin Mountains, just north of Greenhills. You will be safe there. And with luck, Tanner will not be long behind us." Farwen turned her head, pulling her hands away from the flames. Her eyes fell to Faenir, whose head was still draped over Ella's knee. "The wolfpine, you raised it from a cub?"

"We all did," Ella said, scratching the top of Faenir's head, receiving a grumble in response. "Our father found him abandoned in Ölm Forest almost five summers ago. He's been a part of the family since then. I'm sure they're worried sick about him… As they are for me."

Farwen nodded, her eyes fixed on Faenir, unblinking. Something in the elf's stare changed. "In five hundred years, I have only ever known one of your kind."

"My kind?"

"The wolfpine," Farwen said, leaning forward. "He moves with you, feels you. Even now, his heart beats with yours. Don't tell me you can't feel it."

"What in the gods are you talking about?" The elf wasn't making any sense.

In a flash of steel, the elf pulled a knife from somewhere beneath her mantle and lunged towards Ella.

Frantically, Ella threw herself backwards, crashing into the dirt as she pushed herself away. But as she did, Faenir leapt to his feet, snarling and snapping at the elf. But he didn't attack her. The hackles on his back were raised, his teeth were bared, but he didn't move, a deep growl resonating in his chest, inches from Farwen.

The elf didn't move either. She kept her knife raised and her eyes locked on Faenir's. "Incredible…"

Ella's heart pounded, and her throat tightened as she stared at Faenir and Farwen, inches from each other's throats. She looked over towards Yana. The woman still slept, her chest steadily rising and falling.

"What are you doing?" Ella yelled, anger pulsing through her veins as she pushed herself forward onto her knees. As she did, Faenir dropped lower to the ground, the growl in his chest growing deeper, more primal, his eyes locked on Farwen's.

"You truly do not know?" Farwen narrowed her eyes as she looked at Ella, searching her. The elf slid her knife back inside her mantle. She seemed completely unperturbed by the growling wolfpine. "When I pulled my knife free, what did you feel?"

"What do you mean, 'what did I feel?' I was terrified! Why did you do that?"

"And he defended you." The elf said, ignoring Ella's question.

"Of course he did. He is my family. You protect family."

"But he didn't attack me. Does *any* animal hold back when their family is threatened? Has he ever held back when someone has attacked you?"

"I..." Ella turned her gaze to Faenir. The wolfpine stood inches from Farwen, his eyes watching her. "No, but... you weren't attacking me, you stopped."

"Precisely. *You* saw that I stopped. *You* hesitated because I stopped. *You* told Faenir to stop." Walking past Faenir, Farwen reached down and grabbed Ella by the forearm, pulling her to her feet. "Ella, whether you believe it or not, blood of the old druids flows in your veins."

Farda sat on the edge of his cot, his hands laced behind his head, his eyes closed. Outside his tent, the crackling of campfires and the chatter of soldiers filled the night air. With a sigh, he sat up and rolled his neck to the left, then around to the right, then back again, opening his eyes as he did.

Reaching across, he slid his hand into the pocket of his coat, which lay across the back of the chair beside his bed, and pulled the coin free, flipping it back and forth in his hand. "Fate is fluid," he whispered to himself. "It changes with every decision that is made. It is utterly out of our hands and completely within our control at the same time."

Holding the coin out in front of him, Farda bit down on his lip, tasting the slightest hint of iron on his tongue.

He flipped the coin.

Chapter Forty-Two

It is Time

Rist followed Brother Garramon through the embassy, through a set of winding corridors, and down a long staircase that dove further into the ground than Rist would have thought possible. The bottom of the staircase opened into a stone tunnel with oil-burning lanterns set into evenly spaced alcoves in the walls, their dim glow flickering shadows across the stone.

The tunnel didn't look much different from any of the corridors in the embassy of the palace, except there were no windows or doors. Their two sets of footsteps echoed down the long corridor, bouncing off the walls, reverberating in Rist's ears. Sweat slicked his palms and his throat felt as though he had swallowed dust. The trial would have been less intimidating if he had any idea what to expect.

"Brother, I—"

"Today," Garramon said, turning his head to Rist, "you speak only when spoken to. Understood?"

Rist nodded.

"The Battlemage's Trial of Will is one that has been performed by mages for aeons, as far back as the birth of The Order."

"The Order? I thou—" Rist closed his mouth at the sight of a raised eyebrow from Garramon.

"There are some traditions worth keeping. To become an acolyte of the Battlemages is no small thing. Only those with the greatest power over the Spark are chosen, for that power is necessary to defend against the empire's strongest enemies. I need you to understand one thing." Garramon stopped, placing his hand on Rist's shoulder. "Battlemages cannot become Alamants. The emperor granted amnesty to all those who could not pass the trials of their affinity, granting them the title of Alamant. That is, with one exception – Battlemages. Any who are chosen to become apprentices of the Battlemages possess offensive and defensive powers that simply cannot be allowed to roam free in the lands. The ability to touch the Spark is burned from all those who fail the trials of a Battlemage. I am telling you this so you know what is at stake. Do you understand?"

Rist's mouth went dry, and his throat felt as though it were closing in. The idea that the Spark might be taken from him, burned from his body, terrified him to his core. The Spark was as much a part of him as his arms and legs. To lose it… The idea of running flashed across his mind, but he quashed it. They would not allow him to leave for the same reason they would not allow Battlemages to become Alamants. And they would be right, for that kind of power was too dangerous to go unchecked. He would just have to ensure that he passed his trials. That was the only way.

Rist nodded, his palms no longer the only part of his body slicked with sweat.

"Now, come. It is time."

Rist followed Garramon wordlessly, as much from an inability to form coherent sentences as from his instruction not to speak. Eventually, the long tunnel came to an end, and the pair stood in front of an enormous stone door. Great circles and spirals were cut into the stone, forming patterns of such complexity they left Rist awestruck, lost in the intricacy. But he felt Garramon reaching out to the Spark, drawing on threads of Air and Earth. Garramon pushed the threads into the door, weaving them this way and that, in motions equally as complex as those etched in the door. At first, nothing happened except for creaks and groans of stone moving within the door itself. But then the patterns on the door began to shift, sections of the door moving, spinning, turning. The different sections of stone, defined by the ornate patterns, began to separate, pulling apart at the centre, receding into the walls of the tunnel. And as they did, a wash of orange light spilled out from the other side.

A massive circular chamber stood on the other side of the receding doorway. The roof of the chamber stood over fifty feet at its centre, curving in a dome-like shape. Braziers lined the outer edges of the chamber, burning with bright orange flames that cast an incandescent glow across the stone.

At the centre of the chamber was what looked like a large pool of water as black as jet, rippling like the surface of a lake. Fifty mages surrounded the pool, all in long, black hooded cloaks, some with a silver lining, some without.

Directly opposite Rist and Garramon, on the other side of the pool, stood a man with trim of ornate golden thread all along his black cloak, his hood pulled back, his skin pale and wrinkled, his hair white, thin, and frail. But the man himself looked in no way frail. He oozed power. Rist could feel it radiating from him. There was no doubt in Rist's mind who the man was: Andelar Touran, Primarch of the Battlemages.

As Rist and Garramon drew closer to the rippling pool of black, Rist could see it was ringed with smooth grey stone broken into segments about five to six inches long. A glyph was carved into each segment, though they were not any of the glyphs Rist recognised from the books he had read in the library.

Garramon stopped about ten feet from the pool, gesturing for Rist to do the same.

"Who comes before this gathering?" Andelar Touran's voice resounded through the chamber like rolling thunder, amplified by threads of Spirit and Air.

"I, Brother Garramon, and my apprentice, Rist Havel."

"And what is it you seek?" The Primarch's words were slow and purposeful. His lips looked paper thin, as though they might tear if he spoke too swiftly.

"We seek the Trial of Will, so my apprentice may take the first step towards acolyteship of this affinity."

"Step forward, Rist Havel, apprentice." Andelar Touran opened his arms wide, his long sleeves drooping down.

Brother Garramon did not speak, but he gave Rist a look that Rist knew meant he should do as commanded. Swallowing, Rist took a few steps forward, until he was only a foot or so from the ring of stone that ran around the pool's edge. Each of the mages surrounding the pool had their eyes fixed on him, their black hoods drawn up over their heads.

"Speak your name." Again, the Primarch's voice echoed through the chamber.

"Rist Havel." Rist's voice sounded like that of a mouse compared to the Primarch's, but he figured he had good reason.

"And do you understand the consequence of failure in these trials?"

"I do."

"Good. The consequence of failure must always be understood for a Battlemage. It is no more and no less now than it is when you are on the field of battle. For our affinity, failure, at the very least, will result in death. And with the power we wield, some may burn themselves out in search of victory. For most, to never feel the embrace of the Spark again is a fate not worth living. We must never forget the cost of what we do. Apprentice, remove your robes and step forward."

Remove his robes? Rist hesitated for a moment before setting his jaw and removing the brown robes that were draped around his shoulders, leaving him in nothing but his smallclothes and sandals. Deciding to also remove his sandals, Rist took another step forward, until his toes were less than an inch from the glyph-marked stone ring.

"Apprentice, do you wish to start down the path of acolyteship to the affinity of Battlemages? Do you wish to fight on the front lines against the enemies of men and drive back those who would do us harm?"

Rist swallowed. "I do."

"So be it."

The Primarch turned to one of the other mages, who produced a small wooden chest enamelled with gold and silver. From within the chest, the Primarch pulled two metallic discs that glowed with a vibrant blue light. Reaching down, the older man slotted each disc into two ready-made grooves that had been etched into one of the stones. As he did, each of the glyph markings along the ring of segmented stone began to radiate the same blue light, shimmering with life, and the pool of black water pulsed before turning completely still.

"Now, Apprentice, you may step into the Well of Arnen and let the waters take you to your trial."

Rist ran his tongue along his lips, trying desperately to add some moisture to his dry, cracked skin. He took a deep, trembling breath before glancing back at Garramon, who simply stared ahead as though Rist was completely invisible.

There is no turning back now. I am ready. Rist didn't entirely believe his own thoughts, but he didn't have much of a choice. He stepped forward.

As soon as Rist's bare foot touched the surface of the black pool, a wave of energy surged through him. It was as though he had been struck by lightning. The energy permeated every inch of his body, seeping through his skin and into his bones. It hit him so hard that it took a moment for Rist to collect his thoughts before he realised that no matter how much weight he placed down on his foot, it never sank more than an inch into the black liquid, but at the same time, it did not feel as though he was standing on anything solid. It was one of the strangest sensations he had ever felt.

Steadying the tremble in his hands, Rist followed his right foot with his left. His legs shook as he tried to establish some semblance of balance, both his feet resting just below the surface of the black liquid. The surging wave of energy continued to pulse through him from toe to head, numbing all other senses. Then, just as he realised he didn't know what to do next, the black liquid shifted, crawling up over his feet, covering them, then up his lower legs, towards his knees. Immediately, panic set in. Rist wanted to scream, to beg the others to pull him free, but his mouth obeyed no commands, staying firmly shut as fear consumed him.

The black liquid continued to rise, moving past his knees, covering his hips, and pushing on toward his chest. Rist trembled, his lungs scrambling to drag in air as though it would be the last gasps of the precious substance his body would ever consume.

He glanced towards Garramon, but the man stayed firm, his gaze unwavering. *I need to trust him. I need to trust him.*

Rist slowed his breathing, feeling the thrum of his heartbeat. Then, as the black liquid moved up over his throat, Rist closed his eyes.

I need to trust him.

Chapter Forty-Three

Will

Rist convulsed, desperately gasping for air as the black liquid consumed him. He could feel himself screaming, but heard nothing. Not a single sound. Then, a calm washed over him. Everything was still. No sounds, no sensations, no light. He was engulfed by emptiness.

Rist opened his eyes.

He stumbled backwards, completely taken aback by what he saw. He was at the docks where he and Neera had kissed for the first time. But it was different. He couldn't quite put his finger on what exactly it was that was off, but he knew it was not the same as before. The light from the moon was dimmer, and the air held a bitter chill. Not a single sound hung in the night save the gentle crashing of waves against the dock. Not a drunken song, or an overly zealous trader. Not the squeak of axles or the mutterings of an intoxicated sailor. Nothing. It was as though every soul had been plucked from the streets.

"Hello?" Rist's voice echoed unnaturally through the night. He whispered, "What is this place?"

A monstrous roar from behind him caused Rist to turn on his heels. His jaw fell to the floor as he saw the palace, and in turn the embassy, consumed by fire, a large, winged shape soaring in the skies above the inferno.

Without hesitation, he set off as fast as his legs could carry him. Every step echoed in his ears as though he were shouting down a well.

No matter how far he ran or which street he turned down, he did not see a single person – not one. *What is happening? How is this possible?* Rist tried his best to still his racing heart, but it did no good.

Fear is human. Embrace fear. Use it. Words he had read in a book. The concept seemed more easily executed when held within the confines of the page. In the real world, it was not so simple. Yet still, he did find *some* comfort in the words.

"Rist!"

"Neera?" The hairs all over Rist's body stood on end, and his throat went dry. "Neera!"

No matter how loudly he shouted, he got no response. In a panic, he looked around, searching for Neera's voice. Where had it come from? Even in his confusion, something was pulling him towards the palace. And so, he followed that something, whatever it was. It was the only thing giving him any sense of direction.

Rist's lungs burned, and his legs ached in pain as he dashed up the long steps that led to the palace gates. Just like everywhere else, the gates were abandoned. There was no sign of Brother Tharnum and the gold ring that hung from his nose, and no sign of any guards, either. But up ahead, flames engulfed the palace, bursting from windows, climbing up walls, eating away at the supports.

"Neera?" Rist called out, shouting as loud as he could. But he heard no reply. "Brother Garramon? Anybody?"

Another thunderous roar rang out overhead, and a dark shadow swept over the ground, dragging a gust of air behind it, so violent that it pulled all the flames in one direction. *A dragon.* Rist fixed his gaze on the sky, but he could see nothing, as though the sky had purposely darkened once he looked at it.

"Ahh!" Neera's scream echoed through the eerily empty night.

"Neera!" This time, the shout had a direction. It came from the embassy. Rist ran as fast as his legs would carry him, dipping out of the way of billowing flames, weaving through the palace gardens as they collapsed around him. The entrance to the embassy was completely covered in a wall of fire. Stopping in front of it, Rist called out. "Neera?"

No answer.

How do I... Rist reached out to the Spark, feeling it instantly, its power seeping into him. He drew on threads of Air and Fire, using them to part the wall of flames that blocked the entrance to the embassy, then darted in through the opening. "Neera?"

Rist stopped. He was now in the wide-open entrance hall of the embassy. A man stood before him with a long, slightly curved blade in his hands, a crumpled body at his feet. He was tall with broad shoulders, brown leatherwork armour across his torso, arms, and legs. But no matter how hard Rist tried to focus, when he looked at the man's face, he saw nothing but a blur.

Rist cast his eyes down to the body. Raven-black hair was matted with blood. *Neera.*

"Let her go!"

The faceless man tilted his head to the left at Rist's cry, then placed his boot on Neera's shoulder, kicking her over so Rist could see her broken, bloody face. Her clothes were in tatters, burnt and caked with blood. Her skin looked as pale as ice, lips blue. She was dead.

A tremble set into Rist's hand – an involuntary shaking fuelled by pure rage. It was a feeling he had never before experienced. His throat constricted, and a weightlessness set itself in his stomach. Blood rushed through his veins, causing a pressure to build in his head, dulling all sounds to a low, droning buzz. He felt as though he were about to vomit and lose his mind at the same time.

With his chest heaving, Rist let out a roar that rippled through the chamber. He reached out for the Spark, pulling in threads of Fire and Spirit, dragging them into himself with all his might, feeling the Spark burn through him. When it felt like his body was close to tearing itself apart, he unleashed a stream of chain lightning that tore through the chamber. Arcs of lightning ripped stone from the ground and tore panels from the walls, wreaking a path of destruction on their way towards the faceless man, who just stood there, his head tilted to the side.

Rist felt the man draw from the Spark – more threads than he thought possible to control at a single time. A complicated mix of elemental strands that his mind could not even begin to fathom. Most of the lightning simply parted around the faceless man, as though he repulsed it, but some of the arcs reversed their course, streaming back towards Rist.

Rist dove out of the way, a bolt of lightning crashing into the ground where he had stood, shards of stone flying in all directions. Coughing out dust from his lungs, Rist dragged himself to his feet, his brow dripping sweat. Suddenly, he became aware of a sword strapped to his hip. *Was that there before?*

Wrapping his fingers around the hilt, he pulled the sword free as he got to his feet, feeling it shake slightly in his hands. Both Brother Garramon and Sister Anila had instructed him in swordsmanship, but it was by far his weakest area of study. If he lived through this day, it was something he was going to work harder at.

Breathing deep, Rist charged at the faceless man, pulling threads of Earth, Water, Fire, and Air into himself as he did. Pushing the threads of Earth into the ground, he dragged the clay through the areas where lightning had shattered the stone. Severing lengths of clay with threads of Air, he moulded them into spikes, drawing the moisture out with threads of Water, hardening them with threads of Fire.

Then, with a defiant roar, he launched the spears at the faceless man, following in close behind.

Again, the man deflected most of the spears with ease, others simply disintegrating into thin air as they drew close to him. Power radiated from him: more power than Rist thought a single person could ever hold. Rist's throat constricted even more as he lunged at the faceless man, blade first.

The clash of steel on steel rang out through the chamber as the two swords met. Even within a foot of the man's face, it was still a blurred mess, all muddled as though it was a blob of paint that had been half-spread with a brush.

The faceless man pulled on threads of Air, whipping at Rist, sending him sprawling. As soon as Rist hit the ground, he sprang back up, knotting threads of Air together and sending them back towards his attacker. But once again, the threads simply parted around the man as he worked a complicated mixing of threads. Rist had read about some of the mightiest Battlemages the empire had ever seen, including those who had lived in the time of The Order. The books had told of some with this kind of power, but Rist had always been hesitant. He had not truly expected a single person to be capable of holding so much strength.

He panted, dragging air into his lungs. The drain was already beginning to sap at him; he could feel it in his bones. Above him, a crossbeam creaked, consumed by the roaring fire that had begun to snake its way within the chamber from outside. Then he heard a loud crack, and the enormous wooden beam broke away, plummeting to the ground in an eruption of fire and charred splinters.

Rist clenched his jaw, tightening his fingers around the hilt of the sword. He didn't have many choices. He charged.

The man met every stroke of Rist's blade with measured ease before slicing a long gash down the length of Rist's right arm. *He's toying with me.*

Rist charged again. He struck low, before sweeping his blade across, aiming to split the man along the belly. But his opponent was too quick. He caught Rist's blade with threads of Air, holding it firmly in place, then brought his own sword up and swung.

The world faded to black.

Moments passed in the dark emptiness before everything burst to life once more. Rist dropped to one knee, his hand clasped around his throat, his chest heaving, trying desperately to drag air into his lungs. His ears erupted with the sounds of people screaming, mingled with the crackling of fire and the crashing of steel. Rist lifted his head, expecting to see the embassy, but he was no longer there. He was in The Glade. "What… What is happening?"

All around him, people ran like headless chickens, blood smeared across their faces, buckets of water in their hands. The village was on fire, consumed by towering flames as far as the eye could see. Bodies lay strewn about the ground, some human, some Uraks.

Rist froze as his eyes fell on a face he recognised. Dennet Hildom, Fritz and Kurtis's friend. The young man was split from naval to chest, his intestines spilled out on the ground in front of him, steaming into the night. Rist retched, then fell to his knees, emptying the contents of his stomach into the dirt.

Vomit-induced tears burned at the corner of his eyes as he wiped his mouth with the corner of his sleeve, the horrid acidic taste of puke coating his tongue.

"What are you doing on the ground, boy?" Erdhardt Hammersmith's voice boomed, though still somehow sounding as if it were muffled. The man stood over Rist, his enormous hand reaching down.

Rist took Erdhardt's hand, dragging himself to his feet. He looked as though he hadn't slept in weeks. His eyes were ringed with purple, his lips dry and cracked. Blood and ash marred his clothes.

"The inn, boy. They need you at the inn."

"Erdhardt, what is happening?"

"Go to the inn." Erdhardt turned, grabbing a bucket of water from the ground and running towards one of the nearby houses on fire.

"Wait… Gods dammit." Rist tilted his head back, sucking in a breath of air, tainted by the taste of vomit in his mouth. With a sigh, he set off through the village, heading for his father's inn, The Gilded Dragon. As he ran, he saw the bodies of more people he recognised: Lina Styr, her head split open from forehead to crown, an axe still embedded in the bone; Tach Edwin, an enormous arrow protruding from his sternum, his eyes open, cold.

Rist's heart stopped for a beat when he saw the body of Dann's father, Tharn Pimm, hanging from the wall of Iwan Swett's butcher, a massive, blackened blade driven through his chest, pinning him in place.

The man groaned, shifting ever so slightly.

"Tharn!" Rist ran to the Tharn's side, grabbing the man's hands. "Tharn, it's going to be all right."

Blood oozed from around the edges of the blackened blade, streaming down Tharn's clothes, dripping into a thick puddle that had already formed at his feet. Tharn tried to speak, but it mostly just came out as an incomprehensible gargle as the blood caught in his throat.

"No, no!" Rist's entire body shook. "Tharn, please, it's all right..."

Tharn's body sagged completely, his eyelids dropping down.

Rist screamed, fury igniting within him. He drew in threads of Air, feeling them wrap around his body, feeding on his anger. Then, releasing his hold on the threads, he slammed them into the house behind him, shattering the walls into nothing more than splinters.

His entire body trembled. He tried to calm himself, inhaling deeply through his nose, his chest shivering with each breath. Wiping the tears from his eyes, Rist turned back towards Tharn, wrapping threads of Air around the hilt of the blackened blade that pinned the man to the wall. Once he had pulled the blade free, he let it drop to the ground with a clang. Wrapping more threads around Tharn's body, Rist gently lowered the man to the ground.

"I'm sorry," Rist said, kneeling beside Tharn's lifeless body. "May the gods harbour your soul, Tharn Pimm. I will find Dann, I promise you."

His legs shaking, Rist pulled himself to his feet, just about keeping himself upright. Every part of his soul yearned to be sitting by the edge of Ölm forest, resting against the trunk of a tree, a book in his hand, Calen and Dann talking bullshit beside him. He missed his friends. He missed home.

Then he remembered Erdhardt's words. *'They need you at the inn.'*

Settling the slight convulsions that had begun to creep into his chest, Rist pressed on, his fingers wrapping even more tightly around the hilt of the sword.

It seemed The Gilded Dragon was one of the few buildings in the village that was not consumed by flames, but the ground in front of it was another story altogether. Corpses filled the open space in front of the inn, lying face down in the blood-soaked dirt. He recognised all of them. Jorvill Ehrnin, Mara Styr, Rhett Fjorn... The list went on. With each face he saw, another fragment of Rist's heart broke, shattering as he watched the death of his home. Standing in the middle of the corpses was the faceless man, his fingers tangled in a woman's hair, his sword outstretched, blood dripping from its tip.

Rist could only see the back of the woman's head, her long brown hair tumbling through the man's fingers, falling over her shoulders, matted with dirt and blood. There was something familiar about her, though, something Rist couldn't quite put his finger on. It was more a feeling than anything else. That was when he noticed the other body. The one lying at the faceless man's feet.

His father's lifeless eyes stared back at him, empty. Lasch Havel was a proud man, a strong man. But above all else, he was honest and true. The sight of his father's body set a panic in Rist's mind that battled with equal measures of fury and agony, for he now knew why the woman felt so familiar. She was his mother.

"Put her down!" Rist yelled, his voice trembling. "Put her down and take me."

The faceless man tilted his head, just as he had done before, his fingers still firmly wrapped in Elia Havel's hair.

Rist took a step forward, opening himself to the Spark, letting the power of the elemental strands surge through him. He pulled on threads of every element, his mind working of its own volition as it twisted and wove them together. The air rippled, and the ground shook. The blazing fires of the village flickered upwards, as though no longer affected by the push and pull of the wind. All around, dirt, rocks, and bits of debris lifted into the air, hovering off the ground. Rist could see the threads whirling around him, weaving through the fabric of the world. But he could not feel them as he was used to; the iron grate of Earth, or the cool touch of Air. The only thing he felt was raw power, as though lightning seared through his veins. "I said, put her down!"

For a moment, the man stood still, as though contemplating Rist's demand. Then, he raised his blade and dragged it across Rist's mother's throat, releasing her hair and letting her roll on the ground, gasping for air, blood spilling through her fingers.

"Mam, no!" Rist released the Spark, feeling it tear away from his body as the threads dissipated from the world, the bits of hovering rock and debris dropping to the ground. He let go of his sword and leapt to the ground, dropping one hand behind his mother's neck. "No, no."

His stomach lurching, his chest aching, Rist drew in threads of Fire, Spirit, Earth, and Water. *Please no. Please no.* Fumbling over himself, he tried desperately to knit the wound back together, weaving the threads of Spirit into his mother's skin. Water to hold back the blood. Fire to cauterise the wound. "Mam, stay with me. It's all right, it's going to be all right."

Tears streamed down Rist's cheeks as he wove the threads. Nothing was working. Blood simply continued to pour through his mother's fingers, and the energy seeped from his bones at a rate he would not have thought possible.

"Please," Rist whispered, more to the gods than to anyone else. He held one hand behind his mother's head and the other against her cheek. "I love you. I'm sorry I left. I'm sorry."

Rist knelt in the dust, holding his mother in his arms as the light faded in her eyes, her body went limp, and her hands fell away from her throat. He swallowed hard, sniffling as the mixture of snot and tears ran down his face. He knew he should be screaming. He knew his heart should be pouring out over the ground. But instead, he was simply numb.

When he was sure she was gone, Rist lay his mother's head down on the ground, his hands shaking. A rage, the likes of which he had never known, swelled in his chest, burning through the anguish and the loss. It filled every piece of him, seeping into his bones and soaking into his skin.

He stumbled as he pulled himself to his feet. He had never experienced the drain come upon him so rapidly. He had been warned what healing could do to the untrained, but he had thought the warnings to be exaggerated. Now he knew they were not. It felt as though his soul was being pulled, kicking and screaming, from his body.

Gritting his teeth, Rist hobbled towards the faceless man, fury leaking into his voice. "I am going to kill you."

Through the muddled mess of the man's face, Rist thought he saw him smile before he sheathed his sword. Then the entire village shook, an ear-splitting roar resounding through the skies above. A pain burned behind Rist's eyes, and he fell to his knees, once again consumed by darkness as the world faded to black. He knelt there, his hands over his eyes, his chest heaving, his heart broken. "I'm sorry…"

A shiver ran through Rist's body at the touch of the cold wind that rolled over his cheeks. The smell of char and ash was gone, replaced by the scent of pine needles and grass.

A third time, Rist opened his eyes.

He found himself kneeling in a wide-open patch of grass, the sun beaming down over him. A thicket of pine trees ringed the opening, extending out to a sheer cliff edge. A man stood at the edge of the cliff, looking out over what lay beyond. Rist didn't have to think to know who the man was. It was the faceless man. Of that, he had no doubt.

Lifting his sleeves to his face, Rist wiped away the mixture of dirt, snot, and tears that streaked its way down his cheeks, then pulled himself to his feet. He was still weak, stumbling with every second step. But slowly he drew within five feet of the faceless man.

Dropping his hand to his hip, he felt the cold steel of a spherical pommel. He thought he remembered dropping the sword in The Glade, but his memory was hazy, as though something was deliberately fogging it over. Knowing he didn't have the time to dedicate to figuring out the puzzle, Rist slid the sword from its sheath. His throat dry and his chest weak, he held the sword out in front of himself, summoning as strong a voice as he could muster. "Turn around, slowly, and show me your face."

The man turned his head slightly, as though he was not sure what he had heard. Then, after what felt like hours, he faced Rist. Though, this time, his face was not muddled and blurred, it was clear as day. His soft brown hair, his green eyes, his warm smile. It was Calen.

Rist wanted to speak, but he couldn't find the words. This wasn't possible. Calen would never have done those things. He would never have killed all those people…

Another earth-shattering roar tore through the sky above, and an enormous shadow swept over the patch of grass, blotting out the sun, sending a shiver through Rist's skin. Another roar followed, and Rist looked up to find himself staring at the immense, winged shape of a dragon. The creature soared through the sky, its wings spreading so wide that its shadow covered the entire edge of the cliff.

"Calen." Rist turned his attention back to his friend, who now stood facing him. "What are you doing? How…? What is happening?"

"You sided with the enemy," Calen said, stepping closer to Rist. Calen's shoulders had filled out, and his body was laden with muscle. Several scars ran along his arms, one on his right cheek. "What choice did you give me? There can be no mercy in war, Rist. You chose this path."

"The enemy? Calen, I…" Rist stumbled over his words. His brain struggled to form sentences as he looked at his friend, so different, yet still the same. "They taught me about who I am. *What* I am. The empire has done horrible things, but that doesn't mean everyone under its flag is the enemy."

Calen took another step towards Rist, a branch snapping under his foot. The shadow of the dragon was gone, and Rist could see the creature swooping through the sky just behind Calen. *What is that thing doing here?*

"It's us or them, Rist. That's the way it has always been – that's the way they made it. They killed my parents, my family. They take what they want, kill who they want. We can't win unless we fight by their rules."

"You… you killed Neera… my parents… Calen, why? What have you done?" Rist felt himself retch again at the images of Neera, Tharn Pimm, his parents. Tears stung his eyes, and rage set his blood boiling. "You've become a monster."

"I had to become one to defeat one." With Calen's words, a deafening roar erupted from behind him, and the gargantuan shape of the dragon shot up past the edge of the cliff, straight towards the sky. Its body was covered in a glistening ocean of white scales that grew darker towards the base. Ridges of horns framed its face and jaws, over a foot long. It was the largest creature Rist had ever seen, as big as a ship. As the dragon rose, it turned, dropping back down towards Rist and Calen, its enormous wings whipping up gusts of wind that almost sent Rist sprawling to the ground. "You were meant to be my friend." The deafening thump of the dragon's wings almost drowned out Calen's words as Rist struggled to stay upright. "You were meant to be there with me and Dann when the time came. We were meant to be *brothers!* Where were you?"

Rist pulled on thin threads of Air and Spirit, weaving them through the gust around him, parting the air, not stopping it, simply changing its direction. It worked without costing him too much energy. His clothes stopped flapping, and he was able to stand up straight. "I didn't have a choice."

"You always have a choice," Calen retorted, a snarl forming in his throat.

"You murdered my parents!" Rist shouted, anger taking over everything else. He felt himself pulling harder from the Spark. "*You* had a choice!"

"And I made it," Calen said, before shouting something in a language Rist did not understand.

Reacting to the words, the dragon shifted in the air, dropping into a dive, heading straight towards Rist. At the last moment, an arc of purple lightning bolted past Rist's head, colliding with the dragon's chest, sending it reeling off into the sky.

"We need to kill him here, or he will destroy everything." Brother Garramon stood by Rist's side, his black and silver robes flapping behind him. The man was wreathed in threads of Fire, Spirit, and Air. *Where did he come from?*

"I can't, it's Calen. I can't—"

"What more does he have to destroy for you to see the truth? Who else must he kill? End one life to save a million. We need to end this now! I'll hold the dragon off, you take the Draleid!"

The Draleid? Calen? That's not possible. Rist fixed his gaze on his friend, his mouth going dry, his hands slicked with sweat. How could Calen be the Draleid? The one who had been causing so many problems in the South, the one that had stirred the Uraks. How could he be the cause of so much death? Rist asked himself those questions, yet at the same time he remembered the sight of Calen dragging the blade across his mother's throat. He was not the same person Rist once knew. Rist's body shook at the thought of harming his friend. Calen had always been there, *always.* Knots twisted in his stomach, and he felt as though he was on the verge of vomiting. Attempting to steady the tremble in his hand, Rist gripped the hilt of his sword so tightly that his fingers went white, the blood draining. He took in a deep breath, then let it out in a sigh, stepping forward.

"At last, you show your true colours," Calen said, his lip curling and his brow furrowed. "So be it."

Rist froze as Calen charged towards him, only recovering in time to feel a tremor run the length of his arm as his and Calen's swords collided. Then a pang of pain exploded in his chest, Calen's knee crashing into his sternum.

Stumbling backwards, gasping for air, Rist dropped to one knee. Calen didn't allow him any respite. His friend dove after him, the steel of his blade glinting in the sun. Rist was able to deflect the first strike, but he lost his balance as he did, again falling backwards. Calen had always been the better swordsman ever since they were young. There had rarely been a morning where Rist hadn't seen him practising before helping his father in the forge. But this was different; now he moved with an effortless grace, as though the sword were simply an extension of his body.

They traded blows for a few moments before Calen sliced a gash across Rist's thigh, then plunged his sword into Rist's flesh, just below his ribs. Rist howled, pain burning through him. He could feel the cold steel tearing through his flesh with every movement, scraping against bone. He was going to die, and he knew it.

"You should have been by my side," Calen said, his eyes level with Rist's, his stare cold.

Rist glanced towards Garramon. The man lay broken against a large stone, his torso ripped open from groin to neck. Looking back into Calen's eyes, Rist knew what he had to do. "I won't let you become that monster, not more than you already have. You will always be my brother."

Rist reached out to the Spark, opening himself as he had done in The

Glade. But this time, he pulled harder, as hard as his soul would allow, and then harder still. He screamed as the Spark consumed him, ripping through his veins and clawing at his soul. Every fibre of his being told him to let go, and so he pulled even more voraciously. Finally, when he had drawn so heavily he could feel the tethers to his own soul being sheared, he hammered the threads together, and the world erupted in a blinding light.

Rist awoke, convulsing on his side, feeling as though his entire body had been covered in ice. His throat constricted, and his chest heaved as he gasped for air, vaguely aware of someone draping a blanket over him. "I'm sorry," he whispered. "I'm so sorry…"

It took a few moments for Rist to become aware that he was lying on the floor of the enormous chamber he had entered with Brother Garramon. The light of the braziers still cast a warm glow across the stone floor, their flames flickering wildly.

The voice of Andelar Touran rang out through the chamber. "Rist Havel, you have passed your Trial of Will. You have reached within yourself and risen above your own mind. You have taken your first step towards acolyteship."

Hands reached beneath Rist's armpits, lifting him to his feet. It was at that point he realised the blanket around his shoulders was not a blanket at all, but a pair of brown robes with a black line that ran parallel to its edges. Still shivering, he pulled the neck of the robes over his head and slid his arms into the sleeves.

Brother Garramon stood before him, a wide grin on his face. "Very well done, my apprentice. Very well done, indeed."

Rist returned his stare wordlessly, shivering and shaking. 'Well done' were not the words he was telling himself. *How could you?* The images of the dead bodies flashed across his mind. Neera, Tharn, his father, his mother, the look in Calen's eyes. *'You should have been by my side.'*

Rist's stomach turned. Had what he saw been a premonition? It couldn't have been. But what if it was? When he was in there, he had forgotten where he was. It had felt so real.

It was only when Garramon began to lead Rist out of the chamber and back down the tunnel that Rist noticed the throbbing pain below his ribs, along with twinges in his thigh and arm. Reaching up, Rist rubbed his fingers against the outside of his robes, feeling a hard rise in his skin. Stopping, he pulled his robes open and gazed down at a mess of knotted flesh in the same position Calen had driven the sword through. Wide-eyed, Rist lifted his head towards Garramon.

"What happens in the well has consequences," Garramon said, his voice flat. "We had healers standing by."

"Wha… what if I had died in there?"

"It is a good thing that did not happen."

Rist's throat tightened, and he clenched the fingers on his left hand into a fist. "What was that? What happened in there?"

"I do not know what you saw. Each apprentice experiences something different."

"But what *was* it? Was it real? Will what I saw come to pass?"

"Some believe so. Some believe it is a vision from The Saviour, warning us of what will happen if we fail."

Chapter Forty-Four

On a Knife's Edge

Even in the dead of night, the city of Argona was one of the most captivating things Dann had ever seen in his life. Since leaving The Glade, he had seen wonders: Camylin, Midhaven, Belduar, Durakdur. Each of them held their own splendour, and none of them truly compared to any other. But Argona was special. It was the capital city of Illyanara.

When Dann was a child, Belduar was a city of legend, and he had not even heard of Durakdur. He had never had any true desire to see either. But Dann had wanted to see Argona ever since Therin told them the story of the Siege of Argona during the Varsund War.

It was the destruction of the Varsundi vanguard at Argona that turned the tide of the war. He remembered the story as fondly as any he had ever heard. Apparently, one man had challenged the famed Varsundi General, Durin Longfang, to single combat in his own war camp, and won. Then the man simply walked from the camp, leaving the army in disarray. It had taken two days for the Varsundi army to gather themselves, and in that time, reinforcements had arrived from Midhaven, burned the Varsundi supply lines, and forced the army to surrender.

"If you keep gawking like that, somebody is going to think something is wrong with you," Aeson said, his lips pursed and an eyebrow raised.

Aeson had taken Dann with him into Argona to meet one of his informants and collect correspondence. The elves were camped just a few miles south of the city, by the river Marinelle. Dann had never really paid much heed to the fact that, growing up, Therin was the only elf he had ever seen. And it hadn't helped that Therin was so well liked in the villages. But if Dann truly thought about it, he could see how the cities of men could be a dangerous place for elves, particularly after The Fall. People tended to fear what they didn't understand, and fear was a good friend of hate.

"Something probably *is* wrong with me," Dann said with a shrug, gawking up at the enormous rectangular towers that loomed over the city. "In my father's words, 'You're a strange boy, Dann. You're *my* boy, but you're still strange.'"

Aeson looked at Dann as though he were going to say something, but he simply scrunched his eyes and tilted his head, then continued walking.

Dann had found that there was always a simple way to end a conversation with someone. You just had to know what worked for different people. With Rist, you had to agree with him. He never expected you to agree with him. With Calen, the key was to be overly nice. He never really knew how to handle that. All he had to do to end a conversation with Aeson was to act strangely enough that the man felt uncomfortable. It worked like a charm.

As they walked through the flagstone streets, Dann decided Argona was nothing like The Glade, and he didn't mean that in the obvious sense. Yes, Argona was a large city with tall walls and impressive towers, while The Glade was only a small village with a single inn and far too many sheep. But that was not what he meant. There were no homeless in The Glade, or any of the villages. If someone was left without a home, then they would be taken in until a new home could be built. That was what you did. You looked after your own.

Here, homeless men, women, and children lay huddled at every second street corner, wrapped in blankets that looked as though they had passed the point of being useful a decade before. Many of the windows glowed with the lights from candles and lanterns, yet nobody invited these poor souls in to share the warmth of their hearth. It just didn't seem right.

"Pick up the pace," Aeson said, turning to Dann, who had slowed to a pensive walk, his eyes lingering on a small girl huddled into her mother's chest, blankets draped over them both.

Dann felt a hand on his shoulder.

"I know," Aeson said, a melancholy in his voice. "This is the precursor to war, Dann. This will get a lot worse before it gets better. There is nothing we can do for them now."

"And you want this? You want war?"

"It's not as simple as that."

"It's as simple as you make it."

Aeson didn't say anything. He simply gave Dann a weak smile and gestured for them to continue.

It all set an uneasy feeling in Dann's stomach. Aeson wanted to start a rebellion, to bring the empire to its knees. He wanted to start a war between the North and the South. Despite all the silver-tongued excuses and noble reasons of valour, that's what it all boiled down to.

Dann wanted the empire gone as much as anyone. But was there truly no other way? Did all these people really have to suffer? Did so many people have to die? Taking a deep breath, he pushed those thoughts down, letting them fester at the back of his mind. "Who is this we are meeting? We shouldn't be stopping here at all. We should be moving as quickly as we can to Drifaien."

"He is a contact of mine from a while back. He keeps my correspondence here. I need to collect some letters, but we also need to get an accurate lay of the land. The Angan may be capable of communicating information quickly, but they often miss the things that matter."

Dann raised an eyebrow.

"They are not part of our world," Aeson explained. "They do not care for the whims of High Lords, the movement of armies, or the cost of grain. They pay no heed to the civil unrest in cities or the starvation of people. These are things we need to know. We also need to know who stands by our cause."

Aeson yanked Dann into a dark side street at the sound of footsteps, raising his finger to his lips. Six men strode past the street, dressed from head to toe in red and black leather armour with steel breastplates, swords strapped to their hips, and rectangular shields across their backs.

"Why are we hiding? It's not like they'd know who we are." Dann whispered, leaning out to look down the street after the soldiers.

Aeson frowned, pushing Dann back against the wall. "There's no sense in taking unnecessary risks. It's better to be safe. This city is crawling with imperial soldiers. Their garrison usually numbers no more than a hundred or so, just enough to remind Castor Kai who the true ruler is. But I'd say they're closer to around three thousand now."

Checking the coast was clear, Aeson gestured for Dann to follow. Dann adjusted the bow on his back, then followed after Aeson. It wasn't long before they came to an innocuous looking wooden door set into the side of a large, grey building that rose four or five storeys into the air. Aeson rummaged through his pocket, then pulled out a simple iron key, slotting it into the lock and turning it until it elicited a click and the door opened.

"When we meet Arem, don't say a word. Let me do the talking."

"You know me," Dann said with an all too serious look on his face. "Quiet as a mouse at a parade."

Aeson tilted his head, staring at Dann in disbelief. "Dann, what does that even mean?"

"If you don't know, then I can't explain it," Dann said with a shrug. In truth, Dann had no idea what it meant. He had heard an old pedlar say it once when the man had given Dann and Rist some candy and told them not to tell the other children, lest they come begging him for more. But Aeson didn't need to know that.

"Just keep your mouth shut when we're up here."

Dann made a gesture as though he were stitching his mouth shut, then threw away the imaginary needle, which seemed to fetch him an even stranger look from Aeson. The man had little to no sense of humour. And that was being generous.

The inside of the building was just as grey and drab as the outside. As soon as Dann and Aeson stepped through the doorway, a stone staircase stood in front of them, going upwards, then turning around on itself, then upwards again. Wooden doors sat on either side of the foot of the staircase, presumably leading into the homes of residents. Dann had heard about how people in some cities lived in houses stacked atop one another, but he had never seen the inside of one himself. All the homes in the villages were completely detached from the others. He didn't think he'd like to live in these 'tiered houses.' There was absolutely no privacy in them, and nowhere to practise the bow.

Another door sat at the top of the four flights of stairs, thicker than the others, with iron slats across it.

"Remember," Aeson said, pausing at the door.

"Keep my mouth shut," Dann said, cutting across Aeson. "I know, I know. You sound like Rist."

With a sigh, Aeson turned back to the door and pushed it open, revealing a wide-open rooftop trimmed by a low ledge. A large wooden structure ran the length of the left side of the roof, stretching upward about a foot or two over Dann's head, with a green awning that covered it, supported by beams another few feet higher again.

The large wooden structure was broken up into over a dozen segments, each one large enough to house a wolfpine, although maybe not one of Faenir's size, but still. Each of the sections had latched openings latticed with metal wire and were filled with straw. Dann almost leapt out of his skin as something moved inside one of the segments, squawking and flapping its wings.

"Hawks," Dann said, his mouth open. He knew certain breeds of hawk were commonly used to send messages over long distances, but in the villages, most letters were just sent by rider or whenever a well-known merchant was travelling village to village. Nobody really had much need of hawks.

Aeson gave Dann a sidelong glance, which reminded Dann of the only thing Aeson had said. *'Just keep your mouth shut.'*

Aeson sighed. "They're not just any hawks. They're starhawks, after the white feathers that form the shape of a star on their chests. Incredibly intelligent creatures. Capable of remembering multiple locations and associating them with things like colour, smell, and words. Arem's hawks are some of the finest in southern Epheria."

His eyes adjusting to the darkness within the cage, Dann found two gleaming eyes staring back at him, shimmering in the light of the moon. The hawk's gaze locked with his, unyielding, unblinking. Dann couldn't help but smile. He wasn't sure how he knew, but the creature was fascinated by him. "Do they have to be kept in cages?"

"They're not actually cages," a voice said, stepping out from the shadows on the far side of the roof.

Dann had to stop his natural reflex to reach for his bow. If speaking irritated Aeson, shooting his informant would likely not go down well.

The man wore a long black mantle, hood drawn over his head. He moved with a languid gait, almost gliding towards the wooden structure that housed the hawks. "The latches aren't closed, so each of the hawks can leave whenever they wish. Hawks are diurnal animals, so at this time, they usually just sleep. Except for Vela here." The man walked over to the hawk that was still staring straight at Dann and ran his finger along its beak, which was extended out through the latticed metal that fronted of the *'not cage'*. "It seems she has found something worth stirring for."

The man drew his hood down, his gaze, much like the hawk's, fixed on Dann. His head was shaved bald, as was his face. His eyes were a dull grey, barely visible in the dim light. "Starhawks know when they have found a home. And this hawkery provides a safe place for them, away from the large predators. They sleep here, and they eat here, and in exchange they carry messages. It's a mutually beneficial relationship."

Dann focused on Vela, the hawk that had been staring at him. The man was telling the truth. There was no sense of anxiety in the hawk, no panic or worry, only comfort and curiosity. Again, he was not sure how he knew, but he did. The man's voice dragged Dann out of his ponderings.

"Aeson Virandr, I wondered when I would see you next, though I hoped it would be sooner."

Aeson stepped past Dann, pulling the man into an embrace, patting him on the shoulder. "Arem, it has been too long, and for that, I apologise. I won't be staying long, either."

"I did not expect you would," Arem said, pulling back from his embrace with Aeson, patting him fondly on the cheek. "You have come for responses, I assume?"

Aeson nodded. "That, and I would know if you have heard any rumblings."

Arem's mouth drew into a thin line, a soft sigh escaping his nostrils. "First, I will bring you the responses. Then we can talk more."

Without awaiting any form of confirmation from Aeson, Arem strode off, again seeming to almost glide towards a hatch Dann hadn't noticed before that was set into the other side of the roof. That must have been how he had shown up without Dann seeing him.

"He's a bit… peculiar?" Dann said, pulling a face as he walked over to Aeson.

Aeson narrowed his eyes, raising one eyebrow.

"Right, yeah. Shut my mouth."

Aeson nodded.

"Mouth firmly shut."

Aeson's eyes narrowed further.

Dann mouthed the words, "Not gonna say another word."

Aeson just shook his head.

"Here we are," Arem said, lifting himself out of the hatch and handing a cloth bag to Aeson. "Forty-seven in total, I believe."

"That's it?" Aeson held the bag in front of him, looking in at its contents. Dann only managed to catch a glimpse, but it looked like letters.

Arem nodded. "I would expect more to arrive over the next few weeks. But for now, yes. Is that enough?"

"That depends entirely on who has written back." Aeson slung the cloth bag over his shoulder. "Before we go, what news?"

"There is war in Valtara," Arem said, his tone flat. "Though the empire is keeping a tight hold on information coming out of the province. The word is that Skyfell has fallen to rebels."

"Valtara?" Dann hadn't seen Aeson smile often, but at that moment, there was a toothy grin spread across his face. "Dayne must have succeeded. Valtara is a big piece on the board. That is good news indeed, Arem. Very good news. What else?"

The bald man stroked his chin as though he were plucking the bits of news from perches in his mind. "There are rumours floating on the wind that Arkalen, Carvahon, and Varsund are on the verge as well, though the sources are not as solid. My own reckoning is Arkalen and Carvahon are probably close, but Varsund… not so much."

"I would say you are probably correct. The empire's hold on Varsund is too strong. The gold mines in Aonar are crucial to their strength in the South, and the Varsundi Blackthorns are too valuable an asset for the empire to risk losing. How about here in Illyanara?"

Arem sighed. "It's slow to spread here. But I can feel it. A few factions have broken out around the province. A group calling themselves 'The Red Suns' have started raiding farms near Baylomon, and another flying the banner of old Amendel have laid claim to quite a bit of land south of Fearsall. There are others, but those two seem to be gaining the most traction. They have the empire's hackles up. I'd say the empire's garrison here in Argona numbers north of three thousand now, and patrols seem to run night and day between here and the borders with Carvahon, Drifaien, and Arkalen."

Dann stood there, his mouth agape. "How… Aeson—"

A hard glare from Aeson stopped Dann in his tracks.

"Some good news, some bad news," Aeson said, scratching his chin. "Starting a rebellion brings both. What of the North?"

Arem grinned. It was one of the widest grins Dann had ever seen. His snow-white teeth glistened, and the corners of his mouth were just short of touching his eyes. "They are in chaos."

At those words, Dann saw another expression on Aeson's face that he had not seen before – surprise.

"And you didn't think to lead with that news? What has happened?"

"Uraks," Arem said with a shrug. "The raids that are happening here are nothing compared to the goings on in the North. I had a trader pass through only a day ago. He said Fort Harken's gates have been closed for some time now, and a few of the smaller villages at the base of Mar Dorul and Lodhar have been completely overrun. He also heard that Steeple has been sacked, and the northern pass is… well, it's unpassable. The cities along the lightning coast have been completely cut off from the main continent."

Aeson's face was grim. "As happy as I am that the empire will have enough problems to deal with up North, the Uraks are not on our side. Their strength is not our gain."

"Agreed." Arem folded his arms across his chest and nodded his head slightly. He shrugged. "But for now, waste not, want not. Also, now that I think of it. I received a letter just this morning with news that Arisfall was attacked only a couple of days gone. Apparently, the castle was set on fire, and, if the letter is to be believed, a giant wolf and a dragon were involved. Friends of yours?"

"Calen!" Dann snapped his head around to Aeson, unable to hold back the surge that ran through him. "He escaped?"

"I don't know," Aeson replied. "But maybe Baldon will. Come, we need to go. Thank you, Arem."

CHAPTER FORTY-FIVE

ONE DOOR CLOSES

Ella sat on the edge of the opening, her legs dangling over the sheer drop below. The light from the sun felt warm against her skin as it shone down through the jagged peaks of the towering mountains around her. The alcove in which she sat was small, maybe only about thirty feet long and twenty feet wide. It looked as though it had been carved straight from the sandy-brown rock of the mountainside, for the sharp angles and smooth surface of the stone seemed far too perfect to be natural. A small pond sat in the alcove's centre, water glistening in the sun.

It had been a few days since Yana and Farwen had brought her to Tarhelm, a rebel outpost built in the Firnin Mountains, almost a hundred miles from Berona. It appeared Yana and Tanner were more than they had seemed.

Ella let the crisp air fill her lungs, held it for a moment, then exhaled, watching her breath plume out in front of her. It was the first time she had stopped moving since she and Rhett had left The Glade and the first time she had felt even the slightest bit safe since he had died. Ella shook her head as the thought took the air from her lungs. She closed her eyes, trying desperately to stop the tears. She couldn't deal with any more tears.

Ella opened her eyes at the feel of Faenir's coarse fur rubbing against her side. The wolfpine was the only creature within a thousand miles that Ella trusted completely. There was something about him that seemed to fill the holes in her heart, at least for a time. It was as though Rhett himself had sent him to watch over her.

Looking down, Ella stared into Faenir's golden eyes. Farwen's words drifted through her mind. *'Blood of the old druids flows in your veins.'*

The longer Ella stared, it seemed as though the world around her began to fade, dulling at the edges. A warmth touched her mind, a deep feeling of kinship. Just a flash, then it was gone. But she had felt it, as though Faenir's mind had drifted into her own, if only for a moment. Ella whispered, "A druid…" She leaned forward, resting her forehead against the flat of Faenir's snout. "What does that even mean?"

Ella lifted her head to the sound of hurried footsteps echoing into the alcove from the connected system of tunnels. Raising herself to her feet, she brushed down the front of her dress and followed the noise. "Come on, boy."

Each of the caverns, chambers, and alcoves of Tarhelm were linked by a series of interconnecting tunnels that Ella could only think to compare to an ant nest. The tunnels were wide enough for three or four people to walk abreast, and she easily could have stood on her own shoulders twice over without touching her head to the ceilings.

The entire place was essentially one enormous maze.

As Ella drew closer to the hurrying footsteps, she could hear voices. She couldn't make out anything the voices were saying, but they held an urgency that let her know something was wrong.

Picking up her pace, Ella ran down the tunnel, following the sounds. She couldn't be entirely sure, but she thought she had come this direction before. Though, it was not as if she had spent a lot of time exploring Tarhelm since she had arrived. After a few minutes, she emerged into a large, open cavern that held several brown stone buildings. She *had* been there before. It was the medical quarter where Farwen and Yana had taken her when they first arrived at Tarhelm after leaving Berona.

Directly in front of Ella was a small building carved from the same brown stone as all the others, with a red blood drop painted on its wooden door – the infirmary. Beside the door, she saw Yana sitting on the ground, her hands clasped at the back of her head.

Ella dropped to the ground in front of Yana, her breath catching in her throat. "Yana, what's happened? What's wrong?"

Yana lifted her head. Tears marred her cheeks and her eyes were red and raw. In the short time Ella had known her, Yana had been nothing but sharp and fierce. The woman had threatened Ella with physical harm more than once, and Ella had no doubt she would have carried out the threat if needed. She was a force of nature. That is why the sight of her now frightened Ella to her core.

"It's Tanner," Yana said, forcing her voice through a hoarse, sob constricted throat.

"Yana, what happened?"

Yana's eyes grew cold, her breathing slowed, and her sobbing stopped. "I told you I would kill you myself, if he was harmed…" She clasped Ella's shoulder, her fingers digging in so hard it hurt. A slight tremble set into her voice. "Ella, if he dies…"

Ella's throat went dry. Tanner had helped her when he had no cause to do so. It was because of her that he had put himself in danger. *Please be all right. Please be all right.* "Yana, where is he?"

"Inside." Yana said through gritted teeth, her eyes still locked on Ella's.

A shiver ran through Ella's chest as she looked towards the door of the infirmary. She reached down to help Yana to her feet. "Yana, get up. Come on."

"Get your hands off me!" Yana slapped Ella's arm away. But then a tear rolled down her cheek, a crack forming in her walls. "I can't see him like that…"

Ella brought her eyes level with Yana's. She knew the pain she saw there. It was the same as her own. The same pain that stabbed at her with every stone she placed on Rhett's grave. She rested her hands on the woman's shoulders. "He needs you right now. Get up."

Yana returned Ella's gaze, her eyes glistening. She clenched her jaw, her breathing growing deep and heavy. "He's a fool…"

"All men are," Ella said, lifting Yana to her feet. This time, the woman didn't slap her away. She took Ella's arm.

Ella pushed open the infirmary door, Yana following behind her.

The infirmary was double the size of the alcove Ella had been sitting in, with cots lining both the far and near walls interspersed with cabinets full of medicine and herbs and a long stone table in the centre. Most of the cots were empty as Ella and Yana entered, save for a woman who sat at the far end of the room, a bloodied bandage wrapped around her head. Three people stood around another man who lay still on the centre table, his body laced with bloodied cuts and gashes. Tanner.

Farwen stood on the opposite side of the stone table, dirt bedded into her face, her white-streaked hair matted with blood. The elf's chest heaved as she rested her arm against a cot behind her.

Ella also recognised the person tending to Tanner as the infirmerer, the one who had tended to her when she first arrived. A long white cloth apron was draped over her front, and sweat slicked her brow.

The third person who stood beside Tanner had their back to Ella, but her skin was as dark as the petals of a dalya flower, and her long black hair was tied up with a piece of string. Judging by the sword strapped to her hip, she was no infirmerer.

"How is he?" A blend of worry, anxiety, and fear permeated Yana's voice as she pushed past Ella, stopping at the stone table.

"Stable," the infirmerer remarked, not lifting her head from the wounded man. "But it is hard to tell if he will make it through the night."

"I did all I could," the dark-skinned woman said, stumbling slightly to her right. "His wounds were severe, on the very edge of unsavable. Any more, and I would have taken my own life."

"Thank you," Yana said, her hand resting on the woman's shoulder.

"Your thanks are not needed, Yana. He is one worth saving."

Yana nodded, her mouth forming the meekest of smiles before she moved around to Tanner's side, wrapping her hand in his.

The dark-skinned woman sighed and turned towards Ella, the slightest look of surprise on her face. "So, you are the cause of all this trouble, then?"

A knot twisted in Ella's stomach, her throat going dry. "I'm sorry. I didn't mean to cause any of this—"

"No," the woman said, resting her hand on Ella's shoulder. "I will have none of that. Tanner joined us because he saw that every life is worth saving. He knew the risks of what he did. Though, to risk so much, with such little hope of evading detection… For that, there must be a reason. Is there any light you can shed on this?"

Ella shook her head, feeling nauseous at the thought of someone else losing their life for her. "No… His nephew… We were…" Ella paused. "We *are* Ayar Elwyn." *One Heart.*

The woman smiled, the corner of her lips turning upward only slightly. A smile that contained both happiness and loss. "What is your name?"

"Ella. Ella… Fjorn."

The woman reached out her hand. "Well met, Ella Fjorn. I am Coren Valmar. Welcome to the rebellion."

Rist sat in his chambers, the glow of twilight drifting through the windows. His back rested against the wall, his legs stretched out in front of him, feet sticking off the side of the bed. His new robes were draped across his lap, his thumb and forefinger rubbing the edge of the fabric in a semi-dazed repetition.

The heavy robes were woven from a fabric of which Rist had no knowledge. They were brown in colour with a black line running about an inch back from its edge. Black, the colour of the Battlemages. He was officially a second-tier apprentice.

Rist let out a heavy sigh, tilting his head back, letting it rest against the cold stone. As he sat there in his chambers, in the embassy of the Circle of Magii, in the imperial palace, the robes draped over his lap, he was uncertain. Uncertain of who he was, what he wanted, and of who he would become if he stayed on his current path.

He missed home and his family. Calen. Dann. What he had seen in the Trial of Will only made that yearning stronger. It had shaken him to the core. He could still see the lights go out in Tharn's eyes, and the blood streaming from his mother's throat. He could hear Calen's words. *You should have been by my side.*

It had not been real. It had been some kind of illusion created by the well, Rist knew that. But he couldn't lie to himself. When he was inside the well, he had not been able to tell it was not real. He had killed Calen. That thought alone was enough to turn his stomach. There were very few people who had stood by Rist growing up. In fact, he could count them on one hand: Calen and Dann.

When the other children had bullied him for being shy, or skinny, or *different,* it had been Calen and Dann who stood by his side. Dann liked to poke fun at him, but that was simply Dann. It was his way. Calen never did, though.

"I hope you're both all right," Rist muttered, staring out the window at the dim glow of the already-set sun brushing against the dark blue sky.

Rist had thought about asking to go home. Of course he had. But what good would that do? He highly doubted The Circle would agree. The cost of passage from the North to the South was more gold than Rist had ever seen in his lifetime. But even if he did somehow make it back, there was no guarantee he would find Calen and Dann. In fact, it was a near certainty he wouldn't.

The Circle was the right place for him to be. He would be a fool not to glean every ounce of knowledge he could from this place. Not to read every book in the library, not to learn every way to weave the threads of the Spark together, not to learn how to wield a sword properly. With every passing day, he grew stronger. And once he was strong enough, once he had become a Battlemage, he would find them. Maybe, even, Neera could come with him.

Rist laughed, his father's words echoing in his head. *'The best laid plans of mice and men, my boy. They go wrong more often than not.'* Of course, at the time, Lasch Havel was talking about how he and Tharn Pimm had once ended up face first in a pile of cow dung when trying to play a trick on Marlo Egon. But the moral of the story remained. Lay all the plans you want, lay even more, but expect them to fail and plan accordingly.

A slow, soft knock came from the door.

"Come in."

The door creaked open, Neera's head peeking through. "Hey."

Rist gave a lopsided smile, his eyes taking in the beauty of Neera's cheeks. "Hey."

That was when Rist noticed the black line that ran along the length of Neera's brown robes. "Battlemage," he blurted out, almost leaping from the bed. "You passed your Trial of Will, and Sister Ardal chose Battlemage!"

Rist wrapped his arms around Neera, pulling her in close. He wasn't entirely sure why he was so happy that Sister Ardal had chosen Battlemage as Neera's affinity, but he most definitely was happy. Of course, it meant they would get to spend more time together, but to be a Battlemage meant to put your life in danger. It meant Neera would put *her* life in danger. With that thought, Rist felt a pang of guilt in his chest for his selfishness.

"What's wrong?" Neera looked up at him from his chest, her dark eyes glinting.

"Nothing," Rist said, resting his chin on her head. "How was it?"

"How was yours?"

"Fair. Let's not talk about it. Want to celebrate?"

"I know a place."

CHAPTER FORTY-SIX

THE ROAD LESS TRAVELLED

alen bit down into the crusty bread, feeling that satisfying crunch when his teeth finally broke through. Drippings from the pork rolled over his lips, staining the front of his trousers. But he didn't care. For the first two days, he hadn't been able to stomach much food. His stomach had felt as though it had scrunched into a tiny ball. But he had eaten more in the past three days than in the previous month, and he did not intend to stop any time soon. Being deprived of food had given him a new appreciation for it. That morning alone, he had eaten two apples, two bananas, and a sea basset, head to tail. Though he would have to cut back on the fresh fruit. They only had about a week's supply on board, but the cook had said that if it began to rot, then it was first come first served. He had never before hoped for food to rot until now.

Getting up from the bench, Calen hobbled over to the rail of the ship, sunlight bouncing off the surface of the water, icy wind rolling over his skin. He was beginning to feel stronger, but he was still a far cry away from what he had been. His arms and legs were as frail as twigs, and his stomach still pained him, though less than before.

At the very least, Vaeril had regrown the nails on Calen's hands and toes the morning before. Calen had refused at first, but he couldn't argue with

Vaeril's logic – travelling the distance they were planning to travel would be infinitely more difficult with his hands and feet in such bad shape.

Calen reached out his mind to Valerys's. The dragon was a few miles east, soaring along the surface of the water, diving in and out, snatching up fish. He hadn't drifted any further than that since the ship set sail. Valerys never wanted to be more than a few minutes away from Calen, and Calen didn't see that changing for a while, not after what had happened. He could still feel the fear and fury festering in the back of the dragon's mind. That empty loneliness, the absence of half a soul. Calen felt it too, of course, keenly, but it stung him more to feel that hurt in Valerys.

"How are you feeling?" Tarmon asked, stepping up beside Calen at the rail of the ship. "Your appetite has returned, at least."

Calen laughed. "I could do nothing but eat for days."

"Good. You might need to, to regain your strength. You're going to need it."

Calen shoved the last bit of the crusty bread and pork into his mouth, attempting to breathe through the mouthful of food. Once he swallowed it all, he let out a sigh, tilting his head back. "I know," he said, placing his hand over his stomach. "And Tarmon, thank you. Not just for coming with me, but for getting me out of that cell. If you hadn't come, the Dragonguard would have me by now, and more than that. They would have Valerys. We owe you our lives."

Tarmon smiled, patting the palm of his hand on the rough wooden rail. "It was Alleron and Baird who organised the escape. Without them, we would all still be rotting in those cells. Either way, I think we have both saved each other's lives enough at this stage to call it even."

"Alleron and Baird may have organised the escape, but it was you who put me over your shoulders and carried me the entire way out of that city. Don't think I forget that. Most would have left me behind. *I* might have left me behind…"

Tarmon gave a weak smile, staring out at the water. "You think too little of yourself, Calen."

"Hey, you two."

Calen turned at the sound of Erik's voice.

"Captain Kiron asked me to come get you. He wants to talk. Vaeril is already inside."

The captain's cabin was about three times the size of the cabin that Calen, Erik, Vaeril, and Tarmon had been given to share. On the right side, a double bed was set into the wall with ornate bedsheets of vibrant yellow with a red trim.

On the other side of the room, four medium-sized wooden casks were banded against the wall of the ship with strips of iron, small taps jutting out from near the bottom of the casks. A shelf full of wooden mugs ran along the top of the casks. Slats of wood were fastened to the front of the shelf, preventing the mugs from slipping free. And a latch was fitted at the end of the shelf to allow access to the mugs.

Two couches made from a dark oak sat in the middle of the room. Large metal bolts fastened the couches to the floor, which Calen supposed made sense given that ships were prone to tipping side to side. A long, red velvet cushion ran along the seat of each couch, secured with straps of leather.

Past the couches, towards the back of the room, a heavyset oak desk was bolted to the floor in much the same way as the couches. The desk was completely empty, save for four sets of pegs that jutted out along its front and a large map pinned down at each corner with short, flat-headed nails.

Captain Kiron stood behind the table, his right hand resting on the edge, his left hand picking something from between his teeth. He looked up as the three of them entered the room. "Ah, good. Would any of you like a drink?"

"I'm all right," Calen said, holding back a laugh as he looked at Vaeril. The elf's seasickness had only gotten worse with each passing day. He had spent most of his time in the cabin, lying in his cot with a small wooden bucket. The few times he had come above deck, he had stared at the water as though it were an ocean of fire, then promptly returned to his cot. At that moment, he held one hand against the wooden wall and the other cupped over his mouth, tears welling in the corner of his eyes as he no doubt held back vomit.

Captain Kiron shrugged, striding effortlessly across the ever-shifting floor. He undid the latch at the end of the shelf of mugs, snatching one out before fixing the latch in place once more. Sticking the mug under a tap that belonged to one of the kegs, the captain flipped up the knob, letting a clear brown liquid flow freely into the mug. "One hundred percent top quality Karvosi spiced rum. You won't ever taste anything like it in Epheria."

Beside Calen, Tarmon let out a long sigh. "You know what," he said with a shrug, "I will have a drink."

"Me too," Erik jumped in, suddenly eager. "It would be rude not to."

"Quite right," Captain Kiron said with a wide grin. He placed the wooden mug on his desk, nestling it securely into one of the sets of pegs. Calen hadn't noticed it before, but the mugs each had slight grooves moulded into their edges that seemed purpose-made to allow them to be held by the pegs. Dann would have loved them. He was always one for coming up with useful contraptions.

"Draleid, are you sure you wouldn't like one?" The captain grabbed two more mugs from the shelf as he spoke, filling them with rum.

"Thank you, Captain. But I'm all right. I'm not sure my stomach could handle anything like that just yet. And please, call me Calen."

"Sure. Though, if I had a title like that, I'd make sure to keep it." The captain shrugged, turning back towards his desk. He slotted the mugs into two of the remaining sets of pegs, letting them slide down to the bottom on their own. Then, he strode around the other side, opened a drawer that was set into the underside of the desk, and produced a lime, a curved knife, and a small bag of some type of granule.

Slicing the lime into three equal parts, he squeezed the juice into the mugs, then tossed one of the rinds into his mouth, chewing on it as he reached into the bag and poured some of its content into the mugs. "Sugar cane," the captain said when he noticed Calen staring intently. "Balances out the sharpness. I call it Sweet Sea Breeze."

The captain handed a mug each to Tarmon and Erik, taking a hearty swig of his own as he did.

"Divine shit," Erik said, coughing and choking. "That's just a mug full of rum. Why in the gods would you call that a 'Sweet Sea Breeze'?"

Captain Kiron laughed, sipping away at his drink. He shrugged. "Mostly just to see people do that."

Both Calen and Tarmon couldn't help but laugh, Tarmon taking a mouthful of the drink as he did.

"I think it's pretty good," Tarmon said, a mocking smile resting on his lips.

"Right?" The captain winked as he spoke.

The only two people who weren't laughing were Vaeril and Erik, the former because he was too busy holding himself upright and keeping the contents of his stomach firmly within the bounds of his body.

"All right," Kiron said, standing up straight, rolling his shoulders back. "It's time we talk business. It will be another few days before we pass the Arkalen Coast, so best to get our heads straight. Where are we are landing the ship?"

All eyes fell on Calen.

"Well, I…"

"You don't know, do you?"

"In truth, I hadn't thought that far ahead."

The captain let out a sigh, shaking his head. "You landlubbers. You always seem to have it in your head to go somewhere, but never have the foresight to plan anything. How are you not dead yet?"

"There are two options," Tarmon said, moving beside the table, his hand hovering over the map. "We can drop anchor at Kingspass where the river Kilnír meets the Veloran Ocean, then make our way through the Burnt Lands. Or we can sail along the Lightning Coast and drop anchor somewhere between Bromis and Khergan."

"The Burnt Lands or The Lightning Coast. Both of those sound like suicide." Erik stood beside the table, his arms folded across his chest, his eyes scanning the map.

"They are." Captain Kiron said, shrugging.

"Then why are you bringing us?" Calen narrowed his eyes, his gaze fixed on Kiron.

"I have a soft spot for lost causes. It's kind of a kink of mine."

Erik tilted his head back, scrunching his face. "Don't you mean flaw? It's kind of a *flaw* of yours?"

"I meant what I said." A long, awkward pause held in the air for a moment before the captain turned back to the map. "Anyway, if it's all the same to you," Kiron tilted his head towards Calen, "I'd prefer to drop you off at Kingspass. I've lost three ships along the Lightning Coast, and I like this ship. I don't want to see it torn apart. Also, your friend didn't pay me enough to take you along the Lightning Coast."

"Then why are you asking me?" Calen stepped a little closer to the map, gauging the distances of the journey.

"I like to be polite. So Kingspass it is."

"How long will it take to get there?"

The captain puckered out his lower lip. "Another nine days, by my measure. The waters around the Arkalen Coast may not be the Lightning Coast, but they're not plain sailing either. The waters around here are choppy, the rocks are jagged, and the closer we get to the islands, the more whirlpools we'll happen upon."

"Nine days," Calen muttered to himself. "How long to cross the Burnt Lands?"

"You're asking me?" The captain laughed, taking another sip of his drink. "You're a funny one, I'll give you that. I have absolutely no idea. I've never actually heard of someone who has crossed it. Then again, I've never known anyone who had a dragon, so I'd say your odds are better than most. I'm not sure how accurate this map is when it comes to land. The cartographer swore it was accurate, but then again, so would I if I was held at sword point." The captain scrunched his mouth in contemplation as he ran his finger along the map. "It looks like it is about a two hundred miles from nearest point to nearest point. Though that would bring you closer to Copperstille than Berona. Also, there's no chance of you walking in a straight line in that ocean of sand and dust, so I'd say closer to two hundred and fifty miles. Given the terrain and scarcity of food, let's say you can walk twenty miles in a day – it would be painful, but you could do it. That would give you about twelve or thirteen days, two weeks to be safe."

Calen just stared at Kiron. He couldn't quite work out if the man was kooky or just plain mad. The captain carried himself as though he were a well-to-do merchant with his fine clothes, his well-groomed blonde hair, and his clean-cut look. But it was quite clear that he was just a few roses short of a bush.

Calen took a step closer to the table, tracing his finger along the rough cloth map, bringing it from the town of Kingspass, up through the Burnt Lands, stopping at Berona. He lifted his head, moving his gaze between Tarmon and Erik. He had looked to Vaeril, but the elf now leaned against the wooden wall, his eyes closed, taking heavy breaths. "What do you think?"

"I think we'll probably die," Erik said, puckering his lips inward. "But it would be some story to be able to say we crossed the Burnt Lands, and after those tunnels, this is nothing."

Tarmon looked at Erik, his eyebrow raised in amusement. He shook his head. "It's very risky, though it is probably no worse than the Lightning Coast."

"So, it is decided, then?" The captain stood up straight, emptying his mug, then setting his hands on his hips. "We will drop anchor at Kingspass in nine days."

Kallinvar bit the corner of his lip, his hands resting against the cool stone edge of the war table. He and Verathin had been there for hours. But no matter how they played it out, there were not enough knights.

"What if we let the empire fend for itself? The Uraks and the old mages have more than a drop of bad blood between them. Two birds, one stone."

Verathin let out a sigh, his arms folded across his chest, one hand tracing along the bottom of his chin. "You know that is not our way, brother."

"The North is consumed by the Shadow, Verathin. It looms both outside the walls and within. Fane and The Circle have as tight a bond to The Traitor as the Uraks do. If we can let them cull each other's numbers, we will be in a better position."

"And the people? Does the North hold no innocents? Are we to leave them to the Shadow's wrath?"

Kallinvar clenched his jaw, staring down at the carved stone table. Many of the villages along the northern edge of the Burnt Lands had already been overrun, as had quite a few that sat along the foothills of Mar Dorul. The Urak numbers seemed even higher than they had been at The Fall, although they were not all concentrated in a single place. Fane had allied himself to the beasts back then; the fact that they were now at each other's throats gave the knights a better chance. He sighed, rising to his full height. "The duty of the strong is to protect the weak, Grandmaster."

"So, it will always be."

"What of the villages at the base of Wolfpine Ridge?"

"I'm still trying to decide," Verathin said, his brow furrowing as he looked down over the war table. "For now, I have assigned Darmerian and The Fifth to watch over Western Illyanara. The simple fact that we found Bloodmarked there justifies that."

Kallinvar nodded. "Darmerian is a good choice. He is young enough, but he is strong of character. And what of the Draleid?"

Verathin raised an eyebrow. "What of him?"

"We know the empire is looking for him. And I suspect they are not the only ones. We would do well to keep him safe. We need allies, old friend."

Verathin leaned down, pressing his hands against the table, a deep, ruminating look in his eyes. Eventually, lifting his head, Verathin sighed. "Where do our reports last place him?"

"In Drifaien. He has not been seen for weeks. But we received reports that sections of Arisfall castle caught fire only a few days back. I do not believe that was a coincidence."

Verathin lifted his hands and strode around the stone table until he stood directly in front of Kallinvar. "Find him and do whatever it takes to protect him. But for now, keep this only within your own chapter. Some of the other captains will not be happy with this decision. We are not meant to be the arbiters of Epheria. We are its guardians against the Shadow, nothing more."

"And we have failed in that task," Kallinvar said, not moving his gaze from Verathin's. "We must do more."

"Perhaps you are right. Go now. See if you can find the Draleid."

Kallinvar bowed slightly. "Grandmaster."

Chapter Forty-Seven

Water is Thicker

Sweat dripped from Calen's forehead as he moved through the sword forms. He dropped from Howling Wolf into Patient Wind, bringing his elbow in tight as he stepped back onto his left foot. The cool wind tussled his hair, nipped at his skin, and rolled over the rail of the ship as the massive wooden vessel ploughed through the water. The setting sun dipped its toes into the horizon, casting a deep orange-red glow across the sky.

The ship lurched, a particularly high wave crashing into its bow. Calen stumbled, but caught himself, pushing his strength through his back leg. He grimaced, pain shooting through the leg and along his spine. It had been ten days since they boarded the ship. Ten days since Alleron and the others had broken them out of the cells in Arisfall. The pain was ebbing away, though it still lingered. It would take weeks for Calen's full strength to return, probably longer. The time spent locked in that cell with little to no food had stripped his body of a large portion of his muscle.

Calen had never been one for ships. He didn't mind them, but if it were up to him, he would spend as little time aboard one as he could. Though he couldn't complain too much: at least he didn't suffer in the way Vaeril had been suffering. The elf had been bedridden since the start of the journey, only surfacing above deck when his vomit bucket was full to the brim.

Deciding that was all the pain he could endure for the day, Calen slid his sword into the brown and green leather scabbard at his hip. With a heavy sigh, he dropped onto a crate that was strapped to the deck by lengths of rope secured through iron loops. His chest heaving, he snatched his waterskin, unscrewed the cap, and took a deep draught. The water felt cool as ice against his wind-chapped lips, soothing his throat as it went down.

Around him, the deck hands scuttled about. Calen found himself holding more than a little jealousy at the way they moved about the ship with ease, their natural gait taking the ship's motion into account. He supposed after years of seafaring life, even his own muscles would carry the same effortless grace.

The clothing choices for those who worked the deck of the ship varied wildly. Some roamed about shirtless, wearing nothing but baggy trousers and thick-soled sailors' shoes, while others wore cloth or linen shirts. Some even wore heavy doublets not dissimilar to Captain Kiron's. For the most part, though, beneath the clothes – or lack thereof – the deckhands looked as though they could all be brothers and sisters. Each had dark, leathered skin stretched over frames of wiry muscle. Even the women held more muscle on their bodies than most men Calen knew, their shoulders rippling as they hoisted themselves up along nets and ropes.

They wore their long, matted hair in a variety of styles: tied up in knots, nestled in bandanas, draped down over their backs. Most of the men looked as though entire summers had passed since they had last shaved their beards. Much like the seafaring folk of Salme, back in the villages, most wore big looping rings and studs of brass in their ears and noses.

Calen's head spun at the sheer variety of tasks that each of them had to perform. Some climbed up ropes and nets, checking their stability with firm tugs, while others carried buckets and mops, slopping sick – mostly Vaeril's – from the deck. One particularly slim man with no shirt on his back strode about the deck, inspecting each of the iron-banded barrels in turn. Calen figured him for the cooper. Both Vars and Lasch Havel had met with plenty of coopers throughout the years and it was not difficult

CHAPTER FORTY-SEVEN

WATER IS THICKER

Sweat dripped from Calen's forehead as he moved through the sword forms. He dropped from Howling Wolf into Patient Wind, bringing his elbow in tight as he stepped back onto his left foot. The cool wind tussled his hair, nipped at his skin, and rolled over the rail of the ship as the massive wooden vessel ploughed through the water. The setting sun dipped its toes into the horizon, casting a deep orange-red glow across the sky.

The ship lurched, a particularly high wave crashing into its bow. Calen stumbled, but caught himself, pushing his strength through his back leg. He grimaced, pain shooting through the leg and along his spine. It had been ten days since they boarded the ship. Ten days since Alleron and the others had broken them out of the cells in Arisfall. The pain was ebbing away, though it still lingered. It would take weeks for Calen's full strength to return, probably longer. The time spent locked in that cell with little to no food had stripped his body of a large portion of his muscle.

Calen had never been one for ships. He didn't mind them, but if it were up to him, he would spend as little time aboard one as he could. Though he couldn't complain too much: at least he didn't suffer in the way Vaeril had been suffering. The elf had been bedridden since the start of the journey, only surfacing above deck when his vomit bucket was full to the brim.

Deciding that was all the pain he could endure for the day, Calen slid his sword into the brown and green leather scabbard at his hip. With a heavy sigh, he dropped onto a crate that was strapped to the deck by lengths of rope secured through iron loops. His chest heaving, he snatched his waterskin, unscrewed the cap, and took a deep draught. The water felt cool as ice against his wind-chapped lips, soothing his throat as it went down.

Around him, the deck hands scuttled about. Calen found himself holding more than a little jealousy at the way they moved about the ship with ease, their natural gait taking the ship's motion into account. He supposed after years of seafaring life, even his own muscles would carry the same effortless grace.

The clothing choices for those who worked the deck of the ship varied wildly. Some roamed about shirtless, wearing nothing but baggy trousers and thick-soled sailors' shoes, while others wore cloth or linen shirts. Some even wore heavy doublets not dissimilar to Captain Kiron's. For the most part, though, beneath the clothes – or lack thereof – the deckhands looked as though they could all be brothers and sisters. Each had dark, leathered skin stretched over frames of wiry muscle. Even the women held more muscle on their bodies than most men Calen knew, their shoulders rippling as they hoisted themselves up along nets and ropes.

They wore their long, matted hair in a variety of styles: tied up in knots, nestled in bandanas, draped down over their backs. Most of the men looked as though entire summers had passed since they had last shaved their beards. Much like the seafaring folk of Salme, back in the villages, most wore big looping rings and studs of brass in their ears and noses.

Calen's head spun at the sheer variety of tasks that each of them had to perform. Some climbed up ropes and nets, checking their stability with firm tugs, while others carried buckets and mops, slopping sick – mostly Vaeril's – from the deck. One particularly slim man with no shirt on his back strode about the deck, inspecting each of the iron-banded barrels in turn. Calen figured him for the cooper. Both Vars and Lasch Havel had met with plenty of coopers throughout the years and it was not difficult for Calen to tell the practised efficiency with which the man went about his task.

On the other side of the deck, a man and a woman, both shirtless, lounged about, letting the fading sun kiss their already leathered skin. One look at the woman's bare breasts and Calen jerked his head to the side, staring out towards the open water. He was sure his cheeks were glowing red. The woman seemed to care very little that she was completely exposed to the eyes of any man on deck. That did not make Calen's embarrassment any less.

He nearly fell from the crate at the sound of Erik's voice.

"How goes practice?" Erik emerged from a staircase that led below deck, a thick loaf of crusty bread in his hands. He wore a thin cloth shirt and a pair of dark brown trousers tucked into heavy sailor's boots. Erik broke the loaf of bread in half with a snap, tossing one end to Calen.

Calen just about managed to catch the bread; his arms were still heavy from moving through the sword forms.

Erik must have seen something in the way Calen was sitting, because it only took a second for him to start laughing. "What is it with you people raised out in the middle of nowhere? Have you never seen a woman's body before?"

If Calen's cheeks had been glowing red, they were now blazing infernos. He could physically feel the heat radiating from him. "I just… not like that… The women in The Glade always…"

"You're not in The Glade anymore," Erik said, leaning against the rail of the ship, taking a bite out of his half of the bread loaf. "There are all sorts of people in the world, Calen. Do you not find it funny that you have faced down kerathlin and Uraks, yet you shy away from a woman's breasts? Does the man's chest cause you to blush as well?"

"No! I just… leave me alone." Calen took a bite out of the bread, staring out towards the ocean as he chewed it with a fury.

Erik shook his head, still laughing. He pushed Calen's shoulder. "Relax, I'm only teasing you. You will see. The longer you are away from your village, the less these things will cause your cheeks to redden. You village folk are an easy bunch to rattle, I'll tell you that much."

Calen didn't respond. He just kept staring out across the ever-shifting waves, keeping his eyes firmly away from the man and woman lounging on the other side of the ship.

"So," Erik said, a more serious tone entering his voice. "What if we can't find him?"

"What?"

"Rist. What are we going to do if we can't find him? Berona is a big city. We need to be prepared."

"We *will* find him."

Erik sighed, turning around and resting his arms across the ship's rail, staring out over the water with Calen. "What if we don't, Calen? Or what if he's dead?"

Calen gritted his teeth, feeling his anger begin to bubble, partly fuelled by Valerys in the back of his mind. Calen pushed Valerys's thoughts back, just a bit. Anger seemed to be the emotion Valerys fed into more than any other, and Calen didn't want to lose his temper with Erik. "Then we will deal with that as it comes."

"We need to deal with it now." Erik turned to Calen, his mouth a thin line, his eyes locked with Calen's. "You can't control yourself when it comes to Rist and Dann. I know you know that. And we can't afford for something to go wrong here, or for something to go wrong in the heart of Berona. We'll die, Calen. Promise me, if we can't find any sign of him, or something has happened to him, we will leave."

"I can't just—"

"Promise me, Calen."

"Rist is like my brother, Erik. I can't leave him there. I can't let the empire hurt him. I would rather die."

"I know you would, and that's the problem. What about Dann? Are you going to leave him alone? I need you to use your head, all right? We will do everything we can to find Rist. All I want is for you to understand that might not be possible. We are by your side, Calen. And my father is already going to kill me for letting you run right into the empire's grasp, so please, can we *not* get ourselves killed?"

Calen couldn't help but laugh at that. He couldn't argue with Erik. Nothing the man had said was even close to wrong, though Calen was loath to admit it. "All right. I promise."

Erik reached over, draping his arm over Calen's shoulder. "Good. Now, eat up. That was actually Tarmon's loaf. He's a big man. It's best we don't leave any trace."

Chapter Forty-Eight

A Spider's Web

he bustling Heart of Durakdur was a far cry from what it had been the night Belduar fell. The smell of charred skin and the harsh antiseptic tinge of brimlock sap had been replaced by the warm aroma of fresh bread and the bitter-sweet smell of ale. The dark stains of blood had been scrubbed clean from the stone. The screams and wails of the dying no longer filled the chamber, replaced by the din of the busy crowd pierced by the repetitive clink of hammer against steel sounding from the forge on the far side of the square.

But no matter where Dahlen looked, he could not shake the images of the dead and the dying from his mind. The pictures of men with armour fused to their bones, their skin blackened and crackling, deep visceral howls escaping their throats. Clenching his jaw, he tried to push the thoughts away. He used a trick his father had taught him as a child. '*When everything around you gets to be too much, focus on one thing and only one thing. Give your mind a task.*'

Dahlen closed his eyes and took a deep breath, holding it in his lungs as he cast his eyes around the square. The armourer who ran the forge was reasonably tall for a dwarf – just under five and a half feet. His brow was slick with sweat, and his forearms pulsed with every strike. Dahlen watched as blow after blow dropped on a sheet of plate metal, shaping it. *Clink. Clink. Clink.* He let the sound grow ever louder in his mind, consuming all others, expanding until it was like the beating of a drum resounding through his head. Even his heart thumped to the beat of the hammer. He could feel it, pulsing the blood through his veins with each beat. *Thump. Thump. Thump.*

Releasing the breath and opening his eyes, Dahlen brought his hands to his face, digging his fingers into the corner of his eyes and dragging them back over his face. *Push past it. Death is part of life.*

Pushing the thoughts to the back of his head, Dahlen set off again towards the council chamber. The Heart was a never-ending labyrinth of streets and paths. Each street fed into the next and onward into the next again. None was any wider than another, and everything was angles and sharp corners. It would take no more than five minutes for someone to become completely lost in the maze of stone. But Dahlen had memorised each step. He had spent many days taking notes in his mind on which turn led where and which traders occupied which streets on which days at what times. It had taken a day or two of abstract wandering, but he was confident in his memory. When he was a child, his father always used to test him and Erik with word puzzles or small wooden or metal contraptions. He had always enjoyed them more than Erik had. There was something incredibly satisfying about figuring out the solution to a puzzle.

Dahlen stopped at the third corner before the council chamber, where the carapace trader set up shop every second day. Someone was following him. He was sure of it. "What creature does this belong to?" he asked the trader, running his hand along a chitinous slate of carapace that looked as though it was carved from stone. It felt as rough as it looked.

The trader was a stout dwarf just under five feet with a knotted beard that held a gold ring, along with several silver and copper ones. A long, thin scar ran from his hairline down over his right eye – which was a milky white – and continued down over his chin. "That one is kerathlin hide. Freshly harvested only a few days gone." The dwarf continued pulling different segments of carapace from a chest behind him as he spoke. "Three-to-one gold to hide price in weight that is."

Dahlen glanced down the street as the dwarf spoke, catching sight of someone in a black hooded cloak drifting through the crowd, only stopping at a stall when they noticed Dahlen's stare. "Surely not?"

"Gold is pretty, human. But it doesn't tear the flesh from your bones. You're not just paying for the carapace – you're paying for the blood."

Again, Dahlen ran his hand over the piece of carapace he had no intention of purchasing, pretending to appraise its worth.

"As strong as steel," the dwarf said, his lower lip turning up as though he were impressed by his own tidbit of information. "But light as a feather."

Dahlen hefted the piece of carapace in his hand, gauging its weight. In truth, it did feel a lot lighter than it looked, though that would not matter if an arrow pierced straight through it. "Aye, it's impressive," he said, replacing the piece of kerathlin hide. "I have places to be now, but I may well be back."

The dwarf's face contorted into a frown, his brow furrowing and his mouth twisting at the corners. He narrowed his eyes at Dahlen before giving a gruff nod and returning to pulling more sections of carapace from his chest.

Dahlen continued on, stopping at three more stalls as he made his way down the long street. Each time he stopped, he could feel eyes on him. It could be a coincidence. It was possible, but not probable. Reaching inside his coat, he tapped his finger along the pommel of his knife. Ihvon had insisted he leave his swords in his chambers when he travelled about the cities, and Dahlen understood the reasoning. Between the refugees and the tensions between Daymon and the rulers of the Freehold, the people were already balanced on a knife edge. A foreigner walking about the streets with two swords strapped across his back was only asking for trouble. That didn't mean he couldn't keep a few knives hidden away.

Turning the corner onto a side street, Dahlen slipped the knife from its sheath, still holding it beneath his coat. The flow of people on the side street was less, but it still held too many eyes. He took a few more turns, moving further from the main street, until he could no longer hear the buzz of the stalls and the flower lanterns grew sparse enough that their bluish-green light no longer overlapped.

He turned one more corner, then waited in one of those dark spots, pulling the knife free from his coat. Dahlen slowed his breathing, listening to everything around him, letting the sounds drift on the air. Footsteps. They were soft, barely audible as the shoes connected with the stone. Whoever was following him did not want to be heard.

As the footsteps got closer, Dahlen took a deep breath, clenching his jaw and steadying his hand. Once the silhouette turned the corner, Dahlen lunged, grabbing them by the side of the neck and slamming them against the wall. "Who sent you?" he growled, leaning his weight against the person's body. He ripped the hood from their shoulders and pressed the blade of the knife to their neck.

Almond-shaped blue eyes stared back at him, glistening with fear. Locks of dark hair swept down over her shoulders, and a thin scar ran across her neck from side to side.

"I… What are you? Let me go!" The woman's voice trembled as she spoke, her breaths coming in short bursts.

Dahlen stepped back, more in shock than anything else. "I'm sorry. I thought…" He let his words trail off as the woman took off down the street, not so much as stopping to see if he was following her.

With a breath of relief, Dahlen dropped down to his haunches. His heart pounded, and beads of sweat had formed on his brow. He was sure she had been following him, certain of it. But the fear in her eyes had caught him off guard.

Cursing himself, Dahlen stood up, slipped the knife back into its sheath beneath his coat, and made his way back to the main street. Even as he slipped back into the bustling throng of people, he couldn't shake the tingle that set his hairs on end and the rushing of blood through his veins. He licked his lips as he walked, trying to add a bit of moisture to his throat.

It wasn't long before he found himself standing in front of the enormous building that was the council chamber, with its domed roof, gold-cast doors, and innumerable statues set into alcoves halfway up the walls. But it wasn't those things that caught Dahlen's attention. It was the guards.

When he had first arrived in the Heart, after the Battle of Belduar, and had come to the council chamber, no guards had stood at the golden doors. But now, eight dwarves stood guard – two for each kingdom – flanked by a pair of Daymon's Kingsguard, purple cloaks knotted to their shimmering steel pauldrons.

Each of the dwarves was garbed in heavy, sharp-cut plate armour with cloaks around their shoulders in the colours of their kingdom. Crimson for Durakdur, black with a white trim for Ozryn, green with a silver trim for Azmar, and yellow for the kingdom of Volkur. It said a lot to Dahlen about the current tensions that each of the rulers within the chamber felt the need to post official guards at the entrance to the council chamber.

Just as he was about to rest against a nearby wall and wait, the large golden doors swung open, and Daymon stormed out, Ihvon right behind him. Judging by the scowl on Daymon's face, the talks had not gone well. The two Kingsguard fell in line behind him as he marched from the chamber, his long purple cloak drifting behind him, his crown of winding gold resting atop his furrowed brow. Barely a nod passed in Dahlen's direction as the king stalked past him, his jaw set and face reddened.

"I take it the meeting didn't go well," Dahlen said as Ihvon approached. Though more appropriate for talks with kings and queens than armour, the black and purple doublet the man wore sat strangely on his broad shoulders. It's not as though the clothes he wore would fool anybody as to where his true battlefield lay. That was clear by the twisted flesh that constituted the remnants of his left ear, the numerous scars that adorned his face, and the nose that was so broken it was not sure in which direction it was going.

"As well as any other day," Ihvon replied, burying his fingers into his thick beard, scratching away at the skin underneath. "They bicker amongst themselves as much as anything else, but that is to be expected with dwarves. They have once again denied his request for support to retake the city."

"What of the refugee quarters? The food shortages, the sewage?"

"Those talks were tabled for another time." Ihvon sighed, running his hand through the imaginary hair on his head.

"What? How? The people are suffering now. It doesn't matter if we take the city back if the people are half-starved and ready to rebel."

"I know, Dahlen. I know. He is not thinking straight. He sees enemies around every corner. He spends half his time in the chamber trying to make them trip up over their own words and betray their *true intentions*, which is why we need to find out who truly sent the assassin. We need to end this. Can you meet Belina in the Volkur refugee quarters, at the steps in front of the main square? She left me a note saying she found a lead."

"I can. When?"

"Now."

The refugee quarters in Volkur were much the same as those in Durakdur. A single street over a hundred feet wide stretched off into the mountain as far as the eye could see, and even further still. On either side of the street, rows upon rows of doors were set into the smooth stone walls, rising upward, all the way to the ceiling that stood hundreds of feet overhead. Dahlen would have found it breathtaking if the smell of piss and shit didn't hang so heavy in the air.

Leaning back against the stone steps that sat to the side of the main square, Dahlen interlocked his fingers behind his head and blew out his cheeks. He still wasn't sure if he had made the right choice, choosing to stay instead of joining his father in going after Erik. But he could do more good here, and his brother was in safe hands. *He will be all right.*

Dahlen pulled his hands from behind his head, cracked his neck, and rested his elbows on his knees. He looked out over the throngs of refugees that filled the street. Even from where he sat, Dahlen could feel the anger seething in the city. They wouldn't be able to keep going like this. There had been two more small riots in the last week alone.

"Taking in the sights?"

Dahlen almost jumped out of his skin at the sound of Belina Louna's smooth, velvety voice. "Gods dammit, how do you do that?"

The woman always seemed to appear as if from the shadows themselves.

Pulling her hood down over her shoulders, Belina gave Dahlen a wry smile, her dark eyes watching him intently. "The rabbit should never hear the wolf approach," she said with a wink. "Pleasantries aside, the standing guard has been doubled in both Ozryn and Azmar. The same cannot yet be said of Durakdur or Volkur, but I would say it is only a matter of time. Unrest is bubbling, and it will only take a pinprick to set it off."

Dahlen sighed, leaning forward onto his elbows. "This much we already knew. What else?"

The woman's lips pulled back into a knowing grin. "I have found someone. Someone willing to trade information for coin."

"What kind of information does he have?"

"The kind that could topple a kingdom." Belina got to her feet in one graceful motion, the bottom of her cloak just skirting the ground. "Meet me at The Black Forge in Ozryn when the clock strikes twelve. Our informant will be there."

"Wait, why can't you just—" Belina was gone before Dahlen could finish his sentence, drifting off into the crowd of people that swamped the long street before him. "Why couldn't Ihvon have found somebody a little less dramatic?"

The smell of days-old ale and sweat permeated the air in The Black Forge. The inn was as dark and as dingy as any Dahlen had laid eyes on. Only just enough lanterns of Heraya's Ward hung about to cast the slightest of shadows, and patches of a dark green mould made its home across the stone walls.

Dahlen scanned the room as he pushed his way through the crowd. Two entrances: one behind him and one at the far side of the room, likely leading to a back alley. Long tables of grey stone, with barely an inch of free space on their surfaces, lined the open common room. Each of the benches on either side of the tables were crammed with patrons, squeezed in arse-cheek-to-arse-cheek, empty tankards piled high in front of them. The only sound that pierced through the din of drunken revelry was the melodic song from the other side of the inn.

Reaching the bar, Dahlen ordered an ale from the barkeep, passing him three coppers, then took a deep draught from the tankard. He turned his back to the bar, resting his elbows on the stone counter. "Where is the damned woman?" he whispered, the corner of his mouth twisting into a frown.

He had only met Belina a handful of times, but the woman was just that – a handful. She was always late, spoke in riddles, and rarely gave a straight answer. Dahlen was beginning to think she was more trouble than she was worth, even if she was one of the most beautiful women he had ever laid eyes on. Beauty only got you so far.

Taking another draught of ale, Dahlen shoved his way towards the music, almost spilling the contents of his tankard over the head of a particularly short dwarf who apparently didn't have the patience to wait for him to pass. If he was going to stand around waiting, then he might as well enjoy himself.

It was nearly impossible to see the bard through the dense crowd of patrons. Nothing more than a flash of purple clothing or the wood of the lute through the gaps between people as they shifted. But as he drew closer, the words to the song became clearer.

On darkest nights when the moon lies o'erhead,
On stormy seas when creatures stir beneath,
I'll hold you still, I'll hold you tight.
On darkest nights.
On darkest nights.

The words drifted to the back of Dahlen's mind as he pushed to the front of the crowd that surrounded the bard, and his jaw dropped. There, in a deep purple dress with split skirts, a dark violet colouring on her lips, and a lute in her hands, was Belina.

When shadows come and starlight grows so weary,
When mountains move and oceans they run dry,
I'll hold you still, I'll hold you tight.
On those dark nights.
On those dark nights.

The hair on Dahlen's arms stood on end as Belina finished her song to rapturous applause from the gathered crowd.

"Thank you, thank you," Belina said with a half-bow as she held a long cloth sack out with one hand. The clink of metal rang in Dahlen's ears as the other patrons eagerly emptied their pockets. One dwarf actually stumbled over his own feet, his glassy eyes firmly fixed on Belina, as he made to drop the rest of his ale money into the sack.

Dahlen could already picture the smug look Belina was going to give him when he approached her. *I swear to the gods, she better actually have an informant here. If she brought me to this place just to gloat…*

"Ah, young Virandr. Caught the show, did you?" Belina asked with a grin, tying the drawstrings at the end of the cloth sack that was now so chock-full of coin it looked as though it would burst at the seams.

"I did. It was—"

"Fantastic? Wonderful? The only thing that has caused your heart to skip a beat in the last ten years?"

"I was going to say good."

Belina frowned, pursing her lips together before slipping the lute back into the case that lay on the long table behind her and clicking the latches closed. "You're just like your father, you know that?"

"You know my father?"

"I dare say I have known him longer than you have. I doubt I was the only person to receive his letter this past month."

Aeson had sent letters by hawk from The Travellers Rest in Camylin a few months ago. Dahlen was aware of what the letters said, but not to whom they were sent. *"The people who can light the spark"*, was all his father had said. Taking a step outside himself, Dahlen cast his gaze over Belina. Was she someone who could 'light the spark'?

At first glance, she was a beautiful woman with short black hair, dark skin, and gleaming eyes. In her long purple dress, most men wouldn't look far past her beauty, but Dahlen did. He looked into her eyes. His father had always said that at the right moment, you can learn everything you need to know about a person through their eyes. Belina's eyes were hard, her stare unyielding as she looked right back at him.

"Did your father tell you to look into my eyes?"

Dahlen gave a start at the sound of Belina's voice, taking an involuntary step backward.

"He always did blabber on about people's eyes. Good to see the years haven't changed him. Where is he, by the way?"

The woman was relentless; nothing seemed to faze her.

"He's um…"

"He's 'um' what?" Belina leaned in a little closer, raising an eyebrow.

Dahlen's words caught in his throat, and beads of sweat formed on his brow. He was beginning to understand why the woman had received one of his father's letters.

Belina sighed. "Oh, you're no fun. Come, our contact is over there in the corner booth." Slinging her lute case over her shoulder, Belina extended a slender finger towards a stone table set into a corner that Dahlen hadn't noticed when he had entered the inn.

"Let me do the talking," Belina said as she and Dahlen pushed their way through the crowd. More than once, she was forced to stop as men all but drooled on her, telling her how beautiful she was, dropping coins in her hand.

"I have a free room upstairs," a particularly tall man said as he dropped a coin into Belina's hand. He had a scrawny figure with a thick head of curly hair and a reasonably handsome face. "There's more coin where that came from if you—"

Dahlen grimaced as Belina caught the man with a swift knee between the legs. Judging by the twisted agony on his face, she caught him hard.

"Touch me again," she said, patting the man on the side of the cheek as he bent over double, "and I'll burst them open."

Interlocking her hands around the back of the man's head, Belina swung her knee again, so quickly it was barely even a flash. A shiver ran down Dahlen's spine as he heard the crunch of the man's nose and blood sprayed out over the ground.

"Come on," Belina said, pushing Dahlen in the shoulder as she stepped away from the scene as though nothing had happened while a group of men and dwarves crowded around the man who lay rolling on the ground.

Dahlen went to say something, glanced back at the man who held his balls in one hand and his nose in the other, then thought better of it.

The dwarf who sat at the table looked as jittery as a child who had stolen their father's coin purse. Dahlen would know. He was young. At least, he looked young. It was always hard to tell with dwarves. They seemed to come out of the womb with beards down past their chests. But his eyes held a youthfulness, and a distinct lack of rings decorated the dark beard that obscured the majority of his face. That, added to the tremor that ran down his hand and the skittish way his eyes darted around the room before finally settling on Belina and Dahlen, pointed towards his few years. From what Dahlen had learned, most dwarves lived to see just over a hundred summers, or cycles, as they called them, seeing as they never experienced seasons down here below the mountains.

"Jorah. It is good to see you," Belina said, bending down and placing a soft kiss on the dwarf's cheek before taking a seat on the opposite side of the table. "This," she said, gesturing towards Dahlen, "is Dahlen Virandr. He will be joining us today."

"Blessed be The Smith," Jorah said, swallowing hard in between breaths.

"Blessed be The Smith," Dahlen responded, narrowing his eyes as he sat down beside Belina. He wasn't sure if he had ever seen someone as jumpy as the dwarf who sat before him. But he kept his mouth closed, as Belina had asked.

"So, down to business," Belina said, leaning forward towards Jorah, lowering her voice. "Jorah here is an apprentice blacksmith. Aren't you, Jorah?"

The dwarf nodded, a slight tremble in his breathing.

"Why would an apprentice blacksmith—"

"Ah!" Belina cut across Dahlen, raising a finger to her lips.

Dahlen frowned, clicking his tongue. But he kept his mouth shut.

"Excuse me." A young woman stood beside the table, a white apron draped over the front of a dark brown dress with white frills at the bottom of the skirts. She wore a white neckerchief decorated with yellow flowers, her dark hair was tied up in a bun, and she held a wooden tray in her left hand with three tankards atop it. Dahlen couldn't make out much of her face, though. It was difficult in the dim bluish-green flowerlight. "The… ehm, the man over there by the bar bought you these."

The young woman glanced over her shoulder at the man Belina had kneed in the groin. He stood at the bar talking to another man, streaks of blood running down from his nostrils.

"Never say no to a free drink," Belina said, reaching for the tankards.

"Please, allow me." The young woman placed a tankard each in front of Dahlen and Belina before dropping the third down in front of Jorah, giving a slight curtsy, and then disappearing off into the crowd of patrons.

"Well, that is the most unexpected result of kicking somebody in the balls I think I've ever come across."

Dahlen only gave a half nod of agreement as he stared after the young serving girl. Something was niggling at the back of his mind, but he wasn't sure what it was. It danced just out of reach, taunting him.

"Jorah, please continue."

"Well, ehm… The orders for armour and weapons have trebled in the past few weeks. We can barely get them out fast enough. I've heard it's the same in Azmar. There are even rumours that some of the forges in Azmar are burning every waking hour."

Dahlen made the mistake of going to speak, only for Belina to tilt her head to the side and raise a dark eyebrow. She looked back to Jorah, motioning her hand for him to keep talking.

"I'm not sure what it's for," Jorah said, looking at Dahlen, "but I've heard things… I…" The dwarf swallowed, letting out a huff of air. "I'm sorry, I'm not usually this nervous, but I just—"

"It's all right, drink up." Belina put her hands around the back of Jorah's mug, lifting it to his mouth. "Ale will settle the nerves. We're in no rush."

The dwarf nodded as he took a deep draught of the ale, placing the empty tankard on the table and letting out a short breath. "When I was on my way home from the forge, I overheard two people talking on the walkway above me. It was late, and most of the walkways were empty, so their voices carried. I wasn't even going to stop, but then I heard them talking about…" Jorah leaned back a bit, his head darting around the room as though every set of eyes in the inn were now on him. He scratched at his throat and ran his tongue over his dry lips. He leaned in, dropping his chin down so it almost scraped the stone table, his voice barely even a whisper. "The assassination of the king from Belduar."

Dahlen frowned, turning his gaze to Belina. "This is the big news? They already tried that."

Before Belina could respond, Jorah cut across. "What?" His eyes were nearly bulging out of his head. "I didn't… when? This was only last night."

Dahlen froze. Every hair on his body pricked up, and a ball of lead dropped into his stomach. "Last night? Did they mention any names? Jorah, who ordered it?"

"They said…" If the dwarf had seemed nervous before, he now looked as though he were going to empty the contents of his stomach across the table. Sweat dripped from his brow, and red streaks snaked through the whites of his eyes. "I… something doesn't feel—" With a sudden lurch the dwarf spat blood out over the table, his hands coming up to his throat.

"What in the gods?" Dahlen jumped backwards, trying to avoid the spray of blood that splattered across the table.

"Poison," Belina hissed, leaping from the seat quicker than Dahlen would have thought possible, reaching her hand behind the dwarf's head. "Jorah, Jorah. Speak to me."

The only sound that came from the dwarf's throat was a spluttering gurgle as the blood entered his lungs. Dahlen had seen it once before when his father had brought him and Erik to Falstide. That man had been dead within minutes, just as Jorah would be. It was at that moment he realised what had been niggling at the back of his mind. The serving girl. He'd recognised her. The girl with the black cloak who had followed him through the streets in Durakdur. The neckerchief covered up the scar on her neck.

Pulling himself to his feet, Dahlen pushed through the crowd, his eyes scanning every face he passed for a glimpse of the girl. A few of the nearby patrons had rushed over to the table, screaming and gasping in shock, but most of them had yet to notice what had happened. They simply continued on, drinking themselves into a stupor, howling and cheering as they wrapped their arms around each other, dancing to the beat of the bard who had replaced Belina.

Where are you? Where are you?

"Move," he grunted, shoving his way past two elves who looked to be having an intense staring contest. But before he could take a step further, his entire body froze as though the air itself was holding him in place. Panic twisted his way through his stomach. He couldn't move anything. Not his arms, his legs, not even his neck.

"Do they not teach you manners wherever it is you are from?" One of the two elves Dahlen had pushed past now stood in front of him, half bent over, his eyes level with Dahlen's. His coal-black hair, straight as a razor, stopped just short of his shoulders, and his sharp eyes shimmered with a golden hue – like Alea and Lyrei's. His stare sent a shiver down Dahlen's spine. It was cold, calculating. Dahlen could smell the liquor on the elf's breath.

"Let him go, Saleas. This instant!" The other elf now stood beside his companion, hands on his hips and fury carved into his brow. "You know we can't use the Spark like that here. We'll be tossed out come morning."

The black-haired elf – Saleas – stood back to his full height, his jaw clenched. He clicked his tongue off the roof of his mouth, his stare lingering on Dahlen. "Fine."

As the elf spoke, Dahlen felt the force holding him in place dissipate, like vines retreating into the ground. Just as he regained his sense of feeling, Saleas turned to him, a slender finger poking at his chest. "Say *excuse me* next time. Have some manners."

Dahlen's fingers clenched into a fist, and he had to forcefully bite down on the corners of his tongue as the two elves walked away into the crowd, muttering about 'idiot children'. There were very few things in the world that lit a fury in Dahlen like the helplessness of having the Spark used on him. It wasn't right.

Not now. There are more important things. The girl is clearly not here, but which door did she leave through?

Flipping a coin in his head, Dahlen made for the back door. Fifty-fifty chance.

Pushing open the heavy wooden door at the back of the common room, Dahlen stepped out into the dimly lit alley behind The Black Forge. He still hadn't gotten used to the lack of day and night in the dwarven kingdoms. The abundance of clocks was the only thing that stopped him from going completely insane, but it was no true substitute for seeing the sun rise and set.

Reaching into his coat, Dahlen pulled the knife from its loop on his belt, his fingers wrapped around the smooth ash wood handle, feeling the cold touch of steel at its pommel. The alley stretched as far as the eye could see in either direction, backing onto an innumerable number of buildings on either side. It was lined with crates, casks, and small flower lanterns that sat in widely spaced alcoves along the walls.

"Dammit." Dahlen kicked out at bits of stone on the ground. He had lost her. Slipping his knife back into his belt loop, he ran his fingers through his hair, digging the tips into his scalp. He'd had her in his hands in Durakdur, and he let her go. How had he been so naïve?

The slightest of sounds drifted into his ear – a boot shifting over small stones and dust. It was followed by the slicing of steel through air, but Dahlen had already moved by the time it had *whizzed* past where his head had been and clinked off the wall. A small steel knife, top weighted, with a finger ring at the end.

Dahlen dove to the ground as two more knives sliced through the darkness, clinking off the cold stone wall behind him. Rolling to his feet, he pulled his knife from his belt loop. Flipping the handle around, Dahlen pulled the knife into reverse grip – he needed the blade between him and whoever hid in the shadows. His heart beat with slow, methodical thumps as he ducked behind a stack of crates, purposely slowing his breaths.

Dahlen pulled a coin from his pocket, running his fingers over its rounded edges. Releasing a soft puff of air, he tossed the coin against the far wall, hearing the clink as it connected. It was followed by a sharp crack as the blade of another knife was launched towards the sound.

It's now or never. Dahlen tightened his grip around the hilt of the knife and leapt out from behind the crates. A glint of steel shimmered in the flowerlight from the lanterns as the woman charged at him, a black hood now obscuring her face and a cloak fluttering behind her. He caught her first strike between the blade and the cross guard of his knife, just managing to turn the full force of it away. But she kept coming, lunging, stabbing. She was as relentless as she was skilled. Whatever fear she had feigned on the street in Durakdur, she was no stranger to a blade. No stranger to death.

They exchanged blows for what felt like minutes, but in reality was probably only seconds. Dahlen gritted his teeth as her blade sliced a thin gash along the side of his arm, his swift movement the only reason the steel didn't cut any deeper. He cursed himself for listening to Ihvon and leaving his two swords in his chambers.

The alleyway was narrow. She couldn't manage full swings of the blade. He needed to use that to his advantage. He pulled in tighter to her, closing the distance between them. As she brought her blade up into a swing, Dahlen blocked her arm with his elbow before driving his knife into her chest. The woman howled as he dragged the blade free, blood flowing as he plunged the steel back up through her neck.

She stumbled backwards, blood pouring down over her chest, hands clasped around the hilt of the knife. Dahlen watched as she collapsed on the ground, spluttering and choking, coughing up splatters of blood. There was nothing he could do. He knelt beside her as the light went out in her eyes. He took no pleasure in death, but it was something he had become accustomed to. Wrapping his fingers around the wooden handle of the knife, he pulled it free of the woman's neck, wiping off the blood against her cloak and sliding it back into the sheath on his belt.

Letting out a sigh, Dahlen cast his eyes over the woman, running his left hand through his hair. Whoever she was, she knew what she was doing.

Best get to it.

He only found four things on the woman's body: a coin purse, a small piece of paper folded over four times, an empty glass vial, and a solid black obsidian coin with a hole at the centre.

"Dammit."

Dahlen jumped at the sound of Belina's voice. He had not even heard the door to the alleyway opening. "How do you keep doing that?" He let out a sigh, shaking his head. "Jorah?"

"Dead. Just like her. Did she say anything?"

"We didn't exactly have a chat. But I did find these." Dahlen handed the contents of the woman's pockets to Belina, raising a curious eyebrow.

Pulling the small cork from the tip of the empty vial, Belina took one sniff, recoiled, scrunching up her nose, then replaced the cork. "Nightfire," she said, slipping the vial into her pocket. "Nasty stuff."

"Gods dammit. We've got nothing now. She was our only lead." Dahlen let out a sigh of frustration as he dropped back onto his arse, letting his back rest against the stone wall.

"Why did you kill her, then?"

"I didn't mean—" Dahlen stopped at the smirk on Belina's face. The woman delighted in twisting his emotions.

"You're too easy," she said with a laugh. "Anyway, we don't need her."

"We don't?"

"We don't."

Dahlen pulled himself to his feet, lifting one eyebrow. "Are you going to tell me why?"

"Oh, well this coin is a marker of the Thieves Guild here in the Freehold, which raises a few more questions."

"Thieves Guild? That is actually a thing?"

"I know," Belina replied with a shrug. "A bit on the nose, right? Either way, she is not a member of the guild. She is just using them."

"And you know this how?"

"Because," she said, holding up the piece of paper Dahlen had found in the woman's cloak pocket. "I know where she was going next."

"How? From that piece of paper? It's just a bunch of old runes."

"It's an encryption used by the Hand. It needs a cypher."

"The Hand? Why would—Wait, how do you know that cypher?"

"We've all made our mistakes."

Ihvon sat with his back firmly pressed into the leather chair at the corner of Daymon's chambers, watching the king pace back and forth across the room as he had done for the better part of an hour. Although Ihvon's face portrayed a sense of unperturbed calm, his stomach was a bundle of twisted knots. It was not easy for him, seeing Daymon like this.

"They're planning to kill me, Ihvon. How can you not see that?"

It was difficult for Ihvon to truly argue. Someone *had* tried to kill Daymon, and they would most likely try again. Ihvon had no doubt it was one of the dwarves. It was precisely the dirty, underhanded kind of manoeuvre their kind favoured. But he didn't think the kingdoms were working together. They rarely agreed at the best of times. No, it was most likely one of them acting alone. The piece of the puzzle that didn't fit, however, was how killing Daymon would benefit any of them. Hopefully he would know more when Dahlen got back. Though he should have been back already.

What concerned Ihvon more was how completely the paranoia had consumed Daymon.

"My king, I am looking into it as we speak. Leave this matter to me. I will come to the bottom of it. I swear it on my honour."

"Someone is trying to kill me, and you wish me to simply leave it be?" Daymon's voice held a rage that Ihvon knew had been bubbling for a while. He needed to be careful.

"No, my king. I wish you to allow me to protect you."

"The way you protected my father?" Daymon shouted, his face turning a deep red.

Something inside Ihvon snapped. He dragged himself out of the chair, grasped Daymon's collar in both hands, and slammed him against the bookcase that stood against the wall. "Your father was my closest friend. He was a damn good king and an even better man. And he would be ashamed of you!" Ihvon pulled Daymon away from the bookcase, feeling the rough fabric of the king's collar grate against his knuckles, then pushed him back against the wooden frame. "Your people starve and live in squalor while you worry about your own life. You are a king, Daymon. Your needs come second. Your people come first. Did you learn nothing from your father?"

Ihvon's hands trembled as he held Daymon in place, the colour draining from his fingers that gripped the young king's collar. His blood pumped so fiercely through his veins that the pressure in his head dulled all sound to a low throbbing.

Daymon didn't speak. He simply stared at Ihvon, his face expressionless. He didn't fight back. He didn't yell or scream.

"I miss him, Ihvon." A tear rolled down Daymon's cheek and in that moment Ihvon saw the boy he had watched grow up. The boy he had orphaned with his deeds. The boy he would die for.

"I do too," Ihvon said, wrapping his arms around Daymon and pulling him into a tight embrace. "I do too."

Chapter Forty-Nine

Den of Wolves

ahlen pulled the black hooded cloak tighter around himself, the light shirt of chainmail clinking as he rolled his shoulders back and forth. He and Belina stood in the dark alley just around the corner from the meeting place marked out in the assassin's note: an inn in the kingdom of Azmar. "Tell me again why it has to be *me* who does this?"

"Because they would recognise me," Belina said, her dismissive tone suggesting Dahlen's question was a stupid one. "Never mind that I used to be one of them, but you don't see many Narvonans around here, do you? I stick out like a sore thumb."

Dahlen sighed, giving a nod of acquiescence. "Does Ihvon know you used to be a Hand assassin? Does my father know?"

"What do you think? And what does it matter? You kill people. You killed that girl. Why is your blade more noble than mine?" Belina's eyes stayed level with Dahlen's as she spoke, her left eyebrow raised and her hands folded firmly across her chest.

"I didn't mean… I—"

"I'm only trying to make you sweat," Belina said with a wink, her lips curling into a grin. "Of course, they know. I've tried to kill them enough times."

"You what?"

"Not anymore, clearly."

Dahlen stared at the woman in disbelief. Her personality seemed to flip like two sides of a coin. One minute she was as serious as his father, eyes cold and back rigid, the next she was laughing and winking. He had never found someone so difficult to work out. He couldn't even tell how many summers she had seen. Might have been thirty, might have been forty.

"What are you staring at?"

"Nothing," Dahlen said with a laugh. "I'm just trying to figure you out." Dahlen jerked backwards in surprise as the woman burst out laughing hysterically. "Be quiet! What if someone hears us?"

"Oh, I can't stop laughing if you keep telling jokes," she said, holding her hand over her stomach, still chuckling. "Smarter men than you have tried to 'figure me out'. I'll give you a tip – don't. You're not my type anyway. I like a more… *feminine* touch." Belina winked as she said the word 'feminine', as though she thought Dahlen wouldn't pick up on the not-so-subtle emphasis she placed on the word as she spoke.

"What? No… I didn't mean… Gods damn you."

"Come on, lover boy. Let's get back to what we came here for."

Dahlen glared at her, pushing his tongue against the roof of his mouth as he exhaled through his nose. The woman was worse than Dann. He would love to see them both in the same room.

"Now," Belina said, holding up the obsidian coin. It held a smooth edge with a hole at the centre and a thin line that ran around its entire circumference. "This is a mark. Anyone holding one of these will be let into a den. Just show it to the innkeeper, and they will show you the way."

"Is this a good idea? Should we not go back to Ihvon first and tell him what we've just discovered? I mean, The Hand are here, in the Freehold. How? And are they working with one of the dwarven rulers? There are too many unknowns, Belina."

Belina bit the corner of her lip, taking a moment to respond. "The most likely answer is that they snuck onto one of the Wind Runners during the evacuation. They could have been in Belduar ever since the Fade's attack. But that's why we're here, to find out."

"I don't know, maybe we—"

"We don't have time for this. We need to do this now."

Dahlen closed his eyes and let out a sigh. "All right, but won't they be expecting a woman to return?"

"Not necessarily. Often the Hand sends multiple assassins to do a job, particularly if the success rate could be considered low. So, you should be fine."

"Should?"

"Should," Belina repeated with a shrug.

Dahlen again narrowed his eyes at Belina, shaking his head in disbelief.

"What? I can't rightly make that promise, can I? At least I'm being honest. Look, in this particular case, whoever placed the contract had another task after the poisoning. We want to find out what that task is."

Dahlen nodded, going through everything in his head. No matter what way he played it, the whole thing seemed like a stupid idea. But they had no other options. Daymon's paranoia grew with every passing day, and tensions with the dwarves were not getting any better. There was something going on behind the scenes, and if they didn't stop it, there would be blood spilt. A lot of it. "Okay, do I need a password or anything?"

Belina looked at him like he was an idiot. "A password? Are you serious? Go. Get out of my sight before I slap you." She pushed Dahlen out of the alley and into the main street. "Keep your head, get the information, get out. Understood?"

Dahlen clenched his jaw and gave a short nod, pulling the black hood over his head and turning towards the inn that had been named in the note, The Cloak and Dagger. *Very subtle.*

He could hear Belina muttering behind him as he walked towards the inn. "A password? A gods damned password?"

Outside, the inn looked much the same as any he had seen in the Dwarven Freehold. Grey stone, clean angles, and sharp cuts. Even on the inside, it was not much different from The Black Forge – if a little cleaner perhaps, with less mould. Just like The Black Forge, it was crammed with patrons: dwarves, elves, and humans. Though Dahlen had quickly learned that any elves in the

Freehold, and most humans outside of the refugee quarters, were mages on the run from the empire. A shiver ran down his spine at the thought that most of the humans and elves in The Cloak and Dagger were mages. If even a tenth of them had the power the Lorian Battlemages held, this many of them in one place was a terrifying notion.

Pushing his fear into a small compartment at the back of his mind, Dahlen worked his way through the crowd, careful to be a little bit gentler than he had been in The Black Forge. The last thing he needed was one of the mages deciding to start a fight. Most of them, however, took one look at the black hooded cloak and got straight out of his way. Anyone could buy a black hooded cloak and wear it around, but Dahlen supposed these particular patrons were well used to seeing members of the Thieves Guild, or maybe even the Hand, walk through their doors. Probably better to simply assume and play it safe.

The innkeeper was a stout dwarf with a head of thinning hair, a pot belly, a thick knotted black beard, and a greasy apron draped over a bare chest. The dwarf's physique didn't fool Dahlen. Thick calluses were built up on his knuckles, the exposed parts of his chest were marred by a plethora of mottled scars, his nose was too bent to not have been broken, and six small burn marks ran down the side of his neck that were too precise to have been anything but torture.

"Ale?" Dahlen asked, placing his hand on the wooden bar top.

The innkeeper grunted before grabbing a tankard, filling it from the large cask behind him, and placing it down in front of Dahlen.

Dahlen nodded and dropped some coins into the dwarf's open hand. A look of recognition glittered in the innkeeper's eyes as he looked down to find three coppers and an obsidian mark with a hollow centre staring back at him.

The dwarf narrowed his eyes, his gaze lingering on Dahlen for a moment or two before he passed back the obsidian mark, nodded for him to follow, and came out from behind the bar. The innkeeper didn't say a word as he shoved his way through the crowd, being far less careful than Dahlen had been. He brought Dahlen over to a wooden door set into the far wall, slotted a thick iron key into the lock, pushed open the door, and grunted for Dahlen to follow.

The room was small, maybe twenty feet long and ten wide. The musty smell of damp and mould hung in the air, so palpable Dahlen could taste it at the back of his throat. A heavyset table of solid stone occupied the room's centre, while shelves of spirits and liquor ran along the far wall from top to bottom. Besides a few old paintings, nothing hung on the wall. In truth, the 'den' was rather unimpressive and, honestly, a little bit depressing.

The dwarf turned to Dahlen, raising one eyebrow as a silence hung in the air. *Shit. Is he expecting me to do something?*

Dahlen did his best to conceal the panic that tangled in his gut. He nodded his head, gesturing for the man to continue ahead.

The innkeeper grunted, his broken nose flaring as he carried on into the room.

"He will be with you soon," the innkeeper said, turning to Dahlen, his voice sounding as though he had spent his entire childhood gargling rocks. The dwarf walked over to a painting of a large dwarven woman that hung on the wall at the right side of the room and, to Dahlen's surprise, placed the palm of his hand over the artwork and pressed down. As he did, the painting itself depressed into the wall while the frame remained in place. The painting stopped after moving inward about an inch and was followed by a loud click. Dahlen couldn't hear the gears turning, but he could feel them. A low vibration resonated through the stone beneath his feet. Another series of clicks followed the vibration, and a slab of stone that sat beneath the table moved out of place. Lines in the shape of a long rectangle were now visible in what had once been a uniform floor of solid stone.

Dahlen watched, trying his best to keep his mouth from gaping, as the slab of stone dropped out of place and receded into the floor behind it, revealing a long stone staircase that travelled down beneath the inn. An orange glow cast a dim light across the bottom of the steps.

"I need to get back to the bar," the innkeeper said, his voice wrought with impatience, gesturing towards the newly revealed stairwell.

Dahlen nodded, his exterior calm never betraying his interior reluctance. Nothing about that stairwell looked inviting. Once he went down there, he was trapped. *You don't have a choice.*

Again pushing his fear to the back of his mind, Dahlen stepped into the stairwell. The slab of stone moved back into place above his head as he made his way down, the click of his boots on the steps resounding in his ear.

If Dahlen had been surprised by the room upstairs, he was even more so by this new one, and for very different reasons. The den was enormous. It mirrored the length and breadth of the inn above almost exactly, but with far fewer people. None, to be precise. The entire floor was covered with a dark hardwood that did not give even the slightest of creaks as Dahlen brought his weight down upon it. Tapestries of silk and cloth adorned the walls, coloured in vibrant reds, purples, and golds, very clearly crafted by the finest weavers in Vaerleon – Dahlen had spent enough time in the city to know the markers. The chairs and couches were upholstered with an assortment of fine leathers and a deep crimson velvet, all held in place with gold pins. The tables were built from planks of solid oak, and a huge shelving unit covered the entirety of the left wall, stretching over a hundred feet. It was not dissimilar to a bookcase, but instead of books, it held large iron-banded chests with thick heavy locks.

Past the initial 'antechamber', he supposed was the word, though it was far too large to fit that definition, the room was segmented off into multiple nooks, framed by walls of stone adjoined by curtain rails that Dahlen figured offered seclusion for 'discussing business'. Each nook held a low stone table framed by leather couches on either side. A tall flask of clear crystal filled with a golden-brown liquid sat at the centre of each table, two glasses of the same crystal at its side.

But what really caught Dahlen's attention was the source of the orange glow. Small, brass oil lamps were set into the walls all around, their naked flames protected by chimneys of clear glass flecked with black marks. He had grown so accustomed to the bluish-green light of the Heraya's Ward illuminating the city that firelight seemed almost odd. Open flames were banned in the Freehold, save for forges and kitchens. Though, Dahlen supposed, it wasn't as if the people who owned this den abided by any other laws – it would be strange if they adhered to just that particular one. The entire den was a shrine to abundance and greed.

Rolling back his shoulders and letting out a sigh, Dahlen stepped further into the room, past the tapestries and velvet-covered couches, towards the nooks at the back of the room. He needed to look as though he knew what he was doing, as though this wasn't his first time.

He walked past the first two nooks before stepping into the third one on the left and dropping himself onto the leather couch. He shuffled his arse a bit, trying to force the stiff leather to yield to him without much success. He eyed the bottle of golden liquid for a moment – it must have been some spirit or liqueur – but he left it be, unsure as to what the etiquette was.

It wasn't long before he heard the stone slab opening at the top of the staircase, followed by footsteps against the stairs that dissipated once whoever it was reached the wooden floorboards. Dahlen's heart raged like a tempest in his chest, beating and hammering, sending blood surging through his veins. His mouth felt dry, and his chest fluttered with every breath. Put him on his two feet with a sword in his hand and tell him to charge – not a problem. But sitting on that couch with nothing but a knife at his belt, pretending to be somebody he was not? This was an entirely different breed of fear. One he was not familiar with.

Dahlen didn't turn his head as a hooded figure moved in the corner of his eye and then dropped themselves down on the couch opposite.

"It is done?" The voice belonged to a man, but his accent was hard to determine, masked by too many years of smoking tabbac.

Dahlen simply nodded in return.

"Good." The man reached up, drawing back his hood. His hair was grey, almost white, and tied into a tight ponytail. Furrows of time creased his brow and dug into the corner of his eyes. He must have seen at least sixty summers by Dahlen's reckoning, probably more. Despite his age, the man's frame was that of a warrior: broad shoulders, layered muscle on his arms and chest, and a bitter look in his eyes. "We will drink to that. Now that the path has been covered, the second step can be taken."

The man reached over the table and picked up the crystal flask. Removing the stopper from the top, he poured two hefty measures of the spirit into the crystal glasses. "Drifaienin whiskey," he said with a smile. "We're the only providers of it here."

Dahlen picked up his cup, narrowing his eyes at the mellow liquid within.

"To the second step," the man said, holding his glass in the air.

"To the second step." Dahlen clinked his glass off the man's before they both emptied their cups in one mouthful. "I—"

A piercing pain split through Dahlen's head as the other man smashed the crystal glass over his head. Dahlen swayed, his vision blurry, blood streaming into his eyes. His head spinning, he fell from the couch, collapsing onto the floor. He tried to get to his feet but stumbled almost instantly. Something hit him in the gut, causing him to wretch uncontrollably. *Stand up. Fight back.*

Dahlen dug his fingers into the creases of his eyes, blinking furiously as he did, trying to get the blood out of his vision. But as he stood back to his full height, a weight hit him in the chest and sent him sprawling to the ground. A flash of pain burst through him as his back collided with the floor. His head pounded with a fury, and his vision was still clouded with blood and spots of colour.

Dahlen howled as the man dropped down onto his chest and drove a knife into his right shoulder without a moment's hesitation. With a flash of steel, the man pulled a second knife from his coat, a sharp pain letting Dahlen know the blade was pressed against his neck.

"How are you stupid enough to just walk in here?" the man said, a perplexed look on his face. "Honestly, that was one of the stupidest decisions I've seen anyone make. You killed Clara, I take it? Unfortunate. She was effective. Did she speak? Obviously not, you didn't have a clue what you were doing here." The man shrugged. "Enough talk. May Heraya harbour your soul."

Dahlen swung his arm up, aiming a strike at the man's jaw, but he was still weak from the earlier blow to his head, and the man caught his wrist with ease. Still holding the knife, the man punched Dahlen in the face, sending stars flitting across his eyes. But just as he pulled his arm back to deliver the final blow, a shadow flashed over them and something crashed into the man's head, knocking him to the ground.

Blood still streaming into his eyes, Dahlen scrambled backwards on his elbows, just catching sight of Belina as she bounded past him, a long metal staff in her hands.

The man on the floor groaned, swaying from side to side as he pulled himself onto his hands and knees. A swift boot in the face from Belina sent him crashing down onto his back, a spray of blood splattering across the floor. Reaching down, she dragged the man to his feet by the scruff of his neck, slamming him into the stone walls that framed one of the nooks. She held him there, tilting her head to follow the sway of his, looking into his eyes. "Still awake," she muttered, before stretching her palm over his face and slamming his head back into the wall. His body went limp, dropping with a crash to the floor, blood seeping from the back and side of his head.

"What…" Dahlen stopped mid-sentence as he pulled himself to his feet, his fingers running over a ridged cut at the side of his head where the shattered crystal had sliced into his skin. "What are you doing here?"

"Well, I came to save you, of course." Belina shrugged, lodging her hands underneath the unconscious man's armpits. He was alive, but just barely. Dahlen could see the shallow rise and fall of his chest.

"But how did you… You said they wouldn't expect anything. You said they wouldn't have known who she was. He knew her by name!"

"Yeah, I lied. Sorry. Can you help me with him? He's rather heavy."

"You lied?" Dahlen bit his teeth down into the sides of his tongue, stilling the ball of anger that was forming in his chest. "You mean you let me walk in here knowing this would happen?"

"Absolutely not," Belina said, her eyes widening in shock as the man hung limp from her shoulder. Then, she shrugged. "I had no way of knowing they wouldn't just kill you straight away. You got a chatty one. I'll never understand the chatty ones. Just kill your mark. Something always goes wrong when you talk to them."

Dahlen was so taken aback by Belina's candour that he just stood there staring at her, mouth agape. "Why? Why did you send me down here, knowing—"

Tilting her head back, Belina let out a heavy sigh. "Will you stop being a child and help me lift this lug into a nook? You killed our only lead. This was our last way to get a new one. Somebody had to risk it, and it wasn't going to be me. Did I or did I not save you?"

"How did you even get in here? You said they would recognise you!"

"Faruk owed me a favour," Belina said, her face showing strain as she dragged the man's unconscious body over to the nook where Dahlen had been sitting. "Still does, actually. Always gets himself into trouble."

"You know what? Fuck it." Dahlen reached down, grabbed the man's legs, and lifted them up into the air. There was simply no time to try and rationalise anything Belina said. The woman wasn't right in the head. "Where do you want him?"

"On the table, if you please," Belina said, a beaming grin on her face.

With the man's legs grasped firmly in his hands, Dahlen backed into the nook. He dropped himself down onto the leather couch at the same time as he let go of the man's legs.

"Ahh," Dahlen groaned, touching his fingers to the cut at the side of his head. Most of the blood had turned tacky in his hair and dried to the side of his face, but a trickle of fresh crimson still seeped from the cut.

"Why do you keep touching it?" Belina shook her head as she let go of the man's torso, letting it drop onto the stone table with a thud. "Now we just have to wake him up and ask him who hired him and who the next target is."

"And he will just tell us?"

Belina shrugged again. She seemed to do a lot of shrugging. "He will if he wants to die quickly. Oh, don't look at me like that. You can't let men like this live. They will come after you, kill you in your sleep, and leave your ghost ruing your bad choices."

Dahlen went to argue, but he found himself unable to see a flaw in her logic. That didn't mean he agreed with her, he just couldn't argue with her.

A loud slap drew Dahlen out of his own thoughts. "What are you—"

Slap. Belina's hand cracked against the man's face, barely even earning a groan for her efforts.

Slap. She managed to get a groan that time, but that was it.

"Hand me the whiskey." She reached out her hand, raising one eyebrow for Dahlen to pass her the flask of whiskey from the nook opposite them.

Just the sight of the crystal flask sent a sharp pain through the side of Dahlen's head. Shaking the thought from his mind, he shuffled over to the end of the couch, got to his feet, and snatched up the flask of whiskey.

"Here," he said, handing Belina the flask. "What are you going to do?"

Belina pulled the stopper from the whiskey with a practised familiarity, took a long swig of it herself, then proceeded to empty the entire contents of the flask over the man's face.

The man jerked awake, spluttering and coughing as he choked on the harsh spirit. As he sprang up, Belina cracked him in the nose with her fist, spraying blood across her knuckles. "No, no, don't go back asleep on me now," she said, slapping him repeatedly on either side of the face.

"Good. Eyes front." Quicker than Dahlen's eyes could follow, the woman pulled a knife from within her dress and held it against the man's throat. "Not nice, is it?" she turned to Dahlen, a cheeky grin on her face. "See, I've got your back," she said with a wink.

She is crazy. She is genuinely crazy.

"Now," Belina said, pressing the blade of the knife against the man's neck just hard enough to call forth a thin stream of blood that rolled down the side of his neck and onto the table. "I'm going to ask very nicely at first. If you don't tell me what I want to know, then I won't be very nice. If you tell me what I want to know, I'll let you go. Understood?"

"Fuck you." The man leaned his neck into the blade and spat a ball of phlegm mottled with flecks of blood at Belina, catching her in the cheek.

Dahlen grimaced. Assassin or no, the man had no idea who he was dealing with.

With a disconcerting chuckle, Belina tilted her head and used the fingers of her left hand to scoop the phlegm from her face, flicking it onto the ground. "Okay," she said, the corners of her mouth turning upward. "*That* was honesty. We're off to a good start." Belina punched the man in the face once more. Blood burst from his nose and lip, and the back of his head bounced off the table. She pushed the knife back up against his throat. "But don't do that again. Now, who raised the contract on King Daymon?"

"If you think I'm—" *Crack*. Belina's fist flashed. The man's head bounced off the table.

"What did I say? I'm not going to be nice much longer."

This was her being nice? Dahlen shuddered at the thought of what Belina being cruel would look like. He didn't think it was something he would have the stomach to see. Taking a life in the heat of battle was one thing. But torture? Slowly causing pain in cold blood? That was something entirely different. Something that just didn't sit right in his bones, no matter what convoluted, emotionally devoid reason Belina gave.

"I'll ask you again, who raised the contract?"

"It was…" A hesitancy flickered in the man's eyes as he glanced down at the blade pressed against his neck. "It was the—"

The man wailed in pain as Belina plunged the blade into his leg and quick as a flash replaced it in her hand with a second knife she pulled from somewhere on her dress.

"What are you doing?" Dahlen shouted, his eyes wide with shock. "He was telling you!"

Belina pouted, shaking her head. "First interrogation tip. They always lie the first time. Wouldn't you lie if you had a knife to your neck?"

She had a point. Dahlen couldn't help but feel irritated at Belina for always seeming to make sense out of things that just didn't seem right to him.

"One more chance," she said, turning back to the man with a half-grin on her face. "Who raised the contract on the king?" Belina pressed the knife up against the man's neck, slightly widening the trickle of blood.

The assassin's face hardened.

Belina raised the knife again.

"Hold on!" Dahlen yelled, stepping forward. "There has to be another way."

Belina turned towards Dahlen, giving a slight shake of her head. "You should go wait upstairs. This is going to be a few minutes."

"Belina, I'm not—"

"Dahlen, wait upstairs. I know your type. You don't have the constitution for what happens next. Go."

Two sides pulled at Dahlen. He knew what would happen to that man if he walked upstairs and left him alone with Belina. But what was he to do? Convince Belina to let the man live? She was right, he would come straight after them. Fight her, perhaps kill her, to save the man who tried to kill him? There didn't seem to be an option that gave him any happiness.

The world was never black or white, Dahlen knew that. Most decisions were painted with a murky shade of moral grey. But the grey was where he struggled. His mind worked in the split shades the world frowned upon. He had tried all his life to reconcile that, to learn how to think the way the world demanded, but he hadn't yet figured it out. The closest he had come was learning to accept it and grit his teeth. But it still tore at him.

He let a low sigh out through his nostrils, giving a reluctant nod.

A small lever sat at the bottom of the stone staircase that led back up to The Cloak and Dagger. Dahlen pulled the lever and climbed the steps as the slab of stone receded above his head. Each step was heavy, his legs seeming full of lead. Anger burned in his chest. Anger at himself for thinking less of Belina. And he did think less of her, but she was no worse than he was. He had stopped counting the number of lives he had taken. Though there was a key difference between them. Belina was apparently always able to do what needed to be done.

Reaching the top of the stairs, Dahlen crossed the room and opened the door into the common room of the inn.

The innkeeper, Faruk, gave him one look, then furrowed his brow. He placed two small cups on the bar top, filling them to the point of overflow with a blue liquid the colour of the morning sky.

The dwarf picked up his cup, then waited for Dahlen to do the same before giving him a short nod. Dahlen returned the gesture, and they both drained the spirit from their cups. It burned as it went down, and not like any spirit he had ever had before. This was a deep, tangible burn, as though his throat were being set aflame. He bent over double, gripping the wooden bar top with one hand as he coughed viciously. "What in the gods is that?" he asked between choking coughs.

"Dragon's Tears," the dwarf said, his broken nose crinkling as he grinned. That was the only time Dahlen had seen him show any form of emotion whatsoever. "Spirit of Anwar root blended with snapper venom. Not enough to kill, but it will numb the senses."

Standing up straight, Dahlen let out another cough, still feeling the burn in his throat. "Another?"

The dwarf outright laughed, then poured two more cups. Dahlen most definitely didn't *want* another drink, but he did need something to dull his senses.

"Shit," Dahlen said, puffing out his cheeks. The Dragon's Tears burned no less as they ran down his throat for the second time, but their effect was almost instantaneous. He was going to have to find a bottle of that to share with Dann whenever they got back.

Only a few minutes passed before Belina appeared beside him, a panic on her face. "Faruk, there is a cleanup downstairs, my apologies." Reaching into her pocket, Belina produced a small drawstring purse from her pocket and handed it to Faruk, giving the dwarf a nod.

The dwarf frowned but said nothing.

"We need to go, *now*. Elenya's going after them all."

"What?"

"She's trying to take the whole Freehold, Dahlen. She's going to have the others killed, and Daymon for good measure."

CHAPTER FIFTY

SHIFTING SANDS

ick-Tok.

Ihvon was of the mind to rip that clock from the wall and smash it against the ground. He sat in the chair behind Daymon's desk, his feet resting on the hard wood, his hands clasped together at the back of his head. Daymon lay asleep in the leather chair on the other side of the room near the bookcase, his chest rising and falling slowly, his hands crossed over his breast.

Looking at Daymon, it was difficult for Ihvon not to see the child he had helped raise. And with that, guilt flowed through his veins. Daymon had not been ready for this. He was not prepared. Ihvon's actions had led to the fall of Belduar. It was because of him that Arthur had been killed, and the weight of the crown now weighed heavy on Daymon's shoulders. It was Ihvon's weakness that had caused this. He had allowed that Fade to take advantage of Khris and Alyana's death – to use him.

Reaching into his trouser pocket, Ihvon pulled out the slim metal flask that was almost empty. He unscrewed the lid with an ease born of repetition, then drained the last of the flask's fiery contents, feeling the spirit burn its way down his throat. Shaking his head, he pulled his feet from atop the desk, letting out a sigh as he did.

The small table that sat nestled in beside Daymon's desk was home to a crystal flask of Drifaienin whiskey, two crystal glasses, and a small lantern that held some of that luminescent blue flower, Heraya's Ward. Ihvon reached across to the small table, snatched up one of the glasses, and at the same time wrapped his thick fingers around the neck of the flask.

Placing both on the desk before him, he unplugged the stopper, letting the distinctive scents drift from the flask's neck. Drifaienin whiskey, he would know it anywhere. As Ihvon poured a hefty glass of the whiskey, his eyes once again fell on Daymon.

"I will see you honour his memory," Ihvon muttered to himself, tipping the glass against his lips, sighing with satisfaction at the mellow taste of the whiskey.

Turning towards the window, Ihvon looked out over the streets of the Heart of Durakdur. He hated it down here, within the mountain, where the sun never rose nor set, where the light of the moon never glittered across rooftops. The bluish-green light from the Heraya's Ward always washed over Durakdur, making it seem as though the city was nothing but a perpetual dream. Or for him, closer to a nightmare.

Ihvon closed his eyes, stumbling slightly as he did. Now, seeing nothing but darkness, he painted an image of Belduar in his mind. The warm light of the sun drifted down over the city, bouncing off rooftops, glittering off the surface of Haftsfjord lake. In his mind, he stood atop the walls of the Inner Circle, his elbows leaning across the battlements, the cool breeze brushing over the top of his head. That was where he longed to be – not in some cave beneath hundreds of feet of rock, watching his people wither and die.

A light thud came from outside the door. Ihvon snapped his eyes open. He could feel his heart's slow, methodical thumps against his ribs. He listened again but heard nothing. Not so much as a whisper. A chill ran the length of Ihvon's spine, that familiar feeling of something that wasn't right. "Linus? Almin?"

Eight of the Kingsguard were stationed in pairs, between the door to Daymon's office and the main entrance from the street. Linus and Almin were the two who should have been standing directly in front of the office door, but neither of them replied. Ihvon glanced towards his sword where it rested at the side of the leather chair where Daymon sat. He had left it there when he was talking to Daymon earlier that night.

Ihvon took one step closer to the door. "Linus, Alm—"

The door swung open, cracking Ihvon in the nose, sending a bolt of pain bursting through his head. He stumbled backwards, bringing one hand to his nose, once more broken. Through blood-muddied eyes, he made out two shapes bursting into the room, both moving in his direction. Men in black cloaks, hoods draped over their heads, the glint of steel in their hands. *Assassins.*

Ihvon's whiskey-induced grogginess shifted a little, providing some clarity. He caught himself on his back foot and swung his arm through the air, smashing the crystal glass into the cheek of the assassin closest to him. The man reeled back, howling as the glass shattered, slicing into his skin. Unfortunately, the shards of crystal were similarly unkind to Ihvon's hand. He ignored the pain, lunging forward.

Grabbing the side of the assassin's head, Ihvon slammed it as hard as he physically could against the door, a tremor running through his arm at the collision of skull and wood. The man slumped to the floor, his body limp.

Ihvon risked a glance over his shoulder at Daymon, who was now awake, eyes wide, reaching for his sword. Reluctantly, Ihvon dragged his eyes away from his king and charged towards the second man. His sliced hand throbbed as he moved, burning with pain, dripping blood to the floor. He pushed it to the back of his mind. *Deal with the immediate threat first.*

Dropping his shoulder, Ihvon crashed into the second assassin, feeling the connection as bone collided with bone. He howled as the man collected himself and dragged a knife across Ihvon's chest, the cold steel slicing deep into his flesh.

The assassin lunged, only missing Ihvon's neck by a hair's breadth. But he had sacrificed his footing to attempt the strike. Ihvon sidestepped, snatching a hefty-looking hardback book from the shelf to his right.

Swinging the book around, he caught his attacker in the side of the head, setting him into a stumble. As the man fell, Ihvon kicked at his ankles, knocking them together. He crashed to the ground, his face slamming into the stone. Lunging forward, Ihvon rammed the spine of the book into the bridge of the assassin's nose. The man's head shot backward, bouncing off the stone floor. He went still.

The sound of steel on steel exploded in Ihvon's ears. A third assassin had charged into the room and was now going toe to toe with Daymon, moving in a whir of steel. Daymon was no match for him.

A piercing pain throbbed in Ihvon's side as he pulled himself to his feet. He looked down towards the source of the pain, at the same time reaching with his hand. His fingers wrapped around the leather hilt of a short knife, lodged firmly in his side. The battle rush must have concealed the pain when the blade entered, but that rush did little for him now. He would have to leave it in; he would bleed out in minutes if he removed it. Ihvon took as deep a breath as he could manage and clenched his jaw.

He charged at the last assassin as quickly as his body would allow, still clutching the hardback book. Once he was within striking distance, Ihvon slammed the book into the back of the man's head, throwing him off balance.

The man turned, distracted just enough for his thigh to be sliced open by Daymon's blade. He cried out, spinning and cracking Daymon in the chin with the pommel of his sword.

Before he could raise his guard once more, Ihvon rammed the spine of the book into the man's mouth. He could feel a crack as teeth snapped away, blood flowing. Ihvon repeated the strike, breaking more teeth, then hammered the spine into the side of the assassin's head.

Ihvon wrapped his free hand around the back of the man's head, pulling it down onto his rising knee. The manoeuvre sent a horrendous pain through Ihvon's body, but it was worth it as the assassin collapsed to the ground.

Dropping himself down, Ihvon rammed the spine of the book into the man's face with as much force as he could muster. Rage seethed through him, boiling the blood in his veins. Rage at everything. At himself for all that he had done. At Arthur for trusting him. At Daymon for letting his weakness overcome him. Again and again he slammed the book into the man's skull, blood spraying over his face and hands, coating the ground. Even when the man's body went limp, Ihvon didn't stop. He felt bone snap and crack beneath the blows until the book was torn and broken, falling to pieces and stained crimson.

When he finally had no more strength to continue, Ihvon collapsed on the ground beside the assassin's broken body. The pain in his side burned through him. His breathing was short and raspy, each inhalation catching just short of completion.

He lay there, staring up at the ceiling, his throat and chest constricting, his eyes fading to black. He felt cold.

"Ihvon, Ihvon!"

"Ihvon, Ihvon!"

The sound of Daymon's voice echoed down the staircase as Dahlen's feet pounded up the stone stairs, Belina only a few paces behind him.

The bodies of the Kingsguard who had been set to protect Daymon were strewn about the ground, blood seeping from small wounds in the soft spots of their armour: neck, armpits, groins. Not one of them had so much as drawn their swords. Dahlen's heart thumped in his chest, surging the blood through his veins.

Two more Kingsguard lay lifeless at the top of the staircase that led to Daymon's office: Linus and Almin. Good men, both.

Dahlen didn't stop to check them as he passed; they were long gone. He burst into Daymon's office, swords drawn, pushing aside the already half-open door with his shoulder.

"Please, wake up!"

Dahlen's heart stopped, if only for a moment. In the middle of the room, Daymon knelt beside Ihvon, tears streaming down his cheeks. Ihvon's face looked pale, though not yet void of life. The hilt of a knife protruded from his side, just below his ribs.

Three other bodies lay about the room, two dead and one unconscious but breathing.

Dahlen dropped to his knees, pushing the sobbing Daymon away. He called over his shoulder. "Belina, get a healer! Now!" Dahlen pulled back one of Ihvon's eyelids, seeing the man's pupil contract at the light. "Stay with me, Ihvon. Come on."

Belina's footsteps echoed into the room as she charged through the door. "What do—"

"Now, Belina!" Dahlen slapped Ihvon on the side of the cheek, frowning at the thin stream of blood that flowed from around the hilt of the knife in his side. "Come on, you stubborn old fool. We still need you yet. Daymon, what happened?"

The king's eyes were raw red, and tears carved paths down his cheeks. "It wasn't supposed to… Will he be all right? It was just meant to be a distraction. She said only the guards would be hurt."

Dahlen's eyes narrowed, his blood turning to ice in his veins. He reached with one hand and wrapped his fingers around Daymon's gilded collar, dragging the man's face closer to his. "Who said that? What did you do?"

Daymon didn't answer. He just knelt there, blubbering.

Dahlen tightened his fingers on the king's collar and shook him where he knelt. "Answer me or Heraya help me I will gut you and leave your entrails to stain the ground. You might be a king, but you are not *my* king."

Daymon held Dahlen's gaze, his eyes still filled with tears. "Pulroan. She said with Elenya and Hoffnar gone, she and Kira would help us retake Belduar. I'm sorry…"

Chapter Fifty-One

Kingspass

The night was still. The only sounds that broke the heavy silence were the creaking of sails and time-worn wood, along with the gentle crash of the black waters against the hull of *The Enchantress*. To the west, the eldritch woodland of the Darkwood flowed endlessly into the horizon, thunderclouds of etched charcoal dominating the skies above. To the east, the forest of Lynalion sprawled for hundreds of miles, hemmed in on either side by the coastline and the jagged peaks of Mar Dorul. Ahead, the lanterns that hung in the port and along the walls of Kingspass shone in stark contrast to the sheer blackness that surrounded them. An eeriness in the air set an uneasy feeling in Calen's stomach.

"'Tis a place that knows nothing but death." A deckhand stood by Calen's side. The man wore a sleeveless vest of vibrant yellow, along with thick billowy trousers tucked into his boots. His hair was long and scraggy, with a beard to match, and a large brass hoop hung from his right ear.

"And why is that?" Erik asked, a slightly mocking tone in his voice.

The deckhand turned his head sharply, eyes narrowing at Erik for a moment before returning his gaze to the city ahead. "Kingspass lies in the no-man's-land. Edged by the Darkwood on one side, elves on the other. It sits within touching distance of the foothills of Mar Dorul and lies at the mercy of whatever creatures emerge from the Burnt Lands. There be no joke in my words. More dangerous a place in Epheria there does not be."

"Well," Erik said, leaning in close enough so only Calen could hear him, "now I feel much better."

"Faust has a penchant for the dramatic," Captain Kiron said, stepping up beside Calen, nodding towards his deckhand. "But he speaks only the truth. Keep your wits about you. Kingspass and the lands surrounding it are not to be taken lightly. Despite the name, it is not a pass fit for kings, nor is it a pass owned by a king, nor is it a pass that a king has taken in the last four centuries."

Calen looked out at the horizon of blackness that lay in front of them, the swinging lanterns of the port the only beacons in the night. A shiver ran the length of his spine.

He could feel Valerys drifting through the skies above, flitting between the clouds. *If there is an island, or somewhere for you to rest that is off the coast, stay there tonight.*

A rumble of recognition touched the back of Calen's mind. Valerys shared Calen's uneasiness.

By the time the deckhands had begun scurrying about the ship, readying to dock, Tarmon emerged from below deck, his arm draped around Vaeril's shoulders, keeping the elf upright.

"How is he?" Calen asked, his mouth twisting into a frown.

"I've been better," Vaeril answered, lifting his head. Even then, the elf's face was contorted as though he were one lurch away from emptying the contents of his stomach onto the deck. "I will be happy if I never see another ship again."

"He'll live," Tarmon said, throwing Vaeril an amused look.

The sound of voices and clinking mail cut through the silent night as the deckhands lowered the gangplank down onto the dock.

"Let me do the talking," Captain Kiron said as two soldiers in black and red leather armour over coats of black riveted mail strode up the gangplank.

"What business have you in Kingspass?" one of the soldiers asked, his shoulders pulled back, his chest puffed out, and his eyes scanning the deck of the ship. The man's hair was thick and greasy, slicked back over his head. He stood about a match for Calen in height, though it was impossible to determine his build with the amount of armour he wore. The soldier's eyes told Calen all he needed to know. They were dark, cold, and shrewd.

"Simply seeking to trade," Captain Kiron said, holding his hands out wide.

"There's a tariff around here on all that's to be traded." The second soldier was smaller than the first, his bulky mail and leathers making him look a little strange. His blonde hair was cut short, and his skin was leathered bronze.

"Of course." Captain Kiron gave a slight bow at the waist, producing a small pouch from his coat pocket. He held out the pouch, dropping it into the smaller soldier's outstretched hand with a *clink.*

The soldier hefted the purse in his hand for a moment, gauging the weight, then pulled back the drawstrings and peeked inside. "You're light."

"I assure you, I most certainly am not."

The man took a deep phlegm-filled sniff of his nostrils, eyed the captain with a hard glare, then stuffed the purse into his trouser pocket. His eyes fell on Calen, then each of his companions in turn, finally setting on Vaeril. "There's an extra tariff when the goods are alive. Especially when one of them is a dirty fucking *elf.* If you gut him now, I'll waive the extra fee, otherwise pay up."

Calen clenched his jaw, grinding his teeth. He could feel his subconscious reaching out for the Spark, anger rumbling through Valerys's mind. Even as the dragon alighted on a patch of rock about two miles off the coast, his anger flowed like a river.

Captain Kiron coughed, throwing a glance towards Vaeril, then over to Calen, raising a questioning eyebrow and shrugging.

Calen stared back at the captain, tilting his head to the side. Surely there was no way the man was even considering taking the soldier's first option.

The captain rolled his eyes, then reached into the pocket of his doublet, producing another purse, slightly larger, and handed it to the soldier with a very evident reluctance.

"That should do nicely," the man said, hefting the purse in his hand. "Though I still recommend covering the filth's ears or taking them off entirely. They won't do you any good, especially not here." With that, the two soldiers turned and made their way back down the gangplank, the taller man throwing one more cursory glance at the ship before they strode off back down the docks.

"Please, don't tell me—"

"Of course not," Kiron said, cutting Calen off. "Well, maybe for a second."

Calen glared at the captain, shaking his head, his eyes narrowed.

Kiron shrugged. "It was only a second. Look, either way, the soldier did not tell a lie. If you want to stay out of trouble, I would keep the elf's hood up. His kind have not done right by the people in this city. The elves of Lynalion kill as many as the Uraks and the other creatures of the Burnt Lan—"

"They are *not* my kind," Vaeril said, cutting across Kiron, his hand still held against his stomach.

The captain looked over at Vaeril, his eyebrow raised in confusion. "Well, ignoring that strange denial of his elven heritage, my advice remains the same. Many people in this city have lost family to the raids from Lynalion. Keep his ears covered. Also, if you're looking for a place to stay, Madame Olmira down at The Cosy Daisy – believe me, the irony of calling an inn by that name in this city is not lost on me – is about as welcoming as they come around here. Tell her Longhorn sent you. She'll know what you mean."

Calen shuddered involuntarily at the captain's words. There was not a single piece of him that wanted to know what that sentence meant. "I'll look for The Cosy Daisy."

"It's just through the archway with the black lion carved into it, not far from the docks. Can't miss it."

Calen nodded. "Thank you, Captain, for getting us this far."

"Not a problem." Captain Kiron tipped the front of his hat, an acknowledging smile on his face. "After all, you did pay me a lot of money."

After ensuring they had not left anything behind, Calen, Vaeril, Tarmon, and Erik said their last goodbyes to the captain and made their way down the gangplank.

Calen shivered a little as he stepped out onto the dock, pulling his cloak around himself for warmth. At the end of the long jetty, the docks opened into a large empty square that looked as though it was used for fishmongers and traders during the day. But at that moment, the only two souls that inhabited it were the two soldiers who had boarded the ship only minutes before. The two men cast sidelong glances at Calen and his companions as they crossed the square, their eyes narrowing.

Despite himself, Calen did look back to check that Vaeril had in fact pulled his hood up, feeling a sense of relief when he saw the black hood covering the majority of the elf's head. This city did not seem like the kind of place they wanted to draw any unwanted attention.

As they reached the opposite side of the square, Calen noticed a large stone archway with a lion carved across its front, painted black. He tilted his head towards it wordlessly, signalling the others to follow him. Regardless of Calen's disinclination to stay anywhere Captain Kiron was known as 'Longhorn', they needed a place to sleep. The city gates would be closed at this time, and even if they were not, it would do them no good to set off at night. A few hours of sleep in a bed that did not tip to and fro would do them all a world of good, particularly Vaeril. The elf looked more himself with every step he took on solid ground, but he was still a bit wobbly.

One night, then we will set on our way. We're coming for you, Rist. Please be all right.

The streets of Kingspass were so narrow that Calen could stretch out his arms and run his fingertips along the coarse stone walls on either side. Multi-storey stone buildings loomed over the cracked paths, blocking out a vast majority of the pale moonlight that drifted down from the star-speckled sky above. While some windows gave off a dim orange glow, indicating someone within was still awake, most held nothing but darkness, curtains drawn.

The low whistle of the wind was the dominant sound as it streaked through the narrow streets, sweeping up spirals of dust and dried, crumpled leaves. The occasional clinking of mail and heavy steel boots against stone echoed through the city around them, drifting down from the walls. Up ahead, Calen could see silhouettes floating across the battlements like ghosts; he was only able to make out the true forms of the soldiers when they passed through the light of the lanterns that hung at regular intervals along the walls.

It was difficult to tell at night, but Kingspass looked as though it could easily match Camylin for size, and the walls seemed twice again as thick and over a half again as tall. Whatever it was the walls were trying to keep out, Calen did not want to know.

"Anybody else not like this place?" Erik said in a half whisper. "Something about it just feels…"

"Wrong?" Calen suggested.

"Yeah, wrong."

Calen couldn't shake that feeling from his bones. He hadn't quite settled on what it was, but Erik hit the nail on the head. The city felt wrong, as though the very air itself held a certain darkness.

"We need to keep our wits about us," Tarmon said, his hand resting on the pommel of the short sword at his waist.

"Here," Calen said, his eyes catching sight of a building just up to the right with a large rectangular sign hanging from its front that read, 'The Cosy Daisy'. The building had a thatched roof that looked as though it hadn't been tended to in years, and a porch that was held upright by beams of rotting timber.

The wooden door at the front of The Cosy Daisy looked as though it had seen far better days. Rot had set into the wood at multiple points, and the large swathes of rust along the iron bands that held everything together were a clear sign that the metal had not seen even a drop of oil or wax in quite some time.

A shiver ran through Calen's arm as he rested his finger on the iron door handle. He had always hated the texture of rust. With a push, the door creaked inward. It took Calen all of five seconds to decide that the name 'The Cosy Daisy' was the furthest thing from suitable.

The common room of the inn was wide and sweeping, with a miserable looking hearth at the far end that held a small fire which looked as though it was moments from dying. A staircase, close to collapse, was built into the wall just beside where Calen and the others had entered, and small rickety tables were scattered about the floor in such a haphazard manner it looked as though they had been arranged with some strange form of particularity. Two older men sat at a table by the wall near the lumps of crumbled wood that pretended to be a fire, huddled together in deep conversation. Another man sat on his own at a lopsided table in the centre of the room, his face buried in the back of his hands, his empty cup tipped on its side, its contents half-dried into the wood.

"May I be helpin' ya?" a creaky voice said from behind the bar that was set into the wall opposite the entrance. A small, thin woman emerged from the door at the back of the bar that must have led into the kitchen.

'Emerged', Calen decided, was a strong word. The woman was barely five feet tall, with a hooked nose and a scraggy head of white-grey hair. Her eyes seemed to be perpetually narrow, forced down into a glare by years of hard-earned wrinkles. She hobbled along, a walking stick with a fox head handle in her right hand. "Well, don't just stand there starin'. Do ya be needing a room or not?"

"We do," Calen said in as assured a voice as he could muster. "Do you have any?"

"Does it look like I be beatin' away customers with a stick?" The woman's eyes unsettled Calen. He got the feeling she didn't miss much. "Enough babblin'. Follow me."

Without even giving Calen the chance to enquire about price, the woman turned on her heels more spryly than he would have thought possible. She called over her shoulder as she gripped onto the handrail of the dilapidated staircase. "There's no supper left, so you'll have to go hungry till mornin'. And I don't wanna be hearing no complaints about that neither. It is what it is."

Erik looked at Calen, puffing out his cheeks and shaking his head as the woman hobbled up the staircase on her own, talking to herself.

"I suppose she is the 'cosy' part of the daisy?" Tarmon whispered.

Erik burst out laughing. "Did you… did you just make a joke? I didn't know you made jokes!" He patted Tarmon on the shoulder before following the woman up the stairs. "That was actually pretty funny."

Tarmon went to speak, but then shook his head and followed Erik up the staircase.

"How are you feeling now?" Calen asked Vaeril as they followed the others, the rickety old staircase creaking beneath their feet. Calen recoiled as some of the rotting wood along the banister came away at his touch. The place was falling apart.

"Better," the elf said with a sigh, though there was as an intensity in his eyes that made Calen curious.

"What is it?"

"I don't like this place. It's not safe for you here."

"I'll be all right, Vaeril. We will take turns on watch, and Valerys isn't far away. He can be here in minutes." Calen stopped at the top of the staircase, placing his hand on Vaeril's shoulder. "Thank you."

"For what, Draleid?"

"For not trying to stop me when I said I was going after Rist. For being here." Calen had just about given up on trying to get Vaeril to stop referring to him as 'Draleid'.

"I swore to protect you, to go with you wherever you may lead, to the void or beyond. I meant what I said. But I would have come even without the oath."

Calen gave a weak smile as something unspoken passed between him and Vaeril. An understanding.

"Will you two come on?" Erik called from down the hall.

The room was in no better condition than the rest of the inn. The wooden floorboards looked as though they were centuries old, and dark patches of mould clung to every crack, crevice, and corner. A long crack ran through the windowpane, allowing a shivering draft to creep its way into the room. Four beds, two on either side, were set against the walls in an alternating pattern.

"This will do nicely," Calen said, tossing his satchel down on the bed, producing an unexpectedly brittle sound as it crunched against the paper-thin bedsheets. Calen had the feeling that no matter how hard they looked, they wouldn't be finding any better accommodation. "How much for the night?"

"Three silvers – each." The words left the woman's mouth like rusty nails drawn over stone. A lifetime of smoking tabbac and drinking spirits would do that to a person.

"Three silvers?" Erik's eyes widened in disbelief as he sat on the bed beside Tarmon's, at the end of the room. "We could buy a horse and cart for that!"

"Three silvers is the price. No hagglin'. Go sleep in the street if you have a problem with that."

"Here." Calen reached into his pocket, before Erik could say anything else, and produced the purse Alleron had left with Tarmon. His stomach turned at handing the woman twelve pieces of silver. His mind couldn't even begin to process how much food that would have bought back home. But still, he plucked the coins from the pouch and dropped them into the woman's bony, liver-spotted hand.

The woman gave a near toothless grin as she finished counting the coins, then stuck them into her pocket, quick as a flash. "The washroom is down the end of the hall. Breakfast is served from sunrise until it's gone. Oat porridge and goat's milk. Other than that, don't bother me."

"I will take first watch," Tarmon said as soon as the woman had left the room and closed the door behind her.

"No," Vaeril shook his head, tossing his leather sack down on the bed closest to the doorway. "You rest. I don't need as much sleep as you do, and if there are any mages here, I will sense them. You can't. I will wake you in a few hours."

Judging by the look on Tarmon's face, he was about to argue, but then thought better of it. Vaeril and Dann might have been very different in almost every facet of their personalities, but they were similar in one way:

when they made a decision, they both stuck to it, come void or high water.

With the decision agreed upon, Vaeril sat cross-legged on top of his bed, laying his bow down beside him and his sword across his lap, his eyes fixed on the doorway.

Calen tossed from side to side as he set himself into the bed, rolling his shoulders as the rough grate of the old bedsheets sent shivers across his skin. Sleep had once been a safe haven. The land of dreams had been a place he could escape to when the weight of the world grew too heavy. But he didn't dream any more. Artim Valdock had stripped him of that ability, torn it from him like strips of flesh. Now, every time he closed his eyes he was brought back to that cell. The hunger, the agony, the emptiness. Sleep was nothing more than a necessity now.

Closing his eyes, Calen let his mind drift to Valerys. The dragon was nestled on a patch of rock that jutted up from the water a few miles from Kingspass, just off the coast. The patch of rock was small enough to go unnoticed by any passing ships, but large enough for him to curl up comfortably, his tail pulled in towards his chest and his wings folded over himself. Still, Calen always hated the idea of Valerys sleeping alone, as he had done many times as they travelled along the coast. This would be the last time for a while, which did help to add a bit of comfort.

Calen stayed like that a while longer until his tired body begged him for rest and he pulled himself from Valerys's mind. The touch of the dragon's consciousness was the only thing that gave him enough courage to face his nightmares.

Idyn väe, Valerys. Rest well.

CHAPTER FIFTY-TWO

MYIA NITHÍR TIL DIAR

orns bellowed, their sonorous ringing muffled as though underwater. All Calen could see was darkness as the ringing grew louder, broadening, thumping in his ears. Someone grabbed him by the shoulders, shaking him, dragging him into the waking world.

"Calen, wake up."

Calen shot upright, gasping for air as images of Artim Valdock faded from his mind.

Erik stood over him, a serious look in his eyes. In the corner of the room, Tarmon was strapping on his armour. Vaeril stood by the door, his bow across his back, his sword drawn.

"What's going on?" Calen dug his fingers into the creases of his eye, urging his body to wake up faster.

"Not sure," Erik said, turning his head to look out through the cracked glass window. Calen followed Erik's line of sight. More torches had been lit on the walls, and shadows were moving about, back and forth. "It looks like the city is under attack, but whatever it is, we need to get ready."

Calen nodded, pushing his sheets aside and getting dressed, strapping his leather armour across his chest and arms. He held his scabbard out in front of himself, sliding the blade free a few inches, his eyes tracing the intricate pattern of swirls that ornamented the steel. *Death could not be beautiful, but sometimes it was necessary.*

Taking a deep breath, he slid the sword back into the scabbard and strapped the belt around his waist.

In the back of his mind, Calen could feel Valerys, concern permeating the dragon's consciousness. *No. Don't come unless you have to. You need to stay out of sight.*

Even though the dragon was a few miles away on the patch of rock just off the coast, Calen could physically feel the vibrations in the air as Valerys let out a thunderous roar, stamping his forelimbs down against the ground, his claws gouging into the stone.

I'll be all right. The others are here. If I'm in danger, then come.

A low, reluctant grumble resonated through Calen's mind.

Draleid n'aldryr.

With Valerys slightly calmed, Calen turned to Tarmon. "What do you think?"

"The city is under attack. That much is clear, but we need to know by whom, or what."

"Agreed," Erik said, unsheathing his swords from across his back.

Vaeril didn't speak. He just looked at Calen, his gaze hard.

Calen nodded. "Let's see if anyone knows anything downstairs."

The common room of the inn was empty save for Madame Olmira, who stood by the far corner of the room in her shift, her face pressed up against the murky glass window, looking out at the city. There was a noticeable tremble in the woman's bony fingers wrapped around the handle of the fox head walking stick.

"They're back," the woman croaked, not turning her head.

Erik leaned towards Calen, his eyes narrowing. "Is she talking to us?"

"Who else would I be talking to?" Madame Olmira snapped, tapping her walking stick off the wood as she turned, shaking her head. "Idiot."

Erik appeared to be so taken off guard by the comment that he just tilted his head and didn't answer, which was not like him at all. The scene made Calen wish he could introduce Madame Olmira to Dann.

The woman hobbled towards Calen, Tarmon, Vaeril, and Erik, her walking stick clicking against the floor the entire way. "Every night for a week, the Uraks attacked without fail. But not once in the past three days. Why do you think that is?"

Walking straight past the group, Madame Olmira stepped behind the bar, took out four mugs, and proceeded to fill each with a black liquid that came from a brown glass bottle.

"They were testing the defences," Tarmon answered, a worried look on his face.

"That they were." Madame Olmira shoved the stopper back into the bottle and dropped it down behind the bar, pushing each of the mugs across the wooden top.

"Now they have decided they are strong enough to take the city." Tarmon reached over, lifted a mug from the table, and downed its contents in one long swallow.

"Right again," Madame Olmira said, following Tarmon's lead. With a frail hand, she pushed the three remaining cups further across the bar top until they were almost touching the edge. "Drink up, boys. Even you, elf. The city will be needin' all the steel it can get, and the least I can do is be givin' ya some courage."

Erik reached across, snatching up his mug, with Calen and Vaeril following suit.

With a deep sigh, Calen tilted his cup up, felt the worn wood touch his lips, then poured the noxious liquid down his throat. It burned going down, but he didn't choke or cough. He barely even flinched. His bones were weary, and his soul was tired. The time spent in that cell had taken more from him than strength. He didn't want to fight again. He didn't want to watch the people around him die. Calen shuddered involuntarily, images flashing across his mind. Artim Valdock's ice spears ripping through Falmin's body. Lopir's neck snapping.

"Calen, are you all right?"

Calen shivered at the sound of Erik's voice, his mind returning to him. "Yeah… I'll be fine."

Nodding their thanks to Madame Olmira, the group stepped out through the shoddy doorway and into the city.

The sound of the horns still bellowed in the night, resounding through the tightly packed streets of Kingspass. The shouts of men and women hollering to each other blended with the crashing sound of hundreds of steel plated boots colliding against stone paths. Every brazier along the length of the walls was burning at full tilt, and it was easy for Calen to see the rows of archers lined along the battlements, each row alternating, one nocking, one loosing, never allowing the flow of arrows to stop.

"To the walls." Tarmon gestured towards the northern edge of the city where the main gates lay. "These men won't turn down anyone with a sword in their hand."

"Do we really want to help?" Calen stopped as he spoke. It had taken him all the strength in his heart to say those words. "These are empire soldiers, Tarmon. Why should we help them? They are better off dead anyway. Why not let them and the Uraks kill each other? There's still a chance that Kiron is at the port."

Tarmon took a step closer to Calen, his eyes narrowing. Calen could tell by the look on the man's face that he was surprised at what Calen had said. "I'm going to hope you didn't mean that."

"They killed my family." Calen moved closer to Tarmon, his eyes threatening tears as he stared at the giant of a man in the eyes. Calen's stomach twisted, pulling at him. The hair on the back of his neck stood on end. Pain ripped its way through his heart and mind. "The empire murdered my father in front of my eyes. They burned my mother alive. They razed Belduar to the ground. They are our enemies. Now you expect me to help them?"

By the time the words had left Calen's mouth, he was seething. His chest trembled as he took in a deep breath, his hands shaking by his sides. In the back of Calen's mind, Valerys's anger mixed with his own. Every drop of loss and anguish Calen felt stoked the fire of fury within the dragon. Vars and Freis were Valerys's parents, too. They were his family. He had never met them, but he knew them intimately. He loved them. The empire killed them.

To Calen's surprise, Tarmon sheathed his sword and clasped his hand around the back of Calen's neck. The man pulled Calen towards him until their eyes were only inches apart. "You are better than this. I've seen it. I'm standing here with you *because* you are better than this. Tonight, those men and women are not empire soldiers. They are not those who did us harm. They are just people. People who don't want to die. And they need us. They need *you.* They *need* a Draleid." Releasing his hand from the back of Calen's neck, Tarmon stepped away, his gaze still fixed on Calen's. "Show them, Calen. Give them something to believe in."

A wave of shame swept through Calen from head to toe, knotting his stomach and making the hair on his arms and the back of his neck stand on end. His father had always raised him to believe that if you could help, then you did help. He would have been disgusted if he could see Calen now, as would Haem, as would Arthur.

For a long moment, Calen returned Tarmon's stare. "Thank you." Calen turned to look at Vaeril and Erik. "Thank you all."

"It's been a long road from Belduar," Erik said, a sombre expression on his face. "And it's not going to stop here. We are going to get Rist, we are going to get back to Durakdur, and we are going to fight until our last breaths. For Falmin, and Korik, and Lopir."

"For Ellisar," Vaeril said, his face unchanging.

"For Arthur," Tarmon added.

Calen nodded, feeling his fist tighten around the hilt of his sword. "For all those we have lost."

"For all those we have lost," the others chorused.

Calen slowed his breathing as they made their way towards the city gates. He drew the air in through his nose, held it, then released slowly. His sword felt heavy in his hand, and his leather armour weighed down his shoulders as though it were made of lead. Each time he lifted his leg was a struggle, and each deep breath held a rasp in his chest. His body still needed months more food and rest. But he didn't have months, so he gritted his teeth and kept moving, doing his best not to show any outward signs of struggle. He needed to be strong for the others.

In the back of his mind, Calen could feel Valerys standing on the edge of the rocks, his wings spread wide, the sea spray crashing against his scales. Every muscle in Valerys's body was twitching, ready to leap into the air at a moment's notice and fly towards the city.

If they could get through this without revealing Valerys to the empire, then that's what they needed to do. *Not yet. Trust me.*

The only response that flowed through Calen's mind was a wave of anger, but Valerys didn't move. The dragon stayed where he was, claws gouging into the patch of rock in frustration.

Before long, they came to the end of a street lined with Lorian soldiers armoured in thick plate, standing side by side, spears drawn. He couldn't help but be surprised at how young most of them looked. Some couldn't have seen more than sixteen summers.

Behind the soldiers was a large, open plaza that must have been used as a forum during the day. Calen looked past the plaza, at the battlements, and watched as an enormous black spear thrown from the other side of the wall burst straight through a man's skull, lifting him off the ramparts and sending him plummeting to the streets below.

"Who goes there?" A voice called from behind the line of soldiers that blocked the entrance to the plaza.

"Travellers," Tarmon called back. "We want to help."

"I've never seen travellers armed as you are. Speak the truth or die where you stand. We don't have the time to waste on you."

"Can you afford to turn away anyone that carries steel?" Tarmon's voice was firm and unyielding, as though he were commanding his own troops. "Point us to where you need us."

A few moments passed without an answer. Calen swallowed hard, loosening and tightening his grip on the hilt of his sword. Then, some of the soldiers in the middle of the line pulled back and created an opening for the group to pass through.

"We need men before the gate," the Lorian commander said, stepping forward from the mass of soldiers. The woman was a few inches shorter than Calen and had seen at least fifty summers. Her grey-streaked hair was tied at the back, and her eyes held the same steeliness as Tarmon's, the same calm.

"What of the walls?" Tarmon asked, his voice level, an eyebrow raised.

"The walls will not hold. When they break through, we will slow them in the streets with shield lines and pick them off with archers from the rooftops above. This plaza will be our last hold. Everyone will fall back to here. When the walls fall, any time you can give our soldiers to retreat will give us more of a chance. Then, fall back here with them."

Tarmon gave a short nod.

"May The Warrior guide your hand."

"And yours," Tarmon replied, gesturing for Calen and the others to follow him across the plaza.

The plaza was thronged with soldiers. Some wore thick plate over coats of mail and carried heavy shields and spears, while others in red and black leather armour carried short swords or bows. Each group marched about in formation, ushered by a captain at their head, forming into ranks and lines. Calen couldn't help but be impressed by the discipline of it all.

Just as they had neared the other side of the plaza, Calen caught sight of black robes flapping in the night breeze, about twenty feet or so away, near the centre of the plaza. *A Battlemage.* The man's hood was drawn down over his shoulders, exposing a youthful face and fiery red hair. Calen's mind drifted back to the cell in Arisfall. Images flashed across his mind of Artim Valdock standing over him. He could almost feel the cold steel as the man pulled the knife along his skin, the ripping noise as he tore Calen's fingernails free… the emptiness.

"For now," Vaeril said, leaning in, his eyes following Calen's stare, "don't touch the Spark. Once we are in the heat of it, he will not care. There are likely more of them here on the walls, and it will be impossible for them to tell who is touching the Spark once the fighting truly begins."

Calen nodded, Vaeril's voice pulling him back to the present.

Once they had passed through the soldiers on the opposite side of the plaza and entered the street that led to the main gate, Calen could feel the mages on the wall. He had never quite felt anything like it before.

Of course, he had felt the sensation when Aeson had drawn from the Spark, or Therin, or Vaeril. But this was different. He had never felt so many people tapping into the Spark at one time. Even at Belduar, the Belduaran mages were spread thin across the walls, numbering no more than thirty or forty. But here, there had to be more than a hundred Battlemages.

Calen felt a heightened awareness of everything around him as the sensation of the Spark thrummed through the air – like the aftershock of lightning echoing through his skin. Up along the battlements, he could see the threads of Fire, Air, and Spirit. Blinding flashes signalling arcs of lightning being hurled towards the Uraks who besieged the walls. With each passing moment, the sensation grew weaker though, as the imperial mages were torn from the world by bolts of purple lightning or cold black steel.

"If many more of them die, the walls will fall," Vaeril called back to Calen, his eyes fixed on the walls.

"More of who? The soldiers?" Erik looked to Calen, searching for an answer. Calen often forgot the others couldn't sense the Spark like he and Vaeril could, couldn't see the threads of Fire, Air, and Spirit.

"The Battlemages," Calen said. He thought back to Belduar and how the Belduaran mages had manned the battlements, not just to wield the Spark against the imperial soldiers, but also to ensure the imperial mages were not able to bring the walls crashing down.

"There is no sense in worrying about what we can't control," Tarmon said as they reached the end of the long street that opened into a courtyard before the city gates.

The courtyard was mostly built from paved stone. Two rectangular grass areas were set off to the sides, bounded by knee-high walls, stone statues set at each of their corners. Shouts and calls rang out, drowning in the din, as the Lorian forces scrambled to prepare for what was to come. Rows upon rows of soldiers stood in the shadow of the city gates, divided into four columns, each with their shields raised and spears drawn level towards the gates.

Up close, the city walls looked even more gargantuan than they had at first glance. Thick carved stone rising over a hundred feet into the night. Two enormous crenellated bulwarks framed the massive arched gate, which was protected by an interwoven lattice of banded iron.

Calen's heart pounded as he looked over the soldiers, the wails of men and Uraks piercing the air. With every passing moment, the sensation of the Spark grew weaker. It would not be long before the Uraks broke through.

Tarmon turned to look at Vaeril, Erik, and Calen. "No matter what happens. We stay together, understood?"

Calen nodded along with the others.

"If it looks like things—"

A shockwave rippled through the ground, accompanied by an ear-splitting explosion that caused the air itself to tremble. The section of the wall to the left of the gates erupted in a cloud of stone and dust. Massive fragments crashed to the ground, crushing men and women beneath them in plumes of blood mist. All around them, soldiers crashed to the ground, thrown from the top of the walls, their bodies shattering in bursts of blood and bone.

A ringing noise droned through Calen's ears from the explosion, and a thick cloud of dust fell like a blanket over his eyes. The muffled screams of mutilated soldiers drifted through the chaos, accompanied by the rolling and crashing of stone.

Then, a dim red light glowed through the dust that hung in the air. One light became two, then three, turning to many. Calen heard Erik shouting something muffled in his ear, but he couldn't drag his eyes from the red lights. The closer the lights moved, the more they began to take shape, until Calen realised what they were. Uraks.

Only these were not like the ones Calen knew. These monstrosities were easily ten feet tall, with slabs of heavy-set muscle so large it looked as though their skin had been pulled tight across their body to the point of tearing. Sets of glowing red runes covered their flesh, shimmering through the stone dust. A knot of pure dread twisted in Calen's stomach as he stared at the advancing creatures.

"Fall back!" A voice called, piercing through the ringing in Calen's ears. "The walls have fallen! The Uraks have breached the city! Fall back to the plaza!"

Screams and shouts erupted all about the courtyard. Some soldiers broke rank, pushing, shoving, and kicking past anyone who stood in their way, stumbling over the corpses that lay broken on the ground. The more experienced men tightened together, locking their shields, holding their spear arms firm. If only for a second, Calen held a fragile flicker of hope in his chest, but then he watched as one of the enormous, rune-marked Uraks slammed its fists into the ground and sent a shockwave of earth and fire tearing through the ranks of soldiers.

"What in the gods are those creatures?" For the first time, Calen heard fear in Tarmon's voice.

"I… do not know." Vaeril's eyes were wide, his jaw slackened.

"Whatever they are," Erik said. "We can't fight them here. We need to fall back to the plaza where the archers can cover from above."

Erik looked to Calen, expecting a response, but Calen was too focused on these new Uraks tearing through men as though steel were paper and bone were glass. He had seen what had happened in Belduar when men started to break; he had watched the empire cut them down like blades of grass. "We need to hold them here."

"Calen's right," Tarmon said, sliding his great sword from across his back. "If the ranks break here, the rest of the army will rout."

"Am I the only one who thinks this is a bad idea?"

"No," Tarmon said with a shrug. "But it's what we need to do if we want to still be breathing come sunrise. We just need to give the soldiers a chance, then we can fall back."

Calen reached out to Valerys, calling to him. He let their mind flow freely into each other, letting their thoughts, bodies, and spirits become one. He held nothing back. *No matter what, we live together, we die together. Come.*

A surge of energy pulsed through Calen's body as he felt every fibre of Valerys's being burst into life. The dragon kicked his head back and unleashed an earth-shattering roar, so loud and visceral that Calen could hear it from miles away. A thousand thoughts at once cascaded through their mind, colliding, crashing, blending. Every thought, every sensation, and every emotion. The air thrummed around their wings as Valerys lifted into the air. Their heartbeat pulsed through their body. Power flowed through their veins. The weakness in Calen's bones ebbed away, replaced by a strength that felt both alien and familiar. It was all Calen could do not to lose himself in it. Valerys's roar ripped through the night as his powerful wings carried him across the water, towards the city, and his fury ignited within Calen.

"Let's give them something to believe in." Calen tightened his grip on his sword and opened himself to the Spark as he strode towards the rune-marked Uraks that tore through the Lorian soldiers. Two of the creatures spotted him immediately. They snarled and hissed, smoke drifting from the glowing runes etched into their hides. The creatures charged, guttural war cries escaping their throats.

Calen pulled on threads of Fire, Spirit, and Air, knotting them together, feeling the power radiate from them. He had never created lightning before, but he had seen it done enough times. Picking up his pace, he charged towards the nearest of the massive creatures, his sword gripped tightly in his right hand, his heart hammering against his ribs.

The creature unleashed a visceral howl, slamming its fists down against the ground. A spiralling shockwave of fire and stone hurtled through the air. Its magic must have been similar to Artim Valdock's. Calen couldn't sense even the slightest flicker of the Spark from the beast.

With all the strength Calen could muster, he leapt out of the shockwave's path, landing hard, then springing himself back to his feet, unleashing the threads of Fire, Spirit, and Air he had been holding within. Arcs of blue lightning streaked from his fingertips, crashing into the beast's chest, stripping flesh from bone, tearing the creature's torso asunder. The monstrosity collapsed to the ground, howling in pain, blood seeping out onto the stone.

Before Calen could collect his thoughts, the second rune-marked Urak lunged at him, catching him across the shoulder with the back of an outstretched hand. The force of the blow knocked Calen back a few feet, dropping him to one knee. Pulling on threads of Earth and Air, Calen lifted a long fragment of stone from the ground, sharpened its end, then launched it through the beast's gut.

Even with the shard of stone pierced through its stomach, the rune-marked Urak kept moving forward. Stumbling, it swiped out a clawed hand. Valerys's power surging through him, Calen ducked beneath the swipe, slicing his blade across the creature's leg. Crying out, the Urak dropped to its knees. Calen swung. Steel cleaved bone, and the creature's headless body fell to the ground.

Before he could catch his breath, something slammed into Calen's back, sending him hurtling through the air. Instinctively, he wrapped himself in threads of Air, softening the blow as he crashed through a stone statue.

Even with the threads of Air helping break his fall, pain still surged through Calen's body. He coughed and spluttered, dust and blood clinging to his throat as he dragged himself to his feet. He stumbled, catching himself on one knee. His lower back burned in agony, and his ribs pained him with each breath.

Lifting his head, Calen watched as the rune-marked Urak that had thrown him charged towards him with its blood-red eyes shimmering, the light from its runes spraying through the clouds of dust. Calen braced himself, again pulling on threads of Fire, Sprit, and Air. But just as he was ready to strike, an arrow burst through the side of the creature's head. The Urak's body went limp, crashing to the ground with a thud, plumes of dust rising around it.

In seconds, Vaeril was by Calen's side. He clasped Calen's forearm, pulling him to his feet. "Stay closer to me."

Calen nodded, grimacing as he dragged air into his lungs.

"Do you just try your hardest to get yourself killed?" Erik asked, shrugging as he whirled his two blades through the air, slicing through the arm of an Urak before driving cold steel up through its neck and into its head. "Or is it a talent given to you by the gods? By the way, your eyes are glowing purple again. I just thought you should know."

Calen brought his hand up, holding it just in front of his face. A pale purple glow illuminated his palm, shimmering over his blood dappled skin. The sight should have set a panic in his heart, but instead, he smiled. He could feel the blood coursing through Valerys's body, the wind crashing against his scales as the dragon soared towards the city. The light was their bond – Valerys's soul entwined with his. He knew it to be true. "Myia nithír til diar, Valerys." *My soul to yours.*

"Are you all right?" Tarmon asked, his hand clutching Calen's shoulder, his stare fierce.

Calen barely heard Tarmon's words, his mind lost in the bond. He nodded. "I'm fine…"

"Then we need to go. There will be no holding them here." With a nod, Tarmon gestured towards the walls.

Calen followed Tarmon's eyes, feeling his heart drop into his stomach. As the dust around the collapsed section of wall began to settle, he could see the ocean of Uraks that poured into the city, bounding over rubble and corpses, blackened blades and spear gripped in their fists. There had to be thousands of them.

"Go!" Tarmon shouted, pushing Calen back towards the street that led down into the main plaza. Calen's legs moved of their own volition, carrying him across stone, over mutilated bodies, through rubble and shattered bones.

Cries rang out from the soldiers around them who were also retreating towards the enclosed street that led back to the plaza. "Dragon! It's the Dragonguard!"

A thunderous roar rippled through the sky as Valerys swooped overhead, his white scales shimmering in the moonlight.

"Keep going," Calen shouted at Erik, Tarmon, and Vaeril, who had stopped at the soldiers' shouts, eyes fixed on the sky. As he spoke, he saw the realisation spread across each of their faces that it was not, in fact, the Dragonguard. "Get into the street. Valerys will cover our retreat."

As they ran, that familiar pressure built at the back of Calen's mind. Then, in a light so blinding it was as though the sun had re-emerged from beyond the horizon, Valerys unleashed a pillar of dragonfire that ripped through the charging horde of Uraks. In an instant, the air smelled of boiling blood and charred flesh. As the smell hit Calen's nostrils, a fervour rippled within him, a bloodlust that coursed through his body like molten fire. Above him, Valerys let out a roar that shook the air. Their minds were one.

Blood-chilling screams rang out as the Uraks writhed on the ground in pain, howling and clawing at their own skin. But as Calen looked back over his shoulder, the horde kept coming. Those who had fallen, dead or still yet alive, were trampled by those who came after them. The beasts did not give a moment's pause for their fallen. Their eyes, blood-red and hungry, remained fixed on their targets. They howled deep, visceral war cries as they ran, calling out in a language so harsh Calen did not believe it could ever be spoken by a human tongue.

Three more times, Valerys swept over the charging ranks of Uraks. Three more times, he bathed them in dragonfire. And three more times, they kept coming, charging, dragging themselves over charred corpses and broken stone.

Calen's chest heaved, and his limbs ached as he pushed himself as hard as he could. Up ahead, lines of Lorian soldiers formed across the street that led to the main plaza, waiting to hold back the tide of Uraks. There was still a gap in the middle of the Lorian lines where they were letting the retreating soldiers through, but Calen knew they couldn't keep that gap open for long.

Another surge of pressure swept through Calen's mind, and Valerys unleashed a river of dragonfire down on the onrushing Uraks.

One more look over his shoulder. They weren't going to make it.

Arcs of blue lightning peeled over Calen's head, coming from the rooftops of the buildings above, followed by a hail of arrows that momentarily blocked out the moon's light. The lightning ripped into the ground before the Uraks, tearing the stone asunder, creating a small chasm in front of the charging horde. Then the arrows dropped, shredding through the creatures like acid rain.

Looking to the rooftops, Calen could see several figures draped in black robes standing between the archers, threads of Fire, Spirit, and Air whirling around them. Battlemages. A surge of both elation and fear coursed through Calen's veins as he and the others stumbled through the closing ranks of Lorian soldiers, more arrows falling behind them.

More soldiers rushed past Calen as he collapsed to his knees, dragging air into his lungs.

Erik bent over double, panting. "That was too close."

"Agreed." Tarmon stood to his full height, his chest rising and falling in slow, measured breaths, his eyes sweeping over the charging Uraks who had now regained their momentum, and were again charging.

"Are you all right?" Vaeril reached his hand down to Calen as he spoke.

Calen swallowed hard, grasping Vaeril's hand, pulling himself to his feet. He nodded shakily. "I'll be fine. I just feel weak. My lungs, they just…" Calen's voice trailed off as he closed his eyes, giving his lungs a chance to drag in more air. Even with Valerys's strength, his body was still weak.

"You were imprisoned and starved for over a month. Your lungs will take time to recover." Vaeril rested his hand on Calen's back, and Calen felt a wave of relief flood through him.

"Don't," Calen said, pushing Vaeril away. "You need your energy too. I'll be fine."

"You won't be fine," the elf said, ignoring Calen's feeble swipe. "And I have more to spare than you do."

Calen sighed as a warmth washed over him. He straightened his back, filling his lungs with air. He wished he truly understood healing. For whatever Vaeril had done, Calen's lungs felt as though they had been given a week's rest. He gave Vaeril a feeble smile, resting his hand on the elf's arm. "Thank you."

"Din vrai é atuya sin'vala," Vaeril responded, returning Calen's smile. *Your thanks are welcome here.*

The sound of steel on steel blended with the shouts and screams of men and beasts as the Uraks crashed into the ranks of Lorian soldiers who held the street. This time, though, the men did not buckle. With walls on either side of them, their shields locked, and arrows raining down from above, they held their ground.

Cries of 'Hold the line!' and 'For the empire!' rang out, one after another as black steel blades bit into bone, hardened claws rent steel, and the massive beasts with the runes carved into their skin sent shockwaves of earth and fire rippling towards the soldiers.

Calen couldn't help but find his heart stir at the soldiers' implacable courage. To hold a line like that against another man was one thing, but to hold it against this horde was something entirely different.

"You are the last person I expected to find here," came a sharp voice from behind Calen. "*Draleid*."

Calen turned to find himself staring into the azure eyes of a tall woman with hair as black as coal and features as sharp as a knife's edge. Black robes hung from her shoulders, and she held herself with unquestionable authority.

She radiated power.

Calen met the woman's stare, unblinking. His throat felt like parchment, and a coil of dread twisted in his stomach. For a moment, his mind turned back to the cell in Arisfall, a flash of panic in his bones. Calen reached out to the Spark, drawing in threads of Fire. He would not be captured again. He would not let that happen. Out of the corner of his eye, Calen saw Erik take a step towards the Battlemage, his blades held firmly in his fists.

The woman turned her head to look at Erik, her eyes narrowing. "Move and I will crush your heart inside your chest." Pulling her eyes from the now stationary Erik, the woman returned her attention to Calen. "I am Arkana Vardane, imperial Battlemage and commander of the Battlemages of Kingspass. I have no intention of killing you or capturing you."

"I believe you about as far as I could throw you," Erik snapped, a snarl forming in his throat.

Arkana sighed, shaking her head, fixing her gaze on Calen's. "My only concern is surviving this and keeping as many citizens of this city alive as possible. I count my odds as better with a dragon on our side. Have I not already saved you?"

Calen held her gaze for a moment, searching her eyes for something that might betray her true intentions, but he found nothing. Her stare was cold and unyielding. He glanced at Tarmon, who hesitated for a moment, then nodded.

"How do we know we can trust you?" The threads of Fire wrapped themselves around Calen, warming him, calling to him.

"If you could not, you would already be dead."

"And if we do survive?" Tarmon asked, his voice calm and level as he stepped towards the woman, towering over her. "What then?"

To her credit, Arkana met Tarmon's stare with as much confidence as she had met Calen's. Her eyes tracked from Tarmon's boots the whole way up his enormous frame, as though evaluating him, then locked with his. "Then you will leave this place unharmed, and I will say that you escaped in the chaos."

"The Circle will kill you if they find out about your lie."

"The Uraks will kill us all if we don't work together."

"Well spoken." Tarmon stepped back and nodded to Calen.

Erik leaned in, whispering in Calen's ear. "I still don't trust her."

"We don't have a choice," Calen whispered back, turning to Arkana. He let out a sigh, feeling the warmth leave him as he reluctantly released the threads of Fire. "Where do you need us?"

"We're going to retreat to the main plaza. We—"

A cacophony of screams and shouts erupted from the ranks of men who had been holding the street. A number of the giant rune-marked Uraks had crashed through the line, shattering armour and bone as they charged.

"Bloodmarked," Arkana hissed. Calen felt the woman reach for the Spark, whirling threads of Fire, Air, and Spirit around herself before forging them into bolts of blue lightning that she hurled towards the rampaging creatures. Two or three of the Bloodmarked fell, lightning punching through their chests and necks. But more flowed through, snapping bones with swipes of their claws, coating the ground in crimson lifeblood.

"Fall back to the plaza, now!" Arkana shouted, yelling commands at nearby soldiers. She sent one youthful-looking man through the doors of a nearby building to give instructions to the archers and Battlemages who held the rooftops. She turned back to Calen. "We need to get to the plaza."

"What about those men?" Calen instinctively moved towards the ranks of soldiers who were being overrun by the Urak horde.

"They are already dead," Arkana said, not a drop of emotion in her voice. "The best they can do now is cover our retreat."

"No, we can't just leave them here to die."

Calen felt Tarmon's hand on his shoulder. "She's right. We must know when to fight and when to fall back. *This* is when we fall back."

Chapter Fifty-Three

Of Darkness and Light

rrows rained down from the rooftops as Calen and the others retreated back along the street that led to the plaza. Calen kept his eyes forward as he ran. He didn't have the stomach to look back. He knew they had no choice, but leaving those men to die would never sit right with him – nor would he have ever wanted it to.

In front of him, Vaeril spun and dropped to one knee in a single fluid motion, loosing a flurry of arrows into the onrushing swarm of Uraks that bore down on them. Droplets lost in an ocean.

Overhead, Calen could feel Valerys swooping through the sky, circling towards the street, the wind rippling over his armoured body, the pressure building in his mind.

"Get down!" Calen called, sheathing his sword and pushing both Vaeril and Erik to the ground.

Arkana, Tarmon, and the others who had made the retreat with them all followed suit as Valerys dropped low overhead, taking advantage of the narrow street to pour a column of dragonfire down atop the Uraks. A cheer erupted from the soldiers as the beasts were consumed by orange-red fire, screaming, howling, burning. They still believed Valerys to be one of the Dragonguard.

There was a flash of light and a bolt of purple lightning shot into the sky. Calen's heart twisted in on itself, and his body went rigid as the lightning crashed into Valerys's side. The dragon unleashed an earth-shaking roar of pain as it spiralled away, falling towards a nearby rooftop. Calen let out a cry, dropping to his knees, Valerys's pain burning through his veins, piercing his mind.

Erik's hand landed on Calen's shoulder, dragging him to his feet. "Calen, we need to—"

Calen lashed out, whipping a thread of Air at Erik, knocking him to the ground. The only thoughts that echoed through Calen's mind were of Valerys. He was alive. Calen could feel the dragon's heart beating, slow and steady. But there was so much pain. The lightning had struck Valerys in the side, from below his wing up to the joint of his right hind leg.

Calen needed to get to him. He could use the buildings, move across the rooftops. Just as Calen moved for the doorway of a nearby building, a roar of defiance swept through his mind. Images of Erik, Tarmon, and Vaeril, accompanied by the same protective feeling that Valerys always held for Calen. Valerys's intention was clear: 'Protect our family'.

A wave of shame filled Calen from top to bottom for lashing out at Erik. He turned to find himself face-to-face with his friend, who was brushing the dust off his chest. "I'm sorry, I—"

"We'll talk about it later," Erik said, his expression unchanging. "Is he all right?"

"He'll live," Calen replied. "I'm sorry."

Erik simply nodded. Words were not needed.

More howls and war cries signalled that the Uraks had continued their charge, storming through the now dwindling remnants of Valerys's dragonfire. The creatures were relentless. Calen watched some of the larger ones – the Bloodmarked, Arkana had called them – emerge through the smoke and flame, their runes casting a deep red glow through the hazy night.

"We need to move," Arkana said, adjusting her robes. "We need to get into the plaza."

As Calen and the others crossed over the threshold and stepped into the open plaza, the ranks of soldiers closed behind them, forming a wall across the mouth of the street, just as they had done earlier.

Calen hadn't noticed it before, but it looked as though there were only two ways in and out of the main plaza: the street they had just come down and the one at the opposite side leading towards the port. Rows of soldiers stood firm at each entrance, fifty deep but only five wide, so narrow were the streets.

The plaza was just as it had been when they had last passed through, packed with columns of soldiers, some in heavy plate with long spears and rectangular shields, others with chainmail and leather, carrying a variety of ranged weaponry.

Three long rows of crossbowmen stood behind the rows of heavily armoured soldiers at the entrances on either side of the plaza, ready to face whatever beasts might break through the defensive lines.

Up above, lining every single rooftop that framed the plaza, were rows of archers interspersed by dark figures whose black robes flapped in the rising wind.

The only new occupants to the plaza stood at the far side, near the opposite entrance, almost two hundred soldiers astride the largest horses Calen had ever seen in his life. They had to have been eighteen, maybe even nineteen hands in size. Each horse was jet-black, with a thick, powerful neck and hooves that looked as though they could crush steel. He had only seen one once before, but he had heard the stories. "Varsundi Blackthorns."

"There are no greater warhorses in all the continent," Arkana said, her own eyes holding the same sense of recognition as Calen's.

Erik turned to her, his eyes trimming to thin lines. "The empire only *steals* the best." He almost spat his words, turning his gaze from Arkana's as soon as he had spoken.

There was nothing Calen could, or would, say. He despised working with the empire just as much as Erik did. The very idea of it turned his blood to ice. But every time it did, Calen repeated Tarmon's words in his head. *'Tonight, those men and women are not empire soldiers. They are just people. People who don't want to die. And they need us. They need you. They need a Draleid'.*

"Hold!"

Calen turned his head towards the call. The Uraks had reached the soldiers who held the street, crashing into them like a landslide. Above them, arrows rained down, slicing into the onrushing horde below.

"What is your plan?" Tarmon asked Arkana, rolling his shoulders, easing the weight of the greatsword in his hands.

"We stand, and we fight." Calen felt Arkana reaching for the Spark as she spoke, wreathing herself in threads of Air.

"That's your plan?" Erik gasped, glaring at Arkana. "We're all going to die."

"Do you have a better one, oh *wise warrior*?" Arkana lifted a single eyebrow. "I did not think so. My Battlemages on the rooftops, along with the archers, should thin their lines. When they break through into the plaza, the crossbowmen will fire a volley, then we"—Arkana gestured towards Vaeril and Calen—"will push them back with the Spark, giving the spears time to reform the line. If too many get through, the Blackthorns will run them down."

"How long can we maintain that?"

"I don't know," Arkana admitted. "They will break through eventually, but we need to thin them as much as we can. Can the dragon—"

"I'm not risking him in the open like that again," Calen cut across, his voice firm. He reached out to Valerys, grimacing at the pain that burned through the dragon's side. Valerys lay on a rooftop to the west. *Stay there.*

A defiant rumble answered him, sending a tremor through his mind.

"Very well. But you will not be able to keep him out of this fight indefinitely, and the longer he stays away, the greater the chance we will all die."

Calen didn't respond. He simply stood there, holding Arkana's gaze.

A blood-chilling scream rang out, and Calen didn't even have time to turn before a man's body plummeted from the nearby rooftops, bones snapping and bursting through his skin as he hit the ground, blood and gore splattering across the stone. Still in shock, Calen pulled his hand up to his face, his fingers wiping away a thick mixture of blood and bone fragments from his cheek. Looking down, it would not have been possible to tell that the mashed pile of gore, bone, and leather had once been a man. He had to catch the vomit in his mouth.

Another scream rang out, then another, as more soldiers dropped from the rooftops above, crashing down into the plaza. It was not only the soldiers. A woman in a black cloak cracked against the stone beside Tarmon, impaled through the gut by an enormous black spear with a glowing red gem set into its blade.

Calen could feel the panic breaking out, rippling through the soldiers like a stone dropped in a lake. It would not take much for them to break.

"They're jumping!" one of the soldiers cried out, his hand pointing up towards the roof of a nearby building.

At first, Calen wasn't sure what the man meant, surely the men weren't jumping from the rooves; no one could survive that fall. But then his eyes caught sight of an enormous Bloodmarked standing at the parapet of the building, its red runes glimmering. With an almighty leap, the creature threw itself from the roof. The beast crushed two soldiers beneath its feet as it landed, smashing their bones as though they were twigs. Spreading its muscular arms out wide, the enormous creature unleashed a guttural howl, spraying spittle into the air. Its eyes burning with fury, the beast charged at the line of crossbowmen standing before it. More Bloodmarked followed suit, leaping down from the buildings above, tearing through soldiers as though they were nothing.

Then, the men broke.

The horde of Uraks streamed into the plaza, cutting down the Lorian soldiers as they ran. Shouts and cries echoed through the plaza, only surpassed by the howls of the Uraks as they ran down their prey.

"To Calen!" Tarmon called, swinging his greatsword through the air, cleaving an Urak in half across the navel. Within a matter of moments, Tarmon, Erik, and Vaeril were tight by Calen's side. It was only when Calen sensed Arkana reaching for threads of Earth, Spirit, and Air that he realised the Battlemage stood with them. She had not fled or left them to die. Calen still despised her, and all her kind, but at the least, he respected her.

The tide of Uraks was almost upon them.

Twenty feet.

Calen reached out to Valerys. The dragon was already in the air, fighting the agony that seared through his side. Through Valerys's eyes, Calen could see the true enormity of what they faced. The Urak army stretched the whole way back through the long street, out into the courtyard that lay before the gates, and further still, swarming across the rest of the city. There had to be thousands of them, tens of thousands. Calen clenched his jaw. He could not even begin to count the number of times he had thought his life over. But now, as he stood with those he called friends, it truly felt as though this was the end. There was no way out. He would finally get to see his family again. He would finally get to see Haem.

Fifteen feet.

The mass of leathery brown and grey skin hissed as it moved, red eyes and jagged yellow teeth, blackened blades and spears. Mixed amongst the horde were the Bloodmarked, standing at least two feet taller than the rest, red light and smoke drifting from the runes carved into their skin.

Ten feet.

The blood in Calen's veins shivered its way through his body.

The sound of hooves hammering against stone filled Calen's ears, the repetitive thumps drowning out everything else.

"For Loria! For the empire!" came the cry as the regiment of Blackthorn cavalry hammered into the side of the charging Uraks, their formation akin to an arrowhead. Even the Uraks couldn't stand against the enormous black warhorses, their hooves crushing bone and the curved swords of their riders slicing through leathery hide.

The cavalry charge completely collapsed the left flank of the charging beasts, pushing deeper into the centre. But unless they were given relief, the cavalry would be trapped within the encroaching mass.

Overhead, Valerys's white scales shimmered in the moonlight as the dragon dropped low, his lips pulling back, his body ready. Calen could feel the fury that surged through Valerys, seeping into his own mind, igniting the fury of their shared soul. With a roar that caused the dust on the ground to shake, Valerys crashed into the mass of Uraks, crushing bone beneath his talons, cleaving limbs and rending blackened steel.

Then, with a whip of his spearhead tail and a crack of his wings, Valerys lifted himself into the air once more, snatching a Bloodmarked in his jaws as he did. Thrashing his head left to right, the dragon ripped the beast in half, spraying blood down over the fighting below.

Another bolt of purple lightning streaked from somewhere in the mass of Uraks, but Valerys wheeled out of the way at the last second, leaving the lightning to crash into the side of a building, shattering the stone.

As Valerys rose higher into the sky and the soldiers cheered him, Calen weaved the threads of Air and Spirit into his voice, raising it above everything else, Valerys's energy rippling through his body. "To me, warriors of Epheria! Forward!"

Every hair on Calen's body stood on end as he roared his rallying cry. He wasn't brave. Fear thrummed through him with every beat of his heart. But if this was going to be the day he died, he would not go quietly.

As though of their own volition, his legs carried him forward, charging towards the Uraks. He did not have to look to know the others were beside him. Calen clenched his fingers around the hilt of his blade and leaned into the charge, pulling on threads of Air and Earth as he did, feeling Valerys's power pulse through him.

Beside him, Arkana reached out with threads of Earth, pushing them into the jagged steel breastplates worn by a number of the Uraks, forcing them to collapse inward, crushing bones and organs in a series of vicious snaps. The creatures crumpled to the ground, engulfed by the charging horde behind them.

Vaeril stayed tight to Calen's side, weaving threads of Air around them, whipping spears out of the air whenever they got too close.

Holding his breath for a just a moment as he ran, Calen spread his threads of Earth through the fragments of shattered stone that littered the ground in front of him, splitting them into smaller shards, sharp and strong. Lifting the shards from the ground with threads of Air, Calen launched them towards the Uraks like a hundred crossbow bolts. The beasts howled as they dropped. With Valerys's strength flowing through him, Calen could only just feel the drain sapping at the edge of his consciousness, a trickle from an ocean.

Calen's heart stopped for a fraction of a second before he crashed into the thick of the fighting. Without a thought, he dropped into Striking Dragon, letting the forms of the svidarya flow through him. He was the svidarya; he *was* the *burning winds.*

Erik, Vaeril, and Tarmon moved by his side, slicing their way through the Uraks, carving a path to the Blackthorn riders. Imperial soldiers rallied around them, bolstered by their charge, shouting war cries as they moved.

A few of the majestic horses had fallen, torn to pieces by the monstrosities around them, but most still stood, their sheer size and their riders' blades keeping the Uraks at bay.

The head of a black spear sliced across the outside of Calen's left arm. It was only a graze, but the pain burned. Stepping back, he lifted his blade through the air and opened the Urak's throat, watching as the beast fell, spluttering, to the ground. He followed through, his swing carrying him forward. He dragged his sword across the next Urak's chest, then brought it up in two hands to block the downward swing of another, driving his blade through the creature's ribs, burying it to the hilt.

Pulling on threads of Air, Calen pushed the Urak free from his blade, sending its body crashing into more of its companions. To his left, Tarmon moved through the creatures like a pendulum of death, his greatsword swinging in mighty sweeps, cleaving flesh and bone.

As Calen turned, one of the Uraks crashed into him, sending him sprawling to the ground. As he scrambled backwards, trying desperately to get himself to his feet, the creature lunged forward, swinging its blackened blade in a downward arc. *Whoosh.*

An arrow sliced through the air, plunging into the Urak's eye. Calen watched as Vaeril leapt past him, dropping his bow to the ground. The elf slid behind the creature, pulling his sword from its sheath, shearing the Urak's hamstrings in one sweep of his blade. Screaming and flailing its arms in a half-blind rage, the Urak fell to its knees, blood cascading down its face, coating its jagged yellow teeth. Then it went limp as Vaeril drove his blade through its back and out its chest before pulling the sword free and letting the creature drop to the ground.

"We've spoken before about you trying to get yourself killed, haven't we?" Erik stood over Calen, his hand extended.

Calen attempted a half-smile as he took Erik's hand, but he didn't have his friend's ability to smile while those around him were sheared from the world. Part of him envied Erik's ability to detach himself, but an equal part of him never wanted to attain such a skill.

Calen gathered himself, dragging the air back into his lungs. Looking around, he could see that most of the Blackthorns had managed to pull themselves free of the mass and were readying a second charge. Twice more the Blackthorns charged, and twice more they shattered the Urak lines. Calen had never seen such powerful horses and such disciplined riders. No matter how many times they charged towards the Uraks, their courage never faltered.

But as the cavalry manoeuvred to charge once more, Calen saw something he had hoped he would never see again. The world around him grew dimmer, and a chill ran up his spine. Before he could think to shout a warning – not that it would have done any good either way – a shockwave rippled through the air, slamming into the horses' flanks, lifting them off their feet. Some of the Blackthorns escaped the brunt of the blow, but more than half lay crippled on the ground, bones broken and twisted, their riders dead or pinned beneath them.

There, standing at the source of the shockwave, were two figures in black cloaks. The cloaks were not adorned with the same blue spirals as the creature Calen had fought in Belduar, but he did not need to lift their hoods to know what lay underneath: pale skin; thin, brittle lips, icy and cold; dark wells for eyes that drank in the light.

An involuntary shiver ran the length of Calen's body, his throat went dry, and he had to fight hard to keep the feeling of hopelessness at bay. Just one of those creatures had nearly killed them all. They didn't stand a chance against two. Not without Aeson and the others.

A darkness pulsated in one of the Fade's hands, as though the shadows coalesced at its fingertips. Then, within moments, it held a blade of wispy black fire in its grasp. The same weapon the Fade in Belduar had held – a níthral. *Soulblade.*

"I thought they fought *for* the empire?" Erik said, a tremble in his voice.

"Fades fight for no nation," Arkana hissed, her eyes narrowing at the creatures. "They serve Efilatír. No one else. They are his heralds. Though this is the first time I have seen them outwardly opposing the empire."

As Arkana spoke, another creature stepped free from the raging battle around them. An Urak, of sorts. A long, sleeveless robe of grey and silver was draped over its leathery skin. Short, barbed horns grew from its head, and its eyes gleamed crimson. In its right hand, the creature held a long wooden staff, a glowing red gemstone set into its top, held there by twisting branches of wood. A blackened blade was fixed to the bottom of the staff, wicked and slick with blood.

For a few moments, the creature stood there, its eyes fixed on Calen and the others, its stare unblinking. Then, it did something Calen would not have expected in a thousand years. It spoke.

"You… dare… bring… another…" The Urak's words lifted above the din of battle, sifting through the chaos, amplified by some unseen force. Its voice was harsh and broken, each word dragging as though it tasted bitter on the creature's tongue. Pausing, it took a long breath, then spoke again, its lip curling at the corner of its mouth, exposing a row of jagged, yellow teeth. "I… will… bleed… you… all."

Without waiting for a response, the Urak thrust its staff into the air, unleashing a deep, primal roar that scratched at Calen's ears. The gemstone set into the Urak's staff shimmered, its red light growing deeper, more vibrant. As the stone glowed, it poured forth strands of fire that snaked their way around the staff, flickering in the wind. Then the Urak charged, the Fades moving like vipers at its side.

CHAPTER FIFTY-FOUR

THE WARRIOR

Kallinvar leaned forward, breaking off a piece of crusty bread from the loaf. He slathered it in butter, then soaked it in the last of the juices from the pork. With a tired sigh, he tossed the piece of juice-soaked bread into his mouth, closing his eyes as the flavours melted onto his tongue.

"All I'm saying," Lyrin said, leaning back in his chair, holding his arms out wide, "is if you hadn't tricked me, I would've won."

"And all *I'm* saying," Arden replied, "is if you hadn't lost, you would've won."

Tarron, Ruon, and Ildris burst out in fits of laughter, rolling their shoulders back and patting Lyrin across the back.

Kallinvar was truly thankful for nights like these. Nights when his brothers and sisters could put death and blood to the back of their minds. They were few and far between. In truth, he wasn't sure he could remember the last one.

The only blight on the occasion was that the rest of the chapter were not there to enjoy it. Sylven and Mirken had been sent to give aid to the towns along the northern edge of the Lightning Coast, while Varlin and Daynin had gone to investigate a convergence of the Taint at the foot of the Marin Mountains.

"I say you both rematch," Ruon said, creases forming at the corners of her mouth as she continued to laugh. No matter the situation, Ruon had always held onto that laughter. It was something Kallinvar had never stopped admiring in her. "I'll wager tomorrow's rations on Arden. Ildris, care to take that wager?"

Ildris raised both his hands. "I would prefer to eat, thank you very much."

"Hey, hey!" Lyrin shouted. "Let's everybody calm down, okay?"

Another chorus of laughter broke out, but it was soon cut short at the sound of the kitchen's door swinging open, cracking against the stone wall.

Kallinvar's eyes opened wide at the sight of Grandmaster Verathin standing in the doorway, all but his head encased in the overlapping gold-trimmed plates of his Sentinel armour.

"What's happened?" Kallinvar pulled himself to his feet.

"I have sensed another convergence of the Taint," Verathin said, a grim look streaked across his weathered face. "It's the largest I've sensed in a long time."

"Where?"

"Kingspass, just southwest of Lynalion. Multiple Fades and a Shaman."

Kallinvar nodded, his gaze fixed on the floor. "We will follow you to the chamber."

"Be quick about it, brother. I fear we do not have much time."

As Verathin disappeared from the doorway, Kallinvar turned back to his knights. "Lyrin, what is the last report we had on the Draleid?"

Kallinvar saw the realisation dawn in Lyrin's eyes. "Going north, Brother-Captain. Heading along the eastern coast."

Kallinvar gave a slight nod. It was too much of a coincidence. He took a deep breath, then spoke, addressing all his knights. "There is a darkness in this world, my brothers and sisters. A darkness that does not stop, does not sleep, does not tire or wane. It is relentless in its pursuit of all things. It is to stand in the path of this darkness that we were chosen. To stand in Achyron's name. To be his light. Will you join me in this?"

"Yes, Brother-Captain," Ildris shouted, rising to his feet.

"Yes, Brother-Captain," Lyrin, Arden, and Tarron chorused, following Ildris.

Ruon was the last to rise, her deep green eyes finding Kallinvar's as she pushed back her chair. "We would follow you to the void and back, Kallinvar. We would die for you a thousand times over. We would stand before Efilatír himself. We are with you, always."

As Kallinvar stepped into the chamber that was the heart of the great temple of Achyron, the thrum of his Sentinel armour pulsing through his body, his mind drifted back to that night four centuries gone. The night that one hundred of his brothers and sisters had stood in this very chamber. The night when one hundred Knights of Achyron had charged into The Rift, and only seventeen returned.

Looking about the chamber now, the orange candlelight casting shadows across the stone, he counted twenty-eight knights standing within its sacred walls, Verathin and himself included. The rest of the knighthood were on task, holding back the Shadow across the continent.

Most of those who stood in the heart of the temple had not held the Sigil for even a century. Five of the knights were his own. And though they were both fine warriors, Lyrin and Arden had borne the Sigil fewer than ten years between them.

At the far side of the chamber, Kallinvar spotted Sister-Captain Olyria and Brother-Captain Armites – captains of The Third and The Sixth, both survivors of The Fall. Those of their knights who had not been sent on task stood at their side; four from The Sixth, six from The Third. The remaining numbers were made up by The First, Grandmaster Verathin's chapter, all with fewer than four hundred years to the Sigil. Fine warriors, all.

"Your sword, Brother-Captain Kallinvar."

Kallinvar let a soft smile touch his face at the sound of Watcher Gildrick's voice breaking through the otherwise sombre mood that had overcome him. It was sometimes a strange thing for Kallinvar to look upon Gildrick, with his greying temples and ever darkening eyes, and remember him how he was when they had first met – a child of but fourteen summers.

Since then, Gildrick had grown over a foot, his hair had thinned, his face had wisened, and his shoulders had become strong and broad. Thirty summers. Kallinvar had not aged a day in that time, thanks to the Sigil that was fused to his chest.

"Thank you, Gildrick." Kallinvar took his sword from Gildrick and strapped it around his waist. "Last we talked, you and Watcher Poldor thought you might have found a breakthrough in your research into why the dragons stopped hatching. How goes it?"

Gildrick shrugged, taking in a slow sigh, then releasing. "Another dead end, I'm afraid. But if you do happen to encounter this new Draleid, I would very much like to meet him, or even more, his dragon."

"I will keep that in mind." Kallinvar turned to head towards Grandmaster Verathin, who stood at the centre of the chamber.

"Kallinvar?" Gildrick's tone took a sombre tilt.

"What is it, Gildrick?"

"Watch over the others. I feel something tonight. I'm not sure what, but just…"

"I will watch over them, Gildrick, as I always have."

Both men exchanged a slight nod of acknowledgement before Gildrick turned and walked back to where some of the other watchers stood, waiting.

Verathin reached out his hand as Kallinvar approached, grasping Kallinvar's forearm and pulling him into a tight embrace. "Once more into the Rift, my friend."

"Be honest, Verathin," Kallinvar said, pulling back. "How bad is it?"

Verathin took in a slow breath, biting the corner of his lip, then released it even more slowly. "It is not as it was that night in Ilnaen, but the Shadow is strong. It will not be an easy fight."

"It is never an easy fight."

"True enough," Verathin said, giving a half-smile and blowing a short puff of air out his nose.

"Verathin, the Draleid may be on the other side."

"I suspected as much."

"I thought you might."

Verathin held Kallinvar's gaze for a moment; he did not need Kallinvar to ask the question they both knew hung in the air. "Killing any Shaman is the priority, Brother-Captain. But it is in Achyron's best interest if you can keep the Draleid alive."

"Understood, Grandmaster. Do you wish me to lead the way?"

"Not this day, Kallinvar. No, today I will lead."

Kallinvar bowed at the waist, turning to join his fellow knights, giving a slight nod towards Sister-Captain Olyria and Brother-Captain Armites, as he took his place by Ruon's side.

"What did he say?" Ruon whispered, leaning her head towards Kallinvar.

"That it will not be an easy fight."

Ruon struggled to suppress her laugh, that familiar grin spreading across her face. "Oh, is that all?"

"Brothers and Sisters." Grandmaster Verathin's voice echoed through the chamber, the golden ornamentation of his Sentinel armour gleaming in the candlelight. A shiver ran through Kallinvar's body as Verathin spoke.

Four hundred years had passed since the last time Verathin had addressed them so. Many great souls were lost on that night. Men and women whom Kallinvar had loved fiercely, brothers and sisters. So, as he stood there, ready to follow his friend through the Rift once more, he did not chase the fear or sorrow from his heart; he leaned into it, let it feed his anger. If the Traitor wanted blood, Kallinvar would give him blood.

"Achyron calls upon us once more. He calls upon us to shine his light in the darkest of places. To stand steadfast in the path of the Shadow."

As Verathin spoke, a familiar sensation tickled at the back of Kallinvar's neck, signalling that the Grandmaster was opening the Rift.

"I will not stand here and pretend that I have eloquent words that will ease the burden that rests on your shoulders, for I do not. We are Achyron's chosen. Our burden was never meant to be an easy one to bear." Verathin thumped his armoured fist on the breastplate of his Sentinel armour as he spoke. Behind him, a small green orb flickered into existence, floating in the air, sending shivers throughout Kallinvar's body. Expanding outward, the orb spread into a circle, edges a vivid green colour that faded to black closer to the centre. "But we bear it with smiles on our faces, for our brothers and sisters fight by our side. There are men and women on the other side of the Rift who need us. Their lives hang on the tip of our courage. And in that, I do not mean you cannot hold fear in your hearts, for courage is not the absence of fear. It is the will to act in spite of fear."

Verathin slid his sword from the scabbard at his hip, and a series of rasps rang out through the chamber as the other knights, Kallinvar included, did the same. "And now, I ask you, brothers and sisters. Are you with me?"

Every hair on Kallinvar's body stood on end as he roared his response. He looked around, seeing the fervour on the faces of Lyrin and Arden as they, too, chanted their answer to Verathin's question. Young though they might be, Kallinvar had no doubts they would give their lives for the men and women who stood at their side.

Behind Verathin, the Rift continued to spread until it was over twenty feet in diameter, its black, water-like surface rippling with energy, its outer rim shimmering a vivid, green light across the stones.

"The duty of the strong is to protect the weak," Verathin called out.

"The duty of the strong is to protect the weak," Kallinvar shouted, joining the chorus of the other knights.

"Pain is the path to strength," Verathin shouted.

"Pain is the path to strength."

Kallinvar felt a nudge at his left shoulder and turned to see Ruon staring at him with a raised eyebrow, her eyes a brilliant blue. Kallinvar tilted his head slightly.

Ruon gave an almost imperceptible shrug. "I still think your speeches are better."

At first, Kallinvar just stared at her, his eyes narrowed, unsure of how to react. The woman had never cared for what was proper, no matter the situation. But then, against all his better instincts, he smiled.

Ruon matched Kallinvar's smile, giving him another slight nudge. "To the void and back," she said, giving a nod of her head before turning back to Verathin.

To the void and back.

Before them, Verathin turned to face the Rift, the dark green helm of his Sentinel armour forming over his head. "For Achyron!"

The fervorous response of the other knights faded in Kallinvar's ears, all sounds in the chamber capitulating to the thrum of the Rift that resonated through his body. Knots of fear twisted in his stomach as he gazed upon the rippling pool of jet that hung in the air before him. Only a fool held no fear in their heart as they charged to battle, and Kallinvar was no fool. The vibrations of Kallinvar's heart beat through his veins like a war drum, urging him on. Then, before he knew it, he was charging, his brother and sister knights at his side, encased in the dark green plates of their Sentinel armour. *Pain is the path to strength.*

Kallinvar's body shivered as he charged into the icy embrace of the Rift. The black liquid washed over him, seeping through his Sentinel armour, through his skin, through his bones, reaching right down to his soul. It was only for a moment, but in the Rift, time was such that it could feel as though an eternity might pass in the blink of an eye.

Then he was falling.

Air whipped past Kallinvar's helm as he emerged from the icy pool of black, plummeting towards the battlefield below. The Rift had opened in the sky above the city, dropping the knights into the thick of the fighting. The city itself was painted in a mixture of silvery moonlight and the orange-red glow of roaring fire. A massive section of wall beside the main gate had completely collapsed, and the Bloodspawn had flooded into the city. Directly below was an enormous plaza where the fighting was thickest.

As he fell, a shimmering flicker caught Kallinvar's eye. He knew it was a dragon even before the fire spewed forth from its jaws, raking through a cluster of Bloodspawn below. At thirty or so feet, it was far smaller than the dragons he had once known, but it was still young and nothing to be sniffed at. The damage its fire caused was evidence enough of that.

Just before Kallinvar hit the ground, he called to his Sigil, summoning his Soulblade. The spirit of Achyron burned through him, flowing in his veins. Flashes of green light burst to life in the air around him as the other knights did the same, their Soulblades blazing in the dark of night.

Within moments he held his Soulblade in his grasp. Wrought by the warrior god, wielded by the chosen.

A cloud of dust lifted into the air as Kallinvar hit the ground, stone cracking beneath the boots of his Sentinel armour. Resounding hammer blows behind him signalled the landing of his brothers and sisters.

A shiver of repulsion ran through Kallinvar's bones as the sickly Taint of blood magic oozed through the air, seeping into the back of his mind.

"For Achyron!"

Charging forward, Kallinvar carved his way through the mass of Uraks that surrounded him. Amidst the chaos, he could see Lorian soldiers fighting back-to-back, swinging swords and shields, holding Uraks at bay with long spears. Some even rode on the backs of obsidian black mounts that looked as though they could hold a knight in full Sentinel armour. But wherever he looked, the men fell, ripped apart by bloodthirsty beasts.

Kallinvar brought his Soulblade across his body, meeting the blackened blade of an Urak head-on before sidestepping the beast's next strike and driving his shimmering Soulblade through the creature's sternum.

"Not bad," Ruon called, gliding by on Kallinvar's left, leaping through the air, beheading two Uraks with a single wide sweep. Ildris and Tarron surged after her, leaving blood and bodies in their wake.

To his right, Verathin sheared through the Bloodspawn, moving like the harbinger of death, the knights of The First following in his wake. Kallinvar watched as the Grandmaster pulled his Soulblade from the belly of a Bloodmarked, only to take another's head from its shoulders in the same motion.

Arden and Lyrin moved beside the Grandmaster, their Soulblades scintillating as they cut through their enemies, never taking a moment to pause.

Something struck Kallinvar across the back, sending him stumbling forward. Whatever it was had not cracked his armour, but it had certainly left a bruise. Spinning on his heels Kallinvar found himself face-to-face with a Bloodmarked. A corpse encased in heavy plate armour dangled from the beast's right hand, blood dripping from its neck.

The Bloodmarked charged, swinging the corpse through the air as though it were a mace.

Sliding onto his knees, Kallinvar ducked under the creature's swing and extended his Soulblade, cleaving the Bloodmarked's leg in half at the knee. The creature collapsed, howling in pain, the runes that covered its skin burned with a fury, pluming smoke.

Planting his foot on the beast's neck, Kallinvar forced all his might down through his leg until he felt a snap resonate through his Sentinel armour, and the beast's body went limp, the light from its runes fading to nothing.

Around him, Kallinvar could see the flashes of green light drifting in and out of the thick of bodies as the knights carved through the army of Bloodspawn. But he knew they could not keep it up indefinitely. He had seen the sheer number of the creatures when he had emerged from the Rift. They needed to kill the Shaman and any Fades. Only then would they stand a chance.

Kallinvar had only killed four Shamans in his many centuries. But each time he had, the effects of the creature's death had rippled through the Bloodspawn around it, breaking them, sending them into a panicked retreat. *Cut the head off the wyrm and the body will die.*

Reluctantly, Kallinvar opened his mind, sifting through the dense layers of oily darkness that permeated the city. Trying to find the strongest pulses of the Taint amidst the chaos was akin to searching for the hottest point of a blazing inferno. Kallinvar's consciousness recoiled at the Taint's sickly touch, but he pushed onward. Then, just as his mind had reached its breaking point, he felt the epicentre. The pulsing, throbbing heart of darkness amidst the horde of shadow.

"Knights of Achyron, with me!"

With his brothers and sisters at his side, Kallinvar cut a bloody path through the battlefield, his mind following the pulsing core of the Taint.

Leathery hide and dense bone yielded to his Soulblade, the spirit of Achyron surging through him.

Bending at the knee, Kallinvar launched himself through the air, his shoulder hammering into the chest of a Bloodmarked as smoke drifted from the creature's runes. The force of the blow knocked the beast backward, stumbling over the many corpses that littered the ground. As the Bloodmarked dropped, Kallinvar fell with it, driving his Soulblade through the bottom of its jaw and up through the back of its skull. The light of the creature's runes had faded by the time its body crashed to the stone.

As Kallinvar picked himself up, the sickly touch of the Taint throbbed in his mind, pulsing – a thick, visceral oil that leeched at the fabric of the world. *The Shaman.* Scanning the battlefield, he found the creature ripping its way through the Lorian soldiers. It stood at least nine feet tall, horns of bone protruding from its head, whips of fire streaking from its staff.

Two Fades fought by the Shaman's side, their black cloaks billowing in the wind, hoods drawn down, exposing skin as pale as thin parchment stretched over a naked flame. In their hands, they held blades of flickering black flame – abominations. Soulblades wrought from the traitor god. The creatures moved like wyrms, coiled and ready, snapping at their enemies.

Charging towards the Shaman and the Fades, Kallinvar saw a young man, no more than twenty summers, his eyes streaming with a purple light, three companions at his side. They fought like rabid wolves, cornered and desperate. No Draleid Kallinvar had ever known had eyes like that, but he was of no doubt as to who the young man was.

"Verathin, the Draleid!" Kallinvar reached out his Soulblade, pointing towards the young man with the glowing purple eyes.

Verathin's helm turned to liquid metal, receding into his Sentinel armour as his head turned towards the young man, then back to Kallinvar. The Grandmaster gave Kallinvar a nod then raised his Soulblade in the air. "For Achyron!"

The Grandmaster charged towards the Draleid, his helm reforming around his head. Brother-Captain Armites and Sister-Captain Olyria charged after him, their knights in tow.

"Knights of The Second, with me!"

A cry rose out around Kallinvar as his brothers and sisters charged alongside him, their white cloaks streaming behind them, the ground yielding to their Sentinel armour.

The Draleid and his companions fought valiantly, but they were nearing their end. Blood streamed from the many wounds they had sustained, a heaviness held in their movements, and an inevitability hung over them.

Kallinvar watched as one of the Draleid's companions, a man as large as Arden garbed in full plate armour and wielding a mighty greatsword, blocked a strike from a Fade's black-fire blade, dragging his own sword across the creature's chest, then driving it to the hilt into its gut. He watched as the Fade swatted the man to the ground with an unseen force. It had to be the Spark. Kallinvar could not sense the use of the Spark in the way he could with blood magic, but he knew it well enough to know when it had been used.

An imperial Battlemage rushed to the mountain of a man, whips of fire swirling around her. But to Kallinvar's surprise, the mage did not move to drive home the final blow. Instead, she reached out her hand and dragged the man to his feet. It was not a sight Kallinvar had expected to see.

Kallinvar urged his legs onward as the Fade pulled the greatsword from its gut. Bounding over the mutilated corpse of a black horse, he struck out at the Fade, his Soulblade colliding with the creature's black-fire níthral. The Fade hissed, staring at him with those empty black eyes. The Taint that oozed from the creature set a sickly feeling in Kallinvar's stomach.

"I have not seen your kind in a long time, knight." The Fade's voice was harsh and raspy, dripping with malice. It pushed forward, whipping its black-fire blade in short strokes, testing Kallinvar's defences. The creature moved with inhuman speed, matching every swing of Kallinvar's Soulblade with ease before a shockwave erupted from its hand, and Kallinvar crashed to the ground.

Before the Fade could take advantage of Kallinvar's position, Arden and Lyrin surged in from the left, nimbly dashing between the whips of fire the creature hurled at them.

"Try and stay on your feet," Ruon shouted as she reached down, heaving Kallinvar up and forward. "You're no use on your back!"

Kallinvar gritted his teeth and charged after Ruon, Ildris and Tarron at his side. All six of the knights surrounded the Fade, attacking as one, their Soulblades shimmering through the air.

The creature called forth all manner of dark magic, striking out with bolts of purple lightning and whips of fire. But each time one of the knights was pushed back, another slipped into their place. Kallinvar could feel the Fade's fear. For in their hands, the knights held weapons forged with the sole purpose of shearing the dark creatures' very existence from the world: Soulblades.

As Kallinvar moved forward, charging at the creature, a violent shiver pulsated through him, resonating from his Sigil. A knight had been sent to Achyron's halls, one of Olyria's. Kallinvar could feel the man's loss viscerally as it thrummed through him. *Rest easy, Brother.*

Kallinvar pulled his mind from the feeling of loss that pulsed through his Sigil. He could not afford distraction. Stepping forward, he traded blow after blow with the Fade, pushing it back. The Taint pulsated from the creature as it struck out with blood magic, sending an arc of purple lightning crashing into Tarron's chest.

At the sight of his brother hitting the ground, Kallinvar charged forward, sliding past the Fade's defences. Pulling his arm back, he drove his Soulblade through the creature's chest, burying it to the hilt. The Fade unleashed an unnatural shriek as the Soulblade tore its soul from the living world. It thrashed and writhed like a trapped animal, foaming at the mouth. Then it grew still, its arms drooping to its side. The fabric of the world rippled as the Fade's soul was torn from the body it inhabited, and the cord that tethered it to the living world was sheared.

"Go!" Kallinvar shouted to his knights, pulling his blade free of the dark creature's chest, letting its body drop to the floor. "To the Grandmaster!"

Kallinvar and his knights charged towards where Verathin was supporting the Draleid and his companions against the Shaman and the remaining Fade. As they did, a clutch of Bloodmarked and Uraks crashed into them in a frenzy of claws and blackened steel. Kallinvar spun through them, shearing bone in bursts of green light. "Ildris, Tarron, Lyrin, Ruon, hold them off. Arden, with me!"

Arden fell in beside Kallinvar, the other knights holding back the tide of Bloodspawn.

A thunderous roar ripped through the skies overhead, followed by a gust of wind. Its scales gleaming white, shimmering in the silvery light of the moon, the dragon dropped to the ground behind the Draleid.

Even amidst the battle, a shiver ran the length of Kallinvar's spine as he took in the sight. The white dragon's head craned over its Draleid, wings fanned out to its sides, its lips pulled back in a snarl. Beneath the great beast, the Draleid stood tall, his eyes coruscating with a purple light. Then, the dragon's head pulled back, its jaws opened, and a river of dragonfire poured forth, consuming all in its path.

A familiar shriek pierced the din of battle as the dragon's flames washed over the second Fade, scorching its flesh. As the dragonfire flickered from existence, a large patch of blackened earth and charred husks were left in its wake. With its soul still tethered to the living world, the Fade could still return one day, once it found another living host. But for now, it was gone.

"The others are holding back the tide," Verathin said as Kallinvar and Arden reached his side, his eyes still fixed on the Draleid and his dragon. "But if we don't kill that Shaman, this city will be completely overrun."

Kallinvar's eyes fell on the Urak Shaman. A clutch of Bloodmarked surrounded the creature, the shimmering red light of their runes painting the night with an unnatural light.

Verathin turned to Kallinvar. "The duty of the strong is to protect the weak, my brother. Always remember that. No matter what happens here." Before Kallinvar could respond, Verathin turned, charging towards the Shaman, his glowing green Soulblade bursting into life in his hand. "For Achyron!"

"For Achyron!" Kallinvar yelled, following after his old friend. He could hear Arden mimicking the cry as the young knight charged alongside him.

There was a moment while they ran in which Kallinvar's mind took in all that was around him. The guttural war cries of the Uraks. The screams and wails of dying men and women as they defended their home. The shriek of steel colliding with steel. The smell of charred flesh, the iron tang of blood, and the acrid stench of vomit and voided bowels. Around him, flashes of green light meshed with the glowing red runes of the Bloodmarked, the pearlescent shine of the moon, and the incandescent flicker of dragonfire. This was his purpose. *This* was where he was meant to be. Standing against the Shadow, wherever it may rise.

As Kallinvar's shoulder collided with a Bloodmarked's chest, eliciting a resounding crack, his mind was pulled back into the world. The creature reeled backward, unprepared for the force of the blow. Kallinvar did not hesitate. Lunging forward, he drove his Soulblade through the beast's exposed throat, tearing its soul from the world.

A deep *whoosh* tore through the air, and Kallinvar threw himself to the ground just in time as the spear head tip of the dragon's tail whipped above his head and sliced into the belly of a Bloodmarked.

As Kallinvar got to his feet, he found himself face-to-face with the white-scaled dragon, its neck craned down so the tip of its snout hovered just over Kallinvar's head. The dragon's upper lip was pulled back, exposing a row of dagger-like teeth. A tense moment passed where the dragon looked from Kallinvar to the body of the dead Bloodmarked, its warm breath washing over Kallinvar's helm. Then, with a beat of its leathery wings, it pulled away, lifting itself into the air.

As the dragon took flight, the Draleid rushed past Kallinvar, his eyes shimmering with purple light. With a motion of the Draleid's hand, shards of stone and shattered steel lifted into the air and launched towards a clutch of the Bloodmarked, shredding their flesh.

Two of the Draleid's companions moved on either side of him. One was an elf with shoulder-length blonde hair, a curved blade in his grasp and a white bow across his back. The other was a human with a sword in each hand. Both warriors moved with an undisguisable grace, dancing through the Bloodspawn, steel shimmering in their hands.

Kallinvar pushed himself into another charge, the power of his Sentinel armour thrumming through his body. He watched as the Draleid joined Verathin and Arden, the three warriors fighting toe to toe with the Shaman. The hulking beast held its wooden staff in one hand, a dark Soulblade of black fire in the other.

Just as Kallinvar reached Verathin's side, the sensation of blood magic pulsed through the air. The warning came just in time for Kallinvar to leap out of the way, a pillar of black fire scorching the air where he had stood. A rippling shock wave followed the black flames, cracking through the ground beneath Kallinvar's feet, hurling fragments of stone and steel through the air.

Rolling to his side, Kallinvar pulled himself to his feet. The Shaman stood at the epicentre of the blast, the earth around it broken and charred. Once more, Kallinvar summoned his Soulblade – he had released it as he fell – and charged towards the Shaman.

His heart stopped as he realised Verathin had been quicker.

Kallinvar watched as his brother collided with the Shaman, the black-fire blade swallowing the green light from Verathin's Soulblade. The pair exchanged a quick flurry of blows before the Shaman dragged its black-fire blade across Verathin's leg, the unnatural weapon slicing through the Grandmaster's Sentinel armour.

Dread shivered through Kallinvar's veins. Bending at the knee, he launched himself towards his friend. But just as he was within touching distance, something hammered into his shoulder, knocking him off balance and sending him crashing to the ground.

Scrambling to his feet, Kallinvar swept his blade across the throat of the Urak that had charged him and pushed forward, stumbling towards Verathin. He watched in agony as the Shaman drew back its arm before plunging its black-fire blade through Verathin's chest. The twisted Soulblade sheared through Verathin's Sentinel armour and sliced into his heart, ripping his soul from the world, denying him entry into Achyron's halls.

The all-consuming wave of loss that flooded from Kallinvar's Sigil pounded through his chest like a hammer blow, knocking him to his knees. The unyielding torrent of anguish that consumed him was like nothing he had ever felt, not in seven hundred years. It pulled at him, dragging his soul to and fro, tearing at the fabric of his mind. "No... by Achyron... no..."

Verathin had been by Kallinvar's side through everything. He had been the best of them, the light that shone brightest in the darkest of nights. Were it not for Verathin, Kallinvar would have died in Ilnaen. Were it not for Verathin, Kallinvar would probably have died long before that on the fields of Lithwain, where Verathin had first offered him the Sigil. And now the greatest man he had ever known was not even to be granted the respite his soul had so desperately deserved.

Verathin's body collapsed to the ground as the Shaman slid its blade free of his chest. And as Kallinvar watched his friend's body fall, the anguish that flooded his mind was replaced with a blinding fury, a fire so bright it consumed every piece of him, searing through his veins, boiling his blood, igniting his soul. All sounds capitulated to the thrum that resonated through his body.

Kallinvar dragged himself to his feet. Power coursed through his bones, radiating from the Sigil fused with his chest. He threw himself at the Shaman, slamming his armoured fist into the creature's leathered cheek, then swinging his Soulblade down in an arc. A deep vibration resonated through Kallinvar's arm as the creature's blade met his in the air.

"Your... god... abandons... you..." the creature hissed, its lips struggling with the Common Tongue.

"I will rip your soul from this world." Kallinvar's chest heaved as he stared into the creature's crimson eyes. He threw his arms forward, breaking the deadlock, then charged. Bursts of green light rippled through the air as his Soulblade collided with the Shaman's again and again. As the two Soulblades crashed together once more, Kallinvar used the momentum to throw himself backward. The Shaman lunged after him, driving its blade towards his chest. It had taken the bait. Side stepping, Kallinvar twisted his heel into the ground and swept his Soulblade across the creature's back. The Shaman swung back around, crying out in agony, but Kallinvar held no mercy in his heart for the twisted creature. He brought his Soulblade upward, cleaving the Shaman's arm from its body. A harsh, guttural howl escaped the beast's throat as its severed arm fell to the ground, its black-fire blade flickering from existence.

A pulse of Taint seeped from the wailing creature as it extended its staff, arcs of vibrant purple lightning streaming from its tip. The arcs of lightning streaked through the air, ripping chunks of stone from the ground, shredding everything they touched.

Leaping out of the way, Kallinvar pushed forward, his eyes fixed on the Shaman. To his left, Arden charged, forcing the creature back, raking his Soulblade across its shoulder. Kallinvar stormed in beside his brother, fury consuming him.

For a few moments, the three exchanged blows, flashes of green light illuminating the night. Even with one arm the Shaman was formidable, its layers of thick muscle belying a deceptive speed. But then, just as the creature opened itself to block one of Arden's strikes, Kallinvar let out a roar and lunged forward, driving his Soulblade through the Shaman's chest, then pulling it free again in one motion.

The Shaman collapsed to its knees, shrieking, howling, thrashing. With one last swing, Kallinvar took the creature's head from its shoulders. The shrieking stopped.

Releasing his Soulblade, Kallinvar dropped to the ground beside Verathin's body, taking his friend in his arms. Before Kallinvar's eyes, Verathin's Sentinel armour turned to liquid metal, sliding back over his skin, receding into the Sigil that was fused with his chest. Kallinvar watched as the Sigil faded, leaving only a marking of scarred flesh in its place. "I am sorry, brother. I failed you…"

"Brother-Captain, is he…" Arden's voice cracked and faded as his eyes fell on Verathin's lifeless body.

"He's gone."

Calen's chest heaved, his eyes fixed on the two warriors in overlapping green plate. Even with Valerys's strength coursing through him, the drain leached at his bones. A deep wound burned through his thigh, his side ached, and he had lost the feeling in his left arm.

All around him, the Uraks were howling into the night, broken, fleeing. The imperial soldiers that were left cut them down as they ran, showing not even the slightest mercy. Calen couldn't blame them.

When he reached out to Valerys, Calen could feel the dragon's pain searing through him as he flew overhead. Deep wounds and gouges ran the length of Valerys's body, and his side screamed out in agony where the Fade's lightning had struck him.

His heart pounding, Calen approached the two armoured warriors, sheathing his sword as he did. Even if they had been enemies, he had seen the way they fought. He would never have stood a chance. The weapons they wielded reminded him of Asius's axe – a níthral. Soulblade.

One of the warriors knelt on the ground, their companion's body in their arms. Calen had watched the fallen man's armour *melt* away as though it were liquid. He had seen it, and yet he still did not believe it.

The second warrior stood, their armour shimmering in a deep green hue.

"Who are you?" Calen called out, not daring to move any closer.

For a long moment, the warriors did not respond, and dread coiled in Calen's chest. But then he watched as the helmet of the one who stood turned to liquid, just as the fallen man's armour had. Flowing freely, as though it were molten steel, the green helm receded back into the warrior's armour, disappearing as though it had never been.

"We have suffered a great loss," the man said, turning towards Calen. The one who knelt on the ground didn't move, and Calen could see his shoulders convulsing as he wept over his fallen companion.

"I'm sorry." Calen reached out his hand. "I…"

As the armoured man turned, Calen's heart fell into his stomach, every hair on every inch of his body stood on end, and a shiver rippled through his bones. He tried to speak, but his throat constricted, and his mouth went dry. *This is not possible.* Calen's mind felt as though it had been thrown into a whirlpool and left to drown. The man who stood before him had watched over Calen all his childhood. He had been the beacon for Calen's path, the light that guided him. But it was not possible that he stood before him now, for Calen's brother had been dead for two years, and that loss had ached in him ever since.

Feeling tears burn at the corner of his eyes, Calen only managed to push one word past his lips. "Haem?"

"Little brother…"

EPILOGUE

ane Mortem stood before the marble fireplace, his arms folded across his chest, his eyes lost in the dancing flames. He often found solace in fire. It was chaos incarnate. The purest representation of the discordance between the world and the forces that sought to destroy it.

"You had him," Fane said, tilting his head to the side, not shifting his gaze from the fire. "But you thought it better to earn glory for yourself than to put the empire first."

"That was not my intention, Emperor. I—"

Fane raised his right hand, and Artim Valdock shut his mouth. Letting out a sigh, Fane unfolded his arms and turned to meet the Exarch's gaze. Fane didn't say anything. He just took the man in, measuring him. The silver-trimmed black robes of an Exarch adorned his shoulders. He wore the typical brazen attitude that came with being a member of the Battlemages; Fane could see it in the way he held himself, in the puff of his chest, and the starkness of his gaze.

"Tell me, then," Fane said, taking a step closer to Artim. "What *was* your intention?"

"I wanted to extract information, my lord. I—"

"You disobeyed a direct order to bring him to the Dragonguard!" Fane let his anger seep into his words, drawing level with the man. "You sought to gain favour at the expense of your task, and in so doing, you let him escape."

Fane collected himself, unclenching his jaw. He stepped away from Artim and walked towards his desk, which sat at the back of the chamber. Behind his desk hung an enormous red banner that ran all the way down from the top of the wall, falling just short of the ground. At the banner's centre was the symbol of the Lorian empire: the black lion of Loria.

The Exarch stood in silence as Fane's footsteps echoed through the large chamber, his boots tapping off the stone. Fane walked around to the far side of his desk, running his fingertips along the hard oak.

"What is the consequence of failure for a Battlemage, Brother Valdock?" As he spoke, Fane pulled threads of Air into himself, funnelling them into a small chest that lay on his desk. He moved the threads of Air through the chest, pushing and pulling the locking mechanism into place until he heard a *click*. Once the lock was open, he lifted the lid of the chest, revealing a vibrant red glow that emanated from within.

"I..."

"Perhaps you didn't hear me. What is the consequence of failure for a Battlemage?"

"Death, Emperor." Fear permeated the man's words. Fane could hear it in the tremble of his voice.

"Precisely right." Reaching down, Fane wrapped his fingers around the red gemstone that lay nestled atop a bed of crimson satin. The intoxicating power of Blood Essence radiated from the gemstone, pricking at the edge of Fane's consciousness. "Are you ready to die, Exarch?"

Fane lifted his head, fixing his gaze on Artim's. It was a rhetorical question. Rarely was anyone ready to die. Even in the most courageous of hearts, the fear of death held strong. Even in his own heart, Fane could feel that same fear. But for him, it was less a fear of death and more a fear of the things he would leave unfinished if he were to die.

But a question like that, while standing before someone who was capable of carrying out the task, took on a whole new meaning than if it were an abstract pondering.

"I... I would die for the empire, my lord, but I can be of greater use alive."

"I agree." Fane enjoyed the look of surprise on Artim's face. Though he was sure the man had no concept of the use Fane had in mind for him. Closing the lid of the chest, Fane approached the Exarch. "You would do anything for the empire?"

"I would, my lord."

"Good." With slow and purposeful steps, Fane walked back over towards the fireplace, resting his hand on the marble mantelpiece. "You are to ascend, Artim."

"I..." The fear in the man's voice was replaced with dread. "But I..."

"Is there something wrong?" Fane turned his face towards the Exarch, raising an eyebrow. "Do you not believe in The Saviour? Do you not wish to share your soul with one of his heralds? It is the highest honour that can be bestowed."

Fane turned his gaze back towards the flames, letting the man stew in his own dread. In truth, he would have preferred not to force someone to ascend. But he had no choice. The Uraks were pushing harder than he had expected, and Efialtír was aiding their charge. Fane had known this day would come. Only the strongest could act as the recipients of The Saviour's grace. This was a test, and it was one he would not fail. He needed someone powerful enough to host Azrim once more.

"I just don't think—"

"Let me be clear, Artim. The Primarch wants you dead. You not only failed, but you were selfish, and in being so, you have risked the lives of others. I will not offer you this gift twice."

There were many more willing candidates for ascension. But Fane was hesitant to create too many Fades; their loyalties lay with whatever course fed Efialtír's hunger. Azrim was the only spirit Fane could rely on. They had an understanding, of sorts. And the other prospective hosts were not strong enough to receive Azrim's spirit. It would tear their minds asunder.

"What if I am not strong enough? What if—"

"Then you will die, and the circle will be complete. What say you?"

A tense moment passed, the fire crackling through the massive chamber.

Fane watched as Artim stared into the flames, swallowing hard, his tongue wetting his lips.

"I will accept the gift of ascension."

A flicker of relief passed through the back of Fane's mind. It would have been a waste to have killed him. More than a waste, it would have been an inconvenience. "A wise choice. You have a vessel, do you not?"

"I do." The man attempted to hide the tremble in his voice, but Fane had long since learned to see the fear in people.

Reaching within his robes, the man produced a shimmering red gemstone the size of a small apple. *Good, that will do.*

Turning his back on the fire, Fane stared into Artim's eyes. "Open yourself to the Essence within. Let it flow through you. Let it fill every corner of your soul. And when the heralds call to you, answer only for the one who calls himself Azrim."

Artim's eyes widened. "*Now?*"

"Now."

"But… I thought I would have more time."

"There will not be a second chance, Exarch. If this is not what you want, Primarch Touran has sent men to escort you for sentencing."

Artim didn't say anything, but he nodded, closing his eyes, taking in a trembling breath.

A few moments passed before Fane felt the Essence igniting within Artim's gemstone.

His lips curling into a half-smile, Fane tapped into the gemstone he held in his own hand – a vessel for the Essence. The gift given by Efialtír. The power to forge something new from death.

Fane drew the Essence into himself, savouring the sweetness of its touch before pushing it into Artim, feeding his connection to The Saviour.

"Remember his name. Azrim."

Fane smiled as Artim drained both gemstones of their Essence, pulling them into himself with insatiable rapacity. The more Essence he absorbed, the stronger his connection would be. The more spirits would be drawn to him.

A shiver ran through Fane's body as the light in the room dimmed, bathing the chamber in shadow. He watched as the bronze hue of Artim's skin faded, the colour draining from his face and hands. Within moments, the Exarch's cheeks were as pale as porcelain, his lips an icy blue.

With a gasp, he opened his eyes, revealing two deep wells of light-drinking black.

ACKNOWLEDGEMENTS

It's a scary thing, writing a sequel. Well, writing is a scary endeavor all of its own. To pluck the world from the deepest corners of your imagination, sharpen it, sculpt it, twist it, and turn it, then indelibly mark it in ink for the world to journey through. That is a scary thing indeed. But doing it a second time is just that little bit more frightening – expectation is a heavy weight to carry.

Lucky for me, I have a lot of people at my side that make the world a less scary place.

Amy. To put words to how important you have been on this journey would be to sell you short. You believed in me when I didn't believe in myself. You laughed with me when my world needed a bit of joy. You carried me when I felt like stopping. You didn't kill me when I spent sixteen hours a day at the computer. Myia nithír til diar, I denír viël ar altinua. *My soul to yours, in this life and always.*

Séamus. My best friend. My ride or die. Remember when we used to take sticks and go fight imaginary demons? We still fight demons now, real ones sometimes, but the fight is easier with you here, as it always has been.

My parents. You are quite literally responsible for all of this. You brought me into this world after all. But had you stopped there, I wouldn't be who I am. You didn't stop there though. You gave me love, support, inspiration, and compassion. Mam, you read books to me even though dyslexia fought you every step of the way. You taught me determination. Dad, you waited with me in the cold and the rain to buy my favourite books as they came out at midnight. You taught me to do anything and everything for the ones you love.

My brother, Aron. Shithead. You actually read my book. That meant the world to me. You inspire me in the way you pick yourself up every time you fall.

Sarah, my editor – my cheerleader when the need arises. I'm always learning from you and laughing at the crazy things you come out with. Without you, this book simply would not be what it is.

My Beta readers: Mark, Dorothy, Anat, Josie, Mark (again), and Roy. Thank you for trudging through that typo riddled, Frankenstein's monster of a first draft. You are the true heroes here.

My Advance Readers: Anthony, David, Michael, Emma, Johan, Jarred, Donna, Rashmi, Debbie, Nina, Matthew, Arundeepak, Nikki, Cynthia, Dom, Brenda, Jamie, Terry, Sandra, Tianna, Bren, Marie, Beki, Yannick, Steve, Brian, Rob, Nicola, Pat, Graham, Alan, Benny, Viv, Isabelle, John, Adawia, Dale, Josefa, Tom, Eddie, Jenny, Marc, Anj, Jason, Rowena, and Bianca. Thank you for absolutely tearing through the, slightly less typo riddled, advance copy of this book. You assuaged my fears, carried my banner, and kept my torches lit. There are of course many more of you, all of whom hold a place in my heart. May your fires never be extinguished and your blades never dull.

When I wrote *Of Blood and Fire* my loftiest aspiration was that my friends, and maybe a guy with an eReader and too much time to kill on the commute to work, might read it. I was reasonably certain my mam would never read it as books are absolutely not her thing, but then Podium Audio came along and produced the audiobook. My mam still hasn't read the book but she's listened to some of it, so that's a win. Anyway, I digress. What I'm trying to say, is thank you. Thank you to each and every one of you who have read my books. Thank you for joining me on this journey, for passionately shouting at the top of your lungs, and for allowing me to spend my days weaving my imagination into reality.

This is one more step.

Glossary

The Glade

Calen Bryer (Kay-lin BRY-ER): Son of Vars and Freis, brother of Ella and Haem, bound to the dragon Valerys. Aided in defeated the attack on Belduar, led by the Fade.

Haem Bryer (HAYM BRY-ER): Son of Vars and Freis, brother of Ella and Calen. Killed while defending The Glade from Uraks.

Ella Bryer (EL-AH BRY-ER): Daughter of Vars and Freis, sister of Haem and Calen. Presumed dead in the fire of Calen's home. Actually on a ship heading North after the death of her love, Rhett Fjorn.

Freis Bryer (Fr-EHY-s BRY-ER): Wife of Vars, mother of Calen, Haem, and Ella. Herbalist and healer of The Glade. Killed by Farda.

Vars Bryer (VARS BRY-ER): Husband of Freis, father of Calen, Haem, and Ella. Blacksmith of The Glade. Killed by Rendall.

Faenir (FAY-near): A wolfpine who was raised by the Bryer family.

Rhett Fjorn (Ret Fy-orn): Captain of The Glade's town guard. Lover of Ella. Killed on the merchant's road to Gisa.

Erdhardt Hammersmith (ERD-Heart Hammer-smith): Husband of Aela. Village elder of The Glade.

Aela Hammersmith (AY-LAH Hammer-smith): Wife of Erdhardt, jeweller of The Glade.

Dann Pimm (Dan-Pim): Son of Tharn and Ylinda, close friend of Calen's. Leaves The Glade with Calen and Rist, injured in the first battle of Belduar.

Tharn Pimm (TH-ARN Pim): Husband of Ylinda, father of Dann. Fletcher of The Glade.

Ylinda Pimm (Yuh-Lin-Dah Pim): Wife of Tharn, mother of Dann. Weaver of The Glade.

Rist Havel (Ri-st Hah-vul): Son of Lasch and Ylinda, close friend of Calen's. Leaves The Glade with Calen and Dann. Captured by the Fade and brought to the embassy of the Circle of Magii in Al'Nasla.

Lasch Havel (Lash Hah-vul): Husband of Elia, father of Rist. Innkeeper of The Gilded Dragon.

Elia Havel (EH-lee-AH Hah-vul): Wife of Lash, mother of Rist. Bee-keeper.

Verna Gritten (Ver-NAH GRIT-in): Mother of Anya. Village elder of The Glade

Anya Gritten (AHN-YA GRIT-in): Daughter of Verna, close friend of Calen's.

Fritz Netly (F-Ritz Net-lee): Childhood rival of Calen's. Betrays Ella's survival to Farda. Sent to Falstide along with empire soldiers in search of Ella.

Belduar

Arthur Bryne (Are-THUR BRINE): Father of Daymon. Murdered king of Belduar.

Daymon Bryne (DAY-MON BRINE): Son of Arthur, newly crowned king of Belduar.

Ihvon Arnell (EYE-VON ARE-nell): Close friend and advisor to Arthur. Betrayed Arthur and allowed the Fade and the empire into Belduar.

Oleg Marylin (OH-leg Mar-IH-lin): Belduaran emissary to the Dwarven Freehold.

Conal Braker (CUN-UL BRAH-ker): Young porter in Belduar, assigned to Calen to help him around the city.

Dwarven Freehold

Kira (KEE-RAH): Queen of Durakdur.

Pulroan (PULL-ROW-AN): Queen of Azmar.

Elenya (EL-EN-YA): Queen of Ozryn.

Hoffnar (Hoff-NAR): King of Volkur.

Falmin Tain (FAHL-min TAIN): Member of the Wind Runners Guild, navigator of the *Crested Wave.*

Belina Louna (BELL-eena Loo-NAH): A bard that played in the feast tent after The Proving.

Nimara (Nih-MAR-AH): Dwarven warrior from Durakdur who aids in the search for Calen and Erik.

Valtara

Dayne Ateres (DAIN AH-Teer-eece): Son of Arkin and Ilya Ateres, brother of Alina, Baren, and Owain.

Alina Ateres (AH-leen-AH AH-teer-eece): Daughter of Arkin and Ilya Ateres, sister of Dayne, Baren, and Owain.

Baren Ateres (BAH-REN Ah-teer-eece): Son of Arkin and Ilya Ateres, brother of Alina, Dayne, and Owain. Current head of House Ateres.

Owain Ateres (OH-AY-in Ah-teer-eece): Son of Arkin and Ilya Ateres, brother of Alina, Dayne, and Baren. Given over to the empire as a child.

Mera (MEH-RAH): Aligned with House Ateres. Close friend of Alina, past lover of Dayne.

Marlin Arkon (Mar-lin ARE-kon): Steward of House Ateres.

Loren (Loh-REN): High Lord of Valtara.

Rinda (RIN-dah): Consul of the Lorian Empire. Stationed in Valtara.

The North

Farda Kyrana (Far-DAH Kie-RAH-nah): Justicar of the Lorian empire and Exarch of the Imperial Battlemages. Killed Freis Bryer. Currently aboard the same ship as Ella, heading north.

Rendall (REN-DULL): Imperial Inquisitor. Killed Vars Bryer.

Andelar Touran (AN-DEH-LAR TOO-RAN): Primarch of the Imperial Battlemages

Fane Mortem (FAIN MORE-tem): Emperor of Loria.

Karsen Craine (CAR-sin CRAYNE): Grand Consul of the Circle of Magii.

Tanner Fjorn (TAH-ner FY-orn): Uncle to Rhett. High Captain of the Beronan city guard.

Yana (Yah-NAH): Member of the northern rebellion.

Farwen (FAR-win): Member of the northern rebellion.

Coren Valmar (CORE-in Val-MAR): Member of the northern rebellion.

The Circle of Magii

Garramon (GAR-ah-MON): Exarch of the Imperial Battlemages, sponsor of Rist Havel.

Andelar Touran (AN-deh-LAR Too-RAN): Primarch of the Imperial Battlemages.

Neera (Neer-AH): Apprentice to Sister Ardal.

Tommin (TOM-in): Apprentice to Sister Danwar.

Lena (Leh-NAH): Apprentice to brother Halmak.

Elves of the Aravell

Therin Eiltris (Theh-RIN EHL-treece): Former elven ambassador to The Order, powerful mage.

Thalanil (Tha-lah-nil): High Captain of the Aravell Rangers

Faelen (FAY-lin): Elven Warrior.

Gaeleron (GAY-ler-on): An elf from the hidden city of Aravell who swears an oath of honour to protect Calen and Valerys.

Alea (AH-lee-ah): An elf from the hidden city of Aravell who swears an oath of honour to protect Calen and Valerys.

Lyrei (Lie-REE): An elf from the hidden city of Aravell who swears an oath of honour to protect Calen and Valerys.

Ellisar (EHL-is-ARE): An elf from the hidden city of Aravell who swears an oath of honour to protect Calen and Valerys. Killed in the battle of Belduar.

Vaeril (VAY-ril): An elf from the hidden city of Aravell who swears an oath of honour to protect Calen and Valerys. Vaeril has the ability to touch the spark, and is particularly adept at healing.

Aeson's Rebellion

Aeson Virandr (Ay-son VIR-an-DUR): Former Draleid whose dragon was slain, and is now Rakina. Father of Dahlen and Erik. Key member of the rebellion.

Dahlen Virandr (DAH-lin VIR-an-DUR): Son of Aeson, brother of Erik. **Erik Virandr (AIR-ICK VIR-an-DUR):** Son of Aeson, brother of Dahlen.

Asius (AY-see-US): Jotnar, close friends with Aeson, companion of Larion and Senas.

Larion (LAR-eee-ON): Jotnar, companion of Asius and Senas.

Senas (See-NAS): Jotnar, companion of Asius and Larion.

Baldon (BAL-DON): Angan of the clan Fenryr, shapeshifter.

Aneera (AH-Neer-AH): Angan of the clan Fenryr, shapeshifter.

Drifaien

Lothal Helmund (Low-THAL HELL-mund): High Lord of Drifaien.

Orlana Helmund (Or-LAH-NAH HELL-mund): Wife of Lothal.

Artim Valdock (ARE-TIM Val-DOCK): Exarch of the imperial battle-mages sent to Drifaien in search of the Draleid.

Alleron (Al-ER-ON): Warrior of Drifaien. Met Calen, Dann, and Erik in The Two Barges.

Baird (BARE-D): Warrior of Drifaien. Met Calen, Dann, and Erik in The Two Barges.

Kettil (Ket-IL): Warrior of Drifaien. Met Calen, Dann, and Erik in The Two Barges.

Leif (Leaf): Warrior of Drifaien. Met Calen, Dann, and Erik in The Two Barges.

Audun (OW-dun): Warrior of Drifaien. Met Calen, Dann, and Erik in The Two Barges.

Destin (Des-TIN): Warrior of Drifaien. Met Calen, Dann, and Erik in The Two Barges.

The Gods

Achyron (Ack-er-on): The warrior God, or simply The Warrior. The protector against the shadow.

Elyara (El-eee-ARE-AH): The Maiden. The wisest of all the gods, creator of consciousness and free thought.

Varyn (Var-in): The Father. The protector of all things and the provider of the sun.

Heraya (HER-eye-AH): The Mother. The giver of life and receiver of the dead.

Hafaesir (Hah-FYE-SEER): The Smith. The Patron god of the dwarves. Builder of the world.

Neron (NEH-ron): The Sailor. Creator of the seas and provider of safe travel.

Efialtír (Ef-EE-ahl-TIER): The Traitor God. Efialtír betrayed the other six gods at the dawn of creation. He turned his back on their ways, claiming his power through offerings of blood.

The Knights of Achyron

Grandmaster Verathin (Ver-AH-thin): Grandmaster of the knights of Achyron. Leader of The First. Survivor of The Fall.

Brother-Captain Kallinvar (KAL-IN-var): Captain of The Second. Survivor of The Fall.

Arden (AR-DIN): Knight of The Second.

Ildris (ILL-dris): Knight of The Second. Survivor of The Fall.

Ruon (REW-ON): Knight of The Second. Survivor of The Fall.

Tarron (TAR-ON): Knight of The Second. Survivor of The Fall.

Sylven (SILL-VEN): Knight of The Second.

Mirken (MUR-KIN): Knight of The Second.

Daynin (DAY-NIN): Knight of The Second.

Varlin (VAR-LIN): Knight of The Second.

Lyrin (LIH-RIN): Knight of The Second.

Brother-Captain Armites (AR-MIH-teece): Captain of The Sixth. Survivor of The Fall.

Sister-Captain Olyria (OH-LEER-ee-AH): Captain of The Third. Survivor of The Fall.

Brother-Captain Illarin **(ILL-are-IN):** Captain of The Seventh. Survivor of The Fall.

Sister-Captain Valeian (VAL-AY-IN): Captain of The Fourth.

The Dragonguard

Eltoar Daethana (EL-TWAR Die-THA-NAH): Commander of the Dragonguard. Bonded to Helios. Wing commander of Lyina and Pellenor.

Lyina (Lie-eee-NAH): Member of the Dragonguard. Bonded to Karakes. Eltoar's left wing.

Pellenor (Pel-EH-NOR): Member of the Dragonguard. Bonded to Meranth. Eltoar's right wing.

Jormun (JOR-mun): Member of the Dragonguard.

Ilkya (IL-kee-AH): Member of the Dragonguard.

Voranur (VOR-ah-noor): Member of the Dragonguard.

Erdin (ER-DIN): Member of the Dragonguard.

Luka (Loo-KAH): Member of the Dragonguard.

Tivar (Tee-VAR): Member of the Dragonguard.

The Old Tongue

Draleid (Drah-laid): *Dragonbound.* Ancient warriors whose souls were bonded to the dragons that hatched for them.

Rakina (Rah-KEEN-ah): *One who is broken,* or in the elven dialect – '*one who survived*'. When a dragon or their Draleid dies, the other earns the title of 'Rakina'.

Du gryr haydria til myia elwyn (DOO Greer HAY-dree-AH till MAYA EHL-win): *You bring honour to my heart.*

N'aldryr (Nahl-DREAR): *By fire.*

Valerys (Vah-lair-is): *Ice.*

Det være myia haydria (Deh-t VAY-air MAYA HAY-dree-AH): *It would be my honour.*

Du haryn myia vrai (Doo Hah-RIN MAYA VRAY): *You have my thanks.*

Myia elwyn er unira diar *(MAYA EHL-win AIR OO-neer-AH Dee-ARE):* *My heart is always yours.*

Din vrai é atuya sin'vala (DIN VRAY Eh AH-too-YAH Sin-VAH-LAH): *Your thanks are welcome here.*

Draleid n'aldryr, Rakina nai dauva (Drah-laid Nahl-DREAR, Rah-KEEN-ah Nay D-ow-VAH): *Dragonbound by fire, broken by death.*

Det er aldin na vëna du (Deh-t AIR Ahl-DIN Nah VAY-na DOO): *It is good to see you.*

Myia nithír til diar *(MAYA NIH-theer TILL Dee-ARE):* *My soul to yours.*

I denír viël ar altinua (Eee Deh-Neer Vee-EL ARE Al-tin-OO-AH): *In this life and always.*

Vaen (VAY-en): *Truth.*

Drunir (DREW-Neer): *Companion.*

Aldryr (ALL-DREAR): *Fire.*

Níthral (Nee-TH-ral): *Soulblade.*

Svidar'Cia (Svih-DAR-see-AH): *Burnt Lands.*

Svidarya (Svih-DAR-eee-AH): *Burning Winds.*

Valacia (VAH-lay-see-AH): *Icelands.*

Nithír (NIH-Theer): *Soul.*

Din haydria er fyrir (DIN HAY-dree-AH AIR Fih-reer): *Your honour is forfeit.*

Bralgír (Brahl-GEER): *Storyteller.*

Ayar Elwyn (Ay-ARE EHL-win): *One Heart.*

Galdrín (GAHL-DREEN): *Mage.*

Idyn väe (IH-din VAY): *Rest well.*

Races

Humans: Humans first arrived on the continent of Epheria in the year 306 After Doom, fleeing from an unknown cataclysm in their homeland of Terroncia.

Elves: Along with the Jotnar and the dwarves, the elves were one of the first races to inhabit Epheria. After the fall of the Order the elves fought valiantly against the newly formed Lorian Empire, but were eventually defeated and subsequently split into two major factions. One faction blamed the humans for the decimation of Epheria, and retreated into the enormous woodland known as Lynalion, withdrawing themselves from the rest of the continent. The other faction withdrew to the Darkwood, where they built the city of Aravell and continued on the fight in secret by turning the Darkwood into an impassable barrier between the North and South.

Dwarves: Before the fall of The Order, the dwarves occupied territories both above land and below. But after The Fall, the dwarves retreated back to their mountain kingdoms for safety.

Uraks (UH-raks): Creatures whose way of life revolves around bloodshed. Little is known of them outside of battle, other than they serve the traitor God – Efialtir.

Jotnar (Jot-Nar): The Jotnar, known to humans as 'giants', are a race of people who have inhabited Epheria since the dawn of time. They are intrinsically magic, have bluish-white skin, and stand over eight feet tall.

Angan (Ann-GAN): The Angan are a race of humanoid shapeshifters. It is not truly known when they arrived in Epheria, though it is thought that they are as old as the land itself. They are divided into five major factions, each devoted to one of the five Angan Gods: Dvalin, Bjorna, Vethnir, Fenryr, and Kaygan.